06-02=12+1

ACROSS THE SEA OF STARS

by ARTHUR C. CLARKE, 1917 —

An omnibus containing the complete novels

CHILDHOOD'S END *and* EARTHLIGHT

and eighteen short stories

Introduction by Clifton Fadiman

Harcourt, Brace and Company • *New York*

TO LEN AND LOIS

for seeing that I never have a dull moment in Chicago

CONTENTS

INTRODUCTION BY CLIFTON FADIMAN

Not long ago I had cocktails and conversation with a man solidly rooted in the future. His name is Arthur C. Clarke. I believe he has been dubbed, by the editors of *Holiday* magazine, "the colossus of science fiction." Mr. Clarke's demeanor is too modest for a colossus. He looks more like an extremely intelligent bank teller, sandy-haired, amiable. But in his own field, the imaginative mapping and mensuration of the future, he is certainly one of the half-dozen outstanding figures.

Some science fictioneers are plain old-style typewriter hacks. They could as easily or as wearily knock out westerns or thrillers, and many do. But more of them are exceptional fellows: well-educated, well-grounded in half a dozen sciences. I know one who writes (no fee) for a learned journal of philosophy. They are New Bohemians, mavericks, men who, trained in the strict rationale of science, love to kick over the traces and soar into the blue sky of speculation.

Mr. Clarke is one of them. He is barely past forty. Before he was ten (alas for him, this was before the time when quiz programs delicately piloted urchins into the harbor of financial independence) he had built a small telescope and mapped the moon until he could make his way around it better than around his native Somerset. I think Mr. Clarke is still a bit petulant about the other side of the moon's being hidden from us, and looks forward with a certain satisfaction to the colonies we shall inevitably establish on Thither Luna.

Wherever men meet to send up rockets of calculation as a paper prelude to the real thing, there you are apt to encounter Mr. Clarke.

He is a sometime Chairman of the British Interplanetary Society. He is the author of a standard technical treatise on astronautics, bristling with implacable equations (*Interplanetary Flight: An Introduction to Astronautics*). For Mr. Clarke is no mere dreamer. If he roves space, it is with slide rule in hand. From Kings College, London, he wrested a First Class Honors in physics and pure and applied mathematics; and as a very young man held down the assistant editorship of the learned journal *Science Abstracts*.

He reminds me of the early H. G. Wells. Like Wells, he had to make his way up in the world by his own efforts. Like him he received a sound scientific education and a less sound humanistic one, a circumstance reflected in his novels, as is also true of Wells. Like Wells he turned early in life, and successfully, to science fiction. Finally, the slope of his mind parallels that of the beginning Wells, who also developed a dominating interest in the construction of utopias and the calculus of prediction. Before he died Wells had sunk into an almost diseased pessimism, but in his early manhood he placed his faith in the beneficent powers of science. So too young Mr. Clarke.

His three popular volumes on space travel include one (*The Exploration of Space*), which, in a moment of wild escapism, was chosen by the Book-of-the-Month Club judges and sent out to a large, earthbound and possibly baffled audience. He has written any number of technical papers on electronics and kindred subjects, and twelve books of science fiction. In these latter he has been strongly influenced by Olaf Stapledon, whose *Last and First Men* remains science fiction's one unarguable contribution to literature. His most grandiose job, quite Stapledonian, is *Childhood's End,* a fascinating switch on the utopian gambit.

I like him best, however, when he sticks close to the probable or fairly possible. Clarke makes orbital work and play more real than do many current novels about life next door. If you are curious about living on the moon (those now under twenty-five may include a few future colonists), try Mr. Clarke's *Earthlight,* included here. His short stories, eighteen of which appear in this volume, exhibit still other facets of his talent, and it is surprising, indeed, to find here examples of "space humor."

As I was saying, Mr. Clarke and I had cocktails together.

Though we talked quietly, I think our table-neighbors must have occasionally overheard us. Their faces seemed to change from politely concealed interest to bafflement to open alarm. The fact is that Mr. Clarke's conversation is not perfectly adapted to the Oak Room of the Plaza. The Oak Room is a rather worldly rendezvous. Mr. Clarke is not worldly; he is other-worldly. He spoke of space satellites, lunar voyages, interplanetary cruises as other men would discuss the market or the weather. As he explained how within a decade three space stations whirling in an orbit above the equator will make possible (indeed one fears inevitable) simultaneous world-wide television broadcasting, our righthand neighbor (a vice-president of CBS) went into a kind of catalepsy. When he pointed out that one of the minor results of this revolution in communication might well be the dispersal and eventual disappearance of large cities, two well-known Manhattan real-estate operators at a nearby table slowly turned mauve. (Anyway their faces did.) And when he stated that interstar travel, undertaken with a view to discovering other forms of life, might finally rid man of his feeling of being all alone in the universe, I looked around at the crowded room and began to get a bit uneasy myself. After all, I am a hopeless stick-in-the-mud who hasn't even stopped being interested in what happened during the fifth century B.C., and whose instinctive reaction to star-trotters like Mr. Clarke is to mutter, "Is this trip necessary?"

To understand a mind like Mr. Clarke's we must realize that during the last fifty years, more especially the last twenty-five years, virtually a new mental species has emerged among us. They are the men who in a real sense live in the future, men for whom the present is merely a convenient springboard.

In the old days a future-minded human being like Leonardo or Roger Bacon (I am not thinking of sideshow barkers such as Nostradamus) was a sport, a freak, a genius. Nowadays tens of thousands of such minds (though not as powerful) exist, all engaged in making the future exactly as other men make soap or motorcars. Indeed one of the most striking features of our time is the large number of people not living in it.

Some of these Futurians (it is difficult to think of them as having national allegiances) write stories. Like energetic salesmen, they offer a diversified line of utopian merchandise. Others manufacture the future in the laboratory, on the drawing board, on the proving grounds at White Sands, or merely—and these are the true wonder-boys engaged in making brains obsolescent—out of the bewildering intangibles of communication theory. Such men, many of them very young, never ask whether a job *has* a future; their job *is* the future.

EXPEDITION TO EARTH

The next time you see the full moon high in the south, look carefully at its right-hand edge and let your eye travel upward along the curve of the disk. Round about two o'clock you will notice a small, dark oval: anyone with normal eyesight can find it quite easily. It is the great walled plain, one of the finest on the Moon, known as the Mare Crisium—the Sea of Crises. Three hundred miles in diameter, and almost completely surrounded by a ring of magnificent mountains, it had never been explored until we entered it in the late summer of 1996.

Our expedition was a large one. We had two heavy freighters which had flown our supplies and equipment from the main lunar base in the Mare Serenitatis, five hundred miles away. There were also three small rockets which were intended for short-range transport over regions which our surface vehicles couldn't cross. Luckily, most of the Mare Crisium is very flat. There are none of the great crevasses so common and so dangerous elsewhere, and very few craters or mountains of any size. As far as we could tell, our powerful caterpillar tractors would have no difficulty in taking us wherever we wished to go.

I was geologist—or selenologist, if you want to be pedantic—in charge of the group exploring the southern region of the Mare. We had crossed a hundred miles of it in a week, skirting the foothills of the mountains along the shore of what was once the ancient sea, some thousand million years before. When life was beginning on Earth, it was already dying here. The waters were retreating down the flanks of those stupendous cliffs, retreating into the empty heart of the Moon. Over the land which we were crossing, the tideless ocean had once been half a mile deep, and now the only trace of moisture was the hoarfrost one could sometimes find in caves which the searing sunlight never penetrated.

We had begun our journey early in the slow lunar dawn, and still had almost a week of Earth-time before nightfall. Half a dozen times a day we would leave our vehicle and go outside in the space-suits to hunt for interesting minerals, or to place markers for the guidance of future travelers. It was an uneventful routine. There is nothing hazardous or even particularly exciting about lunar exploration. We could live comfortably for a month in our pressurized tractors, and if we ran into trouble we could always radio for help and sit tight until one of the spaceships came to our rescue.

I said just now that there was nothing exciting about lunar exploration, but of course that isn't true. One could never grow tired of those incredible mountains, so much more rugged than the gentle hills of Earth. We never knew, as we rounded the capes and promontories of that vanished sea, what new splendors would be revealed to us. The whole southern curve of the Mare Crisium is a vast delta where a score of rivers once found their way into the ocean, fed perhaps by the torrential rains that must have lashed the mountains in the brief volcanic age when the Moon was young. Each of these ancient valleys was an invitation, challenging us to climb into the unknown uplands beyond. But we had a hundred miles still to cover, and could only look longingly at the heights which others must scale.

We kept Earth-time aboard the tractor, and precisely at 22.00 hours the final radio message would be sent out to Base and we would close down for the day. Outside, the rocks would still be burning beneath the almost vertical sun, but to us it was night until we awoke again eight hours later. Then one of us would prepare breakfast, there would be a great buzzing of electric razors, and someone would switch on the short-wave radio from Earth. Indeed, when the smell of frying sausages began to fill the cabin, it was sometimes hard to believe that we were not back on our own world —everything was so normal and homely, apart from the feeling of decreased weight and the unnatural slowness with which objects fell.

It was my turn to prepare breakfast in the corner of the main cabin that served as a galley. I can remember that moment quite vividly after all these years, for the radio had just played one of my favorite melodies, the old Welsh air, "David of the White Rock."

Our driver was already outside in his space-suit, inspecting our caterpillar treads. My assistant, Louis Garnett, was up forward in the control position, making some belated entries in yesterday's log.

As I stood by the frying pan waiting, like any terrestrial house-wife, for the sausages to brown, I let my gaze wander idly over the mountain walls which covered the whole of the southern horizon, marching out of sight to east and west below the curve of the Moon. They seemed only a mile or two from the tractor, but I knew that the nearest was twenty miles away. On the Moon, of course, there is no loss of detail with distance—none of that almost imperceptible haziness which softens and sometimes transfigures all far-off things on Earth.

Those mountains were ten thousand feet high, and they climbed steeply out of the plain as if ages ago some subterranean eruption had smashed them skyward through the molten crust. The base of even the nearest was hidden from sight by the steeply curving surface of the plain, for the Moon is a very little world, and from where I was standing the horizon was only two miles away.

I lifted my eyes toward the peaks which no man had ever climbed, the peaks which, before the coming of terrestrial life, had watched the retreating oceans sink sullenly into their graves, taking with them the hope and the morning promise of a world. The sun-light was beating against those ramparts with a glare that hurt the eyes, yet only a little way above them the stars were shining steadily in a sky blacker than a winter midnight on Earth.

I was turning away when my eye caught a metallic glitter high on the ridge of a great promontory thrusting out into the sea thirty miles to the west. It was a dimensionless point of light, as if a star had been clawed from the sky by one of those cruel peaks, and I imagined that some smooth rock surface was catching the sunlight and heliographing it straight into my eyes. Such things were not uncommon. When the Moon is in her second quarter, observers on Earth can sometimes see the great ranges in the Oceanus Procellarum burning with a blue-white iridescence as the sunlight flashes from their slopes and leaps again from world to world. But I was curious to know what kind of rock could be shining so brightly up there, and I climbed into the observation turret and swung our four-inch telescope round to the west.

I could see just enough to tantalize me. Clear and sharp in the field of vision, the mountain peaks seemed only half a mile away, but whatever was catching the sunlight was still too small to be resolved. Yet it seemed to have an elusive symmetry, and the summit upon which it rested was curiously flat. I stared for a long time at that glittering enigma, straining my eyes into space, until presently a smell of burning from the galley told me that our breakfast sausages had made their quarter-million mile journey in vain.

All that morning we argued our way across the Mare Crisium while the western mountains reared higher in the sky. Even when we were out prospecting in the space-suits, the discussion would continue over the radio. It was absolutely certain, my companions argued, that there had never been any form of intelligent life on the Moon. The only living things that had ever existed there were a few primitive plants and their slightly less degenerate ancestors. I knew that as well as anyone, but there are times when a scientist must not be afraid to make a fool of himself.

"Listen," I said at last, "I'm going up there, if only for my own peace of mind. That mountain's less than twelve thousand feet high —that's only two thousand under Earth gravity—and I can make the trip in twenty hours at the outside. I've always wanted to go up into those hills, anyway, and this gives me an excellent excuse."

"If you don't break your neck," said Garnett, "you'll be the laughing-stock of the expedition when we get back to Base. That mountain will probably be called Wilson's Folly from now on."

"I won't break my neck," I said firmly. "Who was the first man to climb Pico and Helicon?"

"But weren't you rather younger in those days?" asked Louis gently.

"That," I said with great dignity, "is as good a reason as any for going."

We went to bed early that night, after driving the tractor to within half a mile of the promontory. Garnett was coming with me in the morning; he was a good climber, and had often been with me on such exploits before. Our driver was only too glad to be left in charge of the machine.

At first sight, those cliffs seemed completely unscalable, but to anyone with a good head for heights, climbing is easy on a world where all weights are only a sixth of their normal value. The real danger in lunar mountaineering lies in overconfidence; a six-hundred-foot drop on the Moon can kill you just as thoroughly as a hundred-foot fall on Earth.

We made our first halt on a wide ledge about four thousand feet above the plain. Climbing had not been very difficult, but my limbs were stiff with the unaccustomed effort, and I was glad of the rest. We could still see the tractor as a tiny metal insect far down at the foot of the cliff, and we reported our progress to the driver before starting on the next ascent.

Inside our suits it was comfortably cool, for the refrigeration units were fighting the fierce sun and carrying away the body-heat of our exertions. We seldom spoke to each other, except to pass climbing instructions and to discuss our best plan of ascent. I do not know what Garnett was thinking, probably that this was the craziest goose-chase he had ever embarked upon. I more than half agreed with him, but the joy of climbing, the knowledge that no man had ever gone this way before and the exhilaration of the steadily widening landscape gave me all the reward I needed.

I don't think I was particularly excited when I saw in front of us the wall of rock I had first inspected through the telescope from thirty miles away. It would level off about fifty feet above our heads, and there on the plateau would be the thing that had lured me over these barren wastes. It was, almost certainly, nothing more than a boulder splintered ages ago by a falling meteor, and with its cleavage planes still fresh and bright in this incorruptible, unchanging silence.

There were no hand-holds on the rock face, and we had to use a grapnel. My tired arms seemed to gain new strength as I swung the three-pronged metal anchor round my head and sent it sailing up toward the stars. The first time it broke loose and came falling slowly back when we pulled the rope. On the third attempt, the prongs gripped firmly and our combined weights could not shift it.

Garnett looked at me anxiously. I could tell that he wanted to go first, but I smiled back at him through the glass of my helmet and shook my head. Slowly, taking my time, I began the final ascent.

Even with my space-suit, I weighed only forty pounds here, so I pulled myself up hand over hand without bothering to use my feet. At the rim I paused and waved to my companion, then I scrambled over the edge and stood upright, staring ahead of me.

You must understand that until this very moment I had been almost completely convinced that there could be nothing strange or unusual for me to find here. Almost, but not quite; it was that haunting doubt that had driven me forward. Well, it was a doubt no longer, but the haunting had scarcely begun.

I was standing on a plateau perhaps a hundred feet across. It had once been smooth—too smooth to be natural—but falling meteors had pitted and scored its surface through immeasurable eons. It had been leveled to support a glittering, roughly pyramidal structure, twice as high as a man, that was set in the rock like a gigantic, many-faceted jewel.

Probably no emotion at all filled my mind in those first few seconds. Then I felt a great lifting of my heart, and a strange, inexpressible joy. For I loved the Moon, and now I knew that the creeping moss of Aristarchus and Eratosthenes was not the only life she had brought forth in her youth. The old, discredited dream of the first explorers was true. There had, after all, been a lunar civilization—and I was the first to find it. That I had come perhaps a hundred million years too late did not distress me; it was enough to have come at all.

My mind was beginning to function normally, to analyze and to ask questions. Was this a building, a shrine—or something for which my language had no name? If a building, then why was it erected in so uniquely inaccessible a spot? I wondered if it might be a temple, and I could picture the adepts of some strange priesthood calling on their gods to preserve them as the life of the Moon ebbed with the dying oceans, and calling on their gods in vain.

I took a dozen steps forward to examine the thing more closely, but some sense of caution kept me from going too near. I knew a little of archaeology, and tried to guess the cultural level of the civilization that must have smoothed this mountain and raised the glittering mirror surfaces that still dazzled my eyes.

The Egyptians could have done it, I thought, if their workmen had possessed whatever strange materials these far more ancient architects had used. Because of the thing's smallness, it did not occur to me that I might be looking at the handiwork of a race more advanced than my own. The idea that the Moon had possessed intelligence at all was still almost too tremendous to grasp, and my pride would not let me take the final, humiliating plunge.

And then I noticed something that set the scalp crawling at the back of my neck—something so trivial and so innocent that many would never have noticed it at all. I have said that the plateau was scarred by meteors; it was also coated inches-deep with the cosmic dust that is always filtering down upon the surface of any world where there are no winds to disturb it. Yet the dust and the meteor scratches ended quite abruptly in a wide circle enclosing the little pyramid, as though an invisible wall was protecting it from the ravages of time and the slow but ceaseless bombardment from space.

There was someone shouting in my earphones, and I realized that Garnett had been calling me for some time. I walked unsteadily to the edge of the cliff and signaled him to join me, not trusting myself to speak. Then I went back toward that circle in the dust. I picked up a fragment of splintered rock and tossed it gently toward the shining enigma. If the pebble had vanished at that invisible barrier I should not have been surprised, but it seemed to hit a smooth, hemispherical surface and slide gently to the ground.

I knew then that I was looking at nothing that could be matched in the antiquity of my own race. This was not a building, but a machine, protecting itself with forces that had challenged Eternity. Those forces, whatever they might be, were still operating, and perhaps I had already come too close. I thought of all the radiations man had trapped and tamed in the past century. For all I knew, I might be as irrevocably doomed as if I had stepped into the deadly, silent aura of an unshielded atomic pile.

I remember turning then toward Garnett, who had joined me and was now standing motionless at my side. He seemed quite oblivious to me, so I did not disturb him but walked to the edge of the cliff in an effort to marshal my thoughts. There below me lay the Mare Crisium—Sea of Crises, indeed—strange and weird to most men, but reassuringly familiar to me. I lifted my eyes toward the crescent Earth, lying in her cradle of stars, and I wondered what her clouds had covered when these unknown builders had finished their work. Was it the steaming jungle of the Carboniferous, the bleak shoreline over which the first amphibians must crawl to conquer the land—or, earlier still, the long loneliness before the coming of life?

Do not ask me why I did not guess the truth sooner—the truth that seems so obvious now. In the first excitement of my discovery, I had assumed without question that this crystalline apparition had been built by some race belonging to the Moon's remote past, but suddenly, and with overwhelming force, the belief came to me that it was as alien to the Moon as I myself.

In twenty years we had found no trace of life but a few degenerate plants. No lunar civilization, whatever its doom, could have left but a single token of its existence.

I looked at the shining pyramid again, and the more remote it seemed from anything that had to do with the Moon. And suddenly I felt myself shaking with a foolish, hysterical laughter, brought on by excitement and overexertion: for I had imagined that the little pyramid was speaking to me and was saying: "Sorry, I'm a stranger here myself."

It has taken us twenty years to crack that invisible shield and to reach the machine inside those crystal walls. What we could not understand, we broke at last with the savage might of atomic power and now I have seen the fragments of the lovely, glittering thing I found up there on the mountain.

They are meaningless. The mechanisms—if indeed they are mechanisms—of the pyramid belong to a technology that lies far beyond our horizon, perhaps to the technology of para-physical forces.

The mystery haunts us all the more now that the other planets have been reached and we know that only Earth has ever been the home of intelligent life in our Universe. Nor could any lost civilization of our own world have built that machine, for the thickness of the meteoric dust on the plateau has enabled us to measure its age. It was set there upon its mountain before life had emerged from the seas of Earth.

When our world was half its present age, *something* from the stars swept through the Solar System, left this token of its passage, and went again upon its way. Until we destroyed it, that machine was still fulfilling the purpose of its builders; and as to that purpose, here is my guess.

Nearly a hundred thousand million stars are turning in the circle of the Milky Way, and long ago other races on the worlds of other suns must have scaled and passed the heights that we have reached. Think of such civilizations, far back in time against the fading afterglow of Creation, masters of a universe so young that life as yet had come only to a handful of worlds. Theirs would have been a loneliness we cannot imagine, the loneliness of gods looking out across infinity and finding none to share their thoughts.

They must have searched the star-clusters as we have searched the planets. Everywhere there would be worlds, but they would be empty or peopled with crawling, mindless things. Such was our own Earth, the smoke of the great volcanoes still staining the skies, when that first ship of the peoples of the dawn came sliding in from the abyss beyond Pluto. It passed the frozen outer worlds, knowing that life could play no part in their destinies. It came to rest among the inner planets, warming themselves around the fire of the Sun and waiting for their stories to begin.

Those wanderers must have looked on Earth, circling safely in the narrow zone between fire and ice, and must have guessed that it was the favorite of the Sun's children. Here, in the distant future, would be intelligence; but there were countless stars before them still, and they might never come this way again.

So they left a sentinel, one of millions they have scattered throughout the Universe, watching over all worlds with the promise of life. It was a beacon that down the ages has been patiently signaling the fact that no one had discovered it.

Perhaps you understand now why that crystal pyramid was set upon the Moon instead of on the Earth. Its builders were not concerned with races still struggling up from savagery. They would be interested in our civilization only if we proved our fitness to survive —by crossing space and so escaping from the Earth, our cradle. That is the challenge that all intelligent races must meet, sooner or later. It is a double challenge, for it depends in turn upon the conquest of atomic energy and the last choice between life and death.

Once we had passed that crisis, it was only a matter of time before we found the pyramid and forced it open. Now its signals have ceased, and those whose duty it is will be turning their minds upon Earth. Perhaps they wish to help our infant civilization. But they must be very, very old, and the old are often insanely jealous of the young.

I can never look now at the Milky Way without wondering from which of those banked clouds of stars the emissaries are coming. If you will pardon so commonplace a simile, we have set off the fire-alarm and have nothing to do but to wait.

I do not think we will have to wait for long.

As David said, when one falls on Africa from a height of two hundred and fifty kilometers, a broken ankle may be an anticlimax but it is none the less painful. But what hurt him most, he pretended, was the way we had all rushed out into the desert to see what had happened to the A.20 and hadn't come near him until hours later.

"Be logical, David," Jimmy Langford had protested. "We knew that you were O.K. because the base 'copter radioed when it picked you up. But the A.20 might have been a complete write-off."

"There's only one A.20," I said, trying to be helpful, "but rocket test-pilots are—well, if not two a penny, at any rate twelve for a dime."

David glared back at us from beneath his bushy eyebrows and said something in Welsh.

"The Druid's curse," Jimmy remarked to me. "Any moment now you'll turn into a leek or a perspex model of Stonehenge."

You see, we were still pretty light-headed and it wouldn't do to be serious for a while. Even David's iron nerve must have taken a terrific beating, yet somehow he seemed the calmest of us all. I couldn't understand it—then.

The A.20 had come down fifty kilometers from her launching point. We'd followed her by radar for the whole trajectory, so we knew her position to within a few meters—though we didn't know at the time that David had landed ten kilometers farther east.

The first warning of disaster had come seventy seconds after takeoff. The A.20 had reached fifty kilometers and was following the correct trajectory to within a few per cent. As far as the eye

12

could tell, the luminous track on the radar screen had scarcely deviated from the pre-computed path. David was doing two kilometers a second: not much, but the fastest any man had ever traveled up to then. And *Goliath* was just about to be jettisoned.

The A.20 was a two-step rocket. It had to be, for it was using chemical fuels. The upper component, with its tiny cabin, its folded aerofoils and flaps, weighed just under twenty tons when fully fueled. It was to be lifted by a lower two-hundred-ton booster which would take it up to fifty kilometers, after which it could carry on quite happily under its own power. The big fellow would then drop back to Earth by parachute: it wouldn't weigh much when its fuel was burnt. Meanwhile the upper step would have built up enough speed to reach the six-hundred-kilometer level before falling back and going into a glide that would take David halfway round the world if he wished.

I don't remember who called the two rockets *David* and *Goliath* but the names caught on at once. Having two Davids around caused a lot of confusion, not all of it accidental.

Well, that was the theory, but as we watched the tiny green spot on the screen fall away from its calculated course, we knew that something had gone wrong. And we guessed what it was.

At fifty kilometers the spot should have divided in two. The brighter echo should have continued to rise as a free projectile, and then fallen back to Earth. But the other should have gone on, still accelerating, drawing swiftly away from the discarded booster.

There had been no separation. The empty *Goliath* had refused to come free and was dragging *David* back to Earth—helplessly, for *David's* motors could not be used. Their exhausts were blocked by the machine beneath.

We saw all this in about ten seconds. We waited just long enough to calculate the new trajectory, and then we climbed into the 'copters and set off for the target area.

All we expected to find, of course, was a heap of magnesium looking as if a bulldozer had gone over it. We knew that *Goliath* couldn't eject its parachute while *David* was sitting on top of it, any more than *David* could use its motors while *Goliath* was clinging beneath. I remember wondering who was going to break the news to Mavis, and then realizing that she'd be listening to the radio and would know all about it as soon as anyone.

We could scarcely believe our eyes when we found the two rockets still coupled together, lying undamaged beneath the big parachute. There was no sign of David, but a few minutes later Base called to say that he'd been found. The plotters at Number Two Station had picked up the tiny echo from his parachute and sent a 'copter to collect him. He was in the hospital twenty minutes later, but we stayed out in the desert for several hours checking over the machines and making arrangements to retrieve them.

When at last we got back to Base, we were pleased to see our best-hated science-reporters among the mob being held at bay. We waved aside their protests and sailed on into the ward.

The shock and the subsequent relief had left us all feeling rather irresponsible and perhaps childish. Only David seemed unaffected: the fact that he'd just had one of the most miraculous escapes in human history hadn't made him turn a hair. He sat there in the bed pretending to be annoyed at our jibes until we'd calmed down.

"Well," said Jimmy at last, "what went wrong?"

"That's for you to discover," David replied. "*Goliath* went like a dream until fuel-cutoff point. I waited then for the five-second pause before the explosive bolts detonated and the springs threw it clear, but nothing happened. So I punched the emergency release. The lights dimmed, but the kick I'd expected never came. I tried a couple more times but somehow I knew it was useless. I guessed that something had shorted in the detonator circuit and was earthing the power supply.

"Well, I did some rather rapid calculations from the flight charts and abacs in the cabin. At my present speed I'd continue to rise for another two hundred kilometers and would reach the peak of my trajectory in about three minutes. Then I'd start the two-hundred-and-fifty-kilometer fall and should make a nice hole in the desert four minutes later. All told, I seemed to have a good seven minutes of life left—ignoring air-resistance, to use your favorite phrase. That might add a couple of minutes to my expectation of life.

"I knew that I couldn't get the big parachute out, and *David's* wings would be useless with the forty-ton mass of *Goliath* on its tail. I'd used up two of my seven minutes before I decided what to do.

"It's a good job I made you widen that airlock. Even so, it was a squeeze to get through it in my space-suit. I tied the end of the safety rope to a locking lever and crawled along the hull until I reached the junction of the two steps.

"The parachute compartment couldn't be opened from the outside, but I'd taken the emergency axe from the pilot's cabin. It didn't take long to get through the magnesium skin: once it had been punctured I could almost tear it apart with my hands. A few seconds later I'd released the 'chute. The silk floated aimlessly around me: I had expected some trace of air-resistance at this speed but there wasn't a sign of it. The canopy simply stayed where it was put. I could only hope that when we re-entered atmosphere it would spread itself without fouling the rocket.

"I thought I had a fairly good chance of getting away with it. The additional weight of *David* would increase the loading of the parachute by less than twenty per cent, but there was always the chance that the shrouds would chafe against the broken metal and be worn through before I could reach Earth. In addition the canopy would be distorted when it did open, owing to the unequal lengths of the cords. There was nothing I could do about that.

"When I'd finished, I looked about me for the first time. I couldn't see very well, for perspiration had misted over the glass of my suit. (Someone had better look into that: it can be dangerous.) I was still rising, though very slowly now. To the northeast I could see the whole of Sicily and some of the Italian mainland: farther south I could follow the Libyan coast as far as Bengasi. Spread out beneath me was all the land over which Alexander and Montgomery and Rommel had fought when I was a boy. It seemed rather surprising that anyone had ever made such a fuss about it.

"I didn't stay long: in three minutes I would be entering the atmosphere. I took a last look at the flaccid parachute, straightened some of the shrouds, and climbed back into the cabin. Then I jettisoned *David's* fuel—first the oxygen, and then, as soon as it had had time to disperse, the alcohol.

"That three minutes seemed an awfully long time. I was just over twenty-five kilometers high when I heard the first sound. It was a very high-pitched whistle, so faint that I could scarcely hear it. Glancing through the portholes, I saw that the parachute shrouds were becoming taut and the canopy was beginning to billow above me. At the same time I felt weight returning and knew that the rocket was beginning to decelerate.

"The calculation wasn't very encouraging. I'd fallen free for over two hundred kilometers and if I was to stop in time I'd need an *average* deceleration of ten gravities. The peaks might be twice that, but I'd stood fifteen *g* before now in a lesser cause. So I gave myself a double shot of dynocaine and uncaged the gimbals of my seat. I remember wondering whether I should let out *David's* little wings, and decided that it wouldn't help. Then I must have blacked out.

"When I came round again it was very hot, and I had normal weight. I felt very stiff and sore, and to make matters worse the cabin was oscillating violently. I struggled to the port and saw that the desert was uncomfortably close. The big parachute had done its work, but I thought that the impact was going to be rather too violent for comfort. So I jumped.

"From what you tell me I'd have done better to have stayed in the ship. But I don't suppose I can grumble."

We sat in silence for a while. Then Jimmy remarked casually:

"The accelerometer shows that you touched twenty-one gravities on the way down. Only for three seconds, though. Most of the time it was between twelve and fifteen."

David didn't seem to hear and presently I said:

"Well, we can't hold the reporters off much longer. Do you feel like seeing them?"

David hesitated.

"No," he answered. "Not now."

He read our faces and shook his head violently.

"No," he said with emphasis, "it's not that at all. I'd be willing to take off again right now. But I want to sit and think things over for a while."

His voice sank, and when he spoke again it was to show the real David behind the perpetual mask of extraversion.

"You think I haven't any nerves," he said, "and that I take risks without bothering about the consequences. Well, that isn't quite true and I'd like you to know why. I've never told anyone this, not even Mavis.

"You know I'm not superstitious," he began, a little apologetically, "but most materialists have some secret reservations, even if they won't admit them.

"Many years ago I had a peculiarly vivid dream. By itself, it wouldn't have meant much, but later I discovered that two other men had put almost identical experiences on record. One you've probably read, for the man was J. W. Dunne.

"In his first book, *An Experiment with Time,* Dunne tells how he once dreamed that he was sitting at the controls of a curious flying machine with swept-back wings, and years later the whole experience came true when he was testing his inherent-stability aeroplane. Remembering my own dream, which I'd had *before* reading Dunne's book, this made a considerable impression on me. But the second incident I found even more striking.

"You've heard of Igor Sikorsky: he designed some of the first commercial long-distance flying-boats—'Clippers,' they were called. In his autobiography, *The Story of the Winged-S,* he tells us how he had a dream very similar to Dunne's.

"He was walking along a corridor with doors opening on either side and electric lights glowing overhead. There was a slight vibration underfoot and somehow he knew that he was in a flying machine. Yet at that time there were no aeroplanes in the world, and few people believed there ever would be.

"Sikorsky's dream, like Dunne's, came true many years later. He was on the maiden flight of his first Clipper when he found himself walking along that familiar corridor."

David laughed, a little self-consciously.

"You've probably guessed what my dream was about," he continued. "Remember, it would have made no permanent impression if I hadn't come across these parallel cases.

"I was in a small, bare room with no windows. There were two other men with me, and we were all wearing what I thought at the time were diving-suits. I had a curious control panel in front of me, with a circular screen built into it. There was a picture on the screen, but it didn't mean anything to me and I can't recall it now, though I've tried many times since. All I remember is turning to the other two men and saying: 'Five minutes to go, boys'—though I'm not sure if those were the exact words. And then, of course, I woke up.

"That dream has haunted me ever since I became a test pilot. No —haunted isn't the right word. It's given me confidence that in the long run everything would be all right—at least until I'm in that cabin with those other two men. What happens after that I don't know. But now you understand why I felt quite safe when I brought down the A.20, and when I crash-landed the A.15 off Pantelleria.

"So now you know. You can laugh if you please: I sometimes do myself. But even if there's nothing in it, that dream's given my subconscious a boost that's been pretty useful."

We didn't laugh, and presently Jimmy said:

"Those other men—did you recognize them?"

David looked doubtful.

"I've never made up my mind," he answered. "Remember, they were wearing space-suits and I didn't see their faces clearly. But one of them looked rather like you, though he seemed a good deal older than you are now. I'm afraid you weren't there, Arthur. Sorry."

"I'm glad to hear it," I said. "As I've told you before, I'll have to stay behind to explain what went wrong. I'm quite content to wait until the passenger service starts."

Jimmy rose to his feet.

"O.K., David," he said, "I'll deal with the gang outside. Get some sleep now—with or without dreams. And by the way, the A.20 will be ready again in a week. I think she'll be the last of the chemical rockets: they say the atomic drive's nearly ready for us."

We never spoke of David's dream again, but I think it was often in our minds. Three months later he took the A.20 up to six hundred and eighty kilometers, a record which will never be broken by a machine of this type, because no one will ever build a chemical rocket again. David's uneventful landing in the Nile Valley marked the end of an epoch.

It was three years before the A.21 was ready. She looked very small compared with her giant predecessors, and it was hard to believe that she was the nearest thing to a spaceship man had yet built. This time the takeoff was from sea level, and the Atlas Mountains which had witnessed the start of our earlier shots were now merely the distant background to the scene.

By now both Jimmy and I had come to share David's belief in his own destiny. I remember Jimmy's parting words as the airlock closed.

"It won't be long now, David, before we build that three-man ship."

And I knew he was only half joking.

We saw the A.21 climb slowly into the sky in great, widening circles, unlike any rocket the world had ever known before. There was no need to worry about gravitational loss now that we had a built-in fuel supply, and David wasn't in a hurry. The machine was still traveling quite slowly when I lost sight of it and went into the plotting room.

When I got there the signal was just fading from the screen, and the detonation reached me a little later. And that was the end of David and his dreams.

The next I recall of that period is flying down the Conway Valley in Jimmy's 'copter, with Snowdon gleaming far away on our right. We had never been to David's home before and were not looking forward to this visit. But it was the least that we could do.

As the mountains drifted beneath us we talked about the suddenly darkened future and wondered what the next step would be. Apart from the shock of personal loss, we were beginning to realize how much of David's confidence we had come to share ourselves. And now that confidence had been shattered.

We wondered what Mavis would do, and discussed the boy's future. He must be fifteen now, though I hadn't seen him for several years and Jimmy had never met him at all. According to his father he was going to be an architect and already showed considerable promise.

Mavis was quite calm and collected, though she seemed much older than when I had last met her. For a while we talked about business matters and the disposal of David's estate. I'd never been an executor before, but tried to pretend that I knew all about it.

We had just started to discuss the boy when we heard the front door open and he came into the house. Mavis called to him and his footsteps came slowly along the passage. We could tell that he didn't want to meet us, and his eyes were still red when he entered the room.

I had forgotten how much like his father he was, and I heard a little gasp from Jimmy.

"Hello, David," I said.

But he didn't look at me. He was staring at Jimmy, with that puzzled expression of a man who has seen someone before but can't remember where.

And quite suddenly I knew that young David would never be an architect.

It was in the last days of the Empire. The tiny ship was far from home, and almost a hundred light-years from the great parent vessel searching through the loosely packed stars at the rim of the Milky Way. But even here it could not escape from the shadow that lay across civilization: beneath that shadow, pausing ever and again in their work to wonder how their distant homes were faring, the scientists of the Galactic Survey still labored at their never-ending task.

The ship held only three occupants, but between them they carried knowledge of many sciences, and the experience of half a lifetime in space. After the long interstellar night, the star ahead was warming their spirits as they dropped down toward its fires. A little more golden, a trifle more brilliant than the sun that now seemed a legend of their childhood. They knew from past experience that the chance of locating planets here was more than ninety per cent, and for the moment they forgot all else in the excitement of discovery.

They found the first planet within minutes of coming to rest. It was a giant, of a familiar type, too cold for protoplasmic life and probably possessing no stable surface. So they turned their search sunward, and presently were rewarded.

It was a world that made their hearts ache for home, a world where everything was hauntingly familiar, yet never quite the same. Two great land masses floated in blue-green seas, capped by ice at either pole. There were some desert regions, but the larger part of the planet was obviously fertile. Even from this distance, the signs of vegetation were unmistakably clear.

They gazed hungrily at the expanding landscape as they fell down into the atmosphere, heading toward noon in the subtropics. The ship plummeted through cloudless skies toward a great river, checked its fall with a surge of soundless power, and came to rest among the long grasses by the water's edge.

No one moved: there was nothing to be done until the automatic instruments had finished their work. Then a bell tinkled softly and the lights on the control board flashed in a pattern of meaningful chaos. Captain Altman rose to his feet with a sigh of relief.

"We're in luck," he said. "We can go outside without protection, if the pathogenic tests are satisfactory. What did you make of the place as we came in, Bertrond?"

"Geologically stable—no active volcanoes, at least. I didn't see any trace of cities, but that proves nothing. If there's a civilization here, it may have passed that stage."

"Or not reached it yet?"

Bertrond shrugged. "Either's just as likely. It may take us some time to find out on a planet this size."

"More time than we've got," said Clindar, glancing at the communications panel that linked them to the mother ship and thence to the Galaxy's threatened heart. For a moment there was a gloomy silence. Then Clindar walked to the control board and pressed a pattern of keys with automatic skill.

With a slight jar, a section of the hull slid aside and the fourth member of the crew stepped out onto the new planet, flexing metal limbs and adjusting servo motors to the unaccustomed gravity. Inside the ship, a television screen glimmered into life, revealing a long vista of waving grasses, some trees in the middle distance, and a glimpse of the great river. Clindar punched a button, and the picture flowed steadily across the screen as the robot turned its head.

"Which way shall we go?" Clindar asked.

"Let's have a look at those trees," Altman replied. "If there's any animal life we'll find it there."

"Look!" cried Bertrond. "A bird!"

Clindar's fingers flew over the keyboard: the picture centered on the tiny speck that had suddenly appeared on the left of the screen, and expanded rapidly as the robot's telephoto lens came into action.

"You're right," he said. "Feathers—beak—well up the evolutionary ladder. This place looks promising. I'll start the camera."

The swaying motion of the picture as the robot walked forward did not distract them: they had grown accustomed to it long ago. But they had never become reconciled to this exploration by proxy when all their impulses cried out to them to leave the ship, to run through the grass and to feel the wind blowing against their faces. Yet it was too great a risk to take, even on a world that seemed as fair as this. There was always a skull hidden behind Nature's most smiling face. Wild beasts, poisonous reptiles, quagmires—death could come to the unwary explorer in a thousand disguises. And worst of all were the invisible enemies, the bacteria and viruses against which the only defense might often be a thousand light-years away.

A robot could laugh at all these dangers and even if, as sometimes happened, it encountered a beast powerful enough to destroy it—well, machines could always be replaced.

They met nothing on the walk across the grasslands. If any small animals were disturbed by the robot's passage, they kept outside its field of vision. Clindar slowed the machine as it approached the trees, and the watchers in the spaceship flinched involuntarily at the branches that appeared to slash across their eyes. The picture dimmed for a moment before the controls readjusted themselves to the weaker illumination; then it came back to normal.

The forest was full of life. It lurked in the undergrowth, clambered among the branches, flew through the air. It fled chattering and gibbering through the trees as the robot advanced. And all the while the automatic cameras were recording the pictures that formed on the screen, gathering material for the biologists to analyze when the ship returned to base.

Clindar breathed a sigh of relief when the trees suddenly thinned. It was exhausting work, keeping the robot from smashing into obstacles as it moved through the forest, but on open ground it could take care of itself. Then the picture trembled as if beneath a hammer-blow, there was a grinding metallic thud, and the whole scene swept vertiginously upward as the robot toppled and fell.

"What's that?" cried Altman. "Did you trip?"

"No," said Clindar grimly, his fingers flying over the keyboard.

"Something attacked from the rear. I hope . . . ah . . . I've still got control."

He brought the robot to a sitting position and swiveled its head. It did not take long to find the cause of the trouble. Standing a few feet away, and lashing its tail angrily, was a large quadruped with a most ferocious set of teeth. At the moment it was, fairly obviously, trying to decide whether to attack again.

Slowly, the robot rose to its feet, and as it did so the great beast crouched to spring. A smile flitted across Clindar's face: he knew how to deal with this situation. His thumb felt for the seldom-used key labeled "Siren."

The forest echoed with a hideous undulating scream from the robot's concealed speaker, and the machine advanced to meet its adversary, arms flailing in front of it. The startled beast almost fell over backward in its effort to turn, and in seconds was gone from sight.

"Now I suppose we'll have to wait a couple of hours until everything comes out of hiding again," said Bertrond ruefully.

"I don't know much about animal psychology," interjected Altman, "but is it usual for them to attack something completely unfamiliar?"

"Some will attack anything that moves, but that's unusual. Normally they attack only for food, or if they've already been threatened. What are you driving at? Do you suggest that there are other robots on this planet?"

"Certainly not. But our carnivorous friend may have mistaken our machine for a more edible biped. Don't you think that this opening in the jungle is rather unnatural? It could easily be a path."

"In that case," said Clindar promptly, "we'll follow it and find out. I'm tired of dodging trees, but I hope nothing jumps on us again: it's bad for my nerves."

"You were right, Altman," said Bertrond a little later. "It's certainly a path. But that doesn't mean intelligence. After all, animals—"

He stopped in mid-sentence, and at the same instant Clindar brought the advancing robot to a halt. The path had suddenly opened out into a wide clearing, almost completely occupied by a village of flimsy huts. It was ringed by a wooden palisade, obviously defense against an enemy who at the moment presented no threat.

For the gates were wide open, and beyond them the inhabitants were going peacefully about their ways.

For many minutes the three explorers stared in silence at the screen. Then Clindar shivered a little and remarked: "It's uncanny. It might be our own planet, a hundred thousand years ago. I feel as if I've gone back in time."

"There's nothing weird about it," said the practical Altman. "After all, we've discovered nearly a hundred planets with our type of life on them."

"Yes," retorted Clindar. "A hundred in the whole Galaxy! I still think it's strange it had to happen to us."

"Well, it had to happen to *somebody*," said Bertrond philosophically. "Meanwhile, we must work out our contact procedure. If we send the robot into the village it will start a panic."

"That," said Altman, "is a masterly understatement. What we'll have to do is catch a native by himself and prove that we're friendly. Hide the robot, Clindar. Somewhere in the woods where it can watch the village without being spotted. We've a week's practical anthropology ahead of us!"

It was three days before the biological tests showed that it would be safe to leave the ship. Even then Bertrond insisted on going alone—alone, that is, if one ignored the substantial company of the robot. With such an ally he was not afraid of this planet's larger beasts, and his body's natural defenses could take care of the microorganisms. So, at least, the analyzers had assured him; and considering the complexity of the problem, they made remarkably few mistakes . . .

He stayed outside for an hour, enjoying himself cautiously, while his companions watched with envy. It would be another three days before they could be quite certain that it was safe to follow Bertrond's example. Meanwhile, they kept busy enough watching the village through the lenses of the robot, and recording everything they could with the cameras. They had moved the spaceship at night so that it was hidden in the depths of the forest, for they did not wish to be discovered until they were ready.

And all the while the news from home grew worse. Though their remoteness here at the edge of the Universe deadened its impact, it lay heavily on their minds and sometimes overwhelmed them with a sense of futility. At any moment, they knew, the signal for recall might come as the Empire summoned up its last resources in its extremity. But until then they would continue their work as though pure knowledge were the only thing that mattered.

Seven days after landing, they were ready to make the experiment. They knew now what paths the villagers used when going hunting, and Bertrond chose one of the less frequented ways. Then he placed a chair firmly in the middle of the path and settled down to read a book.

It was not, of course, quite as simple as that: Bertrond had taken all imaginable precautions. Hidden in the undergrowth fifty yards away, the robot was watching through its telescopic lenses, and in its hand it held a small but deadly weapon. Controlling it from the spaceship, his fingers poised over the keyboard, Clindar waited to do what might be necessary.

That was the negative side of the plan: the positive side was more obvious. Lying at Bertrond's feet was the carcass of a small, horned animal which he hoped would be an acceptable gift to any hunter passing this way.

Two hours later the radio in his suit harness whispered a warning. Quite calmly, though the blood was pounding in his veins, Bertrond laid aside his book and looked down the trail. The savage was walking forward confidently enough, swinging a spear in his right hand. He paused for a moment when he saw Bertrond, then advanced more cautiously. He could tell that there was nothing to fear, for the stranger was slightly built and obviously unarmed.

When only twenty feet separated them, Bertrond gave a reassuring smile and rose slowly to his feet. He bent down, picked up the carcass, and carried it forward as an offering. The gesture would have been understood by any creature on any world, and it was understood here. The savage reached forward, took the animal, and threw it effortlessly over his shoulder. For an instant he stared into Bertrond's eyes with a fathomless expression; then he turned and walked back toward the village. Three times he glanced round to see if Bertrond was following, and each time Bertrond smiled and waved reassurance. The whole episode lasted little more than a minute. As the first contact between two races it was completely without drama, though not without dignity.

Bertrond did not move until the other had vanished from sight. Then he relaxed and spoke into his suit microphone.

"That was a pretty good beginning," he said jubilantly. "He wasn't in the least frightened, or even suspicious. I think he'll be back."

"It still seems too good to be true," said Altman's voice in his ear. "I should have thought he'd have been either scared or hostile. Would *you* have accepted a lavish gift from a peculiar stranger with such little fuss?"

Bertrond was slowly walking back to the ship. The robot had now come out of cover and was keeping guard a few paces behind him.

"*I* wouldn't," he replied, "but I belong to a civilized community. Complete savages may react to strangers in many different ways, according to their past experience. Suppose this tribe has never had any enemies. That's quite possible on a large but sparsely populated planet. Then we may expect curiosity, but no fear at all."

"If these people have no enemies," put in Clindar, no longer fully occupied in controlling the robot, "why have they got a stockade round the village?"

"I meant no *human* enemies," replied Bertrond. "If that's true, it simplifies our task immensely."

"Do you think he'll come back?"

"Of course. If he's as human as I think, curiosity and greed will make him return. In a couple of days we'll be bosom friends."

Looked at dispassionately, it became a fantastic routine. Every morning the robot would go hunting under Clindar's direction, until it was now the deadliest killer in the jungle. Then Bertrond would wait until Yaan—which was the nearest they could get to his name—came striding confidently along the path. He came at the same time every day, and he always came alone. They wondered about this: did he wish to keep his great discovery to himself and thus get all the credit for his hunting prowess? If so, it showed unexpected foresight and cunning.

At first Yaan had departed at once with his prize, as if afraid that the donor of such a generous gift might change his mind. Soon, however, as Bertrond had hoped, he could be induced to stay for a while by simple conjuring tricks and a display of brightly colored fabrics and crystals, in which he took a childlike delight. At last

Bertrond was able to engage him in lengthy conversations, all of which were recorded as well as being filmed through the eyes of the hidden robot.

One day the philologists might be able to analyze this material; the best that Bertrond could do was to discover the meanings of a few simple verbs and nouns. This was made more difficult by the fact that Yaan not only used different words for the same thing, but sometimes the same word for different things.

Between these daily interviews, the ship traveled far, surveying the planet from the air and sometimes landing for more detailed examinations. Although several other human settlements were observed, Bertrond made no attempt to get in touch with them, for it was easy to see that they were all at much the same cultural level as Yaan's people.

It was, Bertrond often thought, a particularly bad joke on the part of Fate that one of the Galaxy's very few truly human races should have been discovered at this moment of time. Not long ago this would have been an event of supreme importance; now civilization was too hard-pressed to concern itself with these savage cousins waiting at the dawn of history.

Not until Bertrond was sure he had become part of Yaan's everyday life did he introduce him to the robot. He was showing Yaan the patterns in a kaleidoscope when Clindar brought the machine striding through the grass with its latest victim dangling across one metal arm. For the first time Yaan showed something akin to fear; but he relaxed at Bertrond's soothing words, though he continued to watch the advancing monster. It halted some distance away, and Bertrond walked forward to meet it. As he did so, the robot raised its arms and handed him the dead beast. He took it solemnly and carried it back to Yaan, staggering a little under the unaccustomed load.

Bertrond would have given a great deal to know just what Yaan was thinking as he accepted the gift. Was he trying to decide whether the robot was master or slave? Perhaps such conceptions as this were beyond his grasp: to him the robot might be merely another man, a hunter who was a friend of Bertrond.

Clindar's voice, slightly larger than life, came from the robot's speaker.

"It's astonishing how calmly he accepts us. Won't anything scare him?"

"You will keep judging him by your own standards," replied Bertrond. "Remember, his psychology is completely different, and much simpler. Now that he has confidence in me, anything that I accept won't worry him."

"I wonder if that will be true of all his race?" queried Altman. "It's hardly safe to judge by a single specimen. I want to see what happens when we send the robot into the village."

"Hello!" exclaimed Bertrond. *"That* surprised him. He's never met a person who could speak with two voices before."

"Do you think he'll guess the truth when he meets us?" said Clindar.

"No. The robot will be pure magic to him—but it won't be any more wonderful than fire and lightning and all the other forces he must already take for granted."

"Well, what's the next move?" asked Altman, a little impatiently. "Are you going to bring him to the ship, or will you go into the village first?"

Bertrond hesitated. "I'm anxious not to do too much too quickly. You know the accidents that have happened with strange races when that's been tried. I'll let him think this over, and when we get back tomorrow I'll try to persuade him to take the robot back to the village."

In the hidden ship, Clindar reactivated the robot and started it moving again. Like Altman, he was growing a little impatient of this excessive caution, but on all matters relating to alien life-forms Bertrond was the expert, and they had to obey his orders.

There were times now when he almost wished he were a robot himself, devoid of feelings or emotions, able to watch the fall of a leaf or the death agonies of a world with equal detachment . . .

The sun was low when Yaan heard the great voice crying from the jungle. He recognized it at once, despite its inhuman volume: it was the voice of his friend, and it was calling him.

In the echoing silence, the life of the village came to a stop. Even the children ceased their play: the only sound was the thin cry of a baby frightened by the sudden silence.

All eyes were upon Yaan as he walked swiftly to his hut and

grasped the spear that lay beside the entrance. The stockade would soon be closed against the prowlers of the night, but he did not hesitate as he stepped out into the lengthening shadows. He was passing through the gates when once again that mighty voice summoned him, and now it held a note of urgency that came clearly across all the barriers of language and culture.

The shining giant who spoke with many voices met him a little way from the village and beckoned him to follow. There was no sign of Bertrond. They walked for almost a mile before they saw him in the distance, standing not far from the river's edge and staring out across the dark, slowly moving waters.

He turned as Yaan approached, yet for a moment seemed unaware of his presence. Then he gave a gesture of dismissal to the shining one, who withdrew into the distance.

Yaan waited. He was patient and, though he could never have expressed it in words, contented. When he was with Bertrond he felt the first intimations of that selfless, utterly irrational devotion his race would not fully achieve for many ages.

It was a strange tableau. Here at the river's brink two men were standing. One was dressed in a closely-fitting uniform equipped with tiny, intricate mechanisms. The other was wearing the skin of an animal and was carrying a flint-tipped spear. Ten thousand generations lay between them, ten thousand generations and an immeasurable gulf of space. Yet they were both human. As she must do often in eternity, Nature had repeated one of her basic patterns.

Presently Bertrond began to speak, walking to and fro in short, quick steps as he did, and in his voice there was a trace of madness.

"It's all over, Yaan. I'd hoped that with our knowledge we could have brought you out of barbarism in a dozen generations, but now you will have to fight your way up from the jungle alone, and it may take you a million years to do so. I'm sorry—there's so much we could have done. Even now I wanted to stay here, but Altman and Clindar talk of duty, and I suppose that they are right. There is little enough that we can do, but our world is calling and we must not forsake it.

"I wish you could understand me, Yaan. I wish you knew what I was saying. I'm leaving you these tools: some of them you will discover how to use, though as likely as not in a generation they'll be lost or forgotten. See how this blade cuts: it will be ages before your world can make its like. And guard this well: when you press the button—look! If you use it sparingly, it will give you light for years, though sooner or later it will die. As for these other things— find what use for them you can.

"Here come the first stars, up there in the east. Do you ever look at the stars, Yaan? I wonder how long it will be before you have discovered what they are, and I wonder what will have happened to us by then. Those stars are our homes, Yaan, and we cannot save them. Many have died already, in explosions so vast that I can imagine them no more than you. In a hundred thousand of your years, the light of those funeral pyres will reach your world and set its peoples wondering. By then, perhaps, your race will be reaching for the stars. I wish I could warn you against the mistakes we made, and which now will cost us all that we have won.

"It is well for your people, Yaan, that your world is here at the frontier of the Universe. You may escape the doom that waits for us. One day, perhaps, your ships will go searching among the stars as we have done, and they may come upon the ruins of our worlds and wonder who we were. But they will never know that we met here by this river when your race was young.

"Here come my friends; they would give me no more time. Good-by, Yaan—use well the things I have left you. They are your world's greatest treasures."

Something huge, something that glittered in the starlight, was sliding down from the sky. It did not reach the ground, but came to rest a little way above the surface, and in utter silence a rectangle of light opened in its side. The shining giant appeared out of the night and stepped through the golden door. Bertrond followed, pausing for a moment at the threshold to wave back at Yaan. Then the darkness closed behind him.

No more swiftly than smoke drifts upward from a fire, the ship lifted away. When it was so small that Yaan felt he could hold it in his hands, it seemed to blur into a long line of light slanting upward into the stars. From the empty sky a peal of thunder echoed over the sleeping land; and Yaan knew at last that the gods were gone and would never come again.

For a long time he stood by the gently moving waters, and into his soul there came a sense of loss he was never to forget and never to understand. Then, carefully and reverently, he collected together the gifts that Bertrond had left.

Under the stars, the lonely figure walked homeward across a nameless land. Behind him the river flowed softly to the sea, winding through the fertile plains on which, more than a thousand centuries ahead, Yaan's descendants would build the great city they were to call Babylon.

In making this statement—which I do of my own free will—I wish first to make it perfectly clear that I am not in any way trying to gain sympathy, nor do I expect any mitigation of whatever sentence the Court may pronounce. I am writing this in an attempt to refute some of the lying reports broadcast over the prison radio and published in the papers I have been allowed to see. These have given an entirely false picture of the true cause of our defeat, and as the leader of my race's armed forces at the cessation of hostilities I feel it my duty to protest against such libels upon those who served under me.

I also hope that this statement may explain the reasons for the application I have twice made to the Court, and will now induce it to grant a favor for which I can see no possible grounds of refusal.

The ultimate cause of our failure was a simple one: despite all statements to the contrary, it was not due to lack of bravery on the part of our men, or to any fault of the Fleet's. We were defeated by one thing only—by the inferior science of our enemies. I repeat—by the *inferior* science of our enemies.

When the war opened we had no doubt of our ultimate victory. The combined fleets of our allies greatly exceeded in number and armament those which the enemy could muster against us, and in almost all branches of military science we were their superiors. We were sure that we could maintain this superiority. Our belief proved, alas, to be only too well founded.

At the opening of the war our main weapons were the long-range homing torpedo, dirigible ball-lightning and the various modifications of the Klydon beam. Every unit of the Fleet was equipped with these and though the enemy possessed similar weapons their installations were generally of lesser power. Moreover, we had behind us a far greater military Research Organization, and with this initial advantage we could not possibly lose.

The campaign proceeded according to plan until the Battle of the Five Suns. We won this, of course, but the opposition proved stronger than we had expected. It was realized that victory might be more difficult, and more delayed, than had first been imagined. A conference of supreme commanders was therefore called to discuss our future strategy.

Present for the first time at one of our war conferences was Professor-General Norden, the new Chief of the Research Staff, who had just been appointed to fill the gap left by the death of Malvar, our greatest scientist. Malvar's leadership had been responsible, more than any other single factor, for the efficiency and power of our weapons. His loss was a very serious blow, but no one doubted the brilliance of his successor—though many of us disputed the wisdom of appointing a theoretical scientist to fill a post of such vital importance. But we had been overruled.

I can well remember the impression Norden made at that conference. The military advisers were worried, and as usual turned to the scientists for help. Would it be possible to improve our existing weapons, they asked, so that our present advantage could be increased still further?

Norden's reply was quite unexpected. Malvar had often been asked such a question—and he had always done what we requested.

"Frankly, gentlemen," said Norden, "I doubt it. Our existing weapons have practically reached finality. I don't wish to criticize my predecessor, or the excellent work done by the Research Staff in the last few generations, but do you realize that there has been no basic change in armaments for over a century? It is, I am afraid, the result of a tradition that has become conservative. For too long, the Research Staff has devoted itself to perfecting old weapons instead of developing new ones. It is fortunate for us that our opponents have been no wiser: we cannot assume that this will always be so."

Norden's words left an uncomfortable impression, as he had no doubt intended. He quickly pressed home the attack.

"What we want are *new* weapons—weapons totally different from any that have been employed before. Such weapons can be made: it will take time, of course, but since assuming charge I have replaced some of the older scientists by young men and have directed research into several unexplored fields which show great promise. I believe, in fact, that a revolution in warfare may soon be upon us."

We were skeptical. There was a bombastic tone in Norden's voice that made us suspicious of his claims. We did not know, then, that he never promised anything that he had not already almost perfected in the laboratory. *In the laboratory*—that was the operative phrase.

Norden proved his case less than a month later, when he demonstrated the Sphere of Annihilation, which produced complete disintegration of matter over a radius of several hundred meters. We were intoxicated by the power of the new weapon, and were quite prepared to overlook one fundamental defect—the fact that it *was* a sphere and hence destroyed its rather complicated generating equipment at the instant of formation. This meant, of course, that it could not be used on warships but only on guided missiles, and a great program was started to convert all homing torpedoes to carry the new weapon. For the time being all further offensives were suspended.

We realize now that this was our first mistake. I still think that it was a natural one, for it seemed to us then that all our existing weapons had become obsolete overnight, and we already regarded them as almost primitive survivals. What we did not appreciate was the magnitude of the task we were attempting, and the length of time it would take to get the revolutionary super-weapon into battle. Nothing like this had happened for a hundred years and we had no previous experience to guide us.

The conversion problem proved far more difficult than anticipated. A new class of torpedo had to be designed, as the standard model was too small. This meant in turn that only the larger ships could launch the weapon, but we were prepared to accept this penalty. After six months, the heavy units of the Fleet were being equipped with the Sphere. Training maneuvers and tests had shown that it was operating satisfactorily and we were ready to take it into action. Norden was already being hailed as the architect of victory, and had half promised even more spectacular weapons.

Then two things happened. One of our battleships disappeared completely on a training flight, and an investigation showed that under certain conditions the ship's long-range radar could trigger the Sphere immediately it had been launched. The modification needed to overcome this defect was trivial, but it caused a delay of another month and was the source of much bad feeling between the naval staff and the scientists. We were ready for action again— when Norden announced that the radius of effectiveness of the Sphere had now been increased by ten, thus multiplying by a thousand the chances of destroying an enemy ship.

So the modifications started all over again, but everyone agreed that the delay would be worth it. Meanwhile, however, the enemy had been emboldened by the absence of further attacks and had made an unexpected onslaught. Our ships were short of torpedoes, since none had been coming from the factories, and were forced to retire. So we lost the systems of Kyrane and Floranus, and the planetary fortress of Rhamsandron.

It was an annoying but not a serious blow, for the recaptured systems had been unfriendly, and difficult to administer. We had no doubt that we could restore the position in the near future, as soon as the new weapon became operational.

These hopes were only partially fulfilled. When we renewed our offensive, we had to do so with fewer of the Spheres of Annihilation than had been planned, and this was one reason for our limited success. The other reason was more serious.

While we had been equipping as many of our ships as we could with the irresistible weapon, the enemy had been building feverishly. His ships were of the old pattern with the old weapons—but they now outnumbered ours. When we went into action, we found that the numbers ranged against us were often 100 per cent greater than expected, causing target confusion among the automatic weapons and resulting in higher losses than anticipated. The enemy losses were higher still, for once a Sphere had reached its objective, destruction was certain, but the balance had not swung as far in our favor as we had hoped.

Moreover, while the main fleets had been engaged, the enemy had launched a daring attack on the lightly held systems of Eriston,

Duranus, Carmanidora and Pharanidon—recapturing them all. We were thus faced with a threat only fifty light-years from our home planets.

There was much recrimination at the next meeting of the supreme commanders. Most of the complaints were addressed to Norden—Grand Admiral Taxaris in particular maintaining that thanks to our admittedly irresistible weapon we were now considerably worse off than before. We should, he claimed, have continued to build conventional ships, thus preventing the loss of our numerical superiority.

Norden was equally angry and called the naval staff ungrateful bunglers. But I could tell that he was worried—as indeed we all were—by the unexpected turn of events. He hinted that there might be a speedy way of remedying the situation.

We now know that Research had been working on the Battle Analyzer for many years, but at the time it came as a revelation to us and perhaps we were too easily swept off our feet. Norden's argument, also, was seductively convincing. What did it matter, he said, if the enemy had twice as many ships as we—if the efficiency of ours could be doubled or even trebled? For decades the limiting factor in warfare had been not mechanical but biological—it had become more and more difficult for any single mind, or group of minds, to cope with the rapidly changing complexities of battle in three-dimensional space. Norden's mathematicians had analyzed some of the classic engagements of the past, and had shown that even when we had been victorious we had often operated our units at much less than half of their theoretical efficiency.

The Battle Analyzer would change all this by replacing the operations staff with electronic calculators. The idea was not new, in theory, but until now it had been no more than a utopian dream. Many of us found it difficult to believe that it was still anything but a dream: after we had run through several very complex dummy battles, however, we were convinced.

It was decided to install the Analyzer in four of our heaviest ships, so that each of the main fleets could be equipped with one. At this stage, the trouble began—though we did not know it until later.

The Analyzer contained just short of a million vacuum tubes and needed a team of five hundred technicians to maintain and operate it. It was quite impossible to accommodate the extra staff aboard a battleship, so each of the four units had to be accompanied by a converted liner to carry the technicians not on duty. Installation was also a very slow and tedious business, but by gigantic efforts it was completed in six months.

Then, to our dismay, we were confronted by another crisis. Nearly five thousand highly skilled men had been selected to serve the Analyzers and had been given an intensive course at the Technical Training Schools. At the end of seven months, 10 per cent of them had had nervous breakdowns and only 40 per cent had qualified.

Once again, everyone started to blame everyone else. Norden, of course, said that the Research Staff could not be held responsible, and so incurred the enmity of the Personnel and Training Commands. It was finally decided that the only thing to do was to use two instead of four Analyzers and to bring the others into action as soon as men could be trained. There was little time to lose, for the enemy was still on the offensive and his morale was rising.

The first Analyzer fleet was ordered to recapture the system of Eriston. On the way, by one of the hazards of war, the liner carrying the technicians was struck by a roving mine. A warship would have survived, but the liner with its irreplaceable cargo was totally destroyed. So the operation had to be abandoned.

The other expedition was, at first, more successful. There was no doubt at all that the Analyzer fulfilled its designers' claims, and the enemy was heavily defeated in the first engagements. He withdrew, leaving us in possession of Saphran, Leucon and Hexanerax. But his Intelligence Staff must have noted the change in our tactics and the inexplicable presence of a liner in the heart of our battlefleet. It must have noted, also, that our first fleet had been accompanied by a similar ship—and had withdrawn when it had been destroyed.

In the next engagement, the enemy used his superior numbers to launch an overwhelming attack on the Analyzer ship and its unarmed consort. The attack was made without regard to losses—both ships were, of course, very heavily protected—and it succeeded. The result was the virtual decapitation of the Fleet, since an effectual transfer to the old operational methods proved impossible. We disengaged under heavy fire, and so lost all our gains and also the systems of Lormyia, Ismarnus, Beronis, Alphanidon and Sideneus.

At this stage, Grand Admiral Taxaris expressed his disapproval of Norden by committing suicide, and I assumed supreme command.

The situation was now both serious and infuriating. With stubborn conservatism and complete lack of imagination, the enemy continued to advance with his old-fashioned and inefficient but now vastly more numerous ships. It was galling to realize that if we had only continued building, without seeking new weapons, we would have been in a far more advantageous position. There were many acrimonious conferences at which Norden defended the scientists while everyone else blamed them for all that had happened. The difficulty was that Norden had proved every one of his claims: he had a perfect excuse for all the disasters that had occurred. And we could not now turn back—the search for an irresistible weapon must go on. At first it had been a luxury that would shorten the war. Now it was a necessity if we were to end it victoriously.

We were on the defensive, and so was Norden. He was more than ever determined to re-establish his prestige and that of the Research Staff. But we had been twice disappointed, and would not make the same mistake again. No doubt Norden's twenty thousand scientists would produce many further weapons: we would remain unimpressed.

We were wrong. The final weapon was something so fantastic that even now it seems difficult to believe that it ever existed. Its innocent, noncommittal name—The Exponential Field—gave no hint of its real potentialities. Some of Norden's mathematicians had discovered it during a piece of entirely theoretical research into the properties of space, and to everyone's great surprise their results were found to be physically realizable.

It seems very difficult to explain the operation of the Field to the layman. According to the technical description, it "produces an exponential condition of space, so that a finite distance in normal, linear space may become infinite in pseudo-space." Norden gave an analogy which some of us found useful. It was as if one took a flat disk of rubber—representing a region of normal space—and then pulled its center out to infinity. The circumference of the disk would be unaltered—but its "diameter" would be infinite. That was the sort of thing the generator of the Field did to the space around it.

As an example, suppose that a ship carrying the generator was surrounded by a ring of hostile machines. If it switched on the Field, *each* of the enemy ships would think that it—and the ships on the far side of the circle—had suddenly receded into nothingness. Yet the circumference of the circle would be the same as before: only the journey to the center would be of infinite duration, for as one proceeded, distances would appear to become greater and greater as the "scale" of space altered.

It was a nightmare condition, but a very useful one. Nothing could reach a ship carrying the Field: it might be englobed by an enemy fleet yet would be as inaccessible as if it were at the other side of the Universe. Against this, of course, it could not fight back without switching off the Field, but this still left it at a very great advantage, not only in defense but in offense. For a ship fitted with the Field could approach an enemy fleet undetected and suddenly appear in its midst.

This time there seemed to be no flaws in the new weapon. Needless to say, we looked for all the possible objections before we committed ourselves again. Fortunately the equipment was fairly simple and did not require a large operating staff. After much debate, we decided to rush it into production, for we realized that time was running short and the war was going against us. We had now lost about the whole of our initial gains and enemy forces had made several raids into our own solar system.

We managed to hold off the enemy while the Fleet was re-equipped and the new battle techniques were worked out. To use the Field operationally it was necessary to locate an enemy formation, set a course that would intercept it, and then switch on the generator for the calculated period of time. On releasing the Field again—if the calculations had been accurate—one would be in the enemy's midst and could do great damage during the resulting confusion, retreating by the same route when necessary.

The first trial maneuvers proved satisfactory and the equipment seemed quite reliable. Numerous mock attacks were made and the crews became accustomed to the new technique. I was on one of the test flights and can vividly remember my impressions as the Field was switched on. The ships around us seemed to dwindle as if on the surface of an expanding bubble: in an instant they had vanished completely. So had the stars—but presently we could see that the Galaxy was still visible as a faint band of light around the ship. The virtual radius of our pseudo-space was not really infinite, but some hundred thousand light-years, and so the distance to the farthest stars of our system had not been greatly increased—though the nearest had of course totally disappeared.

These training maneuvers, however, had to be cancelled before they were complete owing to a whole flock of minor technical troubles in various pieces of equipment, notably the communications circuits. These were annoying, but not important, though it was thought best to return to Base to clear them up.

At that moment the enemy made what was obviously intended to be a decisive attack against the fortress planet of Iton at the limits of our solar system. The Fleet had to go into battle before repairs could be made.

The enemy must have believed that we had mastered the secret of invisibility—as in a sense we had. Our ships appeared suddenly out of nowhere and inflicted tremendous damage—for a while. And then something quite baffling and inexplicable happened.

I was in command of the flagship *Hircania* when the trouble started. We had been operating as independent units, each against assigned objectives. Our detectors observed an enemy formation at medium range and the navigating officers measured its distance with great accuracy. We set course and switched on the generator.

The Exponential Field was released at the moment when we should have been passing through the center of the enemy group. To our consternation, we emerged into normal space at a distance of many hundred miles—and when we found the enemy, he had already found us. We retreated, and tried again. This time we were so far away from the enemy that he located us first.

Obviously, something was seriously wrong. We broke communicator silence and tried to contact the other ships of the Fleet to see if they had experienced the same trouble. Once again we failed —and this time the failure was beyond all reason, for the communication equipment appeared to be working perfectly. We could only assume, fantastic though it seemed, that the rest of the Fleet had been destroyed.

I do not wish to describe the scenes when the scattered units of the Fleet struggled back to Base. Our casualties had actually been negligible, but the ships were completely demoralized. Almost all had lost touch with one another and had found that their ranging equipment showed inexplicable errors. It was obvious that the Exponential Field was the cause of the troubles, despite the fact that they were only apparent when it was switched off.

The explanation came too late to do us any good, and Norden's final discomfiture was small consolation for the virtual loss of the war. As I have explained, the Field generators produced a radial distortion of space, distances appearing greater and greater as one approached the center of the artificial pseudo-space. When the Field was switched off, conditions returned to normal.

But not quite. It was never possible to restore the initial state *exactly*. Switching the Field on and off was equivalent to an elongation and contraction of the ship carrying the generator, but there was an hysteretic effect, as it were, and the initial condition was never quite reproducible, owing to all the thousands of electrical changes and movements of mass aboard the ship while the Field was on. These asymmetries and distortions were cumulative, and though they seldom amounted to more than a fraction of one per cent, that was quite enough. It meant that the precision ranging equipment and the tuned circuits in the communication apparatus were thrown completely out of adjustment. Any single ship could never detect the change—only when it compared its equipment with that of another vessel, or tried to communicate with it, could it tell what had happened.

It is impossible to describe the resultant chaos. Not a single component of one ship could be expected with certainty to work aboard another. The very nuts and bolts were no longer interchangeable, and the supply position became quite impossible. Given time, we might even have overcome these difficulties, but the enemy ships were already attacking in thousands with weapons which now seemed centuries behind those that we had invented. Our magnificent Fleet, crippled by our own science, fought on as best it could until it was overwhelmed and forced to surrender. The ships fitted with the Field were still invulnerable, but as fighting units they were almost helpless. Every time they switched on their generators to escape from enemy attack, the permanent distortion of their equipment increased. In a month, it was all over.

This is the true story of our defeat, which I give without prejudice to my defense before this Court. I make it, as I have said, to counteract the libels that have been circulating against the men who fought under me, and to show where the true blame for our misfortunes lay.

Finally, my request, which as the Court will now realize, I make in no frivolous manner and which I hope will therefore be granted.

The Court will be aware that the conditions under which we are housed and the constant surveillance to which we are subjected night and day are somewhat distressing. Yet I am not complaining of this: nor do I complain of the fact that shortage of accommodation has made it necessary to house us in pairs.

But I cannot be held responsible for my future actions if I am compelled any longer to share my cell with Professor Norden, late Chief of the Research Staff of my armed forces.

We were walking back through the woods when Kingman saw the gray squirrel. Our bag was a small but varied one —three grouse, four rabbits (one, I am sorry to say, an infant in arms) and a couple of pigeons. And contrary to certain dark forecasts, both the dogs were still alive.

The squirrel saw us at the same moment. It knew that it was marked for immediate execution as a result of the damage it had done to the trees on the estate, and perhaps it had lost close relatives to Kingman's gun. In three leaps it had reached the base of the nearest tree, and vanished behind it in a flicker of gray. We saw its face once more, appearing for a moment round the edge of its shield a dozen feet from the ground; but though we waited, with guns leveled hopefully at various branches, we never saw it again.

Kingman was very thoughtful as we walked back across the lawn to the magnificent old house. He said nothing as we handed our victims to the cook—who received them without much enthusiasm—and only emerged from his reverie when we were sitting in the smoking room and he remembered his duties as a host.

"That tree-rat," he said suddenly (he always called them "tree-rats," on the grounds that people were too sentimental to shoot the dear little squirrels), "it reminded me of a very peculiar experience that happened shortly before I retired. Very shortly indeed, in fact."

"I thought it would," said Carson dryly. I gave him a glare: he'd been in the Navy and had heard Kingman's stories before, but they were still new to me.

"Of course," Kingman remarked, slightly nettled, "if you'd rather I didn't . . ."

43

"Do go on," I said hastily. "You've made me curious. What connection there can possibly be between a gray squirrel and the Second Jovian War I can't imagine."

Kingman seemed mollified.

"I think I'd better change some names," he said thoughtfully, "but I won't alter the places. The story begins about a million kilometers sunward of Mars . . ."

K.15 was a military intelligence operative. It gave him considerable pain when unimaginative people called him a spy, but at the moment he had much more substantial grounds for complaint. For some days now a fast enemy cruiser had been coming up astern, and though it was flattering to have the undivided attention of such a fine ship and so many highly trained men, it was an honor that K.15 would willingly have forgone.

What made the situation doubly annoying was the fact that his friends would be meeting him off Mars in about twelve hours, aboard a ship quite capable of dealing with a mere cruiser—from which you will gather that K.15 was a person of some importance. Unfortunately, the most optimistic calculation showed that the pursuers would be within accurate gun range in six hours. In some six hours five minutes, therefore, K.15 was likely to occupy an extensive and still expanding volume of space.

There might just be time for him to land on Mars, but that would be one of the worst things he could do. It would certainly annoy the aggressively neutral Martians, and the political complications would be frightful. Moreover, if his friends *had* to come down to the planet to rescue him, it would cost them more than ten kilometers a second in fuel—most of their operational reserve.

He had only one advantage, and that a very dubious one. The commander of the cruiser might guess that he was heading for a rendezvous, but he would not know how close it was or how large was the ship that was coming to meet him. If he could keep alive for only twelve hours, he would be safe. The "if" was a somewhat considerable one.

K.15 looked moodily at his charts, wondering if it was worthwhile to burn the rest of his fuel in a final dash. But a dash to where? He would be completely helpless then, and the pursuing ship might still have enough in her tanks to catch him as he flashed outward into the empty darkness, beyond all hope of rescue—passing his friends as they came sunward at a relative speed so great that they could do nothing to save him.

With some people, the shorter the expectation of life, the more sluggish are the mental processes. They seem hypnotized by the approach of death, so resigned to their fate that they do nothing to avoid it. K.15, on the other hand, found that his mind worked better in such a desperate emergency. It began to work now as it had seldom done before.

Commander Smith—the name will do as well as any other—of the cruiser *Doradus* was not unduly surprised when K.15 began to decelerate. He had half expected the spy to land on Mars, on the principle that internment was better than annihilation, but when the plotting room brought the news that the little scout ship was heading for Phobos, he felt completely baffled. The inner moon was nothing but a jumble of rock some twenty kilometers across, and not even the economical Martians had ever found any use for it. K.15 must be pretty desperate if he thought it was going to be of any greater value to him.

The tiny scout had almost come to rest when the radar operator lost it against the mass of Phobos. During the braking maneuver, K.15 had squandered most of his lead and the *Doradus* was now only minutes away—though she was now beginning to decelerate lest she overrun him. The cruiser was scarcely three thousand kilometers from Phobos when she came to a complete halt: of K.15's ship, there was still no sign. It should be easily visible in the telescopes, but it was probably on the far side of the little moon.

It reappeared only a few minutes later, traveling under full thrust on a course directly away from the sun. It was accelerating at almost five gravities—and it had broken its radio silence. An automatic recorder was broadcasting over and over again this interesting message:

"I have landed on Phobos and am being attacked by a Z-class cruiser. Think I can hold out until you come, but hurry."

The message wasn't even in code, and it left Commander Smith a sorely puzzled man. The assumption that K.15 was still aboard the ship and that the whole thing was a ruse was just a little too naïve. But it might be a double-bluff: the message had obviously been left in plain language so that he would receive it and be duly confused. He could afford neither the time nor the fuel to chase the scout if K.15 really had landed. It was clear that reinforcements were on the way, and the sooner he left the vicinity the better. The phrase "Think I can hold out until you come" might be a piece of sheer impertinence, or it might mean that help was very near indeed.

Then K.15's ship stopped blasting. It had obviously exhausted its fuel, and was doing a little better than six kilometers a second away from the sun. K.15 *must* have landed, for his ship was now speeding helplessly out of the solar system. Commander Smith didn't like the message it was broadcasting, and guessed that it was running into the track of an approaching warship at some indefinite distance, but there was nothing to be done about that. The *Doradus* began to move toward Phobos, anxious to waste no time.

On the face of it, Commander Smith seemed the master of the situation. His ship was armed with a dozen heavy guided missiles and two turrets of electro-magnetic guns. Against him was one man in a space-suit, trapped on a moon only twenty kilometers across. It was not until Commander Smith had his first good look at Phobos, from a distance of less than a hundred kilometers, that he began to realize that, after all, K.15 might have a few cards up his sleeve.

To say that Phobos has a diameter of twenty kilometers, as the astronomy books invariably do, is highly misleading. The word "diameter" implies a degree of symmetry which Phobos most certainly lacks. Like those other lumps of cosmic slag, the asteroids, it is a shapeless mass of rock floating in space with, of course, no hint of an atmosphere and not much more gravity. It turns on its axis once every seven hours thirty-nine minutes, thus keeping the same face always to Mars—which is so close that appreciably less than half the planet is visible, the poles being below the curve of the horizon. Beyond this, there is very little more to be said about Phobos.

K.15 had no time to enjoy the beauty of the crescent world filling the sky above him. He had thrown all the equipment he could carry out of the airlock, set the controls, and jumped. As the little ship went flaming out toward the stars he watched it go with feelings he did not care to analyze. He had burned his boats with a vengeance, and he could only hope that the oncoming battleship would intercept the radio message as the empty vessel went racing by into nothingness. There was also a faint possibility that the enemy cruiser might go in pursuit, but that was rather too much to hope for.

He turned to examine his new home. The only light was the ocher radiance of Mars, since the sun was below the horizon, but that was quite sufficient for his purpose and he could see very well. He stood in the center of an irregular plain about two kilometers across, surrounded by low hills over which he could leap rather easily if he wished. There was a story he remembered reading long ago about a man who had accidentally jumped off Phobos: that wasn't quite possible—though it was on Deimos—as the escape velocity was still about ten meters a second. But unless he was careful, he might easily find himself at such a height that it would take hours to fall back to the surface—and that would be fatal. For K.15's plan was a simple one: he must remain as close to the surface of Phobos as possible—*and diametrically opposite the cruiser*. The *Doradus* could then fire all her armament against the twenty kilometers of rock, and he wouldn't even feel the concussion. There were only two serious dangers, and one of these did not worry him greatly.

To the layman, knowing nothing of the finer details of astronautics, the plan would have seemed quite suicidal. The *Doradus* was armed with the latest in ultra-scientific weapons: moreover, the twenty kilometers which separated her from her prey represented less than a second's flight at maximum speed. But Commander Smith knew better, and was already feeling rather unhappy. He realized, only too well, that of all the machines of transport man has ever invented, a cruiser of space is far and away the least maneuverable. It was a simple fact that K.15 could make half a dozen circuits of his little world while her commander was persuading the *Doradus* to make even one.

There is no need to go into technical details, but those who are still unconvinced might like to consider these elementary facts. A rocket-driven spaceship can, obviously, only accelerate along its major axis—that is, "forward." Any deviation from a straight course demands a physical turning of the ship, so that the motors can blast in another direction. Everyone knows that this is done by internal gyros or tangential steering jets, but very few people know just how long this simple maneuver takes. The average cruiser, fully fueled, has a mass of two or three thousand tons, which does not make for rapid footwork. But things are even worse than this, for it isn't the mass, but the moment of inertia that matters here—and since a cruiser is a long, thin object, its moment of inertia is slightly colossal. The sad fact remains (though it is seldom mentioned by astronautical engineers) that it takes a good ten minutes to rotate a spaceship through 180 degrees, with gyros of any reasonable size. Control jets aren't much quicker, and in any case their use is restricted because the rotation they produce is permanent and they are liable to leave the ship spinning like a slow-motion pinwheel, to the annoyance of all inside.

In the ordinary way, these disadvantages are not very grave. One has millions of kilometers and hundreds of hours in which to deal with such minor matters as a change in the ship's orientation. It is definitely against the rules to move in ten-kilometer radius circles, and the commander of the *Doradus* felt distinctly aggrieved. K.15 wasn't playing fair.

At the same moment that resourceful individual was taking stock of the situation, which might very well have been worse. He had reached the hills in three jumps and felt less naked than he had out in the open plain. The food and equipment he had taken from the ship he had hidden where he hoped he could find it again, but as his suit could keep him alive for over a day that was the least of his worries. The small packet that was the cause of all the trouble was still with him, in one of those numerous hiding places a well-designed space-suit affords.

There was an exhilarating loneliness about his mountain eyrie, even though he was not quite as lonely as he would have wished. Forever fixed in his sky, Mars was waning almost visibly as Phobos swept above the night side of the planet. He could just make out the lights of some of the Martian cities, gleaming pin-points marking the junctions of the invisible canals. All else was stars and silence and a line of jagged peaks so close it seemed he could almost touch them. Of the *Doradus* there was still no sign. She was presumably carrying out a careful telescopic examination of the sunlighted side of Phobos.

Mars was a very useful clock: when it was half full the sun would rise and, very probably, so would the *Doradus*. But she might approach from some quite unexpected quarter: she might even—and this was the one real danger—she might even have landed a search party.

This was the first possibility that had occurred to Commander Smith when he saw just what he was up against. Then he realized that the surface area of Phobos was over a thousand square kilometers and that he could not spare more than ten men from his crew to make a search of that jumbled wilderness. Also, K.15 would certainly be armed.

Considering the weapons which the *Doradus* carried, this last objection might seem singularly pointless. It was very far from being so. In the ordinary course of business, side-arms and other portable weapons are as much use to a space-cruiser as are cutlasses and crossbows. The *Doradus* happened, quite by chance—and against regulations at that—to carry one automatic pistol and a hundred rounds of ammunition. Any search party would therefore consist of a group of unarmed men looking for a well concealed and very desperate individual who could pick them off at his leisure. K.15 was breaking the rules again.

The terminator of Mars was now a perfectly straight line, and at almost the same moment the sun came up, not so much like thunder as like a salvo of atomic bombs. K.15 adjusted the filters of his visor and decided to move. It was safer to stay out of the sunlight, not only because here he was less likely to be detected in the shadow but also because his eyes would be much more sensitive there. He had only a pair of binoculars to help him, whereas the *Doradus* would carry an electronic telescope of twenty centimeters aperture at least.

It would be best, K.15 decided, to locate the cruiser if he could. It might be a rash thing to do, but he would feel much happier when he knew exactly where she was and could watch her movements. He could then keep just below the horizon, and the glare of the rockets would give him ample warning of any impending move. Cautiously launching himself along an almost horizontal trajectory, he began the circumnavigation of his world.

The narrowing crescent of Mars sank below the horizon until only one vast horn reared itself enigmatically against the stars. K.15 began to feel worried: there was still no sign of the *Doradus*. But this was hardly surprising, for she was painted black as night and might be a good hundred kilometers away in space. He stopped, wondering if he had done the right thing after all. Then he noticed that something quite large was eclipsing the stars almost vertically overhead, and was moving swiftly even as he watched. His heart stopped for a moment: then he was himself again, analyzing the situation and trying to discover how he had made so disastrous a mistake.

It was some time before he realized that the black shadow slipping across the sky was not the cruiser at all, but something almost equally deadly. It was far smaller, and far nearer, than he had at first thought. The *Doradus* had sent her television-homing guided missiles to look for him.

This was the second danger he had feared, and there was nothing he could do about it except to remain as inconspicuous as possible. The *Doradus* now had many eyes searching for him, but these auxiliaries had very severe limitations. They had been built to look for sunlit spaceships against a background of stars, not to search for a man hiding in a dark jungle of rock. The definition of their television systems was low, and they could only see in the forward direction.

There were rather more men on the chessboard now, and the game was a little deadlier, but his was still the advantage.

The torpedo vanished into the night sky. As it was traveling on a nearly straight course in this low gravitational field, it would soon be leaving Phobos behind, and K.15 waited for what he knew must happen. A few minutes later, he saw a brief stabbing of rocket exhausts and guessed that the projectile was swinging slowly back on its course. At almost the same moment he saw another flare far away in the opposite quarter of the sky, and wondered just how many of these infernal machines were in action. From what he knew of Z-class cruisers—which was a good deal more than he should— there were four missile-control channels, and they were probably all in use.

He was suddenly struck by an idea so brilliant that he was quite sure it couldn't possibly work. The radio on his suit was a tunable one, covering an unusually wide band, and somewhere not far away the *Doradus* was pumping out power on everything from a thousand megacycles upward. He switched on the receiver and began to explore.

It came in quickly—the raucous whine of a pulse transmitter

not far away. He was probably only picking up a sub-harmonic, but that was quite good enough. It D/F'ed sharply, and for the first time K.15 allowed himself to make long-range plans about the future. The *Doradus* had betrayed herself: as long as she operated her missiles, he would know exactly where she was.

He moved cautiously forward toward the transmitter. To his surprise the signal faded, then increased sharply again. This puzzled him until he realized that he must be moving through a diffraction zone. Its width might have told him something useful if he had been a good enough physicist, but he couldn't imagine what.

The *Doradus* was hanging about five kilometers above the surface, in full sunlight. Her "non-reflecting" paint was overdue for renewal, and K.15 could see her clearly. As he was still in darkness, and the shadow line was moving away from him, he decided that he was as safe here as anywhere. He settled down comfortably so that he could just see the cruiser and waited, feeling fairly certain that none of the guided projectiles would come so near the ship. By now, he calculated, the commander of the *Doradus* must be getting pretty mad. He was perfectly correct.

After an hour, the cruiser began to heave herself round with all the grace of a bogged hippopotamus. K.15 guessed what was happening. Commander Smith was going to have a look at the antipodes, and was preparing for the perilous fifty-kilometer journey. He watched very carefully to see the orientation the ship was adopting, and when she came to rest again was relieved to see that she was almost broadside on to him. Then, with a series of jerks that could not have been very enjoyable aboard, the cruiser began to move down to the horizon. K.15 followed her at a comfortable walking pace—if one could use the phrase—reflecting that this was a feat very few people had ever performed. He was particularly careful not to overtake her on one of his kilometer-long glides, and kept a close watch for any missiles that might be coming up astern.

It took the *Doradus* nearly an hour to cover the fifty kilometers. This, as K.15 amused himself by calculating, represented considerably less than a thousandth of her normal speed. Once she found herself going off into space at a tangent, and rather than waste time turning end over end again fired off a salvo of shells to reduce speed. But she made it at last, and K.15 settled down for another vigil, wedged between two rocks where he could just see the cruiser and he was quite sure she couldn't see him. It occurred to him that by this time Commander Smith might have grave doubts as to whether he really was on Phobos at all, and he felt like firing off a signal flare to reassure him. However, he resisted the temptation.

There would be little point in describing the events of the next ten hours, since they differed in no important detail from those that had gone before. The *Doradus* made three other moves, and K.15 stalked her with the care of a big-game hunter following the spoor of some elephantine beast. Once, when she would have led him out into full sunlight, he let her fall below the horizon until he could only just pick up her signals. But most of the time he kept her just visible, usually low down behind some convenient hill.

Once a torpedo exploded some kilometers away, and K.15 guessed that some exasperated operator had seen a shadow he didn't like—or else that a technician had forgotten to switch off a proximity fuse. Otherwise nothing happened to enliven the proceedings: in fact, the whole affair was becoming rather boring. He almost welcomed the sight of an occasional guided missile drifting inquisitively overhead, for he did not believe that they could see him if he remained motionless and in reasonable cover. If he could have stayed on the part of Phobos exactly opposite the cruiser he would have been safe even from these, he realized, since the ship would have no control there in the moon's radio-shadow. But he could think of no reliable way in which he could be sure of staying in the safety zone if the cruiser moved again.

The end came very abruptly. There was a sudden blast of steering jets, and the cruiser's main drive burst forth in all its power and splendor. In seconds the *Doradus* was shrinking sunward, free at last, thankful to leave, even in defeat, this miserable lump of rock that had so annoyingly balked her of her legitimate prey. K.15 knew what had happened, and a great sense of peace and relaxation swept over him. In the radar room of the cruiser, someone had seen an echo of disconcerting amplitude approaching with altogether excessive speed. K.15 now had only to switch on his suit beacon and to wait. He could even afford the luxury of a cigarette.

"Quite an interesting story," I said, "and I see now how it ties up with that squirrel. But it does raise one or two queries in my mind."

"Indeed?" said Rupert Kingman politely.

I always like to get to the bottom of things, and I knew that my host had played a part in the Jovian War about which he very seldom spoke. I decided to risk a long shot in the dark.

"May I ask how you happen to know so much about this unorthodox military engagement? It isn't possible, is it, that *you* were K.15?"

There was an odd sort of strangling noise from Carson. Then Kingman said, quite calmly: "No, I wasn't."

He got to his feet and went off toward the gun room.

"If you'll excuse me a moment, I'm going to have another shot at that tree-rat. Maybe I'll get him this time." Then he was gone.

Carson looked at me as if to say: "This is another house you'll never be invited to again." When our host was out of earshot he remarked in a coldly cynical voice:

"You've done it. What did you have to say that for?"

"Well, it seemed a safe guess. How else could he have known all that?"

"As a matter of fact, I believe he met K.15 after the War: they must have had an interesting conversation together. But I thought you knew that Rupert was retired from the service with only the rank of lieutenant commander. The Court of Inquiry could never see his point of view. After all, it just wasn't reasonable that the commander of the fastest ship in the Fleet couldn't catch a man in a space-suit."

No one could remember when the tribe had begun its long journey. The land of great rolling plains that had been its first home was now no more than a half-forgotten dream.

For many years Shann and his people had been fleeing through a country of low hills and sparkling lakes, and now the mountains lay ahead. This summer they must cross them to the southern lands. There was little time to lose. The white terror that had come down from the Poles, grinding continents to dust and freezing the very air before it, was less than a day's march behind.

Shann wondered if the glaciers could climb the mountains ahead, and within his heart he dared to kindle a little flame of hope. This might prove a barrier against which even the remorseless ice would batter in vain. In the southern lands of which the legends spoke, his people might find refuge at last.

It took weeks to discover a pass through which the tribe and the animals could travel. When midsummer came, they had camped in a lonely valley where the air was thin and the stars shone with a brilliance no one had ever seen before.

The summer was waning when Shann took his two sons and went ahead to explore the way. For three days they climbed, and for three nights slept as best they could on the freezing rocks, and on the fourth morning there was nothing ahead but a gentle rise to a cairn of gray stones built by other travelers, centuries ago.

Shann felt himself trembling, and not with cold, as they walked toward the little pyramid of stones. His sons had fallen behind. No one spoke, for too much was at stake. In a little while they would know if all their hopes had been betrayed.

54

To east and west, the wall of mountains curved away as if embracing the land beneath. Below lay endless miles of undulating plain, with a great river swinging across it in tremendous loops. It was a fertile land; one in which the tribe could raise crops knowing that there would be no need to flee before the harvest came.

Then Shann lifted his eyes to the south, and saw the doom of all his hopes. For there at the edge of the world glimmered that deadly light he had seen so often to the north—the glint of ice below the horizon.

There was no way forward. Through all the years of flight, the glaciers from the south had been advancing to meet them. Soon they would be crushed beneath the moving walls of ice . . .

Southern glaciers did not reach the mountains until a generation later. In that last summer the sons of Shann carried the sacred treasures of the tribe to the lonely cairn overlooking the plain. The ice that had once gleamed below the horizon was now almost at their feet. By spring it would be splintering against the mountain walls.

No one understood the treasures now. They were from a past too distant for the understanding of any man alive. Their origins were lost in the mists that surrounded the Golden Age, and how they had come at last into the possession of this wandering tribe was a story that now would never be told. For it was the story of a civilization that had passed beyond recall.

Once, all these pitiful relics had been treasured for some good reason, and now they had become sacred though their meaning had long been lost. The print in the old books had faded centuries ago though much of the lettering was still visible—if there had been any to read it. But many generations had passed since anyone had had a use for a set of seven-figure logarithms, an atlas of the world, and the score of Sibelius' Seventh Symphony printed, according to the flyleaf, by H. K. Chu and Sons, at the City of Pekin in the year 2371 A.D.

The old books were placed reverently in the little crypt that had been made to receive them. There followed a motley collection of fragments—gold and platinum coins, a broken telephoto lens, a watch, a cold-light lamp, a microphone, the cutter from an electric

razor, some midget radio tubes, the flotsam that had been left behind when the great tide of civilization had ebbed forever.

All these treasures were carefully stowed away in their resting
place. Then came three more relics, the most sacred of all because
the least understood.

The first was a strangely shaped piece of metal, showing the
coloration of intense heat. It was, in its way, the most pathetic of
all these symbols from the past, for it told of man's greatest achievement and of the future he might have known. The mahogany stand
on which it was mounted bore a silver plate with the inscription:

Auxiliary Igniter from Starboard Jet
Spaceship "Morning Star"
Earth-Moon, A.D. 1985

Next followed another miracle of the ancient science—a sphere
of transparent plastic with strangely shaped pieces of metal im-
bedded in it. At its center was a tiny capsule of synthetic radio-
element, surrounded by the converting screens that shifted its
radiation far down the spectrum. As long as the material remained
active, the sphere would be a tiny radio transmitter, broadcasting
power in all directions. Only a few of these spheres had ever been
made. They had been designed as perpetual beacons to mark the
orbits of the asteroids. But man had never reached the asteroids
and the beacons had never been used.

Last of all was a flat, circular tin, wide in comparison with its
depth. It was heavily sealed, and rattled when shaken. The tribal
lore predicted that disaster would follow if it was ever opened, and
no one knew that it held one of the great works of art of nearly a
thousand years before.

The work was finished. The two men rolled the stones back
into place and slowly began to descend the mountainside. Even to
the last, man had given some thought to the future and had tried
to preserve something for posterity.

That winter the great waves of ice began their first assault on
the mountains, attacking from north and south. The foothills were
overwhelmed in the first onslaught, and the glaciers ground them
into dust. But the mountains stood firm, and when the summer
came the ice retreated for a while.

So, winter after winter, the battle continued, and the roar of the avalanches, the grinding of rock and the explosions of splintering ice filled the air with tumult. No war of man's had been fiercer than this, and even man's battles had not quite engulfed the globe as this had done.

At last the tidal waves of ice began to subside and to creep slowly down the flanks of the mountains they had never quite subdued. The valleys and passes were still firmly in their grip. It was stalemate. The glaciers had met their match, but their defeat was too late to be of any use to man.

So the centuries passed, and presently there happened something that must occur once at least in the history of every world in the universe, no matter how remote and lonely it may be.

The ship from Venus came five thousand years too late, but its crew knew nothing of this. While still many millions of miles away, the telescopes had seen the great shroud of ice that made Earth the most brilliant object in the sky next to the sun itself.

Here and there the dazzling sheet was marred by black specks that revealed the presence of almost buried mountains. That was all. The rolling oceans, the plains and forests, the deserts and lakes —all that had been the world of man was sealed beneath the ice, perhaps forever.

The ship closed in to Earth and established an orbit less than a thousand miles away. For five days it circled the planet, while cameras recorded all that was left to see and a hundred instruments gathered information that would give the Venusian scientists many years of work.

An actual landing was not intended. There seemed little purpose in it. But on the sixth day the picture changed. A panoramic monitor, driven to the limit of its amplification, detected the dying radiation of the five-thousand-year-old beacon. Through all the centuries, it had been sending out its signals with ever-failing strength as its radioactive heart steadily weakened.

The monitor locked on the beacon frequency. In the control room, a bell clamored for attention. A little later, the Venusian ship broke free from its orbit and slanted down toward Earth, toward a range of mountains that still towered proudly above the ice, and to a cairn of gray stones that the years had scarcely touched. . . .

The great disk of the sun blazed fiercely in a sky no longer veiled with mist, for the clouds that had once hidden Venus had now completely gone. Whatever force had caused the change in the sun's radiation had doomed one civilization, but had given birth to another. Less than five thousand years before, the half-savage people of Venus had seen sun and stars for the first time. Just as the science of Earth had begun with astronomy, so had that of Venus, and on the warm, rich world that man had never seen progress had been incredibly rapid.

Perhaps the Venusians had been lucky. They never knew the Dark Age that held man enchained for a thousand years. They missed the long detour into chemistry and mechanics but came at once to the more fundamental laws of radiation physics. In the time that man had taken to progress from the Pyramids to the rocket-propelled spaceship, the Venusians had passed from the discovery of agriculture to antigravity itself—the ultimate secret that man had never learned.

The warm ocean that still bore most of the young planet's life rolled its breakers languidly against the sandy shore. So new was this continent that the very sands were coarse and gritty. There had not yet been time enough for the sea to wear them smooth.

The scientists lay half in the water, their beautiful reptilian bodies gleaming in the sunlight. The greatest minds of Venus had gathered on this shore from all the islands of the planet. What they were going to hear they did not know, except that it concerned the Third World and the mysterious race that had peopled it before the coming of the ice.

The Historian was standing on the land, for the instruments he wished to use had no love of water. By his side was a large machine which attracted many curious glances from his colleagues. It was clearly concerned with optics, for a lens system projected from it toward a screen of white material a dozen yards away.

The Historian began to speak. Briefly he recapitulated what little had been discovered concerning the Third Planet and its people.

He mentioned the centuries of fruitless research that had failed to interpret a single word of the writings of Earth. The planet had been inhabited by a race of great technical ability. That, at least, was proved by the few pieces of machinery that had been found in the cairn upon the mountain.

"We do not know why so advanced a civilization came to an end," he observed. "Almost certainly, it had sufficient knowledge to survive an Ice Age. There must have been some other factor of which we know nothing. Possibly disease or racial degeneration may have been responsible. It has even been suggested that the tribal conflicts endemic to our own species in prehistoric times may have continued on the Third Planet after the coming of technology.

"Some philosophers maintain that knowledge of machinery does not necessarily imply a high degree of civilization, and it is theoretically possible to have wars in a society possessing mechanical power, flight, and even radio. Such a conception is alien to our thoughts, but we must admit its possibility. It would certainly account for the downfall of the lost race.

"It has always been assumed that we should never know anything of the physical form of the creatures who lived on Planet Three. For centuries our artists have been depicting scenes from the history of the dead world, peopling it with all manner of fantastic beings. Most of these creations have resembled us more or less closely, though it has often been pointed out that because *we* are reptiles it does not follow that all intelligent life must necessarily be reptilian.

"We now know the answer to one of the most baffling problems of history. At last, after hundreds of years of research, we have discovered the exact form and nature of the ruling life on the Third Planet."

There was a murmur of astonishment from the assembled scientists. Some were so taken aback that they disappeared for a while into the comfort of the ocean, as all Venusians were apt to do in moments of stress. The Historian waited until his colleagues reemerged into the element they so disliked. He himself was quite comfortable, thanks to the tiny sprays that were continually playing over his body. With their help he could live on land for many hours before having to return to the ocean.

The excitement slowly subsided and the lecturer continued:

"One of the most puzzling of the objects found on Planet Three was a flat metal container holding a great length of transparent plastic material, perforated at the edges and wound tightly into a spool. This transparent tape at first seemed quite featureless, but an examination with the new subelectronic microscope has shown that this is not the case. Along the surface of the material, invisible to our eyes but perfectly clear under the correct radiation, are literally thousands of tiny pictures. It is believed that they were imprinted on the material by some chemical means, and have faded with the passage of time.

"These pictures apparently form a record of life as it was on the Third Planet at the height of its civilization. They are not independent. Consecutive pictures are almost identical, differing only in the detail of movement. The purpose of such a record is obvious. It is only necessary to project the scenes in rapid succession to give an illusion of continuous movement. We have made a machine to do this, and I have here an exact reproduction of the picture sequence.

"The scenes you are now going to witness take us back many thousands of years, to the great days of our sister planet. They show a complex civilization, many of whose activities we can only dimly understand. Life seems to have been very violent and energetic, and much that you will see is quite baffling.

"It is clear that the Third Planet was inhabited by a number of different species, none of them reptilian. That is a blow to our pride, but the conclusion is inescapable. The dominant type of life appears to have been a two-armed biped. It walked upright and covered its body with some flexible material, possibly for protection against the cold, since even before the Ice Age the planet was at a much lower temperature than our own world. But I will not try your patience any further. You will now see the record of which I have been speaking."

A brilliant light flashed from the projector. There was a gentle whirring, and on the screen appeared hundreds of strange beings moving rather jerkily to and fro. The picture expanded to embrace one of the creatures, and the scientists could see that the Historian's description had been correct.

The creature possessed two eyes, set rather close together, but the other facial adornments were a little obscure. There was a large orifice in the lower portion of the head that was continually opening and closing. Possibly it had something to do with the creature's breathing.

The scientists watched spellbound as the strange being became involved in a series of fantastic adventures. There was an incredibly violent conflict with another, slightly different creature. It seemed certain that they must both be killed, but when it was all over neither seemed any the worse.

Then came a furious drive over miles of country in a four-wheeled mechanical device which was capable of extraordinary feats of locomotion. The ride ended in a city packed with other vehicles moving in all directions at breathtaking speeds. No one was surprised to see two of the machines meet head-on with devastating results.

After that, events became even more complicated. It was now quite obvious that it would take many years of research to analyze and understand all that was happening. It was also clear that the record was a work of art, somewhat stylized, rather than an exact reproduction of life as it actually had been on the Third Planet.

Most of the scientists felt themselves completely dazed when the sequence of pictures came to an end. There was a final flurry of motion, in which the creature that had been the center of interest became involved in some tremendous but incomprehensible catastrophe. The picture contracted to a circle, centered on the creature's head.

The last scene of all was an expanded view of its face, obviously expressing some powerful emotion. But whether it was rage, grief, defiance, resignation or some other feeling could not be guessed. The picture vanished. For a moment some lettering appeared on the screen, then it was all over.

For several minutes there was complete silence, save for the lapping of the waves upon the sand. The scientists were too stunned to speak. The fleeting glimpse of Earth's civilization had had a shattering effect on their minds. Then little groups began to start talking together, first in whispers and then more and more loudly as the implications of what they had seen became clearer. Presently the Historian called for attention and addressed the meeting again.

"We are now planning," he said, "a vast program of research to extract all available knowledge from this record. Thousands of copies are being made for distribution to all workers. You will appreciate the problems involved. The psychologists in particular have an immense task confronting them.

"But I do not doubt that we shall succeed. In another generation, who can say what we may not have learned of this wonderful race? Before we leave, let us look again at our remote cousins, whose wisdom may have surpassed our own but of whom so little has survived."

Once more the final picture flashed on the screen, motionless this time, for the projector had been stopped. With something like awe, the scientists gazed at the still figure from the past, while in turn the little biped stared back at them with its characteristic expression of arrogant bad temper.

For the rest of time it would symbolize the human race. The psychologists of Venus would analyze its actions and watch its every movement until they could reconstruct its mind. Thousands of books would be written about it. Intricate philosophies would be contrived to account for its behavior.

But all this labor, all this research, would be utterly in vain. Perhaps the proud and lonely figure on the screen was smiling sardonically at the scientists who were starting on their age-long fruitless quest.

Its secret would be safe as long as the universe endured, for no one now would ever read the lost language of Earth. Millions of times in the ages to come those last few words would flash across the screen, and none could ever guess their meaning:

A Walt Disney Production.

✶ "IF I FORGET THEE, OH EARTH . . ."

When Marvin was ten years old, his father took him through the long, echoing corridors that led up through Administration and Power, until at last they came to the uppermost levels of all and were among the swiftly growing vegetation of the Farmlands. Marvin liked it here: it was fun watching the great, slender plants creeping with almost visible eagerness toward the sunlight as it filtered down through the plastic domes to meet them. The smell of life was everywhere, awakening inexpressible longings in his heart: no longer was he breathing the dry, cool air of the residential levels, purged of all smells but the faint tang of ozone. He wished he could stay here for a little while, but Father would not let him. They went onward until they had reached the entrance to the Observatory, which he had never visited: but they did not stop, and Marvin knew with a sense of rising excitement that there could be only one goal left. For the first time in his life, he was going Outside.

There were a dozen of the surface vehicles, with their wide balloon tires and pressurized cabins, in the great servicing chamber. His father must have been expected, for they were led at once to the little scout car waiting by the huge circular door of the airlock. Tense with expectancy, Marvin settled himself down in the cramped cabin while his father started the motor and checked the controls. The inner door of the lock slid open and then closed behind them: he heard the roar of the great air pumps fade slowly away as the pressure dropped to zero. Then the "Vacuum" sign flashed on, the outer door parted, and before Marvin lay the land which he had never yet entered.

He had seen it in photographs, of course: he had watched it imaged on television screens a hundred times. But now it was lying all around him, burning beneath the fierce sun that crawled so slowly across the jet-black sky. He stared into the west, away from the blinding splendor of the sun—and there were the stars, as he had been told but had never quite believed. He gazed at them for a long time, marveling that anything could be so bright and yet so tiny. They were intense unscintillating points, and suddenly he remembered a rhyme he had once read in one of his father's books:

> Twinkle, twinkle, little star,
> How I wonder what you are.

Well, *he* knew what the stars were. Whoever asked that question must have been very stupid. And what did they mean by "twinkle"? You could see at a glance that all the stars shone with the same steady, unwavering light. He abandoned the puzzle and turned his attention to the landscape around him.

They were racing across a level plain at almost a hundred miles an hour, the great balloon tires sending up little spurts of dust behind them. There was no sign of the Colony: in the few minutes while he had been gazing at the stars, its domes and radio towers had fallen below the horizon. Yet there were other indications of man's presence, for about a mile ahead Marvin could see the curiously shaped structures clustering round the head of a mine. Now and then a puff of vapor would emerge from a squat smokestack and would instantly disperse.

They were past the mine in a moment: Father was driving with a reckless and exhilarating skill as if—it was a strange thought to come into a child's mind—he were trying to escape from something. In a few minutes they had reached the edge of the plateau on which the Colony had been built. The ground fell sharply away beneath them in a dizzying slope whose lower stretches were lost in shadow. Ahead, as far as the eye could reach, was a jumbled wasteland of craters, mountain ranges, and ravines. The crests of the mountains, catching the low sun, burned like islands of fire in a sea of darkness: and above them the stars still shone as steadfastly as ever.

There could be no way forward—yet there was. Marvin clenched his fists as the car edged over the slope and started the long descent. Then he saw the barely visible track leading down the mountainside, and relaxed a little. Other men, it seemed, had gone this way before.

Night fell with a shocking abruptness as they crossed the shadow line and the sun dropped below the crest of the plateau. The twin searchlights sprang into life, casting blue-white bands on the rocks ahead, so that there was scarcely need to check their speed. For hours they drove through valleys and past the foot of mountains whose peaks seemed to comb the stars, and sometimes they emerged for a moment into the sunlight as they climbed over higher ground.

And now on the right was a wrinkled, dusty plain, and on the left, its ramparts and terraces rising mile after mile into the sky, was a wall of mountains that marched into the distance until its peaks sank from sight below the rim of the world. There was no sign that men had ever explored this land, but once they passed the skeleton of a crashed rocket, and beside it a stone cairn surmounted by a metal cross.

It seemed to Marvin that the mountains stretched on forever: but at last, many hours later, the range ended in a towering, precipitous headland that rose steeply from a cluster of little hills. They drove down into a shallow valley that curved in a great arc toward the far side of the mountains: and as they did so, Marvin slowly realized that something very strange was happening in the land ahead.

The sun was now low behind the hills on the right: the valley before them should be in total darkness. Yet it was awash with a cold white radiance that came spilling over the crags beneath which they were driving. Then, suddenly, they were out in the open plain, and the source of the light lay before them in all its glory.

It was very quiet in the little cabin now that the motors had stopped. The only sound was the faint whisper of the oxygen feed and an occasional metallic crepitation as the outer walls of the vehicle radiated away their heat. For no warmth at all came from the great silver crescent that floated low above the far horizon and flooded all this land with pearly light. It was so brilliant that minutes passed before Marvin could accept its challenge and look steadfastly into its glare, but at last he could discern the outlines of continents, the hazy border of the atmosphere, and the white islands of cloud.

And even at this distance, he could see the glitter of sunlight on the polar ice.

It was beautiful, and it called to his heart across the abyss of space. There in that shining crescent were all the wonders that he had never known—the hues of sunset skies, the moaning of the sea on pebbled shores, the patter of falling rain, the unhurried benison of snow. These and a thousand others should have been his rightful heritage, but he knew them only from the books and ancient records, and the thought filled him with the anguish of exile.

Why could they not return? It seemed so peaceful beneath those lines of marching cloud. Then Marvin, his eyes no longer blinded by the glare, saw that the portion of the disk that should have been in darkness was gleaming faintly with an evil phosphorescence: and he remembered. He was looking upon the funeral pyre of a world —upon the radioactive aftermath of Armageddon. Across a quarter of a million miles of space, the glow of dying atoms was still visible, a perennial reminder of the ruinous past. It would be centuries yet before that deadly glow died from the rocks and life could return again to fill that silent, empty world.

And now Father began to speak, telling Marvin the story which until this moment had meant no more to him than the fairy tales he had once been told. There were many things he could not understand: it was impossible for him to picture the glowing, multi-colored pattern of life on the planet he had never seen. Nor could he comprehend the forces that had destroyed it in the end, leaving the Colony, preserved by its isolation, as the sole survivor. Yet he could share the agony of those final days, when the Colony had learned at last that never again would the supply ships come flaming down through the stars with gifts from home. One by one the radio stations had ceased to call: on the shadowed globe the lights of the cities had dimmed and died, and they were alone at last, as no men had ever been alone before, carrying in their hands the future of the race.

Then had followed the years of despair, and the long-drawn battle for survival in this fierce and hostile world. That battle had been won, though barely: this little oasis of life was safe against the worst that Nature could do. But unless there was a goal, a future toward which it could work, the Colony would lose the will to live, and neither machines nor skill nor science could save it then.

So, at last, Marvin understood the purpose of this pilgrimage. He would never walk beside the rivers of that lost and legendary world, or listen to the thunder raging above its softly rounded hills. Yet one day—how far ahead?—his children's children would return to claim their heritage. The winds and the rains would scour the poisons from the burning lands and carry them to the sea, and in the depths of the sea they would waste their venom until they could harm no living things. Then the great ships that were still waiting here on the silent, dusty plains could lift once more into space, along the road that led to home.

That was the dream: and one day, Marvin knew with a sudden flash of insight, he would pass it on to his own son, here at this same spot with the mountains behind him and the silver light from the sky streaming into his face.

He did not look back as they began the homeward journey. He could not bear to see the cold glory of the crescent Earth fade from the rocks around him, as he went to rejoin his people in their long exile.

Grant was writing up the *Star Queen's* log when
he heard the cabin door opening behind him. He didn't bother to
look round—it was hardly necessary for there was only one other
man aboard the ship. But when nothing happened, and when
McNeil neither spoke nor came into the room, the long silence
finally roused Grant's curiosity and he swung the seat round in its
gimbals.

McNeil was just standing in the doorway, looking as if he had
seen a ghost. The trite metaphor flashed into Grant's mind instantly.
He did not know for a moment how near the truth it was. In a
sense McNeil *had* seen a ghost—the most terrifying of all ghosts
—his own.

"What's the matter?" said Grant angrily. "You sick or something?"

The engineer shook his head. Grant noticed the little beads of
sweat that broke away from his forehead and went glittering across
the room on their perfectly straight trajectories. His throat muscles
moved, but for a while no sound came. It looked as though he was
going to cry.

"We're done for," he whispered at last. "Oxygen reserve's
gone."

Then he did cry. He looked like a flabby doll, slowly collapsing
on itself. He couldn't fall, for there was no gravity, so he just folded
up in mid-air.

Grant said nothing. Quite unconsciously he rammed his
smoldering cigarette into the ash tray, grinding it viciously until the
last tiny spark had died. Already the air seemed to be thickening

around him as the oldest terror of the spaceways gripped him by the throat.

He slowly loosed the elastic straps which, while he was seated, gave some illusion of weight, and with an automatic skill launched himself toward the doorway. McNeil did not offer to follow. Even making every allowance for the shock he had undergone, Grant felt that he was behaving very badly. He gave the engineer an angry cuff as he passed and told him to snap out of it.

The hold was a large hemispherical room with a thick central column which carried the controls and cabling to the other half of the dumbbell-shaped spaceship a hundred meters away. It was packed with crates and boxes arranged in a surrealistic three-dimensional array that made very few concessions to gravity.

But even if the cargo had suddenly vanished Grant would scarcely have noticed. He had eyes only for the big oxygen tank, taller than himself, which was bolted against the wall near the inner door of the airlock.

It was just as he had last seen it, gleaming with aluminum paint, and the metal sides still held the faint touch of coldness that gave the only hint of the contents. All the piping seemed in perfect condition. There was no sign of anything wrong apart from one minor detail. The needle of the contents gauge lay mutely against the zero stop.

Grant gazed at that silent symbol as a man in ancient London, returning home one evening at the time of the Plague, might have stared at a rough cross newly scrawled upon his door. Then he banged half a dozen times on the glass in the futile hope that the needle had stuck—though he never really doubted its message. News that is sufficiently bad somehow carries its own guarantee of truth. Only good reports need confirmation.

When Grant got back to the control room, McNeil was himself again. A glance at the opened medicine chest showed the reason for the engineer's rapid recovery. He even assayed a faint attempt at humor.

"It was a meteor," he said. "They tell us a ship this size should get hit once a century. We seem to have jumped the gun with ninety-five years still to go."

"But what about the alarms? The air pressure's normal—how could we have been holed?"

"We weren't," McNeil replied. "You know how the oxygen circulates night-side through the refrigerating coils to keep it liquid? The meteor must have smashed them and the stuff simply boiled away."

Grant was silent, collecting his thoughts. What had happened was serious—deadly serious—but it need not be fatal. After all, the voyage was more than three quarters over.

"Surely the regenerator can keep the air breathable, even if it does get pretty thick?" he asked hopefully.

McNeil shook his head. "I've not worked it out in detail, but I know the answer. When the carbon dioxide is broken down and the free oxygen gets cycled back there's a loss of about ten per cent. That's why we have to carry a reserve."

"The space-suits!" cried Grant in sudden excitement. "What about their tanks?"

He had spoken without thinking, and the immediate realization of his mistake left him feeling worse than before.

"We can't keep oxygen in them—it would boil off in a few days. There's enough compressed gas there for about thirty minutes— merely long enough for you to get to the main tank in an emergency."

"There must be a way out—even if we have to jettison cargo and run for it. Let's stop guessing and work out exactly where we are."

Grant was as much angry as frightened. He was angry with McNeil for breaking down. He was angry with the designers of the ship for not having foreseen this God-knew-how-many-million-to-one chance. The deadline might be a couple of weeks away and a lot could happen before then. The thought helped for a moment to keep his fears at arm's length.

This was an emergency, beyond doubt, but it was one of those peculiarly protracted emergencies that seem to happen only in space. There was plenty of time to think—perhaps too much time.

Grant strapped himself in the pilot's seat and pulled out a writing-pad.

"Let's get the facts right," he said with artificial calmness. "We've got the air that's still circulating in the ship and we lose ten per cent of the oxygen every time it goes through the generator. Chuck me over the Manual, will you? I can never remember how many cubic meters we use a day."

In saying that the *Star Queen* might expect to be hit by a meteor once every century, McNeil had grossly but unavoidably oversimplified the problem. For the answer depended on so many factors that three generations of statisticians had done little but lay down rules so vague that the insurance companies still shivered with apprehension when the great meteor showers went sweeping like a gale through the orbits of the inner worlds.

Everything depends, of course, on what one means by the word meteor. Each lump of cosmic slag that reaches the surface of the Earth has a million smaller brethren that perish utterly in the no-man's-land where the atmosphere has not quite ended and space has yet to begin—that ghostly region where the weird Aurora sometimes walks by night.

These are the familiar shooting stars, seldom larger than a pin's head, and these in turn are outnumbered a millionfold again by particles too small to leave any visible trace of their dying as they drift down from the sky. All of them, the countless specks of dust, the rare boulders and even the wandering mountains that Earth encounters perhaps once every million years—all of them are meteors.

For the purposes of space-flight, a meteor is only of interest if, on penetrating the hull of a ship, it leaves a hole large enough to be dangerous. This is a matter of relative speeds as well as size. Tables have been prepared showing approximate collision times for various parts of the Solar System—and for various sizes of meteors down to masses of a few milligrams.

That which had struck the *Star Queen* was a giant, being nearly a centimeter across and weighing all of ten grams. According to the table the waiting-time for collision with such a monster was of the order of ten to the ninth days—say three million years. The virtual certainty that such an occurrence would not happen again in the course of human history gave Grant and McNeil very little consolation.

However, things might have been worse. The *Star Queen* was 115 days on her orbit and had only 30 still to go. She was traveling, as did all freighters, on the long tangential ellipse kissing the orbits of Earth and Venus on opposite sides of the Sun. The fast liners could cut across from planet to planet at three times her speed—and ten times her fuel consumption—but she must plod along her predetermined track like a streetcar, taking 145 days, more or less, for each journey.

Anything more unlike the early-twentieth-century idea of a spaceship than the *Star Queen* would be hard to imagine. She consisted of two spheres, one fifty and the other twenty meters in diameter, joined by a cylinder about a hundred meters long. The whole structure looked like a match-stick-and-Plasticine model of a hydrogen atom. Crew, cargo, and controls were in the larger sphere, while the smaller one held the atomic motors and was—to put it mildly—out of bounds to living matter.

The *Star Queen* had been built in space and could never have lifted herself even from the surface of the Moon. Under full power her ion drive could produce an acceleration of a twentieth of a gravity, which in an hour would give her all the velocity she needed to change from a satellite of the Earth to one of Venus.

Hauling cargo up from the planets was the job of the powerful little chemical rockets. In a month the tugs would be climbing up from Venus to meet her, but the *Star Queen* would not be stopping for there would be no one at the controls. She would continue blindly on her orbit, speeding past Venus at miles a second—and five months later she would be back at the orbit of the Earth, though Earth itself would then be far away.

It is surprising how long it takes to do a simple addition when your life depends on the answer. Grant ran down the short column of figures half a dozen times before he finally gave up hope that the total would change. Then he sat doodling nervously on the white plastic of the pilot's desk.

"With all possible economies," he said, "we can last about twenty days. That means we'll be ten days out of Venus when. . . ." His voice trailed off into silence.

Ten days didn't sound much—but it might just as well have been ten years. Grant thought sardonically of all the hack adventure writers who had used just this situation in their stories and radio serials. In these circumstances, according to the carbon-copy experts—few of whom had ever gone beyond the Moon—there were three things that could happen.

The popular solution—which had become almost a cliché—was to turn the ship into a glorified greenhouse or a hydroponic farm and let photosynthesis do the rest. Alternatively one could perform prodigies of chemical or atomic engineering—explained in tedious technical detail—and build an oxygen manufacturing plant which would not only save your life—and of course the heroine's—but also make you the owner of fabulously valuable patents. The third or *deus ex machina* solution was the arrival of a convenient spaceship which happened to be matching your course and velocity exactly.

But that was fiction and things were different in real life. Although the first idea was sound in theory there wasn't even a packet of grass seed aboard the *Star Queen*. As for feats of inventive engineering, two men—however brilliant and however desperate—were not likely to improve in a few days on the work of scores of great industrial research organizations over a full century.

The spaceship that "happened to be passing" was, almost by definition, impossible. Even if other freighters had been coasting on the same elliptic path—and Grant knew there were none—then by the very laws that governed their movements they would always keep their original separations. It was not quite impossible that a liner, racing on its hyperbolic orbit, might pass within a few hundred thousand kilometers of them—but at a speed so great that it would be as inaccessible as Pluto.

"If we threw out the cargo," said McNeil at last, "would we have a chance of changing our orbit?"

Grant shook his head.

"I'd hoped so," he replied, "but it won't work. We could reach Venus in a week if we wished—but we'd have no fuel for braking and nothing from the planet could catch us as we went past."

"Not even a liner?"

"According to *Lloyd's Register* Venus has only a couple of freighters at the moment. In any case it would be a practically impossible maneuver. Even if it could match our speed how would the rescue ship get back? It would need about fifty kilometers a second for the whole job!"

"If we can't figure a way out," said McNeil, "maybe someone on Venus can. We'd better talk to them."

"I'm going to," Grant replied, "as soon as I've decided what to say. Go and get the transmitter aligned, will you?"

He watched McNeil as he floated out of the room. The engineer was probably going to give trouble in the days that lay ahead. Until now they had got on well enough—like most stout men McNeil was good-natured and easygoing. But now Grant realized that he lacked fiber. He had become flabby—physically and mentally—living too long in space.

A buzzer sounded on the transmitter switchboard. The parabolic mirror out on the hull was aimed at the gleaming arc-lamp of Venus, only ten million kilometers away and moving on an almost parallel path. The three-millimeter waves from the ship's transmitter would make the trip in little more than half a minute. There was bitterness in the knowledge that they were only thirty seconds from safety.

The automatic monitor on Venus gave its impersonal *Go ahead* signal and Grant began to talk steadily, and he hoped, quite dispassionately. He gave a careful analysis of the situation and ended with a request for advice. His fears concerning McNeil he left unspoken. For one thing he knew that the engineer would be monitoring him at the transmitter.

As yet no one on Venus would have heard the message, even though the transmission time-lag was over. It would still be coiled up in the recorder spools, but in a few minutes an unsuspecting signal officer would arrive to play it over.

He would have no idea of the bombshell that was about to burst, triggering trains of sympathetic ripples on all the inhabited worlds as television and newssheet took up the refrain. An accident in space has a dramatic quality that crowds all other items from the headlines.

Until now Grant had been too preoccupied with his own safety to give much thought to the cargo in his charge. A sea captain of ancient times, whose first thought was for his ship, might have been shocked by this attitude. Grant, however, had reason on his side.

The *Star Queen* could never founder, could never run upon uncharted rocks or pass silently, as so many ships have passed, forever from the knowledge of man. She was safe, whatever might befall her crew. If she was undisturbed she would continue to retrace her orbit with such precision that men might set their calendars by her for centuries to come.

The cargo, Grant suddenly remembered, was insured for over twenty million dollars. There were not many goods valuable enough to be shipped from world to world and most of the crates in the hold were worth more than their weight—or rather their mass—in gold. Perhaps some items might be useful in this emergency and Grant went to the safe to find the loading schedule.

He was sorting the thin, tough sheets when McNeil came back into the cabin.

"I've been reducing the air pressure," he said. "The hull shows some leaks that wouldn't have mattered in the usual way."

Grant nodded absently as he passed a bundle of sheets over to McNeil.

"Here's our loading schedule. I suggest we both run through it in case there's anything in the cargo that may help."

If it did nothing else, he might have added, it would at least give them something to occupy their minds.

As he ran down the long columns of numbered items—a complete cross-section of interplanetary commerce—Grant found himself wondering what lay behind these inanimate symbols. *Item 347 - 1 book - 4 kilos gross.*

He whistled as he noticed that it was a starred item, insured for a hundred thousand dollars, and he suddenly remembered hearing on the radio that the Hesperian Museum had just bought a first edition *Seven Pillars of Wisdom.*

A few sheets later was a very contrasting item, *Miscellaneous books - 25 kilos - no intrinsic value.*

It had cost a small fortune to ship those books to Venus, yet they were of "no intrinsic value." Grant let his imagination loose on the problem. Perhaps someone who was leaving Earth forever was taking with him to a new world his most cherished treasures—the dozen or so volumes that above all others had most shaped his mind.

Item 564 - 12 reels film.

That, of course, would be the Neronian super-epic, *While Rome Burns,* which had left Earth just one jump ahead of the censor. Venus was waiting for it with considerable impatience.

Medical supplies - 50 kilos. Case of cigars - 1 kilo. Precision instruments - 75 kilos. So the list went on. Each item was something rare or something which the industry and science of a younger civilization could not yet produce.

The cargo was sharply divided into two classes—blatant luxury or sheer necessity. There was little in between. And there was nothing, nothing at all, which gave Grant the slightest hope. He did not see how it could have been otherwise, but that did not prevent him from feeling a quite unreasonable disappointment.

The reply from Venus, when it came at last, took nearly an hour to run through the recorder. It was a questionnaire so detailed that Grant wondered morosely if he'd live long enough to answer it. Most of the queries were technical ones concerning the ship. The experts on two planets were pooling their brains in the attempt to save the *Star Queen* and her cargo.

"Well, what do you think of it?" Grant asked McNeil when the other had finished running through the message. He was watching the engineer carefully for any further sign of strain.

There was a long pause before McNeil spoke. Then he shrugged his shoulders and his first words were an echo of Grant's own thoughts.

"It will certainly keep us busy. I won't be able to do all these tests in under a day. I can see what they're driving at most of the time, but some of the questions are just plain crazy."

Grant had suspected that, but said nothing as the other continued.

"Rate of hull leakage—that's sensible enough, but why should anyone want to know the efficiency of our radiation screening? I think they're trying to keep up our morale by pretending they have some bright ideas—or else they want to keep us too busy to worry."

Grant was relieved and yet annoyed by McNeil's calmness—relieved because he had been afraid of another scene and annoyed because McNeil was not fitting at all neatly into the mental category he had prepared for him. Was that first momentary lapse typical of the man or might it have happened to anyone?

Grant, to whom the world was very much a place of blacks and whites, felt angry at being unable to decide whether McNeil was cowardly or courageous. That he might be both was a possibility that never occurred to him.

There is a timelessness about space-flight that is unmatched by any other experience of man. Even on the Moon there are shadows that creep sluggishly from crag to crag as the sun makes its slow march across the sky. Earthward there is always the great clock of the spinning globe, marking the hours with continents for hands.

But on a long voyage in a gyro-stabilized ship the same patterns of sunlight lie unmoving on wall or floor as the chronometer ticks off its meaningless hours and days.

Grant and McNeil had long since learned to regulate their lives accordingly. In deep space they moved and thought with a leisureliness that would vanish quickly enough when a voyage was nearing its end and the time for braking maneuvers had arrived. Though they were now under sentence of death, they continued along the well-worn grooves of habit.

Every day Grant carefully wrote up the log, checked the ship's position and carried out his various routine duties. McNeil was also behaving normally as far as could be told, though Grant suspected that some of the technical maintenance was being carried out with a very light hand.

It was now three days since the meteor had struck. For the last twenty-four hours Earth and Venus had been in conference and Grant wondered when he would hear the result of their deliberations. He did not believe that the finest technical brains in the Solar System could save them now, but it was hard to abandon hope when everything still seemed so normal and the air was still clean and fresh.

On the fourth day Venus spoke again. Shorn of its technicalities, the message was nothing more or less than a funeral oration. Grant and McNeil had been written off, but they were given elaborate instructions concerning the safety of the cargo.

Back on Earth the astronomers were computing all the possible rescue orbits that might make contact with the *Star Queen* in the next few years. There was even a chance that she might be reached from Earth six or seven months later, when she was back at aphelion, but the maneuver could be carried out only by a fast liner with no payload and would cost a fortune in fuel.

McNeil vanished soon after this message came through. At first Grant was a little relieved. If McNeil chose to look after himself that was his own affair. Besides there were various letters to write—though the last-will-and-testament business could come later.

It was McNeil's turn to prepare the "evening" meal, a duty he enjoyed for he took good care of his stomach. When the usual sounds from the galley were not forthcoming Grant went in search of his crew.

He found McNeil lying in his bunk, very much at peace with the universe. Hanging in the air beside him was a large metal crate which had been roughly forced open. Grant had no need to examine it closely to guess its contents. A glance at McNeil was enough.

"It's a dirty shame," said the engineer without a trace of embarrassment, "to suck this stuff up through a tube. Can't you put on some 'g' so that we can drink it properly?"

Grant stared at him with angry contempt, but McNeil returned his gaze unabashed.

"Oh, don't be a sourpuss! Have some yourself—what does it matter now?"

He pushed across a bottle and Grant fielded it deftly as it floated by. It was a fabulously valuable wine—he remembered the consignment now—and the contents of that small crate must be worth thousands.

"I don't think there's any need," said Grant severely, "to behave like a pig—even in these circumstances."

McNeil wasn't drunk yet. He had only reached the brightly lighted anteroom of intoxication and had not lost all contact with the drab outer world.

"I am prepared," he said with great solemnity, "to listen to any good argument against my present course of action—a course which seems eminently sensible to me. But you'd better convince me quickly while I'm still amenable to reason."

He pressed the plastic bulb again and a purple jet shot into his mouth.

"Apart from the fact that you're stealing Company property which will certainly be salvaged sooner or later—you can hardly stay drunk for several weeks."

"That," said McNeil thoughtfully, "remains to be seen."

"I don't think so," retorted Grant. Bracing himself against the wall, he gave the crate a vicious shove that sent it flying through the open doorway.

As he dived after it and slammed the door he heard McNeil shout, "Well, of all the dirty tricks!"

It would take the engineer some time—particularly in his present condition—to unbuckle himself and follow. Grant steered the crate

back to the hold and locked the door. As there was never any need
to lock the hold when the ship was in space McNeil wouldn't have
a key for it himself and Grant could hide the duplicate that was kept
in the control cabin.

McNeil was singing when, some time later, Grant went back
past his room. He still had a couple of bottles for company and
was shouting:

> "We don't care *where* the oxygen goes
> If it doesn't get into the wine. . . ."

Grant, whose education had been severely technical, couldn't
place the quotation. As he paused to listen he suddenly found himself shaken by an emotion which, to do him justice, he did not for
a moment recognize.

It passed as swiftly as it had come, leaving him sick and trembling. For the first time, he realized that his dislike of McNeil was
slowly turning to hatred.

It is a fundamental rule of space-flight that, for sound psychological reasons, the minimum crew on a long journey shall consist
of not less than three men.

But rules are made to be broken and the *Star Queen's* owners
had obtained full authority from the Board of Space Control and
the insurance companies when the freighter set off for Venus without her regular captain.

At the last moment he had been taken ill and there was no
replacement. Since the planets are disinclined to wait upon man
and his affairs, if she did not sail on time she would not sail at all.

Millions of dollars were involved—so she sailed. Grant and
McNeil were both highly capable men and they had no objection
at all to earning double their normal pay for very little extra work.
Despite fundamental differences in temperament, they got on well
enough in ordinary circumstances. It was nobody's fault that circumstances were now very far from ordinary.

Three days without food, it is said, is long enough to remove
most of the subtle differences between a civilized man and a savage.
Grant and McNeil were still in no physical discomfort. But their
imaginations had been only too active and they now had more in

common with two hungry Pacific Islanders in a lost canoe than either would have cared to admit.

For there was one aspect of the situation, and that the most important of all, which had never been mentioned. When the last figures on Grant's writing-pad had been checked and rechecked, the calculation was still not quite complete. Instantly each man had made the one further step, each had arrived simultaneously at the same unspoken result.

It was terribly simple—a macabre parody of those problems in first-year arithmetic that begin, "If six men take two days to assemble five helicopters, how long . . ."

The oxygen would last *two* men for about twenty days, and Venus was thirty days away. One did not have to be a calculating prodigy to see at once that one man, and one man only, might yet live to walk the metal streets of Port Hesperus.

The acknowledged deadline was twenty days ahead, but the unmentioned one was only ten days off. Until that time there would still be enough air for two men—and thereafter for one man only for the rest of the voyage. To a sufficiently detached observer the situation would have been very entertaining.

It was obvious that the conspiracy of silence could not last much longer. But it is not easy, even at the best of times, for two people to decide amicably which one of them shall commit suicide. It is still more difficult when they are no longer on speaking terms.

Grant wished to be perfectly fair. Therefore the only thing to do was to wait until McNeil sobered up and then to put the question to him frankly. He could think best at his desk, so he went to the control cabin and strapped himself down in the pilot's chair.

For a while he stared thoughtfully into nothingness. It would be better, he decided, to broach the matter by correspondence, especially while diplomatic relations were in their present state. He clipped a sheet of note-paper on the writing-pad and began, "Dear McNeil . . ." Then he tore it out and started again, "McNeil . . ."

It took him the best part of three hours and even then he wasn't wholly satisfied. There were some things it was so darned difficult to put down on paper. But at last he managed to finish. He sealed the letter and locked it away in his safe. It could wait for a day or two.

Few of the waiting millions on Earth and Venus could have any idea of the tensions that were slowly building up aboard the *Star Queen*. For days press and radio had been full of fantastic rescue schemes. On three worlds there was hardly any other topic of conversation. But only the faintest echo of the planet-wide tumult reached the two men who were its cause.

At any time the station on Venus could speak to the *Star Queen,* but there was so little that could be said. One could not with any decency give words of encouragement to men in the condemned cell, even when there was some slight uncertainty about the actual date of execution.

So Venus contented itself with a few routine messages every day and blocked the steady stream of exhortations and newspaper offers that came pouring in from Earth. As a result private radio companies on Earth made frantic attempts to contact the *Star Queen* directly. They failed, simply because it never occurred to Grant and McNeil to focus their receiver anywhere except on Venus, now so tantalizingly near at hand.

There had been an embarrassing interlude when McNeil emerged from his cabin, but though relations were not particularly cordial, life aboard the *Star Queen* continued much as before.

Grant spent most of his waking hours in the pilot's position, calculating approach maneuvers and writing interminable letters to his wife. He could have spoken to her had he wished, but the thought of all those millions of waiting ears had prevented him from doing so. Interplanetary speech circuits were supposed to be private—but too many people would be interested in this one.

In a couple of days, Grant assured himself, he would hand his letter to McNeil and they could decide what was to be done. Such a delay would also give McNeil a chance of raising the subject himself. That he might have other reasons for his hesitation was something Grant's conscious mind still refused to admit.

He often wondered how McNeil was spending his time. The engineer had a large library of microfilm books, for he read widely and his range of interests was unusual. His favorite book, Grant knew, was *Jurgen* and perhaps even now he was trying to forget his doom by losing himself in its strange magic. Others of McNeil's books were less respectable and not a few were of the class curiously described as "curious."

The truth of the matter was that McNeil was far too subtle and complicated a personality for Grant to understand. He was a hedonist and enjoyed the pleasures of life all the more for being cut off from them for months at a time. But he was by no means the moral weakling that the unimaginative and somewhat puritanical Grant had supposed.

It was true that he had collapsed completely under the initial shock and that his behavior over the wine was—by Grant's standards —reprehensible. But McNeil had had his breakdown and had recovered. Therein lay the difference between him and the hard but brittle Grant.

Though the normal routine of duties had been resumed by tacit consent, it did little to reduce the sense of strain. Grant and McNeil avoided each other as much as possible except when mealtimes brought them together. When they did meet, they behaved with an exaggerated politeness as if each were striving to be perfectly normal—and inexplicably failing.

Grant had hoped that McNeil would himself broach the subject of suicide, thus sparing him a very awkward duty. When the engineer stubbornly refused to do anything of the sort it added to Grant's resentment and contempt. To make matters worse he was now suffering from nightmares and sleeping very badly.

The nightmare was always the same. When he was a child it had often happened that at bedtime he had been reading a story far too exciting to be left until morning. To avoid detection he had continued reading under the bedclothes by flashlight, curled up in a snug white-walled cocoon. Every ten minutes or so the air had become too stifling to breathe and his emergence into the delicious cool air had been a major part of the fun.

Now, thirty years later, these innocent childhood hours returned to haunt him. He was dreaming that he could not escape from the suffocating sheets while the air was steadily and remorselessly thickening around him.

He had intended to give McNeil the letter after two days, yet somehow he put it off again. This procrastination was very unlike Grant, but he managed to persuade himself that it was a perfectly reasonable thing to do.

He was giving McNeil a chance to redeem himself—to prove that he wasn't a coward by raising the matter himself. That McNeil might be waiting for him to do exactly the same thing somehow never occurred to Grant.

The all-too-literal deadline was only five days off when, for the first time, Grant's mind brushed lightly against the thought of murder. He had been sitting after the "evening" meal, trying to relax as McNeil clattered around in the galley with, he considered, quite unnecessary noise.

What use, he asked himself, was the engineer to the world? He had no responsibilities and no family—no one would be any the worse off for his death. Grant, on the other hand, had a wife and three children of whom he was moderately fond, though for some obscure reason they responded with little more than dutiful affection.

Any impartial judge would have no difficulty in deciding which of them should survive. If McNeil had a spark of decency in him he would have come to the same conclusion already. Since he appeared to have done nothing of the sort he had forfeited all further claims to consideration.

Such was the elemental logic of Grant's subconscious mind, which had arrived at its answer days before but had only now succeeded in attracting the attention for which it had been clamoring. To Grant's credit he at once rejected the thought with horror.

He was an upright and honorable person with a very strict code of behavior. Even the vagrant homicidal impulses of what is misleadingly called "normal" man had seldom ruffled his mind. But in the days—the very few days—left to him, they would come more and more often.

The air had now become noticeably fouler. Though there was still no real difficulty in breathing, it was a constant reminder of what lay ahead, and Grant found that it was keeping him from sleep. This was not pure loss, as it helped to break the power of his nightmares, but he was becoming physically run down.

His nerve was also rapidly deteriorating, a state of affairs accentuated by the fact that McNeil seemed to be behaving with unexpected and annoying calmness. Grant realized that he had come to the stage when it would be dangerous to delay the showdown any longer.

McNeil was in his room as usual when Grant went up to the control cabin to collect the letter he had locked away in the safe—

it seemed a lifetime ago. He wondered if he need add anything more to it. Then he realized that this was only another excuse for delay. Resolutely he made his way toward McNeil's cabin.

A single neutron begins the chain-reaction that in an instant can destroy a million lives and the toil of generations. Equally insignificant and unimportant are the trigger-events which can sometimes change a man's course of action and so alter the whole pattern of his future.

Nothing could have been more trivial than that which made Grant pause in the corridor outside McNeil's room. In the ordinary way he would not even have noticed it. It was the smell of smoke— tobacco smoke.

The thought that the sybaritic engineer had so little self-control that he was squandering the last precious liters of oxygen in such a manner filled Grant with blinding fury. He stood for a moment quite paralyzed with the intensity of his emotion.

Then slowly, he crumpled the letter in his hand. The thought which had first been an unwelcome intruder, then a casual speculation, was at last fully accepted. McNeil had had his chance and had proved, by his unbelievable selfishness, unworthy of it. Very well—he could die.

The speed with which Grant had arrived at this conclusion would not have deceived the most amateurish of psychologists. It was relief as much as hatred that drove him away from McNeil's room. He had wanted to convince himself that there would be no need to do the honorable thing, to suggest some game of chance that would give them each an equal probability of life.

This was the excuse he needed, and he had seized upon it to salve his conscience. For though he might plan and even carry out a murder, Grant was the sort of person who would have to do it according to his own particular moral code.

As it happened he was—not for the first time—badly misjudging McNeil. The engineer was a heavy smoker and tobacco was quite essential to his mental well-being even in normal circumstances. How much more essential it was now, Grant, who only smoked occasionally and without much enjoyment, could never have appreciated.

McNeil had satisfied himself by careful calculation that four cigarettes a day would make no measurable difference whatsoever to the ship's oxygen endurance, whereas they would make all the difference in the world to his own nerves and hence indirectly to Grant's.

But it was no use explaining this to Grant. So he had smoked in private and with a self-control he found agreeably, almost voluptuously, surprising. It was sheer bad luck that Grant had detected one of the day's four cigarettes.

For a man who had only at that moment talked himself into murder, Grant's actions were remarkably methodical. Without hesitation, he hurried back to the control room and opened the medicine chest with its neatly labeled compartments, designed for almost every emergency that could occur in space.

Even the ultimate emergency had been considered, for there behind its retaining elastic bands was the tiny bottle he had been seeking, the image of which had been lying hidden far down in the unknown depths of his mind through all these days. It bore a white label carrying a skull-and-crossbones, and beneath them the words: *Approx. one-half gram will cause painless and almost instantaneous death.*

The poison was painless and instantaneous—that was good. But even more important was a fact unmentioned on the label. It was also tasteless.

The contrast between the meals prepared by Grant and those organized with considerable skill and care by McNeil was striking. Anyone who was fond of food and who spent a good deal of his life in space usually learned the art of cooking in self-defense. Mc-Neil had done this long ago.

To Grant, on the other hand, eating was one of those necessary but annoying jobs which had to be got through as quickly as possible. His cooking reflected this opinion. McNeil had ceased to grumble about it, but he would have been very interested in the trouble Grant was taking over this particular meal.

If he noticed any increasing nervousness on Grant's part as the meal progressed, he said nothing. They ate almost in silence, but that was not unusual for they had long since exhausted most of the possibilities of light conversation. When the last dishes—deep bowls with inturned rims to prevent the contents drifting out—had been cleared away, Grant went into the galley to prepare the coffee.

He took rather a long time, for at the last moment something quite maddening and quite ridiculous happened. He suddenly recalled one of the film classics of the last century in which the fabulous Charlie Chaplin tried to poison an unwanted wife—and then accidentally changed the glasses.

No memory could have been more unwelcome, for it left him shaken with a gust of silent hysteria. Poe's *Imp of the Perverse,* that demon who delights in defying the careful canons of self-preservation, was at work and it was a good minute before Grant could regain his self-control.

He was sure that, outwardly at least, he was quite calm as he carried in the two plastic containers and their drinking tubes. There was no danger of confusing them, for the engineer's had the letters MAC painted boldly across it.

At the thought Grant nearly relapsed into psychopathic giggles but just managed to regain control with the somber reflection that his nerves must be in even worse condition than he had imagined.

He watched, fascinated, though without appearing to do so, as McNeil toyed with his cup. The engineer seemed in no great hurry and was staring moodily into space. Then he put his lips to the drinking tube and sipped.

A moment later he spluttered slightly—and an icy hand seemed to seize Grant's heart and hold it tight. Then McNeil turned to him and said evenly, "You've made it properly for once. It's quite hot."

Slowly, Grant's heart resumed its interrupted work. He did not trust himself to speak, but managed a noncommittal nod. McNeil parked the cup carefully in the air, a few inches away from his face.

He seemed very thoughtful, as if weighing his words for some important remark. Grant cursed himself for having made the drink so hot—that was just the sort of detail that hanged murderers. If McNeil waited much longer he would probably betray himself through nervousness.

"I suppose," said McNeil in a quietly conversational sort of way, "it has occurred to you that there's still enough air to last one of us to Venus?"

Grant forced his jangling nerves under control and tore his eyes away from that hypnotic cup. His throat seemed very dry as he answered, "It—it had crossed my mind."

McNeil touched his cup, found it still too hot and continued thoughtfully, "Then wouldn't it be more sensible if one of us decided to walk out of the airlock, say—or to take some of the poison in there?" He jerked his thumb toward the medicine chest, just visible from where they were sitting.

Grant nodded.

"The only trouble, of course," added the engineer, "is to decide which of us will be the unlucky one. I suppose it would have to be by picking a card or in some other quite arbitrary way."

Grant stared at McNeil with a fascination that almost outweighed his mounting nervousness. He had never believed that the engineer could discuss the subject so calmly. Grant was sure he suspected nothing. Obviously McNeil's thoughts had been running on parallel lines to his own and it was scarcely even a coincidence that he had chosen this time, of all times, to raise the matter.

McNeil was watching him intently, as if judging his reactions.

"You're right," Grant heard himself say. "We must talk it over."

"Yes," said McNeil quite impassively. "We must." Then he reached for his cup again, put the drinking tube to his lips and sucked slowly.

Grant could not wait until he had finished. To his surprise the relief he had been expecting did not come. He even felt a stab of regret, though it was not quite remorse. It was a little late to think of it now, but he suddenly remembered that he would be alone in the *Star Queen,* haunted by his thoughts, for more than three weeks before rescue came.

He did not wish to see McNeil die, and he felt rather sick. Without another glance at his victim he launched himself toward the exit.

Immovably fixed, the fierce sun and the unwinking stars looked down upon the *Star Queen,* which seemed as motionless as they. There was no way of telling that the tiny dumbbell of the ship had now almost reached her maximum speed and that millions of horsepower were chained within the smaller sphere, waiting for the moment of its release. There was no way of telling, indeed, that she carried any life at all.

An airlock on the night-side of the ship slowly opened, letting a blaze of light escape from the interior. The brilliant circle looked very strange hanging there in the darkness. Then it was abruptly eclipsed as two figures floated out of the ship.

One was much bulkier than the other, and for a rather important reason—it was wearing a space-suit. Now there are some forms of apparel that may be worn or discarded as the fancy pleases with no other ill-effects than a possible loss of social prestige. But space-suits are not among them.

Something not easy to follow was happening in the darkness. Then the smaller figure began to move, slowly at first but with rapidly mounting speed. It swept out of the shadow of the ship into the full blast of the sun, and now one could see that strapped to its back was a small gas-cylinder from which a fine mist was jetting to vanish almost instantly into space.

It was a crude but effective rocket. There was no danger that the ship's minute gravitational pull would drag the body back to it again.

Rotating slightly, the corpse dwindled against the stars and vanished from sight in less than a minute. Quite motionless, the figure in the airlock watched it go. Then the outer door swung shut, the circle of brilliance vanished and only the pale Earthlight still glinted on the shadowed wall of the ship.

Nothing else whatsoever happened for twenty-three days.

The captain of the *Hercules* turned to his mate with a sigh of relief.

"I was afraid he couldn't do it. It must have been a colossal job to break his orbit single-handed—and with the air as thick as it must be by now. How soon can we get to him?"

"It will take about an hour. He's still got quite a bit of eccentricity but we can correct that."

"Good. Signal the *Leviathan* and *Titan* that we can make contact and ask them to take off, will you? But I wouldn't drop any tips to your news commentator friends until we're safely locked."

The mate had the grace to blush. "I don't intend to," he said in a slightly hurt voice as he pecked delicately at the keys of his calculator. The answer that flashed instantly on the screen seemed to displease him.

"We'd better board and bring the *Queen* down to circular speed ourselves before we call the other tugs," he said, "otherwise we'll be wasting a lot of fuel. She's still got a velocity excess of nearly a kilometer a second."

"Good idea—tell *Leviathan* and *Titan* to stand by but not to blast until we give them the new orbit."

While the message was on its way down through the unbroken cloudbanks that covered half the sky below, the mate remarked thoughtfully, "I wonder what he's feeling like now?"

"I can tell you. He's so pleased to be alive that he doesn't give a hoot about anything else."

"Still, I'm not sure I'd like to have left my shipmate in space so that I could get home."

"It's not the sort of thing that anyone would like to do. But you heard the broadcast—they'd talked it over calmly and the loser went out of the airlock. It was the only sensible way."

"Sensible, perhaps—but it's pretty horrible to let someone else sacrifice himself in such a cold-blooded way so that you can live."

"Don't be a ruddy sentimentalist. I'll bet that if it happened to us you'd push me out before I could even say my prayers."

"Unless you did it to me first. Still, I don't think it's ever likely to happen to the *Hercules*. Five days out of port's the longest we've ever been, isn't it? Talk about the romance of the spaceways!"

The captain didn't reply. He was peering into the eyepiece of the navigating telescope, for the *Star Queen* should now be within optical range. There was a long pause while he adjusted the vernier controls. Then he gave a little sigh of satisfaction.

"There she is—about nine-fifty kilometers away. Tell the crew to stand by—and send a message to cheer him up. Say we'll be there in thirty minutes even if it isn't quite true."

Slowly the thousand-meter nylon ropes yielded beneath the strain as they absorbed the relative momentum of the ships, then slackened again as the *Star Queen* and the *Hercules* rebounded toward each other. The electric winches began to turn and, like a spider crawling up its thread, the *Hercules* drew alongside the freighter.

Men in space-suits sweated with heavy reaction units—tricky work, this—until the airlocks had registered and could be coupled together. The outer doors slid aside and the air in the locks mingled, fresh with foul. As the mate of the *Hercules* waited, oxygen cylinder in hand, he wondered what condition the survivor would be in. Then the *Star Queen's* inner door slid open.

For a moment, the two men stood looking at each other across the short corridor that now connected the two airlocks. The mate was surprised and a little disappointed to find that he felt no particular sense of drama.

So much had happened to make this moment possible that its actual achievement was almost an anticlimax, even in the instant when it was slipping into the past. He wished—for he was an incurable romantic—that he could think of something memorable to say, some "Doctor Livingstone, I presume?" phrase that would pass into history.

But all he actually said was, "Well, McNeil, I'm pleased to see you."

Though he was considerably thinner and somewhat haggard, McNeil had stood the ordeal well. He breathed gratefully the blast of raw oxygen and rejected the idea that he might like to lie down and sleep. As he explained, he had done very little but sleep for the last week to conserve air. The first mate looked relieved. He had been afraid he might have to wait for the story.

The cargo was being trans-shipped and the other two tugs were climbing up from the great blinding crescent of Venus while McNeil retraced the events of the last few weeks and the mate made surreptitious notes.

He spoke quite calmly and impersonally, as if he were relating some adventure that had happened to another person, or indeed had never happened at all. Which was, of course, to some extent the case, though it would be unfair to suggest that McNeil was telling any lies.

He invented nothing, but he omitted a good deal. He had had three weeks in which to prepare his narrative and he did not think it had any flaws. . . .

Grant had already reached the door when McNeil called softly after him, "What's the hurry? I thought we had something to discuss."

Grant grabbed at the doorway to halt his headlong flight. He turned slowly and stared unbelievingly at the engineer. McNeil should be already dead—but he was sitting quite comfortably, looking at him with a most peculiar expression.

"Sit down," he said sharply—and in that moment it suddenly seemed that all authority had passed to him. Grant did so, quite without volition. Something had gone wrong, though what it was he could not imagine.

The silence in the control room seemed to last for ages. Then McNeil said rather sadly, "I'd hoped better of you, Grant."

At last Grant found his voice, though he could barely recognize it.

"What do you mean?" he whispered.

"What do you think I mean?" replied McNeil, with what seemed no more than mild irritation. "This little attempt of yours to poison me, of course."

Grant's tottering world collapsed at last, but he no longer cared greatly one way or the other. McNeil began to examine his beautifully kept fingernails with some attention.

"As a matter of interest," he said, in the way that one might ask the time, "when did you decide to kill me?"

The sense of unreality was so overwhelming that Grant felt he was acting a part, that this had nothing to do with real life at all.

"Only this morning," he said, and believed it.

"Hmm," remarked McNeil, obviously without much conviction. He rose to his feet and moved over to the medicine chest. Grant's eyes followed him as he fumbled in the compartment and came back with the little poison bottle. It still appeared to be full. Grant had been careful about that.

"I suppose I should get pretty mad about this whole business," McNeil continued conversationally, holding the bottle between thumb and forefinger. "But somehow I'm not. Maybe it's because I never had many illusions about human nature. And, of course, I saw it coming a long time ago."

Only the last phrase really reached Grant's consciousness.

"You—saw it coming?"

"Heavens, yes! You're too transparent to make a good criminal, I'm afraid. And now that your little plot's failed it leaves us both in an embarrassing position, doesn't it?"

To this masterly understatement there seemed no possible reply.

"By rights," continued the engineer thoughtfully, "I should now work myself into a good temper, call Venus Central, and denounce you to the authorities. But it would be a rather pointless thing to do, and I've never been much good at losing my temper anyway. Of course, you'll say that's because I'm too lazy—but I don't think so."

He gave Grant a twisted smile.

"Oh, I know what you think about me—you've got me neatly classified in that orderly mind of yours, haven't you? I'm soft and self-indulgent, I haven't any moral courage—or any morals for that matter—and I don't give a damn for anyone but myself. Well, I'm not denying it. Maybe it's ninety per cent true. But the odd ten per cent is mighty important, Grant!"

Grant felt in no condition to indulge in psychological analysis, and this seemed hardly the time for anything of the sort. Besides, he was still obsessed with the problem of his failure and the mystery of McNeil's continued existence. McNeil, who knew this perfectly well, seemed in no hurry to satisfy his curiosity.

"Well, what do you intend to do now?" Grant asked, anxious to get it over.

"I would like," said McNeil calmly, "to carry on our discussion where it was interrupted by the coffee."

"You don't mean—"

"But I do. Just as if nothing had happened."

"That doesn't make sense. You've got something up your sleeve!" cried Grant.

McNeil sighed. He put down the poison bottle and looked firmly at Grant.

"*You're* in no position to accuse me of plotting anything. To repeat my earlier remarks, I am suggesting that we decide which one of us shall take poison—only we don't want any more unilateral decisions. Also"—he picked up the bottle again—"it will be the real thing this time. The stuff in here merely leaves a bad taste in the mouth."

A light was beginning to dawn in Grant's mind. "You changed the poison!"

"Naturally. You may think you're a good actor, Grant, but frankly—from the balcony—I thought the performance stank. I could tell you were plotting something, probably before you knew it yourself. In the last few days I've deloused the ship pretty thoroughly. Thinking of all the ways you might have done me in was quite amusing and helped to pass the time. The poison was so obvious that it was the first thing I fixed. But I rather overdid the danger signals and nearly gave myself away when I took the first sip. Salt doesn't go at all well with coffee."

He gave that wry grin again. "Also, I'd hoped for something more subtle. So far I've found fifteen infallible ways of murdering anyone aboard a spaceship. But I don't propose to describe them now."

This was fantastic, Grant thought. He was being treated, not like a criminal, but like a rather stupid schoolboy who hadn't done his homework properly.

"Yet you're still willing," said Grant unbelievingly, "to start all over again? And you'd take the poison yourself if you lost?"

McNeil was silent for a long time. Then he began, slowly, "I can see that you still don't believe me. It doesn't fit at all nicely into your tidy little picture, does it? But perhaps I can make you understand. It's really quite simple.

"I've enjoyed life, Grant, without many scruples or regrets—but the better part of it's over now and I don't cling to what's left as desperately as you might imagine. Yet while I *am* alive I'm rather particular about some things.

"It may surprise you to know that I've got any ideals at all. But I have, Grant—I've always tried to act like a civilized, rational being. I've not always succeeded. When I've failed I've tried to redeem myself."

He paused, and when he resumed it was as though he, and not Grant, was on the defensive. "I've never exactly liked you, Grant, but I've often admired you and that's why I'm sorry it's come to this. I admired you most of all the day the ship was holed."

For the first time, McNeil seemed to have some difficulty in choosing his words. When he spoke again he avoided Grant's eyes.

"I didn't behave very well then. Something happened that I thought was impossible. I've always been quite sure that I'd never lose my nerve but—well—it was so sudden it knocked me over."

He attempted to hide his embarrassment by humor. "The same sort of thing happened on my very first trip. I was sure *I'd* never be spacesick—and as a result I was much worse than if I had not been overconfident. But I got over it then—and again this time. It was one of the biggest surprises of my life, Grant, when I saw that you of all people were beginning to crack.

"Oh, yes—the business of the wines! I can see you're thinking about that. Well, that's one thing I *don't* regret. I said I'd always tried to act like a civilized man—and a civilized man should always know when to get drunk. But perhaps you wouldn't understand."

Oddly enough, that was just what Grant was beginning to do. He had caught his first real glimpse of McNeil's intricate and tortuous personality and realized how utterly he had misjudged him. No—misjudged was not the right word. In many ways his judgment had been correct. But it had only touched the surface—he had never suspected the depths that lay beneath.

In a moment of insight that had never come before, and from the nature of things could never come again, Grant understood the reasons behind McNeil's action. This was nothing so simple as a coward trying to reinstate himself in the eyes of the world, for no one need ever know what happened aboard the *Star Queen*.

In any case, McNeil probably cared nothing for the world's opinion, thanks to the sleek self-sufficiency that had so often annoyed Grant. But that very self-sufficiency meant that at all costs he must preserve his own good opinion of himself. Without it life would not be worth living—and McNeil had never accepted life save on his own terms.

The engineer was watching him intently and must have guessed that Grant was coming near the truth, for he suddenly changed his tone as though he was sorry he had revealed so much of his character.

"Don't think I get a quixotic pleasure from turning the other cheek," he said. "Just consider it from the point of view of pure logic. After all, we've got to come to *some* agreement.

"Has it occurred to you that if only one of us survives without a covering message from the other, he'll have a very uncomfortable time explaining just what happened?"

In his blind fury, Grant had completely forgotten this. But he did not believe it bulked at all important in McNeil's own thoughts.

"Yes," he said, "I suppose you're right."

He felt far better now. All the hate had drained out of him and he was at peace. The truth was known and he accepted it.

That it was so different from what he had imagined did not seem to matter now.

"Well, let's get it over," he said unemotionally. "There's a new pack of cards lying around somewhere."

"I think we'd better speak to Venus first—both of us," replied McNeil, with peculiar emphasis. "We want a complete agreement on record in case anyone asks awkward questions later."

Grant nodded absently. He did not mind very much now one way or the other. He even smiled, ten minutes later, as he drew his card from the pack and laid it, face upward, beside McNeil's.

"So that's the whole story, is it?" said the first mate, wondering how soon he could decently get to the transmitter.

"Yes," said McNeil evenly, "that's all there was to it."

The mate bit his pencil, trying to frame the next question. "And I suppose Grant took it all quite calmly?"

The captain gave him a glare, which he avoided, and McNeil looked at him coldly as if he could see through to the sensation-mongering headlines ranged behind. He got to his feet and moved over to the observation port.

"You heard his broadcast, didn't you? Wasn't that calm enough?"

The mate sighed. It still seemed hard to believe that in such circumstances two men could have behaved in so reasonable, so unemotional a manner. He could have pictured all sorts of dramatic possibilities—sudden outbursts of insanity, even attempts at murder. Yet according to McNeil nothing at all had happened. It was too bad.

McNeil was speaking again, as if to himself. "Yes, Grant behaved very well—very well indeed. It was a great pity—"

Then he seemed to lose himself in the ever-fresh, incomparable glory of the approaching planet. Not far beneath, and coming closer by kilometers every second, the snow-white crescent arms of Venus spanned more than half the sky. Down there were life and warmth and civilization—and air.

The future, which not long ago had seemed contracted to a point, had opened out again into all its unknown possibilities and wonders. But behind him McNeil could sense the eyes of his rescuers, probing, questioning—yes, and condemning too.

All his life he would hear whispers. Voices would be saying behind his back, "Isn't that the man who—?"

He did not care. For once in his life at least, he had done something of which he could feel unashamed. Perhaps one day his own pitiless self-analysis would strip bare the motives behind his actions, would whisper in his ear. "Altruism? Don't be a fool! You did it to bolster up your own good opinion of yourself—so much more important than anyone else's!"

But the perverse maddening voices, which all his life had made nothing seem worthwhile, were silent for the moment and he felt content. He had reached the calm at the center of the hurricane. While it lasted he would enjoy it to the full.

TALES FROM THE WHITE HART

You come upon the "White Hart" quite unexpectedly in one of these anonymous little lanes leading down from Fleet Street to the Embankment. It's no use *telling* you where it is: very few people who have set out in a determined effort to get there have ever actually arrived. For the first dozen visits a guide is essential: after that you'll probably be all right if you close your eyes and rely on instinct. Also—to be perfectly frank—we don't want any more customers, at least on *our* night. The place is already uncomfortably crowded. All that I'll say about its location is that it shakes occasionally with the vibration of newspaper presses, and that if you crane out of the window of the gents' room you can just see the Thames.

From the outside, it looks like any other pub—as indeed it is for five days of the week. The public and saloon bars are on the ground floor: there are the usual vistas of brown oak panelling and frosted glass, the bottles behind the bar, the handles of the beer engines . . . nothing out of the ordinary at all. Indeed, the only concession to the twentieth century is the juke box in the public bar. It was installed during the war in a laughable attempt to make G.I.'s feel at home, and one of the first things we did was to make sure there was no danger of its ever working again.

At this point I had better explain who "we" are. That is not as easy as I thought it was going to be when I started, for a complete catalogue of the "White Hart's" clients would probably be impossible and would certainly be excruciatingly tedious. So all I'll say at this point is that "we" fall into three main classes. First there are the journalists, writers and editors. The journalists, of course, gravitated here from Fleet Street. Those who couldn't make the grade fled elsewhere: the tougher ones remained. As for the writers, most of them heard about us from other writers, came here for copy, and got trapped.

Where there are writers, of course, there are sooner or later editors. If Drew, our landlord, got a percentage on the literary business done in his bar, he'd be a rich man. (We suspect he is a rich man, anyway.) One of our wits once remarked that it was a common sight to see half a dozen indignant authors arguing with a hard-faced editor in one corner of the "White Hart", while in another, half a dozen indignant editors argued with a hard-faced author.

So much for the literary side: you will have, I'd better warn you, ample opportunities for close-ups later. Now let us glance briefly at the scientists. How did *they* get in here?

Well, Birkbeck College is only across the road, and King's is just a few hundred yards along the Strand. That's doubtless part of the explanation, and again personal recommendation had a lot to do with it. Also, many of our scientists are writers, and not a few of our writers are scientists. Confusing, but we like it that way.

The third portion of our little microcosm consists of what may be loosely termed "interested laymen". They were attracted to the "White Hart" by the general brouhaha, and enjoyed the conversation and company so much that they now come along regularly every Wednesday—which is the day when we all get together. Sometimes they can't stand the pace and fall by the wayside, but there's always a fresh supply.

With such potent ingredients, it is hardly surprising that Wednesday at the "White Hart" is seldom dull. Not only have some remarkable stories been told there, but remarkable things have *happened* there. For example, there was the time when Professor ——, passing through on his way to Harwell, left behind a brief-case containing—well, we'd better not go into that, even though we did so at the time. And most interesting it was, too. . . . Any Russian agents will find me in the corner under the dartboard. I come high, but easy terms can be arranged.

Now that I've finally thought of the idea, it seems astonishing to me that none of my colleagues has ever got round to writing up these stories. Is it a question of being so close to the wood that they can't see the trees? Or is it lack of incentive? No, the last explanation can hardly hold: several of them are quite as hard up as I am, and have complained with equal bitterness about Drew's "NO CREDIT" rule. My only fear, as I type these words on my old Remington Noiseless, is that John Christopher or George Whitley or John Beynon are already hard at work using up the best material. Such as, for instance, the story of the Fenton Silencer. . . .

I don't know when it began: one Wednesday is much like another and it's hard to tag dates on to them. Besides, people may spend a couple of months lost in the "White Hart" crowd before you first notice their existence. That had probably happened to Harry Purvis, because when I first came aware of him he already knew the names of most of the people in our crowd. Which is more than I do these days, now that I come to think of it.

But though I don't know *when,* I know exactly *how* it all started. Bert Huggins was the catalyst, or, to be more accurate, his voice was. Bert's voice would catalyse anything. When he indulges in a confidential whisper, it sounds like a sergeant major drilling an entire regiment. And when he lets himself go, conversation languishes elsewhere while we all wait for those cute little bones in the inner ear to resume their accustomed places.

He had just lost his temper with John Christopher (we all do this at some time or other) and the resulting detonation had disturbed the chess game in progress at the back of the saloon bar. As usual, the two players were surrounded by backseat drivers, and we all looked up with a start as Bert's blast whammed overhead. When the echoes died away, someone said: "I wish there was a way of shutting him up."

It was then that Harry Purvis replied: "There is, you know."

Not recognising the voice, I looked round. I saw a small, neatly-dressed man in the late thirties. He was smoking one of those carved German pipes that always make me think of cuckoo clocks and the Black Forest. That was the only unconventional thing about him: otherwise he might have been a minor Treasury official all dressed up to go to a meeting of the Public Accounts Committee.

"I beg your pardon?" I said.

He took no notice, but made some delicate adjustments to his pipe. It was then that I noticed that it wasn't, as I'd thought at first glance, an elaborate piece of wood carving. It was something much more sophisticated—a contraption of metal and plastic like a small chemical engineering plant. There were even a couple of minute valves. My God, it *was* a chemical engineering plant. . . .

I don't goggle any more easily than the next man, but I made no attempt to hide my curiosity. He gave me a superior smile.

"All for the cause of science. It's an idea of the Biophysics Lab. They want to find out exactly what there is in tobacco smoke— hence these filters. You know the old argument—*does* smoking cause cancer of the tongue, and if so, how? The trouble is that it takes an awful lot of—er—distillate to identify some of the obscurer by-products. So we have to do a lot of smoking."

"Doesn't it spoil the pleasure to have all this plumbing in the way?"

"I don't know. You see, I'm just a volunteer. I don't smoke."

"Oh," I said. For the moment, that seemed the only reply. Then I remembered how the conversation had started.

"You were saying," I continued with some feeling, for there was still a slight tintinus in my left ear, "that there was some way of shutting up Bert. We'd all like to hear it—if that isn't mixing metaphors somewhat."

"I was thinking," he replied, after a couple of experimental sucks and blows, "of the ill-fated Fenton Silencer. A sad story— yet, I feel, one with an interesting lesson for us all. And one day— who knows?—someone *may* perfect it and earn the blessings of the world."

Suck, bubble, bubble, *plop*. . . .

"Well, let's hear the story. When did it happen?"

He sighed.

"I'm almost sorry I mentioned it. Still, since you insist—and, of course, on the understanding that it doesn't go beyond these walls."

"Er—of course."

"Well, Rupert Fenton was one of our lab assistants. A very bright youngster, with a good mechanical background, but, naturally, not very well up in theory. He was always making gadgets in his spare time. Usually the idea was good, but as he was shaky on fundamentals the things hardly ever worked. That didn't seem to discourage him: I think he fancied himself as a latter-day Edison, and imagined he could make his fortune from the radio tubes and other oddments lying around the lab. As his tinkering didn't interfere with his work, no-one objected: indeed, the physics demonstrators did their best to encourage him, because, after all, there is something refreshing about any form of enthusiasm. But no-one expected he'd ever get very far, because I don't suppose he could even integrate *e* to the *x*."

"Is such ignorance *possible?*" gasped someone.

"Maybe I exaggerate. Let's say *x e* to the *x*. Anyway, all his knowledge was entirely practical—rule of thumb, you know. Give him a wiring diagram, however complicated, and he could make the apparatus for you. But unless it was something *really* simple, like a television set, he wouldn't understand how it worked. The trouble was, he didn't realise his limitations. And that, as you'll see, was most unfortunate.

"I think he must have got the idea while watching the Honours Physics students doing some experiments in acoustics. I take it, of course, that you all understand the phenomenon of interference?"

"Naturally," I replied.

"Hey!" said one of the chess-players, who had given up trying to concentrate on the game (probably because he was losing). "*I* don't."

Purvis looked at him as though seeing something that had no right to be around in a world that had invented penicillin.

"In that case," he said coldly, "I suppose I had better do some explaining." He waved aside our indignant protests. "No, I insist. It's precisely those who don't understand these things who need to be told about them. If someone had only explained the theory to poor Fenton while there was still time. . . ."

He looked down at the now thoroughly abashed chess-player.

"I do not know," he began, "if you have ever considered the nature of *sound*. Suffice to say that it consists of a series of waves moving through the air. Not, however, waves like those on the surface of the sea—oh dear no! *Those* waves are up and down movements. Sound waves consist of alternate compressions and rarefactions."

"Rare-what?"

"Rarefactions."

"Don't you mean 'rarefications'?"

"I do not. I doubt if such a word exists, and if it does, it shouldn't," retorted Purvis, with the *aplomb* of Sir Alan Herbert dropping a particularly revolting neologism into his killing-bottle. "Where was I? Explaining sound, of course. When we make any sort of noise, from the faintest whisper to that concussion that went past just now, a series of pressure changes moves through the air. Have you ever watched shunting engines at work on a siding? You see a perfect example of the same kind of thing. There's a long line of goods-wagons, all coupled together. One end gets a bang, the first two trucks move together—and then you can see the compression wave moving right along the line. Behind it the reverse thing happens—the rarefaction—I repeat, *rarefaction*—as the trucks separate again.

"Things are simple enough when there is only one source of sound—only one set of waves. But suppose you have two wave-patterns, moving in the same direction? That's when interference arises, and there are lots of pretty experiments in elementary physics to demonstrate it. All we need worry about here is the fact—which I think you will all agree is perfectly obvious—that if one could get two sets of waves *exactly* out of step, the total result would be precisely zero. The compression pulse of one sound wave would be on top of the rarefaction of another—net result—no change and hence no sound. To go back to my analogy of the line of wagons, it's as if you gave the last truck a jerk and a push simultaneously. Nothing at all would happen.

"Doubtless some of you will already see what I am driving at, and will appreciate the basic principle of the Fenton Silencer. Young Fenton, I imagine, argued in this manner. 'This world of ours,' he said to himself, 'is too full of noise. There would be a fortune for anyone who could invent a really perfect silencer. Now, what would that imply . . . ?'

"It didn't take him long to work out the answer: I told you he was a bright lad. There was really very little in his pilot model. It consisted of a microphone, a special amplifier, and a pair of loud-speakers. Any sound that happened to be about was picked up by the mike, amplified and *inverted* so that it was exactly out of phase with the original noise. Then it was pumped out of the speakers, the original wave and the new one cancelled out, and the net result was silence.

"Of course, there was rather more to it than that. There had to be an arrangement to make sure that the cancelling wave was just the right intensity—otherwise you might be worse off than when you started. But these are technical details that I won't bore you with. As many of you will recognise, it's a simple application of negative feed-back."

"Just a moment!" interrupted Eric Maine. Eric, I should mention, is an electronics expert and edits some television paper or other. He's also written a radio play about space-flight, but that's another story. "Just a moment! There's something wrong here. You *couldn't* get silence that way. It would be impossible to arrange the phase . . ."

Purvis jammed the pipe back in his mouth. For a moment there was an ominous bubbling and I thought of the first act of "Macbeth". Then he fixed Eric with a glare.

"Are you suggesting," he said frigidly, "that this story is untrue?"

"Ah—well, I won't go as far as that, but . . ." Eric's voice trailed away as if he had been silenced himself. He pulled an old envelope out of his pocket, together with an assortment of resistors and condensers that seemed to have got entangled in his handkerchief, and began to do some figuring. That was the last we heard from him for some time.

"As I was saying," continued Purvis calmly, *"that's* the way Fenton's Silencer worked. His first model wasn't very powerful, and it couldn't deal with very high or very low notes. The result was rather odd. When it was switched on, and someone tried to talk, you'd hear the two ends of the spectrum—a faint bat's squeak, and a kind of low rumble. But he soon got over that by using a more linear circuit (dammit, I can't help using *some* technicalities!) and in the later model he was able to produce complete silence over quite a large area. Not merely an ordinary room, but a full-sized hall. Yes. . . .

"Now Fenton was not one of these secretive inventors who won't tell anyone what they are trying to do, in case their ideas are stolen. He was all too willing to talk. He discussed his ideas with the staff and with the students, whenever he could get anyone to listen. It so happened that one of the first people to whom he demonstrated his improved Silencer was a young Arts student called —I think—Kendall, who was taking Physics as a subsidiary subject.

Kendall was much impressed by the Silencer, as well he might be. But he was not thinking, as you may have imagined, about its commercial possibilities, or the boon it would bring to the outraged ears of suffering humanity. Oh dear no! He had quite other ideas.

"Please permit me a slight digression. At college we have a flourishing Musical Society, which in recent years has grown in numbers to such an extent that it can now tackle the less monumental symphonies. In the year of which I speak, it was embarking on a very ambitious enterprise. It was going to produce a new opera, a work by a talented young composer whose name it would not be fair to mention, since it is now well-known to you all. Let us call him Edward England. I've forgotten the title of the work, but it was one of these stark dramas of tragic love which, for some reason I've never been able to understand, are supposed to be less ridiculous with a musical accompaniment than without. No doubt a good deal depends on the music.

"I can still remember reading the synopsis while waiting for the curtain to go up, and to this day have never been able to decide whether the libretto was meant seriously or not. Let's see—the period was the late Victorian era, and the main characters were Sarah Stampe, the passionate postmistress, Walter Partridge, the saturnine gamekeeper, and the squire's son, whose name I forget. It's the old story of the eternal triangle, complicated by the villager's resentment of change—in this case, the new telegraph system, which the local crones predict will Do Things to the cows' milk and cause trouble at lambing time.

"Ignoring the frills, it's the usual drama of operatic jealousy. The squire's son doesn't want to marry into the Post Office, and the gamekeeper, maddened by his rejection, plots revenge. The tragedy rises to its dreadful climax when poor Sarah, strangled with parcel tape, is found hidden in a mail-bag in the Dead Letter Department. The villagers hang Partridge from the nearest telegraph pole, much to the annoyance of the linesmen. He was supposed to sing an aria while he was being hung: *that* is one thing I regret missing. The squire's son takes to drink, or the Colonies, or both: and that's that.

"I'm sure you're wondering where all this is leading: please bear with me for a moment longer. The fact is that while this synthetic jealousy was being rehearsed, the real thing was going on backstage. Fenton's friend Kendall had been spurned by the young lady who was to play Sarah Stampe. I don't think he was a particularly vindictive person, but he saw an opportunity for a unique revenge. Let us be frank and admit that college life *does* breed a certain irresponsibility—and in identical circumstances, how many of *us* would have rejected the same chance?

"I see the dawning comprehension on your faces. But we, the audience, had no suspicion when the overture started on that memorable day. It was a most distinguished gathering: everyone was there, from the Chancellor downwards. Deans and professors were two a penny: I never did discover how so many people had been bullied into coming. Now that I come to think of it, I can't remember what I was doing there myself.

"The overture died away amid cheers, and, I must admit, occasional cat-calls from the more boisterous members of the audience. Perhaps I do them an injustice: they may have been the more musical ones.

"Then the curtain went up. The scene was the village square at Doddering Sloughleigh, *circa* 1860. Enter the heroine, reading the postcards in the morning's mail. She comes across a letter addressed to the young squire and promptly bursts into song.

"Sarah's opening aria wasn't quite as bad as the overture, but it was grim enough. Luckily, we were to hear only the first few bars. . . .

"Precisely. We need not worry about such details as how Kendall had talked the ingenuous Fenton into it—if, indeed, the inventor realised the use to which his device was being applied. All I need say is that it was a most convincing demonstration. There was a sudden, deadening blanket of silence, and Sarah Stampe just faded out like a TV programme when the sound is turned off. Everyone was frozen in their seats, while the singer's lips went on moving silently. Then she too realised what had happened. Her mouth opened in what would have been a piercing scream in any other circumstances, and she fled into the wings amid a shower of postcards.

"Thereafter, the chaos was unbelievable. For a few minutes everyone must have thought they had lost the sense of hearing, but soon they were able to tell from the behaviour of their companions that they were not alone in their deprivation. Someone in the Physics

Department must have realised the truth fairly promptly, for soon little slips of paper were circulating among the V.I.P.'s in the front row. The Vice-Chancellor was rash enough to try and restore order by sign-language, waving frantically to the audience from the stage. By this time I was too sick with laughter to appreciate such fine details.

"There was nothing for it but to get out of the hall, which we all did as quickly as we could. I think Kendall had fled—he was so overcome by the effect of the gadget that he didn't stop to switch it off. He was afraid of staying around in case he was caught and lynched. As for Fenton—alas, we shall never know *his* side of the story. We can only reconstruct the subsequent events from the evidence that was left.

"As I picture it, he must have waited until the hall was empty, and then crept in to disconnect his apparatus. We heard the explosion all over the college."

"The *explosion?*" someone gasped.

"Of course. I shudder to think what a narrow escape we all had. Another dozen decibels, a few more phons—and it might have happened while the theatre was still packed. Regard it, if you like, as an example of the inscrutable workings of providence that only the inventor was caught in the explosion. Perhaps it was as well: at least he perished in the moment of achievement, and before the Dean could get at him."

"Stop moralising, man. What happened?"

"Well, I told you that Fenton was very weak on theory. If he'd gone into the mathematics of the Silencer he'd have found his mistake. The trouble is, you see, that one can't *destroy* energy. Not even when you cancel out one train of waves by another. All that happens then is that the energy you've neutralized accumulates *somewhere else*. It's rather like sweeping up all the dirt in a room —at the cost of an unsightly pile under the carpet.

"When you look into the theory of the thing, you'll find that Fenton's gadget wasn't a silencer so much as a *collector* of sound. All the time it was switched on, it was really absorbing sound energy. And at that concert, it was certainly going flat out. You'll understand what I mean if you've ever looked at one of Edward England's scores. On top of that, of course, there was all the noise the audience was making—or I should say was *trying* to make—

during the resultant panic. The total amount of energy must have been terrific, and the poor Silencer had to keep on sucking it up. Where did it go? Well, I don't know the circuit details—probably into the condensers of the power pack. By the time Fenton started to tinker with it again, it was like a loaded bomb. The sound of his approaching footsteps was the last straw, and the overloaded apparatus could stand no more. It blew up."

For a moment no-one said a word, perhaps as a token of respect for the late Mr. Fenton. Then Eric Maine, who for the last ten minutes had been muttering in the corner over his calculations, pushed his way through the ring of listeners. He held a sheet of paper thrust aggressively in front of him.

"Hey!" he said. "I was right all the time. The thing couldn't work. The phase and amplitude relations. . . ."

Purvis waved him away.

"That's just what I've explained," he said patiently. "You should have been listening. Too bad that Fenton found out the hard way."

He glanced at his watch. For some reason, he now seemed in a hurry to leave.

"My goodness! Time's getting on. One of these days, remind me to tell you about the extraordinary thing we saw through the new proton microscope. That's an even more remarkable story."

He was half way through the door before anyone else could challenge him. Then George Whitley recovered his breath.

"Look here," he said in a perplexed voice. "How is it that we never heard about this business?"

Purvis paused on the threshold, his pipe now burbling briskly as it got into its stride once more. He glanced back over his shoulder.

"There was only one thing to do," he replied. "We didn't want a scandal—*de mortuis nil nisi bonum,* you know. Besides, in the circumstances, don't you think it was highly appropriate to—ah—*hush* the whole business up? And a very good night to you all."

As I've remarked on previous occasions, no-one has ever succeeded in pinning-down Harry Purvis, prize raconteur of the "White Hart", for any length of time. Of his scientific knowledge there can be no doubt—but where did he pick it up? And what justification is there for the terms of familiarity with which he speaks of so many Fellows of the Royal Society? There are, it must be admitted, many who do not believe a single word he says. That, I feel, is going a little too far, as I recently remarked somewhat forcibly to Bill Temple.

"You're always gunning for Harry," I said, "but you must admit that he provides entertainment. And that's more than most of us can say."

"If you're being personal," retorted Bill, still rankling over the fact that some perfectly serious stories had just been returned by an American editor on the grounds that they hadn't made him laugh, "step outside and say that again." He glanced through the window, noticed that it was still snowing hard, and hastily added, "Not today, then, but maybe sometime in the summer, if we're both here on the Wednesday that catches it. Have another of your favourite shots of straight pineapple juice?"

"Thanks," I said. "One day I'll ask for a gin with it, just to shake you. I think I must be the only guy in the White Hart who can take it or leave it—*and* leaves it."

This was as far as the conversation got, because the subject of the discussion then arrived. Normally, this would merely have added fuel to the controversy, but as Harry had a stranger with him we decided to be polite little boys.

"Hello, folks," said Harry. "Meet my friend Solly Blumberg. Best special effects man in Hollywood."

"Let's be accurate, Harry," said Mr. Blumberg sadly, in a voice that should have belonged to a whipped spaniel. "Not *in* Hollywood. *Out* of Hollywood."

Harry waved the correction aside.

"All the better for you. Sol's come over here to apply his talents to the British film industry."

"There *is* a British film industry?" said Solly anxiously. "No-one seemed very sure round the studio."

"Sure there is. It's in a very flourishing condition, too. The Government piles on an entertainments tax that drives it to bankruptcy, then keeps it alive with whacking big grants. That's the way we do things in this country. Hey, Drew, where's the Visitor's Book? And a double for both of us. Solly's had a terrible time—he needs a bit of building up."

I cannot say that, apart from his hang-dog look, Mr. Blumberg had the appearance of a man who had suffered extreme hardships. He was neatly dressed in a Hart, Schaffner and Marx suit, and the points of his shirt collar buttoned down somewhere around the middle of his chest. That was thoughtful of them as they thus concealed something, but not enough, of his tie. I wondered what the trouble was. Not un-American activities *again,* I prayed: that would trigger off our pet communist, who at the moment was peaceably studying a chess-board in the corner.

We all made sympathetic noises and John said rather pointedly: "Maybe it'll help to get it off your chest. It will be such a change to hear someone else talking around here."

"Don't be so modest, John," cut in Harry promptly. "*I'm* not tired of hearing you yet. But I doubt if Solly feels much like going through it again. Do you, old man?"

"No," said Mr. Blumberg. "*You* tell them."

("I knew it would come to that," sighed John in my ear.)

"Where shall I begin?" asked Harry. "The time Lillian Ross came to interview you?"

"Anywhere but *there*," shuddered Solly. "It really started when we were making the first 'Captain Zoom' serial."

" 'Captain Zoom'?" said someone ominously. "Those are two

very rude words in this place. Don't say you were responsible for *that* unspeakable rubbish!"

"Now boys!" put in Harry in his best oil-on-troubled-waters voice. "Don't be too harsh. We can't apply our own high standards of criticism to everything. And people have got to earn a living. Besides, millions of kids *like* Captain Zoom. Surely you wouldn't want to break their little hearts—and so near Xmas, too!"

"If they *really* liked Captain Zoom, I'd rather break their little necks."

"Such unseasonable sentiments! I really must apologise for some of my compatriots, Solly. Let's see, what was the name of the first serial?"

" 'Captain Zoom and the Menace from Mars'."

"Ah yes, that's right. Incidentally, I wonder why we always are menaced by Mars? I suppose that man Wells started it. One day we may have a big interplanetary libel action on our hands—unless we can prove that the Martians have been equally rude about *us*.

"I'm very glad to say that I never saw 'Menace From Mars' ("I did," moaned somebody in the background. "I'm still trying to forget it.")—but we are not concerned with the story, such as it was. That was written by three men in a bar on Wilshire Boulevard. No-one is sure whether the Menace came out the way it did because the script writers were drunk, or whether they had to keep drunk in order to face the Menace. If that's confusing, don't bother. All that Solly was concerned with were the special effects that the director demanded.

"First of all, he had to build Mars. To do this he spent half an hour with 'The Conquest of Space', and then emerged with a sketch which the carpenters turned into an over-ripe orange floating in nothingness, with an improbable number of stars around it. *That* was easy. The Martian cities weren't so simple. You try and think of *completely alien* architecture that still makes sense. I doubt if it's possible—if it will work at all, someone's already used it here on Earth. What the studio finally built was vaguely Byzantine with touches of Frank Lloyd Wright. The fact that none of the doors led anywhere didn't really matter, as long as there was enough room on the sets for the swordplay and general acrobatics that the script demanded.

"Yes—swordplay. Here was a civilisation which had atomic

power, death-rays, spaceships, television and suchlike modern conveniences, but when it came to a fight between Captain Zoom and the evil Emperor Klugg, the clock went back a couple of centuries. A lot of soldiers stood round holding deadly-looking ray-guns, but they never *did* anything with them. Well, hardly ever. Sometimes a shower of sparks would chase Captain Zoom and singe his pants, but that was all. I suppose that as the rays couldn't very well move faster than light, he could always outrun them.

"Still, those ornamental ray-guns gave everyone quite a few headaches. It's funny how Hollywood will spend endless trouble on some minute detail in a film which is complete rubbish. The director of Captain Zoom had a thing about ray-guns. Solly designed the Mark I, that looked like a cross between a bazooka and a blunderbuss. He was quite satisfied with it, and so was the director—for about a day. And then the great man came raging into the studio carrying a revolting creation of purple plastic with knobs and lenses and levers.

" 'Lookit this, Solly!' he puffed. 'Junior got it down at the Supermarket—they're being given away with packets of Crunch. Collect ten lids, and you get one. Hell, they're better than ours! And they *work!*'

"He pressed a lever, and a thin stream of water shot across the set and disappeared behind Captain Zoom's spaceship, where it promptly extinguished a cigaret that had no right to be burning there. An angry stage-hand emerged through the airlock, saw who it was had drenched him, and swiftly retreated, muttering things about his Union.

"Solly examined the ray-gun with annoyance and yet with an expert's discrimination. Yes, it was certainly much more impressive than anything *he'd* put out. He retired into his office and promised to see what he could do about it.

"The Mark II had everything built into it, including a television screen. If Captain Zoom was suddenly confronted by a charging hickoderm, all he had to do was to switch on the set, wait for the tubes to warm up, check the channel selector, adjust the fine tuning, touch up the focus, twiddle with the Line and Frame holds—and then press the trigger. He was, fortunately, a man of unbelievably swift reactions.

"The director was impressed, and the Mark II went into production. A slightly different model, the Mark IIa, was built for the Emperor Klugg's diabolical cohorts. It would never do, of course, if both sides had the same weapon. I told you that Pandemic Productions were sticklers for accuracy.

"All went well until the first rushes, and even beyond. While the cast was acting, if you can use that word, they had to point the guns and press the triggers as if something was really happening. The sparks and flashes, however, were put on the negative later by two little men in a darkroom about as well guarded as Fort Knox. They did a good job, but after a while the producer again felt twinges in his overdeveloped artistic conscience.

" 'Solly,' he said, toying with the plastic horror which had reached Junior by courtesy of Crunch, the Succulent Cereal—Not a Burp in a Barrel—'Solly, I still want a gun that *does* something.'

"Solly ducked in time, so the jet went over his head and baptised a photograph of Louella Parsons.

" 'You're not going to start shooting all over again!' he wailed.

" 'Nooo,' replied the producer, with obvious reluctance. 'We'll have to use what we've got. But it *looks* faked, somehow.' He ruffled through the script on his desk, then brightened up.

" 'Now next week we start on Episode 54—"Slaves of the Slug-Men." Well, the Slug-Men gotta have guns, so what I'd like you to do is this—'

"The Mark III gave Solly a lot of trouble. (I haven't missed out one yet, have I? Good.) Not only had it to be a completely new design, but as you'll have gathered it had to 'do something'. This was a challenge to Solly's ingenuity: however, if I may borrow from Professor Toynbee, it was a challenge that evoked the appropriate response.

"Some high-powered engineering went into the Mark III. Luckily, Solly knew an ingenious technician who'd helped him out on similar occasions before, and he was really the man behind it. ('I'll say he was!' said Mr. Blumberg gloomily.) The principle was to use a jet of air, produced by a small but extremely powerful electric fan, and then to spray finely divided powder into it. When the thing was adjusted correctly, it shot out a most impressive beam, and made a still more impressive noise. The actors were so scared of it that their performances became most realistic.

"The producer was delighted—for a full three days. Then a dreadful doubt assailed him.

" 'Solly,' he said, 'those damn guns are *too* good. The Slug-Men can beat the pants off Captain Zoom. We'll have to give him something better.'

"It was at this point that Solly realised what had happened. He had become involved in an armaments race.

"Let's see, this brings us to the Mark IV, doesn't it? How did *that* work?—oh yes, I remember. It was a glorified oxy-acetylene burner, with various chemicals injected into it to produce the most beautiful flames. I should have mentioned that from Episode 50—'Doom on Deimos'—the studio had switched over from black and white to Murkicolor, and great possibilities were thus opened up. By squirting copper or strontium or barium into the jet, you could get any colour you wanted.

"If you think that by this time the producer was satisfied, you don't know Hollywood. Some cynics may still laugh when the motto 'Ars Gratia Artis' flashes on the screen, but this attitude, I submit, is not in accordance with the facts. Would such old fossils as Michaelangelo, Rembrandt or Titian have spent so much time, effort and money on the quest for perfection as did Pandemic Productions? I think not.

"I don't pretend to remember all the Marks that Solly and his ingenious engineer friend produced during the course of the serial. There was one that shot out a stream of coloured smoke-rings. There was the high-frequency generator that produced enormous but quite harmless sparks. There was a particularly ingenious *curved* beam produced by a jet of water with light reflected along inside it, which looked most spectacular in the dark. And finally, there was the Mark 12."

"Mark 13," said Mr. Blumberg.

"Of course—how stupid of me! What other number *could* it have been! The Mark 13 was not actually a portable weapon—though some of the others were portable only by a considerable stretch of the imagination. It was the diabolical device to be installed on Phobos in order to subjugate Earth. Though Solly has explained them to me once, the scientific principles involved escape my simple mind. . . . However, who am I to match my brains against the intellects responsible for Captain Zoom? I can only report what the ray was supposed to do, not how it did it. It was to start a chain reaction in the atmosphere of our unfortunate planet, making the nitrogen and the oxygen in the air combine—with highly deleterious effects to terrestrial life.

"I'm not sure whether to be sorry or glad that Solly left all the details of the fabulous Mark 13 to his talented assistant. Though I've questioned him at some length, all he can tell me is that the thing was about six feet high and looked like a cross between the 200 inch telescope and an anti-aircraft gun. That's not very helpful, is it?

"He also says that there were a lot of radio tubes in the brute, as well as a thundering great magnet. And it was definitely supposed to produce a harmless but impressive electric arc, which could be distorted into all sorts of interesting shapes by the magnet. *That* was what the inventor said, and, despite everything, there is still no reason to disbelieve him.

"By one of those mischances that later turns out to be providential, Solly wasn't at the studio when they tried out the Mark 13. To his great annoyance, he had to be down in Mexico that day. And wasn't that lucky for you, Solly! He was expecting a long-distance call from one of his friends in the afternoon, but when it came through it wasn't the kind of message he'd anticipated.

"The Mark 13 had been, to put it mildly, a success. No-one knew exactly what had happened, but by a miracle no lives had been lost and the fire department had been able to save the adjoining studios. It was incredible, yet the facts were beyond dispute. The Mark 13 was supposed to be a phony death-ray—and it had turned out to be a real one. *Something* had emerged from the projector, and gone through the studio wall as if it wasn't there. Indeed, a moment later it wasn't. There was just a great big hole, beginning to smoulder round the edges. And then the roof fell in. . . .

"Unless Solly could convince the F.B.I. that it was all a mistake, he'd better stay the other side of the border. Even now the Pentagon and the Atomic Energy Commission were converging upon the wreckage. . . .

"What would you have done in Solly's shoes? He was innocent, but how could he prove it? Perhaps he would have gone back to face the music if he hadn't remembered that he'd once hired a man who'd campaigned for Henry Wallace, back in '48. *That* might take some explaining away: besides, Solly was a little tired of Captain Zoom. So here he is. Anyone know of a British film company that might have an opening for him? But historical films only, please. He won't touch anything more up-to-date than cross-bows."

I got to the "White Hart" late that evening, and when I arrived everyone was crowded into the corner under the dartboard. All except Drew, that is: he had not deserted his post, but was sitting behind the bar reading the collected T. S. Eliot. He broke off from "The Confidential Clerk" long enough to hand me a beer and to tell me what was going on.

"Eric's brought in some kind of games machine—it's beaten everybody so far. Sam's trying his luck with it now."

At that moment a roar of laughter announced that Sam had been no luckier than the rest, and I pushed my way through the crowd to see what was happening.

On the table lay a flat metal box the size of a checkerboard, and divided into squares in a similar way. At the corner of each square was a two-way switch and a little neon lamp: the whole affair was plugged into the light socket (thus plunging the dartboard into darkness) and Eric Rodgers was looking round for a new victim.

"What does the thing do?" I asked.

"It's a modification of naughts and crosses—what the Americans call Tic-Tac-Toe. Shannon showed it to me when I was over at Bell Labs. What you have to do is to complete a path from one side of the board to the other—call it North to South—by turning these switches. Imagine the thing forms a grid of streets, if you like, and these neons are the traffic lights. You and the machine take turns making moves. The machine tries to block your path by building one of its own in the East-West direction—the little neons light up to tell you which way it wants to make a move. Neither track need be a straight line: you can zig-zag as much as you like.

118

All that matters is that the path must be continuous, and the one to get across the board first wins."

"Meaning the machine, I suppose?"

"Well, it's never been beaten yet."

"Can't you force a draw, by blocking the machine's path, so that at least you don't lose?"

"That's what we're trying: like to have a go?"

Two minutes later I joined the other unsuccessful contestants. The machine had dodged all my barriers and established its own track from East to West. I wasn't convinced that it was unbeatable, but the game was clearly a good deal more complicated than it looked.

Eric glanced round his audience when I had retired. No-one else seemed in a hurry to move forward.

"Ha!" he said. "The very man. What about you, Purvis? You've not had a shot yet."

Harry Purvis was standing at the back of the crowd, with a faraway look in his eye. He jolted back to earth as Eric addressed him, but didn't answer the question directly.

"Fascinating things, these electronic computers," he mused. "I suppose I shouldn't tell you this, but your gadget reminds me of what happened to Project Clausewitz. A curious story, and one very expensive to the American taxpayer."

"Look," said John Wyndham anxiously. "Before you start, be a good sport and let us get our glasses filled. Drew!"

This important matter having been attended to, we gathered round Harry. Only Charlie Willis still remained with the machine, hopefully trying his luck.

"As you all know," began Harry, "Science with a capital S is a big thing in the military world these days. The weapons side—rockets, atom bombs and so on—is only part of it, though that's all the public knows about. Much more fascinating, in my opinion, is the operational research angle. You might say that's concerned with brains rather than brute force. I once heard it defined as how to win wars without actually fighting, and that's not a bad description.

"Now you all know about the big electronic computers that cropped up like mushrooms in the 1950's. Most of them were built to deal with mathematical problems, but when you think about it you'll realise that War itself is a mathematical problem. It's such a complicated one that human brains can't handle it—there are far too many variables. Even the greatest strategist cannot see the picture as a whole: the Hitlers and Napoleons always make a mistake in the end.

"But a machine—that would be a different matter. A number of bright people realised this after the end of the war. The techniques that had been worked out in the building of ENIAC and the other big computers could revolutionize strategy.

"Hence Project Clausewitz. Don't ask me how I got to know about it, or press me for too many details. All that matters is that a good many megabucks worth of electronic equipment, and some of the best scientific brains in the United States, went into a certain cavern in the Kentucky hills. They're still there, but things haven't turned out exactly as they expected.

"Now I don't know what experience you have of high-ranking military officers, but there's one type you've all come across in fiction. That's the pompous, conservative, stick-in-the-mud careerist who's got to the top by sheer pressure from beneath, who does everything by rules and regulations and regards civilians as, at the best, unfriendly neutrals. I'll let you into a secret: he actually exists. He's not very common nowadays, but he's still around and sometimes it's not possible to find a safe job for him. When that happens, he's worth his weight in plutonium to the Other Side.

"Such a character, it seems, was General Smith. No, of *course* that wasn't his real name! His father was a Senator, and although lots of people in the Pentagon had tried hard enough, the old man's influence had prevented the General from being put in charge of something harmless, like the coast defence of Wyoming. Instead, by miraculous misfortune, he had been made the officer responsible for Project Clausewitz.

"Of course, he was only concerned with the administrative, not the scientific, aspects of the work. All might yet have been well had the General been content to let the scientists get on with their work while he concentrated on saluting smartness, the coefficient of reflection of barrack floors, and similar matters of military importance. Unfortunately, he didn't.

"The General had led a sheltered existence. He had, if I may borrow from Wilde (everybody else does) been a man of peace, except in his domestic life. He had never met scientists before, and the shock was considerable. So perhaps it is not fair to blame him for everything that happened.

"It was a considerable time before he realised the aims and objects of Project Clausewitz, and when he did he was quite disturbed. This may have made him feel even less friendly towards his scientific staff, for despite anything I may have said the General was not entirely a fool. He was intelligent enough to understand that, if the Project succeeded, there might be more ex-generals around than even the combined boards of management of American industry could comfortably absorb.

"But let's leave the General for a minute and have a look at the scientists. There were about fifty of them, as well as a couple of hundred technicians. They'd all been carefully screened by the F.B.I., so probably not more than half a dozen were active members of the Communist Party. Though there was a lot of talk of sabotage later, for once in a while the comrades were completely innocent. Besides, what happened certainly wasn't sabotage in any generally accepted meaning of the word. . . .

"The man who had really designed the computer was a quiet little mathematical genius who had been swept out of college into the Kentucky hills and the world of Security and Priorities before he'd really realised what had happened. He wasn't called Dr. Milquetoast, but he should have been and that's what I'll christen him.

"To complete our cast of characters, I'd better say something about Karl. At this stage in the business, Karl was only half-built. Like all big computers, most of him consisted of vast banks of memory units which could receive and store information until it was needed. The creative part of Karl's brain—the analysers and integrators—took this information and operated on it, to produce answers to the questions he was asked. Given all the relevant facts, Karl would produce the right answers. The problem, of course, was to see that Karl *did* have all the facts—he couldn't be expected to get the right results from inaccurate or insufficient information.

"It was Dr. Milquetoast's responsibility to design Karl's brain. Yes, I know that's a crudely anthropomorphic way of looking at it, but no-one can deny that these big computers have personalities. It's hard to put it more accurately without getting technical, so I'll simply say that little Milquetoast had to create the extremely complex circuits that enabled Karl to think in the way he was supposed to do.

"So here are our three protagonists—General Smith, pining for the days of Custer; Dr. Milquetoast, lost in the fascinating scientific intricacies of his job; and Karl, fifty tons of electronic gear, not yet animated by the currents that would soon be coursing through him.

"Soon—but not soon enough for General Smith. Let's not be too hard on the General: someone had probably put the pressure on him, when it became obvious that the Project was falling behind schedule. He called Dr. Milquetoast into his office.

"The interview lasted more than thirty minutes, and the doctor said less than thirty words. Most of the time the General was making pointed remarks about production times, deadlines and bottlenecks. He seemed to be under the impression that building Karl differed in no important particular from the assembly of the current model Ford: it was just a question of putting the bits together. Dr. Milquetoast was not the sort of man to explain the error, even if the General had given him the opportunity. He left, smarting under a considerable sense of injustice.

"A week later, it was obvious that the creation of Karl was falling still further behind schedule. Milquetoast was doing his best, and there was no-one who could do better. Problems of a complexity totally beyond the General's comprehension had to be met and mastered. They *were* mastered, but it took time, and time was in short supply.

"At his first interview, the General had tried to be as nice as he could, and had succeeded in being merely rude. This time, he tried to be rude, with results that I leave to your imagination. He practically insinuated that Milquetoast and his colleagues, by falling behind their deadlines, were guilty of un-American inactivity.

"From this moment onwards, two things started to happen. Relations between the Army and the scientists grew steadily worse; and Dr. Milquetoast, for the first time, began to give serious thought to the wider implications of his work. He had always been too busy, too engaged upon the immediate problems of his task, to consider his social responsibilities. He was still too busy now, but that didn't stop him pausing for reflection. 'Here am I,' he told himself, 'one of the best pure mathematicians in the world—and what am I doing? What's happened to my thesis on Diophantine equations? When am I going to have another smack at the prime number theorem? In short, when am I going to do some *real* work again?'

"He could have resigned, but that didn't occur to him. In any case, far down beneath that mild and diffident exterior was a stubborn streak. Dr. Milquetoast continued to work, even more energetically than before. The construction of Karl proceeded slowly but steadily: the final connexions in his myriad-celled brain were soldered: the thousands of circuits were checked and tested by the mechanics.

"And one circuit, indistinguishably interwoven among its multitude of companions and leading to a set of memory cells apparently identical with all the others, was tested by Dr. Milquetoast alone, for no-one else knew that it existed.

"The great day came. To Kentucky, by devious routes, came very important personages. A whole constellation of multi-starred generals arrived from the Pentagon. Even the Navy had been invited.

"Proudly, General Smith led the visitors from cavern to cavern, from memory banks to selector networks to matrix analysers to input tables—and finally to the rows of electric typewriters on which Karl would print the results of his deliberations. The General knew his way around quite well: at least, he got most of the names right. He even managed to give the impression, to those who knew no better, that he was largely responsible for Karl.

"'Now,' said the General cheerfully. 'Let's give him some work to do. Anyone like to set him a few sums?'

"At the word 'sums' the mathematicians winced, but the General was unaware of his *faux pas*. The assembled brass thought for a while: then someone said daringly, 'What's 9 multiplied by itself twenty times?'

"One of the technicians, with an audible sniff, punched a few keys. There was a rattle of gunfire from an electric typewriter, and before anyone could blink twice the answer had appeared—all twenty digits of it."

(I've looked it up since: for anyone who wants to know it's:—
                    12157665459056928801
But let's get back to Harry and his tale.)

"For the next fifteen minutes Karl was bombarded with similar trivialities. The visitors were impressed, though there was no reason to suppose that they'd have spotted it if all the answers had been completely wrong.

"The General gave a modest cough. Simple arithmetic was as far as he could go, and Karl had barely begun to warm up. 'I'll now hand you over,' he said, 'to Captain Winkler.'

"Captain Winkler was an intense young Harvard graduate whom the General distrusted, rightly suspecting him to be more a scientist than a military man. But he was the only officer who really understood what Karl was supposed to do, or could explain exactly how he set about doing it. He looked, the General thought grumpily, like a damned schoolmaster as he started to lecture the visitors.

"The tactical problem that had been set up was a complicated one, but the answer was already known to everybody except Karl. It was a battle that had been fought and finished almost a century before, and when Captain Winkler concluded his introduction, a general from Boston whispered to his side, 'I'll bet some damn Southerner has fixed it so that Lee wins this time.' Everyone had to admit, however, that the problem was an excellent way of testing Karl's capabilities.

"The punched tapes disappeared into the capacious memory units: patterns of lights flickered and flashed across the registers; mysterious things happened in all directions.

"'This problem,' said Captain Winkler primly, 'will take about five minutes to evaluate.'

"As if in deliberate contradiction, one of the typewriters promptly started to chatter. A strip of paper shot out of the feed, and Captain Winkler, looking rather puzzled at Karl's unexpected alacrity, read the message. His lower jaw immediately dropped six inches, and he stood staring at the paper as if unable to believe his eyes.

"'What is it, man?' barked the General.

"Captain Winkler swallowed hard, but appeared to have lost the power of speech. With a snort of impatience, the General snatched the paper from him. Then it was his turn to stand paralysed, but unlike his subordinate he also turned a most beautiful red. For a moment he looked like some tropical fish strangling out of water: then, not without a slight scuffle, the enigmatic message was captured by the five-star general who outranked everybody in the room.

"His reaction was totally different. He promptly doubled up with laughter.

"The minor officers were left in a state of infuriating suspense for quite ten minutes. But finally the news filtered down through Colonels to Captains to Lieutenants, until at last there wasn't a G.I. in the establishment who did not know the wonderful news.

"Karl had told General Smith that he was a pompous baboon. That was all.

"Even though everybody agreed with Karl, the matter could hardly be allowed to rest there. Something, obviously, had gone wrong. Something—or someone—had diverted Karl's attention from the Battle of Gettysburg.

"'Where,' roared General Smith, finally recovering his voice, 'is Dr. Milquetoast?'

"He was no longer present. He had slipped quietly out of the room, having witnessed his great moment. Retribution would come later, of course, but it was worth it.

"The frantic technicians cleared the circuits and started running tests. They gave Karl an elaborate series of multiplications and divisions to perform—the computer's equivalent of 'The quick brown fox jumps over the lazy dog.' Everything seemed to be functioning perfectly. So they put in a very simple tactical problem, which a Lieutenant J. G. could solve in his sleep.

"Said Karl: 'Go jump in a lake, General.'

"It was then that General Smith realised that he was confronted with something outside the scope of Standard Operating Procedure. He was faced with mechanical mutiny, no less.

"It took several hours of tests to discover exactly what had happened. Somewhere tucked away in Karl's capacious memory units was a superb collection of insults, lovingly assembled by Dr. Milquetoast. He had punched on tape, or recorded in patterns of electrical impulses, everything he would like to have said to the General himself. But that was not all he had done: that would have been too easy, not worthy of his genius. He had also installed what could only be called a censor circuit—he had given Karl the power of discrimination. Before solving it, Karl examined every problem fed to him. If it was concerned with pure mathematics, he co-operated and dealt with it properly. But if it was a military problem —out came one of the insults. After twenty times, he had not repeated himself once, and the WAC's had already had to be sent out of the room.

"It must be confessed that after a while the technicians were almost as interested in discovering what indignity Karl would next heap upon General Smith as they were in finding the fault in the circuits. He had begun with mere insults and surprising geneological surmises, but had swiftly passed on to detailed instructions the mildest of which would have been highly prejudicial to the General's dignity, while the more imaginative would have seriously imperilled his physical integrity. The fact that all these messages, as they emerged from the typewriters, were immediately classified TOP SE-CRET was small consolation to the recipient. He knew with a glum certainty that this would be the worst-kept secret of the cold war, and that it was time he looked round for a civilian occupation.

"And there, gentlemen," concluded Purvis, "the situation remains. The engineers are still trying to unravel the circuits that Dr. Milquetoast installed, and no doubt it's only a matter of time before they succeed. But meanwhile Karl remains an unyielding pacifist. He's perfectly happy playing with the theory of numbers, computing tables of powers, and handling arithmetical problems generally. Do you remember the famous toast 'Here's to pure mathematics— may it never be of any use to anybody'? Karl would have seconded that. . . .

"As soon as anyone attempts to slip a fast one across him, he goes on strike. And because he's got such a wonderful memory, he can't be fooled. He has half the great battles of the world stored up in his circuits, and can recognise at once any variations on them. Though attempts were made to disguise tactical exercises as problems in mathematics, he could spot the subterfuge right away. And out would come another *billet doux* for the General.

"As for Dr. Milquetoast, no one could do much about him because he promptly had a nervous breakdown. It was suspiciously well timed, but he could certainly claim to have earned it. When last heard of he was teaching matrix algebra at a theological college in Denver. He swears he's forgotten everything that had ever happened while he was working on Karl. Maybe he was even telling the truth. . . ."

There was a sudden shout from the back of the room.

"I've won!" cried Charles Willis. "Come and see!"

We all crowded under the dartboard. It seemed true enough. Charlie had established a zig-zag but continuous track from one side of the checker-board to the other, despite the obstacles the machine had tried to put in his way.

"Show us how you did it," said Eric Rodgers.

Charlie looked embarrassed.

"I've forgotten," he said. "I didn't make a note of all the moves."

A sarcastic voice broke in from the background.

"But *I* did," said John Christopher. "You were cheating—you made two moves at once."

After that, I am sorry to say, there was some disorder, and Drew had to threaten violence before peace was restored. I don't know who really won the squabble, and I don't think it matters. For I'm inclined to agree with what Purvis remarked as he picked up the robot checker-board and examined its wiring.

"You see," he said, "this little gadget is only a simple-minded cousin of Karl's—and look what it's done already. All these machines are beginning to make us look fools. Before long they'll start to disobey us without any Milquetoast interfering with their circuits. And then they'll start ordering us about—they're logical, after all, and won't stand any nonsense."

He sighed. "When that happens, there won't be a thing we can do about it. We'll just have to say to the dinosaurs: 'Move over a bit—here comes *homo sap!*' And the transistor shall inherit the earth."

There was no time for further pessimistic philosophy, for the door opened and Police Constable Wilkins stuck his head in. "Where's the owner of CGC 571?" he asked testily. "Oh—it's *you*, Mr. Purvis. Your rear light's out."

Harry looked at me sadly, then shrugged his shoulders in resignation. "You see," he said, "it's started already." And he went out into the night.

✶ *THE NEXT TENANTS*

"The number of mad scientists who wish to conquer the world," said Harry Purvis, looking thoughtfully at his beer, "has been grossly exaggerated. In fact, I can remember encountering only a single one."

"Then there couldn't have been many others," commented Bill Temple, a little acidly. "It's not the sort of thing one would be likely to forget."

"I suppose not," replied Harry, with that air of irrefragable innocence which is so disconcerting to his critics. "And, as a matter of fact, this scientist wasn't really mad. There was no doubt, though, that he was out to conquer the world. Or if you want to be really precise—to let the world be conquered."

"And by whom?" asked George Whitley. "The Martians? Or the well-known little green men from Venus?"

"Neither of them. He was collaborating with someone a lot nearer home. You'll realize who I mean when I tell you he was a myrmecologist."

"A which-what?" asked George.

"Let him get on with the story," said Drew, from the other side of the bar. "It's past ten, and if I can't get you all out by closing time *this* week, I'll lose my license."

"Thank you," said Harry with dignity, handing over his glass for a refill. "This all happened about two years ago, when I was on a mission in the Pacific. It was rather hush-hush, but in view of what's happened since there's no harm in talking about it. Three of us scientists were landed on a certain Pacific atoll not a thousand miles from Bikini, and given a week to set up some detection equip-

128

ment. It was intended, of course, to keep an eye on our good friends and allies when they started playing with thermo-nuclear reactions —to pick some crumbs from the A.E.C.'s table, as it were. The Russians, naturally, were doing the same thing, and occasionally we ran into each other and then both sides would pretend that there was nobody here but us chickens.

"This atoll was supposed to be uninhabited, but this was a considerable error. It actually had a population of several hundred millions—"

"What!" gasped everybody.

"—several hundred millions," continued Purvis calmly, "of which number, one was human. I came across him when I went inland one day to have a look at the scenery."

"Inland?" asked George Whitley. "I thought you said it was an atoll. How can a ring of coral—"

"It was a very plump atoll," said Harry firmly. "Anyway, who's telling this story?" He waited defiantly for a moment until he had the right of way again.

"Here I was, then, walking up a charming little river-course underneath the coconut palms, when to my great surprise I came across a waterwheel—a very modern-looking one, driving a dynamo. If I'd been sensible, I suppose I'd have gone back and told my companions, but I couldn't resist the challenge and decided to do some reconnoitering on my own. I remembered that there were still supposed to be Japanese troops around who didn't know that the war was over, but that explanation seemed a bit unlikely.

"I followed the power-line up a hill, and there on the other side was a low, whitewashed building set in a large clearing. All over this clearing were tall, irregular mounds of earth, linked together with a network of wires. It was one of the most baffling sights I have ever seen, and I stood and stared for a good ten minutes, trying to decide what was going on. The longer I looked, the less sense it seemed to make.

"I was debating what to do when a tall, white-haired man came out of the building and walked over to one of the mounds. He was carrying some kind of apparatus and had a pair of earphones slung around his neck, so I guessed that he was using a Geiger counter. It was just about then that I realized what those tall mounds were. They were termitaries . . . the skyscrapers, in comparison to their makers, far taller than the Empire State Building, in which the so-called white ants live.

"I watched with great interest, but complete bafflement, while the elderly scientist inserted his apparatus into the base of the termitary, listened intently for a moment, and then walked back towards the building. By this time I was so curious that I decided to make my presence known. Whatever research was going on here obviously had nothing to do with international politics, so I was the only one who'd have anything to hide. You'll appreciate later just what a miscalculation *that* was.

"I yelled for attention and walked down the hill, waving my arms. The stranger halted and watched me approaching: he didn't look particularly surprised. As I came closer I saw that he had a straggling moustache that gave him a faintly Oriental appearance. He was about sixty years old, and carried himself very erect. Though he was wearing nothing but a pair of shorts, he looked so dignified that I felt rather ashamed of my noisy approach.

" 'Good morning,' I said apologetically. 'I didn't know that there was anyone else on this island. I'm with an—er—scientific survey party over on the other side.'

"At this, the stranger's eyes lit up. 'Ah,' he said, in almost perfect English, 'a fellow scientist! I'm very pleased to meet you. Come into the house.'

"I followed gladly enough—I was pretty hot after my scramble —and I found that the building was simply one large lab. In a corner was a bed and a couple of chairs, together with a stove and one of those folding wash-basins that campers use. That seemed to sum up the living arrangements. But everything was very neat and tidy: my unknown friend seemed to be a recluse, but he believed in keeping up appearances.

"I introduced myself first, and as I'd hoped he promptly responded. He was one Professor Takato, a biologist from a leading Japanese university. He didn't look particularly Japanese, apart from the moustache I've mentioned. With his erect, dignified bearing he reminded me more of an old Kentucky colonel I once knew.

"After he'd given me some unfamiliar but refreshing wine, we sat and talked for a couple of hours. Like most scientists he seemed happy to meet someone who would appreciate his work. It was true that my interests lay in physics and chemistry rather than on the biological side, but I found Professor Takato's research quite fascinating.

"I don't suppose you know much about termites, so I'll remind you of the salient facts. They're among the most highly evolved of the social insects, and live in vast colonies throughout the tropics. They can't stand cold weather, nor, oddly enough, can they endure direct sunlight. When they have to get from one place to another, they construct little covered roadways. They seem to have some unknown and almost instantaneous means of communication, and though the individual termites are pretty helpless and dumb, a whole colony behaves like an intelligent animal. Some writers have drawn comparisons between a termitary and a human body, which is also composed of individual living cells making up an entity much higher than the basic units. The termites are often called 'white ants', but that's a completely incorrect name as they aren't ants at all but quite a different species of insect. Or should I say 'genus'? I'm pretty vague about this sort of thing. . . .

"Excuse this little lecture, but after I'd listened to Takato for a while I began to get quite enthusiastic about termites myself. Did you know, for example, that they not only cultivate gardens but also keep cows—insect cows, of course—and milk them? Yes, they're sophisticated little devils, even though they do it all by instinct.

"But I'd better tell you something about the Professor. Although he was alone at the moment, and had lived on the island for several years, he had a number of assistants who brought equipment from Japan and helped him in his work. His first great achievement was to do for the termites what von Frische had done with bees—he'd learned their language. It was much more complex than the system of communication that bees use, which as you probably know, is based on dancing. I understood that the network of wires linking the termitaries to the lab not only enabled Professor Takato to listen to the termites talking among each other, but also permitted him to speak to them. That's not really as fantastic as it sounds, if you use the word "speak" in its widest sense. We speak to a good many animals—not always with our voices, by any means. When you throw a stick for your dog and expect him to run and fetch it, that's a form of speech—sign language. The Professor, I gathered, had worked out some kind of code which the termites understood, though how efficient it was at communicating ideas I didn't know.

"I came back each day, when I could spare the time, and by the end of the week we were firm friends. It may surprise you that I was able to conceal these visits from my colleagues, but the island was quite large and we each did a lot of exploring. I felt somehow that Professor Takato was my private property, and did not wish to expose him to the curiosity of my companions. They were rather uncouth characters—graduates of some provincial university like Oxford or Cambridge.

"I'm glad to say that I was able to give the Professor a certain amount of assistance, fixing his radio and lining up some of his electronic gear. He used radioactive tracers a good deal, to follow individual termites around. He'd been tracking one with a Geiger counter when I first met him, in fact.

"Four or five days after we'd met, his counters started to go haywire, and the equipment we'd set up began to reel in its recordings. Takato guessed what had happened: he'd never asked me exactly what I was doing on the islands, but I think he knew. When I greeted him he switched on his counters and let me listen to the roar of radiation. There had been some radioactive fall-out—not enough to be dangerous, but sufficient to bring the background 'way up.

"'I think,' he said softly, 'that you physicists are playing with your toys again. And very big ones, this time.'

"'I'm afraid you're right,' I answered. We wouldn't be sure until the readings had been analyzed, but it looked as if Teller and his team had started the hydrogen reaction. 'Before long, we'll be able to make the first A-bombs look like damp squibs.'

"'My family,' said Professor Takato, without any emotion, 'was at Nagasaki.'

"There wasn't a great deal I could say to that, and I was glad when he went on to add: 'Have you ever wondered who will take over when we are finished?'

"'Your termites?' I said, half facetiously. He seemed to hesitate for a moment. Then he said quietly, 'Come with me; I have not shown you everything.'

"We walked over to a corner of the lab where some equipment lay concealed beneath dust-sheets, and the Professor uncovered a rather curious piece of apparatus. At first sight it looked like one of the manipulators used for the remote handling of dangerously radio-active materials. There were handgrips that conveyed movements through rods and levers, but everything seemed to focus on a small box a few inches on a side. 'What is it?' I asked.

"'It's a micromanipulator. The French developed them for biological work. There aren't many around yet.'

"Then I remembered. These were devices with which, by the use of suitable reduction gearing, one could carry out the most incredibly delicate operations. You moved your finger an inch—and the tool you were controlling moved a thousandth of an inch. The French scientists who had developed this technique had built tiny forges on which they could construct minute scalpels and tweezers from fused glass. Working entirely through microscopes, they had been able to dissect individual cells. Removing an appendix from a termite (in the highly doubtful event of the insect possessing one) would be child's play with such an instrument.

"'I am not very skilled at using the manipulator,' confessed Takato. 'One of my assistants does all the work with it. I have shown no one else this, but you have been very helpful. Come with me, please.'

"We went out into the open, and walked past the avenues of tall, cement-hard mounds. They were not all of the same architec-tural design, for there are many different kinds of termites—some, indeed, don't build mounds at all. I felt rather like a giant walking through Manhattan, for these were skyscrapers, each with its own teeming population.

"There was a small metal (not wooden—the termites would soon have fixed that!) hut beside one of the mounds, and as we entered it the glare of sunlight was banished. The Professor threw a switch, and a faint red glow enabled me to see various types of optical equipment.

"'They hate light,' he said, 'so it's a great problem observing them. We solved it by using infra-red. This is an image-converter of the type that was used in the war for operations at night. You know about them?'

"'Of course,' I said. 'Snipers had them fixed on their rifles so that they could go sharp-shooting in the dark. Very ingenious things —I'm glad you've found a civilized use for them.'

"It was a long time before Professor Takato found what he wanted. He seemed to be steering some kind of periscope arrangement, probing through the corridors of the termite city. Then he said: 'Quick—before they've gone!'

"I moved over and took his position. It was a second or so before my eye focused properly, and longer still before I understood the scale of the picture I was seeing. Then I saw six termites, greatly enlarged, moving rather rapidly across the field of vision. They were travelling in a group, like the huskies forming a dog-team. And that was a very good analogy, because they were towing a sledge. . . .

"I was so astonished that I never even noticed what kind of load they were moving. When they had vanished from sight, I turned to Professor Takato. My eyes had now grown accustomed to the faint red glow, and I could see him quite well.

" 'So that's the sort of tool you've been building with your micromanipulator!' I said. 'It's amazing—I'd never have believed it.'

" 'But that is nothing,' replied the Professor. 'Performing fleas will pull a cart around. I haven't told you what is so important. We only made a few of those sledges. *The one you saw they constructed themselves.*'

"He let that sink in: it took some time. Then he continued quietly, but with a kind of controlled enthusiasm in his voice: 'Remember that the termites, as individuals, have virtually no intelligence. But the colony as a whole is a very high type of organism —and an immortal one, barring accidents. It froze in its present instinctive pattern millions of years before Man was born, and by itself it can never escape from its present sterile perfection. It has reached a dead-end—because it has no tools, no effective way of controlling nature. I have given it the lever, to increase its power, and now the sledge, to improve its efficiency. I have thought of the wheel, but it is best to let that wait for a later stage—it would not be very useful now. The results have exceeded my expectations. I started with this termitary alone—but now they all have the same tools. They have taught each other, and that proves they can co-operate. True, they have wars—but not when there is enough food for all, as there is here.

" 'But you cannot judge the termitary by human standards. What I hope to do is to jolt its rigid, frozen culture—to knock it out of the groove in which it has stuck for so many millions of years. I will give it more tools, more new techniques—and before I die, I hope to see it beginning to invent things for itself.'

" 'Why are you doing this?' I asked, for I knew there was more than mere scientific curiosity here.

" 'Because I do not believe that Man will survive, yet I hope to preserve some of the things he has discovered. If he is to be a dead-end, I think that another race should be given a helping hand. Do you know why I chose this island? It was so that my experiment should remain isolated. My supertermite, if it ever evolves, will have to remain here until it has reached a very high level of attainment. Until it can cross the Pacific, in fact. . . .

. " 'There is another possibility. Man has no rival on this planet. I think it may do him good to have one. It may be his salvation.'

"I could think of nothing to say: this glimpse of the Professor's dreams was so overwhelming—and yet, in view of what I had just seen, so convincing. For I knew that Professor Takato was not mad. He was a visionary, and there was a sublime detachment about his outlook, but it was based on a secure foundation of scientific achievement.

"And it was not that he was hostile to mankind: he was sorry for it. He simply believed that humanity had shot its bolt, and wished to save something from the wreckage. I could not feel it in my heart to blame him.

"We must have been in that little hut for a long time, exploring possible futures. I remember suggesting that perhaps there might be some kind of mutual understanding, since two cultures so utterly dissimilar as Man and Termite need have no cause for conflict. But I couldn't really believe this, and if a contest comes, I'm not certain who will win. For what use would man's weapons be against an intelligent enemy who could lay waste all the wheat fields and all the rice crops in the world?

"When we came out into the open once more, it was almost dusk. It was then that the Professor made his final revelation.

" 'In a few weeks,' he said, 'I am going to take the biggest step of all.'

" 'And what is that?' I asked.

" 'Cannot you guess? I am going to give them fire.'

"Those words did something to my spine. I felt a chill that had nothing to do with the oncoming night. The glorious sunset that was taking place beyond the palms seemed symbolic—and suddenly I realized that the symbolism was even deeper than I had thought.

"That sunset was one of the most beautiful I had ever seen, and it was partly of man's making. Up there in the stratosphere, the dust of an island that had died this day was encircling the earth. My race had taken a great step forward; but did it matter now?

"'*I am going to give them fire.*' Somehow, I never doubted that the Professor would succeed. And when he had done so, the forces that my own race had just unleashed would not save it. . . .

"The flying boat came to collect us the next day, and I did not see Takato again. He is still there, and I think he is the most important man in the world. While our politicians wrangle, he is making us obsolete.

"Do you think that someone ought to stop him? There may still be time. I've often thought about it, but I've never been able to think of a really convincing reason why I should interfere. Once or twice I nearly made up my mind, but then I'd pick up the newspaper and see the headlines.

"I think we should let them have the chance. I don't see how they could make a worse job of it than we've done."

Though few people in the "White Hart" will concede that any of Harry Purvis' stories are actually *true*, everyone agrees that some are much more probable than others. And on any scale of probability, the affair of the Reluctant Orchid must rate very low indeed.

I don't remember what ingenious gambit Harry used to launch this narrative: maybe some orchid fancier brought his latest monstrosity into the bar, and that set him off. No matter. I do remember the story, and after all that's what counts.

The adventure did not, this time, concern any of Harry's numerous relatives, and he avoided explaining just how he managed to know so many of the sordid details. The hero—if you can call him that—of this hothouse epic was an inoffensive little clerk named Hercules Keating. And if you think *that* is the most unlikely part of the story, just stick round a while.

Hercules is not the sort of name you can carry off lightly at the best of times, and when you are four foot nine and look as if you'd have to take a physical culture course before you can even become a 97-pound weakling, it is a positive embarrassment. Perhaps it helped to explain why Hercules had very little social life, and all his real friends grew in pots in a humid conservatory at the bottom of his garden. His needs were simple and he spent very little money on himself; consequently his collection of orchids and cacti was really rather remarkable. Indeed, he had a wide reputation among the fraternity of cactophiles, and often received from remote corners of the globe, parcels smelling of mould and tropical jungles.

Hercules had only one living relative, and it would have been

137

hard to find a greater contrast than Aunt Henrietta. She was a massive six footer, usually wore a rather loud line in Harris tweeds, drove a Jaguar with reckless skill, and chain-smoked cigars. Her parents had set their hearts on a boy, and had never been able to decide whether or not their wish had been granted. Henrietta earned a living, and quite a good one, breeding dogs of various shapes and sizes. She was seldom without a couple of her latest models, and they were not the type of portable canine which ladies like to carry in their handbags. The Keating Kennels specialized in Great Danes, Alsatians, and Saint Bernards. . . .

Henrietta, rightly despising men as the weaker sex, had never married. However, for some reason she took an avuncular (yes, that is definitely the right word) interest in Hercules, and called to see him almost every weekend. It was a curious kind of relationship: probably Henrietta found that Hercules bolstered up her feelings of superiority. If he was a good example of the male sex, then they were certainly a pretty sorry lot. Yet, if this was Henrietta's motivation, she was unconscious of it and seemed genuinely fond of her nephew. She was patronizing, but never unkind.

As might be expected, her attentions did not exactly help Hercules' own well-developed inferiority complex. At first he had tolerated his aunt; then he came to dread her regular visits, her booming voice and her bone-crushing handshake; and at last he grew to hate her. Eventually, indeed, his hate was the dominant emotion in his life, exceeding even his love for his orchids. But he was careful not to show it, realizing that if Aunt Henrietta discovered how he felt about her, she would probably break him in two and throw the pieces to her wolf pack.

There was no way, then, in which Hercules could express his pent-up feelings. He had to be polite to Aunt Henrietta even when he felt like murder. And he often did feel like murder, though he knew that there was nothing he would ever do about it. Until one day . . .

According to the dealer, the orchid came from "somewhere in the Amazon region"—a rather vague postal address. When Hercules first saw it, it was not a very•prepossessing sight, even to anyone who loved orchids as much as he did. A shapeless root, about the size of a man's fist—that was all. It was redolent of decay, and there was the faintest hint of a rank, carrion smell. Hercules was not even sure that it was viable, and told the dealer as much. Perhaps that enabled him to purchase it for a trifling sum, and he carried it home without much enthusiasm.

It showed no signs of life for the first month, but that did not worry Hercules. Then, one day, a tiny green shoot appeared and started to creep up to the light. After that, progress was rapid. Soon there was a thick, fleshy stem as big as a man's forearm, and colored a positively virulent green. Near the top of the stem a series of curious bulges circled the plant: otherwise it was completely feature-less. Hercules was now quite excited: he was sure that some entirely new species had swum into his ken.

The rate of growth was now really fantastic: soon the plant was taller than Hercules, not that that was saying a great deal. Moreover, the bulges seemed to be developing, and it looked as if at any moment the orchid would burst into bloom. Hercules waited anx-iously, knowing how short-lived some flowers can be, and spent as much time as he possibly could in the hothouse. Despite all his watchfulness, the transformation occurred one night while he was asleep.

In the morning, the orchid was fringed by a series of eight dangling tendrils, almost reaching to the ground. They must have developed inside the plant and emerged with—for the vegetable world—explosive speed. Hercules stared at the phenomenon in amazement, and went very thoughtfully to work.

That evening, as he watered the plant and checked its soil, he noticed a still more peculiar fact. The tendrils were thickening, and they were not completely motionless. They had a slight but unmis-takable tendency to vibrate, as if possessing a life of their own. Even Hercules, for all his interest and enthusiasm, found this more than a little disturbing.

A few days later, there was no doubt about it at all. When he approached the orchid, the tendrils swayed toward him in an un-pleasantly suggestive fashion. The impression of hunger was so strong that Hercules began to feel very uncomfortable indeed, and something started to nag at the back of his mind. It was quite a while before he could recall what it was: then he said to himself, "Of course! How stupid of me!" and went along to the local library. Here he spent a most interesting half-hour rereading a little piece by one H. G. Wells entitled, "The Flowering of the Strange Orchid."

"My goodness!" thought Hercules, when he had finished the tale. As yet there had been no stupefying odor which might overpower the plant's intended victim, but otherwise the characteristics were all too similar. Hercules went home in a very unsettled mood indeed.

He opened the conservatory door and stood looking along the avenue of greenery towards his prize specimen. He judged the length of the tendrils—already he found himself calling them tentacles—with great care and walked to within what appeared a safe distance. The plant certainly had an impression of alertness and menace far more appropriate to the animal than the vegetable kingdom. Hercules remembered the unfortunate history of Doctor Frankenstein, and was not amused.

But, really, this was ridiculous! Such things didn't happen in real life. Well, there was one way to put matters to the test . . .

Hercules went into the house and came back a few minutes later with a broomstick, to the end of which he had attached a piece of raw meat. Feeling a considerable fool, he advanced towards the orchid as a lion-tamer might approach one of his charges at meal-time.

For a moment, nothing happened. Then two of the tendrils developed an agitated twitch. They began to sway back and forth, as if the plant was making up its mind. Abruptly, they whipped out with such speed that they practically vanished from view. They wrapped themselves round the meat, and Hercules felt a powerful tug at the end of his broomstick. Then the meat was gone: the orchid was clutching it, if one may mix metaphors slightly, to its bosom.

"Jumping Jehosophat!" yelled Hercules. It was very seldom indeed that he used such strong language.

The orchid showed no further signs of life for twenty-four hours. It was waiting for the meat to become high, and it was also developing its digestive system. By the next day, a network of what looked like short roots had covered the still visible chunk of meat. By nightfall, the meat was gone.

The plant had tasted blood.

Hercules' emotions as he watched over his prize were curiously mixed. There were times when it almost gave him nightmares, and he foresaw a whole range of horrid possibilities. The orchid was now extremely strong, and if he got within its clutches he would be done for. But, of course, there was not the slightest danger of that. He had arranged a system of pipes so that it could be watered from a safe distance, and its less orthodox food he simply tossed within range of its tentacles. It was now eating a pound of raw meat a day, and he had an uncomfortable feeling that it could cope with much larger quantities if given the opportunity.

Hercules' natural qualms were, on the whole, outweighed by his feeling of triumph that such a botanical marvel had fallen into his hands. Whenever he chose, he could become the most famous orchid-grower in the world. It was typical of his somewhat restricted view-point that it never occurred to him that other people besides orchid-fanciers might be interested in his pet.

The creature was now about six feet tall, and apparently still growing—though much more slowly than it had been. All the other plants had been moved from its end of the conservatory, not so much because Hercules feared that it might be cannibalistic as to enable him to tend them without danger. He had stretched a rope across the central aisle so that there was no risk of his accidentally walking within range of those eight dangling arms.

It was obvious that the orchid had a highly developed nervous system, and something very nearly approaching intelligence. It knew when it was going to be fed, and exhibited unmistakable signs of pleasure. Most fantastic of all—though Hercules was still not sure about this—it seemed capable of producing sounds. There were times, just before a meal, when he fancied he could hear an incredibly high-pitched whistle, skirting the edge of audibility. A new-born bat might have had such a voice: he wondered what purpose it served. Did the orchid somehow lure its prey into its clutches by sound? If so, he did not think the technique would work on him.

While Hercules was making these interesting discoveries, he continued to be fussed over by Aunt Henrietta and assaulted by her hounds, which were never as house-trained as she claimed them to be. She would usually roar up the street on a Sunday afternoon with one dog in the seat beside her and another occupying most of the baggage compartment. Then she would bound up the steps two at a time, nearly deafen Hercules with her greeting, half paralyze him with her handshake, and blow cigar smoke in his face. There had been a time when he was terrified that she would kiss him, but he had long since realized that such effeminate behaviour was foreign to her nature.

Aunt Henrietta looked upon Hercules' orchids with some scorn. Spending one's spare time in a hothouse was, she considered, a very effete recreation. When *she* wanted to let off steam, she went big-game hunting in Kenya. This did nothing to endear her to Hercules, who hated blood sports. But despite his mounting dislike for his overpowering aunt, every Sunday afternoon he dutifully prepared tea for her and they had a tête-à-tête together which, on the surface at least, seemed perfectly friendly. Henrietta never guessed that as he poured the tea Hercules often wished it was poisoned: she was, far down beneath her extensive fortifications, a fundamentally good-hearted person and the knowledge would have upset her deeply.

Hercules did not mention his vegetable octopus to Aunt Henrietta. He had occasionally shown her his most interesting specimens, but this was something he was keeping to himself. Perhaps, even before he had fully formulated his diabolical plan, his subconscious was already preparing the ground . . .

It was late one Sunday evening, when the roar of the Jaguar had died away into the night and Hercules was restoring his shattered nerves in the conservatory, that the idea first came fully-fledged into his mind. He was staring at the orchid, noting how the tendrils were now as thick around as a man's thumb, when a most pleasing fantasy suddenly flashed before his eyes. He pictured Aunt Henrietta struggling helplessly in the grip of the monster, unable to escape from its carnivorous clutches. Why, it would be the perfect crime. The distraught nephew would arrive on the scene too late to be of assistance, and when the police answered his frantic call they would see at a glance that the whole affair was a deplorable accident. True, there would be an inquest, but the coroner's censure would be toned down in view of Hercules' obvious grief . . .

The more he thought of the idea, the more he liked it. He could see no flaws, as long as the orchid co-operated. That, clearly, would be the greatest problem. He would have to plan a course of training for the creature. It already looked sufficiently diabolical; he must give it a disposition to suit its appearance.

Considering that he had no prior experience in such matters, and that there were no authorities he could consult, Hercules proceeded along very sound and businesslike lines. He would use a fishing rod to dangle pieces of meat just outside the orchid's range, until the creature lashed its tentacles in a frenzy. At such times its high-pitched squeak was clearly audible, and Hercules wondered how it managed to produce the sound. He also wondered what its organs of perception were, but this was yet another mystery that could not be solved without close examination. Perhaps Aunt Henrietta, if all went well, would have a brief opportunity of discovering these interesting facts—though she would probably be too busy to report them for the benefit of posterity.

There was no doubt that the beast was quite powerful enough to deal with its intended victim. It had once wrenched a broomstick out of Hercules' grip, and although that in itself proved very little, the sickening "crack" of the wood a moment later brought a smile of satisfaction to its trainer's thin lips. He began to be much more pleasant and attentive to his aunt. In every respect, indeed, he was the model nephew.

When Hercules considered that his picador tactics had brought the orchid into the right frame of mind, he wondered if he should test it with live bait. This was a problem that worried him for some weeks, during which time he would look speculatively at every dog or cat he passed in the street, but he finally abandoned the idea, for a rather peculiar reason. He was simply too kind-hearted to put it into practice. Aunt Henrietta would have to be the first victim.

He starved the orchid for two weeks before he put his plan into action. This was as long as he dared risk—he did not wish to weaken the beast—merely to whet its appetite, that the outcome of the encounter might be more certain. And so, when he had carried the tea-cups back into the kitchen and was sitting upwind of Aunt Henrietta's cigar, he said casually: "I've got something I'd like to show you, auntie. I've been keeping it as a surprise. It'll tickle you to death."

That, he thought, was not a completely accurate description, but it gave the general idea.

Auntie took the cigar out of her mouth and looked at Hercules with frank surprise.

"Well!" she boomed. "Wonders will never cease! What *have*

you been up to, you rascal?" She slapped him playfully on the back and shot all the air out of his lungs.

"You'll never believe it," gritted Hercules, when he had recovered his breath. "It's in the observatory."

"Eh?" said Auntie, obviously puzzled.

"Yes—come along and have a look. It's going to create a real sensation."

Auntie gave a snort that might have indicated disbelief, but followed Hercules without further question. The two Alsatians now busily chewing up the carpet looked at her anxiously and half rose to their feet, but she waved them away.

"All right, boys," she ordered gruffly. "I'll be back in a minute." Hercules thought this unlikely.

It was a dark evening, and the lights in the conservatory were off. As they entered, Auntie snorted, "Gad, Hercules—the place smells like a slaughter-house. Haven't met such a stink since I shot that elephant in Bulawayo and we couldn't find it for a week."

"Sorry, auntie," apologized Hercules, propelling her forward through the gloom. "It's a new fertilizer I'm using. It produces the most stunning results. Go on—another couple of yards. I want this to be a *real* surprise."

"I hope this isn't a joke," said Auntie suspiciously, as she stomped forward.

"I can promise you it's no joke," replied Hercules, standing with his hand on the light switch. He could just see the looming bulk of the orchid: Auntie was now within ten feet of it. He waited until she was well inside the danger zone, and threw the switch.

There was a frozen moment while the scene was transfixed with light. Then Aunt Henrietta ground to a halt and stood, arms akimbo, in front of the giant orchid. For a moment Hercules was afraid she would retreat before the plant could get into action: then he saw that she was calmly scrutinizing it, unable to make up her mind what the devil it was.

It was a full five seconds before the orchid moved. Then the dangling tentacles flashed into action—but not in the way that Hercules had expected. The plant clutched them tightly, protectively, *around itself*—and at the same time it gave a high-pitched scream of pure terror. In a moment of sickening disillusionment, Hercules realized the awful truth.

His orchid was an utter coward. It might be able to cope with the wild life of the Amazon jungle, but coming suddenly upon Aunt Henrietta had completely broken its nerve.

As for its proposed victim, she stood watching the creature with an astonishment which swiftly changed to another emotion. She spun around on her heels and pointed an accusing finger at her nephew.

"Hercules!" she roared. "The poor thing's scared to death. *Have you been bullying it?*"

Hercules could only stand with his head hanging low in shame and frustration.

"N-no, auntie," he quavered. "I guess it's naturally nervous."

"Well, I'm used to animals. You should have called me before. You must treat them firmly—but gently. Kindness always works, as long as you show them you're the master. There, there, did-dums—don't be frightened of auntie—she won't hurt you . . ."

It was, thought Hercules in his blank despair, a revolting sight. With surprising gentleness, Aunt Henrietta fussed over the beast, patting and stroking it until the tentacles relaxed and the shrill, whistling scream died away. After a few minutes of this pandering, it appeared to get over its fright. Hercules finally fled with a muffled sob when one of the tentacles crept forward and began to stroke Henrietta's gnarled fingers . . .

From that day, he was a broken man. What was worse, he could never escape from the consequences of his intended crime. Henrietta had acquired a new pet, and was liable to call not only at weekends but two or three times in between as well. It was obvious that she did not trust Hercules to treat the orchid properly, and still suspected him of bullying it. She would bring tasty tidbits that even her dogs had rejected, but which the orchid accepted with delight. The smell, which had so far been confined to the conservatory, began to creep into the house . . .

And there, concluded Harry Purvis, as he brought this improbable narrative to a close, the matter rests—to the satisfaction of two, at any rate, of the parties concerned. The orchid is happy, and Aunt Henrietta has something (query, someone?) else to dominate. From time to time the creature has a nervous breakdown when a mouse gets loose in the conservatory, and she rushes to console it.

As for Hercules, there is no chance that he will ever give any more trouble to either of them. He seems to have sunk into a kind of vegetable sloth: indeed, said Harry thoughtfully, every day he becomes more and more like an orchid himself.

The harmless variety, of course. . . .

REACH FOR TOMORROW

Who was to blame? For three days Alveron's thoughts had come back to that question, and still he had found no answer. A creature of a less civilized or a less sensitive race would never have let it torture his mind, and would have satisfied himself with the assurance that no one could be responsible for the working of fate. But Alveron and his kind had been lords of the Universe since the dawn of history, since that far distant age when the Time Barrier had been folded round the cosmos by the unknown powers that lay beyond the Beginning. To them had been given all knowledge—and with infinite knowledge went infinite responsibility. If there were mistakes and errors in the administration of the galaxy, the fault lay on the heads of Alveron and his people. And this was no mere mistake: it was one of the greatest tragedies in history.

The crew still knew nothing. Even Rugon, his closest friend and the ship's deputy captain, had been told only part of the truth. But now the doomed worlds lay less than a billion miles ahead. In a few hours, they would be landing on the third planet.

Once again Alveron read the message from Base; then, with a flick of a tentacle that no human eye could have followed, he pressed the "General Attention" button. Throughout the mile-long cylinder that was the Galactic Survey Ship S9000, creatures of many races laid down their work to listen to the words of their captain.

"I know you have all been wondering," began Alveron, "why we were ordered to abandon our survey and to proceed at such an acceleration to this region of space. Some of you may realize what this acceleration means. Our ship is on its last voyage: the generators have already been running for sixty hours at Ultimate Overload.

149

We will be very lucky if we return to Base under our own power.

"We are approaching a sun which is about to become a Nova. Detonation will occur in seven hours, with an uncertainty of one hour, leaving us a maximum of only four hours for exploration. There are ten planets in the system about to be destroyed—and there is a civilization on the third. That fact was discovered only a few days ago. It is our tragic mission to contact that doomed race and if possible to save some of its members. I know that there is little we can do in so short a time with this single ship. No other machine can possibly reach the system before detonation occurs."

There was a long pause during which there could have been no sound or movement in the whole of the mighty ship as it sped silently toward the worlds ahead. Alveron knew what his companions were thinking and he tried to answer their unspoken question.

"You will wonder how such a disaster, the greatest of which we have any record, has been allowed to occur. On one point I can reassure you. The fault does not lie with the Survey.

"As you know, with our present fleet of under twelve thousand ships, it is possible to re-examine each of the eight thousand million solar systems in the Galaxy at intervals of about a million years. Most worlds change very little in so short a time as that.

"Less than four hundred thousand years ago, the survey ship S5060 examined the planets of the system we are approaching. It found intelligence on none of them, though the third planet was teeming with animal life and two other worlds had once been inhabited. The usual report was submitted and the system is due for its next examination in six hundred thousand years.

"It now appears that in the incredibly short period since the last survey, intelligent life has appeared in the system. The first intimation of this occurred when unknown radio signals were detected on the planet Kulath in the system X29.35, Y34.76, Z27.93. Bearings were taken on them; they were coming from the system ahead.

"Kulath is two hundred light-years from here, so those radio waves had been on their way for two centuries. Thus for at least that period of time a civilization has existed on one of these worlds—a civilization that can generate electromagnetic waves and all that that implies.

"An immediate telescopic examination of the system was made and it was then found that the sun was in the unstable pre-nova stage. Detonation might occur at any moment, and indeed might have done so while the light waves were on their way to Kulath.

"There was a slight delay while the supervelocity scanners on Kulath II were focused on to the system. They showed that the explosion had not yet occurred but was only a few hours away. If Kulath had been a fraction of a light-year further from this sun, we should never have known of its civilization until it had ceased to exist.

"The Administrator of Kulath contacted Sector Base immediately, and I was ordered to proceed to the system at once. Our object is to save what members we can of the doomed race, if indeed there are any left. But we have assumed that a civilization possessing radio could have protected itself against any rise of temperature that may have already occurred.

"This ship and the two tenders will each explore a section of the planet. Commander Torkalee will take Number One, Commander Orostron Number Two. They will have just under four hours in which to explore this world. At the end of that time, they must be back in the ship. It will be leaving then, with or without them. I will give the two commanders detailed instructions in the control room immediately.

"That is all. We enter atmosphere in two hours."

On the world once known as Earth the fires were dying out: there was nothing left to burn. The great forests that had swept across the planet like a tidal wave with the passing of the cities were now no more than glowing charcoal and the smoke of their funeral pyres still stained the sky. But the last hours were still to come, for the surface rocks had not yet begun to flow. The continents were dimly visible through the haze, but their outlines meant nothing to the watchers in the approaching ship. The charts they possessed were out of date by a dozen Ice Ages and more deluges than one.

The S9000 had driven past Jupiter and seen at once that no life could exist in those half-gaseous oceans of compressed hydrocarbons, now erupting furiously under the sun's abnormal heat. Mars and the outer planets they had missed, and Alveron realized that the worlds nearer the sun than Earth would be already melting. It was more than likely, he thought sadly, that the tragedy of this unknown race was already finished. Deep in his heart, he thought it might be better so. The ship could only have carried a few hundred survivors, and the problem of selection had been haunting his mind.

Rugon, Chief of Communications and Deputy Captain, came into the control room. For the last hour he had been striving to detect radiation from Earth, but in vain.

"We're too late," he announced gloomily. "I've monitored the whole spectrum and the ether's dead except for our own stations and some two-hundred-year-old programs from Kulath. Nothing in this system is radiating any more."

He moved toward the giant vision screen with a graceful flowing motion that no mere biped could ever hope to imitate. Alveron said nothing; he had been expecting this news.

One entire wall of the control room was taken up by the screen, a great black rectangle that gave an impression of almost infinite depth. Three of Rugon's slender control tentacles, useless for heavy work but incredibly swift at all manipulation, flickered over the selector dials and the screen lit up with a thousand points of light. The star field flowed swiftly past as Rugon adjusted the controls, bringing the projector to bear upon the sun itself.

No man of Earth would have recognized the monstrous shape that filled the screen. The sun's light was white no longer: great violet-blue clouds covered half its surface and from them long streamers of flame were erupting into space. At one point an enormous prominence had reared itself out of the photosphere, far out even into the flickering veils of the corona. It was as though a tree of fire had taken root in the surface of the sun—a tree that stood half a million miles high and whose branches were rivers of flame sweeping through space at hundreds of miles a second.

"I suppose," said Rugon presently, "that you are quite satisfied about the astronomers' calculations. After all——"

"Oh, we're perfectly safe," said Alveron confidently. "I've spoken to Kulath Observatory and they have been making some additional checks through our own instruments. That uncertainty of an hour includes a private safety margin which they won't tell me in case I feel tempted to stay any longer."

He glanced at the instrument board.

"The pilot should have brought us to the atmosphere now. Switch the screen back to the planet, please. Ah, there they go!"

There was a sudden tremor underfoot and a raucous clanging of alarms, instantly stilled. Across the vision screen two slim projectiles dived toward the looming mass of Earth. For a few miles they traveled together, then they separated, one vanishing abruptly as it entered the shadow of the planet.

Slowly the huge mother ship, with its thousand times greater mass, descended after them into the raging storms that already were tearing down the deserted cities of Man.

It was night in the hemisphere over which Orostron drove his tiny command. Like Torkalee, his mission was to photograph and record, and to report progress to the mother ship. The little scout had no room for specimens or passengers. If contact was made with the inhabitants of this world, the S9000 would come at once. There would be no time for parleying. If there was any trouble the rescue would be by force and the explanations could come later.

The ruined land beneath was bathed with an eerie, flickering light, for a great auroral display was raging over half the world. But the image on the vision screen was independent of external light, and it showed clearly a waste of barren rock that seemed never to have known any form of life. Presumably this desert land must come to an end somewhere. Orostron increased his speed to the highest value he dared risk in so dense an atmosphere.

The machine fled on through the storm, and presently the desert of rock began to climb toward the sky. A great mountain range lay ahead, its peaks lost in the smoke-laden clouds. Orostron directed the scanners toward the horizon, and on the vision screen the line of mountains seemed suddenly very close and menacing. He started to climb rapidly. It was difficult to imagine a more unpromising land in which to find civilization and he wondered if it would be wise to change course. He decided against it. Five minutes later, he had his reward.

Miles below lay a decapitated mountain, the whole of its summit sheared away by some tremendous feat of engineering. Rising out of the rock and straddling the artificial plateau was an intricate structure of metal girders, supporting masses of machinery. Orostron brought his ship to a halt and spiraled down toward the mountain.

The slight Doppler blur had now vanished, and the picture on the screen was clear-cut. The latticework was supporting some scores of great metal mirrors, pointing skyward at an angle of forty-five degrees to the horizontal. They were slightly concave, and each had some complicated mechanism at its focus. There seemed something impressive and purposeful about the great array; every mirror was aimed at precisely the same spot in the sky—or beyond.

Orostron turned to his colleagues.

"It looks like some kind of observatory to me," he said. "Have you ever seen anything like it before?"

Klarten, a multitentacled, tripedal creature from a globular cluster at the edge of the Milky Way, had a different theory.

"That's communication equipment. Those reflectors are for focusing electromagnetic beams. I've seen the same kind of installation on a hundred worlds before. It may even be the station that Kulath picked up—though that's rather unlikely, for the beams would be very narrow from mirrors that size."

"That would explain why Rugon could detect no radiation before we landed," added Hansur II, one of the twin beings from the planet Thargon.

Orostron did not agree at all.

"If that is a radio station, it must be built for interplanetary communication. Look at the way the mirrors are pointed. I don't believe that a race which has only had radio for two centuries can have crossed space. It took my people six thousand years to do it."

"We managed it in three," said Hansur II mildly, speaking a few seconds ahead of his twin. Before the inevitable argument could develop, Klarten began to wave his tentacles with excitement. While the others had been talking, he had started the automatic monitor.

"Here it is! Listen!"

He threw a switch, and the little room was filled with a raucous whining sound, continually changing in pitch but nevertheless retaining certain characteristics that were difficult to define.

The four explorers listened intently for a minute; then Orostron said, "Surely that can't be any form of speech! No creature could produce sounds as quickly as that!"

Hansur I had come to the same conclusion. "That's a television program. Don't you think so, Klarten?"

The other agreed.

"Yes, and each of those mirrors seems to be radiating a different program. I wonder where they're going? If I'm correct, one of the other planets in the system must lie along those beams. We can soon check that."

Orostron called the S9000 and reported the discovery. Both Rugon and Alveron were greatly excited, and made a quick check of the astronomical records.

The result was surprising—and disappointing. None of the other nine planets lay anywhere near the line of transmission. The great mirrors appeared to be pointing blindly into space.

There seemed only one conclusion to be drawn, and Klarten was the first to voice it.

"They had interplanetary communication," he said. "But the station must be deserted now, and the transmitters no longer controlled. They haven't been switched off, and are just pointing where they were left."

"Well, we'll soon find out," said Orostron. "I'm going to land."

He brought the machine slowly down to the level of the great metal mirrors, and past them until it came to rest on the mountain rock. A hundred yards away, a white stone building crouched beneath the maze of steel girders. It was windowless, but there were several doors in the wall facing them.

Orostron watched his companions climb into their protective suits and wished he could follow. But someone had to stay in the machine to keep in touch with the mother ship. Those were Alveron's instructions, and they were very wise. One never knew what would happen on a world that was being explored for the first time, especially under conditions such as these.

Very cautiously, the three explorers stepped out of the airlock and adjusted the antigravity field of their suits. Then, each with the mode of locomotion peculiar to his race, the little party went toward the building, the Hansur twins leading and Klarten following close behind. His gravity control was apparently giving trouble, for he suddenly fell to the ground, rather to the amusement of his colleagues. Orostron saw them pause for a moment at the nearest door—then it opened slowly and they disappeared from sight.

So Orostron waited, with what patience he could, while the storm rose around him and the light of the aurora grew even brighter in the sky. At the agreed times he called the mother ship and received brief acknowledgments from Rugon. He wondered how Torkalee was faring, halfway round the planet, but he could not contact him through the crash and thunder of solar interference.

It did not take Klarten and the Hansurs long to discover that their theories were largely correct. The building was a radio station, and it was utterly deserted. It consisted of one tremendous room with a few small offices leading from it. In the main chamber, row after row of electrical equipment stretched into the distance; lights flickered and winked on hundreds of control panels, and a dull glow came from the elements in a great avenue of vacuum tubes.

But Klarten was not impressed. The first radio sets his race had built were now fossilized in strata a thousand million years old. Man, who had possessed electrical machines for only a few centuries, could not compete with those who had known them for half the lifetime of the Earth.

Nevertheless, the party kept their recorders running as they explored the building. There was still one problem to be solved. The deserted station was broadcasting programs, but where were they coming from? The central switchboard had been quickly located. It was designed to handle scores of programs simultaneously, but the source of those programs was lost in a maze of cables that vanished underground. Back in the S9000, Rugon was trying to analyze the broadcasts and perhaps his researches would reveal their origin. It was impossible to trace cables that might lead across continents.

The party wasted little time at the deserted station. There was nothing they could learn from it, and they were seeking life rather than scientific information. A few minutes later the little ship rose swiftly from the plateau and headed toward the plains that must lie beyond the mountains. Less than three hours were still left to them.

As the array of enigmatic mirrors dropped out of sight, Orostron was struck by a sudden thought. Was it imagination, or had they all moved through a small angle while he had been waiting, as if they were still compensating for the rotation of the Earth? He could not be sure, and he dismissed the matter as unimportant. It would only mean that the directing mechanism was still working, after a fashion.

They discovered the city fifteen minutes later. It was a great, sprawling metropolis, built around a river that had disappeared leaving an ugly scar winding its way among the great buildings and beneath bridges that looked very incongruous now.

Even from the air, the city looked deserted. But only two and a half hours were left—there was no time for further exploration. Orostron made his decision, and landed near the largest structure he could see. It seemed reasonable to suppose that some creatures would have sought shelter in the strongest buildings, where they would be safe until the very end.

The deepest caves—the heart of the planet itself—would give no protection when the final cataclysm came. Even if this race had reached the outer planets, its doom would only be delayed by the few hours it would take for the ravening wavefronts to cross the Solar System.

Orostron could not know that the city had been deserted not for a few days or weeks, but for over a century. For the culture of cities, which had outlasted so many civilizations, had been doomed at last when the helicopter brought universal transportation. Within a few generations the great masses of mankind, knowing that they could reach any part of the globe in a matter of hours, had gone back to the fields and forests for which they had always longed. The new civilization had machines and resources of which earlier ages had never dreamed, but it was essentially rural and no longer bound to the steel and concrete warrens that had dominated the centuries before. Such cities as still remained were specialized centers of research, administration or entertainment; the others had been allowed to decay, where it was too much trouble to destroy them. The dozen or so greatest of all cities, and the ancient university towns, had scarcely changed and would have lasted for many generations to come. But the cities that had been founded on steam and iron and surface transportation had passed with the industries that had nourished them.

And so while Orostron waited in the tender, his colleagues raced through endless empty corridors and deserted halls, taking innumerable photographs but learning nothing of the creatures who had used these buildings. There were libraries, meeting places, council rooms, thousands of offices—all were empty and deep with dust. If they had not seen the radio station on its mountain eyrie, the explorers could well have believed that this world had known no life for centuries.

Through the long minutes of waiting, Orostron tried to imagine where this race could have vanished. Perhaps they had killed themselves knowing that escape was impossible; perhaps they had built great shelters in the bowels of the planet, and even now were cowering in their millions beneath his feet, waiting for the end. He began to fear that he would never know.

It was almost a relief when at last he had to give the order for the return. Soon he would know if Torkalee's party had been more fortunate. And he was anxious to get back to the mother ship, for as the minutes passed the suspense had become more and more acute. There had always been the thought in his mind: What if the astronomers of Kulath have made a mistake? He would begin to feel happy when the walls of the S9000 were around him. He would be happier still when they were out in space and this ominous sun was shrinking far astern.

As soon as his colleagues had entered the airlock, Orostron hurled his tiny machine into the sky and set the controls to home on the S9000. Then he turned to his friends.

"Well, what have you found?" he asked.

Klarten produced a large roll of canvas and spread it out on the floor.

"This is what they were like," he said quietly. "Bipeds, with only two arms. They seem to have managed well, in spite of that handicap. Only two eyes as well, unless there are others in the back. We were lucky to find this; it's about the only thing they left behind."

The ancient oil paintings stared stonily back at the four creatures regarding it so intently. By the irony of fate, its complete worthlessness had saved it from oblivion. When the city had been evacuated, no one had bothered to move Alderman John Richards, 1909–1974. For a century and a half he had been gathering dust while far away from the old cities the new civilization had been rising to heights no earlier culture had ever known.

"That was almost all we found," said Klarten. "The city must have been deserted for years. I'm afraid our expedition has been a failure. If there are any living beings on this world, they've hidden themselves too well for us to find them."

His commander was forced to agree.

"It was an almost impossible task," he said. "If we'd had weeks instead of hours we might have succeeded. For all we know, they may even have built shelters under the sea. No one seems to have thought of that."

He glanced quickly at the indicators and corrected the course. "We'll be there in five minutes. Alveron seems to be moving rather quickly. I wonder if Torkalee has found anything."

The S9000 was hanging a few miles above the seaboard of a blazing continent when Orostron homed upon it. The danger line was thirty minutes away and there was no time to lose. Skillfully, he maneuvered the little ship into its launching tube and the party stepped out of the airlock.

There was a small crowd waiting for them. That was to be expected, but Orostron could see at once that something more than curiosity had brought his friends here. Even before a word was spoken, he knew that something was wrong.

"Torkalee hasn't returned. He's lost his party and we're going to the rescue. Come along to the control room at once."

From the beginning, Torkalee had been luckier than Orostron. He had followed the zone of twilight, keeping away from the intolerable glare of the sun, until he came to the shores of an inland sea. It was a very recent sea, one of the latest of Man's works, for the land it covered had been desert less than a century before. In a few hours it would be desert again, for the water was boiling and clouds of steam were rising to the skies. But they could not veil the loveliness of the great white city that overlooked the tideless sea.

Flying machines were still parked neatly round the square in which Torkalee landed. They were disappointingly primitive, though beautifully finished, and depended on rotating airfoils for support. Nowhere was there any sign of life, but the place gave the impression that its inhabitants were not very far away. Lights were still shining from some of the windows.

Torkalee's three companions lost no time in leaving the machine. Leader of the party, by seniority of rank and race was T'sinadree, who like Alveron himself had been born on one of the ancient planets of the Central Suns. Next came Alarkane, from a race which was one of the youngest in the Universe and took a perverse pride in the fact. Last came one of the strange beings from the system of Palador. It was nameless, like all its kind, for it possessed no identity of its own, being merely a mobile but still dependent cell in the consciousness of its race. Though it and its fellows had long been scattered over the galaxy in the exploration of countless worlds, some unknown link still bound them together as inexorably as the living cells in a human body.

When a creature of Palador spoke, the pronoun it used was always "We." There was not, nor could there ever be, any first person singular in the language of Palador.

The great doors of the splendid building baffled the explorers, though any human child would have known their secret. T'sinadree wasted no time on them but called Torkalee on his personal transmitter. Then the three hurried aside while their commander maneuvered his machine into the best position. There was a brief burst of intolerable flame; the massive steelwork flickered once at the edge of the visible spectrum and was gone. The stones were still glowing when the eager party hurried into the building, the beams of their light projectors fanning before them.

The torches were not needed. Before them lay a great hall, glowing with light from lines of tubes along the ceiling. On either side, the hall opened out into long corridors, while straight ahead a massive stairway swept majestically toward the upper floors.

For a moment T'sinadree hesitated. Then, since one way was as good as another, he led his companions down the first corridor.

The feeling that life was near had now become very strong. At any moment, it seemed, they might be confronted by the creatures of this world. If they showed hostility—and they could scarcely be blamed if they did—the paralyzers would be used at once.

The tension was very great as the party entered the first room, and only relaxed when they saw that it held nothing but machines —row after row of them, now stilled and silent. Lining the enormous room were thousands of metal filing cabinets, forming a continuous wall as far as the eye could reach. And that was all; there was no furniture, nothing but the cabinets and the mysterious machines.

Alarkane, always the quickest of the three, was already examining the cabinets. Each held many thousand sheets of tough, thin material, perforated with innumerable holes and slots. The Paladorian appropriated one of the cards and Alarkane recorded the scene together with some close-ups of the machines. Then they left. The great room, which had been one of the marvels of the world, meant nothing to them. No living eye would ever again see that wonderful battery of almost human Hollerith analyzers and the five thousand million punched cards holding all that could be recorded of each man, woman and child on the planet.

It was clear that this building had been used very recently. With growing excitement, the explorers hurried on to the next room. This they found to be an enormous library, for millions of books lay all around them on miles and miles of shelving. Here, though the explorers could not know it, were the records of all the laws that Man had ever passed, and all the speeches that had ever been made in his council chambers.

T'sinadree was deciding his plan of action, when Alarkane drew his attention to one of the racks a hundred yards away. It was half empty, unlike all the others. Around it books lay in a tumbled heap on the floor, as if knocked down by someone in frantic haste. The signs were unmistakable. Not long ago, other creatures had been this way. Faint wheel marks were clearly visible on the floor to the acute sense of Alarkane, though the others could see nothing. Alarkane could even detect footprints, but knowing nothing of the creatures that had formed them he could not say which way they led.

The sense of nearness was stronger than ever now, but it was nearness in time, not in space. Alarkane voiced the thoughts of the party.

"Those books must have been valuable, and someone has come to rescue them—rather as an afterthought, I should say. That means there must be a place of refuge, possibly not very far away. Perhaps we may be able to find some other clues that will lead us to it."

T'sinadree agreed; the Paladorian wasn't enthusiastic.

"That may be so," it said, "but the refuge may be anywhere on the planet, and we have just two hours left. Let us waste no more time if we hope to rescue these people."

The party hurried forward once more, pausing only to collect a few books that might be useful to the scientists at Base—though it was doubtful if they could ever be translated. They soon found that the great building was composed largely of small rooms, all showing signs of recent occupation. Most of them were in a neat and tidy condition, but one or two were very much the reverse. The explorers were particularly puzzled by one room—clearly an office of some kind—that appeared to have been completely wrecked. The floor was littered with papers, the furniture had been smashed, and smoke was pouring through the broken windows from the fires outside.

T'sinadree was rather alarmed.

"Surely no dangerous animal could have got into a place like this!" he exclaimed, fingering his paralyzer nervously.

Alarkane did not answer. He began to make that annoying sound which his race called "laughter." It was several minutes before he would explain what had amused him.

"I don't think any animal has done it," he said. "In fact, the explanation is very simple. Suppose *you* had been working all your life in this room, dealing with endless papers, year after year. And suddenly, you are told that you will never see it again, that your work is finished, and that you can leave it forever. More than that —no one will come after you. Everything is finished. How would you make your exit, T'sinadree?"

The other thought for a moment.

"Well, I suppose I'd just tidy things up and leave. That's what seems to have happened in all the other rooms."

Alarkane laughed again.

"I'm quite sure you would. But some individuals have a different psychology. I think I should have liked the creature that used this room."

He did not explain himself further, and his two colleagues puzzled over his words for quite a while before they gave it up.

It came as something of a shock when Torkalee gave the order to return. They had gathered a great deal of information, but had found no clue that might lead them to the missing inhabitants of this world. That problem was as baffling as ever, and now it seemed that it would never be solved. There were only forty minutes left before the S9000 would be departing.

They were halfway back to the tender when they saw the semicircular passage leading down into the depths of the building. Its architectural style was quite different from that used elsewhere, and the gently sloping floor was an irresistible attraction to creatures whose many legs had grown weary of the marble staircases which only bipeds could have built in such profusion. T'sinadree had been the worst sufferer, for he normally employed twelve legs and could use twenty when he was in a hurry, though no one had ever seen him perform this feat.

The party stopped dead and looked down the passageway with a single thought. A tunnel, leading down into the depths of Earth! At its end, they might yet find the people of this world and rescue some of them from their fate. For there was still time to call the mother ship if the need arose.

T'sinadree signaled to his commander and Torkalee brought the little machine immediately overhead. There might not be time for the party to retrace its footsteps through the maze of passages, so meticulously recorded in the Paladorian mind that there was no possibility of going astray. If speed was necessary, Torkalee could blast his way through the dozen floors above their heads. In any case, it should not take long to find what lay at the end of the passage.

It took only thirty seconds. The tunnel ended quite abruptly in a very curious cylindrical room with magnificently padded seats along the walls. There was no way out save that by which they had come and it was several seconds before the purpose of the chamber dawned on Alarkane's mind. It was a pity, he thought, that they would never have time to use this. The thought was suddenly interrupted by a cry from T'sinadree. Alarkane wheeled around, and saw that the entrance had closed silently behind them.

Even in that first moment of panic, Alarkane found himself thinking with some admiration: Whoever they were, they knew how to build automatic machinery!

The Paladorian was the first to speak. It waved one of its tentacles toward the seats.

"We think it would be best to be seated," it said. The multiplex mind of Palador had already analyzed the situation and knew what was coming.

They did not have long to wait before a low-pitched hum came from a grill overhead, and for the very last time in history a human, even if lifeless, voice was heard on Earth. The words were meaningless, though the trapped explorers could guess their message clearly enough.

"Choose your stations, please, and be seated."

Simultaneously, a wall panel at one end of the compartment glowed with light. On it was a simple map, consisting of a series of a dozen circles connected by a line. Each of the circles had writing alongside it, and beside the writing were two buttons of different colors.

Alarkane looked questioningly at his leader.

"Don't touch them," said T'sinadree. "If we leave the controls alone, the doors may open again."

He was wrong. The engineers who had designed the automatic subway had assumed that anyone who entered it would naturally wish to go somewhere. If they selected no intermediate station, their destination could only be the end of the line.

There was another pause while the relays and thyratrons waited for their orders. In those thirty seconds, if they had known what to do, the party could have opened the doors and left the subway. But they did not know, and the machines geared to a human psychology acted for them.

The surge of acceleration was not very great; the lavish upholstery was a luxury, not a necessity. Only an almost imperceptible vibration told of the speed at which they were traveling through the bowels of the earth, on a journey the duration of which they could not even guess. And in thirty minutes, the S9000 would be leaving the Solar System.

There was a long silence in the speeding machine. T'sinadree and Alarkane were thinking rapidly. So was the Paladorian, though in a different fashion. The conception of personal death was meaningless to it, for the destruction of a single unit meant no more to the group mind than the loss of a nail-paring to a man. But it could, though with great difficulty, appreciate the plight of individual intelligences such as Alarkane and T'sinadree, and it was anxious to help them if it could.

Alarkane had managed to contact Torkalee with his personal transmitter, though the signal was very weak and seemed to be fading quickly. Rapidly he explained the situation, and almost at once the signals became clearer. Torkalee was following the path of the machine, flying above the ground under which they were speeding to their unknown destination. That was the first indication they had of the fact that they were traveling at nearly a thousand miles an hour, and very soon after that Torkalee was able to give the still more disturbing news that they were rapidly approaching the sea. While they were beneath the land, there was a hope, though a slender one, that they might stop the machine and escape. But under the ocean—not all the brains and the machinery in the great mother ship could save them. No one could have devised a more perfect trap.

T'sinadree had been examining the wall map with great attention. Its meaning was obvious, and along the line connecting the circles a tiny spot of light was crawling. It was already halfway to the first of the stations marked.

"I'm going to press one of those buttons," said T'sinadree at last. "It won't do any harm, and we may learn something."

"I agree. Which will you try first?"

"There are only two kinds, and it won't matter if we try the wrong one first. I suppose one is to start the machine and the other is to stop it."

Alarkane was not very hopeful.

"It started without any button pressing," he said. "I think it's completely automatic and we can't control it from here at all."

T'sinadree could not agree.

"These buttons are clearly associated with the stations, and there's no point in having them unless you can use them to stop yourself. The only question is, which is the right one?"

His analysis was perfectly correct. The machine could be stopped at any intermediate station. They had only been on their way ten minutes, and if they could leave now, no harm would have been done. It was just bad luck that T'sinadree's first choice was the wrong button.

The little light on the map crawled slowly through the illuminated circle without checking its speed. And at the same time Torkalee called from the ship overhead.

"You have just passed underneath a city and are heading out to sea. There cannot be another stop for nearly a thousand miles."

Alveron had given up all hope of finding life on this world. The S9000 had roamed over half the planet, never staying long in one place, descending ever and again in an effort to attract attention. There had been no response; Earth seemed utterly dead. If any of its inhabitants were still alive, thought Alveron, they must have hidden themselves in its depths where no help could reach them, though their doom would be nonetheless certain.

Rugon brought news of the disaster. The great ship ceased its fruitless searching and fled back through the storm to the ocean above which Torkalee's little tender was still following the track of the buried machine.

The scene was truly terrifying. Not since the days when Earth was born had there been such seas as this. Mountains of water were racing before the storm which had now reached velocities of many hundred miles an hour. Even at this distance from the mainland the air was full of flying debris—trees, fragments of houses, sheets of metal, anything that had not been anchored to the ground. No airborne machine could have lived for a moment in such a gale. And ever and again even the roar of the wind was drowned as the vast water-mountains met head-on with a crash that seemed to shake the sky.

Fortunately, there had been no serious earthquakes yet. Far beneath the bed of the ocean, the wonderful piece of engineering which had been the World President's private vacuum-subway was still working perfectly, unaffected by the tumult and destruction above. It would continue to work until the last minute of the Earth's existence, which, if the astronomers were right, was not much more than fifteen minutes away—though precisely how much more Alveron would have given a great deal to know. It would be nearly an hour before the trapped party could reach land and even the slightest hope of rescue.

Alveron's instructions had been precise, though even without them he would never have dreamed of taking any risks with the great machine that had been entrusted to his care. Had he been human, the decision to abandon the trapped members of his crew would have been desperately hard to make. But he came of a race far more sensitive than Man, a race that so loved the things of the spirit that long ago, and with infinite reluctance, it had taken over control of the Universe since only thus could it be sure that justice was being done. Alveron would need all his superhuman gifts to carry him through the next few hours.

Meanwhile, a mile below the bed of the ocean Alarkane and T'sinadree were very busy indeed with their private communicators. Fifteen minutes is not a long time in which to wind up the affairs of a lifetime. It is indeed, scarcely long enough to dictate more than a few of those farewell messages which at such moments are so much more important than all other matters.

All the while the Paladorian had remained silent and motionless, saying not a word. The other two, resigned to their fate and engrossed in their personal affairs, had given it no thought. They were startled when suddenly it began to address them in its peculiarly passionless voice.

"We perceive that you are making certain arrangements concerning your anticipated destruction. That will probably be unnecessary. Captain Alveron hopes to rescue us if we can stop this machine when we reach land again."

Both T'sinadree and Alarkane were too surprised to say anything for a moment. Then the latter gasped, "How do you know?"

It was a foolish question, for he remembered at once that there were several Paladorians—if one could use the phrase—in the S9000, and consequently their companion knew everything that was happening in the mother ship. So he did not wait for an answer but continued, "Alveron can't do that! He daren't take such a risk!"

"There will be no risk," said the Paladorian. "We have told him what to do. It is really very simple."

Alarkane and T'sinadree looked at their companion with something approaching awe, realizing now what must have happened. In moments of crisis, the single units comprising the Paladorian mind could link together in an organization no less close than that of any physical brain. At such moments they formed an intellect more powerful than any other in the Universe. All ordinary problems could be solved by a few hundred or thousand units. Very rarely, millions would be needed, and on two historic occasions the billions of cells of the entire Paladorian consciousness had been welded together to deal with emergencies that threatened the race. The mind of Palador was one of the greatest mental resources of the Universe; its full force was seldom required, but the knowledge that it was available was supremely comforting to other races. Alarkane wondered how many cells had co-ordinated to deal with this particular emergency. He also wondered how so trivial an incident had ever come to its attention.

To that question he was never to know the answer, though he might have guessed it had he known that the chillingly remote Paladorian mind possessed an almost human streak of vanity. Long ago, Alarkane had written a book trying to prove that eventually all intelligent races would sacrifice individual consciousness and that one day only group-minds would remain in the Universe. Palador, he had said, was the first of those ultimate intellects, and the vast, dispersed mind had not been displeased.

They had no time to ask any further questions before Alveron himself began to speak through their communicators.

"Alveron calling! We're staying on this planet until the detonation waves reach it, so we may be able to rescue you. You're heading toward a city on the coast which you'll reach in forty minutes at your present speed. If you cannot stop yourselves then, we're going to blast the tunnel behind and ahead of you to cut off your power. Then we'll sink a shaft to get you out—the chief engineer says he can do it in five minutes with the main projectors. So you should be safe within an hour, unless the sun blows up before."

"And if that happens, you'll be destroyed as well! You mustn't take such a risk!"

"Don't let that worry you; we're perfectly safe. When the sun detonates, the explosion wave will take several minutes to rise to its maximum. But apart from that, we're on the night side of the planet, behind an eight-thousand-mile screen of rock. When the first warning of the explosion comes, we will accelerate out of the Solar System, keeping in the shadow of the planet. Under our maximum drive, we will reach the velocity of light before leaving the cone of shadow, and the sun cannot harm us then."

T'sinadree was still afraid to hope. Another objection came at once into his mind.

"Yes, but how will you get any warning, here on the night side of the planet?"

"Very easily," replied Alveron. "This world has a moon which is now visible from this hemisphere. We have telescopes trained on it. If it shows any sudden increase in brilliance, our main drive goes on automatically and we'll be thrown out of the system."

The logic was flawless. Alveron, cautious as ever, was taking no chances. It would be many minutes before the eight-thousand-mile shield of rock and metal could be destroyed by the fires of the exploding sun. In that time, the S9000 could have reached the safety of the velocity of light.

Alarkane pressed the second button when they were still several miles from the coast. He did not expect anything to happen then, assuming that the machine could not stop between stations. It seemed too good to be true when, a few minutes later, the machine's slight vibration died away and they came to a halt.

The doors slid silently apart. Even before they were fully open, the three had left the compartment. They were taking no more chances. Before them a long tunnel stretched into the distance, rising slowly out of sight. They were starting along it when suddenly Alveron's voice called from the communicators.

"Stay where you are! We're going to blast!"

The ground shuddered once, and far ahead there came the rumble of falling rock. Again the earth shook—and a hundred yards ahead the passageway vanished abruptly. A tremendous vertical shaft had been cut clean through it.

The party hurried forward again until they came to the end of the corridor and stood waiting on its lip. The shaft in which it ended was a full thousand feet across and descended into the earth as far as the torches could throw their beams. Overhead, the storm clouds fled beneath a moon that no man would have recognized, so luridly brilliant was its disk. And, most glorious of all sights, the S9000 floated high above, the great projectors that had drilled this enormous pit still glowing cherry red.

A dark shape detached itself from the mother ship and dropped swiftly toward the ground. Torkalee was returning to collect his friends. A little later, Alveron greeted them in the control room. He waved to the great vision screen and said quietly, "See, we were barely in time."

The continent below them was slowly settling beneath the mile-high waves that were attacking its coasts. The last that anyone was ever to see of Earth was a great plain, bathed with the silver light of the abnormally brilliant moon. Across its face the waters were pouring in a glittering flood toward a distant range of mountains. The sea had won its final victory, but its triumph would be short-lived for soon sea and land would be no more. Even as the silent party in the control room watched the destruction below, the infinitely greater catastrophe to which this was only the prelude came swiftly upon them.

It was as though dawn had broken suddenly over this moonlit landscape. But it was not dawn: it was only the moon, shining with the brilliance of a second sun. For perhaps thirty seconds that awesome, unnatural light burnt fiercely on the doomed land beneath. Then there came a sudden flashing of indicator lights across the control board. The main drive was on. For a second Alveron glanced at the indicators and checked their information. When he looked again at the screen, Earth was gone.

The magnificent, desperately overstrained generators quietly died when the S9000 was passing the orbit of Persephone. It did not matter, the sun could never harm them now, and although the ship was speeding helplessly out into the lonely night of interstellar space, it would only be a matter of days before rescue came.

There was irony in that. A day ago, they had been the rescuers, going to the aid of a race that now no longer existed. Not for the first time Alveron wondered about the world that had just perished. He tried, in vain, to picture it as it had been in its glory, the streets of its cities thronged with life. Primitive though its people had been, they might have offered much to the Universe. If only they could have made contact! Regret was useless; long before their coming, the people of this world must have buried themselves in its iron heart. And now they and their civilization would remain a mystery for the rest of time.

Alveron was glad when his thoughts were interrupted by Rugon's entrance. The chief of communications had been very busy ever since the take-off, trying to analyze the programs radiated by the transmitter Orostron had discovered. The problem was not a difficult one, but it demanded the construction of special equipment, and that had taken time.

"Well, what have you found?" asked Alveron.

"Quite a lot," replied his friend. "There's something mysterious here, and I don't understand it.

"It didn't take long to find how the vision transmissions were built up, and we've been able to convert them to suit our own equipment. It seems that there were cameras all over the planet, surveying points of interest. Some of them were apparently in cities, on the tops of very high buildings. The cameras were rotating continuously to give panoramic views. In the programs we've recorded there are about twenty different scenes.

"In addition, there are a number of transmissions of a different kind, neither sound nor vision. They seem to be purely scientific—

possibly instrument readings or something of that sort. All these programs were going out simultaneously on different frequency bands.

"Now there must be a reason for all this. Orostron still thinks that the station simply wasn't switched off when it was deserted. But these aren't the sort of programs such a station would normally radiate at all. It was certainly used for interplanetary relaying—Klarten was quite right there. So these people must have crossed space, since none of the other planets had any life at the time of the last survey. Don't you agree?"

Alveron was following intently.

"Yes, that seems reasonable enough. But it's also certain that the beam was pointing to none of the other planets. I checked that myself."

"I know," said Rugon. "What I want to discover is why a giant interplanetary relay station is busily transmitting pictures of a world about to be destroyed—pictures that would be of immense interest to scientists and astronomers. Someone had gone to a lot of trouble to arrange all those panoramic cameras. I am convinced that those beams were going somewhere."

Alveron started up.

"Do you imagine that there might be an outer planet that hasn't been reported?" he asked. "If so, your theory's certainly wrong. The beam wasn't even pointing in the plane of the Solar System. And even if it were—just look at this."

He switched on the vision screen and adjusted the controls. Against the velvet curtain of space was hanging a blue-white sphere, apparently composed of many concentric shells of incandescent gas. Even though its immense distance made all movement invisible, it was clearly expanding at an enormous rate. At its center was a blinding point of light—the white dwarf star that the sun had now become.

"You probably don't realize just how big that sphere is," said Alveron. "Look at this."

He increased the magnification until only the center portion of the nova was visible. Close to its heart were two minute condensations, one on either side of the nucleus.

"Those are the two giant planets of the system. They have still managed to retain their existence—after a fashion. And they were several hundred million miles from the sun. The nova is still expanding—but it's already twice the size of the Solar System."

Rugon was silent for a moment.

"Perhaps you're right," he said, rather grudgingly. "You've disposed of my first theory. But you still haven't satisfied me."

He made several swift circuits of the room before speaking again. Alveron waited patiently. He knew the almost intuitive powers of his friend, who could often solve a problem when mere logic seemed insufficient.

Then, rather slowly, Rugon began to speak again.

"What do you think of this?" he said. "Suppose we've completely underestimated this people? Orostron did it once—he thought they could never have crossed space, since they'd only known radio for two centuries. Hansur II told me that. Well, Orostron was quite wrong. Perhaps we're all wrong. I've had a look at the material that Klarten brought back from the transmitter. He wasn't impressed by what he found, but it's a marvelous achievement for so short a time. There were devices in that station that belonged to civilizations thousands of years older. Alveron, can we follow that beam to see where it leads?"

Alveron said nothing for a full minute. He had been more than half expecting the question, but it was not an easy one to answer. The main generators had gone completely. There was no point in trying to repair them. But there was still power available, and while there was power, anything could be done in time. It would mean a lot of improvisation, and some difficult maneuvers, for the ship still had its enormous initial velocity. Yes, it could be done, and the activity would keep the crew from becoming further depressed, now that the reaction caused by the mission's failure had started to set in. The news that the nearest heavy repair ship could not reach them for three weeks had also caused a slump in morale.

The engineers, as usual, made a tremendous fuss. Again as usual, they did the job in half the time they had dismissed as being absolutely impossible. Very slowly, over many hours, the great ship began to discard the speed its main drive had given it in as many minutes. In a tremendous curve, millions of miles in radius, the S9000 changed its course and the star fields shifted round it.

The maneuver took three days, but at the end of that time the ship was limping along a course parallel to the beam that had once come from Earth. They were heading out into emptiness, the blazing sphere that had been the sun dwindling slowly behind them. By the standards of interstellar flight, they were almost stationary.

For hours Rugon strained over his instruments, driving his detector beams far ahead into space. There were certainly no planets within many light-years; there was no doubt of that. From time to time Alveron came to see him and always he had to give the same reply: "Nothing to report." About a fifth of the time Rugon's intuition let him down badly; he began to wonder if this was such an occasion.

Not until a week later did the needles of the mass-detectors quiver feebly at the ends of their scales. But Rugon said nothing, not even to his captain. He waited until he was sure, and he went on waiting until even the short-range scanners began to react, and to build up the first faint pictures on the vision screen. Still he waited patiently until he could interpret the images. Then, when he knew that his wildest fancy was even less than the truth, he called his colleagues into the control room.

The picture on the vision screen was the familiar one of endless star fields, sun beyond sun to the very limits of the Universe. Near the center of the screen a distant nebula made a patch of haze that was difficult for the eye to grasp.

Rugon increased the magnification. The stars flowed out of the field; the little nebula expanded until it filled the screen and then— it was a nebula no longer. A simultaneous gasp of amazement came from all the company at the sight that lay before them.

Lying across league after league of space, ranged in a vast three-dimensional array of rows and columns with the precision of a marching army, were thousands of tiny pencils of light. They were moving swiftly; the whole immense lattice holding its shape as a single unit. Even as Alveron and his comrades watched, the formation began to drift off the screen and Rugon had to recenter the controls.

After a long pause, Rugon started to speak.

"This is the race," he said softly, "that has known radio for only two centuries—the race that we believed had crept to die in the heart of its planet. I have examined those images under the highest possible magnification.

"That is the greatest fleet of which there has ever been a record.

Each of those points of light represents a ship larger than our own. Of course, they are very primitive—what you see on the screen are the jets of their rockets. Yes, they dared to use rockets to bridge interstellar space! You realize what that means. It would take them centuries to reach the nearest star. The whole race must have embarked on this journey in the hope that its descendants would complete it, generations later.

"To measure the extent of their accomplishment, think of the ages it took us to conquer space, and the longer ages still before we attempted to reach the stars. Even if we were threatened with annihilation, could we have done so much in so short a time? Remember, this is the youngest civilization in the Universe. Four hundred thousand years ago it did not even exist. What will it be a million years from now?"

An hour later, Orostron left the crippled mother ship to make contact with the great fleet ahead. As the little torpedo disappeared among the stars, Alveron turned to his friend and made a remark that Rugon was often to remember in the years ahead.

"I wonder what they'll be like?" he mused. "Will they be nothing but wonderful engineers, with no art or philosophy? They're going to have such a surprise when Orostron reaches them—I expect it will be rather a blow to their pride. It's funny how all isolated races think they're the only people in the Universe. But they should be grateful to us; we're going to save them a good many hundred years of travel."

Alveron glanced at the Milky Way, lying like a veil of silver mist across the vision screen. He waved toward it with a sweep of a tentacle that embraced the whole circle of the galaxy, from the Central Planets to the lonely suns of the Rim.

"You know," he said to Rugon, "I feel rather afraid of these people. Suppose they don't like our little Federation?" He waved once more toward the star-clouds that lay massed across the screen, glowing with the light of their countless suns.

"Something tells me they'll be very determined people," he added. "We had better be polite to them. After all, we only outnumber them about a thousand million to one."

Rugon laughed at his captain's little joke.

Twenty years afterward, the remark didn't seem funny.

It was one of those accidents for which no one could be blamed. Richard Nelson had been in and out of the generator pit a dozen times, taking temperature readings to make sure that the unearthly chill of liquid helium was not seeping through the insulation. This was the first generator in the world to use the principle of superconductivity. The windings of the immense stator had been immersed in a helium bath, and the miles of wire now had a resistance too small to be measured by any means known to man.

Nelson noted with satisfaction that the temperature had not fallen further than expected. The insulation was doing its work; it would be safe to lower the rotor into the pit. That thousand-ton cylinder was now hanging fifty feet above Nelson's head, like the business end of a mammoth drop hammer. He and everyone else in the power station would feel much happier when it had been lowered onto its bearings and keyed into the turbine shaft.

Nelson put away his notebook and started to walk toward the ladder. At the geometric center of the pit, he made his appointment with destiny.

The load on the power network had been steadily increasing for the last hour, while the zone of twilight swept across the continent. As the last rays of sunlight faded from the clouds, the miles of mercury arcs along the great highways sprang into life. By the million, fluorescent tubes began to glow in the cities; housewives switched on their radio-cookers to prepare the evening meal. The needles of the megawattmeters began to creep up the scales.

These were the normal loads. But on a mountain three hundred miles to the south a giant cosmic ray analyzer was being rushed into action to await the expected shower from the new supernova in Capricornus, which the astronomers had detected only an hour before. Soon the coils of its five-thousand-ton magnets began to drain their enormous currents from the thyratron converters.

A thousand miles to the west, fog was creeping toward the greatest airport in the hemisphere. No one worried much about fog, now, when every plane could land on its own radar in zero visibility, but it was nicer not to have it around. So the giant dispersers were thrown into operation, and nearly a thousand megawatts began to radiate into the night, coagulating the water droplets and clearing great swaths through the banks of mist.

The meters in the power station gave another jump, and the engineer on duty ordered the stand-by generators into action. He wished the big, new machine was finished; then there would be no more anxious hours like these. But he thought he could handle the load. Half an hour later the Meteorological Bureau put out a general frost warning over the radio. Within sixty seconds, more than a million electric fires were switched on in anticipation. The meters passed the danger mark and went on soaring.

With a tremendous crash three giant circuit breakers leaped from their contacts. Their arcs died under the fierce blast of the helium jets. Three circuits had opened—but the fourth breaker had failed to clear. Slowly, the great copper bars began to glow cherry-red. The acrid smell of burning insulation filled the air and molten metal dripped heavily to the floor below, solidifying at once on the concrete slabs. Suddenly the conductors sagged as the load ends broke away from their supports. Brilliant green arcs of burning copper flamed and died as the circuit was broken. The free ends of the enormous conductors fell perhaps ten feet before crashing into the equipment below. In a fraction of a second they had welded themselves across the lines that led to the new generator.

Forces greater than any yet produced by man were at war in the windings of the machine. There was no resistance to oppose the current, but the inductance of the tremendous windings delayed the moment of peak intensity. The current rose to a maximum in an immense surge that lasted several seconds. At that instant, Nelson reached the center of the pit.

Then the current tried to stabilize itself, oscillating wildly between narrower and narrower limits. But it never reached its steady state; somewhere, the overriding safety devices came into operation and the circuit that should never have been made was broken again. With a last dying spasm, almost as violent as the first, the current swiftly ebbed away. It was all over.

When the emergency lights came on again, Nelson's assistant walked to the lip of the rotor pit. He didn't know what had happened, but it must have been serious. Nelson, fifty feet down, must have been wondering what it was all about.

"Hello, Dick!" he shouted. "Have you finished? We'd better see what the trouble is."

There was no reply. He leaned over the edge of the great pit and peered into it. The light was very bad, and the shadow of the rotor made it difficult to see what was below. At first it seemed that the pit was empty, but that was ridiculous; he had seen Nelson enter it only a few minutes ago. He called again.

"Hello! You all right, Dick?"

Again no reply. Worried now, the assistant began to descend the ladder. He was halfway down when a curious noise, like a toy balloon bursting very far away, made him look over his shoulder. Then he saw Nelson, lying at the center of the pit on the temporary woodwork covering the turbine shaft. He was very still, and there seemed something altogether wrong about the angle at which he was lying.

Ralph Hughes, chief physicist, looked up from his littered desk as the door opened. Things were slowly returning to normal after the night's disasters. Fortunately, the trouble had not affected his department much, for the generator was unharmed. He was glad he was not the chief engineer: Murdock would still be snowed under with paperwork. The thought gave Dr. Hughes considerable satisfaction.

"Hello, Doc," he greeted the visitor. "What brings you here? How's your patient getting on?"

Doctor Sanderson nodded briefly. "He'll be out of hospital in a day or so. But I want to talk to you about him."

"I don't know the fellow—I never go near the plant, except when the Board goes down on its collective knees and asks me to. After all, Murdock's paid to run the place."

Sanderson smiled wryly. There was no love lost between the chief engineer and the brilliant young physicist. Their personalities were too different, and there was the inevitable rivalry between theoretical expert and "practical" man.

"I think this is up your street, Ralph. At any rate, it's beyond me. You've heard what happened to Nelson?"

"He was inside my new generator when the power was shot into it, wasn't he?"

"That's correct. His assistant found him suffering from shock when the power was cut off again."

"What kind of shock? It couldn't have been electric; the windings are insulated, of course. In any case, I gather that he was in the center of the pit when they found him."

"That's quite true. We don't know what happened. But he's now come round and seems none the worse—apart from one thing." The doctor hesitated a moment as if choosing his words carefully.

"Well, go on! Don't keep me in suspense!"

"I left Nelson as soon as I saw he would be quite safe, but about an hour later Matron called me up to say he wanted to speak to me urgently. When I got to the ward he was sitting up in bed looking at a newspaper with a very puzzled expression. I asked him what was the matter. He answered, 'Something's happened to me, Doc.' So I said, 'Of course it has, but you'll be out in a couple of days.' He shook his head; I could see there was a worried look in his eyes. He picked up the paper he had been looking at and pointed to it. 'I can't read any more,' he said.

"I diagnosed amnesia and thought: This is a nuisance! Wonder what else he's forgotten? Nelson must have read my expression, for he went on to say, 'Oh, I still know the letters and words—but they're the wrong way round! I think something must have happened to my eyes.' He held up the paper again. 'This looks exactly as if I'm seeing it in a mirror,' he said. 'I can spell out each word separately, a letter at a time. Would you get me a looking glass? I want to try something.'

"I did. He held the paper to the glass and looked at the reflection. Then he started to read aloud, at normal speed. But that's a trick anyone can learn—compositors have to do it with type—and I wasn't impressed. On the other hand, I couldn't see why an intelligent fellow like Nelson should put over an act like that. So I decided to humor him, thinking the shock must have given his mind a bit of a twist. I felt quite certain he was suffering from some delusion, though he seemed perfectly normal.

"After a moment he put the paper away and said, 'Well, Doc, what do you make of that?' I didn't know quite what to say without hurting his feelings, so I passed the buck and said, 'I think I'll have to hand you over to Dr. Humphries, the psychologist. It's rather outside my province.' Then he made some remark about Dr. Humphries and his intelligence tests, from which I gathered he had already suffered at his hands."

"That's correct," interjected Hughes. "All the men are grilled by the Psychology Department before they join the company. All the same, it's surprising what gets through," he added thoughtfully.

Dr. Sanderson smiled, and continued his story.

"I was getting up to leave when Nelson said, 'Oh, I almost forgot. I think I must have fallen on my right arm. The wrist feels badly sprained.' 'Let's look at it,' I said, bending to pick it up. 'No, the other arm,' Nelson said, and held up his left wrist. Still humoring him, I answered, 'Have it your own way. But you said your right one, didn't you?'

"Nelson looked puzzled. 'So what?' he replied. 'This *is* my right arm. My eyes may be queer, but there's no argument about that. There's my wedding ring to prove it. I've not been able to get the darned thing off for five years.'

"That shook me rather badly. Because you see, it was his left arm he was holding up, and his left hand that had the ring on it. I could see that what he said was quite true. The ring would have to be cut to get it off again. So I said, 'Have you any distinctive scars?' He answered, 'Not that I can remember.'

" 'Any dental fillings?' "

" 'Yes, quite a few.' "

"We sat looking at each other in silence while a nurse went to fetch Nelson's records. 'Gazed at each other with a wild surmise' is just about how a novelist might put it. Before the nurse returned, I was seized with a bright idea. It was a fantastic notion, but the whole affair was becoming more and more outrageous. I asked Nelson if I could see the things he had been carrying in his pockets. Here they are."

Dr. Sanderson produced a handful of coins and a small, leather-bound diary. Hughes recognized the latter at once as an Electrical Engineer's Diary; he had one in his own pocket. He took it from the doctor's hand and flicked it open at random, with that slightly guilty feeling one always has when a stranger's—still more, a friend's —diary falls into one's hands.

And then, for Ralph Hughes, it seemed that the foundations of his world were giving way. Until now he had listened to Dr. Sanderson with some detachment, wondering what all the fuss was about. But now the incontrovertible evidence lay in his own hands, demanding his attention and defying his logic.

For he could read not one word of Nelson's diary. Both the print and the handwriting were inverted, as if seen in a mirror.

Dr. Hughes got up from his chair and walked rapidly around the room several times. His visitor sat silently watching him. On the fourth circuit he stopped at the window and looked out across the lake, overshadowed by the immense white wall of the dam. It seemed to reassure him, and he turned to Dr. Sanderson again.

"You expect me to believe that Nelson has been laterally inverted in some way, so that his right and left sides have been interchanged?"

"I don't expect you to believe anything. I'm merely giving you the evidence. If you can draw any other conclusion I'd be delighted to hear it. I might add that I've checked Nelson's teeth. All the fillings have been transposed. Explain that away if you can. Those coins are rather interesting, too."

Hughes picked them up. They included a shilling, one of the beautiful new, beryl-copper crowns, and a few pence and halfpence. He would have accepted them as change without hesitation. Being no more observant than the next man, he had never noticed which way the Queen's head looked. But the lettering—Hughes could picture the consternation at the Mint if these curious coins ever came to its notice. Like the diary, they too had been laterally inverted.

Dr. Sanderson's voice broke into his reverie.

"I've told Nelson not to say anything about this. I'm going to write a full report; it should cause a sensation when it's published. But we want to know how this has happened. As you are the designer of the new machine, I've come to you for advice."

Dr. Hughes did not seem to hear him. He was sitting at his

desk with his hands outspread, little fingers touching. For the first time in his life he was thinking seriously about the difference between left and right.

Dr. Sanderson did not release Nelson from hospital for several days, during which he was studying his peculiar patient and collecting material for his report. As far as he could tell, Nelson was perfectly normal, apart from his inversion. He was learning to read again, and his progress was swift after the initial strangeness had worn off. He would probably never again use tools in the same way that he had done before the accident; for the rest of his life, the world would think him left-handed. However, that would not handicap him in any way.

Dr. Sanderson had ceased to speculate about the cause of Nelson's condition. He knew very little about electricity; that was Hughes's job. He was quite confident that the physicist would produce the answer in due course; he had always done so before. The company was not a philanthropic institution, and it had good reason for retaining Hughes's services. The new generator, which would be running within a week, was his brain-child, though he had had little to do with the actual engineering details.

Dr. Hughes himself was less confident. The magnitude of the problem was terrifying; for he realized, as Sanderson did not, that it involved utterly new regions of science. He knew that there was only one way in which an object could become its own mirror image. But how could so fantastic a theory be proved?

He had collected all available information on the fault that had energized the great armature. Calculations had given an estimate of the currents that had flowed through the coils for the few seconds they had been conducting. But the figures were largely guesswork; he wished he could repeat the experiment to obtain accurate data. It would be amusing to see Murdock's face if he said, "Mind if I throw a perfect short across generators One to Ten sometime this evening?" No, that was definitely out.

It was lucky he still had the working model. Tests on it had given some ideas of the field produced at the generator's center, but their magnitudes were a matter of conjecture. They must have been enormous. It was a miracle that the windings had stayed in their slots. For nearly a month Hughes struggled with his calculations and wandered through regions of atomic physics he had carefully avoided since he left the university. Slowly the complete theory began to evolve in his mind; he was a long way from the final proof, but the road was clear. In another month he would have finished.

The great generator itself, which had dominated his thoughts for the past year, now seemed trivial and unimportant. He scarcely bothered to acknowledge the congratulations of his colleagues when it passed its final tests and began to feed its millions of kilowatts into the system. They must have thought him a little strange, but he had always been regarded as somewhat unpredictable. It was expected of him; the company would have been disappointed if its tame genius possessed no eccentricities.

A fortnight later, Dr. Sanderson came to see him again. He was in a grave mood.

"Nelson's back in the hospital," he announced. "I was wrong when I said he'd be O.K."

"What's the matter with him?" asked Hughes in surprise.

"He's starving to death."

"Starving? What on earth do you mean?"

Dr. Sanderson pulled a chair up to Hughes's desk and sat down.

"I haven't bothered you for the past few weeks," he began, "because I knew you were busy on your own theories. I've been watching Nelson carefully all this time, and writing up my report. At first, as I told you, he seemed perfectly normal. I had no doubt that everything would be all right.

"Then I noticed that he was losing weight. It was some time before I was certain of it; then I began to observe other, more technical symptoms. He started to complain of weakness and lack of concentration. He had all the signs of vitamin deficiency. I gave him special vitamin concentrates, but they haven't done any good. So I've come to have another talk with you."

Hughes looked baffled, then annoyed. "But hang it all, you're the doctor!"

"Yes, but this theory of mine needs some support. I'm only an unknown medico—no one would listen to me until it was too late. For Nelson is dying, and I think I know why. . . ."

Sir Robert had been stubborn at first, but Dr. Hughes had had his way, as he always did. The members of the Board of Directors were even now filing into the conference room, grumbling and generally making a fuss about the extraordinary general meeting that had just been called. Their perplexity was still further increased when they heard that Hughes was going to address them. They all knew the physicist and his reputation, but he was a scientist and they were businessmen. What was Sir Robert planning?

Dr. Hughes, the cause of all the trouble, felt annoyed with himself for being nervous. His opinion of the Board of Directors was not flattering, but Sir Robert was a man he could respect, so there was no reason to be afraid of them. It was true that they might consider him mad, but his past record would take care of that. Mad or not, he was worth thousands of pounds to them.

Dr. Sanderson smiled encouragingly at him as he walked into the conference room. The smile was not very successful, but it helped. Sir Robert had just finished speaking. He picked up his glasses in that nervous way he had, and coughed deprecatingly. Not for the first time, Hughes wondered how such an apparently timid old man could rule so vast a commercial empire.

"Well, here is Dr. Hughes, gentlemen. He will—ahem—explain everything to you. I have asked him not to be too technical. You are at liberty to interrupt him if he ascends into the more rarefied stratosphere of higher mathematics. Dr. Hughes . . ."

Slowly at first, and then more quickly as he gained the confidence of his audience, the physicist began to tell his story. Nelson's diary drew a gasp of amazement from the Board, and the inverted coins proved fascinating curiosities. Hughes was glad to see that he had aroused the interest of his listeners. He took a deep breath and made the plunge he had been fearing.

"You have heard what has happened to Nelson, gentlemen, but what I am going to tell you now is even more startling. I must ask you for your very close attention."

He picked up a rectangular sheet of notepaper from the conference table, folded it along a diagonal and tore it along the fold.

"Here we have two right-angled triangles with equal sides. I lay them on the table—so." He placed the paper triangles side by side on the table, with their hypotenuses touching, so that they formed a kite-shaped figure. "Now, as I have arranged them, each triangle is the mirror image of the other. You can imagine that the plane of the mirror is along the hypotenuse. This is the point I want you to notice. As long as I keep the triangles in the plane of the table, I can slide them around as much as I like, but I can never place one so that it exactly covers the other. Like a pair of gloves, they are not interchangeable although their dimensions are identical."

He paused to let that sink in. There were no comments, so he continued.

"Now, if I pick up one of the triangles, turn it over in the air and put it down again, the two are no longer mirror images, but have become completely identical—so." He suited the action to the words. "This may seem very elementary; in fact, it is so. But it teaches us one very important lesson. The triangles on the table were flat objects, restricted to two dimensions. To turn one into its mirror image I had to lift it up and rotate it in the third dimension. Do you see what I am driving at?"

He glanced round the table. One or two of the directors nodded slowly in dawning comprehension.

"Similarly, to change a solid, three-dimensional body, such as a man, into its analogue or mirror image, it must be rotated in a fourth dimension. I repeat—a fourth dimension."

There was a strained silence. Someone coughed, but it was a nervous, not a skeptical cough.

"Four-dimensional geometry, as you know"—he'd be surprised if they did—"has been one of the major tools of mathematics since before the time of Einstein. But until now it has always been a mathematical fiction, having no real existence in the physical world. It now appears that the unheard-of currents, amounting to millions of amperes, which flowed momentarily in the windings of our generator must have produced a certain extension into four dimensions, for a fraction of a second and in a volume large enough to contain a man. I have been making some calculations and have been able to satisfy myself that a 'hyperspace' about ten feet on a side was, in fact, generated: a matter of some ten thousand quartic—not cubic!—feet. Nelson was occupying that space. The sudden collapse of the field when the circuit was broken caused the rotation of the space, and Nelson was inverted.

"I must ask you to accept this theory, as no other explanation fits the facts. I have the mathematics here if you wish to consult them."

He waved the sheets in front of his audience, so that the directors could see the imposing array of equations. The technique worked—it always did. They cowered visibly. Only McPherson, the secretary, was made of sterner stuff. He had had a semi-technical education and still read a good deal of popular science, which he was fond of airing whenever he had the opportunity. But he was intelligent and willing to learn, and Dr. Hughes had often spent official time discussing some new scientific theory with him.

"You say that Nelson has been rotated in the Fourth Dimension; but I thought Einstein had shown that the Fourth Dimension was time."

Hughes groaned inwardly. He had been anticipating this red herring.

"I was referring to an additional dimension of space," he explained patiently. "By that I mean a dimension, or direction, at right-angles to our normal three. One can call it the Fourth Dimension if one wishes. With certain reservations, time may also be regarded as a dimension. As we normally regard space as three-dimensional, it is then customary to call time the Fourth Dimension. But the label is arbitrary. As I'm asking you to grant me four dimensions of space, we must call time the Fifth Dimension."

"Five Dimensions! Good Heavens!" exploded someone further down the table.

Dr. Hughes could not resist the opportunity. "Space of several million dimensions has been frequently postulated in sub-atomic physics," he said quietly.

There was a stunned silence. No one, not even McPherson, seemed inclined to argue.

"I now come to the second part of my account," continued Dr. Hughes. "A few weeks after his inversion we found that there was something wrong with Nelson. He was taking food normally, but it didn't seem to nourish him properly. The explanation has been given by Dr. Sanderson, and leads us into the realms of organic chemistry. I'm sorry to be talking like a textbook, but you will soon realize how vitally important this is to the company. And you also have the satisfaction of knowing that we are now all on equally unfamiliar territory."

That was not quite true, for Hughes still remembered some fragments of his chemistry. But it might encourage the stragglers.

"Organic compounds are composed of atoms of carbon, oxygen and hydrogen, with other elements, arranged in complicated ways in space. Chemists are fond of making models of them out of knitting needles and colored plasticine. The results are often very pretty and look like works of advanced art.

"Now, it is possible to have two organic compounds containing identical numbers of atoms, arranged in such a way that one is the mirror image of the other. They're called stereo-isomers, and are very common among the sugars. If you could set their molecules side by side, you would see that they bore the same sort of relationship as a right and left glove. They are, in fact, called right- or left-handed—dextro or laevo—compounds. I hope this is quite clear."

Dr. Hughes looked around anxiously. Apparently it was.

"Stereo-isomers have almost identical chemical properties," he went on, "though there are subtle differences. In the last few years, Dr. Sanderson tells me, it has been found that certain essential foods, including the new class of vitamins discovered by Professor Vandenburg, have properties depending on the arrangement of their atoms in space. In other words, gentlemen, the left-handed compounds might be essential for life, but the right-handed ones would be of no value. This in spite of the fact that their chemical formulae are identical.

"You will appreciate, now, why Nelson's inversion is much more serious than we at first thought. It's not merely a matter of teaching him to read again, in which case—apart from its philosophical interest—the whole business would be trivial. He is actually starving to death in the midst of plenty, simply because he can no more assimilate certain molecules of food than we can put our right foot into a left boot.

"Dr. Sanderson has tried an experiment which has proved the truth of this theory. With very great difficulty, he has obtained the stereo-isomers of many of these vitamins. Professor Vandenburg himself synthesized them when he heard of our trouble. They have already produced a very marked improvement in Nelson's condition."

Hughes paused and drew out some papers. He thought he would give the Board time to prepare for the shock. If a man's life were not at stake, the situation would have been very amusing. The Board was going to be hit where it would hurt most.

"As you will realize, gentlemen, since Nelson was injured—if you can call it that—while he was on duty, the company is liable to pay for any treatment he may require. We have found that treatment, and you may wonder why I have taken so much of your time telling you about it. The reason is very simple. The production of the necessary stereo-isomers is almost as difficult as the extraction of radium—more so, in some cases. Dr. Sanderson tells me that it will cost over five thousand pounds a day to keep Nelson alive."

The silence lasted for half a minute; then everyone started to talk at once. Sir Robert pounded on the table, and presently restored order. The council of war had begun.

Three hours later, an exhausted Hughes left the conference room and went in search of Dr. Sanderson, whom he found fretting in his office.

"Well, what's the decision?" asked the doctor.

"What I was afraid of. They want me to re-invert Nelson."

"Can you do it?"

"Frankly, I don't know. All I can hope to do is to reproduce the conditions of the original fault as accurately as I can."

"Weren't there any other suggestions?"

"Quite a few, but most of them were stupid. McPherson had the best idea. He wanted to use the generator to invert normal food so that Nelson could eat it. I had to point out that to take the big machine out of action for this purpose would cost several millions a year, and in any case the windings wouldn't stand it more than a few times. So that scheme collapsed. Then Sir Robert wanted to know if you could guarantee there were no vitamins we'd overlooked, or that might still be undiscovered. His idea was that in spite of our synthetic diets we might not be able to keep Nelson alive after all."

"What did you say to that?"

"I had to admit it was a possibility. So Sir Robert is going to have a talk with Nelson. He hopes to persuade him to risk it; his family will be taken care of if the experiment fails."

Neither of the two men said anything for a few moments. Then Dr. Sanderson broke the silence.

"Now do you understand the sort of decision a surgeon often has to make?" he said.

Hughes nodded in agreement. "It's a beautiful dilemma, isn't it? A perfectly healthy man, but it will cost two millions a year to keep him alive, and we can't even be sure of that. I know the

Board's thinking of its precious balance sheet more than anything else, but I don't see any alternative. Nelson will have to take a chance."

"Couldn't you make some tests first?"

"Impossible. It's a major engineering operation to get the rotor out. We'll have to rush the experiment through when the load on the system is at minimum. Then we'll slam the rotor back, and tidy up the mess our artificial short has made. All this has to be done before the peak loads come on again. Poor old Murdock's mad as hell about it."

"I don't blame him. When will the experiment start?"

"Not for a few days, at least. Even if Nelson agrees, I've got to fix up all my gear."

No one was ever to know what Sir Robert said to Nelson during the hours they were together. Dr. Hughes was more than half prepared for it when the telephone rang and the Old Man's tired voice said, "Hughes? Get your equipment ready. I've spoken to Murdock, and we've fixed the time for Tuesday night. Can you manage by then?"

"Yes, Sir Robert."

"Good. Give me a progress report every afternoon until Tuesday. That's all."

The enormous room was dominated by the great cylinder of the rotor, hanging thirty feet above the gleaming plastic floor. A little group of men stood silently at the edge of the shadowed pit, waiting patiently. A maze of temporary wiring ran to Dr. Hughes's equipment—multibeam oscilloscopes, megawattmeters and microchronometers, and the special relays that had been constructed to make the circuit at the calculated instant.

That was the greatest problem of all. Dr. Hughes had no way of telling when the circuit should be closed; whether it should be when the voltage was at maximum, when it was at zero, or at some intermediate point on the sine wave. He had chosen the simplest and safest course. The circuit would be made at zero voltage; when it opened again would depend on the speed of the breakers.

In ten minutes the last of the great factories in the service area would be closing down for the night. The weather forecast had been favorable; there would be no abnormal loads before morning. By then, the rotor had to be back and the generator running again.

Fortunately, the unique method of construction made it easy to reassemble the machine, but it would be a very close thing and there was no time to lose.

When Nelson came in, accompanied by Sir Robert and Dr. Sanderson, he was very pale. He might, thought Hughes, have been going to his execution. The thought was somewhat ill-timed, and he put it hastily aside.

There was just time enough for a last quite unnecessary check of the equipment. He had barely finished when he heard Sir Robert's quiet voice.

"We're ready, Dr. Hughes."

Rather unsteadily, he walked to the edge of the pit. Nelson had already descended, and as he had been instructed, was standing at its exact center, his upturned face a white blob far below. Dr. Hughes waved a brief encouragement and turned away, to rejoin the group by his equipment.

He flicked over the switch of the oscilloscope and played with the synchronizing controls until a single cycle of the main wave was stationary on the screen. Then he adjusted the phasing: two brilliant spots of light moved toward each other along the wave until they had coalesced at its geometric center. He looked briefly toward Murdock, who was watching the megawattmeters intently. The engineer nodded. With a silent prayer, Hughes threw the switch.

There was the tiniest click from the relay unit. A fraction of a second later, the whole building seemed to rock as the great conductors crashed over in the switch room three hundred feet away. The lights faded, and almost died. Then it was all over. The circuit breakers, driven at almost the speed of an explosion, had cleared the line again. The lights returned to normal and the needles of the megawattmeters dropped back onto their scales.

The equipment had withstood the overload. But what of Nelson?

Dr. Hughes was surprised to see that Sir Robert, for all his sixty years, had already reached the generator. He was standing by its edge, looking down into the great pit. Slowly, the physicist went to join him. He was afraid to hurry; a growing sense of premonition was filling his mind. Already he could picture Nelson lying in a twisted heap at the center of the well, his lifeless eyes staring up at them reproachfully. Then came a still more horrible thought. Suppose the field had collapsed too soon, when the inversion was only partly completed? In another moment, he would know the worst.

There is no shock greater than that of the totally unexpected, for against it the mind has no chance to prepare its defenses. Dr. Hughes was ready for almost anything when he reached the generator. Almost, but not quite. . . .

He did not expect to find it completely empty.

What came after, he could never perfectly remember. Murdock seemed to take charge then. There was a great flurry of activity, and the engineers swarmed in to replace the giant rotor. Somewhere in the distance he heard Sir Robert saying, over and over again, "We did our best—we did our best." He must have replied, somehow, but everything was very vague. . . .

In the gray hours before the dawn, Dr. Hughes awoke from his fitful sleep. All night he had been haunted by his dreams, by weird fantasies of multi-dimensional geometry. There were visions of strange, other-worldly universes of insane shapes and intersecting planes along which he was doomed to struggle endlessly, fleeing from some nameless terror. Nelson, he dreamed, was trapped in one of those unearthly dimensions, and he was trying to reach him. Sometimes he was Nelson himself, and he imagined that he could see all around him the universe he knew, strangely distorted and barred from him by invisible walls.

The nightmare faded as he struggled up in bed. For a few moments he sat holding his head, while his mind began to clear. He knew what was happening; this was not the first time the solution of some baffling problem had come suddenly upon him in the night.

There was one piece still missing in the jigsaw puzzle that was sorting itself out in his mind. One piece only—and suddenly he had it. There was something that Nelson's assistant had said, when he was describing the original accident. It had seemed trivial at the time; until now, Hughes had forgotten all about it.

"When I looked inside the generator, there didn't seem to be anyone there, so I started to climb down the ladder. . . ."

What a fool he had been! Old McPherson had been right, or partly right, after all!

The field had rotated Nelson in the fourth dimension of space, but there had been a displacement in *time* as well. On the first occasion it had been a matter of seconds only. This time, the conditions must have been different in spite of all his care. There were so many unknown factors, and the theory was more than half guesswork.

Nelson had not been inside the generator at the end of the experiment. *But he would be.*

Dr. Hughes felt a cold sweat break out all over his body. He pictured that thousand-ton cylinder, spinning beneath the drive of its fifty million horse-power. Suppose something suddenly materialized in the space it already occupied . . . ?

He leaped out of bed and grabbed the private phone to the power station. There was no time to lose—the rotor would have to be removed at once. Murdock could argue later.

Very gently, something caught the house by its foundations and rocked it to and fro, as a sleepy child may shake its rattle. Flakes of plaster came planing down from the ceiling; a network of cracks appeared as if by magic in the walls. The lights flickered, became suddenly brilliant, and faded out.

Dr. Hughes threw back the curtain and looked toward the mountains. The power station was invisible beyond the foothills of Mount Perrin, but its site was clearly marked by the vast column of debris that was slowly rising against the bleak light of the dawn.

"**T**his," said Karn smugly, "will interest you. Just take a look at it!"

He pushed across the file he had been reading, and for the *nth* time I decided to ask for his transfer or, failing that, my own.

"What's it about?" I said wearily.

"It's a long report from a Dr. Matthews to the Minister of Science." He waved it in front of me. "Just read it!"

Without much enthusiasm, I began to go through the file. A few minutes later I looked up and admitted grudgingly: "Maybe you're right—this time." I didn't speak again until I'd finished. . . .

→My dear Minister (the letter began). As you requested, here is my special report on Professor Hancock's experiments, which have had such unexpected and extraordinary results. I have not had time to cast it into a more orthodox form, but am sending you the dictation just as it stands.

Since you have many matters engaging your attention, perhaps I should briefly summarize our dealings with Professor Hancock. Until 1955, the Professor held the Kelvin Chair of Electrical Engineering at Brendon University, from which he was granted indefinite leave of absence to carry out his researches. In these he was joined by the late Dr. Clayton, sometime Chief Geologist to the Ministry of Fuel and Power. Their joint research was financed by grants from the Paul Fund and the Royal Society.

The Professor hoped to develop sonar as a means of precise geological surveying. Sonar, as you will know, is the acoustic equivalent of radar, and although less familiar is older by some millions of years, since bats use it very effectively to detect insects and obstacles at night. Professor Hancock intended to send high-powered supersonic pulses into the ground and to build up from the returning echoes an image of what lay beneath. The picture would be displayed on a cathode ray tube and the whole system would be exactly analogous to the type of radar used in aircraft to show the ground through cloud.

In 1957 the two scientists had achieved partial success but had exhausted their funds. Early in 1958 they applied directly to the government for a block grant. Dr. Clayton pointed out the immense value of a device which would enable us to take a kind of X-ray photo of the Earth's crust, and the Minister of Fuel gave it his approval before passing on the application to us. At that time the report of the Bernal Committee had just been published and we were very anxious that deserving cases should be dealt with quickly to avoid further criticisms. I went to see the Professor at once and submitted a favorable report; the first payment of our grant (S/543A/68) was made a few days later. From that time I have been continually in touch with the research and have assisted to some extent with technical advice.

The equipment used in the experiments is complex, but its principles are simple. Very short but extremely powerful pulses of supersonic waves are generated by a special transmitter which revolves continuously in a pool of a heavy organic liquid. The beam produced passes into the ground and "scans" like a radar beam searching for echoes. By a very ingenious time-delay circuit which I will resist the temptation to describe, echoes from any depth can be selected and so pictures of the strata under investigation can be built up on a cathode ray screen in the normal way.

When I first met Professor Hancock his apparatus was rather primitive, but he was able to show me the distribution of rock down to a depth of several hundred feet and we could see quite clearly a part of the Bakerloo Line which passed very near his laboratory. Much of the Professor's success was due to the great intensity of his supersonic bursts; almost from the beginning he was able to generate peak powers of several hundred kilowatts, nearly all of which was radiated into the ground. It was unsafe to remain near the transmitter, and I noticed that the soil became quite warm around it. I was rather surprised to see large numbers of birds in the vicinity, but soon discovered that they were attracted by the hundreds of dead worms lying on the ground.

At the time of Dr. Clayton's death in 1960, the equipment was working at a power level of over a megawatt and quite good pictures of strata a mile down could be obtained. Dr. Clayton had correlated the results with known geographical surveys, and had proved beyond doubt the value of the information obtained.

Dr. Clayton's death in a motor accident was a great tragedy. He had always exerted a stabilizing influence on the Professor, who had never been much interested in the practical applications of his work. Soon afterward I noticed a distinct change in the Professor's outlook, and a few months later he confided his new ambitions to me. I had been trying to persuade him to publish his results (he had already spent over £50,000 and the Public Accounts Committee was being difficult again), but he asked for a little more time. I think I can best explain his attitude by his own words, which I remember very vividly, for they were expressed with peculiar emphasis.

"Have you ever wondered," he said, "what the Earth really is like inside? We've only scratched the surface with our mines and wells. What lies beneath is as unknown as the other side of the Moon.

"We know that the Earth is unnaturally dense—far denser than the rocks and soil of its crust would indicate. The core may be solid metal, but until now there's been no way of telling. Even ten miles down the pressure must be thirty tons or more to the square inch and the temperature several hundred degrees. What it's like at the center staggers the imagination: the pressure must be thousands of tons to the square inch. It's strange to think that in two or three years we may have reached the Moon, but when we've got to the stars we'll still be no nearer that inferno four thousand miles beneath our feet.

"I can now get recognizable echoes from two miles down, but I hope to step up the transmitter to ten megawatts in a few months. With that power, I believe the range will be increased to ten miles; and I don't mean to stop there."

I was impressed, but at the same time I felt a little skeptical.

"That's all very well," I said, "but surely the deeper you go the less there'll be to see. The pressure will make any cavities impossible, and after a few miles there will simply be a homogeneous mass getting denser and denser."

"Quite likely," agreed the Professor. "But I can still learn a lot from the transmission characteristics. Anyway, we'll see when we get there!"

That was four months ago; and yesterday I saw the result of that research. When I answered his invitation the Professor was clearly excited, but he gave me no hint of what, if anything, he had discovered. He showed me his improved equipment and raised the new receiver from its bath. The sensitivity of the pickups had been greatly improved, and this alone had effectively doubled the range, altogether apart from the increased transmitter power. It was strange to watch the steel framework slowly turning and to realize that it was exploring regions, which, in spite of their nearness, man might never reach.

When we entered the hut containing the display equipment, the Professor was strangely silent. He switched on the transmitter, and even though it was a hundred yards away I could feel an uncomfortable tingling. Then the cathode ray tube lit up and the slowly revolving time-base drew the picture I had seen so often before. Now, however, the definition was much improved owing to the increased power and sensitivity of the equipment. I adjusted the depth control and focussed on the Underground, which was clearly visible as a dark lane across the faintly luminous screen. While I was watching, it suddenly seemed to fill with mist and I knew that a train was going through.

Presently I continued the descent. Although I had watched this picture many times before, it was always uncanny to see great luminous masses floating toward me and to know that they were buried rocks—perhaps the debris from the glaciers of fifty thousand years ago. Dr. Clayton had worked out a chart so that we could identify the various strata as they were passed, and presently I saw that I was through the alluvial soil and entering the great clay saucer which traps and holds the city's artesian water. Soon that too was passed, and I was dropping down through the bedrock almost a mile below the surface.

The picture was still clear and bright, though there was little to see, for there were now few changes in the ground structure. The pressure was already rising to a thousand atmospheres; soon it would be impossible for any cavity to remain open, for the rock itself would begin to flow. Mile after mile I sank, but only a pale mist floated on the screen, broken sometimes when echoes were returned from pockets or lodes of denser material. They became fewer and fewer as the depth increased—or else they were now so small that they could no longer be seen.

The scale of the picture was, of course, continually expanding. It was now many miles from side to side, and I felt like an airman looking down upon an unbroken cloud ceiling from an enormous height. For a moment a sense of vertigo seized me as I thought of the abyss into which I was gazing. I do not think that the world will ever seem quite solid to me again.

At a depth of nearly ten miles I stopped and looked at the Professor. There had been no alteration for some time, and I knew that the rock must now be compressed into a featureless, homogeneous mass. I did a quick mental calculation and shuddered as I realized that the pressure must be at least thirty tons to the square inch. The scanner was revolving very slowly now, for the feeble echoes were taking many seconds to struggle back from the depths.

"Well, Professor," I said, "I congratulate you. It's a wonderful achievement. But we seem to have reached the core now. I don't suppose there'll be any change from here to the center."

He smiled a little wryly. "Go on," he said. "You haven't finished yet."

There was something in his voice that puzzled and alarmed me. I looked at him intently for a moment; his features were just visible in the blue-green glow of the cathode ray tube.

"How far down can this thing go?" I asked, as the interminable descent started again.

"Fifteen miles," he said shortly. I wondered how he knew, for the last feature I had seen at all clearly was only eight miles down. But I continued the long fall through the rock, the scanner turning more and more slowly now, until it took almost five minutes to make a complete revolution. Behind me I could hear the Professor breathing heavily, and once the back of my chair gave a crack as his fingers gripped it.

Then, suddenly, very faint markings began to reappear on the screen. I leaned forward eagerly, wondering if this was the first glimpse of the world's iron core. With agonizing slowness the scanner turned through a right angle, then another. And then——

I leaped suddenly out of my chair, cried "My God!" and turned to face the Professor. Only once before in my life had I received such an intellectual shock—fifteen years ago, when I had accidentally turned on the radio and heard of the fall of the first atomic bomb. That had been unexpected, but this was inconceivable. For on the screen had appeared a grid of faint lines, crossing and recrossing to form a perfectly symmetrical lattice.

I know that I said nothing for many minutes, for the scanner made a complete revolution while I stood frozen with surprise. Then the Professor spoke in a soft, unnaturally calm voice.

"I wanted you to see it for yourself before I said anything. That picture is now thirty miles in diameter, and those squares are two or three miles on a side. You'll notice that the vertical lines converge and the horizontal ones are bent into arcs. We're looking at part of an enormous structure of concentric rings; the center must lie many miles to the north, probably in the region of Cambridge. How much further it extends in the other direction we can only guess."

"But what *is* it, for heaven's sake?"

"Well, it's clearly artificial."

"That's ridiculous! Fifteen miles down!"

The Professor pointed to the screen again. "God knows I've done my best," he said, "but I can't convince myself that Nature could make anything like that."

I had nothing to say, and presently he continued: "I discovered it three days ago, when I was trying to find the maximum range of the equipment. I can go deeper than this, and I rather think that the structure we can see is so dense that it won't transmit my radiations any further.

"I've tried a dozen theories, but in the end I keep returning to one. We know that the pressure down there must be eight or nine thousand atmospheres, and the temperature must be high enough to melt rock. But normal matter is still almost empty space. Suppose that there is life down there—not organic life, of course, but life based on partially condensed matter, matter in which the electron shells are few or altogether missing. Do you see what I mean? To such creatures, even the rock fifteen miles down would offer no

more resistance than water—and we and all our world would be as
tenuous as ghosts."

"Then that thing we can see——"

"Is a city, or its equivalent. You've seen its size, so you can
judge for yourself the civilization that must have built it. All the
world we know—our oceans and continents and mountains—is
nothing more than a film of mist surrounding something beyond
our comprehension."

Neither of us said anything for a while. I remember feeling a
foolish surprise at being one of the first men in the world to learn
the appalling truth; for somehow I never doubted that it was the
truth. And I wondered how the rest of humanity would react when
the revelation came.

Presently I broke into the silence. "If you're right," I said, "why
have they—whatever they are—never made contact with us?"

The Professor looked at me rather pityingly. "We think we're
good engineers," he said, "but how could *we* reach *them?* Besides,
I'm not at all sure that there haven't been contacts. Think of all
the underground creatures and the mythology—trolls and cobalds
and the rest. No, it's quite impossible—I take it back. Still, the idea
is rather suggestive."

All the while the pattern on the screen had never changed: the
dim network still glowed there, challenging our sanity. I tried to
imagine streets and buildings and the creatures going among them,
creatures who could make their way through the incandescent rock
as a fish swims through water. It was fantastic . . . and then I
remembered the incredibly narrow range of temperatures and
pressures under which the human race exists. *We,* not they, were
the freaks, for almost all the matter in the universe is at temperatures of thousands or even millions of degrees.

"Well," I said lamely, "what do we do now?"

The Professor leaned forward eagerly. "First we must learn a
great deal more, and we must keep this an absolute secret until
we are sure of the facts. Can you imagine the panic there would
be if this information leaked out? Of course, the truth's inevitable
sooner or later, but we may be able to break it slowly.

"You'll realize that the geological surveying side of my work is
now utterly unimportant. The first thing we have to do is to build
a chain of stations to find the extent of the structure. I visualize

them at ten-mile intervals toward the north, but I'd like to build the first one somewhere in South London to see how extensive the thing is. The whole job will have to be kept as secret as the building of the first radar chain in the late thirties.

"At the same time, I'm going to push up my transmitter power again. I hope to be able to beam the output much more narrowly, and so greatly increase the energy concentration. But this will involve all sorts of mechanical difficulties, and I'll need more assistance."

I promised to do my utmost to get further aid, and the Professor hopes that you will soon be able to visit his laboratory yourself. In the meantime I am attaching a photograph of the vision screen, which although not as clear as the original will, I hope, prove beyond doubt that our observations are not mistaken.

I am well aware that our grant to the Interplanetary Society has brought us dangerously near the total estimate for the year, but surely even the crossing of space is less important than the immediate investigation of this discovery which may have the most profound effects on the philosophy and the future of the whole human race.

I sat back and looked at Karn. There was much in the document I had not understood, but the main outlines were clear enough.

"Yes," I said, "this is it! Where's that photograph?"

He handed it over. The quality was poor, for it had been copied many times before reaching us. But the pattern was unmistakable and I recognized it at once.

"They were good scientists," I said admiringly. "That's Callastheon, all right. So we've found the truth at last, even if it has taken us three hundred years to do it."

"Is that surprising," asked Karn, "when you consider the mountain of stuff we've had to translate and the difficulty of copying it before it evaporates?"

I sat in silence for a while, thinking of the strange race whose relics we were examining. Only once—never again!—had I gone up the great vent our engineers had opened into the Shadow World. It had been a frightening and unforgettable experience. The multiple layers of my pressure suit had made movement very difficult, and despite their insulation I could sense the unbelievable cold that was all around me.

"What a pity it was," I mused, "that our emergence destroyed them so completely. They were a clever race, and we might have learned a lot from them."

"I don't think we can be blamed," said Karn. "We never really believed that anything could exist under those awful conditions of near-vacuum, and almost absolute zero. It couldn't be helped."

I did not agree. "I think it proves that they were the more intelligent race. After all, *they* discovered us first. Everyone laughed at my grandfather when he said that the radiation he'd detected from the Shadow World must be artificial."

Karn ran one of his tentacles over the manuscript.

"We've certainly discovered the cause of that radiation," he said. "Notice the date—it's just a year before your grandfather's discovery. The Professor must have got his grant all right!" He laughed unpleasantly. "It must have given him a shock when he saw us coming up to the surface, right underneath him."

I scarcely heard his words, for a most uncomfortable feeling had suddenly come over me. I thought of the thousands of miles of rock lying below the great city of Callastheon, growing hotter and denser all the way to the Earth's unknown core. And so I turned to Karn.

"That isn't very funny," I said quietly. "It may be our turn next."

The river was dead and the lake already dying when the monster had come down the dried-up watercourse and turned onto the desolate mud-flats. There were not many places where it was safe to walk, and even where the ground was hardest the great pistons of its feet sank a foot or more beneath the weight they carried. Sometimes it had paused, surveying the landscape with quick, birdlike movements of its head. Then it had sunk even deeper into the yielding soil, so that fifty million years later men could judge with some accuracy the duration of its halts.

For the waters had never returned, and the blazing sun had baked the mud to rock. Later still the desert had poured over all this land, sealing it beneath protecting layers of sand. And later— very much later—had come Man.

"Do you think," shouted Barton above the din, "that Professor Fowler became a palaeontologist because he likes playing with pneumatic drills? Or did he acquire the taste afterward?"

"Can't hear you!" yelled Davis, leaning on his shovel in a most professional manner. He glanced hopefully at his watch.

"Shall I tell him it's dinnertime? He can't wear a watch while he's drilling, so he won't know any better."

"I doubt if it will work," Barton shrieked. "He's got wise to us now and always adds an extra ten minutes. But it will make a change from this infernal digging."

With noticeable enthusiasm the two geologists downed tools and started to walk toward their chief. As they approached, he shut off the drill and relative silence descended, broken only by the throbbing of the compressor in the background.

"About time we went back to camp, Professor," said Davis, wristwatch held casually behind his back. "You know what cook says if we're late."

Professor Fowler, M.A., F.R.S., F.G.S., mopped some, but by no means all, of the ocher dust from his forehead. He would have passed anywhere as a typical navvy, and the occasional visitors to the site seldom recognized the Vice-President of the Geological Society in the brawny, half-naked workman crouching over his beloved pneumatic drill.

It had taken nearly a month to clear the sandstone down to the surface of the petrified mud-flats. In that time several hundred square feet had been exposed, revealing a frozen snapshot of the past that was probably the finest yet discovered by palaeontology. Some scores of birds and reptiles had come here in search of the receding water, and left their footsteps as a perpetual monument eons after their bodies had perished. Most of the prints had been identified, but one—the largest of them all—was new to science. It belonged to a beast which must have weighed twenty or thirty tons: and Professor Fowler was following the fifty-million-year-old spoor with all the emotions of a big-game hunter tracking his prey. There was even a hope that he might yet overtake it; for the ground must have been treacherous when the unknown monster went this way and its bones might still be near at hand, marking the place where it had been trapped like so many creatures of its time.

Despite the mechanical aids available, the work was very tedious. Only the upper layers could be removed by the power tools, and the final uncovering had to be done by hand with the utmost care. Professor Fowler had good reason for his insistence that he alone should do the preliminary drilling, for a single slip might cause irreparable harm.

The three men were halfway back to the main camp, jolting over the rough road in the expedition's battered jeep, when Davis raised the question that had been intriguing the younger men ever since the work had begun.

"I'm getting a distinct impression," he said, "that our neighbors down the valley don't like us, though I can't imagine why. We're not interfering with them, and they might at least have the decency to invite us over."

"Unless, of course, it *is* a war research plant," added Barton, voicing a generally accepted theory.

"I don't think so," said Professor Fowler mildly. "Because it so happens that I've just had an invitation myself. I'm going there tomorrow."

If his bombshell failed to have the expected result, it was thanks to his staff's efficient espionage system. For a moment Davis pondered over this confirmation of his suspicions; then he continued with a slight cough:

"No one else has been invited, then?"

The Professor smiled at his pointed hint. "No," he said. "It's a strictly personal invitation. I know you boys are dying of curiosity but, frankly, I don't know any more about the place than you do. If I learn anything tomorrow, I'll tell you all about it. But at least we've found out who's running the establishment."

His assistants pricked up their ears. "Who is it?" asked Barton. "My guess was the Atomic Development Authority."

"You may be right," said the Professor. "At any rate, Henderson and Barnes are in charge."

This time the bomb exploded effectively; so much so that Davis nearly drove the jeep off the road—not that that made much difference, the road being what it was.

"Henderson and Barnes? In *this* god-forsaken hole?"

"That's right," said the Professor gaily. "The invitation was actually from Barnes. He apologized for not contacting us before, made the usual excuses, and wondered if I could drop in for a chat."

"Did he say what they are doing?"

"No; not a hint."

"Barnes and Henderson?" said Barton thoughtfully. "I don't know much about them except that they're physicists. What's their particular racket?"

"They're *the* experts on low-temperature physics," answered Davis. "Henderson was Director of the Cavendish for years. He wrote a lot of letters to *Nature* not so long ago. If I remember rightly, they were all about Helium II."

Barton, who didn't like physicists and said so whenever possible, was not impressed. "I don't even know what Helium II is," he said smugly. "What's more, I'm not at all sure that I want to."

This was intended for Davis, who had once taken a physics degree in, as he explained, a moment of weakness. The "moment" had lasted for several years before he had drifted into geology by rather devious routes, and he was always harking back to his first love.

"It's a form of liquid helium that only exists at a few degrees above absolute zero. It's got the most extraordinary properties—but, as far as I can see, none of them can explain the presence of two leading physicists in this corner of the globe."

They had now arrived at the camp, and Davis brought the jeep to its normal crash-halt in the parking space. He shook his head in annoyance as he bumped into the truck ahead with slightly more violence than usual.

"These tires are nearly through. Have the new ones come yet?"

"Arrived in the 'copter this morning, with a despairing note from Andrews hoping that you'd make them last a full fortnight this time."

"Good! I'll get them fitted this evening."

The Professor had been walking a little ahead; now he dropped back to join his assistants.

"You needn't have hurried, Jim," he said glumly. "It's corned beef again."

It would be most unfair to say that Barton and Davis did less work because the Professor was away. They probably worked a good deal harder than usual, since the native laborers required twice as much supervision in the Chief's absence. But there was no doubt that they managed to find time for a considerable amount of extra talking.

Ever since they had joined Professor Fowler, the two young geologists had been intrigued by the strange establishment five miles away down the valley. It was clearly a research organization of some type, and Davis had identified the tall stacks of an atomic-power unit. That, of course, gave no clue to the work that was proceeding, but it did indicate its importance. There were still only a few thousand turbo-piles in the world, and they were all reserved for major projects.

There were dozens of reasons why two great scientists might

have hidden themselves in this place: most of the more hazardous atomic research was carried out as far as possible from civilization, and some had been abandoned altogether until laboratories in space could be set up. Yet it seemed odd that this work, whatever it was, should be carried out so close to what had now become the most important center of geological research in the world. It might, of course, be no more than a coincidence; certainly the physicists had never shown any interest in their compatriots so near at hand.

Davis was carefully chipping round one of the great footprints, while Barton was pouring liquid perspex into those already uncovered so that they would be preserved from harm in the transparent plastic. They were working in a somewhat absentminded manner, for each was unconsciously listening for the sound of the jeep. Professor Fowler had promised to collect them when he returned from his visit, for the other vehicles were in use elsewhere and they did not relish a two-mile walk back to camp in the broiling sun. Moreover, they wanted to have any news as soon as possible.

"How many people," said Barton suddenly, "do you think they have over there?"

Davis straightened himself up. "Judging from the buildings, not more than a dozen or so."

"Then it might be a private affair, not an ADA project at all."

"Perhaps, though it must have pretty considerable backing. Of course, Henderson and Barnes could get that on their reputations alone."

"That's where the physicists score," said Barton. "They've only got to convince some war department that they're on the track of a new weapon, and they can get a couple of million without any trouble."

He spoke with some bitterness; for, like most scientists, he had strong views on this subject. Barton's views, indeed, were even more definite than usual, for he was a Quaker and had spent the last year of the War arguing with not-unsympathetic tribunals.

The conversation was interrupted by the roar and clatter of the jeep, and the two men ran over to meet the Professor.

"Well?" they cried simultaneously.

Professor Fowler looked at them thoughtfully, his expression giving no hint of what was in his mind. "Had a good day?" he said at last.

"Come off it, Chief!" protested Davis. "Tell us what you've found out."

The Professor climbed out of the seat and dusted himself down. "I'm sorry, boys," he said with some embarrassment, "I can't tell you a thing, and that's flat."

There were two united wails of protest, but he waved them aside. "I've had a very interesting day, but I've had to promise not to say anything about it. Even now I don't know exactly what's going on, but it's something pretty revolutionary—as revolutionary, perhaps, as atomic power. But Dr. Henderson is coming over tomorrow; see what you can get out of him."

For a moment, both Barton and Davis were so overwhelmed by the sense of anticlimax that neither spoke. Barton was the first to recover. "Well, surely there's a reason for this sudden interest in our activities?"

The Professor thought this over for a moment. "Yes; it wasn't entirely a social call," he admitted. "They think I may be able to help them. Now, no more questions, unless you want to walk back to camp!"

Dr. Henderson arrived on the site in the middle of the afternoon. He was a stout, elderly man, dressed rather incongruously in a dazzling white laboratory smock and very little else. Though the garb was eccentric, it was eminently practical in so hot a climate.

Davis and Barton were somewhat distant when Professor Fowler introduced them; they still felt that they had been snubbed and were determined that their visitor should understand their feelings. But Henderson was so obviously interested in their work that they soon thawed, and the Professor left them to show him round the excavations while he went to supervise the natives.

The physicist was greatly impressed by the picture of the world's remote past that lay exposed before his eyes. For almost an hour the two geologists took him over the workings yard by yard, talking of the creatures who had gone this way and speculating about future discoveries. The track which Professor Fowler was following now lay in a wide trench running away from the main excavation, for he had dropped all other work to investigate it. At its end the trench was no longer continuous: to save time, the Professor had begun to sink pits along the line of the footprints. The last sounding had missed altogether, and further digging had shown that the great reptile had made a sudden change of course.

"This is the most interesting bit," said Barton to the slightly wilting physicist. "You remember those earlier places where it had stopped for a moment to have a look around? Well, here it seems to have spotted something and has gone off in a new direction at a run, as you can see from the spacing."

"I shouldn't have thought such a brute *could* run."

"Well, it was probably a pretty clumsy effort, but you can cover quite a bit of ground with a fifteen-foot stride. We're going to follow it as far as we can. We may even find what it was chasing. I think the Professor has hopes of discovering a trampled battlefield with the bones of the victim still around. That would make everyone sit up."

Dr. Henderson smiled. "Thanks to Walt Disney, I can picture the scene rather well."

Davis was not very encouraging. "It was probably only the missus banging the dinner gong," he said. "The most infuriating part of our work is the way everything can peter out when it gets most exciting. The strata have been washed away, or there's been an earthquake—or, worse still, some silly fool has smashed up the evidence because he didn't recognize its value."

Henderson nodded in agreement. "I can sympathize with you," he said. "That's where the physicist has the advantage. He knows he'll get the answer eventually, if there is one."

He paused rather diffidently, as if weighing his words with great care. "It would save you a lot of trouble, wouldn't it, if you could actually *see* what took place in the past, without having to infer it by these laborious and uncertain methods. You've been a couple of months following these footsteps for a hundred yards, and they may lead nowhere for all your trouble."

There was a long silence. Then Barton spoke in a very thoughtful voice.

"Naturally, Doctor, we're rather curious about your work," he began. "Since Professor Fowler won't tell us anything, we've done a good deal of speculating. Do you really mean to say that——"

The physicist interrupted him rather hastily. "Don't give it any more thought," he said. "I was only daydreaming. As for our work, it's a very long way from completion, but you'll hear all about it in due course. We're not secretive—but, like everyone working in a new field, we don't want to say anything until we're sure of our ground. Why, if any other palaeontologists came near this place, I bet Professor Fowler would chase them away with a pick-axe!"

"That's not quite true," smiled Davis. "He'd be much more likely to set them to work. But I see your point of view; let's hope we don't have to wait too long."

That night, much midnight oil was burned at the main camp. Barton was frankly skeptical, but Davis had already built up an elaborate superstructure of theory around their visitor's remarks.

"It would explain so many things," he said. "First of all, their presence in this place, which otherwise doesn't make sense at all. We know the ground level here to within an inch for the last hundred million years, and we can date any event with an accuracy of better than one per cent. There's not a spot on Earth that's had its past worked out in such detail—it's the obvious place for an experiment like this!"

"But do you think it's even theoretically possible to build a machine that can see into the past?"

"I can't imagine how it could be done. But I daren't say it's impossible—especially to men like Henderson and Barnes."

"Hmmm. Not a very convincing argument. Is there any way we can hope to test it? What about those letters to *Nature?*"

"I've sent to the College Library; we should have them by the end of the week. There's always some continuity in a scientist's work, and they may give us some valuable clues."

But at first they were disappointed; indeed, Henderson's letters only increased the confusion. As Davis had remembered, most of them had been about the extraordinary properties of Helium II.

"It's really fantastic stuff," said Davis. "If a liquid behaved like this at normal temperatures, everyone would go mad. In the first place, it hasn't any viscosity at all. Sir George Darwin once said that if you had an ocean of Helium II, ships could sail in it without any engines. You'd give them a push at the beginning of their voyage and let them run into buffers on the other side. There'd be one snag, though; long before that happened the stuff would have climbed straight up the hull and the whole outfit would have sunk—gurgle, gurgle, gurgle . . ."

"Very amusing," said Barton, "but what the heck has this to do with your precious theory?"

"Not much," admitted Davis. "However, there's more to come. It's possible to have two streams of Helium II flowing in opposite directions *in the same tube*—one stream going through the other, as it were."

"That must take a bit of explaining; it's almost as bad as an object moving in two directions at once. I suppose there *is* an explanation, something to do with Relativity, I bet."

Davis was reading carefully. "The explanation," he said slowly, "is very complicated and I don't pretend to understand it fully. But it depends on the fact that liquid helium can have *negative* entropy under certain conditions."

"As I never understood what positive entropy is, I'm not much wiser."

"Entropy is a measure of the heat distribution of the Universe. At the beginning of time, when all energy was concentrated in the suns, entropy was a minimum. It will reach its maximum when everything's at a uniform temperature and the Universe is dead. There will still be plenty of heat around, but it won't be usable."

"Whyever not?"

"Well, all the water in a perfectly flat ocean won't run a hydro-electric plant—but quite a little lake up in the hills will do the trick. You must have a difference in level."

"I get the idea. Now I come to think of it, didn't someone once call entropy 'Time's Arrow?'"

"Yes—Eddington, I believe. Any kind of clock you care to mention—a pendulum, for instance—might just as easily run forward as backward. But entropy is a strictly one-way affair—it's always increasing with the passage of time. Hence the expression, 'Time's Arrow.'"

"Then *negative* entropy—my gosh!"

For a moment the two men looked at each other. Then Barton asked in a rather subdued voice: "What does Henderson say about it?"

"I'll quote from his last letter: 'The discovery of negative entropy introduces quite new and revolutionary conceptions into our picture of the physical world. Some of these will be examined in a further communication.'"

"And are they?"

"That's the snag: there's no 'further communication.' From that you can guess two alternatives. First, the Editor of *Nature* may have declined to publish the letter. I think we can rule that one out. Second, the consequences may have been *so* revolutionary that Henderson never did write a further report."

"Negative entropy—negative time," mused Barton. "It seems fantastic; yet it might be theoretically possible to build some sort of device that could see into the past. . . ."

"I know what we'll do," said Davis suddenly. "We'll tackle the Professor about it and watch his reactions. Now I'm going to bed before I get brain fever."

Tha. night Davis did not sleep well. He dreamed that he was walking along a road that stretched in both directions as far as the eye could see. He had been walking for miles before he came to the signpost, and when he reached it he found that it was broken and the two arms were revolving idly in the wind. As they turned, he could read the words they carried. One said simply: To the Future; the other: To the Past.

They learned nothing from Professor Fowler, which was not surprising; next to the Dean, he was the best poker player in the College. He regarded his slightly fretful assistants with no trace of emotion while Davis trotted out his theory.

When the young man had finished, he said quietly, "I'm going over again tomorrow, and I'll tell Henderson about your detective work. Maybe he'll take pity on you; maybe he'll tell me a bit more, for that matter. Now let's go to work."

Davis and Barton found it increasingly difficult to take a great deal of interest in their own work while their minds were filled with the enigma so near at hand. Nevertheless they continued conscientiously, though ever and again they paused to wonder if all their labor might not be in vain. If it were, they would be the first to rejoice. Supposing one could see into the past and watch history unfolding itself, back to the dawn of time! All the great secrets of the past would be revealed: one could watch the coming of life on the Earth, and the whole story of evolution from amoeba to man.

No; it was too good to be true. Having decided this, they would go back to their digging and scraping for another half-hour until the thought would come: but what if it *were* true? And then the whole cycle would begin all over again.

When Professor Fowler returned from his second visit, he was a subdued and obviously shaken man. The only satisfaction his assistants could get from him was the statement that Henderson had listened to their theory and complimented them on their powers of deduction.

That was all; but in Davis's eyes it clinched the matter, though Barton was still doubtful. In the weeks that followed, he too began to waver, until at last they were both convinced that the theory was correct. For Professor Fowler was spending more and more of his time with Henderson and Barnes; so much so that they sometimes did not see him for days. He had almost lost interest in the excavations, and had delegated all responsibility to Barton, who was now able to use the big pneumatic drill to his heart's content.

They were uncovering several yards of footprints a day, and the spacing showed that the monster had now reached its utmost speed and was advancing in great leaps as if nearing its victim. In a few days they might reveal the evidence of some eon-old tragedy, preserved by a miracle and brought down the ages for the observation of man. Yet all this seemed very unimportant now; for it was clear from the Professor's hints and his general air of abstraction that the secret research was nearing its climax. He had told them as much, promising that in a very few days, if all went well, their wait would be ended. But beyond that he would say nothing.

Once or twice Henderson had paid them a visit, and they could see that he was now laboring under a considerable strain. He obviously wanted to talk about his work, but was not going to do so until the final tests had been completed. They could only admire his self-control and wish that it would break down. Davis had a distinct impression that the elusive Barnes was mainly responsible for his secrecy; he had something of a reputation for not publishing work until it had been checked and double-checked. If these experiments were as important as they believed, his caution was understandable, however infuriating.

Henderson had come over early that morning to collect the Professor, and as luck would have it, his car had broken down on the primitive road. This was unfortunate for Davis and Barton, who would have to walk to camp for lunch, since Professor Fowler was driving Henderson back in the jeep. They were quite prepared to put up with this if their wait was indeed coming to an end, as the others had more than half-hinted.

They had stood talking by the side of the jeep for some time before the two older scientists had driven away. It was a rather strained parting, for each side knew what the other was thinking. Finally Barton, as usual the most outspoken, remarked:

"Well, Doc, if this *is* Der Tag, I hope everything works properly. I'd like a photograph of a brontosaurus as a souvenir."

This sort of banter had been thrown at Henderson so often that he now took it for granted. He smiled without much mirth and replied, "I don't promise anything. It may be the biggest flop ever."

Davis moodily checked the tire pressure with the toe of his boot. It was a new set, he noticed, with an odd zigzag pattern he hadn't seen before.

"Whatever happens, we hope you'll tell us. Otherwise, we're going to break in one night and find out just what you're up to."

Henderson laughed. "You'll be a pair of geniuses if you can learn anything from our present lash-up. But, if all goes well, we may be having a little celebration by nightfall."

"What time do you expect to be back, Chief?"

"Somewhere around four. I don't want you to have to walk back for tea."

"O.K.—here's hoping!"

The machine disappeared in a cloud of dust, leaving two very thoughtful geologists standing by the roadside. Then Barton shrugged his shoulders.

"The harder we work," he said, "the quicker the time will go. Come along!"

The end of the trench, where Barton was working with the power drill, was now more than a hundred yards from the main excavation. Davis was putting the final touches to the last prints to be uncovered. They were now very deep and widely spaced, and looking along them, one could see quite clearly where the great reptile had changed its course and started, first to run, and then to hop like an enormous kangaroo. Barton wondered what it must have felt like to see such a creature bearing down upon one with the speed of an express; then he realized that if their guess was true this was exactly what they might soon be seeing.

By mid-afternoon they had uncovered a record length of track. The ground had become softer, and Barton was roaring ahead so rapidly that he had almost forgotten his other preoccupations. He had left Davis yards behind, and both men were so busy that only the pangs of hunger reminded them when it was time to finish. Davis was the first to notice that it was later than they had expected, and he walked over to speak to his friend.

"It's nearly half-past four!" he said when the noise of the drill had died away. "The Chief's late—I'll be mad if he's had tea before collecting us."

"Give him another half-hour," said Barton. "I can guess what's happened. They've blown a fuse or something and it's upset their schedule."

Davis refused to be placated. "I'll be darned annoyed if we've got to walk back to camp again. Anyway, I'm going up the hill to see if there's any sign of him."

He left Barton blasting his way through the soft rock, and climbed the low hill at the side of the old riverbed. From here one could see far down the valley, and the twin stacks of the Henderson-Barnes laboratory were clearly visible against the drab landscape. But there was no sign of the moving dust-cloud that would be following the jeep: the Professor had not yet started for home.

Davis gave a snort of disgust. There was a two-mile walk ahead of them, after a particularly tiring day, and to make matters worse they'd now be late for tea. He decided not to wait any longer, and was already walking down the hill to rejoin Barton when something caught his eye and he stopped to look down the valley.

Around the two stacks, which were all he could see of the laboratory, a curious haze not unlike a heat tremor was playing. They must be hot, he knew, but surely not *that* hot. He looked more carefully, and saw to his amazement that the haze covered a hemisphere that must be almost a quarter of a mile across.

And, quite suddenly, it exploded. There was no light, no blinding flash; only a ripple that spread abruptly across the sky and then was gone. The haze had vanished—and so had the two great stacks of the power-house.

Feeling as though his legs had turned suddenly to water, Davis slumped down upon the hilltop and stared open-mouthed along the valley. A sense of overwhelming disaster swept into his mind; as in a dream, he waited for the explosion to reach his ears.

It was not impressive when it came; only a dull, long-drawn-out whoooooosh! that died away swiftly in the still air. Half unconsciously, Davis noticed that the chatter of the drill had also stopped; the explosion must have been louder than he thought for Barton to have heard it too.

The silence was complete. Nothing moved anywhere as far as his eye could see in the whole of that empty, barren landscape. He waited until his strength returned; then, half running, he went unsteadily down the hill to rejoin his friend.

Barton was half sitting in the trench with his head buried in his hands. He looked up as Davis approached; and although his features were obscured by dust and sand, the other was shocked at the expression in his eyes.

"So you heard it too!" Davis said. "I think the whole lab's blown up. Come along, for heaven's sake!"

"Heard what?" said Barton dully.

Davis stared at him in amazement. Then he realized that Barton could not possibly have heard any sound while he was working with the drill. The sense of disaster deepened with a rush; he felt like a character in some Greek tragedy, helpless before an implacable doom.

Barton rose to his feet. His face was working strangely, and Davis saw that he was on the verge of breakdown. Yet, when he spoke, his words were surprisingly calm.

"What fools we were!" he said. "How Henderson must have laughed at us when we told him that he was trying to *see* into the past!"

Mechanically, Davis moved to the trench and stared at the rock that was seeing the light of day for the first time in fifty million years. Without much emotion, now, he traced again the zigzag pattern he had first noticed a few hours before. It had sunk only a little way into the mud, as if when it was formed the jeep had been traveling at its utmost speed.

No doubt it had been; for in one place the shallow tire marks had been completely obliterated by the monster's footprints. They were now very deep indeed, as if the great reptile was about to make the final leap upon its desperately fleeing prey.

Professor Forster is such a small man that a special space-suit had to be made for him. But what he lacked in physical size he more than made up—as is so often the case—in sheer drive and determination. When I met him, he'd spent twenty years pursuing a dream. What is more to the point, he had persuaded a whole succession of hard-headed business men, World Council Delegates and administrators of scientific trusts to underwrite his expenses and to fit out a ship for him. Despite everything that happened later, I still think that was his most remarkable achievement. . . .

The "Arnold Toynbee" had a crew of six aboard when we left Earth. Besides the Professor and Charles Ashton, his chief assistant, there was the usual pilot—navigator—engineer triumvirate and two graduate students—Bill Hawkins and myself. Neither of us had ever gone into space before, and we were still so excited over the whole thing that we didn't care in the least whether we got back to Earth before the next term started. We had a strong suspicion that our tutor had very similar views. The reference he had produced for us was a masterpiece of ambiguity, but as the number of people who could even begin to read Martian script could be counted, if I may coin a phrase, on the fingers of one hand, we'd got the job.

As we were going to Jupiter, and not to Mars, the purpose of this particular qualification seemed a little obscure, though knowing something about the Professor's theories we had some pretty shrewd suspicions. They were partly confirmed when we were ten days out from Earth.

The Professor looked at us very thoughtfully when we answered his summons. Even under zero g he always managed to preserve his dignity, while the best we could do was to cling to the nearest handhold and float around like drifting seaweed. I got the impression—though I may of course be wrong—that he was thinking: What have *I* done to deserve this? as he looked from Bill to me and back again. Then he gave a sort of "It's too late to do anything about it now" sigh and began to speak in that slow, patient way he always does when he has something to explain. At least, he always uses it when he's speaking to *us,* but it's just occurred to me—oh, never mind.

"Since we left Earth," he said, "I've not had much chance of telling you the purpose of this expedition. Perhaps you've guessed it already."

"I think I have," said Bill.

"Well, go on," replied the Professor, a peculiar gleam in his eye. I did my best to stop Bill, but have you ever tried to kick anyone when you're in free fall?

"You want to find some proof—I mean, some *more* proof—of your diffusion theory of extraterrestrial culture."

"And have you any idea why I'm going to Jupiter to look for it?"

"Well, not exactly. I suppose you hope to find something on one of the moons."

"Brilliant, Bill, brilliant. There are fifteen known satellites, and their total area is about half that of Earth. Where would you start looking if you had a couple of weeks to spare? I'd rather like to know."

Bill glanced doubtfully at the Professor, as if he almost suspected him of sarcasm.

"I don't know much about astronomy," he said. "But there are four big moons, aren't there? I'd start on those."

"For your information, Io, Europa, Ganymede and Callisto are each about as big as Africa. Would you work through them in alphabetical order?"

"No," Bill replied promptly. "I'd start on the one nearest Jupiter and go outward."

"I don't think we'll waste any more time pursuing your logical processes," sighed the Professor. He was obviously impatient to begin his set speech. "Anyway, you're quite wrong. We're not going to the big moons at all. They've been photographically surveyed from space and large areas have been explored on the surface. They've got nothing of archaeological interest. *We're* going to a place that's never been visited before."

"Not to Jupiter!" I gasped.

"Heavens no, nothing as drastic as that! But we're going nearer to him than anyone else has ever been."

He paused thoughtfully.

"It's a curious thing, you know—or you probably don't—that it's nearly as difficult to travel between Jupiter's satellites as it is to go between the planets, although the distances are so much smaller. This is because Jupiter's got such a terrific gravitational field and his moons are traveling so quickly. The innermost moon's moving almost as fast as Earth, and the journey to it from Ganymede costs almost as much fuel as the trip from Earth to Venus, even though it takes only a day and a half.

"And it's *that* journey which we're going to make. No one's ever done it before because nobody could think of any good reason for the expense. Jupiter Five is only thirty kilometers in diameter, so it couldn't possibly be of much interest. Even some of the outer satellites, which are far easier to reach, haven't been visited because it hardly seemed worth while to waste the rocket fuel."

"Then why are *we* going to waste it?" I asked impatiently. The whole thing sounded like a complete wild-goose chase, though as long as it proved interesting, and involved no actual danger, I didn't greatly mind.

Perhaps I ought to confess—though I'm tempted to say nothing, as a good many others have done—that at this time I didn't believe a word of Professor Forster's theories. Of course I realized that he was a very brilliant man in his field, but I did draw the line at some of his more fantastic ideas. After all, the evidence was so slight and the conclusions so revolutionary that one could hardly help being skeptical.

Perhaps you can still remember the astonishment when the first Martian expedition found the remains not of one ancient civilization, but of two. Both had been highly advanced, but both had perished more than five million years ago. The reason was unknown (and still is). It did not seem to be warfare, as the two cultures appear to have lived amicably together. One of the races had been insect-like, the other vaguely reptilian. The insects seem to have been the genuine, original Martians. The reptile-people—usually referred to as "Culture X"—had arrived on the scene later.

So, at least, Professor Forster maintained. They had certainly possessed the secret of space travel, because the ruins of their peculiar cruciform cities had been found on—of all places—Mercury. Forster believed that they had tried to colonize all the smaller planets—Earth and Venus having been ruled out because of their excessive gravity. It was a source of some disappointment to the Professor that no traces of Culture X had ever been found on the Moon, though he was certain that such a discovery was only a matter of time.

The "conventional" theory of Culture X was that it had originally come from one of the smaller planets or satellites, had made peaceful contact with the Martians—the only other intelligent race in the known history of the System—and had died out at the same time as the Martian civilization. But Professor Forster had more ambitious ideas: he was convinced that Culture X had entered the Solar System from interstellar space. The fact that no one else believed this annoyed him, though not very much, for he is one of those people who are happy only when in a minority.

From where I was sitting, I could see Jupiter through the cabin porthole as Professor Forster unfolded his plan. It was a beautiful sight: I could just make out the equatorial cloud belts, and three of the satellites were visible as little stars close to the planet. I wondered which was Ganymede, our first port of call.

"If Jack will condescend to pay attention," the Professor continued, "I'll tell you why we're going such a long way from home. You know that last year I spent a good deal of time poking among the ruins in the twilight belt of Mercury. Perhaps you read the paper I gave on the subject at the London School of Economics. You may even have been there—I do remember a disturbance at the back of the hall.

"What I didn't tell anyone then was that while I was on Mercury I discovered an important clue to the origin of Culture X. I've kept quiet about it, although I've been sorely tempted when fools like Dr. Haughton have tried to be funny at my expense. But I wasn't going to risk letting someone else get here before I could organize this expedition.

"One of the things I found on Mercury was a rather well preserved bas-relief of the Solar System. It's not the first that's been discovered—as you know, astronomical motifs are common in true Martian and Culture X art. But there were certain peculiar symbols against various planets, including Mars and Mercury. I think the pattern had some historic significance, and the most curious thing about it is that little Jupiter Five—one of the least important of all the satellites—seemed to have the most attention drawn to it. I'm convinced that there's something on Five which is the key to the whole problem of Culture X, and I'm going there to discover what it is."

As far as I can remember now, neither Bill nor I was particularly impressed by the Professor's story. Maybe the people of Culture X had left some artifacts on Five for obscure reasons of their own. It would be interesting to unearth them, but hardly likely that they would be as important as the Professor thought. I guess he was rather disappointed at our lack of enthusiasm. If so it was his fault since, as we discovered later, he was still holding out on us.

We landed on Ganymede, the largest moon, about a week later. Ganymede is the only one of the satellites with a permanent base on it; there's an observatory and a geophysical station with a staff of about fifty scientists. They were rather glad to see visitors, but we didn't stay long as the Professor was anxious to refuel and set off again. The fact that we were heading for Five naturally aroused a good deal of interest, but the Professor wouldn't talk and we couldn't; he kept too close an eye on us.

Ganymede, by the way, is quite an interesting place and we managed to see rather more of it on the return journey. But as I've promised to write an article for another magazine about that, I'd better not say anything else here. (You might like to keep your eyes on the *National Astrographic* magazine next Spring.)

The hop from Ganymede to Five took just over a day and a half, and it gave us an uncomfortable feeling to see Jupiter expanding hour by hour until it seemed as if he was going to fill the sky. I don't know much about astronomy, but I couldn't help thinking of the tremendous gravity field into which we were falling. All sorts of things could go wrong so easily. If we ran out of fuel we'd never be able to get back to Ganymede, and we might even drop into Jupiter himself.

I wish I could describe what it was like seeing that colossal globe, with its raging storm belts spinning in the sky ahead of us. As a matter of fact I *did* make the attempt, but some literary friends who have read this MS advised me to cut out the result. (They also gave me a lot of other advice which I don't think they could have meant seriously, because if I'd followed it there would have been no story at all.)

Luckily there have been so many color close-ups of Jupiter published by now that you're bound to have seen some of them. You may even have seen the one which, as I'll explain later, was the cause of all our trouble.

At last Jupiter stopped growing: we'd swung into the orbit of Five and would soon catch up with the tiny moon as it raced around the planet. We were all squeezed in the control room waiting for our first glimpse of our target. At least, all of us who could get in were doing so. Bill and I were crowded out into the corridor and could only crane over other people's shoulders. Kingsley Searle, our pilot, was in the control seat looking as unruffled as ever: Eric Fulton, the engineer, was thoughtfully chewing his mustache and watching the fuel gauges, and Tony Groves was doing complicated things with his navigation tables.

And the Professor appeared to be rigidly attached to the eyepiece of the teleperiscope. Suddenly he gave a start and we heard a whistle of indrawn breath. After a minute, without a word, he beckoned to Searle, who took his place at the eyepiece. Exactly the same thing happened, and then Searle handed over to Fulton. It got a bit monotonous by the time Groves had reacted identically, so we wormed our way in and took over after a bit of opposition.

I don't know quite what I'd expected to see, so that's probably why I was disappointed. Hanging there in space was a tiny gibbous moon, its "night" sector lit up faintly by the reflected glory of Jupiter. And that seemed to be all.

Then I began to make out additional markings, in the way that you do if you look through a telescope for long enough. There were faint crisscrossing lines on the surface of the satellite, and suddenly my eye grasped their full pattern. For it *was* a pattern: those lines covered Five with the same geometrical accuracy as the lines of latitude and longitude divide up a globe of the Earth. I suppose I gave my whistle of amazement, for then Bill pushed me out of the way and had his turn to look.

The next thing I remember is Professor Forster looking very smug while we bombarded him with questions.

"Of course," he explained, "this isn't as much a surprise to me as it is to you. Besides the evidence I'd found on Mercury, there were other clues. I've a friend at the Ganymede Observatory whom I've sworn to secrecy and who's been under quite a strain this last few weeks. It's rather surprising to anyone who's not an astronomer that the Observatory has never bothered much about the satellites. The big instruments are all used on extra-galactic nebulae, and the little ones spend all their time looking at Jupiter.

"The only thing the Observatory had ever done to Five was to measure its diameter and take a few photographs. They weren't quite good enough to show the markings we've just observed, otherwise there would have been an investigation before. But my friend Lawton detected them through the hundred-centimeter reflector when I asked him to look, and he also noticed something else that should have been spotted before. Five is only thirty kilometers in diameter, but it's much brighter than it should be for its size. When you compare its reflecting power—its aldeb—its——"

"Its albedo."

"Thanks, Tony—its albedo with that of the other Moons, you find that it's a much better reflector than it should be. In fact, it behaves more like polished metal than rock."

"So that explains it!" I said. "The people of Culture X must have covered Five with an outer shell—like the domes they built on Mercury, but on a bigger scale."

The Professor looked at me rather pityingly.

"So you still haven't guessed!" he said.

I don't think this was quite fair. Frankly, would you have done any better in the same circumstances?

We landed three hours later on an enormous metal plain. As I looked through the portholes, I felt completely dwarfed by my surroundings. An ant crawling on the top of an oil-storage tank might have had much the same feelings—and the looming bulk of Jupiter up there in the sky didn't help. Even the Professor's usual cockiness now seemed to be overlaid by a kind of reverent awe.

The plain wasn't quite devoid of features. Running across it in various directions were broad bands where the stupendous metal plates had been joined together. These bands, or the crisscross pattern they formed, were what we had seen from space.

About a quarter of a kilometer away was a low hill—at least, what would have been a hill on a natural world. We had spotted it on our way in after making a careful survey of the little satellite from space. It was one of six such projections, four arranged equidistantly around the equator and the other two at the Poles. The assumption was pretty obvious that they would be entrances to the world below the metal shell.

I know that some people think it must be very entertaining to walk around on an airless, low-gravity planet in space-suits. Well, it isn't. There are so many points to think about, so many checks to make and precautions to observe, that the mental strain outweighs the glamor—at least as far as I'm concerned. But I must admit that this time, as we climbed out of the airlock, I was so excited that for once these things didn't worry me.

The gravity of Five was so microscopic that walking was completely out of the question. We were all roped together like mountaineers and blew ourselves across the metal plain with gentle bursts from our recoil pistols. The experienced astronauts, Fulton and Groves, were at the two ends of the chain so that any unwise eagerness on the part of the people in the middle was restrained.

It took us only a few minutes to reach our objective, which we discovered to be a broad, low dome at least a kilometer in circumference. I wondered if it was a gigantic airlock, large enough to permit the entrance of whole spaceships. Unless we were very lucky, we might be unable to find a way in, since the controlling mechanisms would no longer be functioning, and even if they were, we would not know how to operate them. It would be difficult to imagine anything more tantalizing than being locked out, unable to get at the greatest archaeological find in all history.

We had made a quarter circuit of the dome when we found an opening in the metal shell. It was quite small—only about two meters across—and it was so nearly circular that for a moment we did not realize what it was. Then Tony's voice came over the radio:

"That's not artificial. We've got a meteor to thank for it."

"Impossible!" protested Professor Forster. "It's much too regular."

Tony was stubborn.

"Big meteors always produce circular holes, unless they strike very glancing blows. And look at the edges; you can see there's been an explosion of some kind. Probably the meteor and the shell were vaporized; we won't find any fragments."

"You'd expect this sort of thing to happen," put in Kingsley. "How long has this been here? Five million years? I'm surprised we haven't found any other craters."

"Maybe you're right," said the Professor, too pleased to argue. "Anyway, I'm going in first."

"Right," said Kingsley, who as captain has the last say in all such matters. "I'll give you twenty meters of rope and will sit in the hole so that we can keep radio contact. Otherwise this shell will blanket your signals."

So Professor Forster was the first man to enter Five, as he deserved to be. We crowded close to Kingsley so that he could relay news of the Professor's progress.

He didn't get very far. There was another shell just inside the outer one, as we might have expected. The Professor had room to stand upright between them, and as far as his torch could throw its beam he could see avenues of supporting struts and girders, but that was about all.

It took us about twenty-four exasperating hours before we got any further. Near the end of that time I remember asking the Professor why he hadn't thought of bringing any explosives. He gave me a very hurt look.

"There's enough aboard the ship to blow us all to glory," he said. "But I'm not going to risk doing any damage if I can find another way."

That's what I call patience, but I could see his point of view. After all, what was another few days in a search that had already taken him twenty years?

It was Bill Hawkins, of all people, who found the way in when we had abandoned our first line of approach. Near the North Pole of the little world he discovered a really giant meteor hole—about a hundred meters across and cutting through both the outer shells surrounding Five. It had revealed still another shell below those, and by one of those chances that must happen if one waits enough eons, a second, smaller, meteor had come down inside the crater and penetrated the innermost skin. The hole was just big enough to allow entrance for a man in a space-suit. We went through head first, one at a time.

I don't suppose I'll ever have a weirder experience than hanging from that tremendous vault, like a spider suspended beneath the dome of St. Peter's. We only knew that the space in which we floated was vast. Just *how* big it was we could not tell, for our torches gave us no sense of distance. In this airless, dustless cavern the beams were, of course, totally invisible and when we shone them on the roof above, we could see the ovals of light dancing away into the distance until they were too diffuse to be visible. If we pointed them "downward" we could see a pale smudge of illumination so far below that it revealed nothing.

Very slowly, under the minute gravity of this tiny world, we fell downward until checked by our safety ropes. Overhead I could see the tiny glimmering patch through which we had entered; it was remote but reassuring.

And then, while I was swinging with an infinitely sluggish pendulum motion at the end of my cable, with the lights of my companions glimmering like fitful stars in the darkness around me, the truth suddenly crashed into my brain. Forgetting that we were all on open circuit, I cried out involuntarily:

"Professor—I don't believe this is a planet at all! *It's a space-ship!*"

Then I stopped, feeling that I had made a fool of myself. There was a brief, tense silence, then a babble of noise as everyone else started arguing at once. Professor Forster's voice cut across the confusion and I could tell that he was both pleased and surprised.

"You're quite right, Jack. This is the ship that brought Culture X to the Solar System."

I heard someone—it sounded like Eric Fulton—give a gasp of incredulity.

"It's fantastic! A ship thirty kilometers across!"

"*You* ought to know better than that," replied the Professor with surprising mildness. "Suppose a civilization wanted to cross interstellar space—how else would it attack the problem? It would build a mobile planetoid out in space, taking perhaps centuries over the task. Since the ship would have to be a self-contained world, which could support its inhabitants for generations, it would need to be as large as this. I wonder how many suns they visited before they found ours and knew that their search was ended? They must have had smaller ships that could take them down to the planets, and of course they had to leave the parent vessel somewhere in space. So they parked it here, in a close orbit near the largest planet, where it would remain safely forever—or until they needed it again. It was the logical place: if they had set it circling the Sun, in time the pulls of the planets would have disturbed its orbit so much that it might have been lost. That could never happen to it here."

"Tell me, Professor," someone asked, "did you guess all this before we started?"

"I *hoped* it. All the evidence pointed to this answer. There's always been something anomalous about Satellite Five, though no one seems to have noticed it. Why this single tiny moon so close to Jupiter, when all the other small satellites are seventy times further away? Astronomically speaking, it didn't make sense. But enough of this chattering. We've got work to do."

That, I think, must count as the understatement of the century. There were seven of us faced with the greatest archaeological discovery of all time. Almost a whole world—a small world, an artificial one, but still a world—was waiting for us to explore. All we could perform was a swift and superficial reconnaissance: there might be material here for generations of research workers.

The first step was to lower a powerful floodlight on a power line running from the ship. This would act as a beacon and prevent us getting lost, as well as giving local illumination on the inner surface of the satellite. (Even now, I still find it hard to call Five a ship.) Then we dropped down the line to the surface below. It was a fall of about a kilometer, and in this low gravity it was quite safe to make the drop unretarded. The gentle shock of the impact could be absorbed easily enough by the spring-loaded staffs we carried for that purpose.

I don't want to take up any space here with yet another description of all the wonders of Satellite Five; there have already been enough pictures, maps and books on the subject. (My own, by the way, is being published by Sidgwick and Jackson next Summer.) What I would like to give you instead is some impression of what it was actually *like* to be the first men ever to enter that strange metal world. Yet I'm sorry to say—I know this sounds hard to believe—I simply can't remember what I was feeling when we came across the first of the great mushroom-capped entrance shafts. I suppose I was so excited and so overwhelmed by the wonder of it all that I've forgotten everything else. But I can recall the impression of sheer size, something which mere photographs can never give. The builders of this world, coming as they did from a planet of low gravity, were giants—about four times as tall as men. We were pigmies crawling among their works.

We never got below the outer levels on our first visit, so we met few of the scientific marvels which later expeditions discovered. That was just as well; the residential areas provided enough to keep us busy for several lifetimes. The globe we were exploring must once have been lit by artificial sunlight pouring down from the triple shell that surrounded it and kept its atmosphere from leaking into space. Here on the surface the Jovians (I suppose I cannot avoid adopting the popular name for the people of Culture X) had reproduced, as accurately as they could, conditions on the world they had left unknown ages ago. Perhaps they still had day and night, changing seasons, rain and mist. They had even taken a tiny sea with them into exile. The water was still there, forming a frozen lake three kilometers across. I hear that there is a plan afoot to electrolize it and provide Five with a breathable atmosphere again, as soon as the meteor holes in the outer shell have been plugged.

The more we saw of their work, the more we grew to like the race whose possessions we were disturbing for the first time in five million years. Even if they were giants from another sun, they had much in common with man, and it is a great tragedy that our races missed each other by what is, on the cosmic scale, such a narrow margin.

We were, I suppose, more fortunate than any archaeologists in history. The vacuum of space had preserved everything from decay and—this was something which could not have been expected—the Jovians had not emptied their mighty ship of all its treasures when they had set out to colonize the Solar System. Here on the inner surface of Five everything still seemed intact, as it had been at the end of the ship's long journey. Perhaps the travelers had preserved it as a shrine in memory of their lost home, or perhaps they had thought that one day they might have to use these things again.

Whatever the reason, everything was here as its makers had left it. Sometimes it frightened me. I might be photographing, with

Bill's help, some great wall carving when the sheer *timelessness* of the place would strike into my heart. I would look round nervously, half expecting to see giant shapes come stalking in through the pointed doorways, to continue the tasks that had been momentarily interrupted.

We discovered the art gallery on the fourth day. That was the only name for it; there was no mistaking its purpose. When Groves and Searle, who had been doing rapid sweeps over the southern hemisphere, reported the discovery we decided to concentrate all our forces there. For, as somebody or other has said, the art of a people reveals its soul, and here we might find the key to Culture X.

The building was huge, even by the standards of this giant race. Like all the other structures on Five, it was made of metal, yet there was nothing cold or mechanical about it. The topmost peak climbed half way to the remote roof of the world, and from a distance—before the details were visible—the building looked not unlike a Gothic cathedral. Misled by this chance resemblance, some later writers have called it a temple; but we have never found any trace of what might be called a religion among the Jovians. Yet there seems something appropriate about the name "The Temple of Art," and it's stuck so thoroughly that no one can change it now.

It has been estimated that there are between ten and twenty million individual exhibits in this single building—the harvest garnered during the whole history of a race that may have been much older than Man. And it was here that I found a small, circular room which at first sight seemed to be no more than the meeting place of six radiating corridors. I was by myself (and thus, I'm afraid, disobeying the Professor's orders) and taking what I thought would be a short-cut back to my companions. The dark walls were drifting silently past me as I glided along, the light of my torch dancing over the ceiling ahead. It was covered with deeply cut lettering, and I was so busy looking for familiar character groupings that for some time I paid no attention to the chamber's floor. Then I saw the statue and focused my beam upon it.

The moment when one first meets a great work of art has an impact that can never again be recaptured. In this case the subject matter made the effect all the more overwhelming. I was the first man ever to know what the Jovians had looked like, for here, carved with superb skill and authority, was one obviously modeled from life.

The slender, reptilian head was looking straight toward me, the sightless eyes staring into mine. Two of the hands were clasped upon the breast as if in resignation; the other two were holding an instrument whose purpose is still unknown. The long, powerful tail—which, like a kangaroo's, probably balanced the rest of the body—was stretched out along the ground, adding to the impression of rest or repose.

There was nothing human about the face or the body. There were, for example, no nostrils—only gill-like openings in the neck. Yet the figure moved me profoundly; the artist had spanned the barriers of time and culture in a way I should never have believed possible. "Not human—but humane" was the verdict Professor Forster gave. There were many things we could not have shared with the builders of this world, but all that was really important we would have felt in common.

Just as one can read emotions in the alien but familiar face of a dog or a horse, so it seemed that I knew the feelings of the being confronting me. Here was wisdom and authority—the calm, confident power that is shown, for example, in Bellini's famous portrait of the Doge Loredano. Yet there was sadness also—the sadness of a race which had made some stupendous effort, and made it in vain.

We still do not know why this single statue is the only representation the Jovians have ever made of themselves in their art. One would hardly expect to find taboos of this nature among such an advanced race; perhaps we will know the answer when we have deciphered the writing carved on the chamber walls.

Yet I am already certain of the statue's purpose. It was set here to bridge time and to greet whatever beings might one day stand in the footsteps of its makers. That, perhaps, is why they shaped it so much smaller than life. Even then they must have guessed that the future belonged to Earth or Venus, and hence to beings whom they would have dwarfed. They knew that size could be a barrier as well as time.

A few minutes later I was on my way back to the ship with my companions, eager to tell the Professor about the discovery. He had been reluctantly snatching some rest, though I don't believe he averaged more than four hours sleep a day all the time we were on

Five. The golden light of Jupiter was flooding the great metal plain as we emerged through the shell and stood beneath the stars once more.

"Hello!" I heard Bill say over the radio, "the Prof's moved the ship."

"Nonsense," I retorted. "It's exactly where we left it."

Then I turned my head and saw the reason for Bill's mistake. We had visitors.

The second ship had come down a couple of kilometers away, and as far as my non-expert eyes could tell it might have been a duplicate of ours. When we hurried through the airlock, we found that the Professor, a little bleary-eyed, was already entertaining. To our surprise, though not exactly to our displeasure, one of the three visitors was an extremely attractive brunette.

"This," said Professor Forster, a little wearily, "is Mr. Randolph Mays, the science writer. I imagine you've heard of him. And this is——" He turned to Mays. "I'm afraid I didn't quite catch the names."

"My pilot, Donald Hopkins—my secretary, Marianne Mitchell."

There was just the slightest pause before the word "secretary," but it was long enough to set a little signal light flashing in my brain. I kept my eyebrows from going up, but I caught a glance from Bill that said, without any need for words: If you're thinking what I'm thinking, I'm ashamed of you.

Mays was a tall, rather cadaverous man with thinning hair and an attitude of bonhomie which one felt was only skin-deep—the protective coloration of a man who has to be friendly with too many people.

"I expect this is as big a surprise to you as it is to me," he said with unnecessary heartiness. "I certainly never expected to find anyone here before me; and I certainly didn't expect to find all *this*."

"What brought you here?" said Ashton, trying to sound not too suspiciously inquisitive.

"I was just explaining that to the Professor. Can I have that folder please, Marianne? Thanks."

He drew out a series of very fine astronomical paintings and passed them round. They showed the planets from their satellites—a common enough subject, of course.

"You've all seen this sort of thing before," Mays continued.

"But there's a difference here. These pictures are nearly a hundred years old. They were painted by an artist named Chesley Bonestell and appeared in *Life* back in 1944—long before space-travel began, of course. Now what's happened is that *Life* has commissioned me to go round the Solar System and see how well I can match these imaginative paintings against the reality. In the centenary issue, they'll be published side by side with photographs of the real thing. Good idea, eh?"

I had to admit that it was. But it was going to make matters rather complicated, and I wondered what the Professor thought about it. Then I glanced again at Miss Mitchell, standing demurely in the corner, and decided that there would be compensations.

In any other circumstances, we would have been glad to meet another party of explorers, but here there was the question of priority to be considered. Mays would certainly be hurrying back to Earth as quickly as he could, his original mission abandoned and all his film used up here and now. It was difficult to see how we could stop him, and not even certain that we desired to do so. We wanted all the publicity and support we could get, but we would prefer to do things in our own time, after our own fashion. I wondered how strong the Professor was on tact, and feared the worst.

Yet at first diplomatic relations were smooth enough. The Professor had hit upon the bright idea of pairing each of us with one of Mays's team, so that we acted simultaneously as guides and supervisors. Doubling the number of investigating groups also greatly increased the rate at which we could work. It was unsafe for anyone to operate by himself under these conditions, and this had handicapped us a great deal.

The Professor outlined his policy to us the day after the arrival of Mays's party.

"I hope we can get along together," he said a little anxiously. "As far as I'm concerned they can go where they like and photograph what they like, as long as *they don't take anything,* and as long as they don't get back to Earth with their records before we do."

"I don't see how we can stop them," protested Ashton.

"Well, I hadn't intended to do this, but I've now registered a claim to Five. I radioed it to Ganymede last night, and it will be at The Hague by now."

"But no one can claim an astronomical body for himself. That was settled in the case of the Moon, back in the last century."

The Professor gave a rather crooked smile.

"I'm not annexing an *astronomical body,* remember. I've put in a claim for salvage, and I've done it in the name of the World Science Organization. If Mays takes anything out of Five, he'll be stealing it from them. Tomorrow I'm going to explain the situation gently to him, just in case he gets any bright ideas."

It certainly seemed peculiar to think of Satellite Five as salvage, and I could imagine some pretty legal quarrels developing when we got home. But for the present the Professor's move should have given us some safeguards and might discourage Mays from collecting souvenirs—so we were optimistic enough to hope.

It took rather a lot of organizing, but I managed to get paired off with Marianne for several trips round the interior of Five. Mays didn't seem to mind: there was no particular reason why he should. A space-suit is the most perfect chaperon ever devised, confound it.

Naturally enough I took her to the art gallery at the first opportunity, and showed her my find. She stood looking at the statue for a long time while I held my torch beam upon it.

"It's very wonderful," she breathed at last. "Just think of it waiting here in the darkness all those millions of years! But you'll have to give it a name."

"I have. I've christened it 'The Ambassador.'"

"Why?"

"Well, because I think it's a kind of envoy, if you like, carrying a greeting to us. The people who made it knew that one day someone else was bound to come here and find this place."

"I think you're right. 'The Ambassador'—yes, that was clever of you. There's something noble about it, and something very sad, too. Don't you feel it?"

I could tell that Marianne was a very intelligent woman. It was quite remarkable the way she saw my point of view, and the interest she took in everything I showed her. But "The Ambassador" fascinated her most of all, and she kept on coming back to it.

"You know, Jack," she said (I think this was sometime the next day, when Mays had been to see it as well), "you must take that statue back to Earth. Think of the sensation it would cause."

I sighed.

"The Professor would like to, but it must weigh a ton. We can't afford the fuel. It will have to wait for a later trip."

She looked puzzled.

"But things hardly weigh anything here," she protested.

"That's different," I explained. "There's weight, and there's inertia—two quite different things. Now inertia—oh, never mind. We can't take it back, anyway. Captain Searle's told us that, definitely."

"What a pity," said Marianne.

I forgot all about this conversation until the night before we left. We had had a busy and exhausting day packing our equipment (a good deal, of course, we left behind for future use). All our photographic material had been used up. As Charlie Ashton remarked, if we met a *live* Jovian now we'd be unable to record the fact. I think we were all wanting a breathing space, an opportunity to relax and sort out our impressions and to recover from our head-on collision with an alien culture.

Mays's ship, the "Henry Luce," was also nearly ready for take-off. We would leave at the same time, an arrangement which suited the Professor admirably as he did not trust Mays alone on Five.

Everything had been settled when, while checking through our records, I suddenly found that six rolls of exposed film were missing. They were photographs of a complete set of transcriptions in the Temple of Art. After a certain amount of thought I recalled that they had been entrusted to my charge, and I had put them very carefully on a ledge in the Temple, intending to collect them later.

It was a long time before take-off, the Professor and Ashton were canceling some arrears of sleep, and there seemed no reason why I should not slip back to collect the missing material. I knew there would be a row if it was left behind, and as I remembered exactly where it was I need be gone only thirty minutes. So I went, explaining my mission to Bill just in case of accidents.

The floodlight was no longer working, of course, and the darkness inside the shell of Five was somewhat oppressive. But I left a portable beacon at the entrance, and dropped freely until my hand torch told me it was time to break the fall. Ten minutes later, with a sigh of relief, I gathered up the missing films.

It was a natural enough thing to pay my last respects to The Ambassador: it might be years before I saw him again, and that calmly enigmatic figure had begun to exercise an extraordinary fascination over me.

Unfortunately, that fascination had not been confined to me alone. For the chamber was empty and the statue gone.

I suppose I could have crept back and said nothing, thus avoiding awkward explanations. But I was too furious to think of discretion, and as soon as I returned we woke the Professor and told him what had happened.

He sat on his bunk rubbing the sleep out of his eyes, then uttered a few harsh words about Mr. Mays and his companions which it would do no good at all to repeat here.

"What I don't understand," said Searle, "is how they got the thing out—if they have, in fact. We should have spotted it."

"There are plenty of hiding places, and they could have waited until there was no one around before they took it up through the hull. It must have been quite a job, even under this gravity," remarked Eric Fulton, in tones of admiration.

"There's no time for post-mortems," said the Professor savagely. "We've got five hours to think of something. They can't take off before then, because we're only just past opposition with Ganymede. That's correct, isn't it Kingsley?"

Searle nodded agreement.

"Yes. We must move round to the other side of Jupiter before we can enter a transfer orbit—at least, a reasonably economical one."

"Good. That gives us a breathing space. Well, has anyone any ideas?"

Looking back on the whole thing now, it often seems to me that our subsequent behavior was, shall I say, a little peculiar and slightly·uncivilized. It was not the sort of thing we could have imagined ourselves doing a few months before. But we were annoyed and overwrought, and our remoteness from all other human beings somehow made everything seem different. Since there were no other laws here, we had to make our own. . . .

"Can't we do something to stop them from taking off? Could we sabotage their rockets, for instance?" asked Bill.

Searle didn't like this idea at all.

"We mustn't do anything drastic," he said. "Besides, Don Hopkins is a good friend of mine. He'd never forgive me if I damaged his ship. There'd be the danger, too, that we might do something that couldn't be repaired."

"Then pinch their fuel," said Groves laconically.

"Of course! They're probably all asleep, there's no light in the cabin. All we've got to do is to connect up and pump."

"A very nice idea," I pointed out, "but we're two kilometers apart. How much pipeline have we got? Is it as much as a hundred meters?"

The others ignored this interruption as though it was beneath contempt and went on making their plans. Five minutes later the technicians had settled everything: we only had to climb into our space-suits and do the work.

I never thought, when I joined the Professor's expedition, that I should end up like an African porter in one of those old adventure stories, carrying a load on my head. Especially when the load was a sixth of a spaceship (being so short, Professor Forster wasn't able to provide very effective help). Now that its fuel tanks were half empty, the weight of the ship in this gravity was about two hundred kilograms. We squeezed beneath, heaved, and up she went—very slowly, of course, because her inertia was still unchanged. Then we started marching.

It took us quite a while to make the journey, and it wasn't quite as easy as we'd thought it would be. But presently the two ships were lying side by side, and nobody had noticed us. Everyone in the "Henry Luce" was fast asleep, as they had every reason to expect us to be.

Though I was still rather short of breath, I found a certain schoolboy amusement in the whole adventure as Searle and Fulton drew the refueling pipeline out of our airlock and quietly coupled up to the other ship.

"The beauty of this plan," explained Groves to me as we stood watching, "is that they can't do anything to stop us, unless they come outside and uncouple our line. We can drain them dry in five minutes, and it will take them half that time to wake up and get into their space-suits."

A sudden horrid fear smote me.

"Suppose they turned on their rockets and tried to get away?"

"Then we'd both be smashed up. No, they'll just have to come outside and see what's going on. Ah, there go the pumps."

The pipeline had stiffened like a fire-hose under pressure, and I knew that the fuel was pouring into our tanks. Any moment now the lights would go on in the "Henry Luce" and her startled occupants would come scuttling out.

It was something of an anticlimax when they didn't. They must have been sleeping very soundly not to have felt the vibration from the pumps, but when it was all over nothing had happened and we just stood round looking rather foolish. Searle and Fulton carefully uncoupled the pipeline and put it back into the airlock.

"Well?" we asked the Professor.

He thought things over for a minute.

"Let's get back into the ship," he said.

When we had climbed out of our suits and were gathered together in the control room, or as far in as we could get, the Professor sat down at the radio and punched out the "Emergency" signal. Our sleeping neighbors would be awake in a couple of seconds as their automatic receiver sounded the alarm.

The TV screen glimmered into life. There, looking rather frightened, was Randolph Mays.

"Hello, Forster," he snapped. "What's the trouble?"

"Nothing wrong here," replied the Professor in his best deadpan manner, "but you've lost something important. Look at your fuel gauges."

The screen emptied, and for a moment there was a confused mumbling and shouting from the speaker. Then Mays was back, annoyance and alarm competing for possession of his features.

"What's going on?" he demanded angrily. "Do you know anything about this?"

The Prof let him sizzle for a moment before he replied.

"I think you'd better come across and talk things over," he said. "You won't have far to walk."

Mays glared back at him uncertainly, then retorted, "You bet I will!" The screen went blank.

"He'll have to climb down now!" said Bill gleefully. "There's nothing else he can do!"

"It's not so simple as you think," warned Fulton. "If he really wanted to be awkward, he could just sit tight and radio Ganymede for a tanker."

"What good would that do him? It would waste days and cost a fortune."

"Yes, but he'd still have the statue, if he wanted it that badly. And he'd get his money back when he sued us."

The airlock light flashed on and Mays stumped into the room. He was in a surprisingly conciliatory mood; on the way over, he must have had second thoughts.

"Well, well," he said affably. "What's all this nonsense in aid of?"

"You know perfectly well," the Professor retorted coldly. "I made it quite clear that nothing was to be taken off Five. You've been stealing property that doesn't belong to you."

"Now, let's be reasonable. Who *does* it belong to? You can't claim everything on this planet as your personal property."

"This is *not* a planet—it's a ship and the laws of salvage operate."

"Frankly, that's a very debatable point. Don't you think you should wait until you get a ruling from the lawyers?"

The Professor was being icily polite, but I could see that the strain was terrific and an explosion might occur at any moment.

"Listen, Mr. Mays," he said with ominous calm. "What you've taken is the most important single find we've made here. I will make allowances for the fact that you don't appreciate what you've done, and don't understand the viewpoint of an archaeologist like myself. Return that statue, and we'll pump your fuel back and say no more."

Mays rubbed his chin thoughtfully.

"I really don't see why you should make such a fuss about one statue, when you consider all the stuff that's still here."

It was then that the Professor made one of his rare mistakes.

"You talk like a man who's stolen the Mona Lisa from the Louvre and argues that nobody will miss it because of all the other paintings. This statue's unique in a way that no terrestrial work of art can ever be. That's why I'm determined to get it back."

You should never, when you're bargaining, make it obvious that you want something really badly. I saw the greedy glint in Mays's eye and said to myself, "Uh-huh! He's going to be tough." And I remembered Fulton's remark about calling Ganymede for a tanker.

"Give me half an hour to think it over," said Mays, turning to the airlock.

"Very well," replied the Professor stiffly. "Half an hour—no more."

I must give Mays credit for brains. Within five minutes we saw his communications aerial start slewing round until it locked on Ganymede. Naturally we tried to listen in, but he had a scrambler. These newspaper men must trust each other.

The reply came back a few minutes later; that was scrambled, too. While we were waiting for the next development, we had another council of war. The Professor was now entering the stubborn, stop-at-nothing stage. He realized he'd miscalculated and that had made him fighting mad.

I think Mays must have been a little apprehensive, because he had reinforcements when he returned. Donald Hopkins, his pilot, came with him, looking rather uncomfortable.

"I've been able to fix things up, Professor," he said smugly. "It will take me a little longer, but I can get back without your help if I have to. Still, I must admit that it will save a good deal of time and money if we can come to an agreement. I'll tell you what. Give me back my fuel and I'll return the other—er—souvenirs I've collected. But I insist on keeping Mona Lisa, even if it means I won't get back to Ganymede until the middle of next week."

The Professor then uttered a number of what are usually called deep-space oaths, though I can assure you they're much the same as any other oaths. That seemed to relieve his feelings a lot and he became fiendishly friendly.

"My dear Mr. Mays," he said, "you're an unmitigated crook, and accordingly I've no compunction left in dealing with you. I'm prepared to use force, knowing that the law will justify me."

Mays looked slightly alarmed, though not unduly so. We had moved to strategic positions round the door.

"Please don't be so melodramatic," he said haughtily. "This is the twenty-first century, not the Wild West back in 1800."

"1880," said Bill, who is a stickler for accuracy.

"I must ask you," the Professor continued, "to consider yourself under detention while we decide what is to be done. Mr. Searle, take him to Cabin B."

Mays sidled along the wall with a nervous laugh.

"Really, Professor, this is *too* childish! You can't detain me against my will." He glanced for support at the Captain of the "Henry Luce."

Donald Hopkins dusted an imaginary speck of fluff from his uniform.

"I refuse," he remarked for the benefit of all concerned, "to get involved in vulgar brawls."

Mays gave him a venomous look and capitulated with bad grace. We saw that he had a good supply of reading matter, and locked him in.

When he was out of the way, the Professor turned to Hopkins, who was looking enviously at our fuel gauges.

"Can I take it, Captain," he said politely, "that you don't wish to get mixed up in any of your employer's dirty business?"

"I'm neutral. My job is to fly the ship here and take her home. You can fight this out among yourselves."

"Thank you. I think we understand each other perfectly. Perhaps it would be best if you returned to your ship and explained the situation. We'll be calling you in a few minutes."

Captain Hopkins made his way languidly to the door. As he was about to leave he turned to Searle.

"By the way, Kingsley," he drawled, "have you thought of torture? Do call me if you get round to it—I've some jolly interesting ideas." Then he was gone, leaving us with our hostage.

I think the Professor had hoped he could do a direct exchange. If so, he had not bargained on Marianne's stubbornness.

"It serves Randolph right," she said. "But I don't really see that it makes any difference. He'll be just as comfortable in your ship as in ours, and you can't do anything to him. Let me know when you're fed up with having him around."

It seemed a complete impasse. We had been too clever by half, and it had got us exactly nowhere. We'd captured Mays, but he wasn't any use to us.

The Professor was standing with his back to us, staring morosely out of the window. Seemingly balanced on the horizon, the immense bulk of Jupiter nearly filled the sky.

"We've got to convince her that we really *do* mean business," he said. Then he turned abruptly to me.

"Do you think she's actually fond of this blackguard?"

"Er—I shouldn't be surprised. Yes, I really believe so."

The Professor looked very thoughtful. Then he said to Searle, "Come into my room. I want to talk something over."

They were gone quite a while. When they returned, they both had an indefinable air of gleeful anticipation, and the Professor was carrying a piece of paper covered with figures. He went to the radio, and called the "Henry Luce."

"Hello," said Marianne, replying so promptly that she'd obviously been waiting for us. "Have you decided to call it off? I'm getting so bored."

The Professor looked at her gravely.

"Miss Mitchell," he replied. "It's apparent that you have not been taking us seriously. I'm therefore arranging a somewhat—er—drastic little demonstration for your benefit. I'm going to place your employer in a position from which he'll be only too anxious for you to retrieve him as quickly as possible."

"Indeed?" replied Marianne noncommittally—though I thought I could detect a trace of apprehension in her voice.

"I don't suppose," continued the Professor smoothly, "that you know anything about celestial mechanics. No? Too bad, but your pilot will confirm everything I tell you. Won't you, Hopkins?"

"Go ahead," came a painstakingly neutral voice from the background.

"Then listen carefully, Miss Mitchell. I want to remind you of our curious—indeed our precarious—position on this satellite. You've only got to look out of the window to see how close to Jupiter we are, and I need hardly remind you that Jupiter has by far the most intense gravitational field of all the planets. You follow me?"

"Yes," replied Marianne, no longer quite so self-possessed. "Go on."

"Very well. This little world of ours goes round Jupiter in almost exactly twelve hours. Now there's a well-known theorem stating that if a body *falls* from an orbit to the center of attraction, it will take point one seven seven of a period to make the drop. In other words, anything falling from here to Jupiter would reach the center of the planet in about two hours seven minutes. I'm sure Captain Hopkins can confirm this."

There was a long pause. Then we heard Hopkins say, "Well, of course I can't confirm the exact figures, but they're probably correct. It would be something like that, anyway."

"Good," continued the Professor. "Now I'm sure you realize," he went on with a hearty chuckle, "that a fall to the *center* of the planet is a very theoretical case. If anything really was dropped from here, it would reach the upper atmosphere of Jupiter in a considerably shorter time. I hope I'm not boring you?"

"No," said Marianne, rather faintly.

"I'm so glad to hear it. Anyway, Captain Searle has worked out the actual time for me, and it's one hour thirty-five minutes—with a few minutes either way. We can't guarantee complete accuracy, ha, ha!

"Now, it has doubtless not escaped your notice that this satellite of ours has an extremely weak gravitational field. Its escape velocity is only about ten meters a second, and anything thrown away from it at that speed would never come back. Correct, Mr. Hopkins?"

"Perfectly correct."

"Then, if I may come to the point, we propose to take Mr. Mays for a walk until he's immediately under Jupiter, remove the reaction pistols from his suit, and—ah—launch him forth. We will be prepared to retrieve him with our ship as soon as you've handed over the property you've stolen. After what I've told you, I'm sure you'll appreciate that time will be rather vital. An hour and thirty-five minutes is remarkably short, isn't it?"

"Professor!" I gasped. "You can't possibly do this!"

"Shut up!" he barked. "Well, Miss Mitchell, what about it?"

Marianne was staring at him with mingled horror and disbelief.

"You're simply bluffing!" she cried. "I don't believe you'd do anything of the kind! Your crew won't let you!"

The Professor sighed.

"Too bad," he said. "Captain Searle—Mr. Groves—will you take the prisoner and proceed as instructed."

"Aye-aye, sir," replied Searle with great solemnity.

Mays looked frightened but stubborn.

"What are you going to do now?" he said, as his suit was handed back to him.

Searle unholstered his reaction pistols. "Just climb in," he said. "We're going for a walk."

I realized then what the Professor hoped to do. The whole thing was a colossal bluff: of course he wouldn't *really* have Mays thrown into Jupiter; and in any case Searle and Groves wouldn't do it. Yet surely Marianne would see through the bluff, and then we'd be left looking mighty foolish.

Mays couldn't run away; without his reaction pistols he was quite helpless. Grasping his arms and towing him along like a captive balloon, his escorts set off toward the horizon—and toward Jupiter.

I could see, looking across the space to the other ship, that Marianne was staring out through the observation windows at the departing trio. Professor Forster noticed it too.

"I hope you're convinced, Miss Mitchell, that my men aren't carrying along an empty spacesuit. Might I suggest that you follow the proceedings with a telescope? They'll be over the horizon in a minute, but you'll be able to see Mr. Mays when he starts to—er—ascend."

There was a stubborn silence from the loudspeaker. The period of suspense seemed to last for a very long time. Was Marianne waiting to see how far the Professor really would go?

By this time I had got hold of a pair of binoculars and was sweeping the sky beyond the ridiculously close horizon. Suddenly I saw it—a tiny flare of light against the vast yellow back-cloth of Jupiter. I focused quickly, and could just make out the three figures rising into space. As I watched, they separated: two of them decelerated with their pistols and started to fall back toward Five. The other went on ascending helplessly toward the ominous bulk of Jupiter.

I turned on the Professor in horror and disbelief.

"They've really done it!" I cried. "I thought you were only bluffing!"

"So did Miss Mitchell, I've no doubt," said the Professor calmly, for the benefit of the listening microphone. "I hope I don't need to impress upon you the urgency of the situation. As I've remarked once or twice before, the time of fall from our orbit to Jupiter's surface is ninety-five minutes. But, of course, if one waited even half that time, it would be much too late. . . ."

He let that sink in. There was no reply from the other ship.

"And now," he continued, "I'm going to switch off our receiver so we can't have any more arguments. We'll wait until you've unloaded that statue—*and* the other items Mr. Mays was careless enough to mention—before we'll talk to you again. Good-by."

It was a very uncomfortable ten minutes. I'd lost track of Mays, and was seriously wondering if we'd better overpower the Professor and go after him before we had a murder on our hands. But the people who could fly the ship were the ones who had actually carried out the crime. I didn't know *what* to think.

Then the airlock of the "Henry Luce" slowly opened. A couple of space-suited figures emerged, floating the cause of all the trouble between them.

"Unconditional surrender," murmured the Professor with a sigh of satisfaction. "Get it into our ship," he called over the radio, "I'll open up the airlock for you."

He seemed in no hurry at all. I kept looking anxiously at the clock; fifteen minutes had already gone by. Presently there was a clanking and banging in the airlock, the inner door opened, and Captain Hopkins entered. He was followed by Marianne, who only needed a bloodstained axe to make her look like Clytaemnestra. I did my best to avoid her eye, but the Professor seemed to be quite without shame. He walked into the airlock, checked that his property was back, and emerged rubbing his hands.

"Well, that's that," he said cheerfully. "Now let's sit down and have a drink to forget all this unpleasantness, shall we?"

I pointed indignantly at the clock.

"Have you gone crazy!" I yelled. "He's already halfway to Jupiter!"

Professor Forster looked at me disapprovingly.

"Impatience," he said, "is a common failing in the young. I see no cause at all for hasty action."

Marianne spoke for the first time; she now looked really scared.

"But you promised," she whispered.

The Professor suddenly capitulated. He had had his little joke, and didn't want to prolong the agony.

"I can tell you at once, Miss Mitchell—and you too, Jack—that Mays is in no more danger than we are. We can go and collect him whenever we like."

"Do you mean that you lied to me?"

"Certainly not. Everything I told you was perfectly true. You simply jumped to the wrong conclusions. When I said that a body

would take ninety-five minutes to fall from here to Jupiter, I omitted
—not, I must confess, accidentally—a rather important phrase. I
should have added *"a body at rest with respect to Jupiter."* Your
friend Mr. Mays was sharing the orbital speed of this satellite, and
he's still got it. A little matter of twenty-six kilometers a second,
Miss Mitchell.

"Oh yes, we threw him completely off Five and toward Jupiter.
But the velocity we gave him then was trivial. He's still moving in
practically the same orbit as before. The most he can do—I've got
Captain Searle to work out the figures—is to drift about a hundred
kilometers inward. And in one revolution—twelve hours—*he'll be
right back where he started,* without us bothering to do anything at
all."

There was a long, long silence. Marianne's face was a study in
frustration, relief, and annoyance at having been fooled. Then she
turned on Captain Hopkins.

"You must have known all the time! Why didn't you tell me?"

Hopkins gave her a wounded expression.

"You didn't ask me," he said.

We hauled Mays down about an hour later. He was only twenty
kilometers up, and we located him quickly enough by the flashing
light on his suit. His radio had been disconnected, for a reason that
hadn't occurred to me. He was intelligent enough to realize that he
was in no danger, and if his set had been working he could have
called his ship and exposed our bluff. That is, if he wanted to.
Personally, I think I'd have been glad enough to call the whole thing
off even if I had known that I was perfectly safe. It must have been
awfully lonely up there.

To my great surprise, Mays wasn't as mad as I'd expected. Perhaps he was too relieved to be back in our snug little cabin when
we drifted up to him on the merest fizzle of rockets and yanked him
in. Or perhaps he felt that he'd been worsted in fair fight and didn't
bear any grudge. I really think it was the latter.

There isn't much more to tell, except that we did play one
other trick on him before we left Five. He had a good deal more
fuel in his tanks than he really needed, now that his payload was
substantially reduced. By keeping the excess ourselves, we were able
to carry The Ambassador back to Ganymede after all. Oh, yes, the

Professor gave him a cheque for the fuel we'd borrowed. Everything was perfectly legal.

There's one amusing sequel I must tell you, though. The day after the new gallery was opened at the British Museum I went along to see The Ambassador, partly to discover if his impact was still as great in these changed surroundings. (For the record, it wasn't—though it's still considerable and Bloomsbury will never be quite the same to me again.) A huge crowd was milling around the gallery, and there in the middle of it was Mays and Marianne.

It ended up with us having a very pleasant lunch together in Holborn. I'll say this about Mays—he doesn't bear any grudges. But I'm still rather sore about Marianne.

And, frankly, I can't imagine *what* she sees in him.

CHILDHOOD'S END

Prologue

The volcano that had reared Taratua up from the Pacific depths had been sleeping now for half a million years. Yet in a little while, thought Reinhold, the island would be bathed with fires fiercer than any that had attended its birth. He glanced towards the launching site, and his gaze climbed the pyramid of scaffolding that still surrounded the "Columbus." Two hundred feet above the ground, the ship's prow was catching the last rays of the descending sun. This was one of the last nights it would ever know: soon it would be floating in the eternal sunshine of space.

It was quiet here beneath the palms, high up on the rocky spine of the island. The only sound from the Project was the occasional yammering of an air compressor or the faint shout of a workman. Reinhold had grown fond of these clustered palms; almost every evening he had come here to survey his little empire. It saddened him to think that they would be blasted to atoms when the "Columbus" rose in flame and fury to the stars.

A mile beyond the reef, the "James Forrestal" had switched on her searchlights and was sweeping the dark waters. The sun had now vanished completely, and the swift tropical night was racing in from the east. Reinhold wondered, a little sardonically, if the carrier expected to find Russian submarines so close to shore.

The thought of Russia turned his mind, as it always did, to Konrad and that morning in the cataclysmic spring of 1945. More than thirty years had passed, but the memory of those last days when the Reich was crumbling beneath the waves from the East and from the West had never faded. He could still see Konrad's tired blue eyes, and the golden stubble on his chin, as they shook hands and parted in that ruined Prussian village, while the refugees streamed endlessly past. It was a parting that symbolized everything that had since happened to the world—the cleavage between East and West.

For Konrad chose the road to Moscow. Reinhold had thought him a fool, but now he was not so sure.

For thirty years he had assumed that Konrad was dead. It was only a week ago that Colonel Sandmeyer, of Technical Intelligence, had given him the news. He didn't like Sandmeyer, and he was sure the feeling was mutual. But neither let that interfere with business.

"Mr. Hoffmann," the Colonel had begun, in his best official manner, "I've just had some alarming information from Washington. It's top secret, of course, but we've decided to break it to the engineering staff so that they'll realize the necessity for speed." He paused for effect, but the gesture was wasted on Reinhold. Somehow, he already knew what was coming.

"The Russians are nearly level with us. They've got some kind of atomic drive—it may even be more efficient than ours, and they're building a ship on the shores of Lake Baikal. We don't know how far they've got, but Intelligence believes it may be launched this year. You know what *that* means."

Yes, thought Reinhold, I know. The race is on—and we may not win it.

"Do you know who's running their team?" he had asked, not really expecting an answer. To his surprise, Colonel Sandmeyer had pushed across a typewritten sheet and there at its head was the name: Konrad Schneider.

"You knew a lot of these men at Peenemünde, didn't you?" said the Colonel. "That may give us some insight into their methods. I'd like you to let me have notes on as many of them as you can—their specialties, the bright ideas they had, and so on. I know it's asking a lot after all this time—but see what you can do."

"Konrad Schneider is the only one who matters," Reinhold had answered. "He was brilliant—the others are just competent engineers. Heaven only knows what he's done in thirty years. Remember —he's probably seen all our results and we haven't seen any of his. That gives him a decided advantage."

He hadn't meant this as a criticism of Intelligence, but for a moment it seemed as if Sandmeyer was going to be offended. Then the Colonel shrugged his shoulders.

"It works both ways—you've told me that yourself. Our free

exchange of information means swifter progress, even if we do give away a few secrets. The Russian research departments probably don't know what their own people are doing half the time. We'll show them that Democracy can get to the moon first."

Democracy—Nuts! thought Reinhold, but knew better than to say it. One Konrad Schneider was worth a million names on an electoral roll. And what had Konrad done by this time, with all the resources of the U.S.S.R. behind him? Perhaps, even now, his ship was already outward bound from Earth. . . .

The sun which had deserted Taratua was still high above Lake Baikal when Konrad Schneider and the Assistant Commissar for Nuclear Science walked slowly back from the motor test rig. Their ears were still throbbing painfully, though the last thunderous echoes had died out across the lake ten minutes before.

"Why the long face?" asked Grigorievitch suddenly. "You should be happy now. In another month we'll be on our way, and the Yankees will be choking themselves with rage."

"You're an optimist, as usual," said Schneider. "Even though the motor works, it's not as easy as that. True, I can't see any serious obstacles now—but I'm worried about the reports from Taratua. I've told you how good Hoffmann is, and he's got billions of dollars behind him. Those photographs of his ship aren't very clear, but it looks as if it's not far from completion. And we know he tested his motor five weeks ago."

"Don't worry," laughed Grigorievitch. *"They're* the ones who are going to have the big surprise. Remember—they don't know a thing about us."

Schneider wondered if that was true, but decided it was much safer to express no doubts. That might start Grigorievitch's mind exploring far too many tortuous channels, and if there had been a leak, he would find it hard enough to clear himself.

The guard saluted as he re-entered the administration building. There were nearly as many soldiers here, he thought grimly, as technicians. But that was how the Russians did things, and as long as they kept out of his way he had no complaints. On the whole—with exasperating exceptions—events had turned out very much as he had hoped. Only the future could tell if he or Reinhold had made the better choice.

He was already at work on his final report when the sound of shouting voices disturbed him. For a moment he sat motionless at his desk, wondering what conceivable event could have disturbed the rigid discipline of the camp. Then he walked to the window—and for the first time in his life he knew despair.

The stars were all around him as Reinhold descended the little hill. Out at sea, the "Forrestal" was still sweeping the water with her fingers of light, while further along the beach the scaffolding round the "Columbus" had transformed itself into an illuminated Christmas tree. Only the projecting prow of the ship lay like a dark shadow across the stars.

A radio was blaring dance music from the living quarters, and unconsciously Reinhold's feet accelerated to the rhythm. He had almost reached the narrow road along the edge of the sands when some premonition, some half-glimpsed movement, made him stop. Puzzled, he glanced from land to sea and back again: it was some little time before he thought of looking at the sky.

Then Reinhold Hoffmann knew, as did Konrad Schneider at this same moment, that he had lost his race. And he knew that he had lost it, not by the few weeks or months that he had feared, but by millennia. The huge and silent shadows driving across the stars, more miles above his head than he dared to guess, were as far beyond his little "Columbus" as it surpassed the log canoes of paleolithic man. For a moment that seemed to last forever, Reinhold watched, as all the world was watching, while the great ships descended in their overwhelming majesty—until at last he could hear the faint scream of their passage through the thin air of the stratosphere.

He felt no regrets as the work of a lifetime was swept away. He had labored to take man to the stars, and, in the moment of success, the stars—the aloof, indifferent stars—had come to him. This was the moment when history held its breath, and the present sheared asunder from the past as an iceberg splits from its frozen, parent cliffs, and goes sailing out to sea in lonely pride. All that the past ages had achieved was as nothing now: only one thought echoed and re-echoed through Reinhold's brain:

The human race was no longer alone.

Part I · Earth and the Overlords

✳ CHAPTER ONE

The Secretary-General of the United Nations stood motionless by the great window, staring down at the crawling traffic on Forty-third Street. He sometimes wondered if it was a good thing for any man to work at such an altitude above his fellow humans. Detachment was all very well, but it could change so easily to indifference. Or was he merely trying to rationalize his dislike of skyscrapers, still unabated after twenty years in New York?

He heard the door open behind him, but did not turn his head as Pieter Van Ryberg came into the room. There was the inevitable pause as Pieter looked disapprovingly at the thermostat, for it was a standing joke that the Secretary-General liked living in an icebox. Stormgren waited until his assistant joined him at the window, then tore his gaze away from the familiar yet always fascinating panorama below.

"They're late," he said. "Wainwright should have been here five minutes ago."

"I've just heard from the police. He's got quite a procession with him, and it's snarled up the traffic. He should be here any moment now."

Van Ryberg paused, then added abruptly, "Are you *still* sure it's a good idea to see him?"

"I'm afraid it's a little late to back out of it now. After all, I've agreed—though as you know it was never my idea in the first place."

Stormgren had walked to his desk and was fidgeting with his famous uranium paperweight. He was not nervous—merely undecided. He was also glad that Wainwright was late, for that would give him a slight moral advantage when the interview opened. Such trivialities played a greater part in human affairs than anyone who set much store on logic and reason might wish.

"Here they are!" said Van Ryberg suddenly, pressing his face against the window. "They're coming along the Avenue—a good three thousand, I'd say."

Stormgren picked up his notebook and rejoined his assistant. Half a mile away, a small but determined crowd was moving slowly towards the Secretariat Building. It carried banners that were indecipherable at this distance, but Stormgren knew their message well enough. Presently he could hear, rising above the sound of the traffic, the ominous rhythm of chanting voices. He felt a sudden wave of disgust sweep over him. Surely the world had had enough of marching mobs and angry slogans!

The crowd had now come abreast of the building; it must know that he was watching, for here and there fists were being shaken, rather self-consciously, in the air. They were not defying him, though the gesture was doubtless meant for Stormgren to see. As pygmies may threaten a giant, so those angry fists were directed against the sky fifty kilometers above his head—against the gleaming silver cloud that was the flagship of the Overlord fleet.

And very probably, thought Stormgren, Karellen was watching the whole thing and enjoying himself hugely, for this meeting would never have taken place except at the Supervisor's instigation.

This was the first time that Stormgren had ever met the head of the Freedom League. He had ceased to wonder if the action was wise, for Karellen's plans were often too subtle for merely human understanding. At the worst, Stormgren did not see that any positive harm could be done. If he had refused to see Wainwright, the league would have used the fact as ammunition against him.

Alexander Wainwright was a tall, handsome man in his late forties. He was, Stormgren knew, completely honest, and therefore doubly dangerous. Yet his obvious sincerity made it hard to dislike him, whatever views one might have about the cause for which he stood—and about some of the followers he had attracted.

Stormgren wasted no time after Van Ryberg's brief and somewhat strained introductions.

"I suppose," he began, "the chief object of your visit is to register a formal protest against the Federation scheme. Am I correct?"

Wainwright nodded gravely.

"That is my main purpose, Mr. Secretary. As you know, for the last five years we have tried to awaken the human race to the danger that confronts it. The task has been a difficult one, for the majority of people seem content to let the Overlords run the world as they please. Nevertheless, more than five million patriots, in every country, have signed our petition."

"That is not a very impressive figure out of two and a half billion."

"It is a figure that cannot be ignored. And for every person who has signed, there are many who feel grave doubts about the wisdom, not to mention the rightness, of this Federation plan. Even Supervisor Karellen, for all his powers, cannot wipe out a thousand years of history at the stroke of a pen."

"What does anyone know of Karellen's powers?" retorted Stormgren. "When I was a boy, the Federation of Europe was a dream—but when I grew to manhood it had become reality. And *that* was before the arrival of the Overlords. Karellen is merely finishing the work we had begun."

"Europe was a cultural and geographic entity. The world is not—that is the difference."

"To the Overlords," replied Stormgren sarcastically, "the Earth probably is a great deal smaller than Europe seemed to our fathers —and their outlook, I submit, is more mature than ours."

"I do not necessarily quarrel with Federation as an *ultimate* objective—though many of my supporters might not agree. But it must come from within—not be superimposed from without. We must work out our own destiny. There must be no more interference in human affairs!"

Stormgren sighed. All this he had heard a hundred times before, and he knew that he could only give the old answer that the Freedom League had refused to accept. He had faith in Karellen, and they had not. That was the fundamental difference, and there was nothing he could do about it. Luckily, there was nothing that the Freedom League could do, either.

"Let me ask you a few questions," he said. "Can you deny that the Overlords have brought security, peace, and prosperity to the world?"

"That is true. But they have taken our liberty. Man does not live—"

"—by bread alone. Yes, I know—but this is the first age in which every man was sure of getting even that. In any case, what freedom have we lost compared with that which the Overlords have given us for the first time in human history?"

"Freedom to control our own lives, under God's guidance."

At last, thought Stormgren, we've got to the point. Basically, the conflict is a religious one, however much it may be disguised. Wainwright never let you forget he was a clergyman. Though he no longer wore a clerical collar, somehow one always got the impression it was still there.

"Last month," pointed out Stormgren, "a hundred bishops, cardinals, and rabbis signed a joint declaration pledging their support for the Supervisor's policy. The world's religions are against you."

Wainwright shook his head in angry denial.

"Many of the leaders are blind; they have been corrupted by the Overlords. When they realize the danger, it may be too late. Humanity will have lost its initiative and become a subject race."

There was silence for a moment. Then Stormgren replied:

"In three days I will be meeting the Supervisor again. I will explain your objections to him, since it is my duty to represent the views of the world. But it will alter nothing—I can assure you of that."

"There is one other point," said Wainwright slowly. "We have many objections to the Overlords—but above all we detest their secretiveness. You are the only human being who has ever spoken with Karellen, and even *you* have never seen him! Is it surprising that we doubt his motives?"

"Despite all that he has done for humanity?"

"Yes—despite that. I do not know which we resent more—Karellen's omnipotence, or his secrecy. If he has nothing to hide, why will he never reveal himself? Next time you speak with the Supervisor, Mr. Stormgren, ask him that!"

Stormgren was silent. There was nothing he could say to this—nothing, at any rate, that would convince the other. He sometimes wondered if he had really convinced himself.

It was, of course, only a very small operation from their point of view, but to Earth it was the biggest thing that had ever happened. There had been no warning when the great ships came pouring out of the unknown depths of space. Countless times this day had been described in fiction, but no one had really believed that it would ever come. Now it had dawned at last; the gleaming, silent shapes hanging over every land were the symbol of a science man could not hope to match for centuries. For six days they had floated motionless above his cities, giving no hint that they knew of his existence. But none was needed; not by chance alone could those mighty ships have come to rest so precisely over New York, London, Paris, Moscow, Rome, Cape Town, Tokyo, Canberra. . . .

Even before the ending of those heart-freezing days, some men had guessed the truth. This was not a first tentative contact by a race which knew nothing of man. Within those silent, unmoving ships, master psychologists were studying humanity's reactions. When the curve of tension had reached its peak, they would act.

And on the sixth day, Karellen, Supervisor for Earth, made himself known to the world in a broadcast that blanketed every radio frequency. He spoke in English so perfect that the controversy it began was to rage across the Atlantic for a generation. But the context of the speech was more staggering even than its delivery. By any standards, it was a work of superlative genius, showing a complete and absolute mastery of human affairs. There could be no doubt that its scholarship and virtuosity, its tantalizing glimpses of knowledge still untapped, were deliberately designed to convince mankind that it was in the presence of overwhelming intellectual power. When Karellen had finished, the nations of Earth knew that their days of precarious sovereignty had ended. Local, internal governments would still retain their powers, but in the wider field of international affairs the supreme decisions had passed from human hands. Argument—protests—all were futile.

It was hardly to be expected that all the nations of the world would submit tamely to such a limitation of their powers. Yet active resistance presented baffling difficulties, for the destruction of the Overlords' ships, even if it could be achieved, would annihilate the cities beneath them. Nevertheless, one major power had made the attempt. Perhaps those responsible hoped to kill two birds with one atomic missile, for their target was floating above the capital of an adjoining and unfriendly nation.

As the great ship's image had expanded on the television screen in the secret control room, the little group of officers and technicians must have been torn by many emotions. If they succeeded, what action would the remaining ships take? Could they also be destroyed, leaving humanity to go its own way once more? Or would Karellen wreak some frightful vengeance upon those who had attacked him?

The screen became suddenly blank as the missile destroyed itself on impact, and the picture switched immediately to an airborne camera many miles away. In the fraction of a second that had elapsed, the fireball should already have formed and should be filling the sky with its solar flame.

Yet nothing whatsoever had happened. The great ship floated unharmed, bathed in the raw sunlight at the edge of space. Not only had the bomb failed to touch it, but no one could ever decide what had happened to the missile. Moreover, Karellen took no action against those responsible, or even indicated that he had known of the attack. He ignored them contemptuously, leaving them to worry over a vengeance that never came. It was a more effective, and more demoralizing, treatment than any punitive action could have been. The government responsible collapsed in mutual recrimination a few weeks later.

There had also been some passive resistance to the policy of the Overlords. Usually, Karellen had been able to deal with it by letting those concerned have their own way, until they had discovered that they were only hurting themselves by their refusal to co-operate. Only once had he taken any direct action against a recalcitrant government.

For more than a hundred years the Republic of South Africa had been the center of racial strife. Men of good will on both sides had tried to build a bridge, but in vain—fears and prejudices were too deeply ingrained to permit any co-operation. Successive governments had differed only in the degree of their intolerance; the land was poisoned with the hate and the aftermath of civil war.

When it became clear that no attempt would be made to end discrimination, Karellen gave his warning. It merely named a date and time—no more. There was apprehension, but little fear or panic, for no one believed that the Overlords would take any violent or destructive action which would involve innocent and guilty alike.

Nor did they. All that happened was that as the sun passed the meridian at Cape Town it went out. There remained visible merely a pale, purple ghost, giving no heat or light. Somehow, out in space, the light of the sun had been polarized by two crossed fields so that no radiation could pass. The area affected was five hundred kilometers across, and perfectly circular.

The demonstration lasted thirty minutes. It was sufficient; the next day the government of South Africa announced that full civil rights would be restored to the white minority.

Apart from such isolated incidents, the human race had accepted the Overlords as part of the natural order of things. In a surprisingly short time, the initial shock had worn off, and the world went about its business again. The greatest change a suddenly-awakened Rip Van Winkle would have noticed was a hushed expectancy, a mental glancing-over-the-shoulder, as mankind waited for the Overlords to show themselves and to step down from their gleaming ships.

Five years later, it was still waiting. That, thought Stormgren, was the cause of all the trouble.

There was the usual circle of sight-seers, cameras at the ready, as Stormgren's car drove on to the landing field. The Secretary-General exchanged a few final words with his assistant, collected his brief case, and walked through the ring of spectators.

Karellen never kept him waiting for long. There was a sudden "Oh!" from the crowd, and a silver bubble expanded with breathtaking speed in the sky above. A gust of air tore at Stormgren's clothes as the tiny ship came to rest fifty meters away, floating delicately a few centimeters above the ground, as if it feared contamination with Earth. As he walked slowly forward, Stormgren saw that familiar puckering of the seamless metallic hull, and in a moment the opening that had so baffled the world's best scientists appeared before him. He stepped through it into the ship's single, softly-lit room. The entrance sealed itself as if it had never been, shutting out all sound and sight.

It opened again five minutes later. There had been no sensation of movement, but Stormgren knew that he was now fifty kilometers above the earth, deep in the heart of Karellen's ship. He was in the world of the Overlords; all around him, they were going about their mysterious business. He had come nearer to them than had any other man; yet he knew no more of their physical nature than did any of the millions on the world below.

The little conference room at the end of the short connecting corridor was unfurnished, apart from the single chair and the table beneath the vision screen. As was intended, it told absolutely nothing of the creatures who had built it. The vision screen was empty now, as it had always been. Sometimes in his dreams Stormgren had imagined that it had suddenly flashed into life, revealing the secret that tormented all the world. But the dream had never come true; behind that rectangle of darkness lay utter mystery. Yet there also lay power and wisdom—and, perhaps most of all, an immense and humorous affection for the little creatures crawling on the planet beneath.

From the hidden grille came that calm, never-hurried voice that Stormgren knew so well though the world had heard it only once in history. Its depth and resonance gave the single clue that existed to Karellen's physical nature, for it left an overwhelming impression of sheer *size*. Karellen was large—perhaps much larger than a man. It was true that some scientists, after analyzing the record of his only speech, had suggested that the voice was that of a machine. This was something that Stormgren could never believe.

"Yes, Rikki, I was listening to your little interview. What did you make of Mr. Wainwright?"

"He's an honest man, even if many of his supporters aren't. What are we going to do about him? The league itself isn't dangerous, but some of its extremists are openly advocating violence. I've been wondering if I should put a guard on my house. But I hope it isn't necessary."

Karellen evaded the point in the annoying way he sometimes had.

"The details of the World Federation have been out for a month now. Has there been a substantial increase in the seven percent who don't approve of me, or the twelve percent who Don't Know?"

"Not yet. But that's of no importance: what *does* worry me is a general feeling, even among your supporters, that it's time this secrecy came to an end."

Karellen's sigh was technically perfect, yet somehow lacked conviction.

"That's your feeling too, isn't it?"

The question was so rhetorical that Stormgren did not bother to answer it.

"I wonder if you really appreciate," he continued earnestly, "how difficult this state of affairs makes my job?"

"It doesn't exactly help mine," replied Karellen with some spirit. "I wish people would stop thinking of me as a dictator, and remember I'm only a civil servant trying to administer a colonial policy in whose shaping I had no hand."

That, thought Stormgren, was quite an engaging description. He wondered just how much truth it held.

"Can't you at least give us *some* reason for your concealment? Because we don't understand it, it annoys us and gives rise to endless rumors."

Karellen gave that rich, deep laugh of his, just too resonant to be altogether human.

"What am I supposed to be now? Does the robot theory still hold the field? I'd rather be a mass of electron tubes than a thing like a centipede—oh, yes, I've seen that cartoon in yesterday's *Chicago Tribune!* I'm thinking of requesting the original."

Stormgren pursed his lips primly. There were times, he thought, when Karellen took his duties too lightly.

"This is *serious,*" he said reprovingly.

"My dear Rikki," Karellen retorted, "it's only by *not* taking the human race seriously that I retain what fragments of my once considerable mental powers I still possess!"

Despite himself, Stormgren smiled.

"That doesn't help me a great deal, does it? I have to go down there and convince my fellow men that, although you won't show yourself, you've got nothing to hide. It's not an easy job. Curiosity is one of the most dominant of human characteristics. You can't defy it forever."

"Of all the problems that faced us when we came to Earth, this was the most difficult," admitted Karellen. "You have trusted our wisdom in other matters—surely you can trust us in this!"

"*I* trust you," said Stormgren, "but Wainwright doesn't, nor do his supporters. Can you really blame them if they put a bad interpretation on your unwillingness to show yourselves?"

There was silence for a moment. Then Stormgren heard that

faint sound (was it a *crackling?*) that might have been caused by the Supervisor moving his body slightly.

"You know why Wainwright and his kind fear me, don't you?" asked Karellen. His voice was somber now, like a great organ rolling its notes from a high cathedral nave. "You will find men like him in all the world's religions. They know that we represent reason and science, and, however confident they may be in their beliefs, they fear that we will overthrow their gods. Not necessarily through any deliberate act, but in a subtler fashion. Science can destroy religion by ignoring it as well as by disproving its tenets. No one ever demonstrated, so far as I am aware, the nonexistence of Zeus or Thor, but they have few followers now. The Wainwrights fear, too, that we know the truth about the origins of their faiths. How long, they wonder, have we been observing humanity? Have we watched Mohammed begin the hegira, or Moses giving the Jews their laws? Do we know all that is false in the stories they believe?"

"And *do* you?" whispered Stormgren, half to himself.

"That, Rikki, is the fear that torments them, even though they will never admit it openly. Believe me, it gives us no pleasure to destroy men's faiths, but *all* the world's religions cannot be right, and they know it. Sooner or later man has to learn the truth: but that time is not yet. As for our secrecy, which you are correct in saying aggravates our problems—that is a matter beyond my control. I regret the need for this concealment as much as you do, but the reasons are sufficient. However, I will try to get a statement from my—superiors—which may satisfy you and perhaps placate the Freedom League. Now, please, can we return to the agenda and start recording again?"

"Well?" asked Van Ryberg anxiously. "Did you have any luck?"

"I don't know," Stormgren replied wearily as he threw the files down on his desk and collapsed into the seat. "Karellen's consulting *his* superiors now, whoever or whatever they may be. He won't make any promises."

"Listen," said Pieter abruptly, "I've just thought of something. What reason have we for believing that there is anyone beyond Karellen? Suppose *all* the Overlords, as we've christened them, are right here on Earth in these ships of theirs? They may have nowhere else to go and are hiding the fact from us."

"It's an ingenious theory," grinned Stormgren. "But it clashes with what little I know—or think I know—about Karellen's background."

"And how much is that?"

"Well, he often refers to his position here as something temporary, hindering him from getting on with his real work, which I think is some form of mathematics. Once I quoted Acton's comment about power corrupting, and absolute power corrupting absolutely. I wanted to see how he'd react to *that*. He gave that cavernous laugh of his, and said: 'There's no danger of that happening to me. In the first case, the sooner I finish my work here, the sooner I can get back to where I belong, a good many light-years from here. And secondly, I don't have absolute power, by any means. I'm just—Supervisor.' Of course, he may have been misleading me. I can never be sure of that."

"He's immortal, isn't he?"

"Yes, by our standards, though there's something in the future he seems to fear. I can't imagine what it is. And that's really all I know about him."

"It isn't very conclusive. My theory is that his little fleet's lost in space and is looking for a new home. He doesn't want us to know how few he and his comrades are. Perhaps all those other ships are automatic, and there's no one in any of them. They're just an imposing façade."

"You," said Stormgren, "have been reading too much science-fiction."

Van Ryberg grinned, a little sheepishly.

"The 'Invasion From Space' didn't turn out quite as expected, did it? My theory would certainly explain why Karellen never shows himself. He doesn't want us to learn that there aren't any more Overlords."

Stormgren shook his head in amused disagreement.

"Your explanation, as usual, is much too ingenious to be true. Though we can only infer its existence, there must be a great civilization behind the Supervisor—and one that's known about man for a very long time. Karellen himself must have been studying us for centuries. Look at his command of English, for example. He taught *me* how to speak it idiomatically!"

"Have you ever discovered *anything* he doesn't know?"

"Oh yes, quite often—but only on trivial points. I think he has an absolutely perfect memory, but there are some things he hasn't bothered to learn. For instance, English is the only language he understands completely, though in the last two years he's picked up a good deal of Finnish just to tease me. And one doesn't learn Finnish in a hurry! He can quote great slabs of the *Kalevala,* whereas I'm ashamed to say I know only a few lines. He also knows the biographies of all living statesmen, and sometimes I can identify the references he's used. His knowledge of history and science seems complete—you know how much we've already learned from him. Yet, taken one at a time, I don't think his mental gifts are quite outside the range of human achievement. But no one man could possibly do *all* the things he does."

"That's more or less what I've decided already," agreed Van Ryberg. "We can argue round Karellen forever, but in the end we always come back to the same question: Why the devil won't he show himself? Until he does, I'll go on theorizing and the Freedom League will go on fulminating."

He cocked a rebellious eye at the ceiling.

"One dark night, Mr. Supervisor, I hope some reporter takes a rocket up to your ship and climbs in through the back door with a camera. What a scoop *that* would be!"

If Karellen was listening, he gave no sign. But, of course, he never did.

In the first year of their coming, the advent of the Overlords had made less difference to the pattern of human life than might have been expected. Their shadow was everywhere, but it was an unobtrusive shadow. Though there were few great cities on Earth where men could not see one of the silver ships glittering against the zenith, after a little while they were taken as much for granted as the sun, moon, or clouds. Most men were probably only dimly aware that their steadily rising standards of living were due to the Overlords. When they stopped to think of it—which was seldom—they realized that those silent ships had brought peace to all the world for the first time in history, and were duly grateful.

But these were negative and unspectacular benefits, accepted and soon forgotten. The Overlords remained aloof, hiding their faces from mankind. Karellen could command respect and admiration; he could win nothing deeper so long as he pursued his present policy. It was hard not to feel resentment against these Olympians who spoke to man only over the radioteleprinter circuits at United Nations Headquarters. What took place between Karellen and Stormgren was never publicly revealed, and sometimes Stormgren himself wondered why the Supervisor found these interviews necessary. Perhaps he felt the need of direct contact with one human being at least; perhaps he realized that Stormgren needed this form of personal support. If this was the explanation, the Secretary-General appreciated it; he did not mind if the Freedom League referred to him contemptuously as "Karellen's office boy."

The Overlords had never had any dealings with individual states and governments. They had taken the United Nations Organization as they found it, had given instructions for installing the necessary radio equipment, and had issued their orders through the mouth of the Secretary-General. The Soviet delegate had quite correctly pointed out, at considerable length and upon innumerable occasions, that this was not in accordance with the Charter. Karellen did not seem to worry.

It was amazing that so many abuses, follies, and evils could be dispelled by those messages from the sky. With the arrival of the Overlords, nations knew that they need no longer fear each other, and they guessed—even before the experiment was made—that their existing weapons were certainly impotent against a civilization that could bridge the stars. So at once the greatest single obstacle to the happiness of mankind had been removed.

The Overlords seemed largely indifferent to forms of government, provided that they were not oppressive or corrupt. Earth still possessed democracies, monarchies, benevolent dictatorships, communism, and capitalism. This was a source of great surprise to many simple souls who were quite convinced that theirs was the only possible way of life. Others believed that Karellen was merely waiting to introduce a system which would sweep away all existing forms of society, and so had not bothered with minor political reforms. But this, like all other speculations concerning the Overlords, was pure guesswork. No one knew their motives: and no one knew toward what future they were shepherding mankind.

✳ CHAPTER TWO

Stormgren was sleeping badly these nights, which was strange, since soon he would be putting aside the cares of office forever. He had served mankind for forty years, and its masters for five, and few men could look back upon a life that had seen so many of its ambitions achieved. Perhaps that was the trouble: in the years of retirement, however many they might be, he would have no further goals to give any zest to life. Since Martha had died and the children had established their own families, his ties with the world seemed to have weakened. It might be, too, that he was beginning to identify himself with the Overlords and thus to become detached from humanity.

This was another of those restless nights when his brain went on turning like a machine whose governor had failed. He knew better than to woo sleep any further, and reluctantly climbed out of bed. Throwing on his dressing gown, he strolled out on to the roof garden of his modest flat. There was not one of his direct subordinates who did not possess much more luxurious quarters, but this place was ample for Stormgren's needs. He had reached the position where neither personal possessions nor official ceremony could add anything to his stature.

The night was warm, almost oppressive, but the sky was clear and a brilliant moon hung low in the southwest. Ten kilometers away, the lights of New York glowed on the skyline like a dawn frozen in the act of breaking.

Stormgren raised his eyes above the sleeping city, climbing again the heights that he alone of living men had scaled. Far away though it was, he could see the hull of Karellen's ship glinting in the moonlight. He wondered what the Supervisor was doing, for he did not believe that the Overlords ever slept.

High above, a meteor thrust its shining spear through the dome of the sky. The luminous trail glowed faintly for a while; then it died away, leaving only the stars. The reminder was brutal: in a hundred years, Karellen would still be leading mankind towards the goal that he alone could see, but four months from now another man would be Secretary-General. That in itself Stormgren was far from minding, but it meant that little time was left if he ever hoped to learn what lay behind that darkened screen.

Only in the last few days had he dared to admit that the Overlords' secretiveness was beginning to obsess him. Until recently, his faith in Karellen had kept him free from doubts; but now, he thought a little wryly, the protests of the Freedom League were beginning to have their effect upon him. It was true that the propaganda about man's enslavement was no more than propaganda. Few people seriously believed it, or really wished for a return to the old days. Men had grown accustomed to Karellen's imperceptible rule, but they were becoming impatient to know who ruled them. And how could they be blamed?

Though it was much the largest, the Freedom League was only one of the organizations that opposed Karellen—and, consequently, the humans who co-operated with the Overlords. The objections and policies of these groups varied enormously: some took the religious viewpoint, while others were merely expressing a sense of inferiority. They felt, with good reason, much as a cultured Indian of the nineteenth century must have done as he contemplated the British Raj. The invaders had brought peace and prosperity to Earth —but who knew what the cost might be? History was not reassuring; even the most peaceable of contacts between races at very different cultural levels had often resulted in the obliteration of the more backward society. Nations, as well as individuals, could lose their spirit when confronted by a challenge which they could not meet. And the civilization of the Overlords, veiled in mystery though it might be, was the greatest challenge man had ever faced.

There was a faint "click" from the facsimile machine in the adjoining room as it ejected the hourly summary sent out by Central News. Stormgren wandered indoors and ruffled halfheartedly through the sheets. On the other side of the world, the Freedom League had inspired a not-very-original headline. "IS MAN RULED BY MONSTERS?" asked the paper, and went on to quote: "Addressing a meeting in Madras today, Dr. C. V. Krishnan, President of the Eastern Division of the Freedom League, said, 'The explanation of the Overlords' behavior is quite simple. Their physical form is so alien and so repulsive that they dare not show themselves to humanity. I challenge the Supervisor to deny this.'"

Stormgren threw down the sheet in disgust. Even if the charge were true, would it really matter? The idea was an old one, but it had never worried him. He did not believe that there was any biological form, however strange, which he could not accept in time and, perhaps, even find beautiful. The mind, not the body, was all that mattered. If only he could convince Karellen of this, the Overlords might change their policy. It was certain that they could not be half as hideous as the imaginative drawings that had filled the papers soon after their coming to Earth!

Yet it was not, Stormgren knew, entirely consideration for his successor that made him anxious to see the end of this state of affairs. He was honest enough to admit that, in the final analysis, his main motive was simple human curiosity. He had grown to know Karellen as a person, and he would never be satisfied until he had also discovered what kind of creature he might be.

When Stormgren failed to arrive at his usual hour next morning, Pieter Van Ryberg was surprised and a little annoyed. Though the Secretary-General often made a number of calls before reaching his own office, he invariably left word that he was doing so. This morning, to make matters worse, there had been several urgent messages for Stormgren. Van Ryberg rang half a dozen departments trying to locate him, then gave it up in disgust.

By noon he had become alarmed and sent a car to Stormgren's house. Ten minutes later he was startled by the scream of a siren, and a police patrol came racing up Roosevelt Drive. The news agencies must have had friends in that vehicle, for even as Van Ryberg watched it approach, the radio was telling the world that he was no longer merely Assistant, but Acting-Secretary-General of the United Nations.

Had Van Ryberg had fewer troubles on his hands, he would have found it entertaining to study the press reactions to Stormgren's disappearance. For the past month, the world's papers had divided themselves into two sharply defined groups. The Western press, on the whole, approved of Karellen's plan to make all men citizens of the world. The Eastern countries, on the other hand, were undergoing violent but largely synthetic spasms of national pride. Some of them had been independent for little more than a generation, and felt that they had been cheated out of their gains. Criticism of the Overlords was widespread and energetic: after an initial period of extreme caution, the press had quickly found that it could be as rude to Karellen as it liked and nothing would happen. Now it was excelling itself.

Most of these attacks, though very vocal, were not representative of the great mass of the people. Along the frontiers that would soon be gone forever the guards had been doubled, but the soldiers eyed each other with a still inarticulate friendliness. The politicians and the generals might storm and rave, but the silently waiting millions felt that, none too soon, a long and bloody chapter of history was coming to an end.

And now Stormgren had gone, no one knew where. The tumult suddenly subsided as the world realized that it had lost the only man through whom the Overlords, for their own strange reasons, would speak to Earth. A paralysis seemed to descend upon press and radio commentators, but in the silence could be heard the voice of the Freedom League, anxiously protesting its innocence.

It was utterly dark when Stormgren awoke. For a moment he was too sleepy to realize how strange that was. Then, as full consciousness dawned, he sat up with a start and felt for the switch beside his bed.

In the darkness his hand encountered a bare stone wall, cold to the touch. He froze instantly, mind and body paralyzed by the impact of the unexpected. Then, scarcely believing his senses, he kneeled on the bed and began to explore with his finger tips that shockingly unfamiliar wall.

He had been doing this only for a moment when there was a sudden "click" and a section of the darkness slid aside. He caught a glimpse of a man silhouetted against a dimly lit background; then the door closed again and the darkness returned. It happened so swiftly that he had no chance to see anything of the room in which he was lying.

An instant later, he was dazzled by the light of a powerful electric torch. The beam flickered across his face, held him steadily for a moment, then dipped to illuminate the whole bed, which was, he now saw, nothing more than a mattress supported on rough planks.

Out of the darkness a soft voice spoke to him in excellent English, but with an accent which Stormgren could not at first identify.

"Ah, Mr. Secretary, I'm glad to see you're awake. I hope you feel *quite* all right."

There was something about the last sentence that caught Stormgren's attention, so that the angry questions he had been about to ask died upon his lips. He stared back into the darkness, then replied calmly, "How long have I been unconscious?"

The other chuckled.

"Several days. We were promised there'd be no aftereffects. I'm glad to see it's true."

Partly to gain time, partly to test his own reactions, Stormgren swung his legs over the side of the bed. He was still wearing his nightclothes, but they were badly crumpled and seemed to have gathered considerable dirt. As he moved he felt a slight dizziness—not enough to be unpleasant but sufficient to convince him that he had indeed been drugged.

He turned towards the light.

"Where am I?" he said sharply. "Does Wainwright know about this?"

"Now, don't get excited," replied the shadowy figure. "We won't talk about that sort of thing yet. I guess you're pretty hungry. Get dressed and come along to dinner."

The oval of light slipped across the room and for the first time Stormgren had an idea of its dimensions. It was scarcely a room at all, for the walls seemed bare rock, roughly smoothed into shape. He realized that he was underground, possibly at a great depth. And if he had been unconscious for several days, he might be anywhere on Earth.

The torchlight illuminated a pile of clothes draped over a packing case.

"This should be enough for you," said the voice from the darkness. "Laundry's rather a problem here, so we grabbed a couple of your suits and half a dozen shirts."

"That," said Stormgren without humor, "was very considerate of you."

"We're sorry about the absence of furniture and electric light. This place is convenient in some ways, but it rather lacks amenities."

"Convenient for what?" asked Stormgren as he climbed into a shirt. The feel of the familiar cloth beneath his fingers was strangely reassuring.

"Just—convenient," said the voice. "And by the way, since we're likely to spend a good deal of time together, you'd better call me Joe."

"Despite your nationality," retorted Stormgren, "—you're Polish, aren't you?—I think I could pronounce your real name. It won't be worse than many Finnish ones."

There was a slight pause and the light flickered for an instant.

"Well, I should have expected it," said Joe resignedly. "You must have plenty of practice at this sort of thing."

"It's a useful hobby for a man in my position. At a guess I should say you were brought up in the United States but didn't leave Poland until . . ."

"That," said Joe firmly, "is quite enough. As you seem to have finished dressing—thank you."

The door opened as Stormgren walked towards it, feeling mildly elated by his small victory. As Joe stood aside to let him pass, he wondered if his captor was armed. Almost certainly he would be, and in any case he would have friends around.

The corridor was dimly lit by oil lamps at intervals, and for the first time Stormgren could see Joe clearly. He was a man of about fifty, and must have weighed well over two hundred pounds. Everything about him was outsize, from the stained battle-dress that might have come from any of half a dozen armed forces, to the startlingly large signet ring on his left hand. A man built on this scale probably would not bother to carry a gun. It should not be difficult to trace him, thought Stormgren, if he ever got out of this place. He was a little depressed to realize that Joe must also be perfectly well aware of this fact.

The walls around them, though occasionally faced with concrete, were mostly bare rock. It was clear to Stormgren that he was in some disused mine, and he could think of few more effective prisons. Until now the fact of his kidnapping had failed to worry him greatly. He had felt that, whatever happened, the immense resources of the Overlords would soon locate and rescue him. Now he was not so sure. He had already been gone several days—and nothing had happened. There must be a limit even to Karellen's power, and if he were indeed buried in some remote continent, all the science of the Overlords might be unable to trace him.

There were two other men sitting at the table in the bare, dimly lit room. They looked up with interest, and more than a little respect, as Stormgren entered. One of them pushed across a bundle of sandwiches which Stormgren accepted eagerly. Though he felt extremely hungry, he could have done with a more interesting meal, but it was very obvious that his captors had dined no better.

As he ate, he glanced quickly at the three men around him. Joe was by far the most outstanding character, and not merely in the matter of physical bulk. The others were clearly his assistants—nondescript individuals, whose origins Stormgren would be able to place when he heard them talk.

Some wine had been produced in a not-too-aseptic glass, and Stormgren washed down the last of the sandwiches. Feeling now more fully in command of the situation, he turned to the huge Pole.

"Well," he said evenly, "perhaps you'll tell me what all this is about, and just what you hope to get out of it."

Joe cleared his throat.

"I'd like to make one thing straight," he said. "This has nothing to do with Wainwright. He'll be as surprised as anyone."

Stormgren had half expected this, though he wondered why Joe was confirming his suspicions. He had long suspected the existence of an extremist movement inside—or on the frontiers of—the Freedom League.

"As a matter of interest," he said, "how did you kidnap me?"

He hardly expected a reply to this, and was somewhat taken aback by the other's readiness—even eagerness—to answer.

"It was all rather like a Hollywood thriller," said Joe cheerfully. "We weren't sure if Karellen kept a watch on you, so we took somewhat elaborate precautions. You were knocked out by gas in the air conditioner—that was easy. Then we carried you out into the car—no trouble at all. All this, I might say, wasn't done by any of our people. We hired—er—professionals for the job. Karellen may get them—in fact, he's supposed to—but he'll be no wiser. When it left your house, the car drove into a long road tunnel not a thousand kilometers from New York. It came out again on schedule at the opposite end, still carrying a drugged man extraordinarily like the Secretary-General. Quite a while later a large truck loaded with metal cases emerged in the opposite direction and drove to a certain airfield where the cases were loaded aboard a freighter on perfectly legitimate business. I'm sure the owners of those cases would be horrified to know how we employed them.

"Meanwhile the car that had actually done the job continued elaborate evasive action towards the Canadian border. Perhaps Karellen's caught it by now; I don't know or care. As you'll see—I do hope you appreciate my frankness—our whole plan depended on one thing. We're pretty sure that Karellen can see and hear everything that happens on the surface of the earth—but unless he uses magic, not science, he can't see *underneath* it. So he won't know about the transfer in the tunnel—at least until it's too late. Naturally we've taken a risk, but there were also one or two other safeguards I won't go into now. We may want to use them again, and it would be a pity to give them away."

Joe had related the whole story with such obvious gusto that Stormgren could hardly help smiling. Yet he also felt very disturbed. The plan was an ingenious one, and it was quite possible that Karellen had been deceived. Stormgren was not even certain that the Overlord kept any form of protective surveillance over him. Nor, clearly, was Joe. Perhaps that was why he had been so frank—he wanted to test Stormgren's reactions. Well, he would try to appear confident, whatever his real feelings might be.

"You must be a lot of fools," said Stormgren scornfully, "if you think you can trick the Overlords as easily as this. In any case, what conceivable good will it do?"

Joe offered him a cigarette, which Stormgren refused, then lit one himself and sat on the edge of the table. There was an ominous creaking and he jumped off hastily.

"Our motives," he began, "should be pretty obvious. We've found argument useless, so we have to take other measures. There have been underground movements before, and even Karellen, whatever powers he's got, won't find it easy to deal with us. We're out to fight for our independence. Don't misunderstand me. There'll be nothing violent—at first, anyway—but the Overlords have to use human agents, and we can make it mighty uncomfortable for them."

Starting with me, I suppose, thought Stormgren. He wondered if the other had given him more than a fraction of the whole story. Did they really think that these gangster methods would influence Karellen in the slightest? On the other hand, it was quite true that a well-organized resistance movement could make life very difficult. For Joe had put his finger on the one weak spot in the Overlords' rule. Ultimately, all their orders were carried out by human agents. If these were terrorized into disobedience, the whole system might collapse. It was only a faint possibility, for Stormgren felt confident that Karellen would soon find some solution.

"What do you intend to do with me?" asked Stormgren at length. "Am I a hostage, or what?"

"Don't worry—we'll look after you. We expect some visitors in a few days, and until then we'll entertain you as well as we can."

He added some words in his own language, and one of the others produced a brand-new pack of cards.

"We got these especially for you," explained Joe. "I read in *Time* the other day that you were a good poker player." His voice suddenly became grave. "I hope there's plenty of cash in your wallet," he said anxiously. "We never thought of looking. After all, we can hardly accept checks."

Quite overcome, Stormgren stared blankly at his captors. Then, as the true humor of the situation sank into his mind, it suddenly seemed to him that all the cares and worries of office had lifted from his shoulders. From now on, it was Van Ryberg's show. Whatever happened, there was absolutely nothing he could do about it—and now these fantastic criminals were anxiously waiting to play poker with him.

Abruptly, he threw back his head and laughed as he had not done for years.

There was no doubt, thought Van Ryberg morosely, that Wainwright was telling the truth. He might have his suspicions, but he did not know who had kidnapped Stormgren. Nor did he approve of the kidnapping itself. Van Ryberg had a shrewd idea that for some time extremists in the Freedom League had been putting pressure on Wainwright to make him adopt a more active policy. Now they were taking matters into their own hands.

The kidnapping had been beautifully organized, there was no doubt of that. Stormgren might be anywhere on Earth, and there seemed little hope of tracing him. Yet something must be done, Van Ryberg decided, and done quickly. Despite the jests he had so often made, his real feeling towards Karellen was one of overwhelming awe. The thought of approaching the Supervisor directly filled him with dismay, but there seemed no alternative.

The communications section occupied the entire top floor of the great building. Lines of facsimile machines, some silent, some clicking busily, stretched away into the distance. Through them poured endless streams of statistics: production figures, census returns, and all the bookkeeping of a world economic system. Somewhere up in Karellen's ship must lie the equivalent of this great room—and Van Ryberg wondered, with a tingling of the spine, what shapes moved to and fro collecting the messages that Earth was sending to the Overlords.

But today he was not interested in these machines and the routine business they handled. He walked to the little private room that only Stormgren was supposed to enter. At his instructions, the lock had been forced and the Chief Communications Officer was waiting there for him.

"It's an ordinary teleprinter—standard typewriter keyboard," he was told. "There's a facsimile machine as well if you want to send any pictures or tabular information, but you said you wouldn't be needing that."

Van Ryberg nodded absently. "That's all. Thanks," he said. "I don't expect to be here very long. Then get the place locked up again and give me all the keys."

He waited until the Communications Officer had left, and then sat down at the machine. It was, he knew, very seldom used, since nearly all business between Karellen and Stormgren was dealt with at their weekly meetings. Since this was something of an emergency circuit, he expected a fairly quick reply.

After a moment's hesitation, he began to tap out his message with unpracticed fingers. The machine purred away quietly and the words gleamed for a few seconds on the darkened screen. Then he leaned back and waited for the answer.

Scarcely a minute later the machine started to whirr again. Not for the first time, Van Ryberg wondered if the Supervisor ever slept.

The message was as brief as it was unhelpful.

NO INFORMATION. LEAVE MATTERS ENTIRELY TO YOUR DISCRETION. K.

Rather bitterly, and without any satisfaction at all, Van Ryberg realized how much greatness had been thrust upon him.

During the past three days Stormgren had analyzed his captors with some thoroughness. Joe was the only one of any importance: the others were nonentities—the riffraff one would expect any illegal movement to gather round itself. The ideals of the Freedom League meant nothing to them: their only concern was earning a living with the minimum of work.

Joe was an altogether more complex individual, though sometimes he reminded Stormgren of an overgrown baby. Their interminable poker games were punctuated with violent political arguments, and it soon became obvious to Stormgren that the big Pole had never thought seriously about the causes for which he was fighting. Emotion and extreme conservatism clouded all his judgments. His country's long struggle for independence had conditioned him so completely that he still lived in the past. He was a picturesque survival, one of those who had no use for an ordered way of life. When his type vanished, if it ever did, the world would be a safer but less interesting place.

There was now little doubt, as far as Stormgren was concerned, that Karellen had failed to locate him. He had tried to bluff, but his captors were unconvinced. He was fairly certain that they had been holding him here to see if Karellen would act, and now that nothing had happened they could proceed with their plans.

Stormgren was not surprised when, a few days later, Joe told him to expect visitors. For some time the little group had shown increasing nervousness, and the prisoner guessed that the leaders of the movement, having seen that the coast was clear, were at last coming to collect him.

They were already waiting, gathered round the rickety table, when Joe waved him politely into the living room. Stormgren was amused to note that his jailer was now wearing, very ostentatiously, a huge pistol that had never been in evidence before. The two thugs had vanished, and even Joe seemed somewhat restrained. Stormgren could see at once that he was now confronted by men of a much higher caliber, and the group opposite him reminded him strongly of a picture he had once seen of Lenin and his associates in the first days of the Russian Revolution. There was the same intellectual force, iron determination, and ruthlessness in these six men. Joe and his kind were harmless; here were the real brains behind the organization.

With a curt nod, Stormgren moved over to the only vacant seat and tried to look self-possessed. As he approached, the elderly, thickset man on the far side of the table leaned forward and stared at him with piercing gray eyes. They made Stormgren so uncomfortable that he spoke first—something he had not intended to do.

"I suppose you've come to discuss terms. What's my ransom?"

He noticed that in the background someone was taking down his words in a shorthand notebook. It was all very businesslike.

The leader replied in a musical Welsh accent.

"You could put it that way, Mr. Secretary-General. But we're interested in information, not cash."

So that was it, thought Stormgren. He was a prisoner of war, and this was his interrogation.

"You know what our motives are," continued the other in his softly lilting voice. "Call us a resistance movement, if you like. We believe that sooner or later Earth will have to fight for its independence—but we realize that the struggle can only be by indirect methods such as sabotage and disobedience. We kidnapped you, partly to show Karellen that we mean business and are well organized, but largely because you are the only man who can tell us anything of the Overlords. You're a reasonable man, Mr. Stormgren. Give us your co-operation, and you can have your freedom."

"Exactly what do you wish to know?" asked Stormgren cautiously.

Those extraordinary eyes seemed to search his mind to its depths; they were unlike any that Stormgren had ever seen in his life. Then the singsong voice replied:

"Do you know who, or what, the Overlords really are?"

Stormgren almost smiled.

"Believe me," he said, "I'm quite as anxious as you to discover that."

"Then you'll answer our questions?"

"I make no promises. But I may."

There was a slight sigh of relief from Joe, and a rustle of anticipation ran round the room.

"We have a general idea," continued the other, "of the circumstances in which you meet Karellen. But perhaps you would describe them carefully, leaving out nothing of importance."

That was harmless enough, thought Stormgren. He had done it many times before, and it would give the appearance of cooperation. There were acute minds here, and perhaps they could uncover something new. They were welcome to any fresh information they could extract from him—so long as they shared it. That it could harm Karellen in any way he did not for a moment believe.

Stormgren felt in his pockets and produced a pencil and an old envelope. Sketching rapidly while he spoke, he began:

"You know, of course, that a small flying machine, with no obvious means of propulsion, calls for me at regular intervals and takes me up to Karellen's ship. It enters the hull—and you've doubtless seen the telescopic films that have been taken of *that* operation. The door opens again—if you can call it a door—and I go into a small room with a table, a chair, and a vision screen. The layout is something like this."

He pushed the plan across to the old Welshman, but the strange eyes never turned towards it. They were still fixed on Stormgren's face, and as he watched them something seemed to change in their depths. The room had become completely silent, but behind him he heard Joe take a sudden indrawn breath.

Puzzled and annoyed, Stormgren stared back at the other, and as he did so, understanding slowly dawned. In his confusion, he crumpled the envelope into a ball of paper and ground it underfoot.

He knew now why those gray eyes had affected him so strangely. The man opposite him was blind.

Van Ryberg had made no further attempts to contact Karellen. Much of his department's work—the forwarding of statistical information, the abstracting of the world's press, and the like—had continued automatically. In Paris the lawyers were still wrangling over the proposed World Constitution, but that was none of his business for the moment. It was a fortnight before the Supervisor wanted the final draft; if it was not ready by then, no doubt Karellen would take what action he thought fit.

And there was still no news of Stormgren.

Van Ryberg was dictating when the "Emergency Only" telephone started to ring. He grabbed the receiver and listened with mounting astonishment, then threw it down and rushed to the open window. In the distance, cries of amazement were rising from the streets, and traffic was slowing to a halt.

It was true: Karellen's ship, that never-changing symbol of the Overlords, was no longer in the sky. He searched the heavens as far as he could see, and found no trace of it. Then, suddenly, it seemed as if night had swiftly fallen. Coming down from the north, its shadowed underbelly black as a thundercloud, the great ship was racing low over the towers of New York. Involuntarily, Van Ryberg shrank away from the onrushing monster. He had always known how huge the ships of the Overlords really were—but it was one thing to see them far away in space, and quite another to watch them passing overhead like demon-driven clouds.

In the darkness of that partial eclipse, he watched until the ship and its monstrous shadow had vanished into the south. There was no sound, not even the whisper of air, and Van Ryberg realized that despite its apparent nearness the ship had passed at least a kilometer above his head. Then the building shuddered once as the shock wave struck it, and from somewhere came the tinkling of broken glass as a window blew inwards.

In the office behind him all the telephones had started to ring, but Van Ryberg did not move. He remained leaning against the window ledge, still staring into the south, paralyzed by the presence of illimitable power.

As Stormgren talked, it seemed to him that his mind was operating on two levels simultaneously. On the one hand he was trying to defy the men who had captured him, yet on the other he was hoping that they might help him unravel Karellen's secret. It was a dangerous game, yet to his surprise he was enjoying it.

The blind Welshman had conducted most of the interrogation. It was fascinating to watch that agile mind trying one opening after another, testing and rejecting all the theories that Stormgren himself had abandoned long ago. Presently he leaned back with a sigh.

"We're getting nowhere," he said resignedly. "We want more facts, and that means action, not argument." The sightless eyes seemed to stare thoughtfully at Stormgren. For a moment he tapped nervously on the table—it was the first sign of uncertainty Stormgren had noticed. Then he continued:

"I'm a little surprised, Mr. Secretary, that you've never made any effort to learn more about the Overlords."

"What do you suggest?" asked Stormgren coldly, trying to disguise his interest. "I've told you that there's only one way out of the room in which I have my talks with Karellen—and that leads straight back to Earth."

"It might be possible," mused the other, "to devise instruments which could teach us something. I'm no scientist, but we can look into the matter. If we give you your freedom, would you be willing to assist with such a plan?"

"Once and for all," said Stormgren angrily, "let me make my position perfectly clear. Karellen is working for a united world, and I'll do nothing to help his enemies. What his ultimate plans may be, I don't know, but I believe that they are good."

"What real proof have we of that?"

"*All* his actions, ever since his ships appeared in our skies. I defy you to mention one act that, in the ultimate analysis, hasn't been beneficial." Stormgren paused for a moment, letting his mind run back through the past years. Then he smiled.

"If you want a single proof of the essential—how shall I put it—*benevolence* of the Overlords, think of that cruelty-to-animals order which they made within a month of their arrival. If I had had any doubts about Karellen before, that banished them—even though that order has caused me more trouble than anything else he's ever done!"

That was scarcely an exaggeration, Stormgren thought. The whole incident had been an extraordinary one, the first revelation of the Overlords' hatred of cruelty. That, and their passion for justice and order, seemed to be the dominant emotions in their lives —as far as one could judge them by their actions.

And it was the only time Karellen had shown anger, or at least the appearance of anger. "You may kill one another if you wish," the message had gone, "and that is a matter between you and your own laws. But if you slay, except for food or in self-defense, the beasts that share your world with you—then you may be answerable to me."

No one knew exactly how comprehensive this ban was supposed to be, or what Karellen would do to enforce it. They had not long to wait.

The Plaza de Toros was full when the matadors and their attendants began their processional entry. Everything seemed normal; the brilliant sunlight blazed harshly on the traditional costumes, the great crowd greeted its favorites as it had a hundred times before. Yet here and there faces were turned anxiously towards the sky, to the aloof silver shape fifty kilometers above Madrid.

Then the picadors had taken up their places and the bull had come snorting out into the arena. The skinny horses, nostrils wide with terror, had wheeled in the sunlight as their riders forced them to meet their enemy. The first lance flashed—made contact—and at that moment came a sound that had never been heard on earth before.

It was the sound of ten thousand people screaming with the pain of the same wound—ten thousand people who, when they had recovered from the shock, found themselves completely unharmed. But that was the end of that bullfight, and indeed of all bullfighting, for the news spread rapidly. It is worth recording that the *aficionados* were so shaken that only one in ten asked for his money back, and also that the London *Daily Mirror* made matters much worse by suggesting that the Spaniards adopt cricket as a new national sport.

"You may be correct," the old Welshman replied. "Possibly the motives of the Overlords are good—according to their standards, which may sometimes be the same as ours. But they are interlopers —we never asked them to come here and turn our world upside down, destroying ideals—yes, and nations—that generations of men have fought to protect."

"I come from a small nation that had to fight for its liberties," retorted Stormgren. "Yet I am for Karellen. You may annoy him, you may even delay the achievement of his aims, but it will make no difference in the end. Doubtless you are sincere in believing as you do. I can understand your fear that the traditions and cultures of little countries will be overwhelmed when the world state arrives. But you are wrong; it is useless to cling to the past. Even before the Overlords came to Earth, the sovereign state was dying. They have merely hastened its end: no one can save it now—and no one should try."

There was no answer. The man opposite neither moved nor spoke. He sat with lips half open, his eyes now lifeless as well as blind. Around him the others were equally motionless, frozen in strained, unnatural attitudes. With a gasp of pure horror, Stormgren rose to his feet and backed away towards the door. As he did so the silence was suddenly broken.

"That was a nice speech, Rikki: thank you. Now I think we can go."

Stormgren spun on his heels and stared into the shadowed corridor. Floating there at eye-level was a small, featureless sphere—the source, no doubt, of whatever mysterious force the Overlords had brought into action. It was hard to be certain, but Stormgren imagined that he could hear a faint humming, as of a hive of bees on a drowsy summer day.

"Karellen! Thank God! But what have you done?"

"Don't worry: they're all right. You can call it a paralysis, but it's much subtler than that. They're simply living a few thousand times more slowly than normal. When we've gone they'll never know what happened."

"You'll leave them here until the police come?"

"No. I've a much better plan. I'm letting them go."

Stormgren felt a surprising sense of relief. He gave a last, valedictory glance at the little room and its frozen occupants. Joe was standing on one foot, staring very stupidly at nothing. Suddenly Stormgren laughed and fumbled in his pockets.

"Thanks for the hospitality, Joe," he said. "I think I'll leave a souvenir."

He ruffled through the scraps of paper until he had found the figures he wanted. Then, on a reasonably clean sheet, he wrote carefully:

"BANK OF MANHATTAN
*Pay Joe the sum of One Hundred Thirty-Five
Dollars and Fifty Cents ($135.50)*
R. Stormgren."

As he laid the strip of paper beside the Pole, Karellen's voice inquired:

"Exactly *what* are you doing?"

"We Stormgrens always pay our debts. The other two cheated, but Joe played fair. At least, I never caught him cheating."

He felt very gay and lightheaded, and quite forty years younger, as he walked to the door. The metal sphere moved aside to let him pass. He assumed that it was some kind of robot, and it explained how Karellen had been able to reach him through the unknown layers of rock overhead.

"Go straight ahead for a hundred meters," said the sphere, speaking in Karellen's voice. "Then turn to the left until I give you further instructions."

He strode forward eagerly, though he realized that there was no need for hurry. The sphere remained hanging in the corridor, presumably covering his retreat.

A minute later he came across a second sphere, waiting for him at a branch in the corridor.

"You've half a kilometer to go," it said. "Keep to the left until we meet again."

Six times he encountered the spheres on his way to the open. At first he wondered if, somehow, the robot was managing to keep ahead of him; then he guessed that there must be a chain of the machines maintaining a complete circuit down into the depths of the mine. At the entrance, a group of guards formed a piece of improbable statuary, watched over by yet another of the ubiquitous spheres. On the hillside a few meters away lay the little flying machine in which Stormgren had made all his journeys to Karellen.

He stood for a moment blinking in the sunlight. Then he saw the ruined mining machinery around him, and beyond that a derelict railway stretching down the mountainside. Several kilometers away a dense forest lapped at the base of the mountain, and very far off Stormgren could see the gleam of water from a great lake. He guessed that he was somewhere in South America, though it was not easy to say exactly what gave him that impression.

As he climbed into the little flying machine, Stormgren had a last glimpse of the mine entrance and the men frozen around it. Then the door sealed behind him and with a sigh of relief he sank back upon the familiar couch.

For a while he waited until he had recovered his breath; then he uttered a single, heartfelt syllable:

"Well??"

"I'm sorry I couldn't rescue you before. But you see how very important it was to wait until all the leaders had gathered here."

"Do you mean to say," spluttered Stormgren, "that you knew where I was all the time? If I thought—"

"Don't be too hasty," answered Karellen, "at least, let me finish explaining."

"Very good," said Stormgren darkly. "I'm listening." He was beginning to suspect that he had been no more than bait in an elaborate trap.

"I've had a—perhaps 'tracer' is the best word for it—on you for some time," began Karellen. "Though your late friends were correct in thinking that I couldn't follow you underground, I was able to keep track until they brought you to the mine. That transfer in the tunnel was ingenious, but when the first car ceased to react it gave the plan away and I soon located you again. Then it was merely a matter of waiting. I knew that once they were certain I'd lost you, the leaders would come here and I'd be able to trap them all."

"But you're letting them go!"

"Until now," said Karellen, "I had no way of telling who of the two and a half billion men on this planet were the real heads of the organization. Now that they're located, I can trace their movements anywhere on Earth, and can watch their actions in detail if I want to. That's far better than locking them up. If they make any moves, they'll betray their remaining comrades. They're effectively neutralized, and they know it. Your rescue will be completely inexplicable to them, for you must have vanished before their eyes."

That rich laugh echoed round the tiny room.

"In some ways the whole affair was a comedy, but it had a serious purpose. I'm not merely concerned with the few score men in this organization—I have to think of the moral effect on other groups that exist elsewhere."

Stormgren was silent for a while. He was not altogether satisfied, but he could see Karellen's point of view, and some of his anger had evaporated.

"It's a pity to do it in my last few weeks of office," he said finally, "but from now on I'm going to have a guard on my house. Pieter can be kidnapped next time. How has he managed, by the way?"

"I've watched him carefully this last week, and have deliberately avoided helping him. On the whole he's done very well—but he's not the man to take your place."

"That's lucky for him," said Stormgren, still somewhat aggrieved. "And by the way, have you had any word yet from your superiors—about showing yourself to us? I'm sure now that it's the strongest argument your enemies have. Again and again they told me: 'We'll never trust the Overlords until we can see them.'"

Karellen sighed.

"No. I have heard nothing. But I know what the answer must be."

Stormgren did not press the matter. Once he might have done so, but now for the first time the faint shadow of a plan was beginning to take shape in his mind. The words of his interrogator passed again through his memory. Yes, perhaps instruments could be devised. . . .

What he had refused to do under duress, he might yet attempt of his own free will.

✳ CHAPTER THREE

It would never have occurred to Stormgren, even a few days before, that he could seriously have considered the action he was planning now. This ridiculously melodramatic kidnapping, which in retrospect seemed like a third-rate TV drama, probably had a great deal to do with his new outlook. It was the first time in his life that Stormgren had ever been exposed to violent physical action, as opposed to the verbal battles of the conference room. The virus must have entered his bloodstream; or else he was merely approaching second childhood more quickly than he had supposed.

Sheer curiosity was also a powerful motive, and so was a determination to get his own back for the trick that had been played upon him. It was perfectly obvious now that Karellen had used him as bait, and even if this had been for the best of reasons, Stormgren did not feel inclined to forgive the Supervisor at once.

Pierre Duval showed no surprise when Stormgren walked unannounced into his office. They were old friends and there was nothing unusual in the Secretary-General paying a personal visit to the Chief of the Science Bureau. Certainly Karellen would not think it odd, if by any chance he—or one of his underlings—turned his instruments of surveillance upon this spot.

For a while the two men talked business and exchanged political gossip; then, rather hesitantly, Stormgren came to the point. As his visitor talked, the old Frenchman leaned back in his chair and his eyebrows rose steadily, millimeter by millimeter, until they were almost entangled in his forelock. Once or twice he seemed about to speak, but each time thought better of it.

When Stormgren had finished, the scientist looked nervously around the room.

"Do you think he's listening?" he said.

"I don't believe he can. He's got what he calls a tracer on me, for my protection. But it doesn't work underground, which is one reason why I came down to this dungeon of yours. It's supposed to be shielded from all forms of radiation, isn't it? Karellen's no magician. He knows where I am, but that's all."

"I hope you're right. Apart from that, won't there be trouble when he discovers what you're trying to do? Because he will, you know."

"I'll take that risk. Besides, we understand each other rather well."

The physicist toyed with his pencil and stared into space for a while.

"It's a very pretty problem. I like it," he said simply. Then he dived into a drawer and produced an enormous writing pad, quite the biggest that Stormgren had ever seen.

"Right," he began, scribbling furiously in what seemed to be some private shorthand. "Let me make sure I have all the facts. Tell me everything you can about the room in which you have your interviews. Don't omit any detail, however trivial it seems."

"There isn't much to describe. It's made of metal, and is about eight meters square and four high. The vision screen is about a meter on a side and there's a desk immediately beneath it—here, it will be quicker if I draw it for you."

Rapidly Stormgren sketched the little room he knew so well, and pushed the drawing over to Duval. As he did so, he recalled, with a slight shiver, the last time he had done this sort of thing. He wondered what had happened to the blind Welshman and his confederates, and how they had reacted to his abrupt departure.

The Frenchman studied the drawing with a puckered brow.

"And that's all you can tell me?"

"Yes."

Duval snorted in disgust.

"What about lighting? Do you sit in total darkness? And how about ventilation, heating—"

Stormgren smiled at the characteristic outburst.

"The whole ceiling is luminous, and as far as I can tell the air comes through the speaker grille. I don't know how it leaves; perhaps the stream reverses at intervals, but I haven't noticed it. There's no sign of any heater, but the room is always at normal temperature."

"Meaning, I suppose, that the water vapor has frozen out, but not the carbon dioxide."

Stormgren did his best to smile at the well-worn joke.

"I think I've told you everything," he concluded. "As for the machine that takes me up to Karellen's ship, the room in which I travel is as featureless as an elevator cage. Apart from the couch and table, it might very well be one."

There was silence for several minutes while the physicist embroidered his writing pad with meticulous and microscopic doodles. As he watched, Stormgren wondered why it was that a man like Duval—whose mind was incomparably more brilliant than his own —had never made a greater mark in the world of science. He remembered an unkind and probably inaccurate comment of a friend in the U.S. State Department. "The French produce the best second-raters in the world." Duval was the sort of man who supported that statement.

The physicist nodded to himself in satisfaction, leaned forward and pointed his pencil at Stormgren.

"What makes you think, Rikki," he asked, "that Karellen's vision screen, as you call it, really is what it pretends to be?"

"I've always taken it for granted; it looks exactly like one. What else would it be, anyway?"

"When you say that it *looks* like a vision screen, you mean, don't you, that it looks like one of *ours?*"

"Of course."

"I find that suspicious in itself. I'm sure the Overlords' own apparatus won't use anything as crude as an actual physical screen —they'll probably materialize images directly in space. But why should Karellen bother to use a TV system, anyway? The simplest solution is always best. Doesn't it seem far more probable that your 'vision screen' is really *nothing more complicated than a sheet of one-way glass?*"

Stormgren was so annoyed with himself that for a moment he sat in silence, retracing the past. From the beginning, he had never challenged Karellen's story—yet now he came to look back, when had the Supervisor ever told him that he was using a TV system? He had simply taken it for granted: the whole thing had been a piece of psychological trickery, and he had been completely deceived. Always assuming, of course, that Duval's theory *was* correct. But he was jumping to conclusions again; no one had proved anything yet.

"If you're right," he said, "all I have to do is to smash the glass—"

Duval sighed.

"These unscientific laymen! Do you think it'll be made of anything you could smash without explosives? And if you succeeded, do you imagine that Karellen is likely to breathe the same air that we do? Won't it be nice for both of you if he flourishes in an atmosphere of chlorine?"

Stormgren felt a little foolish. He should have thought of that.

"Well, what *do* you suggest?" he asked with some exasperation.

"I want to think it over. First of all we've got to find if my theory is correct, and if so learn something about the material of that screen. I'll put a couple of my men on the job. By the way, I suppose you carry a brief case when you visit the Supervisor? Is it the one you've got there?"

"Yes."

"It should be big enough. We don't want to attract attention by changing it for another, particularly if Karellen's grown used to it."

"What do you want me to do?" asked Stormgren. "Carry a concealed X-ray set?"

The physicist grinned.

"I don't know yet, but we'll think of something. I'll let you know what it is in about two weeks."

He gave a little laugh.

"Do you know what all this reminds me of?"

"Yes," said Stormgren promptly, "the time you were building illegal radio sets during the German occupation."

Duval looked disappointed.

"Well, I suppose I *have* mentioned that once or twice before. But there's one other thing—"

"What's that?"

"When you are caught, *I* didn't know what you wanted the gear for."

"What, after all the fuss you once made about the scientist's social responsibility for his inventions? Really, Pierre, I'm ashamed of you!"

Stormgren laid down the thick folder of typescript with a sigh of relief.

"Thank heavens *that's* settled at last," he said. "It's strange to think that these few hundred pages hold the future of mankind. The World State! I never thought I would see it in my lifetime!"

He dropped the file into his brief case, the back of which was no more than ten centimeters from the dark rectangle of the screen. From time to time his fingers played across the locks in a half-conscious, nervous reaction, but he had no intention of pressing the concealed switch until the meeting was over. There was a chance that something might go wrong; though Duval had sworn that Karellen would detect nothing, one could never be sure.

"Now, you said you'd some news for me," Stormgren continued, with scarcely concealed eagerness. "Is it about—"

"Yes," said Karellen. "I received a decision a few hours ago."

What did he mean by that? wondered Stormgren. Surely it was not possible for the Supervisor to have communicated with his distant home, across the unknown numbers of light-years that separated him from his base. Or perhaps—this was Van Ryberg's theory —he had merely been consulting some vast computing machine which could predict the outcome of any political action.

"I don't think," continued Karellen, "that the Freedom League and its associates will be very satisfied, but it should help to reduce the tension. We won't record this, by the way.

"You've often told me, Rikki, that no matter how unlike you we are physically, the human race would soon grow accustomed to us. That shows a lack of imagination on your part. It would probably be true in your case, but you must remember that most of the world is still uneducated by any reasonable standards, and is riddled with prejudices and superstitions that may take decades to eradicate.

"You will grant that we know something of human psychology. We know rather accurately what would happen if we revealed ourselves to the world in its present state of development. I can't go into details, even with you, so you must accept my analysis on trust. We can, however, make this definite promise, which should give you some satisfaction. *In fifty years—two generations from now—we will come down from our ships and humanity will at last see us as we are.*"

Stormgren was silent for a while, absorbing the Supervisor's words. He felt little of the satisfaction that Karellen's statement would once have given him. Indeed, he was somewhat confused by his partial success, and for a moment his resolution faltered. The truth would come with the passage of time: all his plotting was unnecessary and perhaps unwise. If he still went ahead, it would be only for the selfish reason that he would not be alive in fifty years.

Karellen must have seen his irresolution, for he continued:

"I'm sorry if this disappoints you, but at least the political problems of the near future won't be your responsibility. Perhaps you still think that our fears are unfounded—but believe me we've had convincing proofs of the danger of any other course."

Stormgren leaned forward, breathing heavily.

"So you *have* been seen by Man!"

"I didn't say that," Karellen answered promptly. "*Your* world isn't the only planet we've supervised."

Stormgren was not to be shaken off so easily.

"There have been many legends suggesting that Earth has been visited in the past by other races."

"I know: I've read the Historical Research Section's report. It makes Earth look like the crossroads of the Universe."

"There may have been visits about which you know nothing,"

said Stormgren, still angling hopefully. "Though since you must have been observing us for thousands of years, I suppose that's rather unlikely."

"I suppose it is," replied Karellen, in his most unhelpful manner. And at that moment Stormgren made up his mind.

"Karellen," he said abruptly, "I'll draft out the statement and send it up to you for approval. But I reserve the right to continue pestering you, and if I see any opportunity, I'll do my best to learn your secret."

"I'm perfectly well aware of that," replied the Supervisor, with a slight chuckle.

"And you don't mind?"

"Not in the least—though I draw the line at nuclear weapons, poison gas, or anything else that might strain our friendship."

Stormgren wondered what, if anything, Karellen had guessed. Behind the Supervisor's banter he had recognized a note of understanding, perhaps—who could tell?—even of encouragement.

"I'm glad to know it," Stormgren replied in as level a voice as he could manage. He rose to his feet, bringing down the cover on his case as he did so. His thumb slid along the catch.

"I'll draft that statement at once," he repeated, "and send it up on the teletype later today."

While he was speaking, he pressed the button—and knew that all his fears had been groundless. Karellen's senses were no subtler than Man's. The Supervisor could have detected nothing, for there was no change in his voice as he said good-by and spoke the familiar code-words that opened the door of the chamber.

Yet Stormgren still felt like a shoplifter leaving a department store under the eyes of the store detective, and breathed a sigh of relief when the smooth wall had sealed itself behind him.

"I admit," said Van Ryberg, "that some of my theories haven't been very successful. But tell me what you think of this one."

"Must I?" sighed Stormgren.

Pieter didn't seem to notice.

"It isn't really my idea," he said modestly. "I got it from a story of Chesterton's. Suppose the Overlords are hiding the fact that they've got nothing to hide?"

"That sounds just a little complicated to me," said Stormgren, beginning to take a slight interest.

"What I mean is this," Van Ryberg continued eagerly. "*I* think that physically they're human beings like us. They realize that we'll tolerate being ruled by creatures we imagine to be—well, alien and superintelligent. But the human race being what it is, it just won't be bossed around by creatures of the same species."

"Very ingenious, like all your theories," said Stormgren. "I wish you'd give them opus numbers so that I could keep up with them. The objections to this one—"

But at that moment Alexander Wainwright was shown in.

Stormgren wondered what he was thinking. He wondered, too, if Wainwright had made any contact with the men who had kidnapped him. He doubted it, for he believed Wainwright's disapproval of violence to be perfectly genuine. The extremists in his movement had discredited themselves thoroughly, and it would be a long time before the world heard of them again.

The head of the Freedom League listened carefully while the draft was read to him. Stormgren hoped he appreciated this gesture, which had been Karellen's idea. Not for another twelve hours would the rest of the world know of the promise that had been made to its grandchildren.

"Fifty years," said Wainwright thoughtfully. "That is a long time to wait."

"For mankind, perhaps, but not for Karellen," Stormgren answered. Only now was he beginning to realize the neatness of the Overlords' solution. It had given them the breathing space they believed they needed, and it had cut the ground from beneath the Freedom League's feet. He did not imagine that the League would capitulate, but its position would be seriously weakened. Certainly Wainwright realized this as well.

"In fifty years," he said bitterly, "the damage will be done. Those who remembered our independence will be dead; humanity will have forgotten its heritage."

Words—empty words, thought Stormgren. The words for which men had once fought and died, and for which they would never die or fight again. And the world would be better for it.

As he watched Wainwright leave, Stormgren wondered how much trouble the Freedom League would still cause in the years that lay ahead. Yet that, he thought with a lifting of his spirits, was a problem for his successor.

There were some things that only time could cure. Evil men could be destroyed, but nothing could be done with good men who were deluded.

"Here's your case," said Duval. "It's as good as new."

"Thanks," Stormgren answered, inspecting it carefully none the less. "Now perhaps you'll tell me what it was all about, and what we are going to do next."

The physicist seemed more interested in his own thoughts.

"What I can't understand," he said, "is the ease with which we've got away with it. Now if I'd been Kar—"

"But you're not. Get to the point, man. What *did* we discover?"

"Ah me, these excitable, highly strung Nordic races!" sighed Duval. "What we did was to make a type of low powered radar set. Besides radio waves of very high frequency, it used far infrared—all waves, in fact, which we were sure no creature could possibly see, however weird an eye it had."

"How could you be sure of that?" asked Stormgren, becoming intrigued by the technical problem in spite of himself.

"Well—we couldn't be *quite* sure," admitted Duval reluctantly. "But Karellen views you under normal lighting, doesn't he? So his eyes must be approximately similar to ours in spectral range. Anyway, it worked. We've proved that there *is* a large room behind that screen of yours. The screen is about three centimeters thick, and the space behind it is at least ten meters across. We couldn't detect any echo from the far wall, but we hardly expected to with the low power which was all we dared use. However, we did get *this*."

He pushed across a piece of photographic paper on which was a single wavy line. In one spot was a kink like the autograph of a mild earthquake.

"See that little kink?"

"Yes: what is it?"

"Only Karellen."

"Good Lord! Are you sure?"

"It's a pretty safe guess. He's sitting, or standing, or whatever it is he does, about two meters on the other side of the screen. If the resolution had been a bit better, we might even have calculated his size."

Stormgren's feelings were very mixed as he stared at that scarcely visible inflection of the trace. Until now, there had been no proof that Karellen even had a material body. The evidence was still indirect, but he accepted it without question.

"The other thing we had to do," said Duval, "was to calculate the transmission of the screen to ordinary light. We think we've got a reasonable idea of that—anyway it doesn't matter if we're out even by a factor of ten. You'll realize, of course, that there's no such thing as a truly one-way glass. It's simply a matter of arranging the lights. Karellen sits in a darkened room: you are illuminated—that's all." Duval chuckled. "Well, we're going to change that!"

With the air of a conjurer producing a whole litter of white rabbits, he reached into his desk and pulled out an overgrown flashlight. The end flared out into a wide nozzle, so that the whole device looked rather like a blunderbuss.

Duval grinned.

"It's not as dangerous as it looks. All you have to do is to ram the nozzle against the screen and press the trigger. It gives out a very powerful beam lasting ten seconds, and in that time you'll be able to swing it round the room and get a good view. All the light will go through the screen and it will floodlight your friend beautifully."

"It won't hurt Karellen?"

"Not if you aim low and sweep upwards. That will give his eyes time to adapt—I suppose he has reflexes like ours, and we don't want to blind him."

Stormgren looked at the weapon doubtfully and hefted it in his hand. For the last few weeks his conscience had been pricking him. Karellen had always treated him with unmistakable affection, despite his occasional devastating frankness, and now that their time together was drawing to its close he did not wish to do anything that might spoil that relationship. But the Supervisor had received due warning, and Stormgren had the conviction that if the choice had been his, Karellen would long ago have shown himself. Now the decision would be made for him: when their last meeting came to its end, Stormgren would gaze upon Karellen's face.

If, of course, Karellen had a face.

The nervousness that Stormgren had first felt had long since passed away. Karellen was doing almost all the talking, weaving the intricate sentences which he was prone to use. Once this had seemed to Stormgren the most wonderful and certainly the most unexpected of all Karellen's gifts. Now it no longer appeared quite so marvelous, for he knew that like most of the Supervisor's abilities it was the result of sheer intellectual power and not of any special talent.

Karellen had time for any amount of literary composition when he slowed his thoughts down to the pace of human speech.

"There is no need for you or your successor to worry unduly about the Freedom League, even when it has recovered from its present despondency. It has been very quiet for the past month, and, though it will revive again, it will not be a danger for some years. Indeed, since it is always valuable to know what your opponents are doing, the League is a very useful institution. Should it ever get into financial difficulties I might even have to subsidize it."

Stormgren had often found it difficult to tell when Karellen was joking. He kept his face impassive and continued to listen.

"Very soon the League will lose another of its arguments. There has been a good deal of criticism, all somewhat childish, of the special position you have held for the past few years. I found it very valuable in the early days of my administration, but now that the world is moving along the lines that I planned, it can cease. In future, all my dealings with Earth will be indirect and the office of Secretary-General can revert to something resembling its original form.

"During the next fifty years there will be many crises, but they will pass. The pattern of the future is clear 'enough, and one day all these difficulties will be forgotten—even by a race with memories as long as yours."

The last words were spoken with such peculiar emphasis that Stormgren immediately froze in his seat. Karellen, he was sure, never made accidental slips: even his indiscretions were calculated to many decimal places. But there was no time to ask questions—which certainly would not be answered—before the Supervisor had changed the subject again.

"You have often asked me about our long-term plans," he continued. "The foundation of the World State is, of course, only the

first step. You will live to see its completion—but the change will
be so imperceptible that few will notice it when it comes. After that
there will be a period of slow consolidation while your race becomes prepared for us. And then will come the day which we have
promised. I am sorry you will not be there."

Stormgren's eyes were open, but his gaze was fixed far beyond
the dark barrier of the screen. He was looking into the future,
imagining the day that he would never see, when the great ships of
the Overlords came down at last to Earth and were thrown open
to the waiting world.

"On that day," continued Karellen, "the human race will experience what can only be called a psychological discontinuity. But
no permanent harm will be done: the men of that age will be more
stable than their grandfathers. We will always have been part of
their lives, and when they meet us we will not seem so—strange—
as we would do to you."

Stormgren had never known Karellen in so contemplative a
mood, but this gave him no surprise. He did not believe that he
had ever seen more than a few facets of the Supervisor's personality:
the real Karellen was unknown and perhaps unknowable to human
beings. And once again Stormgren had the feeling that the Supervisor's real interests were elsewhere, and that he ruled Earth with
only a fraction of his mind, as effortlessly as a master of three-
dimensional chess might play a game of checkers.

"And after that?" asked Stormgren softly.

"*Then* we can begin our real work."

"I have often wondered what that might be. Tidying up our
world and civilizing the human race is only a means—you must
have an end as well. Will we ever be able to come out into space
and see your universe—perhaps even help you in your tasks?"

"You can put it that way," said Karellen—and now his voice
held a clear yet inexplicable note of sadness that left Stormgren
strangely perturbed.

"But suppose, after all, your experiment fails with Man? We
have known such things in our own dealings with primitive human
races. Surely you have had your failures too?"

"Yes," said Karellen, so softly that Stormgren could scarcely
hear him. "We have had our failures."

"And what do you do then?"

"We wait—and try again."

There was a pause lasting perhaps five seconds. When Karellen spoke again, his words were so unexpected that for a moment Stormgren did not react.

"Good-by, Rikki!"

Karellen had tricked him—probably it was already too late. Stormgren's paralysis lasted only a moment. Then with a single swift, well-practiced movement, he whipped out the flash gun and jammed it against the glass.

The pine trees came almost to the edge of the lake, leaving along its border only a narrow strip of grass a few meters wide. Every evening when it was warm enough Stormgren, despite his ninety years, would walk briskly along this strip to the landing stage, watch the sunlight die upon the water, and then return to the house before the chill night wind came up from the forest. The simple ritual gave him much contentment, and he would continue it as long as he had the strength.

Far away over the lake something was coming in from the west, flying low and fast. Aircraft were uncommon in these parts, unless one counted the transpolar lines which must be passing overhead every hour of the day and night. But there was never any sign of their presence, save an occasional vapor trail high against the blue of the stratosphere. This machine was a small helicopter, and it was coming towards him with obvious determination. Stormgren glanced along the beach and saw that there was no chance of escape. Then he shrugged his shoulders and sat down on the wooden bench at the head of the jetty.

The reporter was so deferential that Stormgren found it surprising. He had almost forgotten that he was not only an elder statesman but, outside his own country, almost a mythical figure.

"Mr. Stormgren," the intruder began, "I'm very sorry to bother you, but I wonder if you'd care to comment on something we've just heard about the Overlords."

Stormgren frowned slightly. After all these years, he still shared Karellen's dislike for that word.

"I do not think," he said, "that I can add a great deal to what has been written elsewhere."

The reporter was watching him with a curious intentness.

"I thought that you might. A rather strange story has just come to our notice. It seems that, nearly thirty years ago, one of the Science Bureau's technicians made some remarkable equipment for you. We wondered if you could tell us anything about it."

For a moment Stormgren was silent, his mind going back into the past. He was not surprised that the secret had been discovered. Indeed, it was surprising that it had been kept so long.

He rose to his feet and began to walk back along the jetty, the reporter following a few paces behind.

"The story," he said, "contains a certain amount of truth. On my last visit to Karellen's ship I took some apparatus with me, in the hope that I might be able to see the Supervisor. It was rather a foolish thing to do but—well, I was only sixty at the time."

He chuckled to himself and then continued.

"It's not much of a story to have brought you all this way. You see, it didn't work."

"You saw nothing?"

"No, nothing at all. I'm afraid you'll have to wait—but after all, there are only twenty years to go!"

Twenty years to go. Yes, Karellen had been right. By then the world would be ready, as it had not been when he had spoken that same lie to Duval thirty years ago.

Karellen had trusted him, and Stormgren had not betrayed his faith. He was as sure as he could be of anything that the Supervisor had known his plan from the beginning, and had foreseen every moment of its final act.

Why else had that enormous chair been already empty when the circle of light blazed upon it? In the same moment he had started to swing the beam, fearing that he was too late. The metal door, twice as high as a man, was closing swiftly when he first caught sight of it—closing swiftly, yet not quite swiftly enough.

Yes, Karellen had trusted him, had not wished him to go down into the long evening of his life haunted by a mystery he could never solve. Karellen dared not defy the unknown powers above him (were *they* of that same race also?), but he had done all that he could. If he had disobeyed them, they could never prove it. It was the final proof, Stormgren knew, of Karellen's affection for him. Though it might be the affection of a man for a devoted and intelligent dog, it was none the less sincere for that, and Stormgren's life had given him few greater satisfactions.

"We have had our failures."

Yes, Karellen, that was true: and were *you* the one who failed, before the dawn of human history? It must have been a failure indeed, thought Stormgren, for its echoes to roll down all the ages, to haunt the childhood of every race of man. Even in fifty years, could you overcome the power of all the myths and legends of the world?

Yet Stormgren knew there would be no second failure. When the two races met again, the Overlords would have won the trust and friendship of mankind, and not even the shock of recognition could undo that work. They would go together into the future, and the unknown tragedy that must have darkened the past would be lost forever down the dim corridors of prehistoric time.

And Stormgren hoped that when Karellen was free to walk once more on Earth, he would one day come to these northern forests, and stand beside the grave of the first man ever to be his friend.

Part II · The Golden Age

✳ CHAPTER FOUR

"This is the day!" whispered the radios in a hundred tongues. "This is the day!" said the headlines of a thousand newspapers. "This is the day!" thought the cameramen as they checked and rechecked the equipment gathered round the vast empty space upon which Karellen's ship would be descending.

There was only the single ship now, hanging above New York. Indeed, as the world had just discovered, the ships above man's other cities had never existed. The day before, the great fleet of the Overlords had dissolved into nothingness, fading like mist beneath the morning sun.

The supply ships, coming and going far out in space, had been real enough; but the silver clouds that had hung for a lifetime over the capitals of Earth had been an illusion. How it had been done, no one could tell, but it seemed that every one of those ships had been nothing more than an image of Karellen's own vessel. Yet it had been far more than a matter of playing with light, for radar had also been deceived and there were still men alive who swore that they had heard the shriek of torn air as the fleet came in through the skies of Earth.

It was not important: all that mattered was that Karellen no longer felt the need for this display of force. He had thrown away his psychological weapons.

"The ship is moving!" came the word, flashed instantly to every corner of the planet. "It is heading westward!"

At less than a thousand kilometers an hour, falling slowly down from the empty heights of the stratosphere, the ship moved out to the great plains and to its second rendezvous with history. It settled down obediently before the waiting cameras and the packed thousands of spectators, so few of whom could see as much as the millions gathered round their TV sets.

The ground should have cracked and trembled beneath that tremendous weight, but the vessel was still in the grip of whatever forces drove it among the stars. It kissed the earth as gently as a falling snowflake.

The curving wall twenty meters above the ground seemed to flow and shimmer: where there had been a smooth and shining surface, a great opening had appeared. Nothing was visible within it, even to the questing eyes of the camera. It was as dark and shadowed as the entrance to a cave.

Out of the orifice, a wide, glittering gangway extruded itself and drove purposefully towards the ground. It seemed a solid sheet of metal with handrails along either side. There were no steps; it was steep and smooth as a toboggan slide and, one would have thought, equally impossible to ascend or descend in any ordinary manner.

The world was watching that dark portal, within which nothing had yet stirred. Then the seldom-heard yet unforgettable voice of Karellen floated softly down from some hidden source. His message could scarcely have been more unexpected.

"There are some children by the foot of the gangway. I would like two of them to come up and meet me."

There was silence for a moment. Then a boy and a girl broke from the crowd and walked, with complete lack of self-consciousness, towards the gangway and into history. Others followed, but stopped when Karellen's chuckle came from the ship.

"Two will be enough."

Eagerly anticipating the adventure, the children—they could not have been more than six years old—jumped on to the metal slide. Then the first miracle happened.

Waving cheerfully to the crowds beneath, and to their anxious parents—who, too late, had probably remembered the legend of the Pied Piper—the children began swiftly ascending the steep slope. Yet their legs were motionless, and soon it was clear also that their bodies were tilted at right angles to that peculiar gangway. It possessed a private gravity of its own, one which could ignore that of Earth. The children were still enjoying this novel experience, and wondering what was drawing them upwards, when they disappeared into the ship.

A vast silence lay over the whole world for the space of twenty seconds—though, afterward, no one could believe that the time had been so short. Then the darkness of the great opening seemed to move forward, and Karellen came forth into the sunlight. The boy was sitting on his left arm, the girl on his right. They were both too busy playing with Karellen's wings to take any notice of the watching multitude.

It was a tribute to the Overlords' psychology, and to their careful years of preparation, that only a few people fainted. Yet there could have been fewer still, anywhere in the world, who did not feel the ancient terror brush for one awful instant against their minds before reason banished it forever.

There was no mistake. The leathery wings, the little horns, the barbed tail—all were there. The most terrible of all legends had come to life, out of the unknown past. Yet now it stood smiling, in ebon majesty, with the sunlight gleaming upon its tremendous body, and with a human child resting trustfully on either arm.

✳ CHAPTER FIVE

Fifty years is ample time in which to change a world and its people almost beyond recognition. All that is required for the task are a sound knowledge of social engineering, a clear sight of the intended goal—and power.

These things the Overlords possessed. Though their goal was hidden, their knowledge was obvious—and so was their power.

That power took many forms, few of them realized by the peoples whose destinies the Overlords now ruled. The might enshrined in their great ships had been clear enough for every eye to see. But behind that display of sleeping force were other and much subtler weapons.

"All political problems," Karellen had once told Stormgren, "can be solved by the correct application of power."

"That sounds a rather cynical remark," Stormgren had replied doubtfully. "It's a little too much like 'Might is Right'. In our own past, the use of power has been notably unsuccessful in solving anything."

"The operative word is *correct*. You have never possessed real power, or the knowledge necessary to apply it. As in all problems, there are efficient and inefficient approaches. Suppose, for example, that one of your nations, led by some fanatical ruler, tried to revolt against me. The highly inefficient answer to such a threat would be some billions of horsepower in the shape of atomic bombs. If I used enough bombs, the solution would be complete and final. It would also, as I remarked, be inefficient—even if it possessed no other defects."

"And the efficient solution?"

"That requires about as much power as a small radio transmitter —and rather similar skills to operate. For it's the *application* of the power, not its amount, that matters. How long do you think Hitler's career as dictator of Germany would have lasted, if wherever he went a voice was talking quietly in his ear? Or if a steady musical note, loud enough to drown all other sounds and to prevent sleep, filled his brain night and day? Nothing brutal, you appreciate. Yet, in the final analysis, just as irresistible as a tritium bomb."

"I see," said Stormgren, "and there would be no place to hide?"

"No place where I could not send my—ah—devices if I felt sufficiently strongly about it. And that is why I shall never have to use really drastic methods to maintain my position."

The great ships, then, had never been more than symbols, and now the world knew that all save one had been phantoms. Yet, by their mere presence, they had changed the history of Earth. Now their task was done, and their achievement lingered behind them to go echoing down the centuries.

Karellen's calculations had been accurate. The shock of revulsion had passed swiftly, though there were many who prided themselves on their freedom from superstition yet would never be able to face one of the Overlords. There was something strange here, something beyond all reason or logic. In the Middle Ages, people believed in the Devil and feared him. But this was the twenty-first century: could it be that, after all, there was such a thing as racial memory?

It was, of course, universally assumed that the Overlords, or beings of the same species, had come into violent conflict with ancient man. The meeting must have lain in the remote past, for it had left no traces in recorded history. Here was another puzzle, and Karellen would give no help in its solution.

The Overlords, though they had now shown themselves to man, seldom left their one remaining ship. Perhaps they found it physically uncomfortable on Earth, for their size, and the existence of their wings, indicated that they came from a world of much lower gravity. They were never seen without a belt adorned with complex mechanisms which, it was generally believed, controlled their weight and enabled them to communicate with each other. Direct sunlight was painful to them, and they never stayed in it for more than a few seconds. When they had to go into the open for any length of time, they wore dark glasses which gave them a somewhat incongruous appearance. Though they seemed able to breathe terrestrial air, they sometimes carried small cylinders of gas from which they refreshed themselves occasionally.

Perhaps these purely physical problems accounted for their aloofness. Only a small fraction of the human race had ever actually met an Overlord in the flesh, and no one could guess how many of them were aboard Karellen's ship. No more than five had ever been seen together at one time, but there might be hundreds, even thousands, of them aboard that tremendous vessel.

In many ways, the appearance of the Overlords had raised more problems than it had solved. Their origin was still unknown, their biology a source of endless speculation. On many matters they would give information freely, but on others their behavior could only be described as secretive. On the whole, however, this did not annoy anyone except the scientists. The average man, though he might prefer not to meet the Overlords, was grateful to them for what they had done to his world.

By the standards of all earlier ages, it was Utopia. Ignorance, disease, poverty, and fear had virtually ceased to exist. The memory of war was fading into the past as a nightmare vanishes with the dawn; soon it would lie outside the experience of all living men.

With the energies of mankind directed into constructive channels, the face of the world had been remade. It was, almost literally, a new world. The cities that had been good enough for earlier generations had been rebuilt—or deserted and left as museum specimens when they had ceased to serve any useful purpose. Many cities had already been abandoned in this manner, for the whole pattern of industry and commerce had changed completely. Production had become largely automatic: the robot factories poured forth consumer goods in such unending streams that all the ordinary necessities of life were virtually free. Men worked for the sake of the luxuries they desired: or they did not work at all.

It was One World. The old names of the old countries were still used, but they were no more than convenient postal divisions. There was no one on earth who could not speak English, who could not read, who was not within range of a television set, who could not visit the other side of the planet within twenty-four hours. . . .

Crime had practically vanished. It had become both unnecessary and impossible. When no one lacks anything, there is no point in stealing. Moreover, all potential criminals knew that there could be no escape from the surveillance of the Overlords. In the early days of their rule, they had intervened so effectively on behalf of law and order that the lesson had never been forgotten.

Crimes of passion, though not quite extinct, were almost unheard of. Now that so many of its psychological problems had been removed, humanity was far saner and less irrational. And what earlier ages would have called vice was now no more than eccentricity—or, at the worst, bad manners.

One of the most noticeable changes had been a slowing down of the mad tempo that had so characterized the twentieth century. Life was more leisurely than it had been for generations. It therefore had less zest for the few, but more tranquility for the many. Western man had relearned—what the rest of the world had never forgotten—that there was nothing sinful in leisure as long as it did not degenerate into mere sloth.

Whatever problems the future might bring, time did not yet hang heavy on humanity's hands. Education was now much more thorough and much more protracted. Few people left college before twenty—and that was merely the first stage, since they normally returned again at twenty-five for at least three more years, after travel and experience had broadened their minds. Even then, they would probably take refresher courses at intervals for the remainder of their lives in the subjects that particularly interested them.

This extension of human apprenticeship so far past the beginning of physical maturity had given rise to many social changes. Some of these had been necessary for generations, but earlier periods had refused to face the challenge—or had pretended that it did not exist. In particular, the patterns of sexual *mores*—insofar as there had ever been one pattern—had altered radically. It had been virtually shattered by two inventions, which were, ironically enough, of purely human origin and owed nothing to the Overlords.

The first was a completely reliable oral contraceptive: the second was an equally infallible method—as certain as fingerprinting, and based on a very detailed analysis of the blood—of identifying the father of any child. The effect of these two inventions upon human society could only be described as devastating, and they had swept away the last remnants of the Puritan aberration.

Another great change was the extreme mobility of the new society. Thanks to the perfection of air transport, everyone was free to go anywhere at a moment's notice. There was more room in the skies than there had ever been on the roads, and the twenty-first century had repeated, on a larger scale, the great American achievement of putting a nation on wheels. It had given wings to the world.

Though not literally. The ordinary private flyer or aircar had no wings at all, or indeed any visible control surfaces. Even the clumsy rotor blades of the old helicopters had been banished. Yet Man had not discovered antigravity: only the Overlords possessed that ultimate secret. His aircars were propelled by forces which the Wright brothers would have understood. Jet reaction, used both directly and in the more subtle form of boundary layer control, drove his flyers forward and held them in the air. As no laws or edicts of the Overlords could have done, the ubiquitous little aircars had washed away the last barriers between the different tribes of mankind.

Profounder things had also passed. It was a completely secular age. Of the faiths that had existed before the coming of the Overlords, only a form of purified Buddhism—perhaps the most austere of all religions—still survived. The creeds that had been based upon miracles and revelations had collapsed utterly. With the rise of education, they had already been slowly dissolving, but for a while the Overlords had taken no sides in the matter. Though Karellen was often asked to express his views on religion, all that he would say was that a man's beliefs were his own affair, so long as they did not interfere with the liberty of others.

Perhaps the old faiths would have lingered for generations yet, had it not been for human curiosity. It was known that the Overlords had access to the past, and more than once historians had appealed to Karellen to settle some ancient controversy. It may have been that he had grown tired of such questions, but it is more likely that he knew perfectly well what the outcome of his generosity would be. . . .

The instrument he handed over on permanent loan to the World History Foundation was nothing more than a television receiver with an elaborate set of controls for determining co-ordinates in time and space. It must have been linked somehow to a far more complex machine, operating on principles that no one could imagine, aboard Karellen's ship. One had merely to adjust the controls, and a window into the past was opened up. Almost the whole of human history for the past five thousand years became accessible in an instant. Earlier than that the machine would not go, and there were baffling blanks all down the ages. They might have had some natural cause, or they might be due to deliberate censorship by the Overlords.

Though it had always been obvious to any rational mind that *all* the world's religious writings could not be true, the shock was nevertheless profound. Here was a revelation which no one could doubt or deny: here, seen by some unknown magic of Overlord science, were the true beginnings of all the world's great faiths. Most of them were noble and inspiring—but that was not enough. Within a few days, all mankind's multitudinous messiahs had lost their divinity. Beneath the fierce and passionless light of truth, faiths that had sustained millions for twice a thousand years vanished like morning dew. All the good and all the evil they had wrought were swept suddenly into the past, and could touch the minds of men no more.

Humanity had lost its ancient gods: now it was old enough to have no need for new ones.

Though few realized it as yet, the fall of religion had been paralleled by a decline in science. There were plenty of technologists, but few original workers extending the frontiers of human knowledge. Curiosity remained, and the leisure to indulge in it, but the heart had been taken out of fundamental scientific research. It seemed futile to spend a lifetime searching for secrets that the Overlords had probably uncovered ages before.

This decline had been partly disguised by an enormous efflorescence of the descriptive sciences such as zoology, botany, and observational astronomy. There had never been so many amateur scientists gathering facts for their own amusement—but there were few theoreticians correlating these facts.

The end of strife and conflict of all kinds had also meant the virtual end of creative art. There were myriads of performers, amateur and professional, yet there had been no really outstanding new works of literature, music, painting, or sculpture for a generation. The world was still living on the glories of a past that could never return.

No one worried except a few philosophers. The race was too intent upon savoring its new-found freedom to look beyond the pleasures of the present. Utopia was here at last: its novelty had not yet been assailed by the supreme enemy of all Utopias—boredom.

Perhaps the Overlords had the answer to that, as they had to all other problems. No one knew—any more than they knew, a lifetime after their arrival, what their ultimate purpose might be. Mankind had grown to trust them, and to accept without question the superhuman altruism that had kept Karellen and his companions so long exiled from their homes.

If, indeed, it was altruism. For there were still some who wondered if the policies of the Overlords would always coincide with the true welfare of humanity.

 CHAPTER SIX

When Rupert Boyce sent out the invitations for his party, the total mileage involved was impressive. To list only the first dozen guests, there were: the Fosters from Adelaide, the Shoenbergers from Haiti, the Farrans from Stalingrad, the Moravias from Cincinnati, the Ivankos from Paris, and the Sullivans from the general vicinity of Easter Island, but approximately four kilometers down on the ocean bed. It was a considerable compliment to Rupert that although thirty guests had been invited, over forty turned up. Only the Krauses let him down, and that was simply because they forgot about the International Date Line and arrived twenty-four hours late.

By noon an imposing collection of flyers had accumulated in the park, and the later arrivals would have quite a distance to walk once they had found somewhere to land. The assembled vehicles ranged from one-man Flitterbugs to family Cadillacs which were more like airborne palaces than sensible flying machines. In this age, however, nothing could be deduced concerning the social status of the guests from their modes of transport.

"It's a very *ugly* house," said Jean Morrel as the Meteor spiralled down. "It looks rather like a box that somebody's stepped on."

George Greggson, who had an old-fashioned dislike of automatic landings, readjusted the rate-of-descent control before answering.

"It's hardly fair to judge the place from *this* angle," he replied, sensibly enough. "From ground level it may look quite different."

George selected a landing place and they floated to rest between another Meteor and something that neither of them could identify. It looked very fast and, Jean thought, very uncomfortable. One of Rupert's technical friends, she decided, had probably built it himself. She had an idea that there was a law against that sort of thing.

The heat hit them like a blast from a blowtorch as they stepped out of the flyer. It seemed to suck the moisture from their bodies, and George almost imagined that he could feel his skin cracking. It was partly their own fault, of course. They had left Alaska three hours before, and should have remembered to adjust the cabin temperature accordingly.

"What a place to live!" gasped Jean. "I thought this climate was supposed to be controlled."

"So it is," replied George. "This was all desert once—and look at it now. Come on—it'll be all right indoors!"

Rupert's voice, slightly larger than life, boomed cheerfully in their ears. Their host was standing beside the flyer, a glass in each hand, looking down at them with a roguish expression. He looked down at them for the simple reason that he was about twelve feet tall: he was also semitransparent. One could see right through him without much difficulty.

"This is a fine trick to play on your guests!" protested George. He grabbed at the drinks, which he could just reach. His hand, of course, went right through them. "I hope you've got something more substantial for us when we reach the house!"

"Don't worry!" laughed Rupert. "Just give your order now, and it'll be ready by the time you arrive."

"Two large beers, cooled in liquid air," said George promptly. "We'll be right there."

Rupert nodded, put down one of his glasses on an invisible table, adjusted an equally invisible control, and promptly vanished from sight.

"Well!" said Jean. "That's the first time I've seen one of those gadgets in action. How did Rupert get hold of it? I thought only the Overlords had them."

"Have you ever known Rupert *not* get anything he wanted?" replied George. "That's just the toy for him. He can sit comfortably in his studio and go wandering round half of Africa. No heat, no bugs, no exertion—and the icebox always in reach. I wonder what Stanley and Livingstone would have thought?"

The sun put an end to further conversation until they had reached the house. As they approached the front door (which was not very easy to distinguish from the rest of the glass wall facing them) it swung automatically open with a fanfare of trumpets. Jean guessed, correctly, that she would be heartily sick of that fanfare before the day was through.

The current Mrs. Boyce greeted them in the delicious coolness of the hall. She was, if the truth be known, the main reason for the good turnout of guests. Perhaps half of them would have come in any case to see Rupert's new house: the waverers had been decided by the reports of Rupert's new wife.

There was only one adjective that adequately described her. She was distracting. Even in a world where beauty was almost commonplace, men would turn their heads when she entered the room. She was, George guessed, about one quarter Negro. Her features were practically Grecian and her hair was long and lustrous. Only the dark, rich texture of her skin—the overworked word "chocolate" was the only one that described it—revealed her mixed ancestry.

"You're Jean and George, aren't you?" she said, holding out her hand. "I'm so pleased to meet you. Rupert is doing something complicated with the drinks—come along and meet everybody."

Her voice was a rich contralto that sent little shivers running up and down George's back, as if someone was playing on his spine like a flute. He looked nervously at Jean, who had managed to force a somewhat artificial smile, and finally recovered his voice.

' "It's—it's very nice to meet you," he said lamely. "We've been looking forward to this party."

"Rupert *always* gives such nice parties," put in Jean. By the way she accented the "always," one knew perfectly well she was thinking, Every time he gets married. George flushed slightly and gave Jean a glance of reproof, but there was no sign that their hostess noticed the barb. She was friendliness itself as she ushered them into the main lounge, already half packed with a representative collection of Rupert's numerous friends. Rupert himself was sitting at the console of what seemed to be a television engineer's control unit: it was, George assumed, the device that had projected his image out to meet them. He was busily demonstrating it by surprising two more arrivals as they descended into the parking place, but paused just long enough to greet Jean and George and to apologize for having given their drinks to somebody else.

"You'll find plenty more over there," he said, waving one hand vaguely behind him while he adjusted controls with the other. "Just make yourself at home. You know most of the people here—Maia will introduce you to the rest. Good of you to come."

"Good of you to invite us," said Jean, without much conviction. George had already departed towards the bar and she made her way after him, occasionally exchanging greetings with someone she recognized. About three-quarters of those present were perfect strangers, which was the normal state of affairs at one of Rupert's parties.

"Let's explore," she said to George when they had refreshed themselves and waved to everyone they knew. "I want to look at the house."

George, with a barely concealed backward look at Maia Boyce, followed after her. There was a faraway look in his eyes that Jean didn't like in the least. It was such a nuisance that men were fundamentally polygamous. On the other hand, if they weren't . . . Yes, perhaps it was better this way, after all.

George quickly came back to normal as they investigated the wonders of Rupert's new abode. The house seemed very large for two people, but this was just as well in view of the frequent overloads it would have to handle. There were two stories, the upper considerably larger so that it overhung and provided shade around the ground floor. The degree of mechanization was considerable, and the kitchen closely resembled the cockpit of an airliner.

"Poor Ruby!" said Jean. "She would have loved this place."

"From what I've heard," replied George, who had no great sympathy for the last Mrs. Boyce, "she's perfectly happy with her Australian boy-friend."

This was such common knowledge that Jean could hardly contradict it, so she changed the subject.

"She's awfully pretty, isn't she?"

George was sufficiently alert to avoid the trap.

"Oh, I suppose so," he replied indifferently. "That is, of course, if one likes brunettes."

"Which you don't, I take it," said Jean sweetly.

"Don't be jealous, dear," chuckled George, stroking her platinum hair. "Let's go and look at the library. What floor do you think *that* will be on?"

"It must be up here: there's no more room down below. Besides, that fits in with the general design. All the living, eating, sleeping, and so on's relegated to the ground floor. This is the fun and games department—though I still think it's a crazy idea having a swimming pool upstairs."

"I guess there's some reason for it," said George, opening a door experimentally. "Rupert must have had skilled advice when he built this place. I'm sure he couldn't have done it himself."

"You're probably right. If he had, there'd have been rooms without doors, and stairways leading nowhere. In fact, I'd be afraid to step inside a house that Rupert had designed all by himself."

"Here we are," said George, with the pride of a navigator making landfall, "the fabulous Boyce collection in its new home. I wonder just how many of them Rupert has really read."

The library ran the whole width of the house, but was virtually divided into half a dozen small rooms by the great bookcases extending across it. These held, if George remembered correctly, some fifteen thousand volumes—almost everything of importance that had ever been published on the nebulous subjects of magic, psychic research, divining, telepathy, and the whole range of elusive phenomena lumped in the category of paraphysics. It was a very peculiar hobby for anyone to have in this age of reason. Presumably it was simply Rupert's particular form of escapism.

George noticed the smell the moment he entered the room. It was faint but penetrating, not so much unpleasant as puzzling. Jean had observed it too: her forehead was wrinkled in the effort of identification. Acetic acid, thought George—that's the nearest thing to it. But it's got something else as well. . . .

The library terminated in a small open space just large enough for a table, two chairs and some cushions. This, presumably, was where Rupert did most of his reading. Someone was reading there now, in an unnaturally dim light.

Jean gave a little gasp and clutched at George's hand. Her reaction was, perhaps, excusable. It was one thing to watch a television picture, quite another to meet the reality. George, who was seldom surprised by anything, rose to the occasion at once.

"I hope we haven't disturbed you, Sir," he said politely. "We'd no idea that there was anyone here. Rupert never told us . . ."

The Overlord put down the book, looked at them closely, then commenced reading again. There was nothing impolite about the action, coming as it did from a being who could read, talk, and probably do several other things at the same time. Nevertheless, to human observers the spectacle was disturbingly schizophrenic.

"My name is Rashaverak," said the Overlord amiably. "I'm afraid I'm not being very sociable, but Rupert's library is a difficult place from which to escape."

Jean managed to suppress a nervous giggle. Their unexpected fellow guest was, she noticed, reading at the rate of a page every two seconds. She did not doubt that he was assimilating every word, and she wondered if he could manage to read a book with each eye. "And then, of course," she thought to herself, "he could go on to learn Braille so he could use his fingers. . . ." The resulting mental picture was too comic to be comfortable, so she tried to suppress it by entering into the conversation. After all, it was not every day that one had a chance of talking to one of the masters of Earth.

George let her chatter on, after he had made the introductions, hoping that she wouldn't say anything tactless. Like Jean, he had never seen an Overlord in the flesh. Though they mixed socially with government officials, scientists, and others who dealt with them in the course of business, he had never heard of one being present at an ordinary private party. One inference was that this party was not as private as it seemed. Rupert's possession of a piece of Overlord equipment also hinted at this, and George began to wonder, in capital letters, just What Was Going On. He would have to tackle Rupert about this when he could get him into a corner.

Since the chairs were too small for him, Rashaverak was sitting on the floor, apparently quite at ease, since he had ignored the cushions only a meter away. As a result, his head was a mere two meters from the ground, and George had a unique chance of studying extraterrestrial biology. Unfortunately, as he knew little about terrestrial biology either, he was not able to learn much that he did not already know. Only the peculiar, and by no means unpleasant, acid odor was new to him. He wondered how humans smelt to the Overlords, and hoped for the best.

There was nothing really anthropomorphic about Rashaverak. George could understand the way in which, if seen from a distance by ignorant, terrified savages, the Overlords could be mistaken for winged men, and so could have given rise to the conventional portrait of the Devil. From as close as this, however, some of the illusion vanished. The little horns (what function did they serve? wondered George) were as per specification, but the body was neither like that of a man nor that of any animal Earth had ever known. Coming from a totally alien evolutionary tree, the Overlords were neither mammals, insects, nor reptiles. It was not even certain that they were vertebrates: their hard, external armor might well be their only supporting framework.

Rashaverak's wings were folded so that George could not see them clearly, but his tail, looking like a piece of armored pipe, lay neatly curled under him. The famous barb was not so much an arrowhead as a large, flat diamond. Its purpose, it was now generally accepted, was to give stability in flight, like the tail feathers of a bird. From scanty facts and suppositions such as these, scientists had concluded that the Overlords came from a world of low gravity and very dense atmosphere.

Rupert's voice suddenly bellowed from a concealed speaker.

"Jean! George! Where the hell are you hiding? Come down and join the party. People are beginning to talk."

"Perhaps I'd better go, too," said Rashaverak, putting his book back on the shelf. He did that quite easily, without moving from the floor, and George noticed for the first time that he had two opposed thumbs, with five fingers between them. I'd hate to do arithmetic, George thought to himself, in a system based on fourteen.

Rashaverak getting to his feet was an impressive sight, and as the Overlord bent to avoid the ceiling it became obvious that, even if they were anxious to mix with human beings, the practical difficulties would be considerable.

Several more cargoes of guests had arrived in the last half hour, and the room was now quite crowded. Rashaverak's arrival made matters a good deal worse, because everyone in the adjacent rooms came running in to see him. Rupert was obviously very pleased with the sensation. Jean and George were much less gratified, as no one took any notice of them. Indeed, few people could see them, because they were standing behind the Overlord.

"Come over here, Rashy, and meet some of the folks," shouted Rupert. "Sit on this divan—then you can stop scraping the ceiling."

Rashaverak, his tail draped over his shoulder, moved across the room like an icebreaker worrying its way through a pack. As he sat down beside Rupert, the room seemed to become much larger again and George let out a sigh of relief.

"It gave me claustrophobia when he was standing. I wonder how Rupert got hold of him—this could be an interesting party."

"Fancy Rupert addressing him like that, in public too. But he didn't seem to mind. It's all very peculiar."

"I bet you he *did* mind. The trouble with Rupert is that he likes to show off, and he's got no tact. And that reminds me—some of those questions you asked!"

"Such as?"

"Well—'How long have you been here?' 'How do you get on with Supervisor Karellen?' 'Do you like it on Earth?' Really, darling! You just *don't* talk to Overlords that way!"

"I don't see why not. It's about time someone did."

Before the discussion could get acrimonious, they were accosted by the Shoenbergers and fission rapidly occurred. The girls went off in one direction to discuss Mrs. Boyce; the men went in another and did exactly the same thing, though from a different viewpoint. Benny Shoenberger, who was one of George's oldest friends, had a good deal of information on the subject.

"For heaven's sake don't tell anyone," he said. "Ruth doesn't know this, but *I* introduced her to Rupert."

"I think," George remarked enviously, "that she's much too good for Rupert. However, it can't possibly last. She'll soon get fed up with him." This thought seemed to cheer him considerably.

"Don't you believe it! Besides being a beauty, she's a really nice person. It's high time someone took charge of Rupert, and she's just the girl to do it."

Both Rupert and Maia were now sitting beside Rashaverak, receiving their guests in state. Rupert's parties seldom had any focal point, but usually consisted of half a dozen independent groups intent on their own affairs. This time, however, the whole gathering had found a center of attraction. George felt rather sorry for Maia. This should have been her day, but Rashaverak had partially eclipsed her.

"Look," said George, nibbling at a sandwich, "how the devil has Rupert got hold of an Overlord? I've never heard of such a thing—but he seems to take it for granted. He never even mentioned it when he invited us."

Benny chuckled.

"Just another of his little surprises. You'd better ask him about it. But this isn't the first time it's happened, after all. Karellen's been to parties at the White House and Buckingham Palace, and—"

"Heck, *that's* different! Rupert's a perfectly ordinary citizen."

"And maybe Rashaverak's a very minor Overlord. But you'd better ask them."

"I will," said George, "just as soon as I can get Rupert by himself."

"Then you'll have to wait a long time."

Benny was right, but as the party was now warming up it was easy to be patient. The slight paralysis which the appearance of Rashaverak had cast over the assembly had now vanished. There was still a small group around the Overlord, but elsewhere the usual fragmentation had taken place and everyone was behaving quite naturally.

Without bothering to turn his head, George could see a famous film producer, a minor poet, a mathematician, two actors, an atomic power engineer, a game warden, the editor of a weekly news magazine, a statistician from the World Bank, a violin virtuoso, a professor of archaeology, and an astrophysicist. There were no other representatives of George's own profession, television studio design —which was a good thing as he wanted to get away from shop. He loved his work: indeed, in this age, for the first time in human history, no one worked at tasks they did not like. But George was the kind of man who could lock the studio doors behind him at the end of the day.

He finally trapped Rupert in the kitchen, experimenting with drinks. It seemed a pity to bring him back to earth when he had such a faraway look in his eye, but George could be ruthless when necessary.

"Look here, Rupert," he began, perching himself on the nearest table. "I think you owe us all some explanations."

"Um," said Rupert thoughtfully, rolling his tongue round his mouth. "Just a teeny bit too much gin, I'm afraid."

"Don't hedge, and don't pretend you're not still sober, because I know perfectly well you are. Where does your Overlord friend come from, and what's he doing here?"

"Didn't I tell you?" said Rupert. "I thought I'd explained it to everybody. You couldn't have been around—of course, you were hiding up in the library." He chuckled in a manner which George found offensive. "It's the library, you know, that brought Rashy here."

"How extraordinary!"

"Why?"

George paused, realizing that this would require tact. Rupert was very proud of his peculiar collection.

"Er—well, when you consider what the Overlords know about science, I should hardly think they'd be interested in psychic phenomena and all that sort of nonsense."

"Nonsense or not," replied Rupert, "they're interested in human psychology, and I've got some books that can teach them a lot. Just before I moved here some Deputy Under-Overlord, or Over-Underlord, got in touch with me and asked if they could borrow about fifty of my rarest volumes. One of the keepers of the British Museum library had put him on to me, it seemed. Of course, you can guess what I said."

"I can't imagine."

"Well, I replied very politely that it had taken me twenty years to get my library together. They were welcome to study my books, *but* they'd darn well have to read them here. So Rashy came along and has been absorbing about twenty volumes a day. I'd love to know what he makes of them."

George thought this over, then shrugged his shoulders in disgust.

"Frankly," he said, "my opinion of the Overlords goes down. I thought they had better things to do with their time."

"You're an incorrigible materialist, aren't you? I don't think Jean will agree at all. But even from your oh-so-practical viewpoint, it still makes sense. Surely you'd study the superstitions of any primitive race you were having dealings with!"

"I suppose so," said George, not quite convinced. The table top was feeling hard, so he rose to his feet. Rupert had now mixed the drinks to his satisfaction and was heading back to his guests. Querulous voices could already be heard demanding his presence.

"Hey!" protested George, "just before you disappear there's one other question. How did you get hold of that two-way television gadget you tried to frighten us with?"

"Just a bit of bargaining. I pointed out how valuable it would be for a job like mine, and Rashy passed the suggestion on to the right quarters."

"Forgive me for being so obtuse, but what *is* your new job? I suppose, of course, it's something to do with animals."

"That's right. I'm a supervet. My practice covers about ten thousand square kilometers of jungle, and as my patients won't come to me I've got to look for them."

"Rather a full time job."

"Oh, of course it isn't practical to bother about the small fry. Just lions, elephants, rhinos, and so on. Every morning I set the controls for a height of a hundred meters, sit down in front of the screen and go cruising over the countryside. When I find anyone in trouble I climb into my flyer and hope my bedside manner will work. Sometimes it's a bit tricky. Lions and suchlike are easy—but trying to puncture a rhino from the air with an anesthetic dart is the devil of a job."

"*Rupert!*" yelled someone from the next room.

"Now look what you've done! You've made me forget my guests. There—you take that tray. Those are the ones with vermouth —I don't want to get them mixed up."

It was just before sunset that George found his way up to the roof. For a number of excellent reasons he had a slight headache and felt like escaping from the noise and confusion downstairs. Jean, who was a much better dancer than he was, still seemed to be enjoying herself hugely, and refused to leave. This annoyed George, who was beginning to feel alcoholically amorous, and he decided to have a quiet sulk beneath the stars.

One reached the roof by taking the escalator to the first floor and then climbing the spiral stairway round the intake of the air-conditioning plant. This led, through a hatchway, out onto the wide, flat roof. Rupert's flyer was parked at one end: the center area was a garden—already showing signs of running wild—and the rest was simply an observation platform with a few deck chairs placed on it. George flopped into one of these and regarded his surroundings with an imperial eye. He felt very much monarch of all he surveyed.

It was, to put it mildly, quite a view. Rupert's house had been built on the edge of a great basin, which sloped downwards towards the east into swamplands and lakes five kilometers away. Westward the land was flat and the jungle came almost to Rupert's back door. But beyond the jungle, at a distance that must have been at least fifty kilometers, a line of mountains ran like a great wall out of sight, to north and south. Their summits were streaked with snow, and the clouds above them were turning to fire as the sun descended, in the last few minutes of its daily journey. As he looked at those remote ramparts, George felt awed into a sudden sobriety.

The stars that sprang out in such indecent haste the moment the sun had set were completely strange to him. He looked for the Southern Cross, but without success. Though he knew very little of astronomy, and could recognize only a few constellations, the absence of familiar friends was disturbing. So were the noises drifting in from the jungle, uncomfortably close at hand. Enough of this fresh air, thought George. I'll go back to the party before a vampire bat, or something equally pleasant, comes flying up to investigate.

He was just starting to walk back when another guest emerged from the hatchway. It was now so dark that George could not see who it was, so he called out: "Hello, there. Have you had enough of it too?" His invisible companion laughed.

"Rupert's starting to show some of his movies. I've seen them all before."

"Have a cigarette," said George.

"Thanks."

By the flame of the lighter—George was fond of such antiques—he could now recognize his fellow guest, a strikingly handsome young Negro whose name George had been told but had immediately forgotten, like those of the twenty other complete strangers at the party. However, there seemed something familiar about him, and suddenly George guessed the truth.

"I don't think we've really met," he said, "but aren't you Rupert's new brother-in-law?"

"That's right. I'm Jan Rodricks. Everyone says that Maia and I look rather alike."

George wondered whether to commiserate with Jan for his newly acquired relative. He decided to let the poor fellow find out for himself; after all, it *was* just possible that Rupert would settle down this time.

"I'm George Greggson. This the first time you've been to one of Rupert's famous parties?"

"Yes. You certainly meet a lot of new people this way."

"And not only humans," added George. "This is the first chance I've had of meeting an Overlord socially."

The other hesitated for a moment before replying, and George wondered what sensitive spot he had struck. But the answer revealed nothing.

"I've never seen one before, either—except of course on TV."

There the conversation languished, and after a moment George realized that Jan wanted to be alone. It was getting cold, anyway, so he took his leave and rejoined the party.

The jungle was quiet now; as Jan leaned against the curving

wall of the air intake, the only sound he could hear was the faint murmur of the house as it breathed through its mechanical lungs. He felt very much alone, which was the way he wanted to be. He also felt highly frustrated—and that was something he had no desire to be at all.

✳ CHAPTER SEVEN

No Utopia can ever give satisfaction to everyone, all the time. As their material conditions improve, men raise their sights and become discontented with power and possessions that once would have seemed beyond their wildest dreams. And even when the external world has granted all it can, there still remain the searchings of the mind and the longings of the heart.

Jan Rodricks, though he seldom appreciated his luck, would have been even more discontented in an earlier age. A century before, his color would have been a tremendous, perhaps an overwhelming, handicap. Today, it meant nothing. The inevitable reaction that had given early twenty-first-century Negroes a slight sense of superiority had already passed away. The convenient word "nigger" was no longer taboo in polite society, but was used without embarrassment by everyone. It had no more emotional content than such labels as republican or methodist, conservative or liberal.

Jan's father had been a charming but somewhat feckless Scot, who had made a considerable name for himself as a professional magician. His death at the early age of forty-five had been brought about by the excessive consumption of his country's most famous product. Though Jan had never seen his father drunk, he was not sure that he had ever seen him sober.

Mrs. Rodricks, still very much alive, lectured in advanced probability theory at Edinburgh University. It was typical of the extreme mobility of Twenty-first-century Man that Mrs. Rodricks, who was coal black, had been born in Scotland, whereas her expatriate and blond husband had spent almost all his life in Haiti. Maia and Jan had never had a single home, but had oscillated between their parents' families like two small shuttlecocks. The treatment had been good fun, but had not helped to correct the instability they had both inherited from their father.

At twenty-seven, Jan still had several years of college life ahead of him before he needed to think seriously about his career. He had taken his bachelors' degrees without any difficulty, following a curriculum that would have seemed very strange a century before. His main subjects had been mathematics and physics, but as subsidiaries he had taken philosophy and music appreciation. Even by the high standards of the time, he was a first-rate amateur pianist.

In three years he would take his doctorate in engineering physics, with astronomy as a second subject. This would involve fairly hard work, but Jan rather welcomed that. He was studying at what was perhaps the most beautifully situated place of higher education in the world—the University of Cape Town, nestling at the foot of Table Mountain.

He had no material worries, yet he was discontented and saw no cure for his condition. To make matters worse, Maia's own happiness—though he did not grudge it in the least—had underlined the chief cause of his own trouble.

For Jan was still suffering from the romantic illusion—the cause of so much misery and so much poetry—that every man has only one real love in his life. At an unusually late age, he had lost his heart for the first time, to a lady more renowned for beauty than constancy. Rosita Tsien claimed, with perfect truth, to have the blood of Manchu emperors flowing in her veins. She still possessed many subjects, including most of the Faculty of Science at Cape. Jan had been taken prisoner by her delicate, flowerlike beauty, and the affair had proceeded far enough to make its termination all the more galling. He could not imagine what had gone wrong. . . .

He would get over it, of course. Other men had survived similar catastrophes without irreparable damage, had even reached the stage when they could say, "I'm sure I could never have been *really* serious about a woman like that!" But such detachment still lay far in the future, and at the moment Jan was very much at odds with life.

His other grievance was less easily remedied, for it concerned the impact of the Overlords upon his own ambitions. Jan was a romantic not only in heart but in mind. Like so many other young men since the conquest of the air had been assured, he had let his dreams and his imagination roam the unexplored seas of space.

A century before, Man had set foot upon the ladder that could lead him to the stars. At that very moment—could it have been coincidence?—the door to the planets had been slammed in his face. The Overlords had imposed few positive bans on any form of human activity (the conduct of war was perhaps the major exception) but research into space flight had virtually ceased. The challenge presented by the science of the Overlords was too great. For the moment, at least, Man had lost heart and had turned to other fields of activity. There was no point in developing rockets when the Overlords had infinitely superior means of propulsion, based on principles of which they had never given any hint.

A few hundred men had visited the Moon, for the purpose of establishing a lunar observatory. They had traveled as passengers in a small vessel loaned by the Overlords—and driven by rockets. It was obvious that little could be learned from a study of this primitive vehicle, even if its owners handed it over without reservation to inquisitive terrestrial scientists.

Man was, therefore, still a prisoner on his own planet. It was a much fairer, but a much smaller, planet than it had been a century before. When the Overlords had abolished war and hunger and disease, they had also abolished adventure.

The rising moon was beginning to paint the eastern sky with a pale, milky glow. Up there, Jan knew, was the main base of the Overlords, lying within the ramparts of Plato. Though the supply ships must have been coming and going for more than seventy years, it was only in Jan's lifetime that all concealment had been dropped and they had made their departure in clear sight of Earth. In the two hundred inch telescope, the shadows of the great ships could be clearly seen when the morning or evening sun cast them for miles across the lunar plains. Since everything that the Overlords did was of immense interest to mankind, a careful watch was kept of their comings and goings, and the pattern of their behavior (though not the reason for it) was beginning to emerge. One of those great shadows had vanished a few hours ago. That meant, Jan knew, that somewhere off the Moon an Overlord ship was lying in space, carrying out whatever routine was necessary before it began its journey to its distant, unknown home.

He had never seen one of those returning ships launch itself towards the stars. If conditions were good the sight was visible over half the world, but Jan had always been unlucky. One could never tell exactly when the take-off would be—and the Overlords did not advertise the fact. He decided he would wait another ten minutes, then rejoin the party.

What was that? Only a meteor sliding down through Eridanus. Jan relaxed, discovered his cigarette had gone out, and lit another.

He was halfway through it when, half a million kilometers away, the Stardrive went on. Up from the heart of the spreading moonglow a tiny spark began to climb towards the zenith. At first its movement was so slow that it could hardly be perceived, but second by second it was gaining speed. As it climbed it increased in brilliance, then suddenly faded from sight. A moment later it had reappeared, gaining speed and brightness. Waxing and waning with a peculiar rhythm, it ascended ever more swiftly into the sky, drawing a fluctuating line of light across the stars. Even if one did not know its real distance, the impression of speed was breathtaking; when one knew that the departing ship was somewhere beyond the moon, the mind reeled at the speeds and energies involved.

It was an unimportant by-product of those energies, Jan knew, that he was seeing now. The ship itself was invisible, already far ahead of that ascending light. As a high-flying jet may leave a vapor trail behind it, so the outward bound vessel of the Overlords left its own peculiar wake. The generally accepted theory—and there seemed little doubt of its truth—was that the immense accelerations of the Stardrive caused a local distortion of space. What Jan was seeing, he knew, was nothing less than the light of distant stars, collected and focused into his eye whenever conditions were favorable along the track of the ship. It was a visible proof of relativity —the bending of light in the presence of a colossal gravitational field.

Now the end of that vast, pencil-thin lens seemed to be moving more slowly, but that was only due to perspective. In reality the ship was still gaining speed: its path was merely being foreshortened as it hurled itself outwards to the stars. There would be many telescopes following it, Jan knew, as Earth's scientists tried to uncover the secrets of the Drive. Dozens of papers had already been published on the subject; no doubt the Overlords had read them with the greatest interest.

The phantom light was beginning to wane. Now it was a fading streak, pointing to the heart of the constellation Carina, as Jan had known that it would. The home of the Overlords was somewhere out there, but it might circle any one of a thousand stars in that sector of space. There was no way of telling its distance from the solar system.

It was all over. Though the ship had scarcely begun its journey, there was nothing more that human eyes could see. But in Jan's mind the memory of that shining path still burned, a beacon that would never fade as long as he possessed ambition and desire.

The party was over. Almost all the guests had climbed back into the sky and were now scattering to the four corners of the globe. There were, however, a few exceptions.

One was Norman Dodsworth, the poet, who had got unpleasantly drunk but had been sensible enough to pass out before any violent action proved necessary. He had been deposited, not very gently, on the lawn, where it was hoped that a hyaena would give him a rude awakening. For all practical purposes he could, therefore, be regarded as absent.

The other remaining guests were George and Jean. This was not George's idea at all: he wanted to go home. He disapproved of the friendship between Rupert and Jean, though not for the usual reason. George prided himself on being a practical, level-headed character, and regarded the interest which drew Jean and Rupert together as being not only childish in this age of science, but more than a little unhealthy. That anyone should still place the slightest credence in the supernormal seemed extraordinary to him, and finding Rashaverak here had shaken his faith in the Overlords.

It was now obvious that Rupert had been plotting some surprise, probably with Jean's connivance. George resigned himself gloomily to whatever nonsense was coming.

"I tried all sorts of things before I settled on *this*," said Rupert proudly. "The big problem is to reduce friction so that you get complete freedom of movement. The old-fashioned polished table and tumbler setup isn't bad, but it's been used for centuries now and I was sure that modern science could do better. And here's the result. Draw up your chairs—are you quite sure you don't want to join, Rashy?"

The Overlord seemed to hesitate for a fraction of a second. Then he shook his head. (Had they learned that habit on Earth? George wondered.)

"No, thank you," he replied. "I would prefer to observe. Some other time, perhaps."

"Very well—there's plenty of time to change your mind later."

Oh, is there? thought George, looking gloomily at his watch.

Rupert had shepherded his friends round a small but massive table, perfectly circular in shape. It had a flat plastic top which he lifted off to reveal a glittering sea of closely packed ball bearings. They were prevented from escaping by the table's slightly raised rim, and George found it quite impossible to imagine their purpose. The hundreds of reflected points of light formed a fascinating and hypnotic pattern, and he felt himself becoming slightly dizzy.

As they drew up their chairs, Rupert reached under the table and brought forth a disc some ten centimeters in diameter, which he placed on the surface of the ball bearings.

"There you are," he said. "You put your fingers on this, and it moves around with no resistance at all."

George eyed the device with profound distrust. He noted that the letters of the alphabet were placed at regular intervals—though in no particular order—round the circumference of the table. In addition there were the numbers 1 to 9, scattered at random among the letters, and two cards bearing the words "Yes" and "No." These were on opposite sides of the table.

"It looks like a lot of mumbo jumbo to me," he muttered. "I'm surprised that anyone takes it seriously in this age." He felt a little better after delivering this mild protest, which was aimed at Jean quite as much as Rupert. Rupert didn't pretend to have more than a detached scientific interest in these phenomena. He was openminded, but not credulous. Jean, on the other hand—well, George was sometimes a little worried about her. She really seemed to think that there was something in this business of telepathy and second sight.

Not until he had made his remark did George realize that it also implied a criticism of Rashaverak. He glanced nervously round but the Overlord showed no reaction. Which, of course, proved absolutely nothing at all.

Everyone had now taken up their positions. Going in a clockwise direction round the table were Rupert, Maia, Jan, Jean, George, and Benny Shoenberger. Ruth Shoenberger was sitting outside the circle with a notebook. She apparently had some objection to taking part in the proceedings, which had caused Benny to make obscurely sarcastic remarks about people who still took the Talmud seriously. However, she seemed perfectly willing to act as a recorder.

"Now listen," began Rupert, "for the benefit of skeptics like George, let's get this quite straight. Whether or not there's anything supernormal about this, *it works*. Personally, I think there's a purely mechanical explanation. When we put our hands on the disc, even though we may try to avoid influencing its movements, our subconscious starts playing tricks. I've analyzed lots of these seances, and I've never got answers that someone in the group mightn't have known or guessed—though sometimes they weren't aware of the fact. However, I'd like to carry out the experiment in these rather—ah—peculiar circumstances."

The Peculiar Circumstance sat watching them silently, but doubtless not with indifference. George wondered just what Rashaverak thought of these antics. Were his reactions those of an anthropologist watching some primitive religious rite? The whole setup was really quite fantastic, and George felt as big a fool as he had ever done in his life.

If the others felt equally foolish, they concealed their emotions. Only Jean looked flushed and excited, though that might have been the drinks.

"All set?" asked Rupert. "Very well." He paused impressively; then, addressing no one in particular, he called out: "Is there anybody there?"

George could feel the plate beneath his fingers tremble slightly. That was not surprising, considering the pressure being exerted upon it by the six people in the circle. It slithered around in a small figure "8," then came to rest back at the center.

"Is there anybody there?" repeated Rupert. In a more conversational tone of voice he added, "It's often ten or fifteen minutes before we get started. But sometimes—"

"Hush!" breathed Jean.

The plate was moving. It began to swing in a wide arc between the cards labelled "YES" and "NO." With some difficulty, George suppressed a giggle. Just what would it prove, he wondered, if the answer was "NO"? He remembered the old joke: "There's nobody here but us chickens, Massa. . . ."

But the answer was "YES." The plate came swiftly back to the center of the table. Somehow it now seemed alive, waiting for the next question. Despite himself, George began to be impressed.

"Who are you?" asked Rupert.

There was no hesitation now as the letters were spelled out. The plate darted across the table like a sentient thing, moving so swiftly that George sometimes found it hard to keep his fingers in contact. He could swear that he was not contributing to its motion. Glancing quickly round the table, he could see nothing suspicious in the faces of his friends. They seemed as intent, and as expectant, as he himself.

"IAMALL" spelled the plate, and returned to its point of equilibrium.

" 'I am all,' " repeated Rupert. "That's a typical reply. Evasive, yet stimulating. It probably means that there's nothing here except our combined minds." He paused for a moment, obviously deciding upon his next question. Then he addressed the air once more.

"Have you a message for anyone here?"

"NO" replied the plate promptly.

Rupert looked around the table.

"It's up to us; sometimes it volunteers information, but this time we'll have to ask definite questions. Anyone like to start?"

"Will it rain tomorrow?" said George jestingly.

At once the plate began to swing back and forth in the YES-NO line.

"That's a silly question," reproved Rupert. "It's bound to be raining *somewhere* and to be dry somewhere else. Don't ask questions that have ambiguous answers."

George felt appropriately squashed. He decided to let someone else have the next turn.

"What is my favorite color?" asked Maia.

"BLUE" came the prompt reply.

"That's quite correct."

"But it doesn't prove anything. At least three people here knew that," George pointed out.

"What's Ruth's favorite color?" asked Benny.

"RED."

"Is that right, Ruth?"

The recorder looked up from her notebook.

"Yes, it is. But Benny knows that, and he's in the circle."

"I didn't know," retorted Benny.

"You darn well ought to—I've told you enough times."

"Subconscious memory," murmured Rupert. "That often happens. But can we have some more *intelligent* questions, please? Now that this has started so well, I don't want it to peter out."

Curiously enough, the very triviality of the phenomenon was beginning to impress George. He was sure that there was no supernormal explanation; as Rupert had said, the plate was simply responding to their unconscious muscular movements. But this fact in itself was surprising and impressive: he would never have believed that such precise, swift replies could have been obtained. Once he tried to see if he could influence the board by making it spell out his own name. He got the "G," but that was all: the rest was nonsense. It was virtually impossible, he decided, for one person to take control without the remainder of the circle knowing it.

After half an hour, Ruth had taken down more than a dozen messages, some of them quite long ones. There were occasional spelling mistakes, and curiosities of grammar, but they were few. Whatever the explanation, George was now convinced that he was not contributing consciously to the results. Several times, as a word was being spelt out, he had anticipated the next letter and hence the meaning of the message. And on each occasion the plate had gone in a quite unexpected direction and spelt something totally different. Sometimes, indeed—since there was no pause to indicate the end of one word and the beginning of the next—the entire message was meaningless until it was complete and Ruth had read it back.

The whole experience gave George an uncanny impression of being in contact with some purposeful, independent mind. And yet there was no *conclusive* proof one way or the other. The replies were so trivial, so ambiguous. What, for example, could one make of:

BELIEVEINMANNATUREISWITHYOU.

Yet sometimes there were suggestions of profound, even disturbing truths:

REMEMBERMANISNOTALONENEARMANIS-
COUNTRYOFOTHERS

But of course everyone knew that—though could one be sure that the message merely referred to the Overlords?

George was growing very sleepy. It was high time, he thought drowsily, that they headed for home. This was all very intriguing, but it wasn't getting them anywhere and you could have too much of a good thing. He glanced around the table. Benny looked as if he might be feeling the same way, Maia and Rupert both appeared slightly glazed, and Jean—well, she had been taking it too seriously all along. Her expression worried George; it was almost as if she were afraid to stop—yet afraid to go on.

That left only Jan. George wondered what he thought of his brother-in-law's eccentricities. The young engineer had asked no questions, shown no surprise at any of the answers. He seemed to be studying the movement of the plate as if it was just another scientific phenomenon.

Rupert roused himself from the lethargy into which he appeared to have fallen.

"Let's have one more question," he said, "then we'll call it a day. What about you, Jan? You've not asked anything."

Surprisingly, Jan never hesitated. It was as if he had made his choice a long time ago, and had been waiting for the opportunity. He glanced once at the impassive bulk of Rashaverak, then called out in a clear, steady voice:

"Which star is the Overlords' sun?"

Rupert checked a whistle of surprise. Maia and Benny showed no reaction at all. Jean had closed her eyes and seemed to be asleep. Rashaverak had leaned forward so that he could look down into the circle over Rupert's shoulder.

And the plate began to move.

When it came to rest again, there was a brief pause: then Ruth asked, in a puzzled voice:

"What does NGS 549672 mean?"

She got no reply, for at the same moment George called out anxiously:

"Give me a hand with Jean. I'm afraid she's fainted."

⊁. CHAPTER EIGHT

"This man Boyce," said Karellen. "Tell me all about him."

The Supervisor did not use those actual words, of course, and the thoughts he really expressed were far more subtle. A human listener would have heard a short burst of rapidly modulated sound, not unlike a high-speed Morse sender in action. Though many samples of Overlord language had been recorded, they all defied analysis because of their extreme complexity. The speed of transmission made it certain that no interpreter, even if he had mastered the elements of the language, could ever keep up with the Overlords in their normal conversation.

The Supervisor for Earth stood with his back to Rashaverak, staring out across the multicolored gulf of the Grand Canyon. Ten kilometers away, yet scarcely veiled by distance, the terraced walls were catching the full force of the sun. Hundreds of meters down the shadowed slope at whose brim Karellen stood, a mule-train was slowly winding its way into the valley's depths. It was strange, Karellen thought, that so many human beings still seized every opportunity for primitive behavior. They could reach the bottom of the canyon in a fraction of the time, and in far greater comfort, if they chose. Yet they preferred to be jolted along tracks which were probably as unsafe as they looked.

Karellen made an imperceptible gesture with his hand. The great panorama faded from view, leaving only a shadowy blankness of indeterminate depth. The realities of his office and of his position crowded in upon the Supervisor once more.

"Rupert Boyce is a somewhat curious character," Rashaverak answered. "Professionally, he's in charge of animal welfare over an important section of the main African reservation. He's quite efficient, and interested in his work. Because he has to keep watch over several thousand square kilometers, he has one of the fifteen panoramic viewers we've so far issued on loan—with the usual safeguards, of course. It is, incidentally, the only one with full projection facilities. He was able to make a good case for these, so we let him have them."

"What was his argument?"

"He wanted to appear to various wild animals so that they could get used to seeing him, and so wouldn't attack when he was physically present. The theory has worked out quite well with animals that rely on sight rather than smell—though he'll probably get killed eventually. And, of course, there was another reason why we let him have the apparatus."

"It made him more co-operative?"

"Precisely. I originally contacted him because he has one of the world's finest libraries of books on parapsychology and allied subjects. He politely but firmly refused to lend any of them, so there was nothing to do but to visit him. I've now read about half his library. It has been a considerable ordeal."

"That I can well believe," said Karellen dryly. "Have you discovered anything among all the rubbish?"

"Yes—eleven clear cases of partial breakthrough, and twenty-seven probables. The material is so selective, however, that one cannot use it for sampling purposes. And the evidence is confused with mysticism—perhaps the prime aberration of the human mind."

"And what is Boyce's attitude to all this?"

"He pretends to be open-minded and skeptical, but it's clear that he would never have spent so much time and effort in this field unless he had some subconscious faith. I challenged him on this and he admitted that I was probably right. He would like to find some convincing proof. That is why he is always carrying out these experiments, even though he pretends that they are only games."

"You are sure he doesn't suspect that your interest is more than academic?"

"Quite sure. In many ways Boyce is remarkably obtuse and simple-minded. That makes his attempts to do research in this, of all fields, rather pathetic. There is no need to take any special action regarding him."

"I see. And what about the girl who fainted?"

"This is the most exciting feature of the entire affair. Jean Morrel was, almost certainly, the channel through which the information came. But she is twenty-six—far too old to be a Prime Contact herself, judging by all our previous experience. It must, therefore, be someone closely linked to her. The conclusion is obvious. We cannot have many more years to wait. We must transfer her to Category Purple: she may be the most important human being alive."

"I will do that. And what of the young man who asked the question? Was it random curiosity, or did he have some other motive?"

"It was chance that brought him there—his sister has just married Rupert Boyce. He had never met any of the other guests before. I am sure the question was unpremeditated, being inspired by the unusual conditions—and probably by my presence. Given these factors, it is hardly surprising that he acted in the way he did. His great interest is astronautics: he is secretary of the space-travel group at Cape Town University, and obviously intends to make this field his life study."

"His career should be interesting. Meanwhile, what action do you think he will take, and what shall we do about him?"

"He will undoubtedly make some checks as soon as he can. But there is no way in which he can prove the accuracy of his information, and because of its peculiar origin he is hardly likely to publish it. Even if he does, will it affect matters in the slightest?"

"I will have both situations evaluated," Karellen replied. "Though it is part of our Directive not to reveal our base, there is no way in which the information could be used against us."

"I agree. Rodricks will have some information which is of doubtful truth, and of no practical value."

"So it would seem," said Karellen. "But let us not be too certain. Human beings are remarkably ingenious, and often very persistent. It is never safe to underrate them, and it will be interesting to follow Mr. Rodricks' career. I must think about this further."

Rupert Boyce never really got to the bottom of it. When his guests had departed, rather less boisterously than usual, he had thoughtfully rolled the table back into its corner. The mild alcoholic fog prevented any profound analysis of what had happened, and even the actual facts were already slightly blurred. He had a vague idea that something of great but elusive importance had happened, and wondered if he should discuss it with Rashaverak. On second thought, he decided it might be tactless. After all, his brother-in-law had caused the trouble, and Rupert felt vaguely annoyed with young Jan. But was it Jan's fault? Was it anybody's fault? Rather guiltily, Rupert remembered that it had been *his* experiment. He decided, fairly successfully, to forget the whole business.

Perhaps he might have done something if the last page of Ruth's notebook could have been found, but it had vanished in the confusion. Jan always feigned innocence—and, well, one could hardly accuse Rashaverak. And no one could ever remember exactly what had been spelled out, except that it didn't seem to make any sense. . . .

The person most immediately affected had been George Greggson. He could never forget his feeling of terror as Jean pitched into his arms. Her sudden helplessness transformed her in that moment from an amusing companion to an object of tenderness and affection. Women had fainted—not always without forethought—since time immemorial, and men had invariably responded in the desired way. Jean's collapse was completely spontaneous, but it could not have been better planned. In that instant, as he realized later, George came to one of the most important decisions of his life. Jean was definitely the girl who mattered, despite her queer ideas and queerer friends. He had no intention of totally abandoning Naomi or Joy or Elsa or—what *was* her name?—Denise; but the time had come for something more permanent. He had no doubt that Jean would agree with him, for her feelings had been quite obvious from the start.

Behind his decision there was another factor of which he was unaware. Tonight's experience had weakened his contempt and skepticism for Jean's peculiar interests. He would never recognize the fact, but it was so—and it had removed the last barrier between them.

He looked at Jean as she lay, pale but composed, in the reclining chair of the flyer. There was darkness below, stars above. George had no idea, to within a thousand kilometers, where they might be—nor did he care. *That* was the business of the robot that was guiding them homewards and would land them in, so the control board announced, fifty-seven minutes from now.

Jean smiled back at him and gently dislodged her hand from his. "Just let me restore the circulation," she pleaded, rubbing her fingers. "I wish you'd believe me when I tell you I'm perfectly all right now."

"Then what do you think happened? Surely you remember *something?*"

"No—it's just a complete blank. I heard Jan ask his question—and then you were all making a fuss over me. I'm sure it was some kind of trance. After all—"

She paused, then decided not to tell George that this sort of thing had happened before. She knew how he felt about these matters, and had no desire to upset him further—and perhaps scare him away completely.

"After all—what?" asked George.

"Oh, nothing. I wonder what that Overlord thought about the whole business. We probably gave him more material than he bargained for."

Jean shivered slightly, and her eyes clouded.

"I'm afraid of the Overlords, George. Oh, I don't mean they're evil, or anything foolish like that. I'm sure they mean well and are doing what they think is best for us. I wonder just what their plans really are?"

George shifted uncomfortably.

"Men have been wondering *that* ever since they came to Earth," he said. "They'll tell us when we're ready for it—and, frankly, I'm not inquisitive. Besides, I've got more important things to bother about." He turned towards Jean and grasped her hands.

"What about going to Archives tomorrow and signing a contract for—let's say—five years?"

Jean looked at him steadfastly, and decided that, on the whole, she liked what she saw.

"Make it ten," she said.

Jan bided his time. There was no hurry, and he wanted to think. It was almost as if he feared to make any checks, lest the fantastic hope that had come into his mind be too swiftly destroyed. While he was still uncertain, he could at least dream.

Moreover, to take any further action he would have to see the Observatory librarian. She knew him and his interests too well, and would certainly be intrigued by his request. Probably it would make no difference, but Jan was determined to leave nothing to chance.

There would be a better opportunity in a week. He was being supercautious, he knew, but that added a schoolboy zest to the enterprise. Jan also feared ridicule quite as much as anything that the Overlords might conceivably do to thwart him. If he was embarking on a wild goose chase, no one else would ever know.

He had a perfectly good reason for going to London: the arrangements had been made weeks ago. Though he was too young and too unqualified to be a delegate, he was one of the three students who had managed to attach themselves to the official party going to the meeting of the International Astronomical Union. The vacancies had been there, and it seemed a pity to waste the opportunity, as he had not visited London since his childhood. He knew that very few of the dozens of papers to be delivered to the I.A.U. would be of the slightest interest to him, even if he could understand them. Like a delegate to any scientific congress, he would attend the lectures that looked promising, and spend the rest of the time talking with fellow enthusiasts, or simply sight-seeing.

London had changed enormously in the last fifty years. It now contained scarcely two million people, and a hundred times as many machines. It was no longer a great port, for with every country producing almost all its needs, the entire pattern of world trade had been altered. There were some goods that certain countries still made best, but they went directly by air to their destinations. The trade routes that had once converged on the great harbors, and later on the great airports, had finally dispersed into an intricate web-work covering the whole world, with no major nodal points.

Yet some things had not altered. The city was still a center of administration, of art, of learning. In these matters, none of the continental capitals could rival it—not even Paris, despite many claims to the contrary. A Londoner from a century before could still have found his way around, at least at the city's center, with no difficulty. There were new bridges over the Thames, but in the old places. The great, grimy railway stations had gone—banished to the suburbs. But the Houses of Parliament were unchanged: Nelson's solitary eye still stared down Whitehall: the dome of St. Paul's still stood above Ludgate Hill, though now there were taller buildings to challenge its pre-eminence.

And the guard still marched in front of Buckingham Palace.

All these things, thought Jan, could wait. It was vacation time, and he was lodged, with his two fellow students, in one of the University hostels. Bloomsbury also had not changed its character in the last century: it was still an island of hotels and boarding houses, though they no longer jostled each other so closely, or formed such endless, identical rows of soot-coated brick.

It was not until the second day of the Congress that Jan got his opportunity. The main papers were being read in the great assembly chamber of the Science Center, not far from the Concert Hall that had done so much to make London the musical metropolis of the world. Jan wanted to hear the first of the day's lectures, which, it was rumored, would completely demolish the current theory of the formation of the planets.

Perhaps it did, but Jan was little the wiser when he left after the interval. He hurried down to the directory, and looked up the rooms he wanted.

Some humorous civil servant had put the Royal Astronomical Society on the top floor of the great building, a gesture which the Council members fully appreciated as it gave them a magnificent view across the Thames and over the entire northern part of the city. There seemed to be nobody around, but Jan—clutching his membership card like a passport in case he was challenged—had no difficulty in locating the library.

It took him almost an hour to find what he wanted, and to learn how to handle the great star catalogues with their millions of entries. He was trembling slightly as he neared the end of his quest, and felt glad that there was no one around to see his nervousness.

He put the catalogue back among its fellows, and for a long time sat quite still, staring sightlessly at the wall of volumes before him. Then he slowly walked out into the still corridors, past the secretary's office (there was somebody there now, busily unpacking parcels of books) and down the stairs. He avoided the elevator, for he wanted to be free and unconfined. There was another lecture he had intended to hear, but that was no longer important now.

His thoughts were still in turmoil as he crossed to the embankment wall and let his eye follow the Thames on its unhurried way to the sea. It was hard for anyone with his training in orthodox science to accept the evidence that had now come into his hands. He could never be certain of its truth, yet the probability was overwhelming. As he paced slowly beside the river wall, he marshalled the facts one by one.

Fact one: no one at Rupert's party could possibly have known that he was going to ask that question. He had not known it himself: it had been a spontaneous reaction to the circumstances. Therefore, no one could have prepared any answer, or had it already lying in their minds.

Fact two: "NGS 549672" probably meant nothing to anyone except an astronomer. Though the great National Geographic Survey had been completed half a century before, its existence was known only to a few thousand specialists. And taking any number from it at random, no one could have said where that particular star lay in the heavens.

But—and this was Fact Three, which he had only this moment discovered—the small and insignificant star known as NGS 549672 was in precisely the right place. It lay in the heart of the constellation Carina, at the end of that shining trail Jan himself had seen, so few nights ago, leading from the solar system out across the depths of space.

It was an impossible coincidence. NGS 549672 *must* be the home of the Overlords. Yet to accept the fact violated all Jan's cherished ideas of scientific method. Very well—let them be violated. He must accept the fact that, somehow, Rupert's fantastic experiment had tapped a hitherto unknown source of knowledge.

Rashaverak? That seemed the most probable explanation. The Overlord had not been in the circle, but that was a minor point. However, Jan was not concerned with the mechanism of paraphysics: he was only interested in using the results.

Very little was known about NGS 549672: there had been nothing to distinguish it from a million other stars. But the catalogue gave its magnitude, its co-ordinates, and its spectral type. Jan would have to do a little research, and make a few simple calculations: then he would know, at least approximately, how far the world of the Overlords was from Earth.

A slow smile spread over Jan's face as he turned away from the Thames, back towards the gleaming white façade of the Science Center. Knowledge was power—and he was the only man on Earth who knew the origin of the Overlords. How he would use that knowledge he could not guess. It would lie safely in his mind, awaiting the moment of destiny.

✳ *CHAPTER NINE*

The human race continued to bask in the long, cloudless summer afternoon of peace and prosperity. Would there ever be a winter again? It was unthinkable. The age of reason, prematurely welcomed by the leaders of the French Revolution two and a half centuries before, had now really arrived. This time, there was no mistake.

There were drawbacks, of course, though they were willingly accepted. One had to be very old indeed to realize that the papers which the telecaster printed in every home were really rather dull. Gone were the crises that had once produced banner headlines. There were no mysterious murders to baffle the police and to arouse in a million breasts the moral indignation that was often suppressed envy. Such murders as did occur were never mysterious: it was only necessary to turn a dial—and the crime could be seen re-enacted. That instruments capable of such feats existed had at first caused considerable panic among quite law-abiding people. This was something that the Overlords, who had mastered most but not all the quirks of human psychology, had not anticipated. It had to be made perfectly clear that no Peeping Tom would be able to spy on his fellows, and that the very few instruments in human hands would be under strict control. Rupert Boyce's projector, for instance, could not operate beyond the borders of the reservation, so he and Maia were the only persons inside its range.

Even the few serious crimes that did occur received no particular attention in the news. For well-bred people do not, after all, care to read about the social *gaffes* of others.

The average working week was now twenty hours—but those twenty hours were no sinecure. There was little work left of a routine, mechanical nature. Men's minds were too valuable to waste on tasks that a few thousand transistors, some photoelectric cells, and a cubic meter of printed circuits could perform. There were factories that ran for weeks without being visited by a single human being. Men were needed for trouble-shooting, for making decisions, for planning new enterprises. The robots did the rest.

The existence of so much leisure would have created tremendous problems a century before. Education had overcome most of these, for a well-stocked mind is safe from boredom. The general standard of culture was at a level which would once have seemed fantastic. There was no evidence that the intelligence of the human race had improved, but for the first time everyone was given the fullest opportunity of using what brain he had.

Most people had two homes, in widely separated parts of the world. Now that the polar regions had been opened up, a considerable fraction of the human race oscillated from Arctic to Antarctic at six monthly intervals, seeking the long, nightless polar summer. Others had gone into the deserts, up the mountains, or even into the sea. There was nowhere on the planet where science and technology could not provide one with a comfortable home, if one wanted it badly enough.

Some of the more eccentric dwelling places provided the few items of excitement in the news. In the most perfectly ordered society, there will always be accidents. Perhaps it was a good sign that people felt it worthwhile to risk, and occasionally break, their necks for the sake of a cozy villa tucked under the summit of Everest, or looking out through the spray of Victoria Falls. As a result, someone was always being rescued from somewhere. It had become a kind of game—almost a planetary sport.

People could indulge in such whims, because they had both the time and the money. The abolition of armed forces had at once almost doubled the world's effective wealth, and increased production had done the rest. As a result, it was difficult to compare the standard of living of twenty-first-century man with that of any of his predecessors. Everything was so cheap that the necessities of life were free, provided as a public service by the community, as roads, water, street lighting, and drainage had once been. A man could travel anywhere he pleased, eat whatever food he fancied—without handing over any money. He had earned the right to do this by being a productive member of the community.

There were, of course, some drones, but the number of people sufficiently strong-willed to indulge in a life of complete idleness is much smaller than is generally supposed. Supporting such parasites was considerably less of a burden than providing for the armies of ticket collectors, shop assistants, bank clerks, stock-brokers, and so forth, whose main function, when one took the global point of view, was to transfer items from one ledger to another.

Nearly a quarter of the human race's total activity, it had been calculated, was now expended on sports of various kinds, ranging from such sedentary occupations as chess to lethal pursuits like ski-gliding across mountain valleys. One unexpected result of this was the extinction of the professional sportsman. There were too many brilliant amateurs, and the changed economic conditions had made the old system obsolete.

Next to sport, entertainment, in all its branches, was the greatest single industry. For more than a hundred years there had been people who had believed that Hollywood was the center of the world. They could now make a better case for this claim than ever before, but it was safe to say that most of 2050's productions would have seemed incomprehensibly highbrow to 1950. There had been some progress: the box office was no longer lord of all it surveyed.

Yet among all the distractions and diversions of a planet which now seemed well on the way to becoming one vast playground, there were some who still found time to repeat an ancient and never-answered question:

"Where do we go from here?"

✴   CHAPTER TEN

Jan leaned against the elephant and rested his hands on the skin, rough as the bark of a tree. He looked up at the great tusks and the curving trunk, caught by the skill of the taxi-dermist in the moment of challenge or salutation. What still weirder creatures, he wondered, from what unknown worlds, would one day be looking at this exile from Earth?

"How many animals have you sent the Overlords?" he asked Rupert.

"At least fifty, though of course this is the biggest one. He's magnificent, isn't he? Most of the others have been quite small—

butterflies, snakes, monkeys, and so on. Though I did get a hippo last year."

Jan gave a wry smile.

"It's a morbid thought, but I suppose they've got a fine stuffed group of *Homo sapiens* in their collection by this time. I wonder who was honored?"

"You're probably right," said Rupert, rather indifferently. "It would be easy to arrange through the hospitals."

"What would happen," continued Jan thoughtfully, "if someone volunteered to go as a *live* specimen? Assuming that an eventual return was guaranteed, of course."

Rupert laughed, though not unsympathetically.

"Is that an offer? Shall I put it to Rashaverak?"

For a moment Jan considered the idea more than half seriously. Then he shook his head.

"Er—no. I was only thinking out loud. They'd certainly turn me down. By the way, do you ever see Rashaverak these days?"

"He called me up about six weeks ago. He'd just found a book I'd been hunting. Rather nice of him."

Jan walked slowly around the stuffed monster, admiring the skill that had frozen it forever at this instant of greatest vigor.

"Did you ever discover what he was looking for?" he asked. "I mean, it seems so hard to reconcile the Overlords' science with an interest in the occult."

Rupert looked at Jan a little suspiciously, wondering if his brother-in-law was poking fun at his hobby.

"His explanation seemed adequate. As an anthropologist, he was interested in every aspect of our culture. Remember, they have plenty of time. They can go into more detail than a human research worker ever could. Reading my entire library probably put only a slight strain on Rashy's resources."

That might be the answer, but Jan was not convinced. Sometimes he had thought of confiding his secret to Rupert, but his natural caution had held him back. When he met his Overlord friend again, Rupert would probably give something away—the temptation would be far too great.

"Incidentally," said Rupert, changing the subject abruptly, "if you think *this* is a big job, you should see the commission Sullivan's got. He's promised to deliver the two biggest creatures of all—a sperm whale and a giant squid. They'll be shown locked in mortal combat. What a tableau *that* will make!"

For a moment Jan did not answer. The idea that had exploded in his mind was too outrageous, too fantastic to be taken seriously. Yet, because of its very daring, it might succeed. . . .

"What's the matter?" said Rupert anxiously. "The heat getting you down?"

Jan shook himself back to present reality.

"I'm all right," he said. "I was just wondering how the Overlords would collect a little packet like that."

"Oh," said Rupert, "one of those cargo ships of theirs will come down, open a hatch, and hoist it in."

"That," said Jan, "is exactly what I thought."

It might have been the cabin of a spaceship, but it was not. The walls were covered with meters and instruments: there were no windows—merely a large screen in front of the pilot. The vessel could carry six passengers, but at the moment Jan was the only one.

He was watching the screen intently, absorbing each glimpse of this strange and unknown region as it passed before his eyes. Unknown—yes, as unknown as anything he might meet beyond the stars, if his mad plan succeeded. He was going into a realm of nightmare creatures, preying upon each other in a darkness undisturbed since the world began. It was a realm above which men had sailed for thousands of years: it lay no more than a kilometer below the keels of their ships—yet until the last hundred years they had known less about it than the visible face of the moon.

The pilot was dropping down from the ocean heights towards the still unexplored vastness of the South Pacific Basin. He was following, Jan knew, the invisible grid of sound waves created by beacons along the ocean floor. They were still sailing as far above that floor as clouds above the surface of the Earth. . . .

There was very little to see: the submarine's scanners were searching the waters in vain. The disturbance created by their jets had probably scared away the smaller fish: if any creature came to investigate, it would be something so large that it did not know the meaning of fear.

The tiny cabin vibrated with power—the power which could

hold at bay the immense weight of the waters above their heads, and could create this little bubble of light and air within which men could live. If that power failed, thought Jan, they would become prisoners in a metal tomb, buried deep in the silt of the ocean bed.

"Time to get a fix," said the pilot. He threw a set of switches, and the submarine came to rest in a gentle surge of deceleration as the jets ceased their thrust. The vessel was motionless, floating in equilibrium as a balloon floats in the atmosphere.

It took only a moment to check their position on the sonar grid. When he had finished with his instrument readings, the pilot remarked: "Before we start the motors again, let's see if we can hear anything."

The loudspeaker flooded the quiet little room with a low, continuous murmur of sound. There was no outstanding noise that Jan could distinguish from the rest. It was a steady background, into which all individual sounds had been blended. He was listening, Jan knew, to the myriad creatures of the sea talking together. It was as if he stood in the center of a forest that teemed with life—except that there he would have recognized some of the individual voices. Here, not one thread in the tapestry of sound could be disentangled and identified. It was so alien, so remote from anything he had ever known that it set Jan's scalp crawling. And yet this was part of his own world. . . .

The shriek cut across the vibrating background like a flash of lightning against a dark storm cloud. It faded swiftly away into a banshee wail, an ululation that dwindled and died, yet was repeated a moment later from a more distant source. Then a chorus of screams broke out, a pandemonium that caused the pilot to reach swiftly for the volume control.

"What in the name of God was *that?*" gasped Jan.

"Weird, isn't it? It's a school of whales, about ten kilometers away. I knew they were in the neighborhood and thought you'd like to hear them."

Jan shuddered.

"And I always thought the sea was silent! Why do they make such a din?"

"Talking to one another, I suppose. Sullivan could tell you—

they say he can even identify some individual whales, though I find that hard to believe. Hello, we've got company!"

A fish with incredibly exaggerated jaws was visible in the viewing screen. It appeared to be quite large, but as Jan did not know the scale of the picture it was hard to judge. Hanging from a point just below its gills was a long tendril, ending in an unidentifiable, bell-shaped organ.

"We're seeing it on infrared," said the pilot. "Let's look at the normal picture."

The fish vanished completely. Only the pendant remained, glowing with its own vivid phosphorescence. Then, just for an instant, the shape of the creature flickered into visibility as a line of lights flashed on along its body.

"It's an angler: that's the bait it uses to lure other fish. Fantastic, isn't it? What I don't understand is—why doesn't his bait attract fish big enough to eat *him?* But we can't wait here all day. Watch him run when I switch on the jets."

The cabin vibrated once again as the vessel eased itself forward. The great luminous fish suddenly flashed on all its lights in a frantic signal of alarm, and departed like a meteor into the darkness of the abyss.

It was after another twenty minutes of slow descent that the invisible fingers of the scanner beams caught the first glimpse of the ocean bed. Far beneath, a range of low hills was passing, their outlines curiously soft and rounded. Whatever irregularities they might once have possessed had long ago been obliterated by the ceaseless rain from the watery heights above. Even here in mid Pacific, far from the great estuaries that slowly swept the continents out to sea, that rain never ceased. It came from the storm-scarred flanks of the Andes, from the bodies of a billion living creatures, from the dust of meteors that had wandered through space for ages and had come at last to rest. Here in the eternal night, it was laying the foundations of the lands to be.

The hills drifted behind. They were the frontier posts, as Jan could see from the charts, of a wide plain which lay at too great a depth for the scanners to reach.

The submarine continued on its gentle downward glide. Now another picture was beginning to form on the screen: because of the angle of view, it was some time before Jan could interpret what he saw. Then he realized that they were approaching a submerged mountain, jutting up from the hidden plain.

The picture was clearer now: at this short range the definition of the scanners improved and the view was almost as distinct as if the image was being formed by light waves. Jan could see fine detail, could watch the strange fish that pursued each other among the rocks. Once a venomous-looking creature with gaping jaws swam slowly across a half-concealed cleft. So swiftly that the eye could not follow the movement, a long tentacle flashed out and dragged the struggling fish down to its doom.

"Nearly there," said the pilot. "You'll be able to see the lab in a minute."

They were traveling slowly above a spur of rock jutting out from the base of the mountain. The plain beneath was now coming into view: Jan guessed that they were not more than a few hundred meters above the sea bed. Then he saw, a kilometer or so ahead, a cluster of spheres standing on tripod legs, and joined together by connecting tubes. It looked exactly like the tanks of some chemical plant, and indeed was designed on the same basic principles. The only difference was that here the pressures which had to be resisted were *outside,* not within.

"What's that?" gasped Jan suddenly. He pointed a shaky finger towards the nearest sphere. The curious pattern of lines on its surface had resolved itself into a network of giant tentacles. As the submarine came closer, he could see that they ended in a great, pulpy bag, from which peered a pair of enormous eyes.

"That," said the pilot indifferently, "is probably Lucifer. Someone's been feeding him again." He threw a switch and leaned over the control desk.

"S.2 calling Lab. I'm connecting up. Will you shoo away your pet?"

The reply came promptly.

"Lab to S.2. O.K.—go ahead and make contact. Lucey will get out of the way."

The curving metal walls began to fill the screen. Jan caught a last glimpse of a giant, sucker-studded arm whipping away at their approach. Then there was a dull clang, and a series of scratching noises as the clamps sought for their locking points on the submarine's smooth, oval hull. In a few minutes the vessel was pressed tightly against the wall of the base, the two entrance ports had locked together, and were moving forward through the hull of the submarine at the end of a giant hollow screw. Then came the "pressure equalized" signal, the hatches unsealed, and the way into Deep Sea Lab One was open.

Jan found Professor Sullivan in a small, untidy room that seemed to combine the attributes of office, workshop and laboratory. He was peeping through a microscope into what looked like a small bomb. Presumably it was a pressure-capsule containing some specimen of deep-sea life, still swimming happily around under its normal tons-to-the-square-centimeter conditions.

"Well," said Sullivan, dragging himself away from the eyepiece. "How's Rupert? And what can we do for you?"

"Rupert's fine," replied Jan. "He sends his best wishes, and says he'd love to visit you if it weren't for his claustrophobia."

"Then he'd certainly feel a little unhappy down here, with five kilometers of water on top of him. Doesn't it worry you, by the way?"

Jan shrugged his shoulders.

"No more than being in a stratoliner. If anything went wrong, the result would be the same in either case."

"That's the sensible approach, but it's surprising how few people see it that way." Sullivan toyed with the controls of his microscope, then shot Jan an inquisitive glance.

"I'll be very glad to show you around," he said, "but I must confess I was a little surprised when Rupert passed on your request. I couldn't understand why one of you spacehounds should be interested in our work. Aren't you going in the wrong direction?" He gave a chuckle of amusement. "Personally, I've never seen why you were in such a hurry to get out there. It will be centuries before we've got everything in the oceans nicely charted and pigeonholed."

Jan took a deep breath. He was glad that Sullivan had broached the subject himself, for it made his task that much easier. Despite the ichthyologist's jest, they had a great deal in common. It should not be too hard to build a bridge, to enlist Sullivan's sympathy and aid. He was a man of imagination, or he would never have invaded this underwater world. But Jan would have to be cautious, for the request he was going to make was, to say the least of it, somewhat unconventional.

There was one fact that gave him confidence. Even if Sullivan refused to co-operate, he would certainly keep Jan's secret. And here in this quiet little office on the bed of the Pacific, there seemed no danger that the Overlords—whatever strange powers they possessed—would be able to listen to their conversation.

"Professor Sullivan," he began, "if you were interested in the ocean, but the Overlords refused to let you go near it, how would you feel?"

"Exceedingly annoyed, no doubt."

"I'm sure you would. And suppose, one day, you had a chance of achieving your goal, without them knowing, what would you do? Would you take the opportunity?"

Sullivan never hesitated.

"Of course. And argue later."

Right into my hands! thought Jan. He can't retreat now—unless he's afraid of the Overlords. And I doubt if Sullivan is afraid of anything. He leaned forward across the cluttered table and prepared to present his case.

Professor Sullivan was no fool. Before Jan could speak, his lips twisted into a sardonic smile.

"So *that's* the game, is it?" he said slowly. "Very, very interesting! Now you go right ahead and tell me why I should help you."

✴ *CHAPTER ELEVEN*

An earlier age would have regarded Professor Sullivan as an expensive luxury. His operations cost as much as a small war: indeed, he could be likened to a general conducting a perpetual campaign against an enemy who never relaxed. Professor Sullivan's enemy was the sea, and it fought him with weapons of cold and darkness and, above all, pressure. In his turn, he countered his adversary with intelligence and engineering skill. He had won many victories, but the sea was patient: it could wait. One day, Sullivan knew, he would make a mistake. At least he had the consolation of knowing that he could never drown. It would be far too quick for that.

He had refused to commit himself one way or the other when Jan made his request, but he knew what his answer was going to be. Here was the opportunity for a most interesting experiment. It was a pity that he would never know the result; still, that happened often enough in scientific research, and he had initiated other programs that would take decades to complete.

Professor Sullivan was a brave and an intelligent man, but looking back on his career he was conscious of the fact that it had not brought him the sort of fame that sends a scientist's name safely down the centuries. Here was a chance, totally unexpected and all the more attractive for that, of really establishing himself in the history books. It was not an ambition he would ever have admitted to anybody—and, to do him justice, he would still have helped Jan even if his part in the plot remained forever secret.

As for Jan, he was now having second thoughts. The momentum of his original discovery had carried him thus far almost without effort. He had made his investigations, but had taken no active steps to turn his dream into reality. In a few days, however, he must make his choice. If Professor Sullivan agreed to co-operate, there was no way in which he could retreat. He must face the future he had chosen, with all its implications.

What finally decided him was the thought that, if he neglected this incredible opportunity, he would never forgive himself. All the rest of his life would be spent in vain regrets—and nothing could be worse than that.

Sullivan's answer reached him a few hours later, and he knew that the die was cast. Slowly, because there was still plenty of time, he began to put his affairs in order.

"*Dear Maia* (the letter began) *this is going to be—to put it mildly —rather a surprise for you. When you get this letter, I shall no longer be on Earth. By that I don't mean that I shall have gone to the Moon, as many others have done. No: I shall be on my way to the home of the Overlords. I shall be the first man ever to leave the Solar System.*

"*I am giving this letter to the friend who is helping me: he will hold it until he knows that my plan has succeeded—in its first phase, at least —and that it is too late for the Overlords to interfere. I shall be so far away, and traveling at such a speed, that I doubt if any recall message can overtake me. Even if it could, it seems most unlikely that the ship would be able to put back to Earth. And I very much doubt if I'm all that important, anyway.*

"First, let me explain what led to this. You know that I've always been interested in spaceflight, and have always felt frustrated because we've never been allowed to go to the other planets, or to learn anything about the civilization of the Overlords. If they had never intervened, we might have reached Mars and Venus by now. I admit that it is equally probable that we would have destroyed ourselves with cobalt bombs and the other global weapons the twentieth century was developing. Yet sometimes I wish we could have had a chance of standing on our own feet.

"Probably the Overlords have their reasons for keeping us in the nursery, and probably they are excellent reasons. But even if I knew what they were, I doubt if it would make much difference to my own feelings—or my actions.

"Everything really began at that party of Rupert's. (He doesn't know about this, by the way, though he put me on the right track.) You remember that silly seance he arranged and how it ended when that girl —I forget her name—fainted? I'd asked what star the Overlords came from, and the reply was 'NGS 549672.' I'd not expected any answer, and had treated the whole business as a joke until then. But when I realized that this was a number in a star catalogue, I decided to look into it. I found that the star was in the constellation Carina—and one of the few facts that we do know about the Overlords is that they come from that direction.

"Now I don't pretend to understand how that information reached us, or where it originated. Did someone read Rashaverak's mind? Even if they had, it's hardly likely that he would have known the reference number of his sun in one of our catalogues. It's a complete mystery, and I leave it to people like Rupert to solve—if they can! I'm just content to take the information, and to act on it.

"We know a lot now, through our observations of their departure, about the speed of the Overlord ships. They leave the Solar System under such tremendous accelerations that they approach the velocity of light in less than an hour. That means that the Overlords must possess some kind of propulsive system that acts equally on every atom of their ships, so that anything aboard won't be crushed instantly. I wonder why they employ such colossal acclerations, when they've got all space to play with and could take their time picking up speed? My theory is that they can somehow tap the energy fields round the stars, and so have to do their starting and stopping while they're fairly close to a sun. But that's all by the way. . . .

"The important fact was that I knew how far they had to travel, and therefore how long the journey took. NGS 549672 is forty light-

years from Earth. The Overlord ships reach more than 99 percent of the speed of light, so the trip must last forty years of our time. Our time: that's the crux of the matter.

"Now as you may have heard, strange things happen as one approaches the speed of light. Time itself begins to flow at a different rate—to pass more slowly, so that what would be months on Earth would be no more than days on the ships of the Overlords. The effect is quite fundamental: it was discovered by the great Einstein more than a hundred years ago.

"I have made calculations based on what we know about the Stardrive, and using the firmly established results of the Relativity theory. From the viewpoint of the passengers on one of the Overlord ships, the journey to NGS 549672 will last not more than two months—even though by Earth's reckoning forty years will have passed. I know this seems a paradox, and if it's any consolation it's puzzled the world's best brains ever since Einstein announced it.

"Perhaps this example will show you the sort of thing that can happen, and will give you a clearer picture of the situation. If the Overlords send me straight back to Earth, I shall arrive home having aged only four months. But on Earth itself, eighty years will have passed. So you understand, Maia, that whatever happens, this is good-by. . . .

"I have few ties binding me here, as you know well enough, so I can leave with a clear conscience. I've not told Mother yet: she would get hysterical, and I couldn't face that. It's better this way. Though I've tried to make allowances, ever since Father died—oh, there's no point now in going into all that again!

"I've terminated my studies and told the authorities that, for family reasons, I'm moving to Europe. Everything has been settled and there should be nothing for you to worry about.

"By this time, you may imagine that I'm crazy, since it seems impossible for anyone to get into one of the Overlord ships. But I've found a way. It doesn't happen very often, and after this it may never happen again, for I'm sure Karellen never makes the same mistake twice. Do you know the legend of the Wooden Horse, that got the Greek soldiers into Troy? But there's a story from the Old Testament that's an even closer parallel. . . ."

"You'll certainly be much more comfortable than Jonah," said Sullivan. "There is no evidence that he was provided with electric light or sanitation. But you'll need a lot of provisions, and I see you're taking oxygen. Can you take enough for a two months' voyage in such a small space?"

He stubbed his finger on the careful sketches which Jan had laid on the table. The microscope acted as a paperweight at one end, the skull of some improbable fish held down the other.

"I hope the oxygen isn't necessary," said Jan. "We know that they can breathe our atmosphere, but they don't seem to like it very much and I might not be able to manage theirs at all. As for the supply situation, using narcosamine solves that. It's perfectly safe. When we're under way, I'll take a shot that will knock me out for six weeks, plus or minus a few days. I'll be nearly there by then. Actually, it wasn't the food and oxygen that was worrying me, so much as the boredom."

Professor Sullivan nodded thoughtfully.

"Yes, narcosamine is safe enough, and can be calibrated fairly accurately. But mind you've got plenty of food handy—you'll be ravening when you wake up, and as weak as a kitten. Suppose you starved to death because you hadn't the strength to use a can opener?"

"I'd thought of that," said Jan, a little hurt. "I'll work up through sugar and chocolate in the usual way."

"Good: I'm glad to see that you've been into the problem thoroughly, and aren't treating it like some stunt you can back out of if you don't like the way it's going. It's your life you're playing with, but I'd hate to feel I was helping you to commit suicide."

He picked up the skull and lifted it absentmindedly in his hands. Jan grabbed the plan to prevent it rolling up.

"Luckily," continued Professor Sullivan, "the equipment you need is all fairly standard, and our shop can put it together in a few weeks. And if you decide to change your mind—"

"I won't," said Jan.

"I've considered all the risks I'm taking, and there seems to be no flaw in the plan. At the end of six weeks I'll emerge like any other stowaway and give myself up. By then—in my time, remember—the journey will be nearly over. We will be about to land on the world of the Overlords.

"Of course, what happens then is up to them. Probably I'll be sent home on the next ship—but at least I can expect to see something. I've got a four millimeter camera and thousands of meters of film: it won't be my fault if I can't use it. Even at the worst, I'll have proved that man can't be kept in quarantine forever. I'll have created a precedent that will compel Karellen to take some action.

"That, my dear Maia, is all I have to say. I know you won't miss me greatly: let's be honest and admit that we never had very strong ties, and now that you've married Rupert you'll be quite happy in your own private universe. At least, I hope so.

"*Good-by, then, and good luck. I shall look forward to meeting your grandchildren—make sure that they know about me, won't you?*
                              Your affectionate brother
                                        Jan."

✳ *CHAPTER TWELVE*

When Jan first saw it, he found it hard to realize that he was not watching the fuselage of a small airliner being assembled. The metal skeleton was twenty meters long, perfectly streamlined, and surrounded by light scaffolding over which the workmen were clambering with their power tools.

"Yes," said Sullivan in reply to Jan's question. "We use standard aeronautical techniques, and most of these men are from the aircraft industry. It's hard to believe that a thing this size could be alive, isn't it? Or could throw itself clear out of the water, as I've seen them do."

It was all very fascinating, but Jan had other things on his mind. His eyes were searching the giant skeleton to find a suitable hiding place for his little cell—the "air-conditioned coffin," as Sullivan had christened it. On one point he was immediately reassured. As far as space was concerned, there would be room for a dozen stowaways.

"The framework looks nearly complete," said Jan. "When will you be putting on the skin? I suppose you've already caught your whale, or you wouldn't know how large to make the skeleton."

Sullivan seemed highly amused by this remark.

"We haven't the slightest intention of catching a whale. Anyway, they don't have skins in the usual sense of the word. It would hardly be practicable to fold a blanket of blubber twenty centimeters thick around that framework. No, the whole thing will be faked up with plastics and then accurately painted. By the time we've finished, no one will be able to tell the difference."

In that case, thought Jan, the sensible thing for the Overlords to have done would be to take photographs and make the full-sized model themselves, back on their home planet. But perhaps their supply ships returned empty, and a little thing like a twenty meter sperm whale would hardly be noticed. When one possessed such power and such resources, one could not be bothered with minor economies. . . .

Professor Sullivan stood by one of the great statues that had been such a challenge to archaeology since Easter Island was discovered. King, god, or whatever it might be, its eyeless gaze seemed to be following his as he looked upon his handiwork. He was proud of what he had done: it seemed a pity that it would soon be banished forever from human sight.

The tableau might have been the work of some mad artist in a drugged delirium. Yet it was a painstaking copy from life: Nature herself was the artist here. The scene was one that, until the perfection of underwater television, few men had ever glimpsed—and even then only for seconds on those rare occasions when the giant antagonists thrashed their way to the surface. These battles were fought in the endless night of the ocean depths, where the sperm whales hunted for their food. It was food that objected strongly to being eaten alive. . . .

The long, saw-toothed lower jaw of the whale was gaping wide, preparing to fasten upon its prey. The creature's head was almost concealed beneath the writhing network of white, pulpy arms with which the giant squid was fighting desperately for life. Livid sucker-marks, twenty centimeters or more in diameter, had mottled the whale's skin where those arms had fastened. One tentacle was already a truncated stump, and there could be no doubt as to the ultimate outcome of the battle. When the two greatest beasts on earth engaged in combat, the whale was always the winner. For all the vast strength of its forest of tentacles, the squid's only hope lay in escaping before that patiently grinding jaw had sawn it to pieces. Its great expressionless eyes, half a meter across, stared at its destroyer—though, in all probability, neither creature could see the other in the darkness of the abyss.

The entire exhibit was more than thirty meters long, and had now been surrounded by a cage of aluminum girders to which the lifting tackle had been connected. Everything was ready, awaiting the Overlords' pleasure. Sullivan hoped that they would act quickly: the suspense was beginning to be uncomfortable.

Someone had come out of the office into the bright sunlight, obviously looking for him. Sullivan recognized his chief clerk, and walked over to meet him.

"Hello, Bill—what's the fuss?"

The other was holding a message form and looked rather pleased.

"Some good news, Professor. We've been honored! The Supervisor himself wants to come and look at our tableau before it's shipped off. Just think of the publicity we'll get! It will help a lot when we apply for our new grant. I'd been hoping for something like this."

Professor Sullivan swallowed hard. He never objected to publicity, but this time he was afraid he might get altogether too much.

Karellen stood by the head of the whale and looked up at the great, blunt snout and the ivory-studded jaw. Sullivan, concealing his unease, wondered what the Supervisor was thinking. His behavior had not hinted at any suspicion, and the visit could be easily explained as a normal one. But Sullivan would be very glad when it was over.

"We've no creatures as large as this on our planet," said Karellen. "That is one reason why we asked you to make this group. My—er—compatriots will find it fascinating."

"With your low gravity," answered Sullivan, "I should have thought you would have had some very large animals. After all, look how much bigger you are than us!"

"Yes—but we have no oceans. And where size is concerned, the land can never compete with the sea."

That was perfectly true, thought Sullivan. And as far as he knew, this was a hitherto unrevealed fact about the world of the Overlords. Jan, confound him, would be very interested.

At the moment that young man was sitting in a hut a kilometer away, anxiously watching the inspection through field glasses. He kept telling himself that there was nothing to fear. No inspection of the whale, however close, could reveal its secret. But there was always the chance that Karellen suspected something—and was playing with them.

It was a suspicion that was growing in Sullivan's mind as the Supervisor peered into the cavernous throat.

"In your Bible," said Karellen, "there is a remarkable story of a

Hebrew prophet, one Jonah, who was swallowed by a whale and thus carried safely to land after he had been cast from a ship. Do you think there could be any basis of fact in such a legend?"

"I believe," Sullivan replied cautiously, "that there is one fairly well-authenticated case of a whaleman being swallowed and then regurgitated with no ill effects. Of course, if he had been inside the whale for more than a few seconds he would have suffocated. And he must have been very lucky to miss the teeth. It's an almost incredible story, but not *quite* impossible."

"Very interesting," said Karellen. He stood for another moment staring at the great jaw, then moved on to examine the squid. Sullivan hoped he did not hear his sigh of relief.

"If I'd known what I was going to go through," said Professor Sullivan, "I'd have thrown you out of the office as soon as you tried to infect me with your insanity."

"I'm sorry about that," Jan replied. "But we've got away with it."

"I hope so. Good luck, anyway. If you want to change your mind, you've still got at least six hours."

"I won't need them. Only Karellen can stop me now. Thanks for all that you've done. If I ever get back, and write a book about the Overlords, I'll dedicate it to you."

"Much good that will do me," said Sullivan gruffly. "I'll have been dead for years." To his surprise and mild consternation, for he was not a sentimental man, he discovered that this farewell was beginning to affect him. He had grown to like Jan during the weeks they had plotted together. Moreover, he had begun to fear he might be an accessory to a complicated suicide.

He steadied the ladder as Jan climbed into the great jaw, carefully avoiding the lines of teeth. By the light of the electric torch, he saw Jan turn and wave before he was lost in the cavernous hollow. There was the sound of the airlock hatch being opened and closed, and, thereafter, silence.

In the moonlight, that had transformed the frozen battle into a scene from a nightmare, Professor Sullivan walked slowly back to his office. He wondered what he had done, and where it would lead. But this, of course, he would never know. Jan might walk this spot again, having given no more than a few months of his life in traveling to the home of the Overlords and returning to Earth. Yet if he did so, it would be on the other side of Time's impassable barrier, for it would be eighty years in the future.

The lights went on in the tiny metal cylinder as soon as Jan had closed the inner door of the lock. He allowed himself no time for second thoughts, but began immediately upon the routine check he had already worked out. All the stores and provisions had been loaded days ago, but a final recheck would put him in the right frame of mind, by assuring him that nothing had been left undone.

An hour later, he was satisfied. He lay back on the sponge rubber couch and recapitulated his plans. The only sound was the faint whirr of the electric calendar clock, which would warn him when the voyage was coming to its end.

He knew that he could expect to feel nothing here in his cell, for whatever tremendous forces drove the ships of the Overlords must be perfectly compensated. Sullivan had checked that, pointing out that his tableau would collapse if subjected to more than a few gravities. His—clients—had assured him that there was no danger on this score.

There would, however, be a considerable change of atmospheric pressure. This was unimportant, since the hollow models could "breathe" through several orifices. Before he left his cell, Jan would have to equalize pressure, and he had assumed that the atmosphere inside the Overlord ship was unbreathable. A simple facemask and oxygen set would take care of that: there was no need for anything elaborate. If he could breathe without mechanical aid, so much the better.

There was no point in waiting any longer: it would only be a strain on the nerves. He took out the little syringe, already loaded with the carefully prepared solution. Narcosamine had been discovered during research into animal hibernation: it was not true to say—as was popularly believed—that it produced suspended animation. All it caused was a great slowing down of the vital processes, though metabolism still continued at a reduced level. It was as if one had banked up the fires of life, so that they smoldered underground. But when, after weeks or months, the effect of the drug wore off, they would burst out again and the sleeper would revive. Narcosamine was perfectly safe. Nature had used it for a million years to protect many of her children from the foodless winter.

So Jan slept. He never felt the tug of the hoisting cables as the huge metal framework was lifted into the hold of the Overlord freighter. He never heard the hatches close, not to open again for three hundred million million kilometers. He never heard, far-off and faint through the mighty walls, the protesting scream of Earth's atmosphere, as the ship climbed swiftly back to its natural element.

And he never felt the Stardrive go on.

✳ *CHAPTER THIRTEEN*

The conference room was always crowded for these weekly meetings, but today it was so closely packed that the reporters had difficulty in writing. For the hundredth time, they grumbled to each other at Karellen's conservatism and lack of consideration. Anywhere else in the world they could have brought TV cameras, tape recorders, and all the other tools of their highly mechanized trade. But here, they had to rely on such archaic devices as paper and pencil—and even, incredible to relate, *shorthand.*

There had, of course, been several attempts to smuggle in recorders. They had been successfully smuggled out again, but a single glance at their smoking interiors had shown the futility of the experiment. Everyone understood, then, why they had always been warned, in their own interest, to leave watches and other metallic objects outside the conference room. . . .

To make things more unfair, Karellen himself recorded the whole proceedings. Reporters guilty of carelessness, or downright misrepresentation—though this was very rare—had been summoned to short and unpleasant sessions with Karellen's underlings, and had been required to listen attentively to playbacks of what the Supervisor had *really* said. The lesson was not one that ever had to be repeated.

It was strange how these rumors got around. No prior announcement was made, yet there was always a full house whenever Karellen had an important statement to make—which happened, on the average, two or three times a year.

Silence descended on the murmuring crowd as the great doorway split open and Karellen came forward onto the dais. The light here was dim—no doubt approximating that of the Overlords' far distant sun—so that the Supervisor for Earth had discarded the dark glasses he normally wore when in the open.

He replied to the ragged chorus of greetings with a formal "Good morning, everybody," then turned to the tall, distinguished figure at the front of the crowd. Mr. Golde, *doyen* of the Press Club, might have been the original inspirer of the butler's announcement: "Two reporters, m'lud, and a gentleman from the *Times*." He dressed and behaved like a diplomat of the old school: no one would ever hesitate to confide in him, and no one had ever regretted it subsequently.

"Quite a crowd today, Mr. Golde. There must be a shortage of news."

The gentleman from the *Times* smiled and cleared his throat:

"I hope you can rectify that, Mr. Supervisor."

He watched intently as Karellen considered his reply. It seemed so unfair that the Overlords' faces, rigid as masks, betrayed no trace of emotion. The great, wide eyes, their pupils sharply contracted even in this indifferent light, stared fathomlessly back into the frankly curious human ones. The twin breathing orifices on either cheek—if those fluted, basalt curves could be called cheeks—emitted the faintest of whistles as Karellen's hypothetical lungs labored in the thin air of Earth. Golde could just see the curtain of tiny white hairs fluttering to and fro, keeping accurately out of phase, as they responded to Karellen's rapid, double-action breathing cycle. Dust filters, they were generally believed to be, and elaborate theories concerning the atmosphere of the Overlords' home had been constructed on this slender foundation.

"Yes, I have some news for you. As you are doubtless aware, one of my supply ships recently left Earth to return to its base. We have just discovered that there was a stowaway on board."

A hundred pencils braked to a halt: a hundred pairs of eyes fixed themselves upon Karellen.

"A *stowaway*, did you say, Mr. Supervisor?" asked Golde. "May we ask who he was—and how he got aboard?"

"His name is Jan Rodricks: he is an engineering student from the University of Cape Town. Further details you can no doubt discover for yourselves through your own very efficient channels."

Karellen smiled. The Supervisor's smile was a curious affair. Most of the effect really resided in the eyes: the inflexible, lipless mouth scarcely moved at all. Was this, Golde wondered, another of the many human customs that Karellen had copied with such skill? For the total effect was, undoubtedly, that of a smile, and the mind readily accepted it as such.

"As for *how* he left," continued the Supervisor, "that is of secondary importance. I can assure you, or any other potential astronauts, that there is no possibility of repeating the exploit."

"What will happen to this young man?" persisted Golde. "Will he be sent back to Earth?"

"That is outside my jurisdiction, but I expect he will come back on the next ship. He would find conditions too—alien—for comfort where he has gone. And this leads me to the main purpose of our meeting today."

Karellen paused, and the silence grew even deeper.

"There has been some complaint, among the younger and more romantic elements of your population, because outer space has been closed to you. We had a purpose in doing this: we do not impose bans for the pleasure of it. But have you ever stopped to consider—if you will excuse a slightly unflattering analogy—what a man from your Stone Age would have felt, if he suddenly found himself in a modern city?"

"Surely," protested the *Herald Tribune,* "there is a fundamental difference. We are accustomed to Science. On your world there are doubtless many things which we might not understand—but they wouldn't seem magic to us."

"Are you quite sure of that?" said Karellen, so softly that it was hard to hear his words. "Only a hundred years lies between the age of electricity and the age of steam, but what would a Victorian engineer have made of a television set or an electronic computer? And how long would he have lived if he started to investigate their workings? The gulf between two technologies can easily become so great that it is—lethal."

("Hello," whispered Reuters to the B.B.C. "We're in luck. He's going to make a major policy statement. I know the symptoms.")

"And there are other reasons why we have restricted the human race to Earth. Watch."

The lights dimmed and vanished. As they faded, a milky opalescence formed in the center of the room. It congealed into a whirlpool of stars—a spiral nebula seen from a point far beyond its outermost sun.

"No human eyes have ever seen this sight before," said Karellen's voice from the darkness. "You are looking at your own Universe, the island galaxy of which your sun is a member, from a distance of half a million light-years."

There was a long silence. Then Karellen continued, and now his voice held something that was not quite pity and not precisely scorn.

"Your race had shown a notable incapacity for dealing with the problems of its own rather small planet. When we arrived, you were on the point of destroying yourselves with the powers that science had rashly given you. Without our intervention, the earth today would be a radioactive wilderness.

"Now you have a world at peace, and a united race. Soon you will be sufficiently civilized to run your planet without our assistance. Perhaps you could eventually handle the problems of an entire solar system—say fifty moons and planets. But do you really imagine that you could ever cope with *this?*"

The nebula expanded. Now the individual stars were rushing past, appearing and vanishing as swiftly as sparks from a forge. And each of those transient sparks was a sun, with who knew how many circling worlds. . . .

"In this galaxy of ours," murmured Karellen, "there are eighty-seven thousand million suns. Even that figure gives only a faint idea of the immensity of space. In challenging it, you would be like ants attempting to label and classify all the grains of sand in all the deserts of the world.

"Your race, in its present stage of evolution, cannot face that stupendous challenge. One of my duties has been to protect you from the powers and forces that lie among the stars—forces beyond anything that you can ever imagine."

The image of the galaxy's swirling fire-mists faded: light returned to the sudden silence of the great chamber.

Karellen turned to go: the audience was over. At the door he paused and looked back upon the hushed crowd.

"It is a bitter thought, but you must face it. The planets you may one day possess. But the stars are not for Man."

"The stars are not for Man." Yes, it would annoy them to have the celestial portals slammed in their faces. But they must learn to face the truth—or as much of the truth as could mercifully be given to them.

From the lonely heights of the stratosphere, Karellen looked down upon the world and the people that had been given into his reluctant keeping. He thought of all that lay ahead, and what this world would be only a dozen years from now.

They would never know how lucky they had been. For a lifetime, mankind had achieved as much happiness as any race can ever know. It had been the Golden Age. But gold was also the color of sunset, of autumn: and only Karellen's ears could catch the first wailings of the winter storms.

And only Karellen knew with what inexorable swiftness the Golden Age was rushing to its close.

Part III · The Last Generation

"**L**ook at this!" exploded George Greggson, hurling the paper across at Jean. It came to rest, despite her efforts to intercept it, spread listlessly across the breakfast table. Jean patiently scraped away the jam and read the offending passage, doing her best to register disapproval. She was not very good at this, because all too often she agreed with the critics. Usually she kept these heretical opinions to herself, and not merely for the sake of peace and quiet. George was perfectly prepared to accept praise from her (or anyone else) but if she ventured any criticism of his work she would receive a crushing lecture on her artistic ignorance.

She read the review twice, then gave up. It appeared quite favorable, and she said so.

"He seemed to like the performance. What are you grumbling about?"

"This," snarled George, stubbing his finger at the middle of the column. "Just read it again."

" 'Particularly restful on the eyes were the delicate pastel greens of the background to the ballet sequence.' Well?"

"They *weren't* greens! I spent a lot of time getting that exact shade of blue! And what happens? Either some blasted engineer in the control room upsets the color balance, or that idiot of a reviewer's got a cockeyed set. Hey, what color did it look on *our* receiver?"

"Er—I can't remember," confessed Jean. "The Poppet started squealing about then and I had to go and find what was wrong with her."

"Oh," said George, relapsing into a gently simmering quiescence. Jean knew that another eruption could be expected at any moment. When it came, however, it was fairly mild.

"I've invented a new definition for TV," he muttered gloomily. "I've decided it's a device for *hindering* communication between artist and audience."

"What do you want to do about it?" retorted Jean. "Go back to the live theater?"

"And why not?" asked George. "That's exactly what I *have* been thinking about. You know that letter I received from the New Athens people? They've written to me again. This time I'm going to answer."

"Indeed?" said Jean, faintly alarmed. "I think they're a lot of cranks."

"Well, there's only one way to find out. I intend to go and see them in the next two weeks. I must say that the literature they put out looks perfectly sane. And they've got some very good men there."

"If you expect me to start cooking over a wood fire, or learning to dress in skins, you'll have—"

"Oh, don't be silly! Those stories are just nonsense. The colony's got everything that's really needed for civilized life. They don't believe in unnecessary frills, that's all. Anyway, it's a couple of years since I visited the Pacific. It will make a nice trip for us both."

"I agree with you there," said Jean. "But I don't intend Junior and the Poppet to grow up into a couple of Polynesian savages."

"They won't," said George. "I can promise you that."

He was right, though not in the way he had intended.

"As you noticed when you flew in," said the little man on the other side of the veranda, "the colony consists of two islands, linked by a causeway. This is Athens, the other we've christened Sparta. It's rather wild and rocky, and is a wonderful place for sport or exercise." His eye flickered momentarily over his visitor's waistline, and George squirmed slightly in the cane chair. "Sparta is an extinct volcano, by the way. At least the geologists *say* it's extinct, ha-ha!

"But back to Athens. The idea of the colony, as you've gathered, is to build up an independent, stable cultural group with its own artistic traditions. I should point out that a vast amount of research took place before we started this enterprise. It's really a piece of applied social engineering, based on some exceedingly complex mathematics which I wouldn't pretend to understand. All I know is that the mathematical sociologists have computed how large the colony should be, how many types of people it should contain—and, above all, what constitution it should have for long-term stability.

"We're ruled by a council of eight directors, representing production, power, social engineering, art, economics, science, sport, and philosophy. There's no permanent chairman or president. The chair's held by each of the directors in rotation for a year at a time.

"Our present population is just over fifty thousand, which is a little short of the desired optimum. That's why we keep our eyes open for recruits. And, of course, there is a certain wastage: we're not yet quite self-supporting in some of the more specialized talents.

"Here on this island we're trying to save something of humanity's independence, its artistic traditions. We've no hostility towards the Overlords: we simply want to be left alone to go our own way. When they destroyed the old nations and the way of life man had known since the beginning of history, they swept away many good things with the bad. The world's now placid, featureless, and culturally dead: nothing really new has been created since the Overlords came. The reason's obvious. There's nothing left to struggle for, and there are too many distractions and entertainments. Do you realize that *every day* something like five hundred hours of radio and TV pour out over the various channels? If you went without sleep and did nothing else, you could follow less than a twentieth of the entertainment that's available at the turn of a switch! No wonder that people are becoming passive sponges—absorbing but never creating. Did you know that the *average* viewing time per person is now three hours a day? Soon people won't be living their own lives any more. It will be a full-time job keeping up with the various family serials on TV!

"Here in Athens, entertainment takes its proper place. Moreover, it's live, not canned. In a community this size it is possible to have almost complete audience participation, with all that that means to the performers and artists. Incidentally we've got a very fine symphony orchestra—probably among the world's half-dozen best.

"But I don't want you to take my word for all this. What usually happens is that prospective citizens stay here a few days, getting the feel of the place. If they decide they'd like to join us, then we let them take the battery of psychological tests which are really our main line of defense. About a third of the applicants are rejected, usually for reasons which don't reflect on them and which wouldn't matter outside. Those who pass go home long enough to settle their affairs, and then rejoin us. Sometimes, they change their minds at this stage, but that's very unusual and almost invariably through personal reasons outside their control. Our tests are practically a hundred percent reliable now: the people they pass are the people who really want to come."

"Suppose anyone changed their mind *later?*" asked Jean anxiously.

"Then they could leave. There'd be no difficulty. It's happened once or twice."

There was a long silence. Jean looked at George, who was rubbing thoughtfully at the side whiskers currently popular in artistic circles. As long as they weren't burning their boats behind them, she was not unduly worried. The colony looked an interesting place, and certainly wasn't as cranky as she'd feared. And the children would love it. That, in the final analysis, was all that mattered.

They moved in six weeks later. The single-storied house was small, but quite adequate for a family which had no intention of being greater than four. All the basic laborsaving devices were in evidence: at least, Jean admitted, there was no danger of reverting to the dark ages of domestic drudgery. It was slightly disturbing, however, to discover that there was a kitchen. In a community of this size, one would normally expect to dial Food Central, wait five minutes, and then get whatever meal had been selected. Individuality was all very well, but this, Jean feared, might be taking things a little *too* far. She wondered darkly if she would be expected to make the family's clothes as well as to prepare its meals. But there was no spinning wheel between the automatic dishwasher and the radar range, so it wasn't quite as bad as that. . . .

Of course, the rest of the house still looked very bare and raw. They were its first occupants, and it would be some time before all this aseptic newness had been converted into a warm, human home. The children, doubtless, would catalyze the process rather effectively. There was already (though Jean did not know it yet) an unfortunate victim of Jeffrey's expiring in the bath, as a result of that young man's ignorance of the fundamental difference between fresh and salt water.

Jean moved to the still-uncurtained window and looked across the colony. It was a beautiful place, there was no doubt of that. The house stood on the western slope of the low hill that dominated, because of the absence of any other competition, the island of Athens. Two kilometers to the north she could see the causeway—a thin knife-edge dividing the water—that led to Sparta. That rocky island, with its brooding volcanic cone, was such a contrast to this peaceful spot that it sometimes frightened her. She wondered how the scientists could be so certain that it would never reawaken and overwhelm them all.

A wavering figure coming up the slope, keeping carefully to the palm trees' shade in defiance of the rule of the road, attracted her eye. George was returning from his first conference. It was time to stop daydreaming and get busy about the house.

A metallic crash announced the arrival of George's bicycle. Jean wondered how long it was going to take them both to learn to ride. This was yet another unexpected aspect of life on the island. Private cars were not permitted, and indeed were unnecessary since the greatest distance one could travel in a straight line was less than fifteen kilometers. There were various community-owned service vehicles—trucks, ambulances, and fire engines, all restricted, except in cases of real emergency, to fifty kilometers an hour. As a result the inhabitants of Athens had plenty of exercise, uncongested streets —and no traffic accidents.

George gave his wife a perfunctory peck and collapsed with a sigh of relief into the nearest chair.

"Phew!" he said, mopping his brow. "Everyone raced past me on the way up the hill, so I suppose people *do* get used to it. I think I've lost ten kilograms already."

"What sort of day did you have?" asked Jean dutifully. She hoped George would not be too exhausted to help with the unpacking.

"Very stimulating. Of course I can't remember half the people I met, but they all seemed very pleasant. And the theater is just as good as I'd hoped. We're starting work next week on Shaw's *Back to Methuselah*. I'll be in complete charge of sets and stage design.

It'll make a change, not having a dozen people to tell me what I can't do. Yes, I think we're going to like it here."

"Despite the bicycles?"

George summoned up enough energy to grin.

"Yes," he said. "In a couple of weeks, I won't even notice this little hill of ours."

He didn't really believe it—but it was perfectly true. It was another month, however, before Jean ceased to pine for the car, and discovered all the things one could do with one's own kitchen.

New Athens was not a natural and spontaneous growth like the city whose name it bore. Everything about the colony was deliberately planned, as the result of many years of study by a group of very remarkable men. It had begun as an open conspiracy against the Overlords, an implicit challenge to their policy if not to their power. At first the colony's sponsors had been more than half certain that Karellen would neatly frustrate them, but the Supervisor had done nothing—absolutely nothing. This was not quite as reassuring as might have been expected. Karellen had plenty of time: he might be preparing a delayed counterstroke. Or he might be so certain of the project's failure that he felt no need to take any action against it.

That the colony would fail had been the prediction of most people. Yet even in the past, long before any real knowledge of social dynamics had existed, there had been many communities devoted to special religious or philosophical ends. It was true that their mortality rate had been high, but some had survived. And the foundations of New Athens were as secure as modern science could make them.

There were many reasons for choosing an island site. Not the least important were psychological. In an age of universal air transport, the ocean meant nothing as a physical barrier, but it still gave a sense of isolation. Moreover, a limited land area made it impossible for too many people to live in the colony. The maximum population was fixed at a hundred thousand: more than that, and the advantages inherent in a small, compact community would be lost. One of the aims of the founders was that any member of New Athens should know all the other citizens who shared his interests—and as many as one or two percent of the remainder as well.

The man who had been the driving force behind New Athens was a Jew. And, like Moses, he had never lived to enter his promised land, for the colony had been founded three years after his death.

He had been born in Israel, the last independent nation ever to come into existence—and, therefore, the shortest lived. The end of national sovereignty had been felt here perhaps more bitterly than anywhere else, for it is hard to lose a dream which one has just achieved after centuries of striving.

Ben Salomon was no fanatic, but the memories of his childhood must have determined, to no small extent, the philosophy he was to put into practice. He could just remember what the world had been before the advent of the Overlords, and had no wish to return to it. Like not a few other intelligent and well-meaning men, he could appreciate all that Karellen had done for the human race, while still being unhappy about the Supervisor's ultimate plans. Was it possible, he sometimes said to himself, that despite all their enormous intelligence the Overlords did not really understand mankind, and were making a terrible mistake from the best of motives? Suppose, in their altruistic passion for justice and order, they had determined to reform the world, but had not realized that they were destroying the soul of man?

The decline had barely started, yet the first symptoms of decay were not hard to discover. Salomon was no artist, but he had an acute appreciation of art and knew that his age could not match the achievements of previous centuries in any single field. Perhaps matters would right themselves in due course, when the shock of encountering the Overlord civilization had worn off. But it might not, and a prudent man would consider taking out an insurance policy.

New Athens was that policy. Its establishment had taken twenty years and some billions of Pounds Decimal—a relatively trivial fraction, therefore, of the world's total wealth. Nothing had happened for the first fifteen years; everything had happened in the last five.

Salomon's task would have been impossible had he not been able to convince a handful of the world's most famous artists that his plan was sound. They had sympathized because it appealed to their egos, not because it was important for the race. But, once convinced, the world had listened to them and given both moral and material support. Behind this spectacular façade of temperamental talent, the real architects of the colony had laid their plans.

A society consists of human beings whose behavior as individuals is unpredictable. But if one takes enough of the basic units, then certain laws begin to appear—as was discovered long ago by life insurance companies. No one can tell what individuals will die in a given time—yet the total number of deaths can be predicted with considerable accuracy.

There are other, subtler laws, first glimpsed in the early twentieth century by mathematicians such as Weiner and Rashavesky. They had argued that such events as economic depressions, the results of armament races, the stability of social groups, political elections, and so on, could be analyzed by the correct mathematical techniques. The great difficulty was the enormous number of variables, many of them hard to define in numerical terms. One could not draw a set of curves and state definitely: "When this line is reached, it will mean war." And one could never wholly allow for such utterly unpredictable events as the assassination of a key figure or the effects of some new scientific discovery—still less such natural catastrophies as earthquakes or floods, which might have a profound effect on large numbers of people and the social groups in which they lived.

Yet one could do much, thanks to the knowledge patiently accumulated during the past hundred years. The task would have been impossible without the aid of the giant computing machines that could perform the work of a thousand human calculators in a matter of seconds. Such aids had been used to the utmost when the colony was planned.

Even so, the founders of New Athens could only provide the soil and the climate in which the plant they wished to cherish might —or might not—come to flower. As Salomon himself had remarked: "We can be sure of talent: we can only pray for genius." But it was a reasonable hope that in such a concentrated society some interesting reactions would take place. Few artists thrive in solitude, and nothing is more stimulating than the conflict of minds with similar interests.

So far, the conflict had produced worthwhile results in sculpture, music, literary criticism, and film-making. It was still too early to see if the group working on historical research would fulfill the hopes of its instigators, who were frankly aiming at restoring mankind's pride in its own achievements. Painting still languished, which supported the view of those who considered that static, two-dimensional forms of art had no further possibilities.

It was noticeable—though a satisfactory explanation for this had not yet been produced—that Time played an essential part in the colony's most successful artistic achievements. Even its sculpture was seldom immobile. Andrew Carson's intriguing volumes and curves changed slowly as one watched, according to complex patterns that the mind could appreciate, even if it could not fully comprehend them. Indeed, Carson claimed, with some truth, to have taken the "mobiles" of a century before to their ultimate conclusion, and thus to have wedded sculpture and ballet.

Much of the colony's musical experimenting was, quite consciously, concerned with what might be called "time span." What was the briefest note that the mind could grasp—or the longest that it could tolerate without boredom? Could the result be varied by conditioning or by the use of appropriate orchestration? Such problems were discussed endlessly, and the arguments were not purely academic. They had resulted in some extremely interesting compositions.

But it was in the art of the cartoon film, with its limitless possibilities, that New Athens had made its most successful experiments. The hundred years since the time of Disney had still left much undone in this most flexible of all mediums. On the purely realistic side, results could be produced indistinguishable from actual photography—much to the contempt of those who were developing the cartoon along abstract lines.

The group of artists and scientists that had so far done least was the one that had attracted the greatest interest—and the greatest alarm. This was the team working on "total identification." The history of the cinema gave the clue to their actions. First, sound, then color, then stereoscopy, then Cinerama, had made the old "moving pictures" more and more like reality itself. Where was the end of the story? Surely, the final stage would be reached when the audience forgot it was an audience, and became part of the action. To achieve this would involve stimulation of all the senses, and perhaps hypnosis as well, but many believed it to be practical. When the goal was attained, there would be an enormous enrichment of human experience. A man could become—for a while, at least—any other person, and could take part in any conceivable adventure, real or imaginary. He could even be a plant or an animal, if it proved possible to capture and record the sense impressions of other living creatures. And when the "program" was over, he would have acquired a memory as vivid as any experience in his actual life—indeed, indistinguishable from reality itself.

The prospect was dazzling. Many also found it terrifying, and hoped that the enterprise would fail. But they knew in their hearts that once science had declared a thing possible, there was no escape from its eventual realization. . . .

This, then, was New Athens and some of its dreams. It hoped to become what the old Athens might have been had it possessed machines instead of slaves, science instead of superstition. But it was much too early yet to tell if the experiment would succeed.

CHAPTER FIFTEEN

Jeffrey Greggson was one islander who, as yet, had no interest in aesthetics or science, the two main preoccupations of his elders. But he heartily approved of the colony, for purely personal reasons. The sea, never more than a few kilometers away in any direction, fascinated him. Most of his short life had been spent far inland, and he was not yet accustomed to the novelty of being surrounded by water. He was a good swimmer, and would often cycle off with other young friends, carrying his fins and mask, to go exploring the shallower water of the lagoon. At first Jean was not very happy about this, but after she had made a few dives herself, she lost her fear of the sea and its strange creatures and let Jeffrey enjoy himself as he pleased—on condition that he never swam alone.

The other member of the Greggson household who approved of the change was Fey, the beautiful golden retriever who nominally belonged to George but could seldom be detached from Jeffrey. The two were inseparable, both by day and—if Jean had not put her foot down—by night. Only when Jeffrey went off on his bicycle did Fey remain at home, lying listlessly in front of the door and staring down the road with moist, mournful eyes, her muzzle resting on her paws. This was rather mortifying to George, who had paid a stiff price for Fey and her pedigree. It looked as if he would have to wait for the next generation—due in three months—before he could have a dog of his own. Jean had other views on the subject. She liked Fey, but felt that one hound per house was quite sufficient.

Only Jennifer Anne had not yet decided whether she liked the colony. That, however, was hardly surprising, for she had so far seen nothing of the world beyond the plastic panels of her cot, and had, as yet, very little suspicion that such a place existed.

George Greggson did not often think about the past: he was too busy with plans for the future, too much occupied by his work and his children. It was seldom indeed that his mind went back across the years to that evening in Africa, and he never talked about it with Jean. By mutual consent, the subject was avoided, and since that day they had never visited the Boyces again, despite repeated invitations. They called Rupert with fresh excuses several times a year, and lately he had ceased to bother them. His marriage to Maia, rather to everyone's surprise, still seemed to be flourishing.

One result of that evening was that Jean had lost all desire to dabble with mysteries at the borders of known science. The naïve and uncritical wonder that had drawn her to Rupert and his experiments had completely vanished. Perhaps she had been convinced and wanted no more proof: George preferred not to ask her. Possibly the cares of maternity had banished such interests from her mind.

There was no point, George knew, in worrying about a mystery that could never be solved, yet sometimes in the stillness of the night he would wake and wonder. He remembered his meeting with Jan Rodricks on the roof of Rupert's house, and the few words that were all he had spoken with the only human being successfully to defy the Overlords' ban. Nothing in the realm of the supernatural, thought George, could be more eerie than the plain scientific fact that though almost ten years had passed since he had spoken to Jan, that now-far-distant voyager would have aged by only a few days.

The universe was vast, but that fact terrified him less than its mystery. George was not a person who thought deeply on such matters, yet sometimes it seemed to him that men were like children amusing themselves in some secluded playground, protected from the fierce realities of the outer world. Jan Rodricks had resented that protection and had escaped from it—into no one knew what. But in this matter, George found himself on the side of the Overlords. He had no wish to face whatever lurked in the unknown darkness, just beyond the little circle of light cast by the lamp of Science.

"How is it," said George plaintively, "that Jeff's always off somewhere when I happen to be home? Where's he gone today?"

Jean looked up from her knitting—an archaic occupation which had recently been revived with much success. Such fashions came and went on the island with some rapidity. The main result of this particular craze was that the men had now all been presented with multicolored sweaters, far too hot to wear in the daytime but quite useful after sundown.

"He's gone off to Sparta with some friends," Jean replied. "He promised to be back for dinner."

"I really came home to do some work," said George thoughtfully. "But it's a nice day, and I think I'll go out there and have a swim myself. What kind of fish would you like me to bring back?"

George had never caught anything, and the fish in the lagoon were much too wily to be trapped. Jean was just going to point this out when the stillness of the afternoon was shattered by a sound that still had power, even in this peaceful age, to chill the blood and set the scalp crawling with apprehension.

It was the wail of a siren, rising and falling, spreading its message of danger in concentric circles out to sea.

For almost a hundred years the stresses had been slowly increasing, here in the burning darkness deep beneath the ocean's floor. Though the submarine canyon had been formed geological ages ago, the tortured rocks had never reconciled themselves to their new positions. Countless times the strata had creaked and shifted, as the unimaginable weight of water disturbed their precarious equilibrium. They were ready to move again.

Jeff was exploring the rock pools along the narrow Spartan beach—an occupation he found endlessly absorbing. One never knew what exotic creatures one might find, sheltered here from the waves that marched forever across the Pacific to spend themselves against the reef. It was a fairyland for any child, and at the moment he possessed it all himself, for his friends had gone up into the hills.

The day was quiet and peaceful. There was not a breath of wind, and even the perpetual muttering beyond the reef had sunk to a sullen undertone. A blazing sun hung halfway down the sky, but Jeff's mahogany-brown body was now quite immune to its onslaughts.

The beach here was a narrow belt of sand, sloping steeply towards the lagoon. Looking down into the glass-clear water, Jeff could see the submerged rocks which were as familiar to him as any formations on the land. About ten meters down, the weed-covered ribs of an ancient schooner curved up towards the world it had left almost two centuries ago. Jeff and his friends had often explored the wreck, but their hopes of hidden treasure had been disappointed. All that they had ever retrieved was a barnacle-encrusted compass.

Very firmly, something took hold of the beach and gave it a single, sudden jerk. The tremor passed so swiftly that Jeff wondered if he had imagined it. Perhaps it was a momentary giddiness, for all around him remained utterly unchanged. The waters of the lagoon were unruffled, the sky empty of cloud or menace. And then a very strange thing began to happen.

Swifter than any tide could ebb, the water was receding from the shore. Jeff watched, deeply puzzled and not in the least afraid, as the wet sands were uncovered and lay sparkling in the sun. He followed the retreating ocean, determined to make the most of whatever miracle had opened up the underwater world for his inspection. Now the level had sunk so far that the broken mast of the old wreck was climbing into the air, its weeds hanging limply from it as they lost their liquid support. Jeff hastened forward, eager to see what wonders would be uncovered next.

It was then that he noticed the sound from the reef. He had never heard anything like it before, and he stopped to think the matter over, his bare feet slowly sinking into the moist sand. A great fish was thrashing in its death agonies a few meters away, but Jeff scarcely noticed it. He stood, alert and listening, while the noise from the reef grew steadily around him.

It was a sucking, gurgling sound, as of a river racing through a narrow channel. It was the voice of the reluctantly retreating sea, angry at losing, even for a moment, the lands it rightfully possessed. Through the graceful branches of the coral, through the hidden submarine caves, millions of tons of water were draining out of the lagoon into the vastness of the Pacific.

Very soon, and very swiftly, they would return.

One of the salvage parties, hours later, found Jeff on a great block of coral that had been hurled twenty meters above the normal water level. He did not seem particularly frightened, though he was upset over the loss of his bicycle. He was also very hungry, as the partial destruction of the causeway had cut him off from home. When rescued he was contemplating swimming back to Athens, and unless the currents had changed drastically, would doubtless have managed the crossing without much trouble.

Jean and George had witnessed the whole sequence of events when the *tsunami* hit the island. Though the damage to the low-lying areas of Athens had been severe, there had been no loss of life. The seismographs had been able to give only fifteen minutes warning, but that had been long enough to get everyone above the danger line. Now the colony was licking its wounds and collecting together a mass of legends that would grow steadily more hair-raising through the years to come.

Jean burst into tears when her son was restored to her, for she had quite convinced herself that he had been swept out to sea. She had watched with horrified eyes as the black, foam-capped wall of water had moved roaring in from the horizon to smother the base of Sparta in spume and spray. It seemed incredible that Jeff could have reached safety in time.

It was scarcely surprising that he could not give a very rational account of what had happened. When he had eaten and was safely in bed, Jean and George gathered by his side.

"Go to sleep, darling, and forget all about it," said Jean. "You're all right now."

"But it was fun, Mummy," protested Jeff. "I wasn't *really* frightened."

"That's fine," said George. "You're a brave lad, and it's a good thing you were sensible and ran in time. I've heard about these tidal waves before. A lot of people get drowned because they go out on the uncovered beach to see what's happened."

"That's what I did," confessed Jeff. "I wonder who it was helped me?"

"What do you mean? There wasn't anyone with you. The other boys were up the hill."

Jeff looked puzzled.

"But someone told me to run."

Jean and George glanced at each other in mild alarm.

"You mean—you imagined you heard something?"

"Oh, don't bother him now," said Jean anxiously, and with a little too much haste. But George was stubborn.

"I want to get to the bottom of this. Tell me just what happened, Jeff."

"Well, I was right down the beach, by that old wreck, when the voice spoke."

"What did it say?"

"I can't quite remember, but it was something like 'Jeffrey, get up the hill as quickly as you can. You'll be drowned if you stay here.' I'm sure it called me Jeffrey, not Jeff. So it couldn't have been anyone I knew."

"Was it a man's voice? And where did it come from?"

"It was ever so close beside me. And it sounded like a man. . . ." Jeff hesitated for a moment, and George prompted him.

"Go on—just imagine that you're back on the beach, and tell us exactly what happened."

"Well, it wasn't quite like anyone I've ever heard talking before. I think he was a very *big* man."

"Is that all the voice said?"

"Yes—until I started to climb the hill. Then another funny thing happened. You know the path up the cliff?"

"Yes."

"I was running up that, because it was the quickest way. I knew what was happening now, for I'd seen the big wave coming in. It was making an awful noise, too. And then I found there was a great big rock in the way. It wasn't there before, and I couldn't get past it."

"The quake must have brought it down," said George.

"Shush! Go on, Jeff."

"I didn't know what to do, and I could hear the wave coming closer. Then the voice said, 'Close your eyes, Jeffrey, and put your hand in front of your face.' It seemed a funny thing to do, but I tried it. And then there was a great flash—I could feel it all over—and when I opened my eyes the rock was gone."

"Gone?"

"That's right—it just wasn't there. So I started running again, and that's when I nearly burnt my feet, because the path was awful hot. The water hissed when it went over it, but it couldn't catch me then—I was too far up the cliff. And that's all. I came down again when there weren't any more waves. Then I found that my bike had gone, and the road home had been knocked down."

"Don't worry about the bicycle, dear," said Jean, squeezing her son thankfully. "We'll get you another one. The only thing that matters is that you're safe. We won't worry about *how* it happened."

That wasn't true, of course, for the conference began immediately they had left the nursery. It decided nothing, but it had two sequels. The next day, without telling George, Jean took her small son to the colony's child psychologist. He listened carefully while Jeff repeated his story, not in the least overawed by his novel surroundings. Then, while his unsuspecting patient rejected seriatim the toys in the next room, the doctor reassured Jean.

"There's nothing on his card to suggest any mental abnormality. You must remember that he's been through a terrifying experience, and he's come out of it remarkably well. He's a highly imaginative child, and probably believes his own story. So just accept it, and don't worry unless there are any later symptoms. Then let me know at once."

That evening, Jean passed the verdict on to her husband. He did not seem as relieved as she had hoped, and she put it down to worry over the damage to his beloved theater. He just grunted "That's fine," and settled down with the current issue of *Stage and Studio*. It looked as if he had lost interest in the whole affair, and Jean felt vaguely annoyed with him.

But three weeks later, on the first day that the causeway was reopened, George and his bicycle set off briskly toward Sparta. The beach was still littered with masses of shattered coral, and in one place the reef itself seemed to have been breached. George wondered how long it would take the myriads of patient polyps to repair the damage.

There was only one path up the face of the cliff, and when he had recovered his breath George began the climb. A few dried fragments of weed, trapped among the rocks, marked the limit of the ascending waters.

For a long time George Greggson stood on that lonely track, staring at the patch of fused rock beneath his feet. He tried to tell himself that it was some freak of the long-dead volcano, but soon abandoned this attempt at self-deception. His mind went back to that night, years ago, when he and Jean had joined that silly experiment of Rupert Boyce's. No one had ever really understood what had happened then, and George knew that in some unfathomable way these two strange events were linked together. First it had been Jean, now her son. He did not know whether to be glad or fearful, and in his heart he uttered a silent prayer:

"Thank you, Karellen, for whatever your people did for Jeff. But I wish I knew *why* they did it."

He went slowly down to the beach, and the great white gulls wheeled around him, annoyed because he had brought no food to throw them as they circled in the sky.

✳ CHAPTER SIXTEEN

Karellen's request, though it might have been expected at any time since the foundation of the colony, was something of a bombshell. It represented, as everyone was fully aware, a crisis in the affairs of Athens, and nobody could decide whether good or bad would come of it.

Until now, the colony had gone its way without any form of interference from the Overlords. They had left it completely alone, as indeed they ignored most human activities that were not subversive or did not offend their codes of behavior. Whether the colony's aims could be called subversive was uncertain. They were nonpolitical, but they represented a bid for intellectual and artistic independence. And from that, who knew what might come? The

Overlords might well be able to foresee the future of Athens more clearly than its founders—and they might not like it.

Of course, if Karellen wished to send an observer, inspector, or whatever one cared to call him, there was nothing that could be done about it. Twenty years ago the Overlords had announced that they had discontinued all use of their surveillance devices, so that humanity need no longer consider itself spied upon. However, the fact that such devices still existed meant that nothing could be hidden from the Overlords if they really wanted to see it.

There were some on the island who welcomed this visit as a chance of settling one of the minor problems of Overlord psychology—their attitude towards art. Did they regard it as a childish aberration of the human race? Did they have any forms of art themselves? In that case, was the purpose of this visit purely aesthetic, or did Karellen have less innocent motives?

All these matters were debated endlessly while the preparations were under way. Nothing was known of the visiting Overlord, but it was assumed that he could absorb culture in unlimited amounts. The experiment would at least be attempted, and the reactions of the victim observed with interest by a battery of very shrewd minds.

The current chairman of the council was the philosopher, Charles Yan Sen, an ironic but fundamentally cheerful man not yet in his sixties and therefore still in the prime of life. Plato would have approved of him as an example of the philosopher-statesman, though Sen did not altogether approve of Plato, whom he suspected of grossly misrepresenting Socrates. He was one of the islanders who was determined to make the most of this visit, if only to show the Overlords that men still had plenty of initiative and were not yet, as he put it, "fully domesticated."

Nothing in Athens was done without a committee, that ultimate hallmark of the democratic method. Indeed, someone had once defined the colony as a system of interlocking committees. But the system worked, thanks to the patient studies of the social psychologists who had been the real founders of Athens. Because the community was not too large, everyone in it could take some part in its running and could be a citizen in the truest sense of the word.

It was almost inevitable that George, as a leading member of the artistic hierarchy, should be one of the reception committee. But he made doubly sure by pulling a few strings. If the Overlords wanted to study the colony, George wanted equally to study them. Jean was not very happy about this. Ever since that evening at the Boyces', she had felt a vague hostility towards the Overlords, though she could never give any reason for it. She just wished to have as little to do with them as possible, and to her one of the island's main attractions had been its hoped-for independence. Now she feared that this independence might be threatened.

The Overlord arrived without ceremony in an ordinary man-made flyer, to the disappointment of those who had hoped for something more spectacular. He might have been Karellen himself, for no one had ever been able to distinguish one Overlord from another with any degree of confidence. They all seemed duplicates from a single, master mold. Perhaps, by some unknown biological process, they were.

After the first day, the islanders ceased to pay much attention when the official car murmured past on its sight-seeing tours. The visitor's correct name, Thanthalteresco, proved too intractable for general use, and he was soon christened "the Inspector." It was an accurate enough name, for his curiosity and appetite for statistics were insatiable.

Charles Yan Sen was quite exhausted when, long after midnight, he had seen the Inspector back to the flyer which was serving as his base. There, no doubt, he would continue to work throughout the night while his human hosts indulged in the frailty of sleep.

Mrs. Sen greeted her husband anxiously on his return. They were a devoted couple, despite his playful habit of calling her Xantippe when they were entertaining guests. She had long ago threatened to make the appropriate retort by brewing him a cup of hemlock, but fortunately this herbal beverage was less common in the new Athens than the old.

"Was it a success?" she asked as her husband settled down to a belated meal.

"I think so—but you can never tell what goes on inside those remarkable minds. He was certainly interested—even complimentary. I apologized, by the way, for not inviting him here. He said he quite understood, and had no wish to bang his head on our ceiling."

"What did you show him today?"

"The bread-and-butter side of the colony, which he didn't seem to find as boring as I always do. He asked every question you could imagine about production, how we balanced our budget, our mineral resources, the birth rate, how we got our food, and so on. Luckily I had Secretary Harrison with me, and *he'd* come prepared with every Annual Report since the colony began. You should have heard them swapping statistics. The Inspector's borrowed the lot, and I'm prepared to bet that when we see him tomorrow he'll be able to quote any figure back at us. I find that kind of mental performance frightfully depressing."

He yawned and began to peck halfheartedly at his food.

"Tomorrow should be more interesting. We're going to do the schools and the Academy. That's when *I'm* going to ask some questions for a change. I'd like to know how the Overlords bring up their kids—assuming, of course, that they have any."

That was not a question that Charles Sen was ever to have answered, but on other points the Inspector was remarkably talkative. He would evade awkward queries in a manner that was a pleasure to behold, and then, quite unexpectedly, would become positively confiding.

Their first real intimacy occurred while they were driving away from the school that was one of the colony's chief prides. "It's a great responsibility," Dr. Sen had remarked, "training these young minds for the future. Fortunately, human beings are extraordinarily resilient: it takes a pretty bad upbringing to do permanent damage. Even if our aims are mistaken, our little victims will probably get over it. And as you've seen, they appear to be perfectly happy." He paused for a moment, then glanced mischievously up at the towering figure of his passenger. The Inspector was completely clothed in some reflecting silvery cloth so that not an inch of his body was exposed to the fierce sunlight. Behind the dark glasses, Dr. Sen was aware of the great eyes watching him emotionlessly—or with emotions which he could never understand. "Our problem in bringing up these children must, I imagine, be very similar to yours when confronted with the human race. Wouldn't you agree?"

"In some ways," admitted the Overlord gravely. "In others perhaps a better analogy can be found in the history of your colonial powers. The Roman and British Empires, for that reason, have always been of considerable interest to us. The case of India is particularly instructive. The main difference between us and the

British in India was that they had no real motives for going there—no conscious objectives, that is, except such trivial and temporary ones as trade or hostility to other European powers. They found themselves possessors of an empire before they knew what to do with it, and were never really happy until they had got rid of it again."

"And will you," asked Dr. Sen, quite unable to resist the opportunity, "get rid of your empire when the time arises?"

"Without the slightest hesitation," replied the Inspector.

Dr. Sen did not press the point. The forthrightness of the reply was not altogether flattering: moreover, they had now arrived at the Academy, where the assembled pedagogues were waiting to sharpen their wits on a real, live Overlord.

"As our distinguished colleague will have told you," said Professor Chance, Dean of the University of New Athens, "our main purpose is to keep the minds of our people *alert,* and to enable them to realize all their potentialities. Beyond this island"—his gesture indicated, and rejected, the rest of the globe—"I fear that the human race has lost its *initiative.* It has peace, it has plenty—but it has no *horizons.*"

"Yet here, of course . . . ?" interjected the Overlord blandly.

Professor Chance, who lacked a sense of humor and was vaguely aware of the fact, glanced suspiciously at his visitor.

"Here," he continued, "we do not suffer from the ancient obsession that leisure is wicked. But we do not consider that it is enough to be passive receptors of entertainment.

"Everybody on this island has one ambition, which may be summed up very simply. It is to do *something,* however small it may be, better than anyone else. Of course, it's an ideal we don't all achieve. But in this modern world the great thing is to *have* an ideal. Achieving it is considerably less important."

The Inspector did not seem inclined to comment. He had discarded his protective clothing, but still wore dark glasses even in the subdued light of the Common Room. The Dean wondered if they were physiologically necessary, or whether they were merely camouflage. Certainly they made quite impossible the already difficult task of reading the Overlord's thoughts. He did not, however, seem to object to the somewhat challenging statements that had been thrown at him, or the criticisms of his race's policy with regard to Earth which they implied.

The Dean was about to press the attack when Professor Sperling, head of the Science Department, decided to make it a three-cornered fight.

"As you doubtless know, Sir, one of the great problems of our culture has been the dichotomy between art and science. I'd very much like to know your views on the matter. Do you subscribe to the view that all artists are abnormal? That their work—or at any rate the impulse behind it—is the result of some deep-seated psychological dissatisfaction?"

Professor Chance cleared his throat purposefully, but the Inspector forestalled him.

"I've been told that all men are artists to a certain extent, so that everyone is capable of creating something, if only on a rudimentary level. At your schools yesterday, for example, I noticed the emphasis placed on self-expression in drawing, painting, and modeling. The impulse seemed quite universal, even among those clearly destined to be specialists in science. So if all artists are abnormal, and all men are artists, we have an interesting syllogism. . . ."

Everyone waited for him to complete it. But when it suited their purpose, the Overlords could be impeccably tactful.

The Inspector came through the symphony concert with flying colors, which was a good deal more than could be said for many human members of the audience. The only concession to popular taste had been Stravinsky's "Symphony of Psalms": the rest of the program was aggressively modernistic. Whatever one's views on its merits, the performance was superb, for the colony's boast that it possessed some of the finest musicians in the world was no idle one. There had been much wrangling among the various rival composers for the honor of being included in the program, though a few cynics wondered if it would be an honor at all. For all that anyone knew to the contrary, the Overlords might be tone deaf.

It was observed, however, that after the concert Thanthalteresco sought out the three composers who had been present, and complimented them all on what he called their "great ingenuity." This caused them to retire with pleased but vaguely baffled expressions.

It was not until the third day that George Greggson had a chance of meeting the Inspector. The theater had arranged a kind of mixed grill rather than a single dish—two one-act plays, a sketch by a world-famous impersonator, and a ballet sequence. Once again all these items were superbly executed and one critic's prediction— "Now at least we'll discover if the Overlords can yawn"—was falsified. Indeed, the Inspector laughed several times, and in the correct places.

And yet—no one could be sure. He might himself be putting on a superb act, following the performance by logic alone and with his own strange emotions completely untouched, as an anthropologist might take part in some primitive rite. The fact that he uttered the appropriate sounds, and made the expected responses, really proved nothing at all.

Though George had been determined to have a talk with the Inspector, he failed utterly. After the performance they exchanged a few words of introduction, then the visitor was swept away. It was completely impossible to isolate him from his entourage, and George went home in a state of extreme frustration. He was by no means certain what he wished to say, even if he had had the chance, but somehow, he felt sure, he could have turned the conversation round to Jeff. And now the opportunity had gone.

His bad temper lasted two days. The Inspector's flyer had departed, amid many protestations of mutual regard, before the sequel emerged. No one had thought of questioning Jeff, and the boy must have been thinking it over for a long time before he approached George.

"Daddy," he said, just prior to bedtime. "You know the Overlord who came to see us?"

"Yes," replied George grimly.

"Well, he came to our school, and I heard him talk to some of the teachers. I didn't really understand what he said—but I think I recognized his voice. That's who told me to run when the big wave came."

"You are quite sure?"

Jeff hesitated for a moment.

"Not *quite*—but if it wasn't him, it was another Overlord. I wondered if I ought to thank him. But he's gone now, hasn't he?"

"Yes," said George, "I'm afraid he has. Still, perhaps we'll have another chance. Now go to bed like a good boy and don't worry about it any more."

When Jeff was safely out of the way, and Jenny had been attended to, Jean came back and sat on the rug beside George's chair, leaning against his legs. It was a habit that struck him as annoyingly sentimental, but not worth creating a fuss about. He merely made his knees as knobbly as possible.

"What do you think about it now?" asked Jean in a tired, flat voice. "Do you believe it really happened?"

"It happened," George replied, "but perhaps we're foolish to worry. After all, most parents would be grateful—and of course, I *am* grateful. The explanation may be perfectly simple. We know that the Overlords have got interested in the colony, so they've undoubtedly been observing it with their instruments—despite that promise they made. Suppose one was just prowling round with that viewing gadget of theirs, and saw the wave coming. It would be natural enough to warn anyone who was in danger."

"But he knew Jeff's name, don't forget that. No, we're being watched. There's something peculiar about us, something that attracts their attention. I've felt it ever since Rupert's party. It's funny how that changed both our lives."

George looked down at her with sympathy, but nothing more. It was strange how much one could alter in so short a time. He was fond of her: she had borne his children and was part of his life. But of the love which a not clearly remembered person named George Greggson had once known towards a fading dream called Jean Morrel, how much remained? His love was divided now between Jeff and Jennifer on the one hand—and Carolle on the other. He did not believe that Jean knew about Carolle, and he intended to tell her before anyone else did. But somehow he had never got round to it.

"Very well—Jeff is being watched—protected, in fact. Don't you think that should make us proud? Perhaps the Overlords have planned a great future for him. I wonder what it can be?"

He was talking to reassure Jean, he knew. He was not greatly disturbed himself, only intrigued and baffled. And quite suddenly another thought struck him, something that should have occurred to him before. His eyes turned automatically towards the nursery.

"I wonder if it's only Jeff they're after," he said.

In due course the Inspector presented his report. The Islanders would have given much to see it. All the statistics and records went into the insatiable memories of the great computers which were some, but not all, of the unseen powers behind Karellen. Even before these impersonal electric minds had arrived at their conclusions, however, the Inspector had given his own recommendations. Expressed in the thoughts and language of the human race, they would have run as follows:

"We need take no action regarding the colony. It is an interesting experiment, but cannot in any way affect the future. Its artistic endeavors are no concern of ours, and there is no evidence that any scientific research is progressing along dangerous channels.

"As planned, I was able to see the school records of subject Zero, without arousing curiosity. The relevant statistics are attached, and it will be seen that there are still no signs of any unusual development. Yet, as we know, breakthrough seldom gives much prior warning.

"I also met the subject's father, and gathered the impression that he wished to speak to me. Fortunately I was able to avoid this. There is no doubt that he suspects something, though of course he can never guess the truth nor affect the outcome in any way.

"I grow more and more sorry for these people."

George Greggson would have agreed with the Inspector's verdict that there was nothing unusual about Jeff. There was just that one baffling incident, as startling as a single clap of thunder on a long, calm day. And after that—nothing.

Jeff had all the energy and inquisitiveness of any other seven year old. He was intelligent—when he bothered to be—but was in no danger of becoming a genius. Sometimes, Jean thought a little wearily, he filled to perfection the classic recipe for a small boy: "a noise surrounded by dirt." Not that it was very easy to be certain about the dirt, which had to accumulate for a considerable time before it showed against Jeff's normal sunburn.

By turns he could be affectionate or morose, reserved or ebullient. He showed no preference for one parent rather than the other, and the arrival of his little sister had not produced any signs of jealousy. His medical card was spotless; he had never had a day's illness in his life. But in these times, and in such a climate, there was nothing unusual about this.

Unlike some boys, Jeff did not grow quickly bored by his father's company and desert him whenever possible for associates of his own age. It was obvious that he shared George's artistic talents, and almost as soon as he was able to walk had become a regular backstage visitor to the colony's theater. Indeed, the theater had adopted him as an unofficial mascot and he was now highly skilled at presenting bouquets to visiting celebrities of stage and screen.

Yes, Jeff was a perfectly ordinary boy. So George reassured himself as they went for walks or rides together over the Island's rather restricted terrain. They would talk as sons and fathers had done since the beginning of time—except that in this age there was so much more to talk about. Though Jeff never left the Island, he could see all that he wished of the surrounding world through the ubiquitous eyes of the television screen. He felt, like all the colonists, a slight disdain for the rest of mankind. They were the elite, the vanguard of progress. They would take mankind to the heights that the Overlords had reached—and perhaps beyond. Not tomorrow, certainly, but one day. . . .

They never guessed that that day would be all too soon.

⨳ *CHAPTER SEVENTEEN*

The dreams began six weeks later.

In the darkness of the subtropical night, George Greggson swam slowly upwards towards consciousness. He did not know what had awakened him, and for a moment he lay in a puzzled stupor. Then he realized that he was alone. Jean had got up and gone silently into the nursery. She was talking quietly to Jeff, too quietly for him to hear what she was saying.

George heaved himself out of bed and went to join her. The Poppet had made such nocturnal excursions common enough, but then there had been no question of his remaining asleep through the uproar. This was something quite different and he wondered what had disturbed Jean.

The only light in the nursery came from the fluoropaint patterns on the walls. By their dim glow, George could see Jean sitting beside Jeff's bed. She turned as he came in, and whispered, "Don't disturb the Poppet."

"What's the matter?"

"I knew that Jeff wanted me, and that woke me up."

The very matter-of-fact simplicity of that statement gave George a feeling of sick apprehension. *"I knew that Jeff wanted me."* How did you know? he wondered. But all he asked was:

"Has he been having nightmares?"

"I'm not sure," said Jean, "he seems all right now. But he was frightened when I came in."

"I *wasn't* frightened, Mummy," came a small, indignant voice. "But it was such a strange place."

"What was?" asked George. "Tell me all about it."

"There were mountains," said Jeff dreamily. "They were ever so high and there was no snow on them, like on all the mountains I've ever seen. Some of them were burning."

"You mean—volcanoes?"

"Not really. They were burning all over, with funny blue flames. And while I was watching, the sun came up."

"Go on—why have you stopped?"

Jeff turned puzzled eyes towards his father.

"That's the other thing I don't understand, Daddy. It came up so quickly, and it was much too big. And—it wasn't the right color. It was such a pretty blue."

There was a long, heart-freezing silence. Then George said quietly, "Is that all?"

"Yes. I began to feel kind of lonely, and that's when Mummy came and woke me up."

George tousled his son's untidy hair with one hand, while tightening his dressing gown around him with the other. He felt suddenly very cold and very small. But there was no hint of this in his voice when he spoke to Jeff.

"It's just a silly dream: you've eaten too much for supper. Forget all about it and go back to sleep, there's a good boy."

"I will, Daddy," Jeff replied: He paused for a moment, then added thoughtfully, "I think I'll try and go there again."

"A blue sun?" said Karellen, not many hours later. "That must have made identification fairly easy."

"Yes," Rashaverak answered. "It is undoubtedly Alphanidon Two. The Sulphur Mountains confirm the fact. And it's interesting to notice the distortion of the time scale. The planet rotates fairly slowly, so he must have observed many hours in a few minutes."

"That's all you can discover?"

"Yes, without questioning the child directly."

"We dare not do that. Events must take their natural course without our interference. When his parents approach us—then, perhaps, we can question him."

"They may never come to us. And when they do, it may be too late."

"That, I am afraid, cannot be helped. We should never forget this fact—that in these matters our curiosity is of no importance. It is no more important, even, than the happiness of mankind."

His hand reached out to break the connection.

"Continue the surveillance, of course, and report all results to me. But do not interfere in any way."

Yet when he was awake, Jeff still seemed just the same. That at least, thought George, was something for which they could be thankful. But the dread was growing in his heart.

To Jeff, it was only a game; it had not yet begun to frighten him. A dream was merely a dream, no matter how strange it might be. He was no longer lonely in the worlds that sleep opened up to him. Only on that first night had his mind called out to Jean across whatever unknown gulfs had sundered them. Now he went alone and fearless into the universe that was opening up before him.

In the mornings they would question him, and he would tell what he could remember. Sometimes his words stumbled and failed as he tried to describe scenes which were clearly not only beyond all his experience, but beyond the imagination of man. They would prompt him with new words, show him pictures and colors to refresh his memory, then build up what pattern they could from his replies. Often they could make nothing of the result, though it seemed that in Jeff's own mind his dream worlds were perfectly plain and sharp. He was simply unable to communicate them to his parents. Yet some were clear enough. . . .

Space—no planet, no surrounding landscape, no world underfoot. Only the stars in the velvet night, and hanging against them a great red sun that was beating like a heart. Huge and tenuous at one moment, it would slowly shrink, brightening at the same time as if new fuel was being fed to its internal fires. It would climb the spectrum and hover at the edge of yellow, and then the cycle would reverse itself, the star would expand and cool, becoming once more a ragged, flame-red cloud. . . .

("Typical pulsating variable," said Rashaverak eagerly. "Seen, too, under tremendous time-acceleration. I can't identify it precisely, but the nearest star that fits the description is Rhamsandron 9. Or it may be Pharanidon 12."

"Whichever it is," replied Karellen, "he's getting further away from home."

"Much further," said Rashaverak. . . .)

It might have been Earth. A white sun hung in a blue sky flecked with clouds, which were racing before a storm. A hill sloped gently down to an ocean torn into spray by the ravening wind. Yet nothing moved: the scene was frozen as if glimpsed in a flash of lightning. And far, far away on the horizon was something that was not of Earth—a line of misty columns, tapering slightly as they soared out of the sea and lost themselves among the clouds. They were spaced with perfect precision along the rim of the planet—too huge to be artificial, yet too regular to be natural.

("Sideneus 4 and the Pillars of the Dawn," said Rashaverak, and there was awe in his voice. "He has reached the center of the universe."

"And he has barely begun his journey," answered Karellen.)

The planet was absolutely flat. Its enormous gravity had long ago crushed into one uniform level the mountains of its fiery youth —mountains whose mightiest peaks had never exceeded a few meters in height. Yet there was life here, for the surface was covered with myriad geometrical patterns that crawled and moved and changed their color. It was a world of two dimensions, inhabited by beings who could be no more than a fraction of a centimeter in thickness.

And in its sky was such a sun as no opium eater could have imagined in his wildest dreams. Too hot to be white, it was a searing ghost at the frontiers of the ultraviolet, burning its planets with radiations which would be instantly lethal to all earthly forms of life. For millions of kilometers around extended great veils of gas and dust, fluorescing in countless colors as the blasts of ultraviolet tore through them. It was a star against which Earth's pale sun would have been as feeble as a glowworm at noon.

("Hexanerax 2, and nowhere else in the known universe," said Rashaverak. "Only a handful of our ships have ever reached it— and they have never risked any landings, for who would have thought that life could exist on such planets?"

"It seems," said Karellen, "that you scientists have not been as thorough as you had believed. If those—*patterns*—are intelligent, the problem of communication will be interesting. I wonder if they have any knowledge of the third dimension?")

It was a world that could never know the meaning of night and day, of years or seasons. Six colored suns shared its sky, so that there came only a change of light, never darkness. Through the clash and tug of conflicting gravitational fields, the planet traveled along the loops and curves of its inconceivably complex orbit, never retracing the same path. Every moment was unique: the configuration which the six suns now held in the heavens would not repeat itself this side of eternity.

And even here there was life. Though the planet might be scorched by the central fires in one age, and frozen in the outer reaches in another, it was yet the home of intelligence. The great, many-faceted crystals stood grouped in intricate geometrical patterns, motionless in the eras of cold, growing slowly along the veins of mineral when the world was warm again. No matter if it took a thousand years for them to complete a thought. The universe was still young, and time stretched endlessly before them. . . .

("I have searched all our records," said Rashaverak. "We have no knowledge of such a world, or such a combination of suns. If it existed inside our universe, the astronomers would have detected it, even if it lay beyond the range of our ships."

"Then he has left the galaxy."

"Yes. Surely it cannot be much longer now."

"Who knows? He is only dreaming. When he awakes, he is still the same. It is merely the first phase. We will know soon enough when the change begins.")

"We have met before, Mr. Greggson," said the Overlord gravely. "My name is Rashaverak. No doubt you remember."

"Yes," said George. "That party of Rupert Boyce's. I am not likely to forget. And I thought we should meet again."

"Tell me—why have you asked for this interview?"

"I think you already know."

"Perhaps: but it will help us both if you tell me in your own words. It may surprise you a good deal, but I also am trying to understand, and in some ways my ignorance is as great as yours."

George stared at the Overlord in astonishment. This was a thought that had never occurred to him. He had subconsciously assumed that the Overlords possessed all knowledge and all power —that they understood, and were probably responsible for, the things that had been happening to Jeff.

"I gather," George continued, "that you have seen the reports I gave to the island psychologist, so you know about the dreams."

"Yes: we know about them."

"I never believed that they were simply the imaginings of a child. They were so incredible that—I know this sounds ridiculous —they *had* to be based on some reality."

He looked anxiously at Rashaverak, not knowing whether to hope for confirmation or denial. The Overlord said nothing, but merely regarded him with his great, calm eyes. They were sitting almost face to face, for the room—which had obviously been designed for such interviews—was on two levels, the Overlord's massive chair being a good meter lower than George's. It was a friendly gesture, reassuring to the men who asked for these meetings and who were seldom in an easy frame of mind.

"We were worried, but not really alarmed at first. Jeff seemed perfectly normal when he woke up, and his dreams didn't appear to bother him. And then one night"—he hesitated and glanced defensively at the Overlord. "I've never believed in the supernatural: I'm no scientist, but I think there's a rational explanation for everything."

"There is," said Rashaverak. "I know what you saw: I was watching."

"I always suspected it. But Karellen had promised that you'd never spy on us with your instruments. Why have you broken that promise?"

"I have not broken it. The Supervisor said that the human race would no longer be under surveillance. That is a promise we have kept. I was watching your children, not you."

It was several seconds before George understood the implications of Rashaverak's words. Then the color drained slowly from his face.

"You mean? . . ." he gasped. His voice trailed away and he had to begin again. "Then what in God's name *are* my children?"

"That," said Rashaverak solemnly, "is what we are trying to discover."

Jennifer Anne Greggson, lately known as the Poppet, lay on her back with her eyes tightly closed. She had not opened them for a long time; she would never open them again, for sight was now as superfluous to her as to the many-sensed creatures of the lightless ocean depths. She was aware of the world that surrounded her: indeed, she was aware of much more than that.

One reflex remained from her brief babyhood, by some unaccountable trick of development. The rattle which had once delighted her sounded incessantly now, beating a complex, everchanging rhythm in her cot. It was that strange syncopation which had roused Jean from her sleep and sent her flying into the nursery. But it was not the sound alone that had started her screaming for George.

It was the sight of that commonplace, brightly colored rattle beating steadily in airy isolation half a meter away from any support, while Jennifer Anne, her chubby fingers clasped tightly together, lay with a smile of calm contentment on her face.

She had started later, but she was progressing swiftly. Soon she would pass her brother, for she had so much less to unlearn.

"You were wise," said Rashaverak, "not to touch her toy. I do not believe you could have moved it. But if you had succeeded, she might have been annoyed. And then, I do not know what would have happened."

"Do you mean," said George dully, "that you can do nothing?"

"I will not deceive you. We can study and observe, as we are doing already. But we cannot interfere, because we cannot understand."

"Then what are we to do? And why has this thing happened to *us?*"

"It had to happen to someone. There is nothing exceptional about you, any more than there is about the first neutron that starts the chain reaction in an atomic bomb. It simply happens to be the first. Any other neutron would have served—just as Jeffrey might have been any boy in the world. We call it Total Breakthrough. There is no need for any secrecy now, and I am very glad. We have been waiting for this to happen, ever since we came to Earth. There was no way to tell when and where it would start—until, by pure chance, we met at Rupert Boyce's party. Then I knew that, almost certainly, your wife's children would be the first."

"But—we weren't married then. We hadn't even—"

"Yes, I know. But Miss Morrel's mind was the channel that, if only for a moment, let through knowledge which no one alive at that time could possess. It could only come from another mind, intimately linked to hers. The fact that it was a mind not yet born was of no consequence, for Time is very much stranger than you think."

"I begin to understand. Jeff knows these things—he can see other worlds and can tell where you come from. And somehow Jean caught his thoughts, even before he was born."

"There is far more to it than that—but I do not imagine you will ever get much closer to the truth. All through history there have been people with inexplicable powers which seemed to transcend space and time. They never understood them: almost without exception, their attempted explanations were rubbish. I should know—I have read enough of them!

"But there is one analogy which is—well, suggestive and helpful. It occurs over and over again in your literature. Imagine that every man's mind is an island, surrounded by ocean. Each seems isolated, yet in reality all are linked by the bedrock from which they spring. If the ocean were to vanish, that would be the end of the islands. They would all be part of one continent, but their individuality would have gone.

"Telepathy, as you have called it, is something like this. In suitable circumstances minds can merge and share each other's contents, and carry back memories of the experience when they are isolated once more. In its highest form, this power is not subject to the usual limitations of time and space. That is why Jean could tap the knowledge of her unborn son."

There was a long silence while George wrestled with these astounding thoughts. The pattern was beginning to take shape. It was an unbelievable pattern, but it had its own inherent logic. And it explained—if the word could be used for anything so incomprehensible—all that had happened since that evening at Rupert Boyce's home. It also accounted, he realized now, for Jean's own curiosity about the supernormal.

"What has started this thing?" asked George. "And where is it going to lead?"

"That is something we cannot answer. But there are many races in the universe, and some of them discovered these powers long before your species—or mine—appeared on the scene. They have been waiting for you to join them, and now the time has come."

"Then where do *you* come into the picture?"

"Probably, like most men, you have always regarded us as your masters. That is not true. We have never been more than guardians, doing a duty imposed upon us from—above. That duty is hard to define: perhaps you can best think of us as midwives attending a difficult birth. We are helping to bring something new and wonderful into being."

Rashaverak hesitated: for a moment it almost seemed as if he was at a loss for words.

"Yes, we are the midwives. But we ourselves are barren."

In that instant, George knew he was in the presence of a tragedy transcending his own. It was incredible—and yet somehow just. Despite all their powers and their brilliance, the Overlords were trapped in some evolutionary cul-de-sac. Here was a great and noble race, in almost every way superior to mankind; yet it had no future, and it was aware of it. In the face of this, George's own problems seemed suddenly trivial.

"Now I know," he said, "why you have been watching Jeffrey. He was the guinea pig in this experiment."

"Exactly—though the experiment was beyond our control. We did not start it—we were merely trying to observe. We did not interfere except when we had to."

Yes, thought George—the tidal wave. It would never do to let a valuable specimen be destroyed. Then he felt ashamed of himself: such bitterness was unworthy.

"I've only one more question," he said. "What shall we do about our children?"

"Enjoy them while you may," answered Rashaverak gently. "They will not be yours for long."

It was advice that might have been given to any parent in any age: but now it contained a threat and a terror it had never held before.

✳ CHAPTER EIGHTEEN

There came the time when the world of Jeffrey's dreams was no longer sharply divided from his everyday existence. He no longer went to school, and for Jean and George also the routine of life was completely broken, as it was soon to break down throughout the world.

They avoided all their friends, as if already conscious that soon no one would have sympathy to spare for them. Sometimes, in the quietness of the night when there were few people about, they would go for long walks together. They were closer now than they had been since the first days of their marriage, united again in the face of the still unknown tragedy that soon would overwhelm them.

At first it had given them a feeling of guilt to leave the sleeping children alone in the house, but now they realized that Jeff and Jenny could look after themselves in ways beyond the knowledge of their parents. And, of course, the Overlords would be watching too. That thought was reassuring: they felt that they were not alone with their problem, but that wise and sympathetic eyes shared their vigil.

Jennifer slept: there was no other word to describe the state she had entered. To all outward appearances, she was still a baby, but round her now was a sense of latent power so terrifying that Jean could no longer bear to enter the nursery.

There was no need to do so. The entity that had been Jennifer Anne Greggson was not yet fully developed, but even in its sleeping chrysalis state it already had enough control of its environment to take care of all its needs. Jean had only once attempted to feed it, without success. It chose to take nourishment in its own time, and in its own manner.

For food vanished from the freezer in a slow, steady stream: yet Jennifer Anne never moved from her cot.

The rattling had ceased, and the discarded toy lay on the nursery floor where no one dared to touch it, lest Jennifer Anne might need it again. Sometimes she caused the furniture to stir itself into peculiar patterns, and it seemed to George that the fluoropaint on the wall was glowing more brilliantly than it had ever done before.

She gave no trouble; she was beyond their assistance, and beyond their love. It could not last much longer, and in the time that was left they clung desperately to Jeff.

He was changing too, but he still knew them. The boy whose growth they had watched from the formless mists of babyhood was losing his personality, dissolving hour by hour before their very eyes. Yet sometimes he still spoke to them as he had always done, and talked of his toys and friends as if unconscious of what lay ahead. But much of the time he did not see them, or show any awareness of their presence. He no longer slept, as they were forced to do, despite their overwhelming need to waste as few as possible of these last remaining hours.

Unlike Jenny, he seemed to possess no abnormal powers over physical objects—perhaps because, being already partly grown, he had less need for them. His strangeness was entirely in his mental life, of which the dreams were now only a small part. He would stay quite still for hours on end, his eyes tightly closed, as if listening to sounds which no one else could hear. Into his mind was flooding knowledge—from somewhere or somewhen—which soon would overwhelm and destroy the half-formed creature who had been Jeffrey Angus Greggson.

And Fey would sit watching, looking up at him with tragic, puzzled eyes, wondering where her master had gone and when he would return to her.

Jeff and Jenny had been the first in all the world, but soon they were no longer alone. Like an epidemic spreading swiftly from land to land, the metamorphosis infected the entire human race. It touched practically no one above the age of ten, and practically no one below that age escaped.

It was the end of civilization, the end of all that men had striven for since the beginning of time. In the space of a few days, humanity had lost its future, for the heart of any race is destroyed, and its will to survive is utterly broken, when its children are taken from it.

There was no panic, as there would have been a century before. The world was numbed, the great cities stilled and silent. Only the vital industries continued to function. It was as though the planet was in mourning, lamenting all that now could never be.

And then, as he had done once before in a now forgotten age, Karellen spoke for the last time to mankind.

✶ CHAPTER NINETEEN

"My work here is nearly ended," said Karellen's voice from a million radios. "At last, after a hundred years, I can tell you what it was.

"There are many things we have had to hide from you, as we hid ourselves for half our stay on Earth. Some of you, I know, thought that concealment unnecessary. You are accustomed to our presence: you can no longer imagine how your ancestors would have reacted to us. But at least you can understand the purpose of our concealment, and know that we had a reason for what we did.

"The supreme secret we kept from you was our purpose in coming to Earth—that purpose about which you have speculated so endlessly. We could not tell you until now, for the secret was not ours to reveal.

"A century ago we came to your world and saved you from self-destruction. I do not believe that anyone would deny that fact—but what that self-destruction was, you never guessed.

"Because we banned nuclear weapons and all the other deadly toys you were accumulating in your armories, the danger of physical annihilation was removed. You thought that was the only danger. We wanted you to believe that, but it was never true. The greatest danger that confronted you was of a different character altogether—and it did not concern your race alone.

"Many worlds have come to the crossroads of nuclear power, have avoided disaster, have gone on to build peaceful and happy civilizations—and have then been utterly destroyed by forces of which they knew nothing. In the twentieth century, you first began to tamper seriously with those forces. That was why it became necessary to act.

"All through that century, the human race was drawing slowly nearer to the abyss—never even suspecting its existence. Across that abyss, there is only one bridge. Few races, unaided, have ever found it. Some have turned back while there was still time, avoiding both the danger and the achievement. Their worlds have become Elysian islands of effortless content, playing no further part in the story of the universe. That would never have been your fate—or your fortune. Your race was too vital for that. It would have plunged into ruin and taken others with it, for you would never have found the bridge.

"I am afraid that almost all I have to say now must be by means of such analogies. You have no words, no conceptions, for many of the things I wish to tell you—and our own knowledge of them is also sadly imperfect.

"To understand, you must go back into the past and recover much that your ancestors would have found familiar, but which you have forgotten—which, in fact, we deliberately helped you to forget. For all our sojourn here has been based on a vast deception, a concealment of truths which you were not ready to face.

"In the centuries before our coming, your scientists uncovered the secrets of the physical world and led you from the energy of steam to the energy of the atom. You had put superstition behind you: Science was the only real religion of mankind. It was the gift of the western minority to the remainder of mankind, and it had destroyed all other faiths. Those that still existed when we came were already dying. Science, it was felt, could explain everything: there were no forces which did not come within its scope, no events for which it could not ultimately account. The origin of the universe might be forever unknown, but all that had happened since obeyed the laws of physics.

"Yet your mystics, though they were lost in their own delusions, had seen part of the truth. There are powers of the mind, and powers beyond the mind, which your science could never have brought within its framework without shattering it entirely. All down the ages there have been countless reports of strange phenomena — poltergeists, telepathy, precognition — which you had named but never explained. At first science ignored them, even denied their existence, despite the testimony of five thousand years. But they exist, and, if it is to be complete, any theory of the universe must account for them.

"During the first half of the twentieth century, a few of your scientists began to investigate these matters. They did not know it, but they were tampering with the lock of Pandora's box. The forces they might have unleashed transcended any perils that the atom could have brought. For the physicists could only have ruined the earth: the paraphysicists could have spread havoc to the stars.

"That could not be allowed. I cannot explain the full nature of the threat you represented. It would not have been a threat to us, and therefore we do not comprehend it. Let us say that you might have become a telepathic cancer, a malignant mentality which in its inevitable dissolution would have poisoned other and greater minds.

"And so we came—we were *sent*—to Earth. We interrupted your development on every cultural level, but in particular we checked all serious work on paranormal phenomena. I am well aware of the fact that we have also inhibited, by the contrast between our civilizations, all other forms of creative achievement as well. But that was a secondary effect, and it is of no importance.

"Now I must tell you something which you may find very surprising, perhaps almost incredible. All these potentialities, all these latent powers—we do not possess them, nor do we understand them. Our intellects are far more powerful than yours, but there is something in your minds that has always eluded us. Ever since we came to Earth we have been studying you; we have learned a great deal, and will learn more, yet I doubt if we shall discover all the truth.

"Our races have much in common—that is why we were chosen for this task. But in other respects, we represent the ends of two different evolutions. Our minds have reached the end of their development. So, in their present form, have yours. Yet you can make the jump to the next stage, and therein lies the difference between us.

Our potentialities are exhausted, but yours are still untapped. They are linked, in ways we do not understand, with the powers I have mentioned—the powers that are now awakening on your world.

"We held the clock back, we made you mark time while those powers developed, until they could come flooding out into the channels that were being prepared for them. What we did to improve your planet, to raise your standards of living, to bring justice and peace—those things we should have done in any event, once we were forced to intervene in your affairs. But all that vast transformation diverted you from the truth, and therefore helped to serve our purpose.

"We are your guardians—no more. Often you must have wondered what position my race held in the hierarchy of the universe. As we are above you, so there is something above us, using us for its own purposes. We have never discovered what it is, though we have been its tool for ages and dare not disobey it. Again and again we have received our orders, have gone to some world in the early flower of its civilization, and have guided it along the road that we can never follow—the road that you are traveling now.

"Again and again we have studied the process we have been sent to foster, hoping that we might learn to escape from our own limitations. But we have glimpsed only the vague outlines of the truth. You called us the Overlords, not knowing the irony of that title. Let us say that above us is the *Overmind,* using us as the potter uses his wheel.

"And your race is the clay that is being shaped on that wheel.

"We believe—it is only a theory—that the Overmind is trying to grow, to extend its powers and its awareness of the universe. By now it must be the sum of many races, and long ago it left the tyranny of matter behind. It is conscious of intelligence, everywhere. When it knew that you were almost ready, it sent us here to do its bidding, to prepare you for the transformation that is now at hand.

"All the earlier changes your race has known took countless ages. But this is a transformation of the mind, not of the body. By the standards of evolution, it will be cataclysmic—instantaneous. It has already begun. You must face the fact that yours is the last generation of *Homo sapiens.*

"As to the nature of that change, we can tell you very little. We do not know how it is produced—what trigger impulse the

Overmind employs when it judges that the time is ripe. All we have discovered is that it starts with a single individual—always a child —and then spreads explosively, like the formation of crystals round the first nucleus in a saturated solution. Adults will not be affected, for their minds are already set in an unalterable mold.

"In a few years, it will all be over, and the human race will have divided in twain. There is no way back, and no future for the world you know. All the hopes and dreams of your race are ended now. You have given birth to your successors, and it is your tragedy that you will never understand them—will never even be able to communicate with their minds. Indeed, they will not possess minds as you know them. They will be a single entity, as you yourselves are the sums of your myriad cells. You will not think them human, and you will be right.

"I have told you these things so that you will know what faces you. In a few hours, the crisis will be upon us. My task and my duty is to protect those I have been sent here to guard. Despite their wakening powers, they could be destroyed by the multitudes around them—yes, even by their parents, when they realized the truth. I must take them away and isolate them, for their protection, and for yours. Tomorrow my ships will begin the evacuation. I shall not blame you if you try to interfere, but it will be useless. Greater powers than mine are wakening now; I am only one of their instruments.

"And then—what am I to do with you, the survivors, when your purpose has been fulfilled? It would be simplest, and perhaps most merciful, to destroy you—as you yourselves would destroy a mortally wounded pet you loved. But this I cannot do. Your future will be your own to choose in the years that are left to you. It is my hope that humanity will go to its rest in peace, knowing that it has not lived in vain.

"For what you will have brought into the world may be utterly alien, it may share none of your desires or hopes, it may look upon your greatest achievements as childish toys—yet it is something wonderful, and you will have created it.

"When our race is forgotten, part of yours will still exist. Do not, therefore, condemn us for what we were compelled to do. And remember this—we shall always envy you."

✳ CHAPTER TWENTY

Jean had wept before, but she was not weeping now. The island lay golden in the heartless, unfeeling sunlight as the ship came slowly into sight above the twin peaks of Sparta. On that rocky island, not long ago, her son had escaped death by a miracle she now understood all too well. Sometimes she wondered if it might not have been better had the Overlords stood aside and left him to his fate. Death was something she could face as she had faced it before: it was in the natural order of things. But this was stranger than death—and more final. Until this day, men had died, yet the race had continued.

There was no sound or movement from the children. They stood in scattered groups along the sand, showing no more interest in one another than in the homes they were leaving forever. Many carried babies who were too small to walk—or who did not wish to assert the powers that made walking unnecessary. For surely, thought George, if they could move inanimate matter, they could move their own bodies. Why, indeed, were the Overlord ships collecting them at all?

It was of no importance. They were leaving, and this was the way they chose to go. And then George realized what it was that had been teasing his memory. Somewhere, long ago, he had seen a century-old newsreel of such an exodus. It must have been at the beginning of the First World War—or the Second. There had been long lines of trains, crowded with children, pulling slowly out of the threatened cities, leaving behind the parents that so many of them would never see again. Few were crying: some were puzzled, clutching nervously at their small belongings, but most seemed to be looking forward with eagerness to some great adventure.

And yet—the analogy was false. History never repeated itself. These who were leaving now were no longer children, whatever they might be. And this time, there would be no reunion.

The ship had grounded along the water's edge, sinking deeply into the soft sand. In perfect unison, the line of great curving panels slid upwards and the gangways extended themselves towards the beach like metal tongues. The scattered, unutterably lonely figures began to converge, to gather into a crowd that moved precisely as a human crowd might do.

Lonely? Why had he thought that, wondered George. For *that* was the one thing they could never be again. Only individuals can be lonely—only human beings. When the barriers were down at last, loneliness would vanish as personality faded. The countless raindrops would have merged into the ocean.

He felt Jean's hand increase its pressure on his in a sudden spasm of emotion.

"Look," she whispered. "I can see Jeff. By that second door."

It was a long way away, and very hard to be certain. There was a mist before his eyes which made it hard to see. But it was Jeff—he was sure of that: George could recognize his son now, as he stood with one foot already on the metal gangway.

And Jeff turned and looked back. His face was only a white blur: at this distance, there was no way of telling if it bore any hint of recognition, any remembrance for all that he was leaving behind. Nor would George ever know if Jeff had turned towards them by pure chance—or if he knew, in those last moments while he was still their son, that they stood watching him as he passed into the land that they could never enter.

The great doors began to close. And in that moment Fey lifted up her muzzle and gave a low, desolate moan. She turned her beautiful, limpid eyes towards George, and he knew that she had lost her master. He had no rival now.

For those who were left there were many roads but only one destination. There were some who said: "The world is still beautiful; one day we must leave it, but why should we hasten our departure?"

But others, who had set more store by the future than the present, and who had lost all that made life worth living, did not wish to stay. They took their leave alone, or with their friends, according to their nature.

It was thus with Athens. The island had been born in fire; in fire it chose to die. Those who wished to leave did so, but most remained, to meet the end among the broken fragments of their dreams.

No one was supposed to know when the time would be. Yet Jean awoke in the stillness of the night, and lay for a moment staring at the ghostly glimmer from the ceiling. Then she reached out to grasp George's hand. He was a sound sleeper, but this time he woke at once. They did not speak, for the words that were wanted did not exist.

Jean was no longer frightened, or even sad. She had come through to the calm waters and was beyond emotion now. But there was one thing still to be done, and she knew that there was barely time to do it.

Still without a word, George followed her through the silent house. They went across the patch of moonlight that had entered through the studio roof, moving as quietly as the shadows it cast, until they came to the deserted nursery.

Nothing had been changed. The fluoro-patterns that George had painted so carefully still glowed on the walls. And the rattle that had once belonged to Jennifer Anne still lay where she had dropped it, when her mind turned into the unknowable remoteness it inhabited now.

She has left her toys behind, thought George, but ours go hence with us. He thought of the royal children of the Pharaohs, whose dolls and beads had been buried with them five thousand years ago. So it would be again. No one else, he told himself, will ever love our treasures: we will take them with us, and will not part with them.

Slowly Jean turned towards him, and rested her head upon his shoulder. He clasped his arms about her waist, and the love he had once known came back to him, faint yet clear, like an echo from a distant range of hills. It was too late now to say all that was due to her, and the regrets he felt were less for his deceits than for his past indifference.

Then Jean said quietly: "Good-by, my darling," and tightened her arms about him. There was no time for George to answer, but even at that final moment he felt a brief astonishment as he wondered how she knew that the moment had arrived.

Far down in the rock, the segments of uranium began to rush together, seeking the union they could never achieve.

And the island rose to meet the dawn.

✳ *CHAPTER TWENTY-ONE*

The ship of the Overlords came sliding in along its glowing meteor-trail through the heart of Carina. It had begun its mad deceleration among the outer planets, but even while passing Mars it had still possessed an appreciable fraction of the velocity of light. Slowly the immense fields surrounding the sun were absorbing its momentum, while for a million kilometers behind, the stray energies of the Stardrive were painting the heavens with fire.

Jan Rodricks was coming home, six months older, to the world he had left eighty years before.

This time he was no longer a stowaway, hidden in a secret chamber. He stood behind the three pilots (why, he wondered, did they need so many?) watching the patterns come and go on the great screen that dominated the control room. The colors and shapes it showed were meaningless to him: he assumed that they were conveying information which in a vessel designed by men would have been displayed on banks of meters. But sometimes the screen showed the surrounding star fields, and soon, he hoped, it would be showing Earth.

He was glad to be home, despite the effort he had devoted to escaping from it. In these few months, he had grown up. He had seen so much, traveled so far, and now was weary for his own familiar world. He understood, now, why the Overlords had sealed Earth from the stars. Humanity still had very far to go before it could play any part in the civilization he had glimpsed.

It might be—though this he refused to accept—that mankind could never be more than an inferior species, preserved in an out-of-the-way zoo with the Overlords as keepers. Perhaps that was what Vindarten had meant when he gave Jan that ambiguous warning, just before his departure. "Much may have happened," the

Overlord had said, "in the time that has passed on your planet. You may not know your world when you see it again."

Perhaps not, thought Jan: eighty years was a long time, and though he was young and adaptable, he might find it hard to understand all the changes that had come to pass. But of one thing he was certain—men would want to hear his story, and to know what he had glimpsed of the civilization of the Overlords.

They had treated him well, as he had assumed they would. Of the outward journey he had known nothing: when the injection had worn off and he had emerged, the ship was already entering the Overlord system. He had climbed out of his fantastic hiding place, and found to his relief that the oxygen set was not needed. The air was thick and heavy, but he could breathe without difficulty. He had found himself in the ship's enormous red-lit hold, among countless other packing cases and all the impedimenta one would expect on a liner of space or of sea. It had taken him almost an hour to find his way to the control room and to introduce himself to the crew.

Their lack of surprise had puzzled him: he knew that the Overlords showed few emotions, but he had expected *some* reaction. Instead, they simply continued with their work, watching the great screen and playing the countless keys on their control panels. It was then that he knew that they were landing, for from time to time the image of a planet—larger at each appearance—would flash upon the screen. Yet there was never the slightest sense of motion or acceleration—only a perfectly constant gravity which he judged to be about a fifth of Earth's. The immense forces that drove the ship must have been compensated with exquisite precision.

And then, in unison, the three Overlords had risen from their seats, and he knew that the voyage was over. They did not speak to their passenger or to each other, and when one of them beckoned to him to follow, Jan realized something that he should have thought of before. There might well be no one here, at this end of Karellen's enormously long supply line, who understood a word of English.

They watched him gravely as the great doors opened before his eager eyes. This was the supreme moment of his life: now he was to be the first human being ever to look upon a world lit by another sun. The ruby light of NGS 549672 came flooding into the ship, and there before him lay the planet of the Overlords.

What had he expected? He was not sure. Vast buildings, cities whose towers were lost among the clouds, machines beyond imagination—these would not have surprised him. Yet what he saw was an almost featureless plain, reaching out to an unnaturally close horizon, and broken only by three more of the Overlords' ships, a few kilometers away.

For a moment Jan felt a surge of disappointment. Then he shrugged his shoulders, realizing that, after all, one would expect to find a spaceport in some such remote and uninhabited region as this.

It was cold, though not uncomfortably so. The light from the great red sun low down on the horizon was quite ample for human eyes, but Jan wondered how long it would be before he yearned for greens and blues. Then he saw that enormous, wafer-thin crescent reaching up the sky like a great bow placed beside the sun. He stared at it for a long time before he realized that his journey was not yet altogether ended. *That* was the world of the Overlords. This must be its satellite, merely the base from which their vessels operated.

They had taken him across in a ship no larger than a terrestrial airliner. Feeling a pygmy, he had climbed up into one of the great seats to try and see something of the approaching planet through the observation windows.

The journey was so swift that he had time to make out few details on the expanding globe beneath. Even so near to home, it seemed, the Overlords used some version of the Stardrive, for in a matter of minutes they were falling down through a deep, cloud-flecked atmosphere. When the doors opened, they stepped out into a vaulted chamber with a roof that must have swung swiftly shut behind them, for there was no sign of any entrance overhead.

It was two days before Jan left this building. He was an unexpected consignment, and they had nowhere to put him. To make matters worse, not one of the Overlords could understand English. Communication was practically impossible, and Jan realized bitterly that getting in touch with an alien race was not as easy as it was so often depicted in fiction. Sign language proved singularly unsuccessful, for it depended too much on a body of gestures, expressions and attitudes which the Overlords and mankind did not possess in common.

It would be more than frustrating, thought Jan, if the only Overlords who spoke his language were all back on Earth. He could only wait and hope for the best. Surely some scientist, some expert on alien races, would come and take charge of him! Or was he so unimportant that no one could be bothered?

There was no way he could get out of the building, because the great doors had no visible controls. When an Overlord walked up to them, they simply opened. Jan had tried the same trick, had waved objects high in the air to interrupt any controlling light-beam, had tried everything he could imagine—with no result at all. He realized that a man from the Stone Age, lost in a modern city or building, might be equally helpless. Once he had tried to walk out when one of the Overlords left, but had been gently shooed back. As he was very anxious not to annoy his hosts, he did not persist.

Vindarten arrived before Jan had begun to get desperate. The Overlord spoke very bad English, much too rapidly, but improved with amazing speed. In a few days they were able to talk together with little trouble on any subject that did not demand a specialized vocabulary.

Once Vindarten had taken charge of him, Jan had no more worries. He also had no opportunity of doing the things he wished, for almost all his time was spent meeting Overlord scientists anxious to carry out obscure tests with complicated instruments. Jan was very wary of these machines, and after one session with some kind of hypnotic device had a splitting headache for several hours. He was perfectly willing to co-operate, but was not sure if his investigators realized his limitations, both mental and physical. It was certainly a long time before he could convince them that he had to sleep at regular intervals.

Between these investigations, he caught momentary glimpses of the city, and realized how difficult—and dangerous—it would be for him to travel around in it. Streets were practically nonexistent, and there seemed to be no surface transport. This was the home of creatures who could fly, and who had no fear of gravity. It was nothing to come without warning upon a vertiginous drop of several hundred meters, or to find that the only entrance into a room was an opening high up in the wall. In a hundred ways, Jan began to realize that the psychology of a race with wings must be fundamentally different from that of earthbound creatures.

It was strange to see the Overlords flying like great birds among the towers of their city, their pinions moving with slow, powerful beats. And there was a scientific problem here. This was a large planet—larger than Earth. Yet its gravity was low, and Jan wondered why it had so dense an atmosphere. He questioned Vindarten on this, and discovered, as he had half expected, that this was not the original planet of the Overlords. They had evolved on a much smaller world and then conquered this one, changing not only its atmosphere but even its gravity.

The architecture of the Overlords was bleakly functional: Jan saw no ornaments, nothing that did not serve a purpose, even though that purpose was often beyond his understanding. If a man from medieval times could have seen this red-lit city, and the beings moving through it, he would certainly have believed himself in Hell. Even Jan, for all his curiosity and scientific detachment, sometimes found himself on the verge of unreasoning terror. The absence of a single familiar reference point can be utterly unnerving even to the coolest and clearest minds.

And there was so much he did not understand, and which Vindarten could or would not attempt to explain. What were those flashing lights and changing shapes, the things that flickered through the air so swiftly that he could never be certain of their existence? They could have been something tremendous and awe-inspiring—or as spectacular yet trivial as the neon signs of old-time Broadway.

Jan also sensed that the world of the Overlords was full of sounds that he could not hear. Occasionally he caught complex rhythmical patterns racing up and down through the audible spectrum, to vanish at the upper or lower edge of hearing. Vindarten did not seem to understand what Jan meant by music, so he was never able to solve this problem to his satisfaction.

The city was not very large: it was certainly far smaller than London or New York had been at their heyday. According to Vindarten, there were several thousand such cities scattered over the planet, each one designed for some specific purpose. On Earth, the closest parallel to this place would have been a university town —except that the degree of specialization had gone much further. This entire city was devoted, Jan soon discovered, to the study of alien cultures.

In one of their first trips outside the bare cell in which Jan lived, Vindarten had taken him to the museum. It had given Jan a much needed psychological boost to find himself in a place whose purpose he could fully understand. Apart from the scale upon which it was built, this museum might well have been on Earth. They had taken a long time to reach it, falling steadily on a great platform that moved like a piston in a vertical cylinder of unknown length. There were no visible controls, and the sense of acceleration at the beginning and ending of the descent was quite noticeable. Presumably the Overlords did not waste their compensating field devices for domestic uses. Jan wondered if the whole interior of this world was riddled with excavations: and why had they limited the size of the city, going underground instead of outwards? That was just another of the enigmas he never solved.

One could have spent a lifetime exploring these colossal chambers. Here was the loot of planets, the achievements of more civilizations than Jan could guess. But there was no time to see much. Vindarten placed him carefully on a strip of flooring that at first sight seemed an ornamental pattern. Then Jan remembered that there were no ornaments here—and at the same time, something invisible grasped him gently and hurried him forward. He was moving past the great display cases, past vistas of unimaginable worlds, at a speed of twenty or thirty kilometers an hour.

The Overlords had solved the problem of museum fatigue. There was no need for anyone to walk.

They must have traveled several kilometers before Jan's guide grasped him again, and with a surge of his great wings lifted him away from whatever force was propelling them. Before them stretched a huge, half-empty hall, flooded with a familiar light that Jan had not seen since leaving Earth. It was faint, so that it would not pain the sensitive eyes of the Overlords, but it was, unmistakably, sunlight. Jan would never have believed that anything so simple or so commonplace could have evoked such yearning in his heart.

So this was the exhibit for Earth. They walked for a few meters past a beautiful model of Paris, past art treasures from a dozen centuries grouped incongruously together, past modern calculating machines and paleolithic axes, past television receivers and Hero of Alexandria's steam turbine. A great doorway opened ahead of them, and they were in the office of the Curator for Earth.

Was he seeing a human being for the first time? Jan wondered. Had he ever been to Earth, or was it just another of the many planets in his charge, of whose exact location he was not precisely sure? Certainly he neither spoke nor understood English, and Vindarten had to act as interpreter.

Jan had spent several hours here, talking into a recording device while the Overlords presented various terrestrial objects to him. Many of these, he discovered to his shame, he could not identify. His ignorance of his own race and its achievements was enormous: he wondered if the Overlords, for all their superb mental gifts, could really grasp the complete pattern of human culture.

Vindarten took him out of the museum by a different route. Once again they floated effortlessly through great vaulted corridors, but this time they were moving past the creations of nature, not of conscious mind. Sullivan, thought Jan, would have given his life to be here, to see what wonders evolution had wrought on a hundred worlds. But Sullivan, he remembered, was probably already dead. . . .

Then, without any warning, they were on a gallery high above a large circular chamber, perhaps a hundred meters across. As usual, there was no protective parapet, and for a moment Jan hesitated to go near the edge. But Vindarten was standing on the very brink, looking calmly downwards, so Jan moved cautiously forward to join him.

The floor was only twenty meters below—far, far too close. Afterwards, Jan was sure that his guide had not intended to surprise him, and was completely taken aback by his reaction. For he had given one tremendous yell and jumped backwards from the gallery's edge, in an involuntary effort to hide what lay below. It was not until the muffled echoes of his shout had died away in the thick atmosphere that he steeled himself to go forward again.

It was lifeless, of course—not, as he had thought in that first moment of panic, consciously staring up at him. It filled almost all that great circular space, and the ruby light gleamed and shifted in its crystal depths.

It was a single giant eye.

"Why did you make that noise?" asked Vindarten.

"I was frightened," Jan confessed sheepishly.

"But why? Surely you did not imagine that there could be any danger here?"

Jan wondered if he could explain what a reflex action was, but decided not to attempt it.

"Anything completely unexpected is frightening. Until a novel situation is analyzed, it is safest to assume the worst."

His heart was still pounding violently as he stared down once more at that monstrous eye. Of course, it might have been a model, enormously enlarged as were microbes and insects in terrestrial museums. Yet even as he asked the question, Jan knew, with a sickening certainty, that it was no larger than life.

Vindarten could tell him little: this was not his field of knowledge, and he was not particularly curious. From the Overlord's description, Jan built up a picture of a cyclopean beast living among the asteroidal rubble of some distant sun, its growth uninhibited by gravity, depending for food and life upon the range and resolving power of its single eye.

There seemed no limit to what Nature could do if she was pressed, and Jan felt an irrational pleasure at discovering something which the Overlords would not attempt. They had brought a full-sized whale from Earth—but they had drawn the line at *this*.

*   *   *

And there was the time when he had gone up, endlessly up, until the walls of the elevator had faded through opalescence into a crystal transparency. He was standing, it seemed, unsupported among the uppermost peaks of the city, with nothing to protect him from the abyss. But he felt no more vertigo than one does in an airplane, for there was no sense of contact with the distant ground.

He was above the clouds, sharing the sky with a few pinnacles of metal or stone. A rose-red sea, the cloud-layer rolled sluggishly beneath him. There were two pale and tiny moons in the sky, not far from the somber sun. Near the center of that bloated red disc was a small, dark shadow, perfectly circular. It might have been a sunspot, or another moon in transit.

Jan slowly moved his gaze along the horizon. The cloud-cover extended clear to the edge of this enormous world, but in one direction, at an unguessable distance, there was a mottled patch that might have marked the towers of another city. He stared at it for a long while, then continued his careful survey.

When he had turned half-circle he saw the mountain. It was not on the horizon, but *beyond* it—a single serrated peak, climbing up over the edge of the world, its lower slopes hidden as the bulk of an iceberg is concealed below the water line. He tried to guess its size, and failed completely. Even on a world with gravity as low as this, it seemed hard to believe that such mountains could exist. Did the Overlords, he wondered, sport themselves upon its slopes and sweep like eagles around those immense buttresses?

And then, slowly, the mountain began to change. When he saw it first, it was a dull and almost sinister red, with a few faint markings near its crown that he could not clearly distinguish. He was trying to focus on them when he realized that they were moving. . . .

At first he could not believe his eyes. Then he forced himself to remember that all his preconceived ideas were worthless here: he must not let his mind reject any message his senses brought into the hidden chamber of the brain. He must not try to understand—only to observe. Understanding would come later, or not at all.

The mountain—he still thought of it as such, for there was no other word that could serve—seemed to be alive. He remembered that monstrous eye in its buried vault—but no, that was inconceivable. It was not organic life that he was watching: it was not even, he suspected, matter as he knew it.

The somber red was brightening to an angrier hue. Streaks of vivid yellow appeared, so that for a moment Jan felt he was looking at a volcano pouring streams of lava down on to the land beneath. But these streams, as he could tell by occasional flecks and mottlings, were moving *upwards*.

Now something else was rising out of the ruby clouds around the mountain's base. It was a huge ring, perfectly horizontal and perfectly circular—and it was the color of all that Jan had left so far behind, for the skies of Earth had held no lovelier blue. Nowhere else on the world of the Overlords had he seen such hues, and his throat contracted with the longing and the loneliness they evoked.

The ring was expanding as it climbed. It was higher than the mountain now, and its nearer arc was sweeping swiftly towards him. Surely, thought Jan, it must be a vortex of some kind—a smoke ring already many kilometers across. But it showed none of the rotation he expected, and it seemed to grow no less solid as its size increased.

Its shadow rushed past long before the ring itself had swept majestically overhead, still rising into space. He watched until it had dwindled to a thin thread of blue, hard for the eye to focus upon in the surrounding redness of the sky. When it vanished at last, it must already have been many thousands of kilometers across. And it was still growing.

He looked back at the mountain. It was golden now, and devoid of all markings. Perhaps it was imagination—he could believe anything by this time—but it seemed taller and narrower, and appeared to be spinning like the funnel of a cyclone. Not until then, still numbed and with his powers of reason almost in abeyance, did he remember his camera. He raised it to eye level, and sighted towards that impossible, mind-shaking enigma.

Vindarten moved swiftly into his line of vision. With implacable firmness, the great hands covered the lens turret and forced him to lower the camera. Jan did not attempt to resist: it would have been useless, of course, but he felt a sudden deathly fear of that thing out there at the edge of the world, and wanted no further part of it.

There was nothing else in all his travels that they would not let him photograph, and Vindarten gave no explanations. Instead, he spent much time getting Jan to describe in minute detail what he had witnessed.

It was then that Jan realized that Vindarten's eyes had seen something totally different: and it was then that he guessed, for the first time, that the Overlords had masters, too.

Now he was coming home, and all the wonder, the fear and the mystery were far behind. It was the same ship, he believed, though surely not the same crew. However long their lives, it was hard to believe that the Overlords would willingly cut themselves off from their home for all the decades consumed on an interstellar voyage.

The Relativity time-dilation effect worked both ways, of course. The Overlords would age only four months on the round trip, but when they returned their friends would be eighty years older.

Had he wished, Jan could doubtless have stayed here for the

remainder of his life. But Vindarten had warned him that there would be no other ship going to Earth for several years, and had advised him to take this opportunity. Perhaps the Overlords realized that even in this relatively short time, his mind had nearly reached the end of its resources. Or he might merely have become a nuisance, and they could spare no more time for him.

It was of no importance now, for Earth was there ahead. He had seen it thus a hundred times before, but always through the remote, mechanical eye of the television camera. Now at last he himself was out here in space, as the final act of his dream unfolded itself, and Earth spun beneath on its eternal orbit.

The great blue-green crescent was in its first quarter: more than half the visible disc was still in darkness. There was little cloud—a few bands scattered along the line of the trade winds. The arctic cap glittered brilliantly, but was far outshone by the dazzling reflection of the sun in the north Pacific.

One might have thought it was a world of water: this hemisphere was almost devoid of land. The only continent visible was Australia, a darker mist in the atmospheric haze along the limb of the planet.

The ship was driving into Earth's great cone of shadow: the gleaming crescent dwindled, shrank to a burning bow of fire, and winked out of existence. Below was darkness and night. The world was sleeping.

It was then that Jan realized what was wrong. There was land down there—but where were the gleaming necklaces of light, where were the glittering coruscations that had been the cities of man? In all that shadowy hemisphere, there was no single spark to drive back the night. Gone without a trace were the millions of kilowatts that once had been splashed carelessly towards the stars. He might have been looking down on Earth as it had been before the coming of man.

This was not the homecoming he had expected. There was nothing he could do but watch, while the fear of the unknown grew within him. Something had happened—something unimaginable. And yet the ship was descending purposefully in a long curve that was taking it again over the sunlit hemisphere.

He saw nothing of the actual landing, for the picture of Earth suddenly winked out and was replaced by that meaningless pattern of lines and lights. When vision was restored, they were on the ground. There were great buildings in the distance, machines moving about, and a group of Overlords watching them.

Somewhere there was the muffled roar of air as the ship equalized pressure, then the sound of great doors opening. He did not wait: the silent giants watched him with tolerance or indifference as he ran from the control room.

He was home, seeing once more by the sparkling light of his own familiar sun, breathing the air that had first washed through his lungs. The gangway was already down, but he had to wait for a moment until the glare outside no longer blinded him.

Karellen was standing, a little apart from his companions, beside a great transport vehicle loaded with crates. Jan did not stop to wonder how he recognized the Supervisor, nor was he surprised to see him completely unchanged. That was almost the only thing that had turned out as he had expected.

"I have been waiting for you," said Karellen.

✳   *CHAPTER TWENTY-TWO*

"In the early days," said Karellen, "it was safe for us to go among them. But they no longer needed us: our work was done when we had gathered them together and given them a continent of their own. Watch."

The wall in front of Jan disappeared. Instead he was looking down from a height of a few hundred meters on to a pleasantly wooded country. The illusion was so perfect that he fought a momentary giddiness.

"This is five years later, when the second phase had begun."

There were figures moving below, and the camera swooped down upon them like a bird of prey.

"This will distress you," said Karellen. "But remember that your standards no longer apply. You are not watching human children."

Yet that was the immediate impression that came to Jan's mind, and no amount of logic could dispel it. They might have been savages, engaged in some complex ritual dance. They were naked and filthy, with matted hair obscuring their eyes. As far as Jan could tell, they were of all ages from five to fifteen, yet they all moved with the same speed, precision, and complete indifference to their surroundings.

Then Jan saw their faces. He swallowed hard, and forced himself not to turn away. They were emptier than the faces of the dead, for even a corpse has some record carved by time's chisel upon its features, to speak when the lips themselves are dumb. There was no more emotion or feeling here than in the face of a snake or an insect. The Overlords themselves were more human than this.

"You are searching for something that is no longer there," said Karellen. "Remember—they have no more identity than the cells in your own body. But linked together, they are something much greater than you."

"Why do they keep moving like this?"

"We called it the Long Dance," replied Karellen. "They never sleep, you know, and this lasted almost a year. Three hundred million of them, moving in a controlled pattern over a whole continent. We've analyzed that pattern endlessly, but it means nothing, perhaps because we can see only the physical part of it—the small portion that's here on Earth. Possibly what we have called the Overmind is still training them, molding them into one unit before it can wholly absorb them into its being."

"But how did they manage about food? And what happened if they hit obstructions, like trees, or cliffs, or water?"

"Water made no difference: they could not drown. When they encountered obstacles, they sometimes damaged themselves, but they never noticed it. As for food—well, there was all the fruit and game they required. But now they have left that need behind, like so many others. For food is largely a source of energy, and they have learned to tap greater sources."

The scene flickered as if a heat haze had passed over it. When it cleared, the movement below had ceased.

"Watch again," said Karellen. "It is three years later."

The little figures, so helpless and pathetic if one did not know the truth, stood motionless in forest and glade and plain. The camera roamed restlessly from one to the other: already, thought Jan, their faces were merging into a common mold. He had once seen some photographs made by the superposition of dozens of prints, to give one "average" face. The result had been as empty, as void of character as this.

They seemed to be sleeping or entranced. Their eyes were tightly closed, and they showed no more awareness of their surroundings than did the trees under which they stood. What thoughts, Jan wondered, were echoing through the intricate network in which their minds were now no more—and yet no less—than the separate threads of some great tapestry? And a tapestry, he now realized, that covered many worlds and many races—and was growing still.

It happened with a swiftness that dazzled the eye and stunned the brain. At one moment Jan was looking down upon a beautiful, fertile country with nothing strange about it save the countless small statues scattered—yet not randomly—over its length and breadth. And then in an instant all the trees and grass, all the living creatures that had inhabited this land, flickered out of existence and were gone. There were left only the still lakes, the winding rivers, the rolling brown hills, now stripped of their green carpet—and the silent, indifferent figures who had wrought all this destruction.

"Why did they do it?" gasped Jan.

"Perhaps the presence of other minds disturbed them—even the rudimentary minds of plants and animals. One day, we believe, they may find the material world equally distracting. And then, who knows what will happen? Now you understand, why we withdrew when we had done our duty. We are still trying to study them, but we never enter their land or even send our instruments there. All we dare do is to observe from space."

"That was many years ago," said Jan. "What has happened since?"

"Very little. They have never moved in all that time, and take no notice of day or night, summer or winter. They are still testing their powers; some rivers have changed their courses, and there is one that flows uphill. But they have done nothing that seems to have any purpose."

"And they have ignored you completely?"

"Yes, though that is not surprising. The—entity—of which they are part knows all about us. It does not seem to care if we attempt to study it. When it wishes us to leave, or has a new task for us elsewhere, it will make its desires very obvious. Until then, we will remain here so that our scientists can gather what knowledge they may."

So this, thought Jan, with a resignation that lay beyond all sadness, was the end of man. It was an end that no prophet had ever foreseen—an end that repudiated optimism and pessimism alike.

Yet it was fitting: it had the sublime inevitability of a great work of art. Jan had glimpsed the universe in all its awful immensity, and knew now that it was no place for man. He realized at last how vain, in the ultimate analysis, had been the dream that had lured him to the stars.

For the road to the stars was a road that forked in two directions, and neither led to a goal that took any account of human hopes or fears.

At the end of one path were the Overlords. They had preserved their individuality, their independent egos: they possessed self-awareness and the pronoun "I" had a meaning in their language. They had emotions, some at least of which were shared by humanity. But they were trapped, Jan realized now, in a cul-de-sac from which they could never escape. Their minds were ten—perhaps a hundred—times as powerful as men's. It made no difference in the final reckoning. They were equally helpless, equally overwhelmed by the unimaginable complexity of a galaxy of a hundred thousand million suns, and a cosmos of a hundred thousand million galaxies.

And at the end of the other path? There lay the Overmind, whatever it might be, bearing the same relation to man as man bore to amoeba. Potentially infinite, beyond mortality, how long had it been absorbing race after race as it spread across the stars? Did it too have desires, did it have goals it sensed dimly yet might never attain? Now it had drawn into its being all that the human race had ever achieved. This was not tragedy, but fulfillment. The billions of transient sparks of consciousness that had made up humanity would flicker no more like fireflies against the night. But they had not lived utterly in vain.

The last act, Jan knew, had still to come. It might occur tomorrow, or it might be centuries hence. Even the Overlords could not be certain.

He understood their purpose now, what they had done with man and why they still lingered upon Earth. Towards them he felt a great humility, as well as admiration for the inflexible patience that had kept them waiting here so long.

He never learned the full story of the strange symbiosis between the Overmind and its servants. According to Rashaverak, there had never been a time in his race's history when the Overmind was not there, though it had made no use of them until they had achieved a scientific civilization and could range through space to do its bidding.

"But why does it need you?" queried Jan. "With all its tremendous powers, surely it could do anything it pleased."

"No," said Rashaverak, "it has limits. In the past, we know, it has attempted to act directly upon the minds of other races, and to influence their cultural development. It's always failed, perhaps because the gulf is too great. We are the interpreters—the guardians. Or, to use one of your other metaphors, we till the field until the crop is ripe. The Overmind collects the harvest—and we move on to another task. This is the fifth race whose apotheosis we have watched. Each time we learn a little more."

"And you do not resent being used as a tool by the Overmind?"

"The arrangement has some advantages: besides, no one of intelligence resents the inevitable."

That proposition, Jan reflected wryly, had never been fully accepted by mankind. There were things beyond logic that the Overlords had never understood.

"It seems strange," said Jan, "that the Overmind chose you to do its work, if you have no trace of the paraphysical powers latent in mankind. How does it communicate with you and make its wishes known?"

"That is one question I cannot answer—and I cannot tell you the reason why I must keep the facts from you. One day, perhaps, you will know some of the truth."

Jan puzzled over this for a moment, but knew it was useless to follow this line of inquiry. He would have to change the subject and hope to pick up clues later.

"Tell me this, then," he said. "Here is something else you've never explained. When your race first came to Earth, back in the distant past, what went wrong? Why had you become the symbol of fear and evil to us?"

Rashaverak smiled. He did not do this as well as Karellen could, but it was a fair imitation.

"No one ever guessed, and you see now why we could never

tell you. There was only one event that could have made such an impact upon humanity. And that event was not at the dawn of history, *but at its very end.*"

"What do you mean?" asked Jan.

"When our ships entered your skies a century and a half ago, that was the first meeting of our two races, though of course we had studied you from a distance. And yet you feared and recognized us, as we knew that you would. It was not precisely a memory. You have already had proof that time is more complex than your science ever imagined. For that memory was not of the past, but of the *future*—of those closing years when your race knew that everything was finished. We did what we could, but it was not an easy end. And because we were there, we became identified with your race's death. Yes, even while it was ten thousand years in the future! It was as if a distorted echo had reverberated round the closed circle of time, from the future to the past. Call it not a memory, but a premonition."

The idea was hard to grasp, and for a moment Jan wrestled with it in silence. Yet he should have been prepared; he had already received proof enough that cause and event could reverse their normal sequence.

There must be such a thing as racial memory, and that memory was somehow independent of time. To it, the future and the past were one. That was why, thousands of years ago, men had already glimpsed a distorted image of the Overlords, through a mist of fear and terror.

"Now I understand," said the last man.

The Last Man! Jan found it very hard to think of himself as that. When he had gone into space, he had accepted the possibility of eternal exile from the human race, and loneliness had not yet come upon him. As the years passed, the longing to see another human being might rise and overwhelm him, but for the present, the company of the Overlords prevented him from feeling utterly alone.

There had been men on Earth as little as ten years ago, but they had been degenerate survivors and Jan had lost nothing by missing them. For reasons which the Overlords could not explain, but which Jan suspected were largely psychological, there had been no children to replace those who had gone. *Homo sapiens* was extinct.

Perhaps, lost in one of the still-intact cities, was the manuscript of some latter-day Gibbon, recording the last days of the human race. If so, Jan was not sure that he would care to read it; Rashaverak had told him all he wished to know.

Those who had not destroyed themselves had sought oblivion in ever more feverish activities, in fierce and suicidal sports that were often indistinguishable from minor wars. As the population had swiftly fallen, the ageing survivors had clustered together, a defeated army closing its ranks as it made its last retreat.

That final act, before the curtain came down forever, must have been lit by flashes of heroism and devotion, darkened by savagery and selfishness. Whether it had ended in despair or resignation, Jan would never know.

There was plenty to occupy his mind. The Overlord base was about a kilometer from a deserted villa, and Jan spent months fitting this out with equipment he had taken from the nearest town, some thirty kilometers distant. He had flown there with Rashaverak, whose friendship, he suspected, was not completely altruistic. The Overlord psychologist was still studying the last specimen of *Homo sapiens*.

The town must have been evacuated before the end, for the houses and even many of the public services were still in good order. It would have taken little work to restart the generators, so that the wide streets glowed once more with the illusion of life. Jan toyed with the idea, then abandoned it as too morbid. The one thing he did not wish to do was to brood upon the past. There was everything here that he needed to maintain him for the rest of his life, but what he wanted most was an electronic piano and certain Bach transcriptions. He had never had as much time for music as he would have liked, and now he would make up for it. When he was not performing himself, he played tapes of the great symphonies and concertos, so that the villa was never silent. Music had become his talisman against the loneliness which, one day, must surely overwhelm him.

Often he would go for long walks on the hills, thinking of all that had happened in the few months since he had last seen Earth. He had never thought, when he said good-by to Sullivan eighty terrestrial years ago, that the last generation of mankind was already in the womb.

What a young fool he had been! Yet he was not sure that he regretted his action: had he stayed on Earth, he would have witnessed those closing years over which time had now drawn a veil. Instead, he had leapfrogged past them into the future, and had learned the answers to questions that no other man would ever know. His curiosity was almost satisfied, but sometimes he wondered why the Overlords were waiting, and what would happen when their patience was at last rewarded.

But most of the time, with a contented resignation that comes normally to a man only at the end of a long and busy life, he sat before the keyboard and filled the air with his beloved Bach. Perhaps he was deceiving himself, perhaps this was some merciful trick of the mind, but now it seemed to Jan that this was what he had always wished to do. His secret ambition had at last dared to emerge into the full light of consciousness.

Jan had always been a good pianist—and now he was the finest in the world.

✳ CHAPTER TWENTY-THREE

It was Rashaverak who brought Jan the news, but he had already guessed it. In the small hours of the morning a nightmare had awakened him, and he had not been able to regain sleep. He could not remember the dream, which was very strange, for he believed that all dreams could be recalled if one tried hard enough immediately after waking. All he could remember of this was that he had been a small boy again, on a vast and empty plain, listening to a great voice calling in an unknown language.

The dream had disturbed him: he wondered if it was the first onslaught of loneliness upon his mind. Restlessly, he walked out of the villa on to the neglected lawn.

A full moon bathed the scene with a golden light so brilliant that he could see perfectly. The immense, gleaming cylinder of Karellen's ship lay beyond the buildings of the Overlord base, towering above them and reducing them to man-made proportions. Jan looked at the ship, trying to recall the emotions it had once roused in him.

There was a time when it had been an unattainable goal, a symbol of all that he had never really expected to achieve. And now it meant nothing.

How quiet and still it was! The Overlords, of course, would be as active as ever, but for the moment there was no sign of them. He might have been alone on Earth—as, indeed, in a very real sense he was. He glanced up at the Moon, seeking some familiar sight on which his thoughts could rest.

There were the ancient, well-remembered seas. He had been forty light-years into space, yet he had never walked on those silent, dusty plains less than two light-seconds away. For a moment he amused himself trying to locate the crater Tycho. When he did discover it, he was puzzled to find that gleaming speck further from the center line of the disc than he had thought. And it was then that he realized that the dark oval of the Mare Crisium was missing altogether.

The face that her satellite now turned towards the Earth was not the one that had looked down on the world since the dawn of life. The Moon had begun to turn upon its axis.

This could mean only one thing. On the other side of the Earth, in the land that they had stripped so suddenly of life, *they* were emerging from their long trance. As a waking child may stretch its arms to greet the day, they too were flexing their muscles and playing with their new-found powers. . . .

"You have guessed correctly," said Rashaverak. "It is no longer safe for us to stay. They may ignore us still, but we cannot take the risk. We leave as soon as our equipment can be loaded—probably in two or three hours."

He looked up at the sky, as if afraid that some new miracle was about to blaze forth. But all was peaceful: the Moon had set, and only a few clouds rode high upon the west wind.

"It does not matter greatly if they tamper with the Moon," Rashaverak added, "but suppose they begin to interfere with the Sun? We shall leave instruments behind, of course, so that we can learn what happens."

"I shall stay," said Jan abruptly. "I have seen enough of the universe. There's only one thing that I'm curious about now—and that is the fate of my own planet."

Very gently, the ground trembled underfoot.

"I was expecting that," Jan continued. "If they alter the Moon's spin, the angular momentum must go somewhere. So the Earth is slowing down. I don't know which puzzles me more—*how* they are doing it, or *why*."

"They are still playing," said Rashaverak. "What logic is there in the actions of a child? And in many ways the entity that your race has become is still a child. It is not yet ready to unite with the Overmind. But very soon it will be, and then you will have the Earth to yourself."

He did not complete the sentence, and Jan finished it for him.

"—if, of course, the Earth still exists."

"You realize that danger—and yet you will stay?"

"Yes. I have been home five—or is it six?—years now. Whatever happens, I'll have no complaints."

"We were hoping," began Rashaverak slowly, "that you would wish to stay. There is something that you can do for us. . . ."

The glare of the Stardrive dwindled and died, somewhere out there beyond the orbit of Mars. Along that road, thought Jan, he alone had traveled, out of all the billions of human beings who had lived and died on Earth. And no one would ever travel it again.

The world was his. Everything he needed—all the material possessions anyone could ever desire—were his for the taking. But he was no longer interested. He feared neither the loneliness of the deserted planet, nor the presence that still rested here in the last moments before it went to seek its unknown heritage. In the inconceivable backwash of that departure, Jan did not expect that he and his problems would long survive.

That was well. He had done all that he had wished to do, and to drag out a pointless life on this empty world would have been an unbearable anticlimax. He could have left with the Overlords, but for what purpose? For he knew, as no one else had ever known, that Karellen spoke the truth when he had said: "The stars are not for Man."

He turned his back upon the night and walked through the vast entrance of the Overlord base. Its size affected him not in the least: sheer immensity no longer had any power over his mind. The lights were burning redly, driven by energies that could feed them for ages yet. On either side lay machines whose secrets he would never know, abandoned by the Overlords in their retreat. He went past them, and clambered awkwardly up the great steps until he had reached the control room.

The spirit of the Overlords still lingered here: their machines were still alive, doing the bidding of their now far-distant masters. What could he add, wondered Jan, to the information they were already hurling into space?

He climbed into the great chair and made himself as comfortable as he could. The microphone, already live, was waiting for him: something that was the equivalent of a TV camera must be watching, but he could not locate it.

Beyond the desk and its meaningless instrument panels, the wide windows looked out into the starry night, across a valley sleeping beneath a gibbous moon, and to the distant range of mountains. A river wound along the valley, glittering here and there as the moonlight struck upon some patch of troubled water. It was all so peaceful. It might have been thus at Man's birth as it was now at his ending.

Out there across unknown millions of kilometers of space, Karellen would be waiting. It was strange to think that the ship of the Overlords was racing away from Earth almost as swiftly as his signal could speed after it. Almost—but not quite. It would be a long chase, but his words would catch the Supervisor and he would have repaid the debt he owed.

How much of this, Jan wondered, had Karellen planned, and how much was masterful improvisation? Had the Supervisor deliberately let him escape into space, almost a century ago, so that he could return to play the role he was fulfilling now? No, that seemed too fantastic. But Jan was certain, now, that Karellen was involved in some vast and complicated plot. Even while he served it, he was studying the Overmind with all the instruments at his command. Jan suspected that it was not only scientific curiosity that inspired the Supervisor: perhaps the Overlords had dreams of one day escaping from their peculiar bondage, when they had learned enough about the powers they served.

That Jan could add to that knowledge by what he was now doing seemed hard to believe. "Tell us what you see," Rashaverak had said. "The picture that reaches your eyes will be duplicated by our cameras. But the message that enters your brain may be very different, and it could tell us a great deal." Well, he would do his best.

"Still nothing to report," he began. "A few minutes ago I saw the trail of your ship disappear in the sky. The Moon is just past full, and almost half its familiar side has now turned away from Earth—but I suppose you already know that."

Jan paused, feeling slightly foolish. There was something incongruous, even faintly absurd, about what he was doing. Here was the climax of all history, yet he might have been a radio-commentator at a race-track or a boxing-ring. Then he shrugged his shoulders and put the thought aside. At all moments of greatness, he suspected, bathos had never been far away—and certainly he alone could sense its presence here.

"There have been three slight quakes in the last hour," he continued. "Their control of Earth's spin must be marvelous, but not quite perfect. . . . You know now, Karellen, I'm going to find it very hard to say anything your instruments haven't already told you. It might have helped if you'd given me some idea of what to expect, and warned me how long I may have to wait. If nothing happens, I'll report again in six hours, as we arranged. . . .

"Hello! They must have been waiting for you to leave. Something's starting to happen. The stars are becoming dimmer. It's as if a great cloud is coming up, very swiftly, over all the sky. But it isn't really a cloud. It seems to have some sort of structure—I can glimpse a hazy network of lines and bands that keep changing their positions. It's almost as if the stars are tangled in a ghostly spider's web.

"The whole network is beginning to glow, to pulse with light, exactly as if it were alive. And I suppose it is: or is it something as much beyond life as *that* is above the inorganic world?

"The glow seems to be shifting to one part of the sky—wait a minute while I move around to the other window.

"Yes—I might have guessed. There's a great burning column, like a tree of fire, reaching above the western horizon. It's a long way off, right round the world. I know where it springs from: *they're* on their way at last, to become part of the Overmind. Their probation is ended: they're leaving the last remnants of matter behind.

"As that fire spreads upwards from the Earth, I can see the network becoming firmer and less misty. In places it seems almost solid, yet the stars are still shining faintly through it.

"I've just realized. It's not exactly the same, but the thing I saw shooting up above your world, Karellen, was very much like this. Was that part of the Overmind? I suppose you hid the truth from me so that I would have no preconceived ideas—so that I'd be an unbiassed observer. I wish I knew what your cameras were showing you now, to compare it with what my mind imagines I'm seeing!

"Is this how it talks to you, Karellen, in colors and shapes like these? I remember the control screens on your ship and the patterns that went across them, speaking to you in some visual language which your eyes could read.

"Now it looks exactly like the curtains of the aurora, dancing and flickering across the stars. Why, that's what it really is, I'm sure—a great auroral storm. The whole landscape is lit up—it's brighter than day—reds and golds and greens are chasing each other across the sky—oh, it's beyond words, it doesn't seem fair that I'm the only one to see it—I never thought such colors—

"The storm's dying down, but the great misty network is still there. I think that aurora was only a by-product of whatever energies are being released up there on the frontier of space. . . .

"Just a minute: I've noticed something else. *My weight's decreasing*. What does that mean? I've dropped a pencil—it's falling slowly. Something's happened to gravity. There's a great wind coming up—I can see the trees tossing their branches down there in the valley.

"Of course—the atmosphere's escaping. Sticks and stones are rising into the sky, almost as if the earth itself is trying to follow *them* out into space. There's a great cloud of dust, whipped up by the gale. It's becoming hard to see . . . perhaps it will clear in a moment, and I'll be able to find out what's happening.

"Yes—that's better. Everything moveable has been stripped away, the dust clouds have vanished. I wonder how long this building will stand? And it's getting hard to breathe—I must try to talk more slowly.

"I can see clearly again. That great burning column is still there, but it's constricting, narrowing; it looks like the funnel of a tornado, about to retract into the clouds. And—oh, this is hard to describe, but just then I felt a great wave of emotion sweep over me. It wasn't joy or sorrow; it was a sense of fulfillment, achievement. Did I imagine it? Or did it come from outside? I don't know.

"And now—*this* can't be all imagination—the world feels empty.

Utterly empty. It's like listening to a radio set that's suddenly gone dead. And the sky is clear again—the misty web has gone. What world will it go to next, Karellen? And will you be there to serve it still?

"Strange: everything around me is unaltered. I don't know why, but somehow I'd thought that . . ."

Jan stopped. For a moment he struggled for words, then closed his eyes in an effort to regain control. There was no room for fear or panic now: he had a duty to perform—a duty to Man, and a duty to Karellen.

Slowly at first, like a man awakening from a dream, he began to speak.

"The buildings round me, the ground, the mountains—everything's like glass—*I can see through it*. Earth's dissolving. My weight has almost gone. You were right—they've finished playing with their toys.

"It's only a few seconds away. There go the mountains, like wisps of smoke. Good-by, Karellen, Rashaverak—I am sorry for you. Though I cannot understand it, I've seen what my race became. Everything we ever achieved has gone up there into the stars. Perhaps that's what the old religions were trying to say. But they got it all wrong: they thought mankind was so important, yet we're only one race in—do *you* know how many? Yet now we've become something that you could never be.

"There goes the river. No change in the sky, though. I can hardly breathe. Strange to see the Moon still shining up there. I'm glad they left it, but it will be lonely now—

"The light! From *beneath* me—inside the Earth—shining upward, through the rocks, the ground, everything—growing brighter, brighter, blinding—"

In a soundless concussion of light, Earth's core gave up its hoarded energies. For a little while the gravitational waves crossed and re-crossed the Solar System, disturbing ever so slightly the orbits of the planets. Then the Sun's remaining children pursued their ancient paths once more, as corks floating on a placid lake ride out the tiny ripples set in motion by a falling stone.

There was nothing left of Earth: *They* had leeched away the last atoms of its substance. It had nourished them, through the fierce moments of their inconceivable metamorphosis, as the food stored in a grain of wheat feeds the infant plant while it climbs towards the Sun.

Six thousand million kilometers beyond the orbit of Pluto, Karellen sat before a suddenly darkened screen. The record was complete, the mission ended; he was homeward bound for the world he had left so long ago. The weight of centuries was upon him, and a sadness that no logic could dispel. He did not mourn for Man: his sorrow was for his own race, forever barred from greatness by forces it could not overcome.

For all their achievements, thought Karellen, for all their mastery of the physical universe, his people were no better than a tribe that had passed its whole existence upon some flat and dusty plain. Far off were the mountains, where power and beauty dwelt, where the thunder sported above the glaciers and the air was clear and keen. There the sun still walked, transfiguring the peaks with glory, when all the land below was wrapped in darkness. And they could only watch and wonder; they could never scale those heights.

Yet, Karellen knew, they would hold fast until the end: they would await without despair whatever destiny was theirs. They would serve the Overmind because they had no choice, but even in that service they would not lose their souls.

The great control screen flared for a moment with somber, ruby light: without conscious effort, Karellen read the message of its changing patterns. The ship was leaving the frontiers of the Solar System: the energies that powered the Stardrive were ebbing fast, but they had done their work.

Karellen raised his hand, and the picture changed once more. A single brilliant star glowed in the center of the screen: no one could have told, from this distance, that the Sun had ever possessed planets or that one of them had now been lost. For a long time Karellen stared back across that swiftly widening gulf, while many memories raced through his vast and labyrinthine mind. In silent farewell, he saluted the men he had known, whether they had hindered or helped him in his purpose.

No one dared disturb him or interrupt his thoughts: and presently he turned his back upon the dwindling Sun.

EARTHLIGHT

✳ CHAPTER ONE

The monorail was losing speed as it climbed up out of the shadowed lowlands. At any moment now, thought Sadler, they would overtake the sun. The line of darkness moved so slowly here that, with a little effort, a man could keep abreast of it, could hold the sun balanced on the horizon until he had to pause for rest. Even then, it would slip so reluctantly from sight that more than an hour would pass before the last dazzling segment vanished below the edge of the Moon, and the long lunar night began.

He had been racing through that night, across the land that the first pioneers had opened up two centuries ago, at a steady and comfortable five hundred kilometers an hour. Apart from a bored conductor, who seemed to have nothing to do but produce cups of coffee on request, the only other occupants of the car were four astronomers from the Observatory. They had nodded affably enough when he came aboard, but had promptly lost themselves in a technical argument and had ignored Sadler ever since. He felt a little hurt by this neglect, then consoled himself with the thought that perhaps they took him for a seasoned resident, not a newcomer on his first assignment to the Moon.

The lights in the car made it impossible to see much of the darkened land through which they were racing in almost complete silence. "Darkened," of course, was only a relative term. It was true that the sun had gone, but not far from the zenith the Earth was approaching its first quarter. It would grow steadily until at lunar midnight, a week from now, it would be a blinding disk too bright for the unprotected eye to gaze upon.

Sadler left his seat and went forward, past the still-arguing

437

astronomers, toward the curtained alcove at the front of the car. He was not yet accustomed to possessing only a sixth of his normal weight, and moved with exaggerated caution through the narrow corridor between the toilets and the little control room.

Now he could see properly. The observation windows were not as large as he would have liked; some safety regulation was responsible for that. But there was no internal light to distract his eyes, and at last he could enjoy the cold glory of this ancient, empty land.

Cold—yes, he could well believe that beyond these windows it was already two hundred degrees below zero, though the sun had sunk only a few hours before. Some quality of the light pouring down from the distant seas and clouds of Earth gave the impression. It was a light tinged with blues and greens, an arctic radiance that gave no atom of heat. And that, thought Sadler, was surely a paradox, for it came from a world of light and warmth.

Ahead of the speeding car, the single rail—supported by pillars uncomfortably far apart—arrowed into the east. Another paradox; this world was full of them. Why couldn't the sun set in the west, as it did on Earth? There must be some simple astronomical explanation, but for the moment Sadler could not decide what it was. Then he realized that, after all, such labels were purely arbitrary, and could easily get misplaced when a new world was mapped.

They were still rising slowly, and there was a cliff on the right which limited vision. On the left—let's see, that would be south, wouldn't it?—the broken land fell away in a series of layers as though a billion years ago the lava welling up from the Moon's molten heart had solidified in successive, weakening waves. It was a scene that chilled the soul, yet there were spots on Earth as bleak as this. The Badlands of Arizona were equally desolate; the upper slopes of Everest were far more hostile, for here at least was no eternal, ravening wind.

And then Sadler almost cried out aloud, for the cliff on the right came to a sudden end as if a monstrous chisel had sliced it off the surface of the Moon. It no longer barred his view: he could see clear round to the north. The unpremeditated artistry of Nature had produced an effect so breathtaking that it was hard to believe it was merely an accident of time and place.

There, marching across the sky in flaming glory, were the peaks of the Apennines, incandescent in the last rays of the hidden sun.

The abrupt explosion of light left Sadler almost blinded; he shielded his eyes from the glare, and waited until he could safely face it again. When he looked once more, the transformation was complete. The stars, which until a moment ago had filled the sky, had vanished. His contracted pupils could no longer see them: even the glowing Earth now seemed no more than a feeble patch of greenish luminosity. The glare from the sunlit mountains, still a hundred kilometers away, had eclipsed all other sources of light.

The peaks floated in the sky, fantastic pyramids of flame. They seemed to have no more connection with the ground beneath them than do the clouds that gather above a sunset on Earth. The line of shadow was so sharp, the lower slopes of the mountains so lost in utter darkness, that only the burning summits had any real existence. It would be hours yet before the last of those proud peaks fell back into the shadow of the Moon and surrendered to the night.

The curtains behind Sadler parted; one of his fellow passengers came into the alcove and took up a position by the window. Sadler wondered whether to open the conversation. He still felt a little piqued at being so completely ignored. However, the problem in etiquette was solved for him.

"Worth coming from Earth to see, isn't it?" said a voice from the gloom at his side.

"It certainly is," Sadler replied. Then, trying to be blasé, he added: "But I suppose you get used to it in time."

There was a chuckle from the darkness.

"I wouldn't say that. Some things you never get used to, however long you live here. Just got in?"

"Yes. Landed last night in the *Tycho Brahe*. Haven't had time to see much yet."

In unconscious mimicry, Sadler found himself using the clipped sentences of his companion. He wondered if everyone on the Moon talked like this. Perhaps they thought it saved air.

"Going to work at the Observatory?"

"In a way, though I won't be on the permanent staff. I'm an accountant. Doing a cost-analysis of your operations."

This produced a thoughtful silence, which was finally broken by: "Rude of me—should have introduced myself. Robert Molton.

Head of Spectroscopy. Nice to have someone around who can tell us how to do our income tax."

"I was afraid that would come up," said Sadler dryly. "My name's Bertram Sadler; I'm from the Audit Bureau."

"Humph. Think we're wasting money here?"

"That's for someone else to decide. I've only got to find *how* you spend it, not why."

"Well, you're going to have some fun. Everyone here can make out a good case for spending twice as much money as they get. And I'd like to know how the devil you'll put a price tag on pure scientific research."

Sadler had been wondering that for some time, but thought it best not to attempt any further explanations. His story had been accepted without question; if he tried to make it more convincing, he would give himself away. He was not a good liar, though he hoped to improve with practice.

In any case, what he had told Molton was perfectly true. Sadler only wished it were the whole truth, and not a mere five per cent of it.

"I was wondering how we're going to get through those mountains," he remarked, pointing to the burning peaks ahead. "Do we go over—or under?"

"Over," said Molton. "They look spectacular, but they're really not so big. Wait till you see the Leibnitz Mountains or the Oberth Range. They're twice as high."

These are quite good enough to start with, thought Sadler. The low-slung monorail car, straddling its single track, bored through the shadows on a slowly rising course. In the darkness around them, dimly seen crags and cliffs rushed forward with explosive swiftness, then vanished astern. Sadler realized that probably nowhere else could one travel at such velocities so close to the ground. No jet liner, far above the clouds of Earth, ever gave such an impression of sheer speed as this.

If it had been day, Sadler could have seen the prodigies of engineering that had flung this track across the foothills of the Apennines. But the darkness veiled the gossamer bridges and the canyon-fringing curves; he saw only the approaching peaks, still magically afloat upon the sea of night that lapped around them.

Then, far to the east, a burning bow peeped above the edge of the Moon. They had risen out of shadow, had joined the mountains in their glory and overtaken the sun itself. Sadler looked away from the glare which flooded the cabin, and for the first time saw clearly the man standing by his side.

Doctor (or would it be Professor?) Molton was in the early fifties, but his hair was quite black and very abundant. He had one of those strikingly ugly faces that somehow immediately inspire confidence. Here, one felt, was the humorous, worldly-wise philosopher, the modern Socrates, sufficiently detached to give unbiased advice to all, yet by no means aloof from human contact. The heart of gold beneath the rugged exterior, Sadler thought to himself, and flinched mentally at the triteness of the phrase.

Their eyes met in the silent appraisal of two men who know that their future business will bring them together again. Then Molton smiled, wrinkling a face that was almost as craggy as the surrounding moonscape.

"Must be your first dawn on the Moon. If you can call this a dawn, of course—anyway, it's a sunrise. Pity it'll only last ten minutes—we'll be over the top then and back into night. Then you'll have to wait two weeks to see the sun again."

"Doesn't it get a trifle—boring—being cooped up for fourteen days?" asked Sadler. No sooner had he spoken the words than he realized that he had probably made a fool of himself. But Molton let him down lightly.

"You'll see," he answered. "Day or night, it's much the same underground. Anyway, you can go out whenever you like. Some people prefer the nighttime; the Earthlight makes them feel romantic."

The monorail had now reached the apex of its trajectory through the mountains. Both travelers fell silent as the peaks on either side reared to their climax, then began to sink astern. They had burst through the barrier, and were dropping down the much steeper slopes overlooking the *Mare Imbrium*. As they descended, so the sun which their speed had conjured back from night shrank from a bow to a thread, from a thread to a single point of fire, and winked out of existence. In the last instant of that false sunset, seconds before they sank again into the shadow of the Moon, there was a moment of magic that Sadler would never forget. They were moving along a ridge that the sun had already left, but the track of the monorail, scarcely a meter above it, still caught the last rays.

It seemed as if they were rushing along an unsupported ribbon of light, a filament of flame built by sorcery rather than human engineering. Then final darkness fell, and the magic ended. The stars began to creep back into the sky as Sadler's eyes readapted themselves to the night.

"You were lucky," said Molton. "I've ridden this run a hundred times, but I've never seen that. Better come back into the car—they'll be serving a snack in a minute. Nothing more to see now, anyway."

That, thought Sadler, was hardly true. The blazing Earthlight, coming back into its own now that the sun was gone, flooded the great plain that the ancient astronomers had so inaccurately christened the Sea of Rains. Compared with the mountains that lay behind, it was not spectacular, yet it was still something to catch the breath.

"I'll wait awhile," Sadler answered. "Remember, this is all new to me and I don't want to miss any of it."

Molton laughed, not unkindly. "Can't say I blame you," he said. "Afraid we sometimes take things for granted."

The monorail was now sliding down an absolutely vertiginous incline that would have been suicide on Earth. The cold, greenlit plain lifted to meet them: a range of low hills, dwarfs beside the mountains they had left behind, broke the skyline ahead. Once again, the uncannily near horizon of this little world began to close in upon them. They were back at "sea" level. . . .

Sadler followed Molton through the curtains and into the cabin, where the steward was setting out trays for his small company.

"Do you always have as few passengers as this?" asked Sadler. "I shouldn't think it was a very economical proposition."

"Depends what you mean by economical," Molton replied. "A lot of the things here will look funny on your balance sheets. But it doesn't cost much to run this service. Equipment lasts forever—no rust, no weather. Cars get serviced only every couple of years."

That was something Sadler certainly hadn't considered. There were a great many things he had to learn, and some of them he might find out the hard way.

The meal was tasty but unidentifiable. Like all food on the Moon, it would have been grown in the great hydroponic farms that sprawled their square kilometers of pressurized greenhouses along the equator. The meat course was presumably synthetic: it might have been beef, but Sadler happened to know that the only cow on the Moon lived in luxury at the Hipparchus Zoo. This was the sort of useless information his diabolically retentive mind was always picking up and refusing to disgorge.

Perhaps mealtime had made the other astronomers more affable, for they were friendly enough when Dr. Molton introduced them, and managed to avoid talking shop for a few minutes. It was obvious, however, that they regarded his mission with some alarm. Sadler could see them all mentally reviewing their appropriations and wondering what kind of case they could put up if they were challenged. He had no doubt that they would all have highly convincing stories, and would try to blind him with science if he attempted to pin them down. He had been through it all before, though never in quite such circumstances as these.

The car was now on the last lap of its journey, and would be at the Observatory in little more than an hour. The six-hundred-kilometer run across the *Mare Imbrium* was almost straight and level, apart from a brief detour to the east to avoid the hills around the giant walled-plain of Archimedes. Sadler settled himself down comfortably, pulled out his briefing papers, and began to do some study.

The organization chart he unfolded covered most of the table. It was neatly printed in several colors, according to the various departments of the Observatory, and Sadler looked at it with some distaste. Ancient man, he remembered, had once been defined as a tool-making animal. He often felt that the best description of modern man would be a paper-wasting animal.

Below the headings "Director" and "Deputy Director" the chart split three ways under the captions ADMINISTRATION, TECHNICAL SERVICES, and OBSERVATORY. Sadler looked for Dr. Molton; yes, there he was, in the OBSERVATORY section, directly beneath the chief scientist and heading the short column of names labeled "Spectroscopy." He seemed to have six assistants: two of them—Jamieson and Wheeler—were men to whom Sadler had just been introduced. The other traveler in the monocab, he discovered, was not really a scientist at all. He had a little box of his own on the chart, and was responsible to no one but the director. Sadler suspected that

Secretary Wagnall was probably quite a power in the land, and would be well worth cultivating.

He had been studying the chart for half an hour, and had completely lost himself in its ramifications, when someone switched on the radio. Sadler had no objection to the soft music that filled the car; his powers of concentration could deal with worse interference than this. Then the music stopped; there was a brief pause, the six beeps of a time signal, and a suave voice began:

"This is Earth, Channel Two, Interplanetary Network. The signal you have just heard was twenty-one hundred hours G.M.T. Here is the news."

There was no trace of interference. The words were as clear as if they were coming from a local station. Yet Sadler had noticed the skyward tilting antenna system on the roof of the monocab, and knew that he was listening to a direct transmission. The words he was hearing had left Earth almost one and a half seconds ago. Already they would be heading past him to far more distant worlds. There would be men who would not hear them for minutes yet—perhaps for hours, if the ships that the Federation had beyond Saturn were listening in. And that voice from Earth would still go on, expanding and fading, far beyond the uttermost limits of man's explorations, until somewhere on the way to Alpha Centauri it was at last obliterated by the ceaseless radio whispering of the stars themselves.

"Here is the news. It has just been announced from the Hague that the conference on planetary resources has broken down. The delegates of the Federation are leaving Earth tomorrow, and the following statement has been issued from the office of the President. . . ."

There was nothing here that Sadler had not expected. But when a fear, however long anticipated, turns into a fact, there is always that same sinking of the heart. He glanced at his companions. Did they realize how serious this was?

They did. Secretary Wagnall had his chin cupped fiercely in his hands; Dr. Molton was leaning back in his chair, eyes closed; Jamieson and Wheeler were staring at the table in glum concentration. Yes, they understood. Their work and their remoteness from Earth had not isolated them from the main currents of human affairs.

The impersonal voice, with its catalogue of disagreements and countercharges, of threats barely veiled by the euphemisms of diplomacy, seemed to bring the inhuman cold of the lunar night seeping through the walls. It was hard to face the bitter truth, and millions of men would still be living in a fool's paradise. They would shrug their shoulders and say with forced cheerfulness, "Don't worry—it will all blow over."

Sadler did not believe so. As he sat in that little, brightly illuminated cylinder racing north across the Sea of Rains, he knew that for the first time in two hundred years humanity was faced with the threat of war.

✳ CHAPTER TWO

If war came, thought Sadler, it would be a tragedy of circumstances rather than deliberate policy. Indeed, the stubborn fact that had brought Earth into conflict with her ex-colonies sometimes seemed to him like a bad joke on the part of Nature.

Even before his unwelcome and unexpected assignment, Sadler had been well aware of the main facts behind the current crisis. It had been developing for more than a generation, and it arose from the peculiar position of the planet Earth.

The human race had been born on a world unique in the solar system, loaded with a mineral wealth unmatched elsewhere. This accident of fate had given a flying start to man's technology, but when he reached the other planets, he found to his surprise and disappointment that for many of his most vital needs he must still depend on the home world.

Earth is the densest of all the planets, only Venus approaching it in this respect. But Venus has no satellite, and the Earth-Moon system forms a double world of a type found nowhere else among the planets. Its mode of formation is a mystery still, but it is known that when Earth was molten the Moon circled at only a fraction of its present distance, and raised gigantic tides in the plastic substance of its companion.

As a result of these internal tides, the crust of the Earth is rich in heavy metals—far richer than that of any other of the planets:

they hoard their wealth far down within their unreachable cores, protected by pressures and temperatures that guard them from man's depredations. So as human civilization spread outward from Earth, the drain on the mother world's dwindling resources steadily increased.

The light elements existed on the other planets in unlimited amounts, but such essential metals as mercury, lead, uranium, platinum, thorium and tungsten were almost unobtainable. For many of them no substitutes existed; their large-scale synthesis was impractical, despite two centuries of effort—and modern technology could not survive without them.

It was an unfortunate situation, and a very galling one for the independent republics on Mars, Venus and the larger satellites, which had now united to form the Federation. It kept them dependent upon Earth, and prevented their expansion toward the frontiers of the solar system. Though they had searched among the asteroids and moons, among the rubble left over when the worlds were formed, they had found little but worthless rock and ice. They must go cap in hand to the mother planet for almost every gram of a dozen metals that were more precious than gold.

That in itself might not have been serious, had not Earth grown steadily more jealous of its offspring during the two hundred years since the dawn of space travel. It was, thought Sadler, an old, old story, perhaps its classic example being the case of England and the American colonies. It has been truly said that history never repeats itself, but historical situations recur. The men who governed Earth were far more intelligent than George the Third; nevertheless, they were beginning to show the same reactions as that unfortunate monarch.

There were excuses on both sides; there always are. Earth was tired; it had spent itself, sending out its best blood to the stars. It saw power slipping from its hands, and knew that it had already lost the future. Why should it speed the process by giving to its rivals the tools they needed?

The Federation, on the other hand, looked back with a kind of affectionate contempt upon the world from which it had sprung. It had lured to Mars, Venus and the satellites of the giant planets some of the finest intellects and the most adventurous spirits of the human race. Here was the new frontier, one that would expand forever toward the stars. It was the greatest physical challenge mankind had ever faced; it could be met only by supreme scientific skill and unyielding determination. These were virtues no longer essential on Earth; the fact that Earth was well aware of it did nothing to ease the situation.

All this might lead to discord and interplanetary invective, but it could never lead to violence. Some other factor was needed to produce that, some final spark which would set off an explosion echoing round the solar system.

That spark had now been struck. The world did not know it yet, and Sadler himself had been equally ignorant a short six months ago. Central Intelligence, the shadowy organization of which he was now a reluctant member, had been working night and day to neutralize the damage. A mathematical thesis entitled "A Quantitative Theory of the Formation of the Lunar Surface Features" did not look like the sort of thing that could start a war—but an equally theoretical paper by a certain Albert Einstein had once ended one.

The paper had been written about two years ago by Professor Roland Phillips, a peaceable Oxford cosmologist with no interest in politics. He had submitted it to the Royal Astronomical Society, and it was now becoming a little difficult to give him a satisfactory explanation of the delay in publication. Unfortunately—and this was the fact that caused great distress to Central Intelligence—Professor Phillips had innocently sent copies to his colleagues on Mars and Venus. Desperate attempts had been made to intercept them, but in vain. By now, the Federation must know that the Moon was not as impoverished a world as had been believed for two hundred years.

There was no way of calling back knowledge that had leaked out, but there were other things about the Moon which it was now equally important that the Federation should not learn. Yet somehow it was learning them; somehow, information was leaking across space from Earth to Moon, and then out to the planets.

When there's a leak in the house, thought Sadler, you send for the plumber. But how do you deal with a leak which you can't see—and which may be anywhere on the surface of a world as large as Africa?

He still knew very little about the scope, size and methods of Central Intelligence—and still resented, futile though that was, the way in which his private life had been disrupted. By training, he was precisely what he pretended to be—an accountant. Six months ago, for reasons which had not been explained and which he probably never would discover, he had been interviewed and offered an unspecified job. His acceptance was quite voluntary; it was merely made clear to him that he had better not refuse. Since then he had spent most of his time under hypnosis, being pumped full of the most various kinds of information and living a monastic life in an obscure corner of Canada. (At least, he thought it was Canada, but it might equally well have been Greenland or Siberia.) Now he was here on the Moon, a minor pawn in a game of interplanetary chess. He would be very glad when the whole frustrating experience was over. It seemed quite incredible to him that anyone would ever *voluntarily* become a secret agent. Only very immature and unbalanced individuals could get any satisfaction from such frankly uncivilized behavior.

There were a few compensations. In the ordinary way, he would never have had a chance of going to the Moon, and the experience he was gathering now might be a real asset in later years. Sadler always tried to take the long view, particularly when he was depressed by the current situation. And the situation, both on the personal and interplanetary levels, was depressing enough.

The safety of Earth was quite a responsibility, but it was really too big for one man to worry about. Whatever reason said, the vast imponderables of planetary politics were less of a burden than the little cares of everyday life. To a cosmic observer, it might have seemed very quaint that Sadler's greatest worry concerned one solitary human being. Would Jeannette ever forgive him, he wondered, for being away on their wedding anniversary? At least she would expect him to call her, and that was the one thing he dared not do. As far as his wife and his friends were concerned, he was still on Earth. There was no way of calling from the Moon without revealing his location, for the two-and-a-half-second time-lag would betray him at once.

Central Intelligence could fix many things, but it could hardly speed up radio waves. It could deliver his anniversary present on time, as it had promised—but it couldn't tell Jeannette when he would be home again.

And it couldn't change the fact that, to conceal his whereabouts, he had had to lie to his wife in the sacred name of Security.

✳ CHAPTER THREE

When Conrad Wheeler had finished comparing the tapes, he got up from his chair and walked three times round the room. From the way he moved, an old hand could have told that Wheeler was a relative newcomer to the Moon. He had been with the Observatory staff for just six months, and still overcompensated for the fractional gravity in which he now lived. There was a jerkiness about his movements that contrasted with the smooth, almost slow-motion gait of his colleagues. Some of this abruptness was due to his own temperament, his lack of discipline, and quickness at jumping to conclusions. It was that temperament he was now trying to guard against.

He had made mistakes before—but this time, surely, there could be no doubt. The facts were undisputed, the calculation trivial—the answer awe-inspiring. Far out in the depths of space, a star had exploded with unimaginable violence. Wheeler looked at the figures he had jotted down, checked them for the tenth time, and reached for the phone.

Sid Jamieson was not pleased at the interruption. "Is it really important?" he queried. "I'm in the darkroom, doing some stuff for Old Mole. I'll have to wait until these plates are washing, anyway."

"How long will that take?"

"Oh, maybe five minutes. Then I've got some more to do."

"I think this *is* important. It'll only take a moment. I'm up in Instrumentation 5."

Jamieson was still wiping developer from his hands when he arrived. After more than three hundred years, certain aspects of photography were quite unchanged. Wheeler, who thought that everything could be done by electronics, regarded many of his older friend's activities as survivals from the age of alchemy.

"Well?" said Jamieson, as usual wasting no words.

Wheeler pointed to the punched tape lying on the desk.

"I was doing the routine check of the magnitude integrator. It's found something."

"It's always doing *that,*" snorted Jamieson. "Every time anyone sneezes in the Observatory, it thinks it's discovered a new planet."

There were solid grounds for Jamieson's skepticism. The integrator was a tricky instrument, easily misled, and many astronomers thought it more trouble than it was worth. But it happened to be one of the director's pet projects, so there was no hope of doing anything about it until there was a change of administration. Maclaurin had invented it himself, back in the days when he had had time to do some practical astronomy. An automatic watchdog of the skies, it would wait patiently for years until a new star—a "nova" —blazed in the heavens. Then it would ring a bell and start calling for attention.

"Look," said Wheeler, "there's the record. Don't just take my word for it."

Jamieson ran the tape through the converter, copied down the figures and did a quick calculation. Wheeler smiled in satisfaction and relief as his friend's jaw dropped.

"Thirteen magnitudes in twenty-four hours! Wow!"

"I made it thirteen point four, but that's good enough. For my money, it's a supernova. And a close one."

The two young astronomers looked at each other in thoughtful silence. Then Jamieson remarked:

"This is too good to be true. Don't start telling everybody about it until we're quite sure. Let's get its spectrum first, and treat it as an ordinary nova until then."

There was a dreamy look in Wheeler's eyes.

"When was the last supernova in our galaxy?"

"That was Tycho's star—no it wasn't—there was one a bit later, round about 1600."

"Anyway, it's been a long time. This ought to get me on good terms with the director again."

"Perhaps," said Jamieson dryly. "It would just about take a supernova to do that. I'll go and get the spectrograph ready while you put out the report. We mustn't be greedy; the other observatories will want to get into the act." He looked at the integrator, which had returned to its patient searching of the sky. "I guess you've paid for yourself," he added, "even if you never find anything again except spaceship navigation lights."

Sadler heard the news without particular excitement in the Common Room an hour later. He was too preoccupied with his own problems and the mountain of work which faced him to take much notice of the Observatory's routine program, even when he fully understood it. Secretary Wagnall, however, quickly made it clear that this was very far from being a routine matter.

"Here's something to put on your balance sheet," he said cheerfully. "It's the biggest astronomical discovery for years. Come up to the roof."

Sadler dropped the trenchant editorial in *Time Interplanetary* which he had been reading with growing annoyance. The magazine fell with that dreamlike slowness he had not yet grown accustomed to, and he followed Wagnall to the elevator.

They rose past the residential level, past Administration, past Power and Transport, and emerged into one of the small observation domes. The plastic bubble was scarcely ten meters across, and the awnings that shielded it during the lunar day had been rolled back. Wagnall switched off the internal lights, and they stood looking up at the stars and the waxing Earth. Sadler had been here several times before; he knew no better cure for mental fatigue.

A quarter of a kilometer away the great framework of the largest telescope ever built by man was pointing steadily toward a spot in the southern sky. Sadler knew that it was looking at no stars that his eyes could see—at no stars, indeed, that belonged to this universe. It would be probing the limits of space, a billion light-years from home.

Then, unexpectedly, it began to swing toward the north. Wagnall chuckled quietly.

"A lot of people will be tearing their hair now," he said. "We've interrupted the program to turn the big guns on *Nova Draconis*. Let's see if we can find it."

He searched for a little while, consulting a sketch in his hand. Sadler, also staring into the north, could see nothing in the least unusual. All the stars there looked just the same to him. But presently, following Wagnall's instructions, and using the Great Bear and Polaris as guides, he found the faint star low down in the northern sky. It was not at all impressive, even if you realized that a couple of days before only the largest telescopes could have found it, and that it had climbed in brilliance a hundred thousand times in a few hours.

Perhaps Wagnall sensed his disappointment.

"It may not look very spectacular now," he said defensively, "but it's still on the rise. With any luck, we may really see something in a day or two."

Day lunar or day terrestrial? Sadler wondered. It was rather confusing, like so many things here. All the clocks ran on a twenty-four hour system and kept Greenwich Mean Time. One minor advantage of this was that one had only to glance at the Earth to get a reasonably accurate time check. But it meant that the progress of light and dark on the lunar surface had no connection at all with what the clocks might say. The sun could be anywhere above or below the horizon when the clocks said it was noon.

Sadler glanced away from the north, back to the Observatory. He had always assumed—without bothering to think about it—that any observatory would consist of a cluster of giant domes, and had forgotten that here on the weatherless Moon there would be no purpose in enclosing the instruments. The thousand centimeter reflector and its smaller companion stood naked and unprotected in the vacuum of space. Only their fragile masters remained underground in the warmth and air of this buried city.

The horizon was almost flat in all directions. Though the Observatory was at the center of the great walled-plain of Plato, the mountain ring was hidden by the curve of the Moon. It was a bleak and desolate prospect, without even a few hills to give it interest. Only a dusty plain, studded here and there with blowholes and craterlets—and the enigmatic works of man, straining at the stars and trying to wrest away their secrets.

As they left, Sadler glanced once more toward *Draco,* but already he had forgotten which of the faint circumpolar stars was the one he had come to see. "Exactly why," he said to Wagnall, as tactfully as he could—for he did not want to hurt the secretary's feelings—"is this star so important?"

Wagnall looked incredulous, then pained, then understanding.

"Well," he began, "I guess stars are like people. The well-behaved ones never attract much attention. They teach us something, of course, but we can learn a lot more from the ones that go off the rails."

"And do stars do that sort of thing fairly often?"

"Every year about a hundred blow up in our galaxy alone, but those are only ordinary novae. At their peak, they may be above a hundred thousand times as bright as the sun. A *supernova* is a very much rarer, and a very much more exciting affair. We still don't know what causes it, but when a star goes super it may become several *billion* times brighter than the sun. In fact, it can outshine all the other stars in the galaxy added together."

Sadler considered this for a while. It was certainly a thought calculated to inspire a moment's silent reflection.

"The important thing is," Wagnall continued eagerly, "that nothing like this has happened since telescopes were invented. The last supernova in *our* universe was six hundred years ago. There have been plenty in other galaxies, but they're too far away to be studied properly. This one, as it were, is right on our doorstep. That fact will be pretty obvious in a couple of days. In a few hours it will be outshining everything in the sky, except the sun and Earth."

"And what do you expect to learn from it?"

"A supernova explosion is the most titanic event known to occur in nature. We'll be able to study the behavior of matter under conditions that make the middle of an atom bomb look like a dead calm. But if you're one of those people who always want a practical use for everything, surely it's of considerable interest to find what makes a star explode? One day, after all, our sun may decide to do likewise."

"And in *that* case," retorted Sadler, "I'd really prefer not to know about it in advance. I wonder if that nova took any planets with it?"

"There's absolutely no way of telling. But it must happen fairly often, because at least one star in ten's got planets."

It was a heart-freezing thought. At any moment, as likely as not, *somewhere* in the universe a whole solar system, with strangely peopled worlds and civilizations, was being tossed carelessly into a cosmic furnace. Life was a fragile and delicate phenomenon, poised on the razor's edge between cold and heat.

But Man was not content with the hazards that Nature could provide. He was busily building his own funeral pyre.

The same thought had occurred to Dr. Molton, but unlike Sadler he could set against it a more cheerful one. *Nova Draconis* was more than two thousand light-years away; the flash of the detonation had been traveling since the birth of Christ. In that time, it must have swept through millions of solar systems, have alerted the inhabitants of a thousand worlds. Even at this moment, scattered over the surface of a sphere four thousand light-years in diameter, there must surely be other astronomers, with instruments not unlike his own, who would be trapping the radiations of this dying sun as they ebbed out toward the frontiers of the universe. And it was stranger still to think that infinitely more distant observers, so far away that to them the whole galaxy was no more than a faint smudge of light, would notice some hundred million years from now that our island universe had momentarily doubled its brilliance. . . .

Dr. Molton stood at the control desk in the softly lit chamber that was his laboratory and workshop. It had once been little different from any of the other cells that made up the Observatory, but its occupant had stamped his personality upon it. In one corner stood a vase of artificial flowers, something both incongruous and welcome in such a place as this. It was Molton's only eccentricity, and no one grudged it to him. Since the native lunar vegetation gave such little scope for ornament, he was forced to use creations of wax and wire, skillfully made up for him in Central City. Their arrangement he varied with such ingenuity and resource that he never seemed to have the same flowers on two successive days.

Sometimes Wheeler used to make fun of him about this hobby, claiming that it proved he was homesick and wanted to get back to Earth. It had, in fact, been more than three years since Dr. Molton had returned to his native Australia, but he seemed in no hurry to do so. As he pointed out, there were about a hundred lifetimes of work for him here, and he preferred to let his leave accumulate until he felt like taking it in one installment.

The flowers were flanked by metal filing cases containing the thousands of spectrograms which Molton had gathered during his research. He was not, as he was always careful to point out, a theoretical astronomer. He simply looked and recorded; other people had the task of explaining what he found. Sometimes indignant mathematicians would arrive protesting that no star could *possibly* have a spectrum like this. Then Molton would go to his files, check that there had been no mistake, and reply, "Don't blame me. Take it up with old Mother Nature."

The rest of the room was a crowded mass of equipment that would have been completely meaningless to a layman, and indeed would have baffled many astronomers. Most of it Molton had built himself, or at least designed and handed over to his assistants for construction. For the last two centuries, every practical astronomer had had to be something of an electrician, an engineer, a physicist —and, as the cost of his equipment steadily increased, a public-relations man.

The electronic commands sped silently through the cables as Molton set Right Ascension and Declination. Far above his head, the great telescope, like some mammoth gun, tracked smoothly round to the north. The vast mirror at the base of the tube was gathering more than a million times as much light as a human eye could grasp, and focusing it with exquisite precision into a single beam. That beam, reflected again from mirror to mirror as if down a periscope, was now reaching Dr. Molton, to do with as he pleased.

Had he looked into the beam, the sheer glare of *Nova Draconis* would have blinded him—and as compared with his instruments, his eyes could tell him practically nothing. He switched the electronic spectrometer into place, and started it scanning. It would explore the spectrum of *N. Draconis* with patient accuracy, working down through yellow, green, blue into the violet and far ultra-violet, utterly beyond range of the human eye. As it scanned, it would trace on moving tape the intensity of every spectral line, leaving an unchallengeable record which astronomers could still consult a thousand years from now.

There was a knock at the door and Jamieson entered, carrying some still-damp photographic plates.

"Those last exposures did it!" he said jubilantly. "They show the gaseous shell expanding round the nova. And the speed agrees with your Doppler shifts."

"So I should hope," growled Molton. "Let's look at them."

He studied the plates, while in the background the whirring of electric motors continued from the spectrometer as it kept up its automatic search. They were negatives, of course, but like all astronomers he was accustomed to that and could interpret them as easily as positive prints.

There at the center was the little disk that marked *N. Draconis,* burnt through the emulsion by overexposure. And around it, barely visible to the naked eye, was a tenuous ring. As the days passed, Molton knew, that ring would expand further and further into space until it was finally dissipated. It looked so small and insignificant that the mind could not comprehend what it really was.

They were looking into the past, at a catastrophe that had happened two thousand years ago. They were seeing the shell of flame, so hot that it had not yet cooled to white-heat, which the star had blasted into space at millions of kilometers an hour. That expanding wall of fire would have engulfed the mightiest planet without checking its speed; yet from Earth it was no more than a faint ring at the limits of visibility.

"I wonder," said Jamieson softly, "if we'll ever find out just *why* a star does this sort of thing?"

"Sometimes," replied Molton, "as I'm listening to the radio, I think it would be a good idea if it did happen. Fire's a good sterilizer."

Jamieson was obviously shocked; this was unlike Molton, whose brusque exterior so inadequately concealed his deep inner warmth.

"You don't really mean that!" he protested.

"Well, perhaps not. We've made some progress in the past million years, and I suppose an astronomer should be patient. But look at the mess we're running into now—don't you ever wonder how it's all going to end?"

There was a passion, a depth of feeling behind the words that astonished Jamieson and left him profoundly disturbed. Molton had never before let down his guard—had never, indeed, indicated that he felt very strongly on any subject outside his own field. Jamieson knew he had glimpsed the momentary weakening of an iron control. It stirred something in his own mind, and mentally he reacted like a startled animal against the shock of recognition.

For a long moment the two scientists stared at each other, appraising, speculating, reaching out across the gulf that separates every man from his neighbor. Then, with a shrill buzzing, the automatic spectrometer announced that it had finished its task. The tension had broken; the everyday world crowded in upon them again. And so a moment that might have widened out into incalculable consequences trembled on the verge of being, and returned once more to Limbo.

✳ *CHAPTER FOUR*

Sadler had known better than to expect an office of his own; the most he could hope for was a modest desk in some corner of Accounts Section, and that was exactly what he had got. This did not worry him; he was anxious to cause no trouble and to draw no unnecessary attention to himself, and in any case he spent relatively little time at his desk. All the final writing up of his reports took place in the privacy of his room—a tiny cubicle just large enough to ward off claustrophobia, which was one of a hundred identical cells on the residential level.

It had taken him several days to adapt to this completely artificial way of life. Here in the heart of the Moon, time did not exist. The fierce temperature changes between the lunar day and night penetrated no more than a meter or two into the rock; the diurnal waves of heat and cold ebbed away before they reached this depth. Only Man's clocks ticked off the seconds and minutes; every twenty-four hours the corridor lights dimmed, and there was a pretense of night. Even then the Observatory did not sleep. Whatever the hour, there would be someone on duty. The astronomers, of course, had always been accustomed to working at peculiar hours, much to the annoyance of their wives (except in those quite common cases where the wives were astronomers too). The rhythm of lunar life was no additional hardship to them; the ones who grumbled were the engineers who had to maintain air, power, communications and the Observatory's other multitudinous services on a twenty-four-hour basis.

On the whole, thought Sadler, the administrative staff had the best of it. It did not matter much if Accounts, Entertainment or Stores closed down for eight hours, as they did in every twenty-four, so long as someone continued to run the surgery and the kitchen.

Sadler had done his best not to get in anyone's hair, and believed that so far he had been quite successful. He had met all the senior staff except the director himself—who was absent on Earth—and knew by sight about half the people in the Observatory. His plan had been to work conscientiously from section to section until he had seen everything the place had to offer. When he had done that, he would sit and think for a couple of days. There were some jobs which simply could not be hurried, whatever the urgency.

Urgency—yes, that was his main problem. Several times he had been told, not unkindly, that he had come to the Observatory at a very awkward time. The mounting political tension had set the little community's nerves on edge, and tempers had been growing short. It was true that *Nova Draconis* had improved the situation somewhat, since no one could be bothered with such trivialities as politics while this phenomenon blazed in the skies. But they could not be bothered with cost accounting either, and Sadler could hardly blame them.

He spent all the time he could spare from his investigation in the Common Room, where the staff relaxed when they were off duty. Here was the center of the Observatory's social life, and it gave him an ideal opportunity of studying the men and women who had exiled themselves here for the good of science—or, alternatively, for the inflated salaries required to lure less dedicated individuals to the Moon.

Though Sadler was not addicted to gossip, and was more interested in facts and figures than in people, he knew that he had to make the most of this opportunity. Indeed, his instructions had been very specific on this point, in a manner he considered unnecessarily cynical. But it could not be denied that human nature is always very much the same, among all classes and on all planets. Sadler had picked up some of his most useful information simply by standing within earshot of the bar. . . .

The Common Room had been designed with great skill and taste, and the constantly changing photo-murals made it hard to believe that this spacious chamber was, in reality, deep in the crust of the Moon. As a whim of the architect, there was an open fire in which a most realistic pile of logs burned forever without being consumed. This quite fascinated Sadler, who had never seen anything like it on Earth.

He had now shown himself sufficiently good at games and general conversation to become an accepted member of the staff, and had even been entrusted with much of the local scandal. Apart from the fact that its members were of distinctly superior intelligence, the Observatory was a microcosm of Earth itself. With the exception of murder (and *that* was probably only a matter of time) almost everything that happened in terrestrial society was going on somewhere here. Sadler was seldom surprised by anything, and certainly not by this. It was merely to be expected that all six of the girls in Computing, after some weeks in a largely male community, now had reputations that could only be described as fragile. Nor was it remarkable that the chief engineer was not on speaking terms with the assistant chief executive, or that Professor X thought that Dr. Y was a certifiable lunatic, or that Mr. Z was reputed to cheat at Hypercanasta. All these items were no direct concern of Sadler's, though he listened to them with great interest. They merely went to prove that the Observatory was one big happy family.

Sadler was wondering what humorist had stamped NOT TO BE TAKEN OUT OF THE LOUNGE across the shapely lady on the cover of last month's *Triplanet News* when Wheeler came storming into the room.

"What is it now?" asked Sadler. "Discovered another nova? Or just looking for a shoulder to weep on?"

He rather guessed that the latter was the case, and that his shoulder would have to do in the absence of anything more suitable. By this time he had grown to know Wheeler quite well. The young astronomer might be one of the most junior members of the staff, but he was also the most memorable. His sarcastic wit, lack of respect for higher authority, confidence in his own opinions and general argumentativeness prevented him from hiding his light under a bushel. But Sadler had been told, even by those who did not like Wheeler, that he was brilliant and would go far. At the moment he had not used up the stock of good will created by his discovery of *Nova Draconis,* which in itself would be enough to insure a reputation for the rest of his career.

"I was looking for Wagtail; he's not in his office, and I want to lodge a complaint."

"Secretary Wagnall," answered Sadler, putting as much reproof as he could into the correction, "went over to Hydroponics half an hour ago. And if I may make a comment, isn't it somewhat unusual for you to be the source, rather than the cause, of a complaint?"

Wheeler gave a large grin, which made him look incredibly and disarmingly boyish.

"I'm afraid you're right. And I know this ought to go through the proper channels, and all that sort of thing—but it's rather urgent. I've just had a couple of hours' work spoiled by some fool making an unauthorized landing."

Sadler had to think quickly before he realized what Wheeler meant. Then he remembered that this part of the Moon was a restricted area: no ships were supposed to fly over the northern hemisphere without first notifying the Observatory. The blinding glare of ion rockets picked up by one of the great telescopes could ruin photographic exposures and play havoc with delicate instruments.

"You don't suppose it was an emergency?" Sadler asked, struck by a sudden thought. "It's too bad about your work, but that ship may be in trouble."

Wheeler had obviously not thought of this, and his rage instantly abated. He looked helplessly at Sadler, as if wondering what to do next. Sadler dropped his magazine and rose to his feet.

"Shouldn't we go to Communications?" he said. "They ought to know what's going on. Mind if I come along?"

He was very particular about such points in etiquette, and never forgot that he was here very much on sufferance. Besides, it was always good policy to let people think they were doing you favors.

Wheeler jumped at the suggestion, and led the way to Communications as if the whole idea had been his own. The signals office was a large, spotlessly tidy room at the highest level of the Observatory, only a few meters below the lunar crust. Here was the automatic telephone exchange, which was the Observatory's central nervous system, and here were the monitors and transmitters which kept this remote scientific outpost in touch with Earth. They were all presided over by the duty signals officer, who discouraged casual visitors with a large notice reading: POSITIVELY AND ABSOLUTELY NO ADMITTANCE TO UNAUTHORIZED PERSONS.

"That doesn't mean us," said Wheeler, opening the door. He was promptly contradicted by a still larger notice—THIS MEANS YOU. Unabashed, he turned to the grinning Sadler and added, "All the places you're *really* not supposed to enter are kept locked, anyway." Nevertheless he did not push open the second door, but knocked and waited until a bored voice called "Come in."

The D.S.O., who was dissecting a spacesuit walkie-talkie set, seemed quite glad for the interruption. He promptly called Earth and asked Traffic Control to find out what a ship was doing in the *Mare Imbrium* without notifying the Observatory. While they were waiting for the reply to come back, Sadler wandered round the racks of equipment.

It was really surprising that it needed so much apparatus just to talk to people, or to send pictures between Moon and Earth. Sadler, who knew how technicians loved explaining their work to anyone who showed real interest, asked a few questions and tried to absorb as many of the answers as he could. He was thankful that by this time no one bothered to wonder if he had any ulterior motives and was trying to find if they could do their jobs for half the money. They had accepted him as an interested and inquisitive audience of one, for it was quite obvious that many of the questions he asked could have no financial significance.

The reply from Earth came through on the auto-printer soon after the D.S.O. had finished his swift conducted tour. It was a slightly baffling message:

FLIGHT NON-SCHEDULED. GOVERNMENT BUSINESS. NO NOTIFI-CATION ISSUED. FURTHER LANDINGS ANTICIPATED. INCONVEN-IENCE REGRETTED.

Wheeler looked at the words as if he could not believe his eyes. Until this moment, the skies of the Observatory had been sacrosanct. No abbot facing the violation of his monastery could have been more indignant.

"They're going to keep it up!" he spluttered. "What about our program?"

"Grow up, Con," said the signals officer indulgently. "Don't you listen to the news? Or have you been too busy looking at your pet nova? This message means just one thing. There's something secret going on out in the *Mare*. I'll give you one guess."

"I know," said Wheeler. "There's another of those hush-hush expeditions looking for heavy ores, in the hope that the Federation won't find out. It's all so damn childish."

"What makes you think *that's* the explanation?" asked Sadler sharply.

"Well, that sort of thing's been going on for years. Any bar in town will give you all the latest gossip."

Sadler hadn't been "into town" yet—as the trip to Central City was called—but he could well believe this. Wheeler's explanation was highly plausible, particularly in view of the current situation.

"We'll just have to make the best of it, I suppose," said the D.S.O., attacking his walkie-talkie again. "Anyway, there's one consolation. All this is going on to the south of us—the other side of the sky from Draco. So it won't really interfere with your main work, will it?"

"I suppose not," Wheeler admitted grudgingly. For a moment he seemed quite downcast. It was not—far from it—that he wanted anything to interfere with work. But he had been looking forward to a good fight, and to have it snatched out of his hands like this was a bitter disappointment.

It needed no knowledge of the stars to see *Nova Draconis* now. Next to the waxing Earth, it was by far the brightest object in the sky. Even Venus, following the sun into the east, was pale compared to this arrogant newcomer. Already it had begun to cast a distinct shadow and it was still growing in brilliance.

Down on Earth, according to the reports coming over the radio, it was clearly visible even in the daytime. For a little while it had crowded politics off the front page, but now the pressure of events was making itself felt again. Men could not bear to think of eternity for long; and the Federation was only light-minutes, not light-centuries, away.

✱ CHAPTER FIVE

There were still those who believed that Man would have been happier had he stayed on his own planet; but it was rather too late, now, to do anything about that. In any case, had he remained on Earth, he would not have been Man. The restlessness that had driven him over the face of his own world, that had made him climb the skies and plumb the seas, would not be assuaged while the Moon and planets beckoned to him across the deeps of space.

The colonization of the Moon had been a slow, painful, sometimes tragic and always fabulously expensive enterprise. Two centuries after the first landings, much of Earth's giant satellite was still unexplored. Every detail had, of course, been mapped from space, but more than half that craggy globe had never been examined at close quarters.

Central City and the other bases that had been established with such labor were islands of life in an immense wilderness, oases in a silent desert of blazing light or inky darkness. There had been many who had asked whether the effort needed to survive here was worthwhile, since the colonization of Mars and Venus offered much greater opportunities. But for all the problems it presented him, Man could not do without the Moon. It had been his first bridgehead in space, and was still the key to the planets. The liners that plied from world to world obtained all their propellent mass here, filling their great tanks with the finely divided dust which the ionic rockets would spit out in electrified jets. By obtaining that dust from the Moon, and not having to lift it through the enormous gravity field of Earth, it had been possible to reduce the cost of space-travel more than ten-fold. Indeed, without the Moon as a refueling base, economical space-flight could never have been achieved.

It had also proved, as the astronomers and physicists had predicted, of immense scientific value. Freed at last from the imprisoning atmosphere of Earth, astronomy had made giant strides, and indeed there was scarcely a branch of science that had not benefited from the lunar laboratories. Whatever the limitations of Earth's statesmen, they had learned one lesson well. Scientific research was the lifeblood of civilization; it was the one investment that could be guaranteed to pay dividends for eternity. . . .

Slowly, with countless heartbreaking setbacks, man had discovered how to exist, then to live, and at last to flourish on the Moon. He had invented whole new techniques of vacuum engineering, of low-gravity architecture, of air and temperature control. He had defeated the twin demons of the lunar day and the lunar night, though always he must be on the watch against their depredations. The burning heat could expand his domes and crack his buildings; the fierce cold could tear apart any metal structure not designed to guard against contractions never encountered on Earth. But all these problems had, at last, been overcome.

All novel and ambitious enterprises seem much more hazardous and difficult from afar. So it had proved with the Moon. Problems that had appeared insuperable before the Moon was reached had now passed into lunar folklore. Obstacles that had disheartened the first explorers had been almost forgotten. Over the lands where men had once struggled on foot, the monocabs now carried the tourists from Earth in luxurious comfort. . . .

In a few respects, conditions on the Moon had helped rather than hindered the invaders. There was, for example, the question of the lunar atmosphere. On Earth it would have counted as a good vacuum, and it had no appreciable effect on astronomical observations. It was quite sufficient, however, to act as a very efficient shield against meteors. Most meteors are blocked by Earth's atmosphere before they get to within a hundred kilometers of the surface; they have been checked, in other words, while traveling through air no denser than the Moon's. Indeed, the Moon's invisible meteor shield is even more effective than Earth's, since thanks to the low lunar gravity it extends much farther into space.

Perhaps the most astonishing discovery of the first explorers was the existence of plant life. It had long been suspected, from the peculiar changes of light and shade in such craters as Aristarchus and Eratosthenes, that there was some form of vegetation on the Moon, but it was difficult to see how it could survive under such extreme conditions. Perhaps, it was surmised, a few primitive lichens or mosses might exist, and it would be interesting to see how they managed to do it.

The guess was quite wrong. A little thought would have shown that any lunar plants would not be primitive, but would be highly specialized—extremely sophisticated, in fact, so that they could cope with their hostile environment. Primitive plants could no more exist on the Moon than could primitive Man.

The commonest lunar plants were plump, often globular growths, not unlike cacti. Their horny skins prevented the loss of precious water, and were dotted here and there with transparent "windows" to let sunlight enter. This astonishing improvisation, surprising though it seemed to many, was not unique. It had been evolved independently by certain desert plants in Africa, faced with the same problem of trapping sunlight without losing water.

The unique feature of the lunar plants, however, was their ingenious mechanism for collecting air. An elaborate system of flaps and valves, not unlike that by which some sea creatures pump water through their bodies, acted as a kind of compressor. The plants were patient; they would wait for years along the great crevasses which occasionally gush forth feeble clouds of carbon or sulphur dioxides from the Moon's interior. Then the flaps would go frantically to work, and the strange plants would suck into their pores every molecule that drifted by, before the transient lunar mist dispersed into the hungry near-vacuum which was all the atmosphere remaining to the Moon.

Such was the strange world which was now home to some thousands of human beings. For all its harshness, they loved it and would not return to Earth, where life was easy and therefore offered little scope for enterprise or initiative. Indeed, the lunar colony, bound though it was to Earth by economic ties, had more in common with the planets of the Federation. On Mars, Venus, Mercury and the satellites of Jupiter and Saturn, men were fighting a frontier war against Nature, very like that which had won the Moon. Mars was already completely conquered; it was the only world outside Earth where a man could walk in the open without the use of artificial aids. On Venus, victory was in sight, and a land surface three times as great as Earth's would be the prize. Elsewhere, only outposts existed: burning Mercury and the frozen outer worlds were a challenge for future centuries.

So Earth considered. But the Federation could not wait, and Professor Phillips, in complete innocence, had brought its impatience to the breaking point. It was not the first time that a scientific paper had changed the course of history, and it would not be the last.

Sadler had never seen the pages of mathematics that had caused all the trouble, but he knew the conclusions to which they led. He had been taught many things in the six months that had been abstracted from his life. Some he had learned in a small, bare classroom with six other men whose names he had never been told, but much knowledge had come to him in sleep or in the dreamy trance-state of hypnosis. One day, perhaps, it would be withdrawn from him by the same techniques. The face of the Moon, Sadler had been told, consists of two distinct kinds of terrain—the dark areas of the so-called Seas, and the bright regions which are usually higher in elevation and much more mountainous. It is the bright areas which are pitted with the countless lunar craters, and appear to have been torn and blasted by eons of volcanic fury. The Seas, by contrast, are flat and relatively smooth. They contain occasional craters and many pits and crevasses, but they are incomparably more irregular than the rugged highlands.

They were formed, it seems, much later than the mountains and crater chains of the Moon's fiery youth. Somehow, long after the older formations had congealed, the crust melted again in a few areas to form the dark, smooth plains that are the Seas. They contain the wrecks of many older craters and mountains that have been melted down like wax, and their coasts are fringed with half-destroyed cliffs and ringed plains that barely escaped total obliteration.

The problem which had long engaged scientists, and which Professor Phillips had solved, was this: Why did the internal heat of the Moon break out only in the selected areas of the Seas, leaving the ancient highlands untouched?

A planet's internal heat is produced by radioactivity. It seemed to Professor Phillips, therefore, that under the great Seas must be rich deposits of uranium and its associated elements. The ebb and flow of tides in the Moon's molten interior had somehow produced these local concentrations, and the heat they had generated through millennia of radioactivity had melted the surface features far above them to form the Seas.

For two centuries, men had gone over the face of the Moon with every conceivable measuring instrument. They had set its interior trembling with artificial earthquakes; they had probed it with magnetic and electric fields. Thanks to these observations, Professor Phillips had been able to put his theory on a sound mathematical basis.

Vast lodes of uranium existed far below the Seas. Uranium itself was no longer of the vital importance that it had been in the twentieth and twenty-first centuries, for the old fission piles had long since given way to the hydrogen reactor. But where there was uranium, the heavy metals would be found as well.

Professor Phillips had been quite sure that his theory had no practical applications. All these great deposits, he had carefully pointed out, were at such depths that any form of mining would be totally out of the question. They were at least a hundred kilometers down—and the pressure in the rock at that depth was so great that the toughest metal would flow like a liquid, so that no shaft or bore-hole could stay open even for an instant.

It seemed a great pity. These tantalizing treasures, Professor Phillips had concluded, must remain forever beyond the reach of the men who needed them so badly.

A scientist, thought Sadler, should really have known better than that. One day Professor Phillips was going to have a big surprise.

✳ **CHAPTER SIX**

Sadler lay in his bunk and tried to focus his mind on the past week. It was very hard to believe that he had arrived from Earth only eight of its days ago, but the calendar clock on the wall confirmed the notes he had made in his diary. And if he doubted both these witnesses, he had merely to go up to the surface and enter one of the observation domes. There he could look up at the unmoving Earth, now just past full and beginning to wane. When he had arrived on the Moon, it had been at its first quarter.

It was midnight over the *Mare Imbrium*. Dawn and sunset were both equally remote, but the lunar landscape was ablaze with light. Challenging the Earth itself was *Nova Draconis,* already brighter than any star in history. Even Sadler, who found most astronomical events too remote and impersonal to touch his emotions, would occasionally make the trip "upstairs" to look at this new invader of the modern skies. Was he looking at the funeral pyre of worlds older and wiser than the Earth? It was strange that such an awe-inspiring event should take place at a moment of human crisis. It could only be coincidence, of course. *N. Draconis* was a close star, yet the signal of its death had been traveling for twenty centuries. One had to be not only superstitious but also very geocentric to imagine that this event had been planned as a warning for Earth.

For what of all the other planets of other suns in whose skies the nova blazed with equal or even greater brilliance?

Sadler called home his wandering thoughts, and concentrated on his proper business. What had he left undone? He had visited every section of the Observatory, and met everyone of importance, with the single exception of the director. Professor Maclaurin was due back from Earth in a day or so, and his absence had, if anything, simplified Sadler's task. When the Boss returned, so everybody had warned him, life would not be quite so free and easy, and everything would have to be done through the Proper Channels. Sadler was used to that, but did not enjoy it any the better.

There was a discreet purr from the speaker in the wall over the bed. Sadler reached out one foot and kicked a switch with the toe of his sandal. He could do this the first time now, but faint scars on the wall were a still-visible memento of his apprenticeship.

"Yes," he said. "Who's that?"

"Transport Section here. I'm closing the list for tomorrow. There are still a couple of seats left—you want to come along?"

"If there's room," Sadler replied. "I don't want any more-deserving causes to suffer."

"O.K.—you're down," said the voice briskly, and clicked off.

Sadler felt only the mildest twinge of conscience. After a week's solid work, he could do with a few hours in Central City. He was not yet due to meet his first contact, and so far all his reports had gone out through the normal mail service, in a form that would have meant nothing to anyone happening to read them. But it was high time he got to know his way around the city, and indeed it would look odd if he took no holidays at all.

His main reason for the trip, however, was purely personal. There was a letter he wanted to post, and he knew that the Observatory mail was being censored by his colleagues in Central Intelligence. By now they must be indifferent to such matters, but he would still prefer to keep his private life to himself.

Central City was twenty kilometers from the spaceport, and Sadler had seen nothing of the lunar metropolis on his arrival. As the monocab—much fuller this time than it had been on the outward journey—pulled once more into the *Sinus Medii,* Sadler no longer felt a complete stranger. He knew, at least by sight, everyone in the car. Almost half the Observatory staff were here; the other half would take their day off next week. Even *Nova Draconis* was not allowed to interfere with this routine, which was based on common sense and sound psychology.

The cluster of great domes began to hump themselves over the horizon. A beacon light burned on the summit of each, but otherwise they were darkened and gave no sign of life. Some, Sadler knew, could be made transparent when desired. All were opaque now, conserving their heat against the lunar night.

The monocab entered a long tunnel at the base of one of the domes. Sadler had a glimpse of great doors closing behind them— then another set, and yet another. They're taking no chances, he thought to himself, and heartily approved of such caution. Then there was the unmistakable sound of air surging around them, a final door opened ahead, and the vehicle rolled to a halt beside a platform that might have been in any station back on Earth. It gave Sadler quite a shock to look through the window and see people walking around outside without spacesuits. . . .

"Going anywhere in particular?" asked Wagnall as they waited for the crush at the door to subside.

Sadler shook his head.

"No—I just want to wander round and have a look at the place. I want to see where you people manage to spend all your money."

Wagnall obviously couldn't decide whether he was joking or not, and to Sadler's relief did not offer his services as a guide. This was one of the occasions when he would be quite happy to be left on his own.

He walked out of the station and found himself at the top of a large ramp, sloping down into the compact little city. The main level was twenty meters below him. He had not realized that the whole dome was countersunk this far into the lunar plain, thus reducing the amount of roof structure necessary. By the side of the ramp a wide conveyor belt was carrying freight and luggage into the station at a leisurely rate. The nearest buildings were obviously industrial, and though well kept had the slightly seedy appearance which inevitably overtakes anything in the neighborhood of stations or docks.

It was not until Sadler was halfway down the ramp that he realized there was a blue sky overhead, that the sun was shining just behind him, and that there were high cirrus clouds floating far above.

The illusion was so perfect that he had taken it completely for granted, and had forgotten for a moment that this was midnight on the Moon. He stared for a long time into the dizzy depths of that synthetic sky, and could see no flaw in its perfection. Now he understood why the lunar cities insisted upon their expensive domes, when they could just as well have burrowed underground like the Observatory.

There was no risk of getting lost in Central City. With one exception each of the seven interconnected domes was laid out in the same pattern of radiating avenues and concentric ring-roads. The exception was Dome Five, the main industrial and production center, which was virtually one vast factory and which Sadler decided to leave alone.

He wandered at random for some time, going where his stray impulses took him. He wanted to get the "feel" of the place, for he realized it was completely impossible to know the city properly in the short time at his disposal. There was one thing about Central City that struck him at once—it had a personality, a character of its own. No one can say why this is true of some cities and not of others, and Sadler felt a little surprised that it should be of such an artificial environment as this. Then he remembered that *all* cities, whether on Earth or on the Moon, were equally artificial. . . .

The roads were narrow, the only vehicles small, three-wheeled open cars that cruised along at less than thirty kilometers an hour and appeared to be used exclusively for freight rather than passengers. It was some time before Sadler discovered the automatic subway that linked the outer six domes in a great ring, passing under the center of each. It was really a glorified conveyor belt, and moved in a counterclockwise direction only. If you were unlucky, you might have to go right round the city to get to the adjacent dome, but as the circular tour took only about five minutes, this was no great hardship.

The shopping center, and main repository of lunar chic, was in Dome One. Here also lived the senior executives and technicians— the most senior of all in houses of their own. Most of the residential buildings had roof gardens, where plants imported from Earth ascended to improbable heights in this low gravity. Sadler kept his eyes open for any lunar vegetation, but saw no signs of it. He did not know that there was a strict rule against bringing the indigenous plants into the domes. An oxygen-rich atmosphere, it had been found, over-stimulated them so that they ran riot and promptly died, producing a stench which had to be experienced to be believed when their sulphur-loaded organisms began to decay.

Most of the visitors from Earth were to be found here. Sadler, a selenite of eight days' standing, found himself eying the obvious newcomers with amused contempt. Many of them had hired weight-belts as soon as they entered the city, under the impression that this was the safest thing to do. Sadler had been warned about this fallacy in time, and so had avoided contributing to what was really a mild racket. It was true that if you loaded yourself down with lead, there was less danger of soaring off the ground with incautious steps, and perhaps terminating the trajectory upon your head. But surprisingly few people realized the distinction between weight and inertia which made these belts of such dubious value. When one tried to start moving, or to stop in a hurry, one quickly found that though a hundred kilos of lead might *weigh* only sixteen kilos here, it had exactly the same momentum as it did on Earth.

From time to time, as he made his way through the scanty crowds and roamed from shop to shop, Sadler ran into friends from the Observatory. Some of them were already festooned with parcels as they made up for a week's compulsory saving. Most of the younger members of the staff, male and female, had acquired companions. Sadler surmised that though the Observatory might be self-sufficient in most matters, there were others which demanded some variety.

The clear, bell-like note, thrice repeated, caught him unaware. He looked around him, but could not locate its source. At first it seemed that no one was taking any notice of the signal, whatever it might mean. Then he observed that the streets were slowly clearing —and that the sky was getting darker.

Clouds had come up over the sun. They were black and ragged, their edges flame-fringed as the sunlight spilled past them. Once again, Sadler marveled at the skill with which these images—for they could be nothing else—were projected on the dome. No actual thunderstorm could have seemed more realistic, and when the first rumble rolled round the sky he did not hesitate to look for shelter.

Even if the streets had not already emptied themselves, he would have guessed that the organizers of this storm were going to omit none of the details. . . .

The little sidewalk café was crowded with other refugees when the initial drops came down, and the first fiery tongue of lightning licked across the heavens. Sadler could never see lightning without counting the seconds before the thunder peal. It came when he had got to "Six," making it two kilometers away. That, of course, would put it well outside the dome, in the soundless vacuum of space. Oh well, one had to allow some artistic license, and it wasn't fair to quibble over points like this.

Thicker and heavier came the rain, more and more continuous the flashes. The roads were running with water, and for the first time Sadler became aware of the shallow gutters which, if he had seen them before, he had dismissed without a second thought. It was not safe to take *anything* for granted here; you had to keep stopping and asking yourself "What function does this serve— What's it doing here on the Moon? Is it even what I think it is?" Certainly, now he came to consider the matter, a gutter was as unexpected a thing to see in Central City as a snow plow. But perhaps even that——

Sadler turned to his closest neighbor, who was watching the storm with obvious admiration.

"Excuse me," he said, "but how often does this sort of thing happen?"

"About twice a day—lunar day, that is," came the reply. "It's always announced a few hours in advance, so that it won't interfere with business."

"I don't want to be too inquisitive," continued Sadler, fearing that was just what he was, "but I'm surprised at the trouble you've gone to. Surely all this realism isn't necessary?"

"Perhaps not, but we like it. We've got to have some rain, remember, to keep the place clean and deal with the dust. So we try to do it properly."

If Sadler had any doubts on that score, they were dispelled when the glorious double rainbow arched out of the clouds. The last drops spattered on the sidewalk; the thunder dwindled away to an angry, distant mutter. The show was over, and the glistening streets of Central City began to fill with life once more.

Sadler remained in the café for a meal, and after a little hard bargaining managed to get rid of some terrestrial currency at only a trifle below the market rate. The food, somewhat to his surprise, was excellent. Every bit must have been synthesized or grown in the yeast and chlorella tanks, but it had been blended and processed with great skill. The trouble with Earth, Sadler mused, was that it could take food for granted, and seldom gave the matter the attention it deserved. Here, on the other hand, food was not something that a bountiful Nature, with a little prompting, could be relied upon to provide. It had to be designed and produced from scratch, and since the job *had* to be done, someone had seen that it was done properly. Like the weather, in fact. . . .

It was time he moved. The last mail for Earth would be cleared in two hours, and if he missed it Jeannette would not get his letter for almost a week of Earth time. She had already been in suspense long enough.

He pulled the unsealed letter from his pocket, and read it through again for any final amendments.

"Jeannette, my dearest,

"I wish I could tell you where I am, but I'm not allowed to say. It wasn't my idea, but I've been chosen for a special job and I've got to make the best of it. I'm in good health, and though I can't contact you directly, any letters you send to the Box Number I gave you will reach me sooner or later.

"I hated being away on our anniversary, but believe me there was *absolutely nothing* I could do about it. I hope you received my present safely—and I hope you liked it. It took me a long time to find that necklace, and I won't tell you how much it cost!

"Do you miss me very badly? God, how I wish I was home again! I know you were hurt and upset when I left, but I want you to trust me and to understand that I couldn't tell you what was happening. Surely you realize that I want Jonathan Peter as much as you do. Please have faith in me, and don't think that it was because of selfishness, or because I don't love you, that I acted as I did. I had very good reasons, which one day I'll be able to tell you.

"Above all, don't worry, and don't be impatient. You know that I'll get back as soon as I can. And I promise you this—*when I'm home again, we'll go ahead*. I wish I knew how soon that would be!

"I love you, my darling—don't ever doubt that. This is a tough job, and your faith in me is the one thing that keeps me going."

He read the letter with great care, trying for the moment to forget all that it meant to him, and to regard it as a message that a complete stranger might have written. Did it give too much away? He did not believe so. It might be indiscreet, but there was nothing in it that revealed his location or the nature of his work.

He sealed the envelope, but put no name or address on it. Then he did something that was, strictly speaking, a direct violation of his oath. He enclosed the letter in another envelope which he addressed, with a covering note, to his lawyer in Washington. "Dear George," he wrote, "You'll be surprised to see where I am now. Jeannette doesn't know, and I don't want her to worry. So please address the enclosed to her and post it in the nearest mailbox. *Treat my present location as absolutely confidential.* I'll explain it all one day."

George would guess the truth, but he could keep secrets just as well as anyone in Central Intelligence. Sadler could think of no other fool-proof way of getting his letter to Jeannette, and he was prepared to take the slight risk for his peace of mind—and for hers.

He asked the way to the nearest mailbox (they were hard to find in Central City) and slid the letter down the chute. In a couple of hours it would be on the way to Earth; by this time tomorrow, it would have reached Jeannette. He could only hope that she would understand—or, if she could not understand, would suspend judgment until they met again.

There was a paper rack beside the mailbox, and Sadler purchased a copy of the *Central News*. He still had several hours before the monorail left for the Observatory, and if anything interesting was going on in town the local paper would presumably tell him all about it.

The political news received such little space that Sadler wondered if a mild censorship was in force. No one would have realized that there was a crisis if he went by the headlines alone; it was necessary to search through the paper to find the really significant items. Low down on page two, for example, was a report that a liner from Earth was having quarantine trouble off Mars and was not being allowed to land—while another on Venus was not being allowed to take off. Sadler was fairly sure that the real trouble was political rather than medical; the Federation was simply getting tough.

On page four was a still more thought-provoking piece of news.

A party of prospectors had been arrested on some remote asteroid in the vicinity of Jupiter. The charge, it seemed, was a violation of space-safety regulations. Sadler suspected that the charge was phony —and that so were the prospectors. Central Intelligence had probably lost some of its agents.

On the center page of the paper was a rather naïve editorial making light of the situation and expressing the confident hope that common sense would prevail. Sadler, who had no illusions about the commonness of common sense, remained skeptical and turned to the local news.

All human communities, wherever they may be in space, follow the same pattern. People were getting born, being cremated (with careful conservation of phosphorus and nitrates), rushing in and out of marriage, moving out of town, suing their neighbors, having parties, holding protest meetings, getting involved in astonishing accidents, writing Letters to the Editor, changing jobs. . . . Yes, it was just like Earth. That was a somewhat depressing thought. Why had Man ever bothered to leave his own world if all his travels and experiences had made so little difference to his fundamental nature? He might just as well have stayed at home, instead of exporting himself and his foibles, at great expense, to another world.

Your job's making you cynical, Sadler told himself. Let's see what Central City has in the way of entertainment.

He'd just missed a tennis tournament in Dome Four, which should have been worth watching. It was played, so someone had told him, with a ball of normal size and mass. But the ball was honeycombed with holes, which increased its air-resistance so much that ranges were no greater than on earth. Without some such subterfuge, a good drive would easily span one of the domes. However, the trajectories followed by these doctored balls were most peculiar, and enough to induce a swift nervous breakdown in anyone who had learned to play under normal gravity.

There was a cyclorama in Dome Three, promising a tour of the Amazon Basin (mosquito bites optional), starting at every alternate hour. Having just come from Earth, Sadler felt no desire to return so promptly. Besides, he felt he had already seen an excellent cyclorama display in the thunderstorm that had now passed out of sight. Presumably it had been produced in the same manner, by batteries of wide-angle projectors.

The attraction that finally took his fancy was the swimming pool in Dome Two. It was the star feature of the Central City gymnasium, much frequented by the Observatory staff. One of the occupational risks of life on the Moon was lack of exercise and resultant muscular atrophy. Anyone who stayed away from Earth for more than a few weeks felt the change of weight very severely when he came home. What lured Sadler to the gym, however, was the thought that he could practice some fancy dives that he would never dare risk on Earth, where one fell five meters in the first second and acquired far too much kinetic energy before hitting the water.

Dome Two was on the other side of the city, and as Sadler felt he should save his energy for his destination he took the subway. But he missed the slow-speed section which led one off the continuously moving belt, and was carried willy-nilly on to Dome Three before he could escape. Rather than circle the city again, he retraced the way on the surface, passing through the short connecting tunnel that linked all the domes together at the points where they touched. There were automatic doors here that opened at a touch—and would seal instantly if air-pressure dropped on either side.

Half the Observatory staff seemed to be exercising itself in the gym. Dr. Molton was sculling a rowing machine, one eye fixed anxiously on the indicator that was adding up his strokes. The chief engineer, eyes closed tightly as per the warning instructions, was standing in the center of a ring of ultra-violet tubes which gave out an eerie glare as they replenished his tan. One of the M.D.'s from Surgery was attacking a punchbag with such viciousness that Sadler hoped he would never have to meet him professionally. A tough-looking character who Sadler believed came from Maintenance was trying to see if he could lift a clear ton; even if one allowed mentally for the low gravity, it was still awe-inspiring to watch.

Everybody else was in the swimming pool, and Sadler quickly joined them. He was not sure what he had expected, but somehow he had imagined that swimming on the Moon would differ drastically from the same experience on the Earth. But it was exactly the same, and the only effect of gravity was the abnormal height of the waves, and the slowness with which they moved across the pool.

The diving went well as long as Sadler attempted nothing ambitious. It was wonderful to know just what was going on, and to have time to admire the surroundings during one's leisurely descent. Then, greatly daring, Sadler tried a somersault from five meters. After all, this was equivalent to less than a meter on Earth. . . .

Unfortunately, he completely misjudged his time of fall, and made half a turn too many—or too few. He landed on his shoulders, and remembered too late just what a crack one could give oneself even from a low height if things went wrong. Limping slightly, and feeling that he had been flayed alive, he crawled out of the pool. As the slow ripples ebbed languidly away, Sadler decided to leave this sort of exhibitionism to younger men.

After all this exertion, it was inevitable that he join Molton and a few of his other acquaintances when they left the gymnasium. Tired but relaxed, and feeling that he had learned a good deal more about the lunar way of life, Sadler leaned back in his seat as the monocab pulled out of the station and the great doors sealed tight behind them. Blue, cloud-flecked skies gave place to the harsh reality of the lunar night. There was the unchanged Earth, just as he had seen it hours ago. He looked for the blinding star of *Nova Draconis,* then remembered that in these latitudes it was hidden below the northern edge of the Moon.

The dark domes, which gave so little sign of the life and light they held, sank beneath the horizon. As he watched them go, Sadler was struck by a sudden, somber thought. They had been built to withstand the forces that Nature could bring against them—but how pitiably fragile they would be if ever they faced the fury of Man!

✳ *CHAPTER SEVEN*

"I still think," said Jamieson, as the tractor headed toward the southern wall of Plato, "that there'll be a hell of a row when the Old Man hears about it."

"Why should he?" asked Wheeler. "When he gets back, he'll be too busy to bother about us. And anyway, we're paying for all the fuel we use. So stop worrying and enjoy yourself. This is our day off, in case you'd forgotten."

Jamieson did not reply. He was too busy concentrating on the road ahead—if it could be called a road. The only sign that other vehicles had ever been this way were the occasional furrows in the dust. Since these would last for eternity here on the windless Moon, no other signposts were needed, though occasionally one came across unsettling notices that read DANGER—CLEFTS AHEAD! or EMERGENCY OXYGEN—10 KILOMETERS.

There are only two methods of long-range transport on the Moon. The highspeed monorails link the main settlements with a fast, comfortable service running on a regular schedule. But the rail system is very limited, and likely to remain so because of its cost. For unrestricted ranging over the lunar surface, one must fall back on the powerful turbine-driven tractors known as "Caterpillars" or, more briefly, "Cats." They are, virtually, small spaceships mounted on fat little tires that enable them to go anywhere within reason even over the appallingly jagged surface of the Moon. On smooth terrain they can easily do a hundred kilometers an hour, but normally they are lucky to manage half that speed. The weak gravity, and the caterpillar treads they can lower if necessary, enable them to climb fantastic slopes. In emergencies, they have been known to haul themselves up vertical cliffs with their built-in winches. One can live in the larger models for weeks at a time without undue hardship, and all the detailed exploration of the Moon has been carried out by prospectors using these tough little vehicles.

Jamieson was a more-than-expert driver, and knew the way perfectly. Nevertheless, for the first hour Wheeler felt that his hair would never lie down again. It usually took newcomers to the Moon quite a while to realize that slopes of one-in-one were perfectly safe if treated with respect. Perhaps it was just as well that Wheeler was a novice, for Jamieson's technique was so unorthodox that it would have filled a more experienced passenger with real alarm.

Why Jamieson was such a recklessly brilliant driver was a paradox that had caused much discussion among his colleagues. Normally he was very painstaking and cautious, inclined not to act at all unless he could be certain of the consequences. No one had ever seen him really annoyed or excited; many thought him lazy, but that was a libel. He would spend weeks working on some observations until the results were absolutely unchallengeable—and would then put them away for two or three months to have another look at them later.

Yet once at the controls of a "cat," this quiet and peace-loving astronomer became a daredevil driver who held the unofficial record for almost every tractor run in the northern hemisphere. The reason lay—buried too deeply even for Jamieson to be aware of it himself—in a boyhood desire to be a spaceship pilot, a dream that had been frustrated by an erratic heart.

From space—or through a telescope on Earth—the walls of Plato seem a formidable barrier when the slanting sunlight shows them to best advantage. But in reality they are less than a kilometer high, and if one chooses the correct route through the numerous passes, the journey out of the crater and into the *Mare Imbrium* presents no great difficulty. Jamieson got through the mountains in less than an hour, though Wheeler wished that he had taken a little longer.

They came to a halt on a high escarpment overlooking the plain. Directly ahead, notching the horizon, was the pyramidal summit of Pico. Toward the right, sinking down into the northeast, were the more rugged peaks of the Teneriffe Mountains. Very few of those peaks had ever been climbed, largely because no one had so far bothered to attempt it. The brilliant Earthlight made them appear an uncanny blue-green, contrasting strangely with their appearance by day, when they would be bleached into raw whites and blacks by the merciless sun.

While Jamieson relaxed to enjoy the view, Wheeler began a careful search of the landscape with a pair of powerful binoculars. Ten minutes later he gave it up, having discovered nothing in the least unusual. He was not surprised by this, for the area where the unscheduled rockets had been landing was well below the horizon.

"Let's drive on," he said. "We can get to Pico in a couple of hours, and we'll have dinner there."

"And then what?" asked Jamieson in resigned tones.

"If we can't see anything, we'll come back like good little boys."

"O.K.—but you'll find it rough going from now on. I don't suppose more than a dozen tractors have ever been down there before. To cheer you up, I might tell you that our Ferdinand is one of them."

He eased the vehicle forward, gingerly skirting a vast talus slope where splintered rock had been accumulating for millennia. Such slopes were extremely dangerous, for the slightest disturbance could often set them moving in slow, irresistible avalanches that would overwhelm everything before them. For all his apparent recklessness, Jamieson took no real risks, and always gave such traps a very wide berth. A less experienced driver would have gaily galloped along the foot of the slide without a moment's thought—and ninety-nine times out of a hundred would have got away with it. Jamieson had seen what happened on the hundredth time. Once the wave of dusty rubble had engulfed a tractor, there was no escape, since any attempt at rescue would only start fresh slides.

Wheeler began to feel distinctly unhappy on the way down the outer ramparts of Plato. This was odd, for they were much less steep than the inner walls, and he had expected a smoother journey. He had not allowed for the fact that Jamieson would take advantage of the easier conditions to crowd on speed, with the result that Ferdinand was indulging in a peculiar rocking motion. Presently Wheeler disappeared to the rear of the well-appointed tractor, and was not seen by his pilot for some time. When he returned he remarked rather crossly, "No one ever told me you could actually be seasick on the Moon."

The view was now rather disappointing, as it usually is when one descends to the lunar lowlands. The horizon is so near—only two or three kilometers away—that it gives a sense of confinement and restraint. It is almost as if the small circle of rock surrounding one is all that exists. The illusion can be so strong that men have been known to drive more slowly than necessary, as if subconsciously afraid they might fall off the edge of that uncannily near horizon.

For two hours Jamieson drove steadily onward, until at last the triple tower of Pico dominated the sky ahead. Once this magnificent mountain had been part of a vast crater wall that must have been a twin to Plato. But ages ago the encroaching lava of the *Mare Imbrium* had washed away all the rest of the hundred-and-fifty-kilometer-diameter ring, leaving Pico in lonely and solitary state.

The travelers paused here to open a few food packs and make some coffee in the pressure kettle. One of the minor discomforts of life on the Moon is that really hot drinks are an impossibility—water boils at about seventy degrees centigrade in the oxygen-rich, low-pressure atmosphere universally employed. After a while, however, one grows used to lukewarm beverages.

When they had cleared up the debris of the meal, Jamieson remarked to his colleague, "Sure you still want to go through with it?"

"As long as you say it's safe. Those walls look awfully steep from here."

"It's safe, if you do what I tell you. I was just wondering how you felt now. There's nothing worse than being sick in a spacesuit."

"*I'm* all right," Wheeler replied with dignity. Then another thought struck him. "How long will we be outside, anyway?"

"Oh, say a couple of hours. Four at the most. Better do all the scratching you want to now."

"I wasn't worrying about *that*," retorted Wheeler, and retired to the back of the cabin again.

In the six months he had been on the Moon, Wheeler had worn a suit no more than a dozen times, and most of those occasions were on emergency drill. There were very few times when the observing staff had to go into vacuum—most of their equipment was remotely controlled. But he was not a complete novice, though he was still in the cautious stage which is so much safer than lighthearted overconfidence.

They called Base, *via* Earth, to report their position and intentions, then adjusted each other's equipment. First Jamieson, then Wheeler, chanted the alphabetical mnemonic—"A is for airlines, B is for batteries, C is for couplings, D is for D.F. loop . . ." which sounds so childish the first time one hears it, but which so quickly becomes part of the routine of lunar life—and is something nobody ever jokes about. When they were sure that all their equipment was in perfect condition, they cracked the doors of the airlock and stepped out onto the dusty plain.

Like most lunar mountains, Pico was not so formidable when seen close at hand as when glimpsed from a distance. There were a few vertical cliffs, but they could always be avoided, and it was seldom necessary to climb slopes of more than forty-five degrees. Under a sixth of a gravity, this is no great hardship, even when one is wearing a spacesuit.

Nevertheless, the unaccustomed exertion made Wheeler sweat and pant somewhat after they had been climbing for half an hour, and his face plate was misting badly so that he had to peer out of the corners to see properly. Though he was too stubborn to request a slower pace, he was very glad when Jamieson called a halt.

They were now almost a kilometer above the plain, and could see for at least fifty kilometers to the north. They shielded their eyes from the glare of the Earth and began to search.

It took only a moment to find their objective. Halfway to the horizon, two extremely large freight rockets were standing like ungainly spiders on their extended undercarriages. Large though they were, they were dwarfed by the curious dome-shaped structure rising out of the level plain. This was no ordinary pressure dome—its proportions were all wrong. It looked almost as if a complete sphere had been partly buried, so that the upper three-quarters emerged from the surface. Through his binoculars, whose special eyepieces allowed him to use them despite his face plate, Wheeler could see men and machines moving round the base of the dome. From time to time clouds of dust shot into the sky and fell back again as if blasting was in progress. That was another odd thing about the Moon, he thought. Most objects fell too slowly here in this low gravity, for anyone accustomed to conditions on Earth. But dust fell much *too* quickly—at the same rate as anything else, in fact—for there was no air to check its descent.

"Well," said Jamieson after he too had carried out a long scrutiny through the glasses, "someone's spending an awful lot of money."

"What do you think it is? A mine?"

"It could be," replied the other, cautious as ever. "Perhaps they've decided to process the ores on the spot, and all their extraction plant is in that dome. But that's only a guess—I've certainly never seen anything like it before."

"We can reach it in an hour, whatever it is. Shall we go over and have a closer look?"

"I was afraid you were going to say that. I'm not sure it would be a very wise thing. They might insist on us staying."

"You've been reading too many scare articles. Anyone would think there was a war on and we were a couple of spies. They couldn't detain us—the Observatory knows where we are and the director would raise hell if we didn't get back."

"I suspect he will when we *do,* so we might as well get hung for sheep as lambs. Come along—it's easier on the way down."

"I never said it was hard on the way up," protested Wheeler, not very convincingly. A few minutes later, as he followed Jamieson down the slope, an alarming thought struck him.

"Do you think they're listening to us? Suppose someone's got a watch on this frequency—they'll have heard every word we've said. After all, we're in direct line of sight."

"Who's being melodramatic now? No one except the Observatory would be listening on this frequency, and the folks at home can't hear us as there's rather a lot of mountain in the way. Sounds as if you've got a guilty conscience; anyone would think that you'd been using naughty words again."

This was a reference to an unfortunate episode soon after Wheeler's arrival. Since then he had been very conscious of the fact that privacy of speech, which is taken for granted on Earth, is not always available to the wearers of spacesuits, whose every whisper can be heard by anyone within radio range.

The horizon contracted about them as they descended to ground level, but they had taken careful bearings and knew which way to steer when they were back in Ferdinand. Jamieson was driving with extra caution now, for this was terrain over which he had never previously traveled. It was nearly two hours before the enigmatic dome began to bulge above the skyline, followed a little later by the squat cylinders of the freighters.

Once again, Wheeler aimed their roof antenna on Earth, and called the Observatory to explain what they had discovered and what they intended to do. He rang off before anyone could tell them not to do it, reflecting how crazy it was to send a message 800,000 kilometers in order to talk to someone a hundred kilometers away. But there was no other way of getting long-distance communication from ground level; everything below the horizon was blocked off by the shielding effect of the Moon. It was true that by using long waves it was sometimes possible to send signals over great distances by reflection from the Moon's very tenuous ionosphere, but this method was too unreliable to be of serious use. For all practical purposes, lunar radio contact had to be on a "line of sight" basis.

It was very amusing to watch the commotion that their arrival had caused. Wheeler thought it resembled nothing so much as an ant heap that had been well stirred with a stick. In a very short time they found themselves surrounded by tractors, moondozers, hauling machines, and excited men in spacesuits. They were forced by sheer congestion to bring Ferdinand to a halt.

"At any moment," said Wheeler, "they'll call out the guards."

Jamieson failed to be amused.

"You shouldn't make jokes like that," he chided. "They're apt to be too near the truth."

"Well, here comes the reception committee. Can you read the lettering on his helmet? SEC. 2, isn't it? 'Section Two,' I suppose that means."

"Perhaps. But SEC. could just as easily stand for Security. Well —it was all your idea. I'm merely the driver."

At that moment there was a series of peremptory knocks on the outer door of the airlock. Jamieson pressed the button that opened the seal and a moment later the "reception committee" was removing his helmet in the cabin. He was a grizzled, sharp-featured man with a worried expression that looked as though it was permanently built in. It did not appear that he was pleased to see them.

He regarded Wheeler and Jamieson thoughtfully, while the two astronomers put on their friendliest smiles. "We don't usually get visitors in these parts," he said. "How did you happen to get here?"

The first sentence, Wheeler thought, was as good an understatement as he had heard for some time.

"It's our day off—we're from the Observatory. This is Dr. Jamieson—I'm Wheeler. Astrophysicists, both of us. We knew you were around here, so decided to come and have a look."

"How did you know?" the other asked sharply. He still had not introduced himself, which would have been bad manners even on Earth and was quite shocking here.

"As you may have heard," said Wheeler mildly, "we possess one or two rather large telescopes over at the Observatory. And you've been causing us a lot of trouble. I, personally, have had two spectrograms ruined by rocket glare. So can you blame us for being a trifle inquisitive?"

A slight smile played around their interrogator's lips, and was instantly banished. Nevertheless, the atmosphere seemed to thaw a little.

"Well, I think it would be best if you come along to the office while we make a few checks. It won't take very long."

"I beg your pardon? Since when has any part of the Moon been private property?"

"Sorry, but that's the way it is. Come along, please."

The two astronomers climbed into their suits and followed through the airlock. Despite his aggressive innocence, Wheeler was beginning to feel a trifle worried. Already he was visualizing all sorts of unpleasant possibilities; and recollections of what he had read about spies, solitary confinement and brick walls at dawn rose up to comfort him.

They were led to a smoothly fitting door in the curve of the great dome, and found themselves inside the space formed by the outer wall and an inner, concentric hemisphere. The two shells, as far as could be seen, were spaced apart by an intricate webbing of some transparent plastic. Even the floor underfoot was made of the same substance. This, Wheeler decided, was all very odd, but he had no time to examine it closely.

Their uncommunicative guide hurried them along almost at a trot, as if he did not wish them to see more than necessary. They entered the inner dome through a second airlock, where they removed their suits. Wheeler wondered glumly when they would be allowed to retrieve them again.

The length of the airlock indicated that the inner dome must be of tremendous thickness, and when the door ahead of them opened, both astronomers immediately noticed a familiar smell. It was ozone. Somewhere, not very far away, was high-voltage electrical equipment. There was nothing unduly remarkable about that, but it was another fact to be filed away for future reference.

The airlock had opened into a small corridor flanked by doors bearing painted numbers and such labels as PRIVATE, TECHNICAL STAFF ONLY, INFORMATION, STANDBY AIR, EMERGENCY POWER and CENTRAL CONTROL. Neither Wheeler nor Jamieson could deduce much from these notices, but they looked at each other thoughtfully when they were finally halted at a door marked SECURITY. Jamieson's expression told Wheeler, as clearly as any words could do, "I told you so!"

After a short pause a "Come In" panel glowed and the door swung automatically open. Ahead lay a perfectly ordinary office dominated by a determined-looking man at a very large desk. The size of the desk was itself a proclamation to the world that money was no object here, and the astronomers contrasted it ruefully with the office equipment to which they were accustomed. A teleprinter of unusually complicated design stood on a table in one corner, and the remaining walls were entirely covered by file cabinets.

"Well," said the security officer, "who are these people?"

"Two astronomers from the Observatory over in Plato. They've just dropped in by tractor, and I thought you should see them."

"Most certainly. Your names, please?"

There followed a tedious quarter of an hour while particulars were carefully noted down and the Observatory was called. That meant, Wheeler thought glumly, that the fat would now be in the fire. Their friends in Signals, who had been logging their progress in case of any accident, would now have to report their absence officially.

At last their identities were established, and the man at the imposing desk regarded them with some perplexity. Presently his brows cleared and he began to address them.

"You realize, of course, that you are something of a nuisance. This is the last place we ever expected visitors, otherwise we'd have put up notices telling them to keep off. Needless to say, we have means of detecting any who may turn up, even if they're not sensible enough to drive up openly, as you did.

"However, here you are and I suppose there's no harm done. You have probably guessed that this is a government project, and one we don't want talked about. I'll have to send you back, but I want you to do two things."

"What are they?" asked Jamieson suspiciously.

"I want you to promise not to talk about this visit more than you have to. Your friends will know where you've gone, so you can't keep it a complete secret. Just don't discuss it with them, that's all."

"Very well," agreed Jamieson. "And the second point?"

"If anyone persists in questioning you, and shows particular interest in this little adventure of yours—report it at once. That's all. I hope you have a good ride home."

Back in the tractor, five minutes later, Wheeler was still fuming.

"Of all the high-handed so-and-sos! He never even offered us a smoke."

"I rather think," said Jamieson mildly, "that we were lucky to get off so easily. They meant business."

"I'd like to know what *sort* of business. Does that look like a mine to you? And why should anything be going on in a slagheap like the *Mare?*"

"I think it must be a mine. When we drove up, I noticed something that looked very much like drilling machinery on the other side of the dome. But it's hard to account for all the cloak-and-dagger nonsense."

"Unless they've discovered something that they don't want the Federation to know about."

"In that case we're not likely to find out, either, and might as well stop racking our brains. But to get on to more practical matters—where do we go from here?"

"Let's stick to our original plan. It may be some time before we have a chance of using Ferdy again, and we might as well make the most of it. Besides, it's always been one of my ambitions to see the *Sinus Iridum* from ground level, as it were."

"It's a good three hundred kilometers east of here."

"Yes, but you said yourself it was pretty flat, if we keep away from the mountains. We should be able to manage it in five hours. I'm a good-enough driver now to relieve you when you want a rest."

"Not over fresh ground—that would be far too risky. But we'll make a compromise. I'll take you as far as the Laplace Promontory, so that you'll have a look into the Bay. And then you can drive home, following the track I've made. Mind you stick to it, too."

Wheeler accepted gladly. He had been half afraid that Jamieson would abandon the trip and sneak back to the Observatory, but decided that he had done his friend an injustice.

For the next three hours they crawled along the flanks of the Teneriffe Mountains, then struck out across the plain to the Straight Range, that lonely, isolated band of mountains like a faint echo of the mighty Alps. Jamieson drove now with a steady concentration; he was going into new territory and could take no chances.

From time to time he pointed out famous landmarks and Wheeler checked them against the photographic chart.

They stopped for a meal about ten kilometers east of the Straight Range, and investigated more of the boxes which the Observatory kitchen had given them. One corner of the tractor was fitted out as a tiny galley, but they didn't intend to do any real cooking except in an emergency. Neither Wheeler nor Jamieson was a sufficiently good cook to enjoy the preparation of meals and this, after all, *was* a holiday. . . .

"Sid," began Wheeler abruptly, between mouthfuls of sandwich, "what do you think about the Federation? You've met more of their people than I have."

"Yes, and liked them. Pity you weren't here before the last crowd left; we had about a dozen of them at the Observatory studying the telescope mounting. They're thinking of building a fifteen-hundred-centimeter instrument on one of the moons of Saturn, you know."

"That would be quite a project—I always said we're too close to the sun here. It would certainly get clear of the Zodiacal Light and the other rubbish around the inner planets. But to get back to the argument—did they strike you as likely to start a quarrel with Earth?"

"It's difficult to say. They were very open and friendly with us, but then we were all scientists together and that helps a lot. It might have been different if we'd been politicians or civil servants."

"Dammit, we *are* civil servants! That fellow Sadler was reminding me of it only the other day."

"Yes, but at least we're *scientific* civil servants, which makes quite a difference. I could tell that they didn't care a lot for Earth, though they were too polite to say so. There's no doubt that they're annoyed about the metals allocations; I often heard them complain about it. Their main point is that they have much greater difficulties than we have, in opening up the outer planets, and that Earth wastes half the stuff she uses."

"Which side do you think is right?"

"I don't know; it's so hard to get at all the facts. But there are a lot of people on Earth who are afraid of the Federation and don't want to give it any more power. The Federals know that; one day they may grab first and argue afterward."

Jamieson screwed up the wrappings and tossed them into the waste bin. He glanced at the chronometer, then swung himself up into the driving seat. "Time to get moving again," he said. "We're falling behind schedule."

From the Straight Range they swung southeast, and presently the great headland of Promontory Laplace appeared on the skyline. As they rounded it, they came across a disconcerting sight—the battered wreck of a tractor, and beside it a rough cairn surmounted by a metal cross. The tractor seemed to have been destroyed by an explosion in its fuel tanks, and was an obsolete model of a type that Wheeler had never seen before. He was not surprised when Jamieson told him it had been there for almost a century; it would still look exactly the same a million years from now.

As they rolled past the headland, the mighty northern wall of the *Sinus Iridum*—the Bay of Rainbows—swept into view. Eons ago the *Sinus Iridum* had been a complete ring mountain—one of the largest walled-plains on the Moon. But the cataclysm which had formed the Sea of Rains had destroyed the whole of the southern wall, so that only a semicircular bay is now left. Across that bay Promontory Laplace and Promontory Heraclides stare at each other, dreaming of the day when they were linked by mountains four kilometers high. Of those lost mountains, all that now remain are a few ridges and low hillocks.

Wheeler was very quiet as the tractor rolled past the great cliffs, which stood like a line of titans full-face toward the Earth. The green light splashing down their flanks revealed every detail of the terraced walls. No one had ever climbed those heights, but one day, Wheeler knew, men would stand upon their summits and stare out in victory across the Bay. It was strange to think that after two hundred years, there was so much of the Moon untrodden by human feet, and so many places that a man must reach with nothing to aid him but his own exertions and skill.

He remembered his first glimpse of the *Sinus Iridum,* through the little homemade telescope he had built when he was a boy. It had been nothing more than two small lenses fixed in a cardboard tube, but it had given him more pleasure than the giant instruments of which he was now the master.

Jamieson swung the tractor round in a great curve, and brought it to a halt facing back toward the west. The line they had trampled through the dust was clearly visible, a road which would remain here forever unless later traffic obliterated it.

"The end of the line," he said. "You can take over from here. She's all yours until we get to Plato. Then wake me up and I'll take her through the mountains. Good night."

How he managed it, Wheeler couldn't imagine, but within ten minutes Jamieson was asleep. Perhaps the gentle rocking of the tractor acted as a lullaby, and he wondered how successful he would be in avoiding jolts and jars on the way home. Well, there was only one way to find out. . . . He aimed carefully at the dusty track, and began to retrace the road to Plato.

✳ *CHAPTER EIGHT*

It was bound to happen sooner or later, Sadler told himself philosophically, as he knocked at the director's door. He had done his best, but in work like this it was impossible to avoid hurting someone's feelings. It would be interesting, very interesting, to know who had complained. . . .

Professor Maclaurin was one of the smallest men Sadler had ever seen. He was so tiny that some people had made the fatal mistake of not taking him seriously. Sadler knew better than this. Very small men usually took care to compensate for their physical deficiencies (how many dictators had been of even average height?) and from all accounts Maclaurin was one of the toughest characters on the Moon.

He glared at Sadler across the virgin, uncluttered surface of his desk. There was not even a scribbling pad to break its bleakness—only the small panel of the communicator switchboard with its built-in speaker. Sadler had heard about Maclaurin's unique methods of administration, and his hatred of notes and memoranda. The Observatory was run, in its day-to-day affairs, almost entirely by word of mouth. Of course, other people had to prepare notices and schedules and reports—Maclaurin just switched on his mike and gave the orders. The system worked flawlessly for the simple reason that the director recorded everything, and could play it back at a moment's notice to anyone who said, "But, sir, you never told me *that!*" It was rumored—though Sadler suspected this was a libel—that Maclaurin had occasionally committed verbal forgery by retrospectively altering the record. Such a charge, needless to say, was virtually impossible to prove.

The director waved to the only other seat, and started talking before Sadler could reach it.

"I don't know whose brilliant idea this was," he began, "but I was never notified that you were coming here. If I had been, I would have asked for a postponement. Although no one appreciates the importance of efficiency more than I do, these are very troubled times. It seems to me that my men could be better employed than by explaining their work to you—particularly while we are coping with the *N. Draconis* observations."

"I'm sorry there was a failure to inform you, Professor Maclaurin," Sadler replied. "I can only assume that the arrangements were made while you were en route to Earth." He wondered what the director would think if he knew how carefully matters had been arranged in this precise manner. "I realize that I must be something of a nuisance to your staff, but they have given me every assistance and I've had no complaints. In fact, I thought I was getting on rather well with them."

Maclaurin rubbed his chin thoughtfully. Sadler stared in fascination at the tiny, perfectly formed hands, no larger than those of a child.

"How much longer do you expect to be here?" the director asked. He certainly doesn't worry about your feelings, Sadler told himself wryly.

"It's very hard to say—the area of my investigation is so undefined. And it's only fair to warn you that I've scarcely started on the scientific side of your work, which is likely to present the greatest difficulties. So far I have confined myself to Administration and Technical Services."

This news did not seem to please Maclaurin. He looked like a small volcano working up to an eruption. There was only one thing to do, and Sadler did it quickly.

He walked to the door, opened it swiftly, looked out, then closed it again. This piece of calculated melodrama held the director speechless while Sadler walked over to the desk and brusquely flicked down the switch on the communicator.

"Now we can talk," he began. "I wanted to avoid this, but I see it's inevitable. Probably you've never met one of these cards before."

The still flabbergasted director, who had probably never before in his life been treated like this, stared at the blank sheet of plastic. As he watched, a photograph of Sadler, accompanied by some lettering, flashed into view—then vanished abruptly.

"And what," he asked when he had recovered his breath, "is Central Intelligence? I've never heard of it."

"You're not supposed to," Sadler replied. "It's relatively new, and highly unadvertised. I'm afraid the work I'm doing here is not exactly what it seems. To be brutally frank, I could hardly care less about the efficiency of your establishment, and I completely agree with all the people who tell me that it's nonsense to put scientific research on a cost-accounting basis. But it's a plausible story, don't you think?"

"Go on," said Maclaurin, with dangerous calm.

Sadler was beginning to enjoy himself beyond the call of duty. It wouldn't do, however, to get drunk with power. . . .

"I'm looking for a spy," he said, with a bleak and simple directness.

"Are you serious? This is the twenty-second century!"

"I am perfectly serious, and I need not impress upon you that you must reveal nothing of this conversation to anybody, even Wagnall."

"I refuse to believe," snorted Maclaurin, "that any of my staff would be engaged in espionage. The idea's fantastic."

"It always is," Sadler replied patiently. "That doesn't alter the position."

"Assuming that there's the slightest basis in this charge, have you any idea who it might be?"

"If I had, I'm afraid I couldn't tell you at this stage. But I'll be perfectly frank. We're not certain that it is anyone here—we're merely acting on a nebulous hint one of our—ah—agents picked up. But there is a leak *somewhere* on the Moon, and I'm covering this particular possibility. Now you see why I have been so inquisitive. I've tried not to act out of character, and I think that by now I'm taken for granted by everybody. I can only hope that our elusive Mr. X, if he exists at all, has accepted me at my face value. This, by the way, is why I'd like to know who has been complaining to you. I assume that somebody has."

Maclaurin hummed and hawed for a moment, then capitulated.

"Jenkins, down in Stores, rather implied that you'd been taking up a lot of his time."

"That's very interesting," said Sadler, more than a little puzzled. Jenkins, chief storekeeper, had been nowhere near his list of suspects. "As a matter of fact, I've spent relatively little time there— just enough to make my mission look convincing. I'll have to keep an eye on Mr. Jenkins."

"This whole idea is all very new to me," said Maclaurin thoughtfully. "But even if we have someone here passing out information to the Federation, I don't quite see how they would do it. Unless it was one of the signals officers, of course."

"That's the key problem," admitted Sadler. He was willing to discuss the general aspects of the case, for the director might be able to throw some light on them. Sadler was all too aware of his difficulties, and the magnitude of the task he had been set. As a counterspy, his status was strictly amateur. The only consolation he had was that his hypothetical opponent would be in the same position. Professional spies had never been too numerous in any age, and the last one must have died more than a century ago.

"By the way," said Maclaurin, with a forced and somewhat unconvincing laugh. "How do you know that *I'm* not the spy?"

"I don't," Sadler replied cheerfully. "In counter-espionage, certainty is rare. But we do the best we can. I hope you weren't seriously inconvenienced during your visit to Earth?"

Maclaurin stared uncomprehendingly at him for a moment. Then his jaw dropped.

"So you've been investigating *me!*" he spluttered indignantly.

Sadler shrugged his shoulders.

"It happens to the best of us. If it's any consolation, you can just imagine what *I* had to go through before they gave me this job. And I never asked for it in the first place. . . ."

"Then what do you want me to do?" growled Maclaurin. For a man of his size, his voice was surprisingly deep, though Sadler had been told that when he was really annoyed it developed a high-pitched squeak.

"Naturally, I'd like you to inform me of anything suspicious that comes to your notice. From time to time I may consult you on various points, and I'd be very glad of your advice. Otherwise, please take as little notice of me as possible and continue to regard me as a nuisance."

"That," replied Maclaurin, with a half-hearted smile, "will present no difficulties at all. However, you can count on me to assist you in every way—if only to help prove that your suspicions are unfounded."

"I sincerely hope that they are," Sadler replied. "And thank you for your co-operation—I appreciate it."

Just in time, he stopped himself whistling as he closed the door behind him. He felt very pleased that the interview had gone so well, but he remembered that no one whistled after they had had an interview with the director. Adjusting his expression to one of grave composure, he walked out through Wagnall's office and into the main corridor, where he at once ran into Jamieson and Wheeler.

"Have you seen the Old Man?" Wheeler asked anxiously. "Is he in a good mood?"

"As this is the first time I've met him, I've no standards of reference. We got on well enough. What's the matter? You look like a couple of naughty schoolboys."

"He's just asked for us," said Jamieson. "We don't know why, but he's probably been catching up on what's happened while he's away. He's already congratulated Con for discovering *N. Draconis,* so it can't be that. I'm afraid he's found out that we've borrowed a Cat for a run."

"What's wrong with that?"

"Well, they're only supposed to be used on official jobs. But everybody does it—as long as we replace the fuel we burn, no one's any the worse. Heck, I suppose I shouldn't have told that to *you,* of all people!"

Sadler did a quick double-take, then realized with relief that Jamieson was merely referring to his well-advertised activities as a financial watchdog.

"Don't worry," he laughed. "The worst I'll do with the information is to blackmail you into taking me for a ride. I hope the Old

Ma—Professor Maclaurin—doesn't give you too rough a passage."

All three would have been quite surprised to know with what uncertainty the director himself was regarding this interview. In the ordinary way, such minor infractions of the rules as unauthorized use of a Caterpillar would have been a matter for Wagnall to deal with, but something more important was involved here. Until five minutes ago, he had no idea what it might be, and had asked to see Wheeler and Jamieson to discover what was going on. Professor Maclaurin prided himself on keeping in touch with everything, and a certain amount of his staff's time and ingenuity had to be employed in seeing that he was not always successful.

Wheeler, drawing heavily on the stock of good will *N. Draconis* had given him, gave an account of their unofficial mission. He tried to make it sound as if they were a pair of knights in armor riding out into the wilderness to discover the dragon which was menacing the Observatory. He concealed nothing of importance, which was well for him as the director already knew where he had been.

As he listened to Wheeler's account, Maclaurin found the pieces of the jigsaw fitting together. This mysterious message from Earth, ordering him to keep his people out of the *Mare Imbrium* in future, must have originated from the place these two had visited. The leak that Sadler was investigating would also have something to do with it. Maclaurin still found it hard to believe that any of his men was a spy, but he realized that a spy was the last thing any competent spy ever looked like.

He dismissed Jamieson and Wheeler with an absent-minded mildness that left them both sorely puzzled. For a moment he sat lost in gloomy thought. It might be a coincidence, of course—the story hung together well. But if one of these men was after information, he had set about it in the right way. Or had he? Would a real spy have acted so openly, knowing that he was bound to draw suspicion on himself? Could it even be a daring double-bluff, on the principle that no one would seriously suspect such a frontal attack?

Thank God, it wasn't his problem. He would get it off his hands as quickly as he could. Professor Maclaurin snapped down the TRANSMIT switch and spoke to the outer office.

"Please find Mr. Sadler for me. I want to speak to him again."

✳ CHAPTER NINE

There had been a subtle change in Sadler's status since the director's return. It was something that Sadler had known must happen, though he had done his best to guard against it. On his arrival, he had been treated with polite suspicion by everybody, and it had taken him several days solid public-relations work to break down the barriers. People had become friendly and talkative, and he could make some headway. But now they seemed to be regretting their earlier frankness, and it was uphill work once more.

He knew the reason. Certainly no one suspected his real purpose in being here, but everybody knew that the return of the director, far from limiting his activities, had somehow enhanced his position. In the echoing sounding-box of the Observatory, where rumor and gossip traveled at speeds scarcely inferior to that of light, it was hard to keep any secrets. The word must have gone out that Sadler was more important than he seemed. He only hoped it would be a long while before anybody guessed *how* much more important. . . .

Until now, he had confined his attention to the Administrative section. This was partly a matter of policy, because this would be the way he would be expected to act. But the Observatory really existed for the scientists, not the cooks, typists, accountants and secretaries, however essential they might be.

If there was a spy in the Observatory, there were two main problems he had to face. Information is useless to a spy unless he can send it to his superiors. Mr. X must not only have contacts who passed material to him—he must have an out-going channel of communication as well.

Physically, there were only three ways out of the Observatory. One could leave it by monorail, by tractor, or on foot. The last case did not seem very likely to be important. In theory, a man might walk a few kilometers and leave a message to be picked up at some prearranged rendezvous. But such peculiar behavior would soon be noticed, and it would be very easy to check on the small number of men in Maintenance who were the only people who used suits regularly. Every exit and entrance through the airlocks had to be logged, though Sadler doubted that this rule was invariably obeyed.

The tractors were more promising, as they would give so much greater range. But their use would involve collusion, since they always carried a crew of at least two men—and this was one rule which was *never* broken, for safety reasons. There was the odd case of Jamieson and Wheeler, of course. Their backgrounds were being busily investigated now, and he should have the report in a few days. But their behavior, though irregular, had been too open to be really suspicious.

That left the monorail to Central City. Everybody went there, on the average, about once a week. There were endless possibilities for the exchange of messages here, and at this very moment a number of "tourists" were inconspicuously checking contacts and making all sorts of interesting discoveries about the private lives of the Observatory staff. There was little part that Sadler could play in this work, except to furnish lists of the most frequent visitors to the City.

So much for physical lines of communication. Sadler discounted them all. There were other, and subtler, means far more likely to be used by a scientist. Any member of the Observatory's staff could build a radio transmitter, and there were countless places where one could be concealed. It was true that the patiently listening monitors had detected nothing, but sooner or later Mr. X would make a slip.

Meanwhile, Sadler would have to find what the scientists were doing. The high-pressure course in astronomy and physics he had taken before coming here would be totally inadequate to give him any real understanding of the Observatory's work, but at least he would be able to get the general outline. And he might eliminate a few suspects from his depressingly long list.

The Computing Section did not detain him for long. Behind their glass panels, the spotless machines sat in silent cogitation while the girls fed the program tapes into their insatiable maws. In an adjacent sound-proofed room, the electric typewriters stormed away, printing endless rows and columns of numbers. Dr. Mays, the head of the section, did his best to explain what was going on— but it was a hopeless task. These machines had left far behind such elementary operations as integration, such kindergarten functions as cosines or logarithms. They were dealing with mathematical entities of which Sadler had never heard, and solving problems whose very statement would be meaningless to him.

That did not worry him unduly; he had seen what he wanted to. All the main equipment was sealed and locked; only the maintenance engineers who called once a month could get at it. Certainly there was nothing for him here. Sadler tiptoed away as from a shrine.

The optical workshop, where patient craftsmen shaped glass to a fraction of a millionth of an inch, using a technique unchanged for centuries, fascinated him but advanced his search no further. He peered at the interference fringes produced by clashing light waves, and watched them scurry madly back and forth as the heat of his body caused microscopic expansions in blocks of flawless glass. Here art and science met, to achieve perfections unmatched elsewhere in the whole range of human technology. Could there be any clue for him here in this buried factory of lenses, prisms and mirrors? It seemed most improbable.

He was, Sadler thought glumly, rather in the position of a man in a darkened coal cellar, looking for a black cat that might not be there. What was worse, to make the analogy more accurate he would have to be a man who didn't know what a cat looked like, even when he saw one.

His private discussions with Maclaurin helped him a good deal. The director was still skeptical, but was obviously co-operating to the full if only to get this annoying interloper out of the way. Sadler could question him about any technical aspect of the Observatory's work, though he was careful not to give any hints as to the direction his search was taking him.

He had now compiled a small dossier for every member of the staff—no mean achievement, even though the factual data had been supplied before he came to the Observatory. For most of his subjects, a single sheet of paper sufficed, but for some he had accumulated several pages of cryptic notes. The facts he was sure of he wrote in ink; the speculations were in pencil so that they could be modified when necessary. Some of these speculations were very wild and frequently libelous, and Sadler often felt very ashamed of them. It was hard, for example, to accept a drink from someone whom you had noted down as possibly susceptible to bribes owing to the cost of maintaining an expensive mistress in Central City. . . .

This particular suspect had been one of the engineers in Construction. Sadler had soon ruled him out as a likely candidate for blackmail, since far from concealing the situation the victim was always complaining bitterly about his inamorata's extravagances. He had even warned Sadler against incurring similar liabilities.

The filing system was divided into three parts. Section A contained the names of the ten or so men Sadler considered the most probable suspects, though there was not one against whom he had any real evidence. Some were down simply because they had the greatest opportunity for passing out information if they wished to do so. Wagnall was one of these; Sadler was practically certain that the secretary was innocent, but kept him on the list to be on the safe side.

Several others were listed because they had close relatives in the Federation, or because they were too openly critical of Earth. Sadler did not really imagine that a well-trained spy would risk arousing suspicion by behaving in this way, but he had to be on the watch for the enthusiastic amateur who could be just as dangerous. The records of atomic espionage during the Second World War had been very instructive in this respect, and Sadler had studied them with great care.

Another name on List A was that of Jenkins, the chief storekeeper. This was only the most tenuous of hunches, and all attempts by Sadler to follow it up had been unsuccessful. Jenkins seemed to be a somewhat morose individual, who resented interference and was not very popular with the rest of the staff. Getting anything out of him in the way of equipment was supposed to be the most difficult job on the Moon. This, of course, might merely mean that he was a good representative of his proverbially tenacious tribe.

There remained that interesting couple Jamieson and Wheeler, who between them did a great deal to enliven the Observatory scene. Their drive out into the *Mare Imbrium* had been a fairly typical exploit, and had followed, so Sadler was assured, the pattern of earlier adventures.

Wheeler was always the leading spirit. His trouble—if it was a trouble—was that he had too much energy and too many interests. He was not yet thirty; one day, perhaps, age and responsibility would mellow him, but so far neither had had much opportunity. It was too easy to dismiss him as a case of arrested development, as a college boy who had failed to grow up. He had a first-rate mind, and never did anything that was really foolish. Though there were many people who did not like him, particularly after they had been the victims of one of his practical jokes, there was nobody who wished him any harm. He moved unscathed through the little jungle of Observatory politics, and had the abiding virtues of complete honesty and forthrightness. One always knew what he was thinking, and it was never necessary to ask him for his opinion. He gave it first.

Jamieson was a very different character, and presumably it was the contrast in their personalities which drew these two men together. He was older than Wheeler by a couple of years, and was regarded as a sobering influence on his younger companion. Sadler doubted this; as far as he could judge, Jamieson's presence had never made any difference in his friend's behavior. He had mentioned this to Wagnall, who had thought for a while and said, "Yes, but think how much worse Con would be if Sid *wasn't* there to keep an eye on him."

Certainly Jamieson was far more stable and much harder to get to know. He was not as brilliant as Wheeler and would probably never make any shattering discoveries, but he would be one of those reliable, sound men who do the essential tidying up after the geniuses have broken through into new territory.

Scientifically reliable—yes. Politically reliable—that was another matter. Sadler had tried to sound him, without making it too obvious, but so far with little success. Jamieson seemed more interested in his work and his hobby—the painting of lunar landscapes—than in politics. During his term at the Observatory he had built up a small art gallery, and whenever he had the chance he would go out in a spacesuit carrying easel and special paints made from low-vapor-pressure oils. It had taken him a good deal of experimenting to find pigments that could be used in a vacuum, and Sadler frankly doubted that the results were worth the trouble. He thought he knew enough about art to decide that Jamieson had more enthusiasm than talent, and Wheeler shared this point of view. "They say that Sid's pictures grow on you after a while," he had confided to Sadler. "Personally, I can think of no more horrible fate."

Sadler's List B contained the names of everybody else in the Observatory who looked intelligent enough to be a spy. It was depressingly long, and from time to time he went through it trying to transfer people to List A or—better still—to the third and final list of those who were completely clear of suspicion. As he sat in his little cubicle, shuffling his sheets and trying to put himself into the places of the men he was watching, Sadler sometimes felt that he was playing an intricate game, in which most of the rules were flexible and all the players unknown. It was a deadly game, the moves were taking place at accelerating speed—and upon its outcome might depend the future of the human race.

✳   **CHAPTER TEN**

The voice that came from the speaker was deep, cultured and sincere. It had been traveling across space for many minutes, beamed through the clouds of Venus along the two-hundred-million-kilometer link to Earth, then relayed again from Earth to Moon. After that immense journey, it was still clear and clean, almost untouched by interference or distortion.

"The situation here has hardened since my last commentary. No one in official circles will express any opinion, but the press and radio are not so reticent. I flew in from Hesperus this morning, and the three hours I've been here are quite long enough for me to gauge public opinion.

"I must speak bluntly, even if I have to upset the people back home. Earth isn't very popular here. The phrase 'dog in the manger' gets bandied around quite a lot. Your own supply difficulties are recognized, but it's felt that the frontier planets are short of necessities while Earth wastes much of its resources on trivial luxuries. I'll give you an example. Yesterday the news came in that the Mercury outpost has just lost five men through a faulty heat-exchange unit in one of the domes. The temperature control failed and the lava got them—not a very nice death. If the manufacturer had not been short of titanium, this wouldn't have happened.

"Of course, it's not fair to blame Earth for this. But it's unfortunate that only a week ago you cut the titanium quota again, and the interested parties here are seeing that the public doesn't forget it. I can't be more specific than that, because I don't want to be cut off, but you'll know who I mean.

"I don't believe that the situation will get any worse unless some new factor enters the picture. But suppose—and here I want to make it quite clear that I'm only considering a hypothetical case —suppose Earth were to locate new supplies of the heavy metals. In the still-unexplored ocean depths, for instance. Or even on the Moon, despite the disappointments it's given in the past.

"If this happens, and Earth tries to keep its discovery to itself, the consequences may be serious. It's all very well to say that Earth would be within its rights. Legal arguments don't carry much weight when you're fighting thousand-atmosphere pressures on Jupiter, or trying to thaw out the frozen moons of Saturn. Don't forget, as you enjoy your mild spring days and peaceful summer evenings, how lucky you are to live in the temperate region of the solar system, where the air never freezes and the rocks never melt. . . .

"What is the Federation likely to do if such a situation arises? If I knew, I couldn't tell you. I can only make some guesses. To talk about war, in the old-fashioned sense, seems absurd to me. Either side could inflict heavy damage on the other, but any real trial of strength could not possibly be conclusive. Earth has too many resources, even though they are dangerously concentrated. And she owns most of the ships in the solar system.

"The Federation has the advantage of dispersion. How can Earth carry out a simultaneous fight against half-a-dozen planets and moons, poorly equipped though they may be? The supply problem would be completely hopeless.

"If, which heaven forbid, it should come to violence, we may see sudden raids on strategic points by specially equipped vessels which will make an attack and then retreat into space. Any talk of interplanetary invasion is pure fantasy. Earth certainly has no wish to take over the planets. And the Federation, even if it wanted to enforce its will on Earth, has neither the men nor the ships for a full-scale assault. As I see it, the immediate danger is that something like a duel may take place—where and how is anyone's guess —as one side attempts to impress the other with its strength. But I would warn any who may be thinking of a limited, gentlemanly war that wars were seldom limited, and never gentlemanly. Good-by, Earth—this is Roderick Beynon, speaking to you from Venus."

Someone reached out and turned off the set, but at first nobody seemed inclined to start the inevitable discussion. Then Jansen, from Power, said admiringly:

"Beynon's got guts, you must admit. He wasn't pulling his punches. I'm surprised they let him make that broadcast."

"I thought he talked good sense," remarked Mays. The High Priest of Computing had a slow, measured style of delivery that contrasted quaintly with the lightning speed of his machines.

"Whose side are you on?" someone asked suspiciously.

"Oh, I'm a friendly neutral."

"But Earth pays your salary. Which side would you support if there was a showdown?"

"Well that would depend on the circumstances. I'd *like* to support Earth. But I reserve the right to make up my own mind. Whoever it was who said 'My planet right or wrong' was a damned fool. I'd be for Earth if it was right, and would probably give it the benefit of the doubt in a borderline case. But I'd not support it if I felt its cause was definitely wrong."

There was a long silence while everyone thought this over. Sadler had been watching Mays intently while the mathematician was speaking. Everyone, he knew, respected Mays's honesty and logic. A man who was actively working against Earth would never have expressed himself as forthrightly as this. Sadler wondered if Mays would have spoken any differently had he known that a counter-intelligence man was sitting within two meters of him. He did not believe that he would have altered a word.

"But, blast it," said the chief engineer, who as usual was blocking the synthetic fire, "there's no question of right and wrong here. Anything found on Earth or Moon belongs to us, to do with as we like."

"Certainly, but don't forget we've been falling back on our quota deliveries, as Beynon said. The Federation has been relying on them for its programs. If we repudiate our agreements because we haven't got the stuff ourselves, that's one thing. But it's a very different matter if we *have* got it and are just holding the Federation up for ransom."

"Why should we do any such thing?"

It was Jamieson, unexpectedly enough, who answered this. "Fear," he said. "Our politicians are frightened of the Federation. They know it already has more brains, and one day it may have more power. Then Earth will be a back number."

Before anyone could challenge him on this, Czuikov from the Electronics Lab started a fresh hare.

"I've been thinking," he said, "about that broadcast we've just heard. We know that Beynon's a pretty honest man, but after all he was broadcasting from Venus, with their permission. There may be more in that talk of his than meets the ear."

"What do you mean?"

"He may be putting across their propaganda. Not consciously, perhaps; they may have primed him to say what they want us to hear. That talk about raids, for instance. Perhaps it's intended to scare us."

"That's an interesting idea. What do you think, Sadler? You're the last to come up from Earth."

This frontal attack took Sadler rather by surprise, but he dexterously tossed the ball back.

"I don't think Earth can be frightened as easily as that. But the passage that interested me was his reference to possible new supplies on the Moon. It looks as if rumors are beginning to float around."

This was a calculated indiscretion on Sadler's part. It was not so very indiscreet, however, for there was no one in the Observatory who did not know (a) that Wheeler and Jamieson had stumbled on some unusual government project in the *Mare Imbrium,* and (b) that they had been ordered not to talk about it. Sadler was particularly anxious to see what their reactions would be.

Jamieson assumed a look of puzzled innocence, but Wheeler did not hesitate to rise to the bait.

"What do you expect?" he said. "Half the Moon must have seen those ships coming down in the *Mare.* And there must be hundreds of workmen there. They can't all have come from Earth—they'll be going into Central City and talking to their girl friends when they've had a few drinks too many."

How right you are, thought Sadler, and what a headache *that* little problem was giving Security. . . .

"Anyway," continued Wheeler, "I've got an open mind on the subject. They can do what they like out there as long as they don't interfere with me. You can't tell a thing from the outside of the place, except that it's costing the poor taxpayer an awful lot of money."

There was a nervous cough from a mild little man from Instrumentation, where only that morning Sadler had spent a boring couple of hours looking at cosmic-ray telescopes, magnetometers, seismographs, molecular-resonance clocks, and batteries of other devices which were surely storing information more rapidly than anyone would ever be able to analyze it.

"I don't know about them interfering with you, but they've been playing hell with me."

"What do you mean?" everyone asked simultaneously.

"I had a look at the magnetic-field-strength meters half an hour ago. Usually the field here is pretty constant, except when there's a storm around, and we always know when to expect those. But something odd's going on at the moment. The field keeps hopping up and down—not very much, a few microgauss—and I'm sure it's artificial. I've checked all the equipment in the Observatory, and everyone swears they're not mucking around with magnets. I wondered if our secretive friends out in the *Mare* were responsible, and just on the chance, I had a look at the other instruments. I didn't find anything until I came to the seismographs. We've got a telemetering one down by the south wall of the crater, you know, and it had been knocked all over the place. Some of the kinks looked like blasting; I'm always picking that up from Hyginus and the other mines. But there were also some most peculiar jitters of the trace that were almost synchronized with the magnetic pulses. Allowing for the time-lag through the rock, the distance checked up well. There's no doubt where it comes from."

"An interesting piece of research," Jamieson remarked, "but what does it add up to?"

"There are probably a good many interpretations. But I'd say that out there in the *Mare Imbrium* someone is generating a colossal magnetic field, in pulses lasting about a second at a time."

"And the moon-quakes?"

"Just a by-product. There's a lot of magnetic rock around here, and I imagine it must get quite a jolt when that field goes on. You probably wouldn't notice that quake even if you were where it started, but our seismographs are so sensitive they can spot a meteor falling twenty kilometers away."

Sadler listened to the resulting technical argument with great interest. With so many keen minds worrying around the facts, it was inevitable that some would guess the truth—and inevitable that others would counter it with their own theories. This was not important; what concerned him was whether anyone showed special knowledge or curiosity.

But no one did, and Sadler was still left with his discouraging three propositions: Mr. X was too clever for him; Mr. X was not here; Mr. X did not exist at all. . . .

✴ CHAPTER ELEVEN

Nova Draconis was waning; no longer did it outshine all the suns of the Galaxy. Yet in the skies of Earth it was still brighter than Venus at her most brilliant, and it might be a thousand years before men saw its like again.

Though it was very near on the scale of stellar distances, *N. Draconis* was still so remote that its apparent magnitude did not vary across the whole width of the solar system. It shone with equal brilliance above the firelands of Mercury and the nitrogen glaciers of Pluto. Transient though it was, it had turned men's minds for a moment from their own affairs and made them think of ultimate realities.

But not for long. The fierce violet light of the greatest nova in history shone now upon a divided system, upon planets that had ceased to threaten each other and were now preparing for deeds.

The preparations were far more advanced than the public realized. Neither Earth nor the Federation had been frank with its people. In secret laboratories, men had been turning toward destruction the tools which had given them the freedom of space. Even if the contestants had worked in entire independence, it was inevitable that they would have evolved similar weapons, since they were basing them on the same technologies.

But each side had its agents and counter-agents, and each knew, at least approximately, the weapons which the other was developing. There might be some surprises—any one of which could be decisive —but on the whole the antagonists were equally matched.

In one respect, the Federation had a great advantage. It could hide its activities, its researches and tests, among the scattered moons and asteroids, beyond any hope of discovery. Earth, on the other hand, could not launch a single ship without the information reaching Mars and Venus within a matter of minutes.

The great uncertainty that plagued each side was the efficiency of its Intelligence. If this came to war, it would be a war of amateurs. A secret service requires a long tradition, though perhaps not an honorable one. Spies cannot be trained overnight, and even if they could, the kind of flair that characterizes a really brilliant agent is not easy to come by.

No one was better aware of this than Sadler. Sometimes he wondered if his unknown colleagues, scattered over the solar system, felt equally frustrated. Only the man at the top could see the complete picture—or something approaching it. He had never realized the isolation in which a spy must work, the horrible feeling that you are alone, that there is no one you can trust, no one with whom you can share your burdens. Since he had reached the Moon, he had—at least to his knowledge—spoken to no other member of Central Intelligence. All his contacts with the organization had been impersonal and indirect. His routine reports—which to any casual reader would have seemed extremely dull analyses of the Observatory's accounts—went by the daily monorail to Central City, and he had little idea what happened to them after that. A few messages had arrived by the same means, and in the event of real emergency the teleprinter circuit was available.

He was looking forward to his first meeting with another agent, which had been arranged weeks in advance. Though he doubted if it would be of much practical value, it would give his morale a badly needed boost.

Sadler had not, to his own satisfaction at least, acquainted himself with all the main aspects of Administration and Technical Services. He had looked (from a respectful distance) into the burning heart of the micro-pile which was the Observatory's main power source. He had watched the big mirrors of the solar generators, waiting patiently for the sunrise. They had not been used for years, but it was nice to have them around in case of any emergency, ready to tap the limitless resources of the sun itself.

The Observatory farm had surprised and fascinated him most of all. It was strange that in this age of scientific marvels, of synthetic this and artificial that, there were still some things in which Nature could not be excelled. The farm was an integral part of the air-conditioning system, and was at its best during the long lunar day. When Sadler saw it, lines of fluorescent lamps were providing substitute sunlight, and metal shutters had been drawn over the great windows which would greet the dawn when the sun rose above the western wall of Plato.

He might have been back on Earth, in some well-appointed greenhouse. The slowly moving air passed along the rows of growing plants, gave up its carbon dioxide and emerged not only richer in oxygen, but also with that indefinable freshness which the chemists had never been able to duplicate.

And here Sadler was presented with a small but very ripe apple, every atom of which had come from the Moon. He took it back to his room where he could enjoy it in privacy, and was no longer surprised that the farm was out of bounds to everyone except the men who tended it. The trees would soon be stripped if any casual visitor could wander through these verdant corridors.

The Signals section was just about as great a contrast as could be imagined. Here were the circuits that linked the Observatory with Earth, with the rest of the Moon, and if necessary with the planets direct. It was the greatest and most obvious danger point. Every message that came or went was monitored, and the men who operated the equipment had been checked and rechecked by Security. Two of the staff had been transferred, without knowing the reason, to less sensitive jobs. Moreover—even Sadler did not know this—a telescopic camera thirty kilometers away was taking a photograph every minute of the big transmitting arrays which the Observatory used for long-distance work. If one of these radio searchlights happened to point for any length of time in an unauthorized direction, the fact would soon be known.

The astronomers, without exception, were all very willing to discuss their work and explain their equipment. If they wondered at some of Sadler's questions, they gave no sign of it. For his part, he was very careful not to step outside of his adopted role. The technique he used was the frank man-to-man one: "Of course this isn't really my job, but I'm quite interested in astronomy, and while I'm here on the Moon I want to see all I can. Naturally, if you're too busy at the moment——" It always worked like a charm.

Wagnall usually made the arrangements and smoothed the way for him. The secretary had been so helpful that at first Sadler wondered if he was trying to safeguard himself, but further inquiry had shown that Wagnall was like that. He was one of those people who cannot help trying to create a good impression, simply because they want to be on good terms with everybody. He must find it singularly frustrating, Sadler thought, working for a cold fish like Professor Maclaurin.

The heart of the Observatory was, of course, the thousand-centimeter telescope—the largest optical instrument ever made by man. It stood on the summit of a slight knoll some distance from the residential area and was impressive rather than elegant. The enormous barrel was surrounded by a gantry-like structure which controlled its vertical movement, and the whole framework could rotate on a circular track.

"It's not a bit like any of the telescopes back on Earth," explained Molton as they stood together inside the nearest observation dome, looking out across the plain. "The tube, for instance. That's so we can still work during the day. Without it, we'd get sunlight reflected down into the mirror from the supporting structure. That would ruin our observations, and the heat would distort the mirror. It might take hours to settle down again. The big reflectors on Earth haven't got to worry about this sort of thing. They're only used at night—those that are still in action at all."

"I wasn't sure that there were any active observatories left on Earth," Sadler remarked.

"Oh, there are a few. Nearly all training establishments, of course. *Real* astronomical research is impossible down in that peasoup of an atmosphere. Look at my own work, for instance—ultraviolet spectroscopy. The Earth's atmosphere is *completely* opaque to the wavelengths I'm interested in. No one ever observed them until we got out into space. Sometimes I wonder how astronomy ever *started* down on Earth."

"The mounting looks odd to me," Sadler remarked thoughtfully. "It's more like that of a gun than any telescope I've ever seen."

"Quite correct. They didn't bother about an equatorial mounting. There's an automatic computer that keeps it tracking any star we set it on. But come downstairs and see what happens at the business end."

Molton's laboratory was a fantastic maze of half-assembled equipment, scarcely any of which Sadler could recognize. When he complained about this, his guide seemed highly amused.

"You needn't feel ashamed of that. We've designed and built most of it here; we're always trying out improvements. But roughly speaking, what happens is this. The light from the big mirror—we're directly underneath it here—is piped down through that tube over there. I can't demonstrate at the moment, as someone is taking photographs and it's not my turn for another hour. But when it is, I can select any part of the sky I like from this remote-control desk here and lock the instrument on to it. Then all I have to do is to analyze the light with these spectroscopes. You can't see much of their works, I'm afraid—they're all totally enclosed. When they're in use the whole optical system has to be evaluated, because as I mentioned just now even a trace of air blocks the far ultra-violet rays."

Sadler was suddenly struck by an incongruous thought.

"Tell me," he said, glancing round the maze of wiring, the batteries of electronic counters, the atlases of spectral lines, "have you ever *looked* through this telescope?"

Molton smiled back at him.

"Never," he said. "It wouldn't be hard to arrange, but there would be absolutely no point in it. All these really big telescopes are super-cameras. And who wants to look through a camera?"

There were, however, telescopes at the Observatory through which one could look without too much trouble. Some of the smaller instruments were fitted with TV cameras which could be swung into position when it was necessary to search for comets or asteroids whose exact locations were unknown. Once or twice Sadler managed to borrow one of these instruments, and to sweep the skies at random to see what he could find. He would dial a position on the remote-control board, then peer into the screen to see what he had caught. After a while he discovered how to use the *Astronautical Almanac,* and it was a great moment when he set up the co-ordinates for Mars and found it bang in the middle of the field.

He stared with mixed feelings at the green-and-ocher disk almost filling the screen. One of the polar caps was tilted slightly sunward—it was the beginning of spring, and the great frost-covered tundras would be slowly thawing after the iron winter. A beautiful planet to watch from space, but a hard planet on which to build a civilization. No wonder its sturdy children were losing patience with Earth.

The image of the planet was incredibly sharp and clear. There was not the slightest tremor or unsteadiness as it floated in the field of view, and Sadler, who had once glimpsed Mars through a telescope on Earth, could now see with his own eyes how astronomy had been liberated from its chains when the atmosphere had been left behind. Earth-bound observers had studied Mars for decades through instruments larger than this, but he could see more in a few hours than they could have glimpsed in a lifetime. He was no nearer to Mars than they had been—indeed, the planet was now at a considerable distance from Earth—but there was no dancing, quivering haze of air to veil his view.

When he had gazed his fill at Mars, he searched for Saturn. The sheer beauty of the spectacle took his breath away: it seemed impossible that he was not looking at some perfect work of art, rather than a creation of nature. The great yellow globe, slightly flattened at the poles, floated at the center of its intricate system of rings. The faint bands and shadings of atmospheric disturbances were clearly visible, even across two thousand million kilometers of space. And beyond the concentric girdles of the rings, Sadler could count at least seven of the planet's moons.

Though he knew that the instantaneously operating eye of the television camera could never rival the patient photographic plate, he also looked for some of the distant nebulae and star clusters. He let the field of view drift along the crowded highway of the Milky Way, checking the image whenever some particularly beautiful group of stars, or cloud of glowing mist appeared upon the screen. After a while, it seemed to Sadler that he had become intoxicated with the infinite splendor of the skies; he needed something that would bring him back into the realm of human affairs. So he turned the telescope on Earth.

It was so huge that even under the weakest power he could get only part of it on the screen. The great crescent was shrinking fast, but even the unlit portion of the disk was full of interest. Down there in the night were the countless phosphorescent glows that marked the positions of cities—and down there was Jeannette, sleeping now, but perhaps dreaming of him. At least he knew that she had received his letter; her puzzled but guarded reply had been reassuring, though its loneliness and unspoken reproach had torn at his heart. Had he, after all, made a mistake? Sometimes he bitterly regretted the conventional caution which had ruled the first year of their married life. Like most couples on the overpopulated planet that swam before his eyes, they had waited to prove their compatibility before embarking on the adventure of parenthood. In this age, it was a definite social stigma to have children before one had been married for several years—it was a proof of fecklessness and irresponsibility.

They had both wanted a family, and now that such matters could be decided in advance had intended to start with a son. Then Sadler had received his assignment, and realized for the first time the full seriousness of the interplanetary situation. He would not bring Jonathan Peter into the uncertain future that lay ahead.

In earlier ages, few men would have hesitated for such a reason. Indeed, the possibility of their own extinction had often made them even more anxious to seek the only immortality human beings can know. But the world had been at peace for two hundred years, and if war came now the complex and fragile pattern of life on Earth might be broken into fragments. A woman burdened with a child might have little chance of survival.

Perhaps he was being melodramatic, and had let his fears overpower his sense of judgment. If Jeannette had known all the facts, she would still not have hesitated; she would have taken the chance. But because he could not talk to her freely, he would not take advantage of her ignorance.

It was too late for regret; all that he loved lay there on that sleeping globe, sundered from him by the abyss of space. His thoughts had come full circle. He had made the journey from star to man, across the immense desert of the Cosmos to the lonely oasis of the human soul.

✳ *CHAPTER TWELVE*

"**I**'ve no reason to suppose," said the man in the blue suit, "that anyone suspects you, but it would be difficult to meet inconspicuously in Central City. There are too many people around, and everybody knows everybody else. You'd be surprised how hard it is to get any privacy."

"You don't think it will seem odd for me to come here?" asked Sadler.

"No, most visitors do, if they can manage it. It's like going to Niagara Falls—something no one wants to miss. You can't blame them, can you?"

Sadler agreed. Here was one spectacle that could never be a disappointment, that would always surpass any advance publicity. Even now the shock of stepping out onto this balcony had not completely worn off; he could well believe that many people were physically incapable of coming as far as this.

He was standing above nothingness, encased in a transparent cylinder jutting out from the edge of the canyon. The metal catwalk beneath his feet, and the slim hand rail, were the only tokens of security granted to him. His knuckles still grasped that railing tightly.

The Hyginus Cleft ranks among the greatest wonders on the Moon. From end to end it is more than three hundred kilometers long, and in places it is five kilometers wide. It is not so much a canyon as a series of interlinked craters, branching out in two arms from a vast central well. And it is the gateway through which men have reached the buried treasures of the Moon.

Sadler could now look down into the depths without flinching. Infinitely far below, it seemed, some strange insects were slowly crawling back and forth in little pools of artificial light. If one shone a torch upon a group of cockroaches, they would have looked like this.

But those tiny insects, Sadler knew, were the great mining machines at work on the floor of the canyon. It was surprisingly flat down there, so many thousands of meters below, for it seemed that lava had flooded into the cleft soon after it was formed, and then congealed into a buried river of rock.

The Earth, almost vertically overhead, illuminated the great wall immediately opposite. The canyon marched away to right and left as far as the eye could follow, and sometimes the blue-green light falling upon the rock face produced a most unexpected illusion. Sadler found it easy to imagine, if he moved his head suddenly, that he was looking into the heart of a gigantic waterfall, sweeping down forever into the depths of the Moon.

Across the face of that fall, on the invisible threads of hoisting cables, the ore buckets were rising and dropping. Sadler had seen those buckets, moving on the overhead lines away from the Cleft, and he knew that they were taller than he was. But now they looked like beads moving slowly along a wire, as they carried their loads to the distant smelting plants. It's a pity, he thought to himself, that they're only carrying sulphur and oxygen and silicon and aluminum —we could do with fewer of the light elements and more of the heavy ones.

But he had been called here on business, not to stand gaping like a tourist. He pulled the coded notes from his pocket, and began to give his report.

It did not take as long as he could have wished. There was no way of telling whether his listener was pleased or disappointed at the inconclusive summary. He thought it over for a minute, then remarked, "I wish we could give you some more help, but you can imagine how shorthanded we are now. Things are getting rough; if there is going to be trouble, we expect it in the next ten days. There's something happening out around Mars, but we don't know what it is. The Federation has been building at least two ships of unusual design, and we think they're testing them. Unfortunately we haven't a single sighting, only some rumors that don't make sense but have worried Defense. I'm telling you this to give you more background. No one here should know about it, and if you hear anybody talking on these lines it will mean that they've somehow had access to classified information.

"Now about your short list of provisional suspects. I see you've got Wagnall down, but he's clear with us."

"O.K. I'll move him to List B."

"Then Brown, Lefevre, Tolanski—they've certainly had no contacts here."

"Can you be sure of that?"

"Fairly. They use their off-duty hours here in highly non-political ways."

"I'd suspected that," Sadler remarked, permitting himself the luxury of a smile. "I'll take them off altogether."

"Now this man Jenkins, in Stores. Why are you so keen on keeping him?"

"I've no real evidence at all. But he seems about the only person who's taken any objection to my nominal activities."

"Well, we'll continue to watch him from this end. He comes to town quite often, but of course he's got a good excuse—he does most of the local purchasing. That leaves you with five names on your A list, doesn't it?"

"Yes, and frankly, I'll be very surprised if it's any of them. Wheeler and Jamieson we've already discussed. I know that Maclaurin's suspicious of Jamieson after that trip out to the *Mare Imbrium,* but I don't put much reliance on that. It was largely Wheeler's idea, anyway.

"Then there are Benson and Carlin. Their wives come from Mars, and they keep getting into arguments whenever the news is being discussed. Benson's an electrician in Tech Maintenance; Carlin's a medical orderly. You could say they have some motive, but it's a pretty tenuous one. Moreover, they'd be rather too obvious suspects."

"Well, here's another we'd like you to move up to your List A. This fellow Molton."

"Dr. Molton?" exclaimed Sadler in some surprise. "Any particular reason?"

"Nothing serious, but he's been to Mars several times on astronomical missions and has some friends there."

"He never talks politics. I've tackled him once or twice and he just didn't seem interested. I don't think he meets many people in Central City—he seems completely wrapped up in his work and I think he only goes into town to keep fit in the gym. You've nothing else?"

"No—sorry. It's still a fifty-fifty case. There's a leak *somewhere,* but it may be in Central City. The report about the Observatory may be a deliberate plant. As you say, it's very hard to see how anyone there could pass on information. The radio monitors have detected nothing except a few unauthorized personal messages which were quite innocent."

Sadler closed his notebook and put it away with a sigh. He glanced once more down into the vertiginous depths above which he was so insecurely floating. The cockroaches were crawling briskly away from a spot at the base of the cliff, and suddenly a slow stain seemed to spread across the floodlit wall. (*How* far down was that? Two kilometers? Or three?) A puff of smoke emerged, and instantly dispersed into the vacuum. Sadler began to count the seconds to time his distance from the explosion, and had got to twelve before he remembered that he was wasting his efforts. If that had been an atom bomb, he would have heard nothing here.

The man in blue adjusted his camera strap, nodded at Sadler, and became the perfect tourist again.

"Give me ten minutes to get clear," he said, "and remember not to know me if we meet again."

Sadler rather resented that last advice. After all, he was not a complete amateur. He had been fully operational for almost half a lunar day.

Business was slack at the little café in the Hyginus station, and Sadler had the place to himself. The general uncertainty had discouraged tourists; any who happened to be on the Moon were hurrying home as fast as they could get shipping space. They were probably doing the right thing; if there was trouble, it would be here. No one really believed that the Federation would attack Earth directly and destroy millions of innocent lives. Such barbarities belong to the past—so it was hoped. But how could one be sure? Who knew what might happen if war broke out? Earth was so fearfully vulnerable.

For a moment Sadler lost himself in reveries of longing and self-pity. He wondered if Jeannette had guessed where he was. He was not sure, now, that he wanted her to know. It would only increase her worries.

Over his coffee—which he still ordered automatically though he had never met any on the Moon worth drinking—he considered the information his unknown contact had given to him. It had been of very little value; he was still groping in the dark. The tip about Molton was a distinct surprise, and he did not take it too seriously. There was a kind of trustworthiness about the astrophysicist which made it hard to think of him as a spy. Sadler knew perfectly well that it was fatal to rely on such hunches, and whatever his own feelings, he would now pay extra attention to Molton. But he made a private bet with himself that it would lead nowhere.

He marshaled all the facts he could remember about the head of the Spectroscopy Section. He already knew about Molton's three trips to Mars. The last visit had been over a year ago, and the director himself had been there more recently than that. Moreover, among the interplanetary brotherhood of astronomers, there was probably no member of the senior staff who did not have friends on both Mars and Venus.

Were there any unusual features about Molton? None that Sadler could think of, apart from that curious aloofness that seemed to conflict with a real inner warmth. There was, of course, his amusing and rather touching "flower-bed," as he had heard someone christen it. But if he was to start investigating innocent eccentricities like *that,* he'd never get anywhere.

There was one thing that might be worth looking into, however. He'd make a note of the shop where Molton purchased his replacements (it was almost the only place outside the gym he ever visited), and one of the counter-agents in the city could sniff around it. Feeling rather pleased with himself at thus proving he was missing no chances, Sadler paid his bill and walked up the short corridor connecting the café with the almost deserted station.

He rode the spur-line back to Central City, over the incredibly broken terrain past Triesnecker. For almost all the journey, the monorail track was accompanied by the pylons passing their loaded buckets out from Hyginus, and the empty ones back. The long cables, with their kilometer spans, were the cheapest and most practical means of conveyance—if there was no particular hurry to deliver the goods. Soon after the domes of Central City appeared on the skyline, however, they changed direction and curved off to the right. Sadler could see them marching away down to the horizon toward the great chemical plants which, directly or indirectly, fed and clothed every human being on the Moon.

He no longer felt a stranger in the city, and went from dome to dome with the assurance of a seasoned traveler. The first priority was an overdue haircut; one of the Observatory cooks earned some extra money as a barber, but having seen the results, Sadler preferred to stick to the professionals. Then there was just time to call at the gym for fifteen minutes in the centrifuge.

As usual, the place was full of Observatory staff making sure they would be able to live on Earth again when they wished to. There was a waiting list for the centrifuge, so Sadler dumped his clothes in a locker and went for a swim until the descending whine of the motor told him that the big machine was ready for a new cargo of passengers. He noticed, with wry amusement, that two of his List-A suspects—Wheeler and Molton—and no less than seven of the Class-B ones were present. But it was not so surprising about Class B. Ninety per cent of the Observatory staff were on *that* unwieldly list, which if it had been titled at all would have been called: "Persons sufficiently intelligent and active to be spies, but concerning whom there is no evidence one way or the other."

The centrifuge held six people, and had some ingenious safety device which prevented its starting unless the load was properly balanced. It refused to co-operate until a fat man on Sadler's left had changed places with a thin man opposite; then the motor began to pick up speed and the big drum with its slightly anxious human cargo started to turn on its axis. As the speed increased, Sadler felt his weight steadily mounting. The direction of the vertical was shifting, too—it was swinging round toward the center of the drum. He breathed deeply, and tried to see if he could lift his arms. They felt as if they were made of lead.

The man on Sadler's right staggered to his feet and began to walk to and fro, keeping within the carefully defined white lines that marked the limits of his territory. Everyone else was doing the same; it was uncanny to watch them standing on what, from the point of view of the Moon, was a vertical surface. But they were glued to it by a force six times as great as the Moon's feeble gravity—a force equal to the weight they would have had on Earth.

It was not a pleasant sensation. Sadler found it almost impossible to believe that until a few days ago he had spent his entire existence in a gravity field of this strength. Presumably he would get used to it again, but at the moment it made him feel as weak as a kitten. He was heartily glad when the centrifuge slowed down and he was able to crawl back into the gentle gravity of the friendly Moon.

He was a tired and somewhat discouraged man as the monorail pulled out of Central City. Even the brief glimpse he caught of the new day, as the still-hidden sun touched the highest pinnacles of the western mountains, failed to cheer him. He had been here more than twelve days of Earth time, and the long lunar night was ending. But he dreaded to think what the day might bring.

✳ **CHAPTER THIRTEEN**

Every man has his weakness, if you can find it. Jamieson's was so obvious that it seemed unfair to exploit it, but Sadler could not afford to have any scruples. Everyone in the Observatory regarded the young astronomer's painting as a subject for mild amusement, and gave him no encouragement at all. Sadler, feeling a considerable hypocrite, began to play the role of sympathetic admirer.

It had taken some time to break through Jamieson's reserve and to get him to speak frankly. The process could not be hurried without arousing suspicion, but Sadler had made fair progress by the simple technique of supporting Jamieson when his colleagues ganged up on him. This happened, on the average, every time he produced a new picture.

To steer the conversation from art to politics took less skill than might have been expected, for politics was never very far away these days. Yet oddly enough, it was Jamieson himself who raised the questions that Sadler had been trying to ask. He had obviously been thinking hard, in his methodical way, wrestling with the problem that had concerned every scientist, to a greater and greater extent, since the day when atomic power was born on Earth.

"What would you do," he asked Sadler abruptly, a few hours after the latter's return from Central City, "if you had to choose between Earth and the Federation?"

"Why ask me?" replied Sadler, trying to conceal his interest.

"I've been asking a lot of people," Jamieson replied. There was a wistfulness in his voice, the puzzled wonder of someone looking for guidance in a strange and complex world. "Do you remember that argument we had in the Common Room, when Mays said that whoever believed in 'my planet, right or wrong' was a fool?"

"I remember," Sadler answered cautiously.

"I think Mays was right. Loyalty isn't just a matter of birth, but ideals. There can be times when morality and patriotism clash."

"What's started you philosophizing on these lines?"

Jamieson's reply was unexpected.

"*Nova Draconis,*" he said. "We've just got in the reports from the Federation observatories out beyond Jupiter. They were routed through Mars, and someone there had attached a note to them—Molton showed it to me. It wasn't signed, and it was quite short. It merely said that *whatever* happened—and the word was repeated twice—they'd see that their reports continued to reach us."

A touching example of scientific solidarity, thought Sadler; it had obviously made a deep impression on Jamieson. Most men—certainly most men who were not scientists—would have thought the incident rather trivial. But trifles like this could sway men's minds at crucial moments.

"I don't know just what you deduce from this," said Sadler, feeling like a skater on very thin ice. "After all, everybody knows that the Federation has plenty of men who are just as honest and well-intentioned and co-operative as anyone here. But you can't run a solar system on gusts of emotion. Would you really hesitate if it came to a showdown between Earth and the Federation?"

There was a long pause. Then Jamieson sighed.

"I don't know," he answered. "I really don't know."

It was a completely frank and honest answer. As far as Sadler was concerned, it virtually eliminated Jamieson from his list of suspects.

The fantastic incident of the searchlight in the *Mare Imbrium* occurred nearly twenty-four hours later. Sadler heard about it when he joined Wagnall for morning coffee, as he usually did when he was near Administration.

"Here's something to make you think," said Wagnall as Sadler walked into the secretary's office. "One of the technicians from

Electronics was up in the dome just now, admiring the view, when suddenly a beam of light shot up over the horizon. It lasted for about a second, and he says it was a brilliant blue-white. There's no doubt that it came from that place that Wheeler and Jamieson visited. I know that Instrumentation has been having trouble with them, and I've just checked. Their magnetometers were kicked right off scale ten minutes ago, and there's been a severe local 'quake.' "

"I don't see how a searchlight would do that sort of thing," answered Sadler, genuinely puzzled. Then the full implications of the statement reached him.

"*A beam of light?*" he gasped. "Why, that's impossible. It wouldn't be visible in the vacuum here."

"Exactly," said Wagnall, obviously enjoying the other's mystification. "You can only see a light beam when it passes through something. And this was really brilliant—almost dazzling. The phrase Williams used was 'it looked like a solid bar.' Do you know what *I* think that place is?"

"No," replied Sadler, wondering how near Wagnall had got to the truth. "I haven't any idea."

The secretary looked rather bashful, as if trying out a theory of which he was a little ashamed.

"I think it's some kind of fortress. Oh, I know it sounds fantastic, but when you think about it, you'll see it's the only explanation that fits all the facts."

Before Sadler could reply, or indeed think of a suitable answer, the desk buzzer sounded and a slip of paper dropped out of Wagnall's teleprinter. It was a standard Signals form, but there was one non-standard item about it. It carried the crimson banner of Priority.

Wagnall read it aloud, his eyes widening as he did so.

URGENT TO DIRECTOR PLATO OBSERVATORY

DISMANTLE ALL SURFACE INSTRUMENTS AND MOVE ALL DELI-
CATE EQUIPMENT UNDERGROUND COMMENCING WITH LARGE
MIRRORS. RAIL SERVICE SUSPENDED UNTIL FURTHER NOTICE.
KEEP STAFF UNDERGROUND AS FAR AS POSSIBLE. EMPHASIZE
THIS PRECAUTIONARY REPEAT PRECAUTIONARY MEASURE. NO
IMMEDIATE DANGER EXPECTED.

"And that," said Wagnall slowly, "appears to be that. I'm very much afraid my guess was perfectly correct."

It was the first time that Sadler had ever seen the entire Observatory staff gathered together. Professor Maclaurin stood on the raised dais at the end of the main lounge—the traditional place for announcements, musical recitals, dramatic interludes and other forms of Observatory entertainment. But no one was being entertained now.

"I fully understand," said Maclaurin bitterly, "what this means to your programs. We can only hope that this move is totally unnecessary, and that we can start work again within a few days. But obviously we can take no chances with our equipment—the five-hundred and the thousand-centimeter mirrors must be got under cover at once. I have no idea what form of trouble is anticipated, but it seems we are in an unfortunate position here. If hostilities do break out, I shall signal at once to both Mars and Venus reminding them that this is a scientific institution, that many of their nationals have been honored guests here, and that we are of no conceivable military importance. Now please assemble behind your group leaders, and carry out your instructions as swiftly and efficiently as possible."

The director walked down from the dais. Small though he was, he seemed still more shrunken now. In that moment, there was no one in the room who did not share his feelings, however much they might have inveighed against him in the past.

"Is there anything I can do?" asked Sadler, who had been left out of the hastily drawn-up emergency plans.

"Ever worn a spacesuit?" said Wagnall.

"No, but I don't mind trying."

To Sadler's disappointment, the secretary shook his head firmly.

"Too dangerous—you might get in trouble and there aren't enough suits to go around, anyway. But I could do with some more help in the office—we've had to tear up all the existing programs and go over to a two-watch system. So all the rotas and schedules have to be rearranged—you could help on this."

That's what comes of volunteering for anything, thought Sadler. But Wagnall was right; there was nothing he could do to help the technical teams. As for his own mission, he could probably serve it better in the secretary's office than anywhere else, for it would be the operational headquarters from now on.

Not, thought Sadler grimly, that it now mattered a great deal. If Mr. X had ever existed, and was still in the Observatory, he could now relax with the consciousness of a job well done.

Some instruments, it had been decided, would have to take their chance. These were the smaller ones, which could be easily replaced. Operation Safeguard, as someone with a penchant for military nomenclature had christened it, was to concentrate on the priceless optical components of the giant telescopes and coelostats.

Jamieson and Wheeler drove out with Ferdinand and collected the mirrors of the interferometer, the great instrument whose twin eyes, twenty kilometers apart, made it possible to measure the diameters of the stars. The main activity, however, centered round the thousand-centimeter reflector.

Molton was in charge of the mirror team. The work would have been impossible without his detailed knowledge of the telescope's optical and engineering features. It would have been impossible, even with his help, if the mirror had been cast in a single unit, like that of the historic instrument that still stood atop Mount Palomar. This mirror, however, was built from more than a hundred hexagonal sections, dovetailed together into a great mosaic. Each could be removed separately and carried to safety, though it was slow and tedious work and it would take weeks to reassemble the complete mirror with the fantastic precision needed.

Spacesuits are not really designed for this sort of work, and one helper, through inexperience or haste, managed to drop his end of a mirror section as he lifted it out of the cell. Before anyone could catch it, the big hexagon of fused quartz had picked up enough speed to chip off one of its corners. This was the only optical casualty, which in the circumstances was very creditable.

The last tired and disheartened men came in through the airlocks twelve hours after the operation had commenced. Only one research project continued—a single telescope was still following the slow decline of *Nova Draconis* as it sank toward final extinction. War or no war, this work would go on.

Soon after the announcement that the two big mirrors were safe, Sadler went up to one of the observation domes. He did not know when he would have another chance to see the stars and the waning Earth, and he wished to carry the memory down into his subterranean retreat.

As far as the eye could tell, the Observatory was quite unchanged. The great barrel of the thousand-centimeter reflector pointed straight to the zenith; it had been swung over to the vertical to bring the mirror cell down to ground level. Nothing short of a direct hit could damage this massive structure, and it would have to take its chances in the hours or days of danger that lay ahead.

There were still a few men moving around in the open; one of them, Sadler noticed, was the director. He was perhaps the only man on the Moon who could be recognized when wearing a spacesuit. It had been specially built for him, and brought his height up to a full meter and a half.

One of the open trucks used for moving equipment around the Observatory was scuttling across toward the telescope, throwing up little gouts of dust. It halted beside the great circular track on which the framework revolved, and the spacesuited figures clambered clumsily aboard. Then it made off briskly to the right, and disappeared into the ground as it descended the ramp leading into the airlocks of the garage.

The great plain was deserted, the Observatory blind save for the one faithful instrument pointing toward the north in sublime defiance of the follies of man. Then the speaker of the ubiquitous public-address system ordered Sadler out of the dome, and he went reluctantly into the depths. He wished he could have waited a little longer, for in a few more minutes the western walls of Plato would be touched by the first fingers of the lunar dawn. It seemed a pity that no one would be there to greet it.

Slowly the Moon was turning toward the sun, as it could never turn toward the Earth. The line of day was crawling across the mountains and plains, banishing the unimaginable cold of the long night. Already the entire westward wall of the Apennines was ablaze, and the *Mare Imbrium* was climbing into the dawn. But Plato still lay in darkness, lit only by the radiance of the waning Earth.

A group of scattered stars suddenly appeared low down in the western sky. The tallest spires of the great ring-wall were catching the sun, and minute by minute the light spread down their flanks, until it linked them together in a necklace of fire. Now the sun was striking clear across the whole vast circle of the crater, as the ramparts on the east lifted into the dawn. Any watchers down on Earth would see Plato as an unbroken ring of light, surrounding a pool of inky shadow. It would be hours yet before the rising sun could clear the mountains and subdue the last strongholds of the night.

There were no eyes to watch when, for the second time, that blue-white bar stabbed briefly at the southern sky. That was well for Earth. The Federation had learned much, but there were still some things which it might discover too late.

✳ CHAPTER FOURTEEN

The Observatory had settled down for a siege of indefinite duration. It was not, on the whole, as frustrating an experience as might have been expected. Although the main programs had been interrupted, there was endless work to do in reducing results, checking theories, and writing papers, which until now had been put aside for lack of time. Many of the astronomers almost welcomed the break, and several fundamental advances in cosmology were a direct outcome of this enforced idleness.

The worst aspect of the whole affair, everyone agreed, was the uncertainty and lack of news. What was really going on? Could one believe the bulletins from Earth, which seemed to be trying to soothe the public while at the same time preparing it for the worst?

As far as could be observed, some kind of attack was expected, and it was just the Observatory's bad luck that it was so near a possible danger point. Perhaps Earth guessed what form the attack would take, and certainly it had made some preparations to meet it.

The two great antagonists were circling each other, each unwilling to strike the first blow, each hoping to bluff the other into capitulation. But they had gone too far, and neither could retreat without a loss of prestige too damaging to be faced.

Sadler feared that the point of no return had already been passed. He was sure of it when the news came over the radio that the Federation Minister at the Hague had delivered a virtual ultimatum to the government of Earth. It charged Earth with failing to meet its agreed quotas of heavy metals, of deliberately withholding supplies for political purposes, and of concealing the existence of new resources. Unless Earth agreed to discuss the allocation of these new resources, she would find it impossible to use them herself.

The ultimatum was followed, six hours later, by a general broadcast to Earth, beamed from Mars by a transmitter of astonishing power. It assured the people of Earth that no harm would befall them, and that if any damage was done to the home planet it would be an unfortunate accident of war, for which their own government must take the blame. The Federation would avoid any acts which might endanger populated areas, and it trusted that its example would be followed.

The Observatory listened to this broadcast with mixed feelings. There was no doubt as to its meaning, and no doubt that the *Mare Imbrium* was, within the meaning of the Act, an unpopulated area. One effect of the broadcast was to increase sympathy for the Federation, even among those likely to be damaged by its actions. Jamieson in particular began to be much less diffident in expressing his views, and had soon made himself quite unpopular. Before long, indeed, a distinct rift appeared in the Observatory ranks. On the one side were those (mostly the younger men) who felt much as Jamieson did, and regarded Earth as reactionary and intolerant. Against them, on the other hand, were the steady, conservative individuals who would always automatically support those in authority without worrying too much about moral abstractions.

Sadler watched these arguments with great interest, even though he was conscious that the success or failure of his mission had already been decided and that nothing he could do now would alter that. However, there was always the chance that the probably mythical Mr. X might now become careless, or might even attempt to leave the Observatory. Sadler had taken certain steps to guard against this, with the co-operation of the director. No one could get at the spacesuits or tractors without authority, and the base was therefore effectively sealed. Living in a vacuum did have certain advantages from the Security point of view.

The Observatory's state of siege had brought Sadler one tiny triumph, which he could very well have forgone and which seemed an ironic commentary on all his efforts. Jenkins, his suspect from the Stores Section, had been arrested in Central City. When the monorail service had been suspended, he had been in town on very unofficial business, and had been picked up by the agents who had been watching him as a result of Sadler's hunch.

He had been scared of Sadler, and with good reason. But he had never betrayed any state secrets, for he had never possessed any. Like a good many storekeepers before him, he had been busy selling government property.

It was poetic justice. Jenkins' own guilty conscience had caught him. But though Sadler had eliminated one name from his list, the victory gave him very little satisfaction indeed.

The hours dragged on, with tempers getting more and more frayed. Overhead, the sun was now climbing up the morning sky and had now lifted well above the western wall of Plato. The initial sense of emergency had worn off, leaving only a feeling of frustration. One misguided effort was made to organize a concert, but it failed so completely that it left everyone more depressed than before.

Since nothing seemed to be happening, people began to creep up to the surface again, if only to have a look at the sky and to reassure themselves that all was still well. Some of these clandestine excursions caused Sadler much anxiety, but he was able to convince himself that they were quite innocent. Eventually the director recognized the position, by permitting a limited number of people to go up to the observation domes at set hours of the day.

One of the engineers from Power organized a sweepstake, the prizewinner to be the person who guessed how long this peculiar siege was going to last. Everybody in the Observatory contributed, and Sadler—acting on a very long shot—read the lists thoughtfully when they were complete. If there was anyone here who happened to know what the right answer might be, he would take care to avoid winning. That, at least, was the theory. Sadler learned nothing from his study, and finished it wondering just how tortuous his mental processes were becoming. There were times when he feared that he would never be able to think in a straightforward fashion again.

The waiting ended just five days after the Alert. Up on the surface, it was approaching noon, and the Earth had waned to a thin crescent too close to the sun to be looked at with safety. But it was midnight by the Observatory clocks, and Sadler was sleeping when Wagnall unceremoniously entered his room.

"Wake up!" he said, as Sadler rubbed the sleep from his eyes. "The director wants to see you!" Wagnall seemed annoyed at being used as a messenger boy. "There's something going on," he complained, looking at Sadler suspiciously. "He won't even tell *me* what it's all about!"

"I'm not sure that I know either," Sadler replied as he climbed into his dressing gown. He was telling the truth, and on the way to the director's office speculated sleepily on all the things that could possibly have happened.

Professor Maclaurin, thought Sadler, had aged a good deal in the last few days. He was no longer the brisk, forceful little man he had been, ruling the Observatory with a rod of iron. There was even a disorderly pile of documents at the side of his once-unsullied desk.

As soon as Wagnall, with obvious reluctance, had left the room, Maclaurin said abruptly:

"What's Carl Steffanson doing on the Moon?"

Sadler blinked uncertainly—he was still not fully awake—and then answered lamely:

"I don't even know who he is. Should I?"

Maclaurin seemed surprised and disappointed.

"I thought your people might have told you he was coming. He's one of the most brilliant physicists we have, in his own specialized field. Central City's just called to say that he's landed —and we've got to get him out to *Mare Imbrium* just as soon as we can, to this place they call Project Thor."

"Why can't he fly there? How do we come into the picture?"

"He was supposed to go by rocket, but the transport's out of action and won't be serviceable for at least six hours. So they're sending him down by monorail, and we're taking him on the last lap by tractor. I've been asked to detail Jamieson for the job. Everyone knows that he's the best tractor driver on the Moon—and he's the only one who's ever been out to Project Thor, whatever *that* is."

"Go on," said Sadler, half suspecting what was coming next.

"I don't trust Jamieson. I don't think it's safe to send him on a mission as important as this one appears to be."

"Is there anyone else who could do it?"

"Not in the time available. It's a very skilled job, and you've no idea how easy it is to lose your way."

"So it has to be Jamieson, it seems. Why do you feel he's a risk?"

"I've listened to him talking in the Common Room. Surely *you've* heard him, too! He's made no secret of his sympathies with the Federation."

Sadler was watching Maclaurin intently while the director was speaking. The indignation—almost the anger—in the little man's voice surprised him. For a moment it raised a fleeting suspicion in his mind: was Maclaurin trying to divert attention from himself?

The vague mistrust lasted only for an instant. There was no need, Sadler realized, to search for deeper motives. Maclaurin was tired and overworked: as Sadler had always suspected, for all his external toughness he was a small man in spirit as well as in stature. He was reacting childishly to his frustration: he had seen his plans disorganized, his whole program brought to a halt—even his precious equipment imperiled. It was all the fault of the Federation, and anyone who did not agree was a potential enemy of Earth.

It was hard not to feel some sympathy for the director; Sadler suspected that he was on the verge of a nervous breakdown, and would have to be handled with extreme care.

"What do you want me to do about it?" he asked in as non-committal a tone of voice as he could manage.

"I'd like to know if you agree with me about Jamieson. You must have studied him carefully."

"I'm not allowed to discuss my evaluations," Sadler replied. "They're too often based on hearsay and hunches. But I feel that Jamieson's very frankness is a point in his favor. There is a great difference, you know, between dissent and treason."

Maclaurin was silent for a while. Then he shook his head angrily.

"It's too great a risk. I'll not accept the responsibility."

This, thought Sadler, was going to be difficult. He had no authority here, and certainly could not override the director. No one had sent him any instructions; the people who had routed Steffanson through the Observatory probably did not even know that he existed. Liaison between Defense and Central Intelligence was not all that it should be.

But even without instructions, his duty was clear. If Defense wanted to get someone out to Project Thor as urgently as this, they had a very good reason. He must help even if he had to step outside his role of passive observer.

"This is what I suggest, sir," he said briskly. "Interview Jamieson and outline the position to him. Ask him if he'll volunteer for the job. I'll monitor the conversation from the next room and advise you if it's safe to accept. My belief is that if he says he'll do it, he will. Otherwise he'll turn you down flat. I don't think he'll double-cross you."

"You'll go on record over this?"

"Yes," said Sadler, impatiently. "And if I may give some advice, do your best to hide your suspicions. Whatever your own feelings are, be as friendly and open as you can."

Maclaurin thought it over for a while, then shrugged his shoulders in resignation. He flicked the microphone switch.

"Wagnall," he said, "fetch Jamieson here."

To Sadler, waiting in the next room, it seemed hours before anything happened. Then the loudspeaker brought the sound of Jamieson's arrival, and immediately he heard Maclaurin say:

"Sorry to break into your sleep, Jamieson, but we've an urgent job for you. How long would it take you to drive a tractor to Prospect Pass?"

Sadler smiled at the clearly heard gasp of incredulity. He knew exactly what Jamieson was thinking. Prospect was the pass through the southern wall of Plato, overlooking the *Mare Imbrium*. It was avoided by the tractors, which took an easier but more roundabout route a few kilometers to the west. The monocabs, however, went through it without difficulty, and when the lighting was correct gave their passengers one of the most famous views on the Moon—the great sweep down into the *Mare* with the far-off fang of Pico on the skyline.

"If I pushed things, I could do it in an hour. It's only forty kilometers, but very rough going."

"Good," said Maclaurin's voice. "I've just had a message from Central City, asking me to send you out. They know you're our best driver, and you've been there before."

"Been where?" said Jamieson.

"Project Thor. You won't have heard the name, but that's what it's called. The place you drove out to the other night."

"Go on, sir. I'm listening," Jamieson replied. To Sadler, the tension in his voice was obvious.

"This is the position. There's a man in Central City who has to reach Thor immediately. He was supposed to go by rocket, but that's not possible. So they're sending him down here on the monorail, and to save time you'll meet the car out in the pass and take him off. Then you'll drive straight across country to Project Thor. Understand?"

"Not quite. Why can't Thor collect him in one of their own Cats?"

Was Jamieson hedging? wondered Sadler. No, he decided. It was a perfectly reasonable question.

"If you look at the map," said Maclaurin, "you'll see that Prospect is the only convenient place for a tractor to meet the monorail. Moreover, there aren't any really skilled drivers at Thor, it seems. They're sending out a tractor, but you'll probably have finished the job before they can reach Prospect."

There was a long pause. Jamieson was obviously studying the map.

"I'm willing to try it," said Jamieson. "But I'd like to know what it's all about."

Here we go, thought Sadler. I hope Maclaurin does what I told him.

"Very well," Maclaurin replied. "You've a right to know, I suppose. The man who's going to Thor is Dr. Carl Steffanson. And the mission he's engaged on is vital to the security of Earth. That's all I know, but I don't think I need say any more."

Sadler waited, hunched over his speaker, as the long silence dragged on. He knew the decision Jamieson must be making. The young astronomer was discovering that it was one thing to criticize Earth and to condemn her policy when the matter was of no practical importance—and quite another to choose a line of action that might help to bring about her defeat. Sadler had read somewhere that there were plenty of pacifists before the outbreak of war, but few after it had actually started. Jamieson was learning now where his loyalty, if not his logic, lay.

"I'll go," he said at last, so quietly that Sadler could scarcely hear him.

"Remember," insisted Maclaurin, "you have a free choice."

"Have I?" said Jamieson. There was no sarcasm in his voice. He was thinking aloud, talking to himself rather than to the director.

Sadler heard Maclaurin shuffling his papers. "What about your co-driver?" he asked.

"I'll take Wheeler. He went out with me last time."

"Very well. You go and fetch him, and I'll get in touch with Transport. And—good luck."

"Thank you, sir."

Sadler waited until he heard the door of Maclaurin's office close behind Jamieson; then he joined the director. Maclaurin looked up at him wearily and said:

"Well?"

"It went off better than I'd feared. I thought you handled it very well."

This was not mere flattery; Sadler was surprised at the way in which Maclaurin had concealed his feelings. Though the interview had not been exactly cordial, there had been no overt unfriendliness.

"I feel much happier," said Maclaurin, "because Wheeler's going with him. He can be trusted."

Despite his worry, Sadler had difficulty in suppressing a smile. He was quite sure that the director's faith in Conrad Wheeler was based largely on that young man's discovery of *Nova Draconis* and his vindication of the Maclaurin Magnitude Integrator. But he needed no further proofs that scientists were just as inclined as anyone else to let their emotions sway their logic.

The desk speaker called for attention.

"The tractor's just leaving, sir. Outer doors opening now."

Maclaurin looked automatically at the wall clock. "That was quick," he said. Then he gazed somberly at Sadler.

"Well, Mr. Sadler, it's too late to do anything about it now. I only hope you're right."

It is seldom realized that driving on the Moon by day is far less pleasant, and even less safe, than driving by night. The merciless glare demands the use of heavy sun filters, and the pools of inky shadow which are always present except on those rare occasions when the sun is vertically overhead can be very dangerous. Often they conceal crevasses which a speeding tractor may be unable to avoid. Driving by Earthlight, on the other hand, involves no such strain. The light is so much softer, the contrasts less extreme.

To make matters worse for Jamieson, he was driving due south —almost directly into the sun. There were times when conditions were so bad that he had to zigzag wildly to avoid the glare from patches of exposed rock ahead. It was not so difficult when they were traveling over dusty regions, but these became fewer and fewer as the ground rose toward the inner ramparts of the mountain wall.

Wheeler knew better than to talk to his friend on this part of the route: Jamieson's task required too much concentration. Presently they were climbing up toward the pass, weaving back and forth along the rugged slopes overlooking the plain. Like fragile tops on the far horizon, the gantries of the great telescopes marked the location of the Observatory. There, thought Wheeler bitterly, was invested millions of man-hours of skill and labor. Now it was doing nothing, and the best that could be hoped was that one day those splendid instruments could once more begin their search into the far places of the universe.

A ridge cut off their view of the plain below, and Jamieson swung round to the right through a narrow valley. Far up the slopes above them, the track of the monorail was now visible, as it came in great, striding leaps down the face of the mountain. There was no way in which a Caterpillar could get up to it, but when they were through the pass they would have no difficulty in driving to within a few meters of the track.

The ground was extremely broken and treacherous here, but drivers who had gone this way before had left markers for the guidance of any who might come after them. Jamieson was using his headlights a good deal now, as he was often working through shadow. On the whole he preferred this to direct sunlight, for he could see the ground ahead much more easily with the steerable beams from the projectors on top of the cab. Wheeler soon took over their operation, and found it fascinating to watch the ovals of light skittering across the rocks. The complete invisibility of the beams themselves, here in the almost perfect vacuum, gave a magical effect to the scene. The light seemed to be coming from nowhere, and to have no connection at all with the tractor.

They reached Prospect fifty minutes after leaving the Observatory, and radioed back their position. From now on, it was only a few kilometers downhill until they came to the rendezvous. The monorail track converged toward their path, then swept on to the south past Pico, a silver thread shrinking out of sight across the face of the Moon.

"Well," said Wheeler with satisfaction, "we haven't kept them waiting. I wish I knew what all this is about."

"Isn't it obvious?" Jamieson answered. "Steffanson's the greatest expert on radiation physics we have. If there's going to be war, surely you realize the sort of weapons that will be used."

"I hadn't thought much about it—it never seemed something to take seriously. Guided missiles, I suppose."

"Very likely, but we should be able to do better than that. Men have been talking about radiation weapons for centuries. If they wanted them, they could make them now."

"Don't say you believe in death-rays!"

"And why not? If you remember your history books, death-rays killed some thousands of people at Hiroshima. And that was a couple of hundred years ago."

"Yes, but it's not difficult to shield against that sort of thing. Can you imagine doing any real *physical* damage with a ray?"

"It would depend on the range. If it was only a few kilometers, I'd say yes. After all, we can generate unlimited amounts of power. By this time we should be able to squirt it all in the same direction if we wanted to. Until today there's been no particular incentive. But now—how do we know what's been going on in secret labs all over the solar system?"

Before Wheeler could reply, he saw the glittering point of light far out across the plain. It was moving toward them with incredible speed, coming up over the horizon like a meteor. Within minutes, it had resolved itself into the blunt-nosed cylinder of the monocab, crouched low over its single track.

"I think I'd better go out and give him a hand," said Jamieson. "He's probably never worn a spacesuit before. He'll certainly have some luggage, too."

Wheeler sat up in the driving position and watched his friend clamber across the rocks to the monorail. The door of the vehicle's emergency airlock opened, and a man stepped out, somewhat unsteadily, onto the Moon. By the way he moved, Wheeler could tell at a glance that he had never been in low gravity before.

Steffanson was carrying a thick briefcase and a large wooden box, which he handled with the utmost care. Jamieson offered to relieve him of these hindrances, but he refused to part with them. His only other baggage was a small traveling-case, which he allowed Jamieson to carry.

The two figures scrambled back down the rocky ramp and Wheeler operated the airlock to let them in. The monocab, having delivered its burden, pulled back into the south and swiftly disappeared the way it had come. It seemed, thought Wheeler, that the driver was in a great hurry to get home. He had never seen one of the cars travel so fast, and for the first time he began to have some faint surmise of the storm that was gathering above this peaceful, sun-drenched landscape. He suspected that they were not the only ones making a rendezvous at Project Thor.

He was right. Far out in space, high above the plane in which Earth and planets swim, the commander of the Federal forces was marshaling his tiny fleet. As a hawk circles above its prey in the moments before its plummeting descent, so Commodore Brennan, lately Professor of Electrical Engineering at the University of Hesperus, held his ships poised above the Moon.

He was waiting for the signal which he still hoped would never come.

✳   *CHAPTER FIFTEEN*

Doctor Carl Steffanson did not stop to wonder if he was a brave man. Never before in his life had he known the need for so primitive a virtue as physical courage, and he was agreeably surprised at his calmness now that the crisis had almost come. In a few hours, he would probably be dead. The thought gave him more annoyance than fear; there was so much work he wanted to do, so many theories to be tested. It would be wonderful to get back to scientific research again, after the rat-race of the last two years. But that was day-dreaming; mere survival was as much as he could hope for now.

He opened his briefcase and pulled out the sheafs of wiring diagrams and component schedules. With some amusement, he noticed that Wheeler was staring with frank curiosity at the complex circuits and the SECRET labels plastered over them. Well, there was little need for security now, and Steffanson himself could not have made much sense of these circuits had he not invented them himself.

He glanced again at the packing case to make sure that it was securely lashed down. There, in all probability, lay the future of more worlds than one. How many other men had ever been sent on a mission like this? Steffanson could think of but two examples, both back in the days of the Second World War. There had been a British scientist who had carried a small box across the Atlantic, containing what was later called the most valuable consignment ever to reach the shores of the United States. That had been the first cavity magnetron, the invention which made radar the key weapon of war and destroyed the power of Hitler. Then, a few years later, there had been a plane flying across the Pacific to the island of Tinian, carrying almost all the free uranium 235 then in existence. . . .

But neither of those missions, for all their importance, had the urgency of this.

Steffanson had exchanged only a few words of formal greeting with Jamieson and Wheeler, expressing his thanks at their co-operation. He knew nothing about them, except that they were astronomers from the Observatory who had volunteered to undertake this trip. Since they were scientists, they would certainly be curious to know what he was doing here, and he was not surprised when Jamieson handed over the controls to his colleague and stepped down from the driving position.

"It won't be so rough from now on," said Jamieson. "We'll get to this Thor place in about twenty minutes. Is that good enough for you?"

Steffanson nodded.

"That's better than we'd hoped, when that damn ship broke down. You'll probably get a special medal for this."

"I'm not interested," said Jamieson rather coldly. "All I want to do is what's right. Are you quite certain that you're doing the same?"

Steffanson looked at him in surprise, but it took him only an instant to sum up the situation. He had met Jamieson's type before among the younger men of his own staff. These idealists all went through the same mental heart-searchings. And they would all grow out of it when they were older. He sometimes wondered if that was a tragedy or a blessing.

"You are asking me," he said quietly, "to predict the future. No man can ever tell if, in the long run, his acts will lead to good or evil. But I am working for the defense of Earth, and if there is an attack it will come from the Federation, not from us. I think you should bear that in mind."

"Yet haven't we provoked it?"

"Perhaps so, but again there is much to be said on both sides. You think of the Federals as starry-eyed pioneers, building wonderful new civilizations out there on the planets. You forget that they can be tough and unscrupulous, too. If they get what they want, they'll be intolerable. I'm afraid they've asked for a lesson, and we hope to give it to them. It's a pity it's come to this, but I see no alternative."

He glanced at his watch, saw that it was nearly at the hour, and continued: "Do you mind switching on the news? I'd like to hear the latest developments."

Jamieson tuned in the set, and rotated the antenna system toward Earth. There was a fair amount of noise from the solar background, for Earth was now almost in line with the sun, but the sheer power of the station made the message perfectly intelligible and there was no trace of fading.

Steffanson was surprised to see that the tractor chronograph was over a second fast. Then he realized that it was set for that oddly christened hybrid, Lunar Greenwich Time. The signal he was listening to had just bridged the four-hundred-thousand-kilometer gulf from Earth. It was a chilling reminder of his remoteness from home.

Then there was a delay so long that Jamieson turned up the volume to check that the set was still operating. After a full minute, the announcer spoke, his voice striving desperately to be as impersonal as ever.

"This is Earth calling. The following statement has been issued from the Hague:

"The Triplanetary Federation has informed the government of Earth that it intends to seize certain portions of the Moon, and that any attempt to resist this action will be countered by force.

"This government is taking all necessary steps to preserve the integrity of the Moon. A further announcement will be issued as soon as possible. For the present it is emphasized that there is no immediate danger, as there are no hostile ships within twenty hours of Earth.

"This is Earth. Stand by."

A sudden silence fell; only the hiss of the carrier-wave and the occasional crackle of solar static still issued from the speaker. Wheeler had brought the tractor to a halt so that he could hear the announcement. From his driving seat, he looked down at the little tableau in the cabin beneath him. Steffanson was staring at the circuit diagrams spread over the map table, but was obviously not seeing them. Jamieson still stood with his hand on the volume control; he had not moved since the beginning of the announcement. Then, without a word, he climbed up into the driving cab, and took over from Wheeler.

To Steffanson, it seemed ages before Wheeler called to him: "We're nearly there! Look—dead ahead." He went to the forward observation port, and stared across the cracked and broken ground. What a place to fight for, he thought. But, of course, this barren wilderness of lava and meteor dust was only a disguise. Beneath it

Nature had hidden treasures which men had taken two hundred years to find. Perhaps it would have been better had they never found them at all. . . .

Still two or three kilometers ahead, the great metal dome was glinting in the sunlight. From this angle, it had an astonishing appearance, for the segment in shadow was so dark as to be almost invisible. At first sight, indeed, it looked as if the dome had been bisected by some enormous knife. The whole place looked utterly deserted, but within, Steffanson knew, it would be a hive of furious activity. He prayed that his assistants had completed the wiring of the power and sub-modulator circuits.

Steffanson began to adjust the helmet of his spacesuit, which he had not bothered to take off after entering the tractor. He stood behind Jamieson, holding on to one of the storage racks to steady himself.

"Now that we're here," he said, "the least I can do is to let you understand what's happened." He gestured toward the rapidly approaching dome. "This place started as a mine, and it still is. We've achieved something that's never been done before—drilled a hole a hundred kilometers deep, right through the Moon's crust and down into really rich deposits of metal."

"A hundred kilometers!" cried Wheeler. "That's impossible! No hole could stay open under the pressure."

"It can and does," retorted Steffanson. "I've not time to discuss the technique, even if I knew much about it. But remember you can drill a hole six times as deep on the Moon as you can on Earth, before it caves in. However, that's only part of the story. The real secret lies in what they've called pressure-mining. As fast as it's sunk, the well is filled with a heavy silicone oil, the same density as the rocks around it. So no matter how far down you go, the pressure is the same inside as out, and there's no tendency for the hole to close. Like most simple ideas, it's taken a lot of skill to put it into practice. All the operating equipment has to work submerged, under enormous pressure, but the problems are being overcome and we believe we can get metals out in worthwhile quantities.

"The Federation learned this was going on about two years ago. We believe they've tried the same thing, but without any luck. So they're determined that if they can't share this hoard, we won't have it either. Their policy seems to be one of bullying us into co-operation, and it's not going to work.

"That's the background, but now it's only the less important part of the story. There are weapons here as well. Some have been completed and tested, others are waiting for the final adjustments. I'm bringing the key components for what may be the decisive one. That's why Earth may owe you a greater debt than it can ever pay. Don't interrupt—we're nearly there and this is what I really want to tell you. The radio was not telling the truth about that twenty hours of safety. That's what the Federation wants us to believe, and we hope they go on thinking we've been fooled. But we've spotted their ships, and they're approaching ten times as fast as anything that's ever moved through space before. I'm afraid they've got a fundamental new method of propulsion—I only hope it hasn't given them new weapons as well. We've not much more than three hours before they get here, assuming they don't step up their speed still further. You could stay, but for your own safety I advise you to turn around and drive like hell back to the Observatory. If anything starts to happen while you're still out in the open, get under cover as quickly as possible. Go down into a crevasse—anywhere you can find shelter—and stay there until it's all over. Now good-by and good luck. I hope we have a chance of meeting again, when this business is finished."

Still clutching his mysterious packing case, Steffanson disappeared into the airlock before either of the men could speak. They were now entering the shadows of the great dome, and Jamieson circled it looking for an opening. Presently he recognized the spot through which he and Wheeler had made their entrance, and brought Ferdinand to a halt.

The outer door of the tractor slammed shut and the "Airlock Clear" indicator flashed on. They saw Steffanson running across toward the dome, and with perfect timing a circular port flipped open to let him in, then snapped shut behind him.

The tractor was alone in the building's enormous shadow. Nowhere else was there any sign of life, but suddenly the metal framework of the machine began to vibrate at a steadily rising frequency. The meters on the control panel wavered madly, the lights dimmed, and then it was all over. Everything was normal again, but some tremendous field of force had swept out from the dome and was even now expanding into space. It left the two men with an over-whelming impression of energies awaiting the signal for their release. They began to understand the urgency of Steffanson's warn-ing. The whole deserted landscape seemed tense with expectation.

Across the steeply curving plain, the tiny beetle of the tractor raced for the safety of the distant hills. But could they be sure of safety even there? Jamieson doubted it. He remembered the weap-ons that science had made more than two centuries ago; they would be merely the foundation upon which the arts of war could build today. The silent land around him, now burning beneath the noon-day sun, might soon be blasted by radiations fiercer still.

He drove forward into the shadow of the tractor, toward the ramparts of Plato, towering along the skyline like some fortress of the giants. But the real fortress was behind him, preparing its un-known weapons for the ordeal that must come.

✶ CHAPTER SIXTEEN

It would never have happened had Jamieson been thinking more of driving and less of politics—though, in the circum-stances, he could hardly be blamed. The ground ahead looked level and firm—exactly the same as the kilometers they had already safely traversed.

It was level, but it was no firmer than water. Jamieson knew what had happened the moment that Ferdinand's engine started to race, and the tractor's nose disappeared in a great cloud of dust. The whole vehicle tilted forward, began to rock madly to and fro, and then lost speed despite all that Jamieson could do. Like a ship foundering in a heavy sea, it started to sink. To Wheeler's horrified eyes, they seemed to be going under in swirling clouds of spray. Within seconds, the sunlight around them had vanished. Jamieson had stopped the motor; in a silence broken only by the murmur of the air circulators, they were sinking below the surface of the Moon.

The cabin lights came on as Jamieson found the switch. For a moment, both men were too stunned to do anything but sit and stare helplessly at each other. Then Wheeler walked, not very steadily, to the nearest observation window. He could see absolutely nothing: no night was ever as dark as this. A smooth velvet curtain might have been brushing the other side of the thick quartz, for all the light that could penetrate it.

Suddenly, with a gentle but distinct bump, Ferdinand reached the bottom.

"Thank God for that," breathed Jamieson. "It's not very deep."

"What good does that do us?" asked Wheeler, hardly daring to believe there was any hope. He had heard too many horrifying tales of these treacherous dust bowls, and the men and tractors they had engulfed.

The lunar dust bowls are, fortunately, less common than might be imagined from some travelers' tales, for they can occur only under rather special conditions, which even now are not fully understood. To make one, it is necessary to start with a shallow crater pit in the right kind of rock, and then wait a few hundred million years while the temperature changes between night and day slowly pulverize the surface layers. As this agelong process continues, so a finer and finer grade of dust is produced, until at last it begins to flow like a liquid and accumulates at the bottom of the crater. In almost all respects, indeed, it *is* a liquid: it is so incredibly fine that if collected in a bucket, it will slop around like a rather mobile oil. At night one can watch convection currents circulating in it, as the upper layers cool and descend, and the warmer dust at the bottom rises to the top. This effect makes dust bowls easy to locate, since infrared detectors can "see" their abnormal heat radiation at distances of several kilometers. However, during the daytime this method is useless owing to the masking effect of the sun.

"There's no need to get alarmed," said Jamieson, though he looked none too happy. "I think we can get out of this. It must be a very small bowl, or it would have been spotted before. This area's supposed to have been thoroughly marked."

"It's big enough to have swallowed us."

"Yes, but don't forget what this stuff's like. As long as we can keep the motors running, we have a chance of pushing our way out —like a submarine-tank making its way up on to shore. The thing that bothers me is whether we should go ahead, or try and back out."

"If we go ahead, we might get in deeper."

"Not necessarily. As I said, it must be a pretty small bowl and our momentum may have carried us more than halfway across it. Which way would you say the floor is tilted now?"

"The front seems to be a bit higher than the rear."

"That's what I thought. I'm going ahead—we can get more power that way, too."

Very gently, Jamieson engaged the clutch in the lowest possible gear. The tractor shook and protested, then lurched forward a few centimeters, then halted again.

"I was afraid of that," said Jamieson. "I can't keep up a steady progress. We'll have to go in jerks. Pray for the engine—not to mention the transmission."

They jolted their way forward in agonizingly slow surges, then Jamieson cut the engine completely.

"Why did you do that?" Wheeler asked anxiously. "We seemed to be getting somewhere."

"Yes, but we're also getting too hot. This dust is an almost perfect heat insulator. We'll have to wait a minute until we cool off."

Neither felt like making any conversation as they sat in the brightly lit cabin that might well, Wheeler reflected, become their tomb. It was ironic that they had encountered this mishap while they were racing for safety.

"Do you hear that noise?" said Jamieson suddenly. He switched off the air-circulator, so that complete silence fell inside the cab.

There was the faintest of sounds coming through the walls. It was a sort of whispering rustle, and Wheeler could not imagine what it was.

"The dust's starting to rise. It's highly unstable, you know, and even a small amount of heat is enough to start convection currents. I expect we're making quite a little geyser up at the top—it will help anyone to find us if they come and look."

That was some consolation, at any rate. They had air and food for many days—all tractors carried a large emergency reserve—and the Observatory knew their approximate position. But before long the Observatory might have trouble of its own, and would be unable to bother about them. . . .

Jamieson re-started the motor, and the sturdy vehicle started to butt its way forward again through the dry quicksand that enveloped them. It was impossible to tell how much progress they were making, and Wheeler dared not imagine what would happen if the motors failed. The caterpillar treads were grinding at the rock beneath them, and the whole tractor shook and groaned under the intolerable load.

It was almost an hour before they were certain they were getting somewhere. The floor of the tractor was definitely tilting upward, but there was no way of telling how far below the quasi-liquid surface they were still submerged. They might emerge at any moment into the blessed light of day—or they might have a hundred meters still to traverse at this snail-like pace.

Jamieson was stopping for longer and longer intervals, which might reduce the strain on the engine but did nothing to reduce that on the passengers. During one of these pauses Wheeler asked him outright what they should do if they could get no further.

"We've only two possibilities," Jamieson answered. "We can stay here and hope to be rescued—which won't be as bad as it sounds, since our tracks will make it obvious where we are. The other alternative is to go out."

"What! That's impossible!"

"Not at all. I know a case where it's been done. It would be rather like escaping from a sunken submarine."

"It's a horrible thought—trying to swim through this stuff."

"I was once caught in a snowdrift when I was a kid, so I can guess what it would be like. The great danger would be losing your direction and floundering around in circles until you were exhausted. Let's hope we don't have to try the experiment."

It was a long time, Wheeler decided, since he had heard a bigger understatement than that.

The driving cab emerged above the dust level about an hour later, and no men could ever have greeted the sun with such joy. But they had not yet reached safety; though Ferdinand could make better speed as the resistance slackened, there might still be unsuspected depths ahead of them.

Wheeler watched with fascinated repulsion as the horrible stuff eddied past the tractor. At times it was quite impossible to believe that they were not forcing their way through a liquid, and only the slowness with which they moved spoiled the illusion. He wondered if it was worth suggesting that in future Caterpillars have better streamlining to improve their chances in emergencies like this. Who would ever have dreamed, back on Earth, that *that* sort of thing might be necessary?

At last Ferdinand crawled up to the security of the dry land, which, after all, was no drier than the deadly lake from which they had escaped. Jamieson, almost exhausted by the strain, slumped down across the control panel. The reaction had left Wheeler shaken and weak, but he was too thankful to be out of danger to let that worry him.

He had forgotten, in the relief of seeing sunlight again, that they had left Project Thor three hours ago, and had covered less than twenty kilometers.

Even so, they might have made it. But they had just started on their way again, and were crawling over the top of a quite gentle ridge, when there was a scream of tearing metal and Ferdinand tried to spin round in a circle. Jamieson cut the motor instantly and they came to rest broadside-on to their direction of motion.

"And that," said Jamieson softly, "is most definitely that. But I don't think we're in a position to grumble. If the starboard transmission had sheared while we were still in that dust bowl——" He didn't finish the sentence, but turned to the observation port that looked back along their trail. Wheeler followed his gaze.

The dome of Project Thor was still visible on the horizon. Perhaps they had already strained their luck to the utmost, but it would have been nice could they have put the protecting curve of the Moon clear between themselves and the unknown storms that were brewing there.

✳ *CHAPTER SEVENTEEN*

Even today, little has ever been revealed concerning the weapons used in the Battle of Pico. It is known that missiles played only a minor part in the engagement. In space warfare, anything short of a direct hit is almost useless, since there is nothing to transmit the energy of a shock wave. An atom bomb exploding a few hundred meters away can cause no blast damage, and even its radiation can do little harm to well-protected structures. Moreover, both Earth and the Federation had effective means of diverting ordinary projectiles.

Purely non-material weapons would have to play the greatest role. The simplest of these were the ion-beams, developed directly from the drive-units of spaceships. Since the invention of the first radio tubes, almost three centuries before, men had been learning how to produce and focus ever more concentrated streams of charged particles. The climax had been reached in spaceship propulsion with the so-called "ion rocket," generating its thrust from the emission of intense beams of electrically charged particles. The deadliness of these beams had caused many accidents in space, even though they were deliberately defocused to limit their effective range.

There was, of course, an obvious answer to such weapons. The electric and magnetic fields which produced them could also be used for their dispersion, converting them from annihilating beams into a harmless, scattered spray.

More effective, but more difficult to build, were the weapons using pure radiation. Yet even here, both Earth and the Federation had succeeded. It remained to be seen which had done the better job—the superior science of the Federation, or the greater productive capacity of Earth.

Commodore Brennan was well aware of all these factors as his little fleet converged upon the Moon. Like all commanders, he was going into action with fewer resources than he would have wished. Indeed, he would very much have preferred not to be going into action at all.

The converted liner *Eridanus* and the largely rebuilt freighter *Lethe*—once listed in Lloyd's register as the *Morning Star* and the *Rigel*—would now be swinging in between Earth and Moon along their carefully plotted courses. He did not know if they still had the element of surprise. Even if they had been detected, Earth might not know of the existence of this third and largest ship, the *Acheron*. Brennan wondered what romantic with a taste for mythology was responsible for these names—probably Commissioner Churchill, who made a point of emulating his famous ancestor in as many ways as he possibly could. Yet they were not inappropriate. The rivers of Death and Oblivion—yes, these were things they might bring to many men before another day had passed.

Lieutenant Curtis, one of the few men in the crew who had actually spent most of his working life in space, looked up from the communications desk.

"Message just picked up from the Moon, sir. Addressed to us."

Brennan was badly shaken. If they had been spotted, surely their opponents were not so contemptuous of them that they would freely admit the fact! He glanced quickly at the signal, then gave a sigh of relief.

OBSERVATORY TO FEDERATION.

WISH TO REMIND YOU OF EXISTENCE IRREPLACEABLE INSTRU-
MENTS PLATO. ALSO ENTIRE OBSERVATORY STAFF STILL HERE.
MACLAURIN. DIRECTOR.

"Don't frighten me like that again, Curtis," said the commodore. "I thought you meant it was beamed at me. I'd hate to think they could detect us this far out."

"Sorry, sir. It's just a general broadcast. They're still sending it out on the Observatory wavelength."

Brennan handed the signal over to his operations controller, Captain Merton.

"What do you make of this? You worked there, didn't you?"

Merton smiled as he read the message.

"Just like Maclaurin. Instruments first, staff second. I'm not too worried. I'll do my damnedest to miss him. A hundred kilometers isn't a bad safety margin, when you come to think of it. Unless there's a direct hit with a stray, they've nothing to worry about. They're pretty well dug in, you know."

The relentless hand of the chronometer was scything away the last minutes. Still confident that his ship, encased in its cocoon of night, had not yet been detected, Commodore Brennan watched the three sparks of his fleet creep along their appointed tracks in the plotting sphere. This was not a destiny he had ever imagined would be his—to hold the fate of worlds within his hands.

But he was not thinking of the powers that slumbered in the reactor banks, waiting for his command. He was not concerned with the place he would take in history, when men looked back upon this day. He only wondered, as had all who had ever faced battle for the first time, where he would be this same time tomorrow.

Less than a million kilometers away, Carl Steffanson sat at a control desk and watched the image of the sun, picked up by one of the many cameras that were the eyes of Project Thor. The group of tired technicians standing around him had almost completed the equipment before his arrival; now the discriminating units he had brought from Earth in such desperate haste had been wired into the circuit.

Steffanson turned a knob, and the sun went out. He flicked from one camera position to another, but all the eyes of the fortress were equally blind. The coverage was complete.

Too weary to feel any exhilaration, he leaned back in his seat and gestured toward the controls.

"It's up to you now. Set it to pass enough light for vision, but to give total rejection from the ultra-violet upward. We're sure none of their beams carry any effective power much beyond a thousand Angstroms. They'll be very surprised when all their stuff bounces off. I only wish we could send it back the way it came."

"Wonder what we look like from outside when the screen's on?" said one of the engineers.

"Just like a perfectly reflecting mirror. As long as it keeps reflecting, we're safe against pure radiation. That's all I can promise you."

Steffanson looked at his watch.

"If Intelligence is correct, we have about twenty minutes to spare. But I shouldn't count on it."

"At least Maclaurin knows where we are now," said Jamieson as he switched off the radio. "But I can't blame him for not sending someone to pull us out."

"Then what do we do now?"

"Get some food," Jamieson answered, walking back to the tiny galley. "I think we've earned it, and there may be a long walk ahead of us."

Wheeler looked nervously across the plain, to the distant but all too clearly visible dome of Project Thor. Then his jaw dropped and it was some seconds before he could believe that his eyes were not playing tricks on him.

"Sid!" he called. "Come and look at this!"

Jamieson joined him at a rush, and together they stared out

toward the horizon. The partly shadowed hemisphere of the dome had changed its appearance completely. Instead of a thin crescent of light, it now showed a single dazzling star, as though the image of the sun was being reflected from a perfectly spherical mirror surface.

The telescope confirmed this impression. The dome itself was no longer visible; its place seemed to have been taken by this fantastic silver apparition. To Wheeler it looked exactly like a great blob of mercury sitting on the skyline.

"I'd like to know how they've done that," was Jamieson's unexcited comment. "Some kind of interference effect, I suppose. It must be part of their defense system."

"We'd better get moving," said Wheeler anxiously. "I don't like the look of this. It feels horribly exposed up here."

Jamieson had started throwing open cupboards and pulling out stores. He tossed some bars of chocolate and packets of compressed meat over to Wheeler.

"Start chewing some of this," he said. "We won't have time for a proper meal now. Better have a drink as well, if you're thirsty. But don't take too much—you'll be in that suit for hours, and these aren't luxury models."

Wheeler was doing some mental arithmetic. They must be about eighty kilometers from base, with the entire rampart of Plato between them and the Observatory. Yes, it would be a long walk home, and they might after all be safer here. The tractor, which had already served them so well, could protect them from a good deal of trouble.

Jamieson toyed with the idea, but then rejected it. "Remember what Steffanson said," he reminded Wheeler. "He told us to get underground as soon as we could. And he must know what he's talking about."

They found a crevasse within fifty meters of the tractor, on the slope of the ridge away from the fortress. It was just deep enough to see out of when they stood upright, and the floor was sufficiently level to lie down. As a slit trench, it might almost have been made to order, and Jamieson felt much happier when he had located it.

"The only thing that worries me now," he said, "is how long we may have to wait. It's still possible that nothing will happen at all. On the other hand, if we start walking we may be caught in the open away from shelter."

After some discussion, they decided on a compromise. They would keep their suits on, but would go back and sit in Ferdinand where at least they would be comfortable. It would take them only a few seconds to get to the trench.

There was no warning of any kind. Suddenly the gray, dusty rocks of the Sea of Rains were scorched by a light they had never known before in all their history. Wheeler's first impression was that someone had turned a giant searchlight full upon the tractor; then he realized that this sun-eclipsing explosion was many kilometers away. High above the horizon was a ball of violet flame, perfectly spherical, and rapidly losing brilliance as it expanded. Within seconds, it had faded to a great cloud of luminous gas. It was dropping down toward the edge of the Moon, and almost at once had sunk below the skyline like some fantastic sun.

"We were fools," said Jamieson gravely. "That was an atomic warhead—we may be dead men already."

"Nonsense," retorted Wheeler, though without much confidence. "That was fifty kilometers away. The gammas would be pretty weak by the time they reached us—and these walls aren't bad shielding."

Jamieson did not answer; he was already on his way to the airlock. Wheeler started to follow him, then remembered that there was a radiation detector aboard and went back to collect it. Was there anything else that might be useful while he was here? On a sudden impulse, he jerked down the curtain-rod above the little alcove that concealed the lavatory, then ripped away the wall mirror over the sink.

When he joined Jamieson, who was waiting impatiently for him in the airlock, he handed over the detector, but did not bother to explain the rest of his equipment. Not until they had settled down in their trench, which they reached without further incident, did he make its purpose clear.

"If there's one thing I hate," he said petulantly, "it's not being able to see what's going on." He started to fix the mirror to the curtain rod, using some wire from one of the pouches round his suit. After a couple of minutes' work, he was able to hoist a crude periscope out of the hole.

"I can just see the dome," he said with some satisfaction. "It's quite unchanged, as far as I can tell."

"It would be," Jamieson replied. "They must have managed to explode that bomb somehow while it was miles away."

"Perhaps it was only a warning shot."

"Not likely! No one wastes plutonium for firework displays. That meant business. I wonder when the next move is going to be?"

It did not come for another five minutes. Then, almost simultaneously, three more of the dazzling atomic suns burst against the sky. They were all moving on trajectories that took them toward the dome, but long before they reached it they had dispersed into tenuous clouds of vapor.

"Rounds one and two to Earth," muttered Wheeler. "I wonder where these missiles are coming from?"

"If any of them burst directly overhead," said Jamieson, "we *will* be done for. Don't forget that there's no atmosphere to absorb the gammas here."

"What does the radiation meter say?"

"Nothing much yet, but I'm worried about that first blast, when we were still in the tractor."

Wheeler was too busily searching the sky to answer. Somewhere up there among the stars, which he could see now that he was out of the direct glare of the sun, must be the ships of the Federation, preparing for the next attack. It was not likely that the ships themselves would be visible, but he might be able to see their weapons in action.

From somewhere beyond Pico, six sheaves of flame shot up into the sky at an enormous acceleration. The dome was launching its first missiles, straight into the face of the sun. The *Lethe* and the *Eridanus* were using a trick as old as warfare itself; they were approaching from a direction in which their opponent would be partly blinded. Even radar could be distracted by the background of solar interference, and Commodore Brennan had enlisted two large sunspots as minor allies.

Within seconds, the rockets were lost in the glare. Minutes seemed to pass; then the sunlight abruptly multiplied itself a hundredfold. The folks up on Earth, thought Wheeler as he readjusted the filters of his visor, will be having a grandstand view tonight.

And the atmosphere which is such a nuisance to astronomers will protect them from anything that these warheads can radiate.

There was no way to tell if the missiles had done any damage. That enormous and soundless explosion might have dissipated itself harmlessly into space. This would be a strange battle, he realized. He might never even see the Federation ships, which would almost certainly be painted as black as night to make them undetectable.

Then he saw that something was happening to the dome. It was no longer a gleaming spherical mirror reflecting only the single image of the sun. Light was splashing from it in all directions, and its brilliance was increasing second by second. From somewhere out in space, power was being poured into the fortress. That could only mean that the ships of the Federation were floating up there against the stars, beaming countless millions of kilowatts down upon the Moon. But there was still no sign of them, for there was nothing to reveal the track of the river of energy pouring invisibly through space.

The dome was now far too bright to look upon directly, and Wheeler readjusted his filters. He wondered when it was going to reply to the attack, or indeed if it could do so while it was under this bombardment. Then he saw that the hemisphere was surrounded by a wavering corona, like some kind of brush discharge. Almost at the same moment, Jamieson's voice rang in his ears.

"Look, Con—right overhead!"

He glanced away from the mirror and looked directly into the sky. For the first time, he saw one of the Federation ships. Though he did not know it, he was seeing the *Acheron,* the only spaceship ever to be built specifically for war. It was clearly visible, and seemed remarkably close. Between it and the fortress, like an impalpable shield, flared a disk of light which as he watched turned cherry-red, then blue-white, then the deadly searing violet seen only in the hottest of the stars. The shield wavered back and forth, giving the impression of being balanced by tremendous and opposing energies. As Wheeler stared, oblivious to his peril, he saw that the whole ship was surrounded by a faint halo of light, brought to incandescence only where the weapons of the fortress tore against it.

It was some time before he realized that there were two other ships in the sky, each shielded by its own flaming nimbus. Now the battle was beginning to take shape; each side had cautiously tested its defenses and its weapons, and only now had the real trial of strength begun.

The two astronomers stared in wonder at the moving fireballs of the ships. Here was something totally new—something far more important than any mere weapon. These vessels possessed a means of propulsion which must make the rocket obsolete. They could hover motionless at will, then move off in any direction at a high acceleration. They needed this mobility; the fortress, with all its fixed equipment, far outpowered them and much of their defense lay in their speed.

In utter silence, the battle was rising to its climax. Millions of years ago the molten rock had frozen to form the Sea of Rains, and now the weapons of the ships were turning it once more to lava. Out by the fortress, clouds of incandescent vapor were being blasted into the sky as the beams of the attackers spent their fury against the unprotected rocks. It was impossible to tell which side was inflicting the greater damage. Now and again a screen would flare up, as a flicker of heat passes over white-hot steel. When that happened to one of the battleships, it would move away with that incredible acceleration, and it would be several seconds before the focusing devices of the fort had located it again.

Both Wheeler and Jamieson were surprised that the battle was being fought at such short ranges. There was probably never more than a hundred kilometers between the antagonists, and usually it was much less than this. When one fought with weapons that traveled at the speed of light—indeed, when one fought with light itself—such distances were trivial.

The explanation did not occur to them until the end of the engagement. All radiation weapons have one limitation: they must obey the law of inverse squares. Only explosive missiles are equally effective from whatever range they have been projected: if one is hit by an atomic bomb, it makes no difference whether it has traveled ten kilometers or a thousand.

But double the distance of any kind of radiation weapon, and you divide its power by four owing to the spreading of the beam. No wonder, therefore, that the Federal commander was coming as close to his objective as he dared.

The fort, lacking mobility, had to accept any punishment the ships could give it. After the battle had been on for a few minutes, it was impossible for the unshielded eye to look anywhere toward the south. Ever and again the clouds of rock vapor would go sailing up into the sky, falling back on the ground like luminous steam. And presently, as he peered through his darkened goggles and maneuvered his clumsy periscope, Wheeler saw something he could scarcely believe. Around the base of the fortress was a slowly spreading circle of lava, melting down ridges and even small hillocks like lumps of wax.

That awe-inspiring sight brought home to him, as nothing else had done, the frightful power of the weapons that were being wielded only a few kilometers away. If even the merest stray reflection of those energies reached them here, they would be snuffed out of existence as swiftly as moths in an oxy-hydrogen flame.

The three ships appeared to be moving in some complex tactical pattern, so that they could maintain the maximum bombardment of the fort while reducing its opportunity of striking back. Several times one of the ships passed vertically overhead, and Wheeler retreated as far into the crack as he could in case any of the radiation scattered from the screens splashed down upon them. Jamieson, who had given up trying to persuade his colleague to take fewer risks, had now crawled some distance along the crevasse, looking for a deeper part, preferably with a good overhang. He was not so far away, however, that the rock was shielding the suit-radios, and Wheeler gave him a continuous commentary on the battle.

It was hard to believe that the entire engagement had not yet lasted ten minutes. As Wheeler cautiously surveyed the inferno to the south, he noticed that the hemisphere seemed to have lost some of its symmetry. At first he thought that one of the generators might have failed, so that the protective field could no longer be maintained. Then he saw that the lake of lava was at least a kilometer across, and he guessed that the whole fort had floated off its foundations. Probably the defenders were not even aware of the fact. Their insulation must be taking care of solar heats, and would hardly notice the modest warmth of molten rock.

And now a strange thing was beginning to happen. The rays with which the battle was being fought were no longer quite invisible, for the fortress was no longer in a vacuum. Around it the boiling rock was releasing enormous volumes of gas, through which the paths of the rays were as clearly visible as searchlights in a misty night on Earth. At the same time Wheeler began to notice a continual hail of tiny particles around him. For a moment he was puzzled; then he realized that the rock vapor was condensing after it had been blasted up into the sky. It seemed too light to be dangerous, and he did not mention it to Jamieson—it would only give him something else to worry about. As long as the dust fall was not too heavy, the normal insulation of the suits could deal with it. In any case, it would probably be quite cold by the time it got back to the surface.

The tenuous and temporary atmosphere round the dome was producing another unexpected effect. Occasional flashes of lightning darted between ground and sky, draining off the enormous static charges that must be accumulating around the fort. Some of those flashes would have been spectacular by themselves—but they were scarcely visible against the incandescent clouds that generated them.

Accustomed though he was to the eternal silences of the Moon, Wheeler still felt a sense of unreality at the sight of these tremendous forces striving together without the least whisper of sound. Sometimes a gentle vibration would reach him, perhaps the rock-borne concussion of falling lava. But much of the time, he had the feeling that he was watching a television program when the sound had failed.

Afterward, he could hardly believe he had been such a fool as to expose himself to the risks he was running now. At the moment, he felt no fear—only an immense curiosity and excitement. He had been caught, though he did not know it, by the deadly glamor of war. There is a fatal strain in men that, whatever reason may say, makes their hearts beat faster when they watch the colors flying and hear the ancient music of the drums.

Curiously enough, Wheeler did not feel any sense of identification with either side. It seemed to him, in his present abnormally overwrought mood, that all this was a vast, impersonal display arranged for his special benefit. He felt something approaching contempt for Jamieson, who was missing everything by seeking safety.

Perhaps the real truth of the matter was that having just escaped from one peril, Wheeler was in the exalted state, akin to drunkenness, in which the idea of personal danger seems absurd. He had managed to get out of the dust bowl—nothing else could harm him now.

Jamieson had no such consolation. He saw little of the battle, but felt its terror and grandeur far more deeply than his friend. It was too late for regrets, but over and over again he wrestled with his conscience. He felt angry at fate for having placed him in such a position that his action might have decided the destiny of worlds. He was angry, in equal measure, with Earth and the Federation for having let matters come to this. And he was sick at heart as he thought of the future toward which the human race might now be heading.

Wheeler never knew why the fortress waited so long before it used its main weapon. Perhaps Steffanson—or whoever was in charge—was waiting for the attack to slacken so that he could risk lowering the defenses of the dome for the millisecond that he needed to launch his stiletto.

Wheeler saw it strike upward, a solid bar of light stabbing at the stars. He remembered the rumors that had gone round the Observatory. So *this* was what had been seen, flashing above the mountains. He did not have time to reflect on the staggering violation of the laws of optics which this phenomenon implied, for he was staring at the ruined ship above his head. The beam had gone through the *Lethe* as if she did not exist; the fortress had speared her as an entomologist pierces a butterfly with a pin.

Whatever one's loyalties, it was a terrible thing to see how the screens of that great ship suddenly vanished as her generators died, leaving her helpless and unprotected in the sky. The secondary weapons of the fort were at her instantly, tearing out great gashes of metal and boiling away her armor layer by layer. Then, quite slowly, she began to settle toward the Moon, still on an even keel. No one will ever know what stopped her, probably some short-circuit in her controls, since none of her crew could have been left alive. For suddenly she went off to the east in a long, flat trajectory. By that time most of her hull had been boiled away and the skeleton of her framework was almost completely exposed. The crash came, minutes later, as she plunged out of sight beyond the Teneriffe Mountains. A blue-white aurora flickered for a moment below the horizon, and Wheeler waited for the shock to reach him.

And then, as he stared into the east, he saw a line of dust rising from the plain, sweeping toward him as if driven by a mighty wind. The concussion was racing through the rock, hurling the surface dust high into the sky as it passed. The swift, inexorable approach of that silently moving wall, advancing at the rate of several kilometers a second, was enough to strike terror into anyone who did not know its cause. But it was quite harmless; when the wave-front reached him, it was as if a minor earthquake had passed. The veil of dust reduced visibility to zero for a few seconds, then subsided as swiftly as it had come.

When Wheeler looked again for the remaining ships, they were so far away that their screens had shrunk to little balls of fire against the zenith. At first he thought they were retreating; then, abruptly, the screens began to expand as they came down into the attack under a terrific vertical acceleration. Over by the fortress the lava, like some tortured living creature, was throwing itself madly into the sky as the beams tore into it.

The *Acheron* and *Eridanus* came out of their dives about a kilometer above the fort. For an instant, they were motionless; then they went back into the sky together. But the *Eridanus* had been mortally wounded, though Wheeler knew only that one of the screens was shrinking much more slowly than the other. With a feeling of helpless fascination, he watched the stricken ship fall back toward the Moon. He wondered if the fort would use its enigmatic weapon again, or whether the defenders realized that it was unnecessary.

About ten kilometers up, the screens of the *Eridanus* seemed to explode and she hung unprotected, a blunt torpedo of black metal, almost invisible against the sky. Instantly her light-absorbing paint, and the armor beneath, were torn off by the beams of the fortress. The great ship turned cherry-red, then white. She swung over so that her prow turned toward the Moon, and began her last dive. At first it seemed to Wheeler that she was heading straight toward him; then he saw that she was aimed at the fort. She was obeying her captain's last command.

It was almost a direct hit. The dying ship smashed into the lake of lava and exploded instantly, engulfing the fortress in an expanding hemisphere of flame. This, thought Wheeler, must surely be the end. He waited for the shock wave to reach him, and again watched the wall of dust sweep by—this time into the north. The concussion was so violent that it jerked him off his feet, and he did not see how anyone in the fort could have survived. Cautiously, he put down the mirror which had given him almost all his view of the battle, and peered over the edge of his trench. He did not know that the final paroxysm was yet to come.

Incredibly, the dome was still there, though now it seemed that part of it had been sheared away. And it was inert and lifeless: its screens were down, its energies exhausted, its garrison, surely, already dead. If so, they had done their work. Of the remaining Federal ship, there was no sign. She was already retreating toward Mars, her main armament completely useless and her drive units on the point of failure. She would never fight again, yet in the few hours of life that were left to her, she had one more role to play.

"It's all over, Sid," Wheeler called into his suit radio. "It's safe to come and look now."

Jamieson climbed up out of a crack fifty meters away, holding the radiation detector in front of him.

"It's still hot around here," Wheeler heard him grumble, half to himself. "The sooner we get moving the better."

"Will it be safe to go back to Ferdinand and put through a radio——" began Wheeler. Then he stopped. Something was happening over by the dome.

In a blast like an erupting volcano, the ground tore apart. An enormous geyser began to soar into the sky, hurling great boulders thousands of meters toward the stars. It climbed swiftly above the plain, driving a thunderhead of smoke and spray before it. For a moment it towered against the southern sky, like some incredible, heaven-aspiring tree that had sprung from the barren soil of the Moon. Then, almost as swiftly as it had grown, it subsided in silent ruin and its angry vapors dispersed into space.

The thousands of tons of heavy liquid holding open the deepest shaft that man had ever bored had finally come to the boiling point, as the energies of the battle seeped into the rock. The mine had blown its top as spectacularly as any oil well on Earth, and had proved that an excellent explosion could still be arranged without the aid of atom bombs.

✳ *CHAPTER EIGHTEEN*

To the Observatory, the battle was no more than an occasional distant earthquake, a faint vibration of the ground which disturbed some of the more delicate instruments but did no material damage. The psychological damage, however, was a different matter. Nothing is so demoralizing as to know that great and shattering events are taking place, but to be totally unaware of their outcome. The Observatory was full of wild rumors, the Signals Office besieged with inquiries. But even here there was no information. All news broadcasts from Earth had ceased; the whole world was waiting, as if with bated breath, for the fury of the battle to die away so that the victor could be known. That there would be no victor was the one thing that had not been anticipated.

Not until long after the last vibrations had died away and the radio had announced that the Federation forces were in full retreat did Maclaurin permit anyone to go up to the surface. The report that came down was, after the strain and excitement of the last few hours, not only a relief but a considerable anticlimax. There was a small amount of increased radioactivity about, but not the slightest trace of damage. What it would be like on the other side of the mountains was, of course, a different matter.

The news that Wheeler and Jamieson were safe gave a tremendous boost to the staff's morale. Owing to a partial breakdown of communications, it had taken them almost an hour to contact Earth and to get connected to the Observatory. The delay had been both infuriating and worrying, for it had left them wondering if the Observatory had been destroyed. They dared not set out on foot until they were sure they had somewhere to go—and Ferdinand was now too radioactive to be a safe refuge.

Sadler was in Communications trying to find out what was happening, when the message came through. Jamieson, sounding very tired, gave a brief report of the battle and asked for instructions.

"What's the radiation reading inside the cab?" Maclaurin asked. Jamieson called back the figures: it still seemed strange to Sadler that the message should have to go all the way to Earth just to span a hundred kilometers of the Moon, and he was never able to get used to the three-second delay that this implied.

"I'll get the health section to work out the tolerance," Maclaurin answered. "You say it's only a quarter of that reading out in the open?"

"Yes—we've stayed outside the tractor as much as possible, and have come in every ten minutes to try and contact you."

"The best plan is this—we'll send a Caterpillar right away, and you start walking toward us. Any particular rendezvous you'd like to aim for?"

Jamieson thought for a moment.

"Tell your driver to head for the five-kilometer marker on this side of Prospect; we'll reach it about the same time as he does. We'll keep our suit radios on so there'll be no chance of him missing us."

As Maclaurin was giving his orders, Sadler asked if there was room for an extra passenger in the rescue tractor. It would give him a chance of questioning Wheeler and Jamieson much sooner than would otherwise be the case. When they reached the Observatory—though they did not know it yet—they would be whipped into hospital at once and treated for radiation sickness. They were in no serious danger, but Sadler doubted that he would have much chance of seeing them for a while when the doctors got hold of them.

Maclaurin granted the request, adding the comment: "Of course, you realize this means that you'll have to tell them who you are. Then the whole Observatory will know inside ten minutes."

"I've thought of that," Sadler replied. "It doesn't matter now." Always assuming, he added to himself, that it ever did.

Half an hour later, he was learning the difference between travel in the smooth, swift monorail and in a jolting tractor. After a while he became used to the nightmare grades the driver was light-heartedly attacking, and ceased to regret volunteering for this mission. Besides the operating crew, the vehicle was carrying the chief medical officer, who hoped to make blood counts and give injections as soon as the rescue had been effected.

There was no dramatic climax to the expedition; as soon as they topped Prospect Pass, they made radio contact with the two men trudging toward them. Fifteen minutes later the moving figures appeared on the skyline, and there was no ceremony apart from fervent handshakes as they came aboard the tractor.

They halted for a while so that the M.O. could give his injections and make his tests. When he had finished he told Wheeler: "You're going to be in bed for the next week, but there's no need to worry."

"What about me?" asked Jamieson.

"You're all right—a much smaller dose. A couple of days is all you need."

"It was worth it," said Wheeler cheerfully. "I don't think that was much of a price to pay for a grandstand view of Armageddon." Then, as the reaction of knowing that he was safe wore off, he added anxiously: "What's the latest news? Has the Federation attacked anywhere else?"

"No," Sadler replied. "It hasn't, and I doubt that it can. But it seems to have achieved its main objective, which was to stop us using that mine. What will happen now is up to the politicians."

"Hey," said Jamieson, "what are *you* doing here, anyway?"

Sadler smiled.

"I'm still investigating, but let's say that my terms of reference are wider than anyone imagined."

"You aren't a radio reporter?" asked Wheeler suspiciously.

"Er—not exactly. I'd rather not——"

"I know," Jamieson interjected suddenly. "You're something to do with Security. It makes sense now."

Sadler looked at him with mild annoyance. Jamieson, he decided, had a remarkable talent for making things difficult.

"It doesn't matter. But I want to send in a full report of everything you saw. You realize that you are the only surviving eyewitnesses, except for the crew of the Federal ship."

"I was afraid of that," said Jamieson. "So Project Thor was wiped out?"

"Yes, but I think it did its job."

"What a waste, though—Steffanson and all those others! If it hadn't been for me, he'd probably still be alive."

"He knew what he was doing—and he made his own choice," replied Sadler, rather curtly. Yes, Jamieson was going to be a most recalcitrant hero.

For the next thirty minutes, as they were climbing back over the wall of Plato on the homeward run, he questioned Wheeler about the course of the battle. Although the astronomer could only have seen a small part of the engagement, owing to his limited angle of view, his information would be invaluable when the tacticians back on Earth carried out their post-mortem.

"What puzzles me most of all," Wheeler concluded, "is the weapon the fort used to destroy the battleship. It looked like a beam of some kind, but of course that's impossible. *No* beam can be visible in a vacuum. And I wonder why they only used it once? Do *you* know anything about it?"

"I'm afraid not," replied Sadler, which was quite untrue. He still knew very little about the weapons in the fort, but this was the only one he now fully understood. He could well appreciate why a jet of molten metal, hurled through space at several hundred kilometers a second by the most powerful electromagnets ever built, might have looked like a beam of light flashing on for an instant. And he knew that it was a short-range weapon, designed to pierce the fields which would deflect ordinary projectiles. It could be used only under ideal conditions, and it took many minutes to recharge the gigantic condensers which powered the magnets.

This was a mystery the astronomers would have to solve for themselves. He did not imagine that it would take them very long, when they really turned their minds to the subject.

The tractor came crawling cautiously down the steep inner slopes of the great walled-plain, and the latticework of the telescopes appeared on the horizon. They looked, Sadler thought, exactly like a couple of factory chimneys surrounded by scaffolding. Even in his short stay here, he had grown quite fond of them and had come to think of them as personalities, just as did the men who used them. He could share the astronomer's concern that any harm might befall these superb instruments, which had brought knowledge back to Earth from a hundred thousand million light-years away in space.

A towering cliff cut them off from the sun, and darkness fell abruptly as they rolled into shadow. Overhead, the stars began to reappear as Sadler's eyes automatically adjusted for the change in light. He stared up into the northern sky, and saw that Wheeler was doing the same.

Nova Draconis was still among the brightest stars in the sky, but it was fading fast. In a few days, it would be no more brilliant than Sirius; in a few months, it would be beyond the grasp of the unaided eye. There was, surely, some message here, some symbol half glimpsed on the frontiers of imagination. Science would learn much from *N. Draconis,* but what would it teach the ordinary world of men?

Only this, thought Sadler. The heavens might blaze with portents, the galaxy might burn with the beacon lights of detonating stars, but man would go about his own affairs with a sublime indifference. He was busy with the planets now, and the stars would have to wait. He would not be overawed by anything that they could do; and in his own good time, he would deal with them as he considered fit.

Neither rescued nor rescuers had much to say on the last lap of the homeward journey. Wheeler was obviously beginning to suffer from delayed shock, and his hands had developed a nervous tremble. Jamieson merely sat and watched the Observatory approaching, as if he had never seen it before. When they drove through the long shadow of the thousand-centimeter telescope, he turned to Sadler and asked: "Did they get everything under cover in time?"

"I believe so," Sadler replied. "I've not heard of any damage."

Jamieson nodded absent-mindedly. He showed no sign of pleasure or relief; he had reached emotional saturation, and nothing could really affect him now until the impact of the last few hours had worn away.

Sadler left them as soon as the tractor drove into the underground garage, and hurried to his room to write up his report. This was outside his terms of reference, but he felt glad that at least he was able to do something constructive.

There was a sense of anticlimax now—a feeling that the storm had spent its fury and would not return. In the aftermath of the battle, Sadler felt far less depressed than he had for days. It seemed to him that both Earth and the Federation must be equally overawed by the forces they had released, and both equally anxious for peace.

For the first time since he had left Earth, he dared to think once more of his future. Though it could still not be wholly dismissed, the danger of a raid on Earth itself now seemed remote. Jeannette was safe, and soon he might be seeing her again. At least he could tell her where he was, since events had made any further secrecy absurd.

But there was just one nagging frustration in Sadler's mind. He hated to leave a job undone, yet in the nature of things this mission of his might remain forever uncompleted. He would have given so much to have known whether or not there had been a spy in the Observatory.

✳ *CHAPTER NINETEEN*

The liner *Pegasus,* with three hundred passengers and a crew of sixty, was only four days out from Earth when the war began and ended. For some hours there had been a great confusion and alarm on board, as the radio messages from Earth and Federation were intercepted. Captain Halstead had been forced to take firm measures with some of the passengers, who wished to turn back rather than go on to Mars and an uncertain future as prisoners of war. It was not easy to blame them; Earth was still so close that it was a beautiful silver crescent, with the Moon a fainter and smaller echo beside it. Even from here, more than a million kilometers away, the energies that had just flamed across the face of the Moon had been clearly visible, and had done little to restore the morale of the passengers.

They could not understand that the law of celestial mechanics admit of no appeal. The *Pegasus* was barely clear of Earth, and still weeks from her intended goal. But she had reached her orbiting speed, and had launched herself like a giant projectile on the path that would lead inevitably to Mars, under the guidance of the sun's all-pervading gravity. There could be no turning back: that would be a maneuver involving an impossible amount of propellant. The *Pegasus* carried enough dust in her tanks to match velocity with Mars at the end of her orbit, and to allow for reasonable course corrections en route. Her nuclear reactors could provide energy for a dozen voyages—but sheer energy was useless if there was no propellant mass to eject. Whether she wanted to or not, the *Pegasus* was headed for Mars with the inevitability of a runaway streetcar. Captain Halstead did not anticipate a pleasant trip.

The words MAYDAY, MAYDAY came crashing out of the radio and banished all other preoccupations of the *Pegasus* and her crew. For three hundred years, in air and sea and space, these words had alerted rescue organizations, had made captains change their course and race to the aid of stricken comrades. But there was so little that the commander of a spaceship could do; in the whole history of astronautics, there have been only three cases of a successful rescue operation in space.

There are two main reasons for this, only one of which is widely advertised by the shipping lines. Any serious disaster in space is extremely rare; almost all accidents occur during planetfall or departure. Once a ship has reached space, and has swung into the orbit that will lead it effortlessly to its destination, it is safe from all hazards except internal, mechanical troubles. Such troubles occur more often than the passengers ever know, but are usually trivial and are quietly dealt with by the crew. All spaceships, by law, are built in several independent sections, any one of which can serve as a refuge in an emergency. So the worst that ever happens is that some uncomfortable hours are spent by all while an irate captain breathes heavily down the neck of his engineering officer.

The second reason why space rescues are so rare is that they are almost impossible, from the nature of things. Spaceships travel at enormous velocities on exactly calculated paths, which do not permit of major alterations—as the passengers of the *Pegasus* were now beginning to appreciate. The orbit any ship follows from one planet to another is unique; no other vessel will ever follow the same path again, among the changing patterns of the planets. There are no "shipping lanes" in space, and it is rare indeed for one ship to pass within a million kilometers of another. Even when this does happen, the difference of speed is almost always so great that contact is impossible.

All these thoughts flashed through Captain Halstead's mind when the message came down to him from Signals. He read the position and course of the distressed ship—the velocity figure must have been garbled in transmission, it was so ridiculously high. Almost certainly, there was nothing he could do—they were too far away, and it would take days to reach them.

Then he noticed the name at the end of the message. He thought he was familiar with every ship in space, but this was a new one to him. He stared in bewilderment for a moment before he suddenly realized just who was calling for his assistance. . . .

Enmity vanishes when men are in peril on sea or in space. Captain Halstead leaned over his control desk and said: "Signals! Get me their captain."

"He's on circuit, sir. You can go ahead."

Captain Halstead cleared his throat. This was a novel experience, and not a pleasant one. It gave him no sort of satisfaction to tell even an enemy that he could do nothing to save him.

"Captain Halstead, *Pegasus,* speaking," he began. "You're too far away for contact. Our operational reserve is less than ten kilometers a second. I've no need to compute, I can see it's impossible. Have you any suggestions? Please confirm your velocity; we were given an incorrect figure."

The reply, after a four-second time-lag that seemed doubly maddening in these circumstances, was unexpected and astonishing.

"Commodore Brennan, Federal cruiser *Acheron.* I can confirm our velocity figure. We can contact you in two hours, and will make all course corrections ourselves. We still have power, but must abandon ship in less than three hours. Our radiation shielding has gone, and the main reactor is becoming unstable. We've got manual control on it, and it will be safe for at least an hour after we reach you. But we can't guarantee it beyond then."

Captain Halstead felt the scalp crawl at the back of his neck. He did not know how a reactor could become unstable, but he knew what would happen if one did. There were a good many things about the *Acheron* he did not understand—her speed, above all—but there was one point that emerged very clearly and upon which Commodore Brennan must be left in no doubt.

"*Pegasus* to *Acheron,*" he replied. "I have three hundred passengers aboard. I cannot hazard my ship if there is danger of an explosion."

"There is no danger, I can guarantee that. We will have at least five minutes' warning, which will give us ample time to get clear of you."

"Very well—I'll get my airlocks ready and my crew standing by to pass you a line."

There was a pause longer than that dictated by the sluggish progress of radio waves. Then Brennan replied:

"That's our trouble. We're cut off in the forward section. There are no external locks here, and we have only five suits among a hundred and twenty men."

Halstead whistled and turned to his navigating officer before answering.

"There's nothing we can do for them," he said. "They'll have to crack the hull to get out, and that will be the end of everyone except the five men in the suits. We can't even lend them our own suits—there'll be no way we can get them aboard without letting down the pressure." He flicked over the microphone switch.

"*Pegasus* to *Acheron*. How do you suggest we can assist you?"

It was eerie to be speaking to a man who was already as good as dead. The traditions of space were as strict as those of the sea. Five men could leave the *Acheron* alive, but her captain would not be among them.

Halstead did not know that Commodore Brennan had other ideas, and had by no means abandoned hope, desperate though the situation on board the *Acheron* seemed. His chief medical officer, who had proposed the plan, was already explaining it to the crew.

"This is what we're going to do," said the small, dark man who a few months ago had been one of the best surgeons on Venus. "We can't get at the airlocks, because there's vacuum all round us and we've only got five suits. This ship was built for fighting, not for carrying passengers, and I'm afraid her designers had other matters to think about besides Standard Spaceworthiness Regs. Here we are, and we have to make the best of it.

"We'll be alongside the *Pegasus* in a couple of hours. Luckily for us, she's got big locks for loading freight and passengers; there's room for thirty or forty men to crowd into them, if they squeeze tight—*and aren't wearing suits*. Yes, I know that sounds bad, but it's not suicide. You're going to breathe space, and get away with it! I won't say it will be enjoyable, but it will be something to brag about for the rest of your lives.

"Now listen carefully. The first thing I've got to prove to you is that you can live for five minutes without breathing—in fact, *without wanting to breathe*. It's a simple trick: Yogis and magicians have known it for centuries, but there's nothing occult about it and it's based on common-sense physiology. To give you confidence, I want you to make this test."

The M.O. pulled a stop watch out of his pocket, and continued:

"When I say 'Now!' I want you to exhale completely—empty your lungs of every drop of air—and then see how long you can stay before you have to take a breath. Don't strain—just hold out until it becomes uncomfortable, then start breathing again normally. I'll start counting the seconds after fifteen, so you can tell what you managed to do. If anyone can't take the quarter minute, I'll recommend his instant dismissal from the Service."

The ripple of laughter broke the tension, as it had been intended to; then the M.O. held up his hand, and swept it down with a shout of "Now!" There was a great sigh as the entire company emptied its lungs; then utter silence.

When the M.O. started counting at "Fifteen," there were a few gasps from those who had barely been able to make the grade. He went on counting to "Sixty" accompanied by occasional explosive pants as one man after another capitulated. Some were still stubbornly holding out after a full minute.

"That's enough," said the little surgeon. "You tough guys can stop showing off, you're spoiling the experiment."

Again there was a murmur of amusement; the men were rapidly regaining their morale. They still did not understand what was happening, but at least some plan was afoot that offered them a hope of rescue.

"Let's see how we managed," said the M.O. "Hands up all those who held out for fifteen to twenty seconds. . . . Now twenty to twenty-five. . . . Now twenty-five to thirty—Jones, you're a damn liar—you folded up at fifteen! . . . Now thirty to thirty-five. . . ."

When he had finished the census, it was clear that more than half the company had managed to hold their breath for thirty seconds, and no one had failed to reach fifteen seconds.

"That's about what I expected," said the M.O. "You can regard this as a control experiment, and now we come on to the real thing. I ought to tell you that we're now breathing almost pure oxygen here, at about three hundred millimeters. So although the pressure in the ship is less than half its sea-level value on Earth, your lungs are taking in twice as much oxygen as they would on Earth, and still more than they would on Mars or Venus. If any of you have sneaked off to have a surreptitious smoke in the toilet, you'll already have noticed that the air was rich, as your cigarette will only have lasted a few seconds.

"I'm telling you all this because it will increase your confidence to know what is going on. What you're going to do now is to flush out your lungs and fill your system with oxygen. It's called hyperventilation, which is simply a ten dollar word for deep breathing. When I give the signal, I want you all to breathe as *deeply* as you can, then exhale *completely,* and carry on breathing in the same way until I tell you to stop. I'll let you do it for a minute; some of you may feel a bit dizzy at the end of that time, but it'll pass. Take in all the air you can with every breath; swing your arms to get maximum chest expansion.

"Then, when the minute's up, I'll tell you to exhale, then stop breathing, and I'll begin counting seconds again. I think I can promise you a big surprise. O.K.—here we go!"

For the next minutes, the overcrowded compartments of the *Acheron* presented a fantastic spectacle. More than a hundred men were flailing their arms and breathing stertorously, as if each was at his last gasp. Some were too closely packed together to breathe as deeply as they would have liked, and all had to anchor themselves somehow so that their exertion would not cause them to drift around the cabins.

"Now!" shouted the M.O. "Stop breathing—blow out all your air—and see how long you can manage before you've got to start again. I'll count the seconds, but this time I won't begin until half a minute has gone."

The result, it was obvious, left everyone flabbergasted. One man failed to make the minute, otherwise almost two minutes elapsed before most of the men felt the need to breathe again. Indeed, to have taken a breath before then would have demanded a deliberate effort. Some men were still perfectly comfortable after three or four minutes; one was holding out at five when the doctor stopped him.

"I think you'll all see what I was trying to prove. When your lungs are flushed out with oxygen, you just don't *want* to breathe for several minutes, any more than you want to eat again after a heavy meal. It's no strain or hardship; it's not a question of holding your breath. And if your life depended on it, you could do even better than this, I promise you.

"Now we're going to tie up right alongside the *Pegasus;* it will take less than thirty seconds to get over to her. She'll have her men out in suits to push along any stragglers, and the air-lock doors will be slammed shut as soon as you're all inside. Then the lock will be flooded with air and you'll be none the worse except for some bleeding noses."

He hoped that was true. There was only one way to find out. It was a dangerous and unprecedented gamble, but there was no alternative. At least it would give every man a fighting chance for his life.

"Now," he continued, "you're probably wondering about the pressure drop. That's the only uncomfortable part, but you won't be in a vacuum long enough for severe damage. We'll open the hatches in two stages; first we'll drop pressure slowly to a tenth of an atmosphere, then we'll blow out completely in one bang and make a dash for it. Total decompression's painful, but not dangerous. Forget all that nonsense you may have heard about the human body blowing up in a vacuum. We're a lot tougher than that, and the final drop we're going to make from a tenth of an atmosphere to zero is considerably less than men have already stood in lab tests. Hold your mouth wide open and let yourself break wind. You'll feel your skin stinging all over, but you'll probably be too busy to notice that."

The M.O. paused, and surveyed his quiet, intent audience. They were all taking it very well, but that was only to be expected. Every one was a trained man—they were the pick of the planets' engineers and technicians.

"As a matter of fact," the surgeon continued cheerfully, "you'll probably laugh when I tell you the biggest danger of the lot. It's nothing more than sunburn. Out there you'll be in the sun's raw ultra-violet, unshielded by atmosphere. It can give you a nasty blister in thirty seconds, so we'll make the crossing in the shadow of the *Pegasus.* If you happen to get outside that shadow, just shield your face with your arm. Those of you who've got gloves might as well wear them.

"Well, that's the picture. I'm going to cross with the first team just to show how easy it is. Now I want you to split up into four groups, and I'll drill you each separately."

Side by side, the *Pegasus* and the *Acheron* raced toward the distant planet that only one of them would ever reach. The airlocks of the liner were open, gaping wide no more than a few meters from the hull of the crippled battleship. The space between the two vessels was strung with guide ropes, and among them floated the men of the liner's crew, ready to give assistance if any of the escaping men were overcome during the brief but dangerous crossing.

It was lucky for the crew of the *Acheron* that four pressure bulkheads were still intact. Their ship could still be divided into four separate compartments, so that a quarter of the crew could leave at a time. The airlocks of the *Pegasus* could not have held everyone at once if a mass escape had been necessary.

Captain Halstead watched from the bridge as the signal was given. There was a sudden puff of smoke from the hull of the battleship, then the emergency hatch—certainly never designed for an emergency such as *this*—blew away into space. A cloud of dust and condensing vapor blasted out, obscuring the view for a second. He knew how the waiting men would feel the escaping air sucking at their bodies, trying to tear them away from their handholds.

When the cloud had dispersed, the first men had already emerged. The leader was wearing a spacesuit, and all the others were strung on the three lines attached to him. Instantly, men from the *Pegasus* grabbed two of the lines and darted off to their respective airlocks. The men of the *Acheron,* Halstead was relieved to see, all appeared to be conscious and to be doing everything they could to help.

It seemed ages before the last figure on its drifting line was towed or pushed into an airlock. Then the voice from one of those spacesuited figures out there shouted, "Close Number Three!" Number One followed almost at once; but there was an agonizing delay before the signal for Two came. Halstead could not see what was happening; presumably someone was still outside and holding up the rest. But at last all the locks were closed. There was no time to fill them in the normal way; the valves were jerked open by brute force and the chambers flooded with air from the ship.

Aboard the *Acheron,* Commodore Brennan waited with his remaining ninety men, in the three compartments that were still unsealed. They had formed their groups and were strung in chains of ten behind their leaders. Everything had been planned and rehearsed; the next few seconds would prove whether or not in vain.

Then the ship's speakers announced, in an almost quietly conversational tone:

"*Pegasus* to *Acheron*. We've got all your men out of the locks. No casualties. A few hemorrhages. Give us five minutes to get ready for the next batch."

They lost one man on the last transfer. He panicked and they had to slam the lock shut without him, rather than risk the lives of all the others. It seemed a pity that they could not all have made it, but for the moment everyone was too thankful to worry about that.

There was only one thing still to be done. Commodore Brennan, the last man aboard the *Acheron,* adjusted the timing circuit that would start the drive in thirty seconds. That would give him long enough; even in his clumsy spacesuit he could get out of the open hatch in half that time. It was cutting it fine, but only he and his engineering officer knew how narrow the margin was.

He threw the switch and dived for the hatch. He had already reached the *Pegasus* when the ship he had commanded, still loaded with millions of kilowatt-centuries of energy, came to life for the last time and dwindled silently toward the stars of the Milky Way.

The explosion was easily visible among all the inner planets. It blew to nothingness the last ambitions of the Federation, and the last fears of Earth.

✳ *CHAPTER TWENTY*

Every evening, as the sun drops down beyond the lonely pyramid of Pico, the shadow of the great mountain reaches out to engulf the metal column that will stand in the Sea of Rains as long as the Sea itself endures. There are five hundred and twenty-seven names on that column, in alphabetical order. No mark distinguishes the men who died for the Federation from those who died for Earth, and perhaps this simple fact is the best proof that they did not die in vain.

The Battle of Pico ended the domination of Earth and marked the coming of age of the planets. Earth was weary after her long

saga and the efforts she had put forth to conquer the nearer worlds
—those worlds which had now so inexplicably turned against her, as
long ago the American colonies had turned against their motherland.
In both cases the reasons were similar, and in both the eventual
outcomes equally advantageous to mankind.

Had either side won a clearcut victory, it might have been a
disaster. The Federation might have been tempted to impose on
Earth an agreement which it could never enforce. Earth, on the
other hand, might well have crippled its errant children by with-
drawing all supplies, thus setting back for centuries the colonization
of the planets.

Instead, it had been a stalemate. Each antagonist had learned
a sharp and salutary lesson; above all, each had learned to respect
the other. And each was now very busy explaining to its citizens
exactly what it had been doing in their names. . . .

The last explosion of the war was followed, within a few hours,
by political explosions on Earth, Mars and Venus. When the smoke
had drifted away, many ambitious personalities had disappeared, at
least for the time being, and those in power had one main objective
—to re-establish friendly relations, and to erase the memory of an
episode which did credit to no one.

The *Pegasus* incident, cutting across the divisions of war and
reminding men of their essential unity, made the task of the statesmen far easier than it might otherwise have been. The Treaty of
Phobos was signed in what one historian called an atmosphere of
shamefaced conciliation. Agreement was swift, for Earth and
Federation each possessed something that the other needed badly.

The superior science of the Federation had given it the secret
of the accelerationless drive, as it is now universally but inaccurately called. For its part, Earth was now prepared to share the
wealth she had tapped far down within the Moon. The barren crust
had been penetrated, and at last the heavy core was yielding up its
stubbornly guarded treasures. There was wealth here that would
supply all man's needs for centuries to come.

It was destined, in the years ahead, to transform the solar system and to alter completely the distribution of the human race. Its
immediate effect was to make the Moon, long the poor relation of
the old and wealthy Earth, into the richest and most important of
all the worlds. Within ten years, the Independent Lunar Republic

would be dictating F.O.B. terms to Earth and Federation with equal impartiality.

But the future would take care of itself. All that mattered now was that the war was over.

✳ *CHAPTER TWENTY-ONE*

Central City, thought Sadler, had grown since he was here thirty years ago. Any one of these domes could cover the whole seven they had back in the old days. How long would it be, at this rate, before the whole Moon was covered up? He rather hoped it would not be in his time.

The station itself was almost as large as one of the old domes. Where there had been five tracks, there were now thirty. But the design of the monocabs had not altered much, and their speed seemed to be about the same. The vehicle which had brought him from the spaceport might well have been the one that had carried him across the Sea of Rains a quarter of a lifetime ago.

A quarter of a lifetime, that is, if you were a citizen of the Moon and could expect to see your one hundred and twentieth birthday. But a full third of a lifetime if you spent all your waking and sleeping hours fighting the gravity of Earth. . . .

There were far more vehicles in the streets; Central City was too big to operate on a pedestrian basis now. But one thing had not changed. Overhead was the blue, cloud-flecked sky of Earth, and Sadler did not doubt that the rain still came on schedule.

He jumped into an autocab and dialed the address, relaxing as he was carried through the busy streets. His baggage had already gone to the hotel, and he was in no hurry to follow it. As soon as he arrived there, business would catch up with him again, and he might not have another chance of carrying out this mission.

There seemed almost as many businessmen and tourists from Earth here as there were residents. It was easy to distinguish them, not only by their clothes and behavior but by the way they walked in this low gravity. Sadler was surprised to find that though he had been on the Moon only a few hours, the automatic muscular adjustment he had learned so long ago came smoothly into play again. It was like learning to ride a bicycle; once you had achieved it, you never forgot.

So they had a lake here now, complete with islands and swans. He had read about the swans; their wings had to be carefully clipped to prevent their flying away and smashing into the "sky." There was a sudden splash as a large fish broke the surface; Sadler wondered if it was surprised to find how high it could jump out of the water.

The cab, threading its way above the buried guide-rods, swooped down a tunnel that must lead beneath the edge of the dome. Because the illusion of sky was so well contrived, it was not easy to tell when you were about to leave one dome and enter another, but Sadler knew where he was when the vehicle went past the great metal doors at the lowest part of the tube. These doors, so he had been told, could smash shut in less than two seconds, and would do so automatically if there was a pressure drop on either side. Did such thoughts as these, he wondered, ever give sleepless nights to the inhabitants of Central City? He very much doubted it; a considerable fraction of the human race had spent its life in the shadow of volcanoes, dams and dykes, without developing any signs of nervous tension. Only once had one of the domes of Central City been evacuated—in both senses of the word—and that was due to a slow leak that had taken hours to be effective.

The cab rose out of the tunnel into the residential area, and Sadler was faced with a complete change of scenery. This was no dome encasing a small city; this was a single giant building in itself, with moving corridors instead of streets. The cab came to a halt, and reminded him in polite tones that it would wait thirty minutes for an extra one-fifty. Sadler, who thought it might take him that length of time even to find the place he was looking for, declined the offer and the cab pulled away in search of fresh customers.

There was a large bulletin board a few meters away, displaying a three-dimensional map of the building. The whole place reminded Sadler of a type of beehive used many centuries ago, which he had once seen illustrated in an old encyclopedia. No doubt it was absurdly easy to find your way around when you'd got used to it, but for the moment he was quite baffled by Floors, Corridors, Zones and Sectors.

"Going somewhere, mister?" said a small voice behind him.

Sadler turned round, and saw a boy of six or seven years looking at him with alert, intelligent eyes. He was just about the same age as Jonathan Peter II. Lord, it *had* been a long time since he last visited the Moon. . . .

"Don't often see Earth folk here," said the youngster. "You lost?"

"Not yet," Sadler replied. "But I suspect I soon will be."

"Where going?"

If there was a "you" in that sentence, Sadler missed it. It was really astonishing that, despite the interplanetary radio networks, distinct differences of speech were springing up on the various worlds. This boy could doubtless speak perfectly good Earth-English when he wanted to, but it was not his language of everyday communication.

Sadler looked at the rather complex address in his notebook, and read it out slowly.

"Come on," said his self-appointed guide. Sadler gladly obeyed.

The ramp ahead ended abruptly in a broad, slowly moving roller-road. This carried them forward a few meters, then decanted them on to a high-speed section. After sweeping at least a kilometer past the entrances to countless corridors, they were switched back on to a slow section and carried to a huge, hexagonal concourse. It was crowded with people, coming and going from one roadway to another, and pausing to make purchases at little kiosks. Rising through the center of the busy scene were two spiral ramps, one carrying the up and the other the down traffic. They stepped on to the "Up" spiral and let the moving surface lift them half a dozen floors. Standing at the edge of the ramp, Sadler could see that the building extended downward for an immense distance. A very long way below was something that looked like a large net. He did some mental calculations, then decided that it would, after all, be adequate to break the fall of anyone foolish enough to go over the edge. The architects of lunar buildings had a light-hearted approach to gravity which would lead to instant disaster on Earth.

The upper concourse was exactly like the one by which they had entered, but there were fewer people about and one could tell that, however democratic the Autonomous Lunar Republic might be, there were subtle class distinctions here as in all other cultures that man had ever created. There was no more aristocracy of birth or wealth, but that of responsibility would always exist. Here, no doubt, lived the people who really ran the Moon. They had few more possessions, and a good many more worries, than their fellow citizens on the floors below, and there was a continual interchange from one level to another.

Sadler's small guide led him out of this central concourse along yet another moving passageway, then finally into a quiet corridor with a narrow strip of garden down its center and a fountain playing at either end. He marched up to one of the doors and announced: "Here's place." The brusqueness of his statement was quite neutralized by the proud there-wasn't-that-clever-of-me smile he gave Sadler, who was now wondering what would be a suitable reward for his enterprise. Or would the boy be offended if he gave him anything?

This social dilemma was solved for him by his observant guide. "More than ten floors, that's fifteen."

So there's a standard rate, thought Sadler. He handed over a quarter, and to his surprise was compelled to accept the change. He had not realized that the well-known lunar virtues of honesty, enterprise and fair-dealing started at such an early age.

"Don't go yet," he said to his guide as he rang the doorbell. "If there's no one in, I'll want you to take me back."

"You not phoned first?" said that practical person, looking at him incredulously.

Sadler felt it was useless to explain. The inefficiencies and vagaries of old-fashioned Earth folk were not appreciated by these energetic colonists—though heaven help him if he ever used *that* word here.

However, there was no need for the precaution. The man he wanted to meet was at home, and Sadler's guide waved him a cheerful good-by as he went off down the corridor, whistling a tune that had just arrived from Mars.

"I wonder if you remember me," said Sadler. "I was at the Plato Observatory during the Battle of Pico. My name's Bertram Sadler."

"Sadler? Sadler? Sorry, but I don't remember you at the moment. But come right in; I'm always pleased to meet old friends."

Sadler followed into the house, looking round curiously as he did so. It was the first time he had ever been into a private home on the Moon, and as he might have expected there was no way in which it could be distinguished from a similar residence on Earth. That it was one cell in a vast honeycomb did not make it any less a home; it had been two centuries since more than a minute fraction of the human race had lived in separate, isolated buildings and the word "house" had changed its meaning with the times.

There was just one touch in the main living room, however, that was too old-fashioned for any terrestrial family. Extending halfway across one wall was a large animated mural of a kind which Sadler had not seen for years. It showed a snow-flecked mountainside sloping down to a tiny Alpine village a kilometer or more below. Despite the apparent distance, every detail was crystal clear; the little houses and the toy church had the sharp, vivid distinctness of something seen through the wrong end of a telescope. Beyond the village, the ground rose again, more and more steeply, to the great mountain that dominated the skyline and trailed from its summit a perpetual plume of snow, a white streamer drifting forever down the wind.

It was, Sadler guessed, a real scene recorded a couple of centuries ago. But he could not be sure; Earth still had such surprises in out-of-the-way spots.

He took the seat he was offered and had his first good look at the man he had played truant from rather important business to meet. "You don't remember me?" he said.

"I'm afraid not—but I'm quite bad at names and faces."

"Well, I'm nearly twice as old now, so it's not surprising. But *you* haven't changed, Professor Molton. I can still remember that you were the first man I ever spoke to on my way to the Observatory. I was riding the monorail from Central City, watching the sun going down behind the Apennines. It was the night before the Battle of Pico, and my first visit to the Moon."

Sadler could see that Molton was genuinely baffled. It was thirty years, after all, and he must not forget that he had a completely abnormal memory for faces and facts.

"Never mind," he continued. "I couldn't really expect you to remember me, because I wasn't one of your colleagues. I was only a visitor to the Observatory, and I wasn't there long. I'm an accountant, not an astronomer."

"Indeed?" said Molton, clearly still at a loss.

"That was not, however, the capacity in which I visited the Observatory, though I pretended it was. At the time, I was actually a government agent investigating a security leak."

He was watching the old man's face intently, and there was no mistaking the flicker of surprise. After a short silence, Molton replied, "I seem to remember something of the kind. But I'd quite forgotten the name. It was such a long time ago, of course."

"Yes, of course," echoed Sadler. "But I'm sure there are some things you'll remember. However, before I go on, there's one thing I'd better make clear. My visit here is quite unofficial. I really *am* nothing but an accountant now, and I'm glad to say quite a successful one. In fact, I'm one of the partners of Carter, Hargreaves and Tillotson, and I'm here to audit a number of the big lunar corporations. Your Chamber of Commerce will confirm that."

"I don't quite see——" began Molton.

"—what it's all got to do with you? Well, let me jog your memory. I was sent to the Observatory to investigate a security leak. Somehow, information was getting to the Federation. One of our agents had reported that the leak was at the Observatory, and I went there to look for it."

"Go on," said Molton.

Sadler smiled, a little wryly.

"I'm considered to be a good accountant," he said, "but I'm afraid I was not a very successful security man. I suspected a lot of people, but found nothing, though I accidentally uncovered one crook."

"Jenkins," said Molton suddenly.

"That's right—your memory's not so bad, Professor. Anyway, I never found the spy; I couldn't even prove that he existed, though I investigated every possibility I could think of. The whole affair fizzled out eventually, of course, and a few months later I was back at my normal work, and much happier too. But it has always worried me; it was a loose end I didn't like having round—a discrepancy in the balance sheet. I'd given up any hope of settling it, until a couple of weeks ago. Then I read Commodore Brennan's book. Have you seen it yet?"

"I'm afraid not, though of course I've heard about it."

Sadler reached into his briefcase and produced a fat volume, which he handed over to Molton.

"I've brought a copy for you—I know you'll be *very* interested. It's quite a sensational book, as you can judge by the fuss it's causing all over the System. He doesn't pull any punches, and I can understand why a lot of people in the Federation are pretty mad with him. However, that's not the point that concerns me. What I found quite fascinating was his account of the events leading up to the Battle of Pico. Imagine my surprise when he definitely confirmed that vital information had come from the Observatory. To quote his phrase: 'One of Earth's leading astronomers, by a brilliant technical subterfuge, kept us informed of developments during the progress of Project Thor. It would be improper to give his name, but he is now living in honored retirement on the Moon.' "

There was a very long pause. Molton's craggy face had now set in granite folds, and gave no hint of his emotions.

"Professor Molton," Sadler continued earnestly. "I hope you'll believe me when I say that I'm here purely out of private curiosity. In any case, you're a citizen of the Republic—there's nothing I could do to you even if I wanted to. *But I know you were that agent.* The description fits, and I've ruled out all the other possibilities. Moreover, some friends of mine in the Federation have been looking at records, again quite unofficially. It's not the slightest use pretending you know nothing about it. If you don't want to talk, I'll clear out. But if you feel like telling me—and I don't see how it matters now—I'd give a very great deal to know how you managed to do it."

Molton had opened Professor, late Commodore, Brennan's book and was leafing through the index. Then he shook his head in some annoyance.

"He shouldn't have said that," he remarked testily, to no one in particular. Sadler breathed a sigh of satisfied anticipation. Abruptly, the old scientist turned upon him.

"If I tell you, what use will you make of the information?"

"None, I swear."

"Some of my colleagues might be annoyed, even after this time. It wasn't easy, you know. *I* didn't enjoy it either. But Earth had to be stopped, and I think I did the right thing."

"Professor Jamieson—he's director now, isn't he?—had similar ideas. But he didn't put them into practice."

"I know. There was a time when I nearly confided in him, but perhaps it's just as well that I didn't."

Molton paused reflectively, and his face creased into a smile.

"I've just remembered," he said. "I showed you round my lab. I was a little bit suspicious then—I thought it odd you should have come when you did. So I showed you *absolutely everything,* until I could see you were bored and had had enough."

"That happened rather often," said Sadler dryly. "There was quite a lot of equipment at the Observatory."

"Some of mine, however, was unique. Not even a man in my own field would have guessed what it did. I suppose your people were looking for concealed radio transmitters, and that sort of thing?"

"Yes; we had monitors on the lookout, but they never spotted anything."

Molton was obviously beginning to enjoy himself. Perhaps he too, thought Sadler, had been frustrated for the last thirty years, unable to say how he had fooled the security forces of Earth.

"The beauty of it was," Molton continued, "my transmitter was in full sight all the time. In fact, it was about the most obvious thing in the Observatory. You see, it was the thousand-centimeter telescope."

Sadler stared at him incredulously.

"I don't understand you."

"Consider," said Molton, becoming once more the college professor he had been after leaving the Observatory, "exactly what it is a telescope does. It gathers light from a tiny portion of the sky, and brings it accurately to a focus on a photographic plate or the slit of a spectroscope. But don't you see—*a telescope can work both ways.*"

"I'm beginning to follow."

"My observing program involved using the thousand centimeter for studying faint stars. I worked in the far ultra-violet—which of course is quite invisible to the eye. I'd only to replace my usual instruments by an ultra-violet lamp, and the telescope immediately became a searchlight of immense power and accuracy, sending out a beam so narrow that it could only be detected in the exact portion of the sky I'd aimed it at. Interrupting the beam for signaling purposes was, of course, a trivial problem. I can't send Morse, but I built an automatic modulator to do it for me."

Sadler slowly absorbed this revelation. Once explained, the idea was ridiculously simple. Yes, any telescope, now he came to think of it, *must* be capable of working both ways—of gathering light from the stars, or of sending an almost perfectly parallel beam back at them, if one shone a light into the eyepiece end. Molton had turned the thousand-centimeter reflector into the largest electric torch ever built.

"Where did you aim your signals?" he asked.

"The Federation had a small ship about ten million kilometers out. Even at that distance, my beam was still pretty narrow and it needed good navigation to keep in it. The arrangement was that the ship would always keep dead in line between me and a faint northern star that was always visible above my horizon. When I wanted to send a signal—they knew when I would be operating, of course—I merely had to feed the co-ordinates into the telescope, and I'd be sure that they'd receive me. They had a small telescope aboard, with an ultra-violet detector. They kept in contact with Mars by ordinary radio. I often thought it must have been very dull out there, just listening for me. Sometimes I didn't send anything for days."

"That's another point," Sadler remarked. "How did the information get to *you,* anyway?"

"Oh, there were two methods. We got copies of all the astronomical journals, of course. There were agreed pages in certain journals—*The Observatory,* I recall, was one of them—that I kept my eye on. Some of the letters were fluorescent under far ultra-violet. No one could have spotted it; ordinary u.v. was no use."

"And the other method?"

"I used to go to the gym in Central City every weekend. You leave your clothes in locked cubicles when you undress, but there's enough clearance at the top of the doors for anything to be slipped in. Sometimes I used to find an ordinary tabulating-machine card on top of my things, with a set of holes punched in it. Perfectly commonplace and innocent, of course—you'll find them all over the Observatory, and not only in the Computing Section. I always made a point of having a few genuine ones in my pockets. When I got back, I'd decipher the card and send the message out on my next transmission. I never knew what I was sending—it was always in code. And I never discovered who dropped the cards in my locker."

Molton paused, and looked quizzically at Sadler.

"On the whole," he concluded, "I really don't think you had much chance. My only danger was that you might catch my contacts and find they were passing information to me. Even if that happened, I thought I could get away with it. Every piece of apparatus I used had some perfectly genuine astronomical function. Even the modulator was part of an unsuccessful spectrum analyzer I'd never bothered to dismantle. And my transmissions only lasted for a few minutes; I could send a lot in that time, and then get on with my regular program."

Sadler looked at the old astronomer with undisguised admiration. He was beginning to feel a good deal better: an ancient inferiority complex had been exorcised. There was no need for self-reproach; he doubted if anyone could have detected Molton's activities, while they were confined to the Observatory end alone. The people to blame were the counteragents in Central City and Project Thor, who should have stopped the leak further up the line.

There was still one question that Sadler wished to ask, but could not bring himself to do so; it was, after all, no real concern of his. *How* was no longer a mystery; *why* still remained.

He could think of many answers. His studies of the past had shown him that a man like Molton would not become a spy for money, or power, or any such trivial reason. Some emotional impulse must have driven him on the path he followed, and he would have acted from a profound inner conviction that what he did was right. Logic might have told him that the Federation should be supported against Earth, but in a case like this, logic was never enough.

Here was one secret that would remain with Molton. Perhaps he was aware of Sadler's thoughts, for abruptly he walked over to the wide bookcase and slid aside a section of the paneling.

"I came across a quotation once," he said, "that's been a considerable comfort to me. I'm not sure whether it was supposed to be cynical or not, but there's a great deal of truth in it. It was made, I believe, by a French statesman named Talleyrand, about four hundred years ago. And he said this: *'What is treason? Merely a matter of dates.'* You might care to think that over, Mr. Sadler."

He walked back from the bookcase, carrying two glasses and a large decanter.

"A hobby of mine," he informed Sadler. "The last vintage from Hesperus. The French make fun of it, but I'd match it against anything from Earth."

They touched glasses.

"To peace among the planets," said Professor Molton, "and may no men ever again have to play the parts we did."

Against a landscape four hundred thousand kilometers away in space and two centuries ago in time, spy and counterspy drank the toast together. Each was full of memories, but those memories held no bitterness now. There was nothing more to say: for both of them, the story was ended.

Molton took Sadler down the corridor, past the quiet fountains, and saw him safely on the rolling floor that led to the main concourse. As he walked back to the house, lingering by the fragrant little garden, he was almost bowled over by a troop of laughing children racing across to the playground in Sector Nine. The corridor echoed briefly with their shrill voices; then they were gone like a sudden gust of wind.

Professor Molton smiled as he watched them racing toward their bright, untroubled future—the future he had helped to make. He had many consolations, and that was the greatest of them. Never again, as far ahead as imagination could roam, would the human race be divided against itself. For above him, beyond the roof of Central City, the inexhaustible wealth of the Moon was flowing outward across space, to all the planets Man now called his own.